THE DEVIL'S THIEF

ALSO BY LISA MAXWELL

The Last Magician
Unhooked

THE DEVIL'S THIEF

BOOK TWO IN THE *NEW YORK TIMES* BESTSELLING LAST MAGICIAN SERIES

BY LISA MAXWELL

SIMON PULSE

NEW YORK   LONDON   TORONTO   SYDNEY   NEW DELHI

SIMON PULSE

An imprint of Simon & Schuster Children's Publishing Division
1230 Avenue of the Americas, New York, New York 10020
First Simon Pulse hardcover edition October 2018
Text copyright © 2018 by Lisa Maxwell
Jacket title typography and photo-illustration copyright © 2018 by Craig Howell
Map illustrations copyright © 2017 (pages vi–vii) and 2018 (pages viii–ix) by Drew Willis
All rights reserved, including the right of reproduction in whole or in part in any form.
SIMON PULSE and colophon are registered trademarks of Simon & Schuster, Inc.
For information about special discounts for bulk purchases, please contact
Simon & Schuster Special Sales at 1-866-506-1949 or business@simonandschuster.com.
The Simon & Schuster Speakers Bureau can bring authors to your live event.
For more information or to book an event contact the Simon & Schuster Speakers Bureau
at 1-866-248-3049 or visit our website at www.simonspeakers.com.
Jacket designed by Russell Gordon
Interior designed by Brad Mead
The text of this book was set in Bembo Std.
Manufactured in the United States of America
2 4 6 8 10 9 7 5 3 1
Library of Congress Cataloging-in-Publication Data
Names: Maxwell, Lisa, 1979– author.
Title: The devil's thief / by Lisa Maxwell.
Description: New York : Simon Pulse, [2018] | Series: The last magician ; 2 |
Summary: "Esta and Harte set off on a cross-country chase through time to steal back the
elemental stones they need to save the future of magic"—Provided by publisher.
Identifiers: LCCN 2018013470 (print) | LCCN 2018020872 (eBook) |
ISBN 9781481494472 (eBook) | ISBN 9781481494458 (hardcover)
Subjects: | CYAC: Magic—Fiction. | Time travel—Fiction. | Stealing—Fiction. |
Gangs—Fiction. | New York (N.Y.)—History—20th century—Fiction.
Classification: LCC PZ7.M44656 (eBook) | LCC PZ7.M44656 Dev 2018 (print) |
DDC [Fic]—dc23
LC record available at https://lccn.loc.gov/2018013470

To Olivia and Danielle

~

It is not often that someone comes along
who is a true friend and a good writer.
—E. B. WHITE

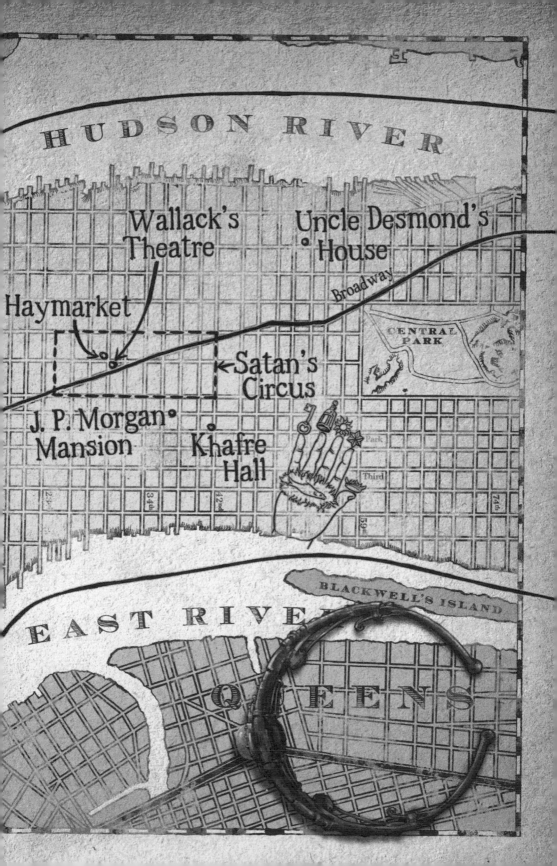

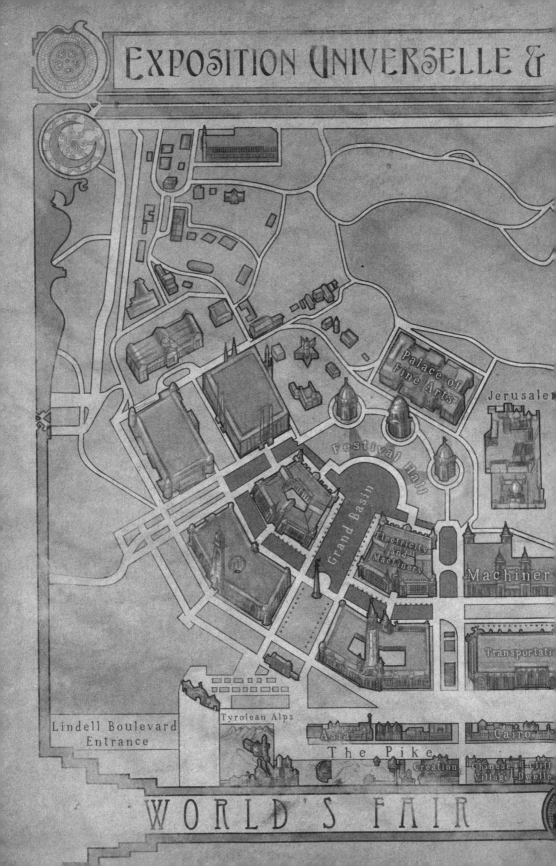

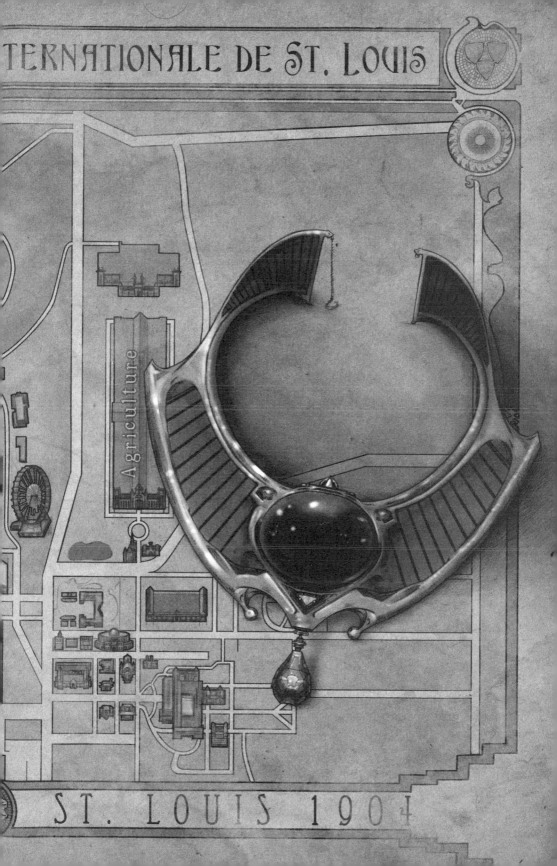

INTERNATIONALE DE ST. LOUIS

Agriculture

ST. LOUIS 1904

THE THIEF

1902—New York

The Thief turned her back on the city—on everything she had once been and on all the lies she had once believed. The ache of loss had honed her, and the weight of memory had pressed her into something new—hard and cold as a diamond. The Thief carried the memory of those losses as a weapon against what was to come as she faced the span of the great bridge.

The dark road spooled out before her, leading onward to where night had already bruised the horizon, its shadow falling over the low-slung buildings and the bare treetops of a land she'd never thought to visit. Measured in steps, the distance wasn't all that great, but between her and that other shore stood the Brink, with all its devastating power.

At her side stood the Magician. Once he had been her enemy. Always he had been her equal. Now he was her ally, and she had risked everything to come back for him. He shuddered, but whether it was from the cold evening air on his bare arms or from the reality of what they needed to do—the *impossibility* of it—the Thief couldn't be sure.

His voice came to her, a hushed whisper in the wind. "A day ago I had planned to die. I *thought* I was ready, but . . ." He glanced over at her, his storm-cloud eyes revealing everything he wasn't saying.

"This will work," she reassured him, not because she knew it was true but because there was no other option. She might not be able to change the past, might not be able to save the innocent or rewrite her mistakes and regrets, but she *would* change the future.

Behind them, a streetcar approached, sending vibrations through the track beneath their feet.

They couldn't be seen there.

"Give me your hand," the Thief commanded.

The Magician glanced at her, a question in his eyes, but she held out her bare hand, ready. With one touch he would be able read her every hope and fear. With one touch he could turn her from this path. Better to know where his heart stood now.

A moment later his hand caught hers, palm to palm.

The coolness of his skin barely registered, because when her skin touched his, power sizzled against her palm. She'd felt his affinity's warmth before, but what she felt now was something new. A wave of unfamiliar energy licked against her skin, testing her boundaries as though searching for a way *into* her.

The Book.

He'd tried to explain—tried to warn her after she had returned from the future he'd sent her to, a future he'd thought was safe. *All that power is in me,* he'd said.

She hadn't understood. Until now.

Now the familiar warmth of his affinity was overwhelmed by a stronger magic, a power that had once been contained in the pages of the Ars Arcana the Thief had tucked into her skirts—a book that people she loved had lied and fought and died for. Now its power was beginning to creep upward, wrapping around her wrist, solid and heavy as the silver cuff she wore on her arm.

At the edges of her consciousness, the Thief thought she heard voices whispering.

"Stop it," she told him through clenched teeth.

His response came out clipped, strained. "I'm trying."

When she looked over at him, his expression was pained, but his eyes were bright, their irises flashing with colors she could not have named. He drew in a breath, his nostrils flaring slightly with the effort, and a moment later the colors in his eyes faded until they were his usual stormy gray. The warmth vining around her arm receded, and the voices she'd heard scratching at the boundaries of her mind went quiet.

Together they began to walk. Away from their city, their only home. Away from her regrets and failures.

As they passed the first set of brick and steel arches, each step was one more toward their possible end. This close to the Brink, its cold energy warned anyone with an affinity for the old magic to stay away. The Thief could feel it, could sense those icy tendrils of corrupted power clawing at her, at the very heart of what she was.

But the warning didn't stop her.

Too much had happened. Too many people had been lost, and all because she had been willing to believe in the comfort of lies and too easily led. It was a mistake she wouldn't repeat. The truth of who and what she was had seared her, burning away all the lies she'd once accepted. About her world. About *herself*.

That blaze had cauterized her aching regrets and left her a girl of fire. A girl of ash and scars. She carried a taste in her mouth that made her think of vengeance. It stiffened her resolve and kept her feet moving. Because after everything that had happened, all that she had learned, she had nothing left to lose.

She had *everything* left to lose.

Brushing aside the dark thought, the Thief took a deep, steadying breath and found the spaces between the seconds that hung suspended around her. Once she had not thought of time, or her ability to manipulate it, as anything particularly special. She knew better now. Time was the quintessence of existence—Aether—the substance that held the world together. Now she appreciated the way she could sense *everything*—the air and the light, matter itself—tugging against the net of time.

How could she have missed this? It was all so startlingly clear.

The streetcar's bell clanged out its warning again, and this time she didn't hesitate to use her affinity to pull the seconds until they ran slow. As the world went still around her, the rumble of the streetcar died away into silence. And the Thief's breath caught in a strangled gasp.

"Esta?" the Magician asked, fear cracking his voice. "What's wrong?"

"Can't you see it?" she asked, not bothering to hide her wonder.

Before her the Brink shimmered in the light of the setting sun, its power fluctuating haphazardly in ribbons of energy. *Visible.* Almost solid. They were every color she had ever imagined and some she didn't have names for. Like the colors that had flashed in the Magician's eyes, they were beautiful. *Terrible.*

"Come on," she told the Magician, leading him toward the barrier. She could see the path they would take, the spaces between the coiling tendrils of power that would let them slide through untouched.

They were in the middle of the swirling colors, the Magician's hand like a vise around hers, cold and damp with his fear, when she noticed the darkness. It started at the edges of her vision, like the black spots you see after a flash of light. Nothing more than wisps at first, the darkness slowly bled into her vision like ink in water.

Before, the spaces between the seconds had been easy to find and grab hold of, but now they seemed to be slipping away, the substance of them dissolving as if eaten by the same darkness filling her vision.

"Run," she said as she felt her hold on time slipping.

"What?" The Magician looked over at her, his eyes now shadowed with the creeping blackness as well.

She stumbled, her legs suddenly like rubber beneath her. The cold power of the Brink was sliding against her skin like a blade. Everything was going dark, and the world around her was fading into nothing.

"Run!"

PART

I

THE WHITE LADY

1902—New York

The white lady was dying, and there wasn't a thing that Cela Johnson could do about it. Cela's nose wrinkled as she approached the lump of rags and filth in the corner. The smell of sweat and piss and something like decay was thick in the air. It was the decay—the sweet ripeness of it—that told Cela the woman wouldn't make it through the week. Maybe not even through the night. Felt like Death himself had already arrived in the room and was just sitting around, waiting for the right moment.

Cela wished Death would hurry up already. Her brother, Abel, was due home the next evening, and if he found the woman in the house, there'd be hell to pay.

She'd been damned stupid for agreeing to keep the woman, not that she could fathom what had possessed her to accept Harte Darrigan's request two nights before. Cela liked the magician well enough—he was one of the few at the theater who bothered to looked her in the eye when he talked to her—and she supposed she did owe him for making Esta that gown of stars behind his back. But she certainly didn't owe him enough to be putting up with his dope fiend of a mother.

But Harte had always been too slick for his own good. He was like the paste stones she fixed to the performers' costumes: To the audience, her creations sparkled like they were covered in precious gems—but that was all lights and smoke. Her garments may have been well made, her seams straight and her stitching true, but there was nothing real about the sparkle and shine. Up close, you could tell easy enough that the stones were nothing but polished glass.

Harte was a little like that. The problem was, most people couldn't see past the shine.

Though she probably shouldn't think so uncharitably of the dead. She'd heard about what happened at the Brooklyn Bridge earlier that day. He'd attempted some fool trick and ended up jumping to his death instead. Which meant he wouldn't be coming back for his mother, as he'd told her he would.

Still . . . As much as Darrigan might have been all spit and polish on the surface, like the straight, evenly stitched seams in her costumes, there was something beneath that was sturdy and true. Cela had suspected that much all along, but she knew it for the truth when he'd appeared on her doorstep, cradling the filthy woman like she was the most precious of cargo. She supposed she owed it to him now to honor his last wishes by seeing his mother through to the other side.

Two days ago the woman had been so deep in an opium dream that nothing would rouse her. But it wasn't long before the opium had worn off and the moaning had begun. The laudanum-laced wine Harte had left had lasted less than a day, but the woman's pain had lasted far longer. At least she seemed to be peaceful now.

With a sigh, Cela knelt next to her, careful not to get her skirts too dirty on the cellar's floor. The old woman wasn't sleeping, as Cela had first thought. Her eyes were glassy, staring into the darkness of the ceiling above, and her chest rose and fell unevenly. There was a wet-sounding rattle in her shallow breaths that confirmed Cela's suspicions. Harte's mother would be dead by morning.

Maybe she should have felt worse about that, but she'd promised Harte that she'd look after the old woman and make her comfortable, not that she'd save her. After all, Cela was a seamstress, not a miracle worker, and Harte's mother—Molly O'Doherty, he'd called her—was far past saving. Anyone could see that.

Still, the woman—no matter how low life had laid her or how much she stank—deserved a bit of comfort in her final moments. Cela took the bowl of clean, warm water she'd brought with her to the cellar and gently mopped the woman's brow and the crusted spittle around her mouth, but the woman didn't so much as stir.

As Cela finished cleaning the woman up as well as she could without disturbing her, she heard footsteps at the top of the wooden stairs.

"Cela?" It was Abel, her older brother, who shouldn't have been home yet. He was a Pullman porter on the New York Central line, and he should have been on his way back from Chicago, not standing in their stairwell.

"That you, Abe?" she called, easing herself up from the floor and smoothing her hair back from her face. The dampness of the cellar was surely making it start to curl up around her temples. "I thought your train wasn't due until tomorrow?"

"Switched with someone for an earlier berth." She heard him start down the steps. "What're you doing down there?"

"I'm coming up now." She grabbed a jar of peaches—an excuse for being down in the cellar—and started up the steps before he could come all the way down. "I was just getting some fruit for tonight's dinner."

Above her, Abe was still dressed in his uniform. His eyes were ringed with fatigue—probably from taking a back-to-back shift to get home—but he was smiling at her with their father's smile.

Abel Johnson Sr. had been a tall, wiry man with the build of someone who used his hands for a living. He'd been killed in the summer of 1900, when the city had erupted in riots after Arthur Harris had been arrested for stabbing some white man who'd turned out to be a plainclothes policeman. Her father didn't have anything to do with it, but that hadn't stopped him from being caught up in the hate and the fury that had swept through the city during those hot months.

Some days Cela thought she could hardly remember her father's voice or the sound of his laugh, as though he was already fading from her memory. But it helped that Abe wore her father's smile almost every day.

Times like this, it struck her just how much her brother resembled her father. Same tall, wiry build. Same high forehead and square chin. Same lines of worry and exhaustion etched into his too-young face from the long hours of working on the rail lines. But he wasn't *exactly* the spitting image of his namesake. The deep-set eyes that were a warm chestnut brown flecked with gold, and the red undertones of his skin—those features were from their mother. Cela's own skin was a good bit darker, more like the burnished brown of her father's.

Abel's expression brightened at her mention of food. "You making me something good?"

She frowned. Because she'd been too wrapped up in caring for the old woman to go to the market, she didn't have anything but the jar of peaches in her hand. "Considering that I wasn't planning on you being home until tomorrow night? You'll have to settle for porridge with peaches, same as what I was planning on making for myself."

His expression fell, and he looked so forlorn that she had to hold back her laugh. She gathered up her skirts and took a few more steps. "Oh, don't look so—"

Before she could finish, a soft moaning came from the darkness of the cellar.

Abe went completely still. "You hear that?"

"What?" Cela asked, inwardly cursing herself and the old woman just the same. "I didn't hear nothing at all." She took another step up toward where Abel was waiting. But the stupid old woman let out another moan, which had Abel's expression bunching. Cela pretended that she didn't hear it. "You know this old building . . . probably just a rat or something."

Abel started to descend the narrow staircase. "Rats don't make that kind of noise."

"Abe," she called, but he already had the lamp out of her hand and was pushing past her. She closed her eyes and waited for the inevitable outburst, and when it came, she gave herself—and Abel—a moment before trudging back to the cellar.

"What the hell is going on, Cela?" he asked, crouched over the woman in the corner. The material of his navy porter's uniform was pulled tight across his shoulders, and he had his nose tucked into his shirt. She couldn't blame him—the woman stank. There was nothing for it.

"You don't need to worry about it," Cela told him, crossing her arms. Maybe it was a stupid decision to help out the magician, but it had been *her* decision. As much as Abe thought it was his duty to take up where their father left off, Cela wasn't a child anymore. She didn't need her older brother to approve every little thing she did, especially when five days of seven he wasn't even around.

"I don't need to worry about it?" Abe asked, incredulous. "There's a white woman unconscious in my cellar, and I don't need to *worry* about it? What have you gotten yourself into this time?"

"It's *our* cellar," she told him, emphasizing the word. Left to them *both* by their parents. "And I haven't gotten myself into anything. I'm helping a friend," she answered, her shoulders squared.

"She your friend?" Abe's face shadowed with disbelief.

"No. I promised a friend I'd keep her comfortable, until she . . ." But it seemed wrong, somehow, to speak Death's name when he was sitting in the room with them. "It's not like she's got much time left."

"That doesn't help anything, Cela. Do you know what could happen to us if someone found out she was here?" Abel asked. "How are we supposed to explain a white woman dying in our cellar? We could lose this building. We could lose *everything*."

"Nobody knows she's here," Cela said, even as her insides squirmed. *Why* had she agreed to do this? She wished she could go back and slap herself to the other side of tomorrow for even considering to help Harte. "You and I, we're the only ones with keys to the cellar. None of the tenants upstairs know anything about this. They don't *need* to know anything. She'll be gone before the night is over, and then you won't have to worry about it. You weren't even supposed to be home," she told him, as though that made any difference at all.

"So you were going behind my back?"

"It's my house too," Cela said, squaring her shoulders. "And I'm not a complete idiot. I got compensated for my trouble."

"You got compensated." Abe's voice was hollow.

She told him about the ring she had stitched into her skirts. The setting held an enormous clear stone, probably worth a fortune.

Abel was shaking his head. "You're just gonna walk up to some fancy East Side jeweler and sell it, are you?"

Cela's stomach sank. He was right. *How did I not think of that?* There was no way to sell the ring without raising suspicion. Not that she was going to admit it to him at that particular moment. "It's security. That's all."

"Security is this here building," Abel told her, lifting his eyes as though he could see through the ceiling above him, to the first floor where they lived, to the second floor the Brown family rented, clear up to the attic, which held a row of cots they leased out to down-on-their-luck single men in the dead of winter. "Security is what our parents gave us when they left us *this*."

He wasn't wrong. Their house had been bought and paid for with their father's hard work. It meant that no one could turn them away or raise their rent because of the color of their skin. More, it was a testament every day that their mother's choice in their father had been a good one, no matter what her mother's family had believed.

The woman moaned again, her breath rattling like Death himself was pulling the air from her chest. The sound had such a forlorn helplessness to it that Cela couldn't help but crouch over her.

"Cela, are you even hearing me?" Abel asked.

Somehow, the woman's skin was even more colorless. Her eyes were dull, lifeless. Cela reached out tentatively and touched the woman's cool hand, taking it in hers. The fingertips beneath the nails were already blue. "She's dying, Abe. This is her time, and whatever mistakes I might have made in bringing her here, I'm not leaving a dying woman alone, no matter what she is or what she isn't." Cela looked up at her brother. "Are you?"

His expression was creased in frustration, but a moment later his eyes closed and his shoulders sank. "No, Rabbit," he said softly, using her childhood nickname. "I suppose not." He opened his eyes again. "How long do you think she has?"

Cela frowned, staring at the fragile woman. She wasn't exactly sure. When their mother had passed on from consumption five years before, Cela had been barely twelve years old. Her father had kept her from the sickroom until the very last moments, trying to protect her. He'd always been trying to protect all of them.

"Can't you hear the death rattle? She's got hours . . . maybe minutes. I don't know. Not long, though." Because the rattle in the old woman's throat was the one thing she did remember of watching her mother pass on. That sickly, paper-thin rattle that sounded nothing like her sunshine-and-laughter mother. "She'll be gone before this night is through."

Together they waited silently for the moment when the woman's chest would cease to rise or fall.

"What are we going to do when she finally dies?" Abel asked after they'd watched for a long while. "We can't exactly call someone."

"When she passes, we'll wait for the dead of night, and then we'll take her to St. John's over on Christopher Street," Cela said, not really understanding where the impulse came from. But the moment the words were out, she felt sure they were right. "They can care for her there."

Abel was shaking his head, but he didn't argue. She could tell he was trying to think of a better option when a loud pounding sounded from the floor above.

Abel's dark eyes met hers in the flickering lamplight. It was well past ten, too late for a social call. "Someone's here," he said, as though Cela couldn't have figured that out on her own. But his voice held the same worry she felt.

"Maybe just a boarder needing a bed for the night," she told him.

"Weather's too nice for that," he said almost to himself as he stared up at the ceiling. The pounding came again, harder and more urgent than before.

"Just let it be," she told him. "They'll go away eventually."

But Abel shook his head. His eyes were tight. "You wait here, and I'll see what they want."

"Abe—"

He never did listen, she thought as he disappeared into the darkness of the staircase that led up to their apartment above. At least he'd left her the lamp.

Cela waited as Abe's footsteps crossed the floor above her. The pounding stopped, and she could just barely hear the low voices of men.

Then the voices grew into shouts.

The sudden sound of a scuffle had Cela on her feet. But before she could take even a step, the crack of a gun split the silence of the night and the thud of a body hitting the floor pressed the air from her lungs.

No.

There were more footsteps above now. Heavy footsteps made by heavy boots. There were men in their house. In *her* house.

Abel.

She started to go toward the steps, desperate to get to her brother, but something within her clicked, some primal urge that she could not understand and she could not fight. It was as though her feet had grown roots.

She had to get to her brother. But *she could not move.*

The papers had been filled with news of the patrols that were combing the city, ransacking private homes and burning them to the ground. The fires had been contained in the immigrant quarters close to the Bowery. The blocks west of Greenwich Village, where her father had bought the building they lived in, had been safe. But Cela knew enough about how quickly things could change that she understood last week's safety didn't mean anything today.

There were men in her house.

She could hear their voices, could feel their footfalls vibrating through her as they spread out like they were searching the rooms above. *Robbing us? Looking for something?*

Abe.

Cela didn't particularly care. She only needed to make sure Abel was okay. She needed to be upstairs, but her will no longer seemed to be her own.

Without knowing why she did it or what drove her, she turned from the steps that led up into the house her parents had bought ten years before with their hard-earned money and went to the white lady, now clearly lifeless. With the pads of her fingers, Cela closed the newly dead woman's eyes, saying a short prayer for both of their souls, and then she was climbing the short ramp to the coal chute.

Cela pushed open the doors and climbed out into the cool freshness of the night. Her feet were moving before she could make herself stop, before she could think *Abe* or *No* or any of the things that she *should* have been thinking. She couldn't have stopped herself from running if she tried, so she was already around the corner and out of sight when the flames started to lick from the windows of the only home she had ever known.

THE BOWERY AFIRE

1902—New York

By the time Jianyu Lee made it from the Brooklyn Bridge to the Bowery, his mind had turned to murder. Ironic that he was set on killing to avenge the man who had once saved him from a life of violence. Jianyu supposed that Dolph Saunders would have been amused by the turn of events. But Dolph was dead. The leader of the Devil's Own and the one sāi yàn who had never looked at Jianyu with the suspicion that shimmered in the eyes of so many others had been shot in the back by one of his own—by someone he had trusted. Someone they *all* had trusted.

Nibsy Lorcan.

For Jianyu, it did not matter whether Esta and Harte made it through the Brink, as they planned. If their wild scheme to get through its devastating power worked, he doubted they would ever return. Why should they, if they found freedom on the other side? If *he* were able to escape from this trap of a city, he would certainly never look back. He would find the first ship heading to the East, to the home he never should have left.

He would see the land that had borne him once again.

He would breathe the clean air of the village where his family lived in Sānnìng and forget his ambitions.

Once he had been *so* young. So innocent in his headstrong confidence. After his parents had died, his older brother, Siu-Kao, had raised him. Siu-Kao was nearly a decade older and had a wife who, though beautiful, was cunning as a fox. She had married his brother as much for the magic that ran in their family as for the benefit of the family's farmlands. But when their first child seemed not to have any affinity at all, she began to make clear that Jianyu was no longer welcome in her house. By the time he started to sprout hair beneath his arms, he was so angry at his place in his older brother's home, so desperate to strike out on his own, that he had decided to leave.

He saw now that his youth had blinded him and his magic had made him reckless. Drawn into one of the packs of roving bandits that were so common in the more impoverished villages throughout Gwóng-dūng, he had lived freely for a time, repudiating his older brother's control and choosing his own path. But then, he had lingered too long in one town, a tiny hamlet close to the banks of the Zyū Gōng, and had forgotten that magic was not a panacea for stupidity. He had been barely thirteen years of age when he was caught breaking into a local merchant's home.

Then, he could not have gone back to face his brother. He *refused*.

Then, he had believed that leaving his homeland and starting anew was his only recourse.

He had not realized that there were places in the world where magic was caged. Now, he knew too well. There was a safety in fealty that he had failed to understand and freedom in the constraints of family duty that he had not appreciated as a boy.

Once, he had thought that, given the chance, he would repent and live the life that had been demanded of him, a life he had once run from. He would not make the same mistakes again.

Why else would he have given his loyalty to Dolph Saunders if not for the promise that one day the Brink would be brought down? Why else would he have kept the queue so many others had already discarded, if not for the hope that one day he would find a way to return to his homeland? Certainly, it would have been easier to cut the long braid that drew curious glances and wary stares—many of his countrymen already had. But cutting his hair would mean a final admission that he would never return.

From what Esta had told him, though, going back to Sānnìng would be pointless if the danger she foresaw ever came to pass. If Nibsy Lorcan managed to obtain the Ars Arcana, the Book that contained the very source of magic, or if he retrieved the Order's five artifacts—ancient stones that the Order had used to create the Brink and maintain their power—the boy would be unstoppable. No land, no people—Mageus or Sundren—would be safe from the power Nibsy would wield. He would subjugate the Sundren, and he would use his control over Mageus to do so.

Jianyu saw it as his duty now to make sure that future could never be realized. If he could not return to his homeland, he would protect it from Nibsy Lorcan and his like.

Darrigan had left him with very specific instructions: Jianyu must protect the first of the Order's artifacts—and the woman who carried it. But he did not have much time. Soon the boy Esta had warned them about would arrive—a boy with the power to find lost objects and with knowledge of the future to come. A boy who was loyal to Nibsy. That boy could not be allowed to reach Nibsy, especially not so long as somewhere in the city, one of the Order's stones lay waiting to be found.

Jianyu would rather risk dying on foreign shores, his bones far from his ancestors, than allow Nibsy Lorcan to win. He would find the artifact and stop this "Logan." And then Jianyu would kill Nibsy and avenge his murdered friend. Or he would die trying.

As Jianyu made his way through the Bowery, toward his destination in the Village, the scent of ash and soot was heavy in the air. For the last week—ever since Dolph Saunders' team had robbed the Order of its most powerful artifacts and Khafre Hall had burned to the ground—much of the Lower East Side had been shrouded with smoke. In retaliation for the theft, one fire after another had erupted through the most impoverished neighborhoods of the city. The Order, after all, had a point to make.

Where Hester Street met the wide boulevard that was the Bowery, Jianyu passed the burned-out remains of a tenement. The sidewalk was heaped with the detritus of destroyed lives. The building had once housed Mageus, people who had lived under Dolph's care. Jianyu wondered where they had gone and who they would depend upon now that Dolph was dead.

As Jianyu walked, he noticed a clutch of dark shadows lurking just beyond the circle of lamplight across from the remains of the building. *Paul Kelly's men.* Sundren, all of them, the Five Pointers had nothing to fear from the Order.

Once, the Five Pointers wouldn't have dared cross Elizabeth Street or come within four blocks of the Bella Strega, Dolph's saloon. But now they walked the streets Dolph had once protected, their presence a declaration of their intent to occupy. To conquer.

It wasn't unexpected. As news of Dolph's death spread, the other gangs would begin to take the territory the Devil's Own once held. It was no more surprising to see the Five Pointers in the neighborhood than it would be to see Eastman's gang or any of the rest. If Jianyu had to guess, he suspected that even Tom Lee, the leader of the most powerful tong in Chinatown, would try to take what territory he could.

The Five Pointers were different, though. More dangerous. More ruthless.

They were a newer faction in the Bowery, and because of that they fought like they had something to prove. But unlike the other gangs, Kelly's boys had managed to procure the protection of Tammany Hall. The year before, the Five Pointers had broken heads and flooded polling places to elect a Tammany puppet to the city council, and ever since, the police overlooked whatever crimes the Five Pointers committed.

It had been bad enough that Kelly had been working in league with the corrupt bosses at Tammany, but during the days preceding Dolph's death, they had grown more brazen than ever. It had been an unmistakable sign that something was afoot. Everyone in the Strega had known that unrest was stirring in the Bowery, but it was a sign read too poorly and too late.

Feeling exposed, Jianyu drew on his affinity and opened the threads of light cast by the streetlamps. He bent them around himself like a cloak so that the Five Pointers wouldn't see him pass. Invisible to their predatory vigilance, he allowed himself to relax into the comfort of his magic, the certainty of it when everything else was so uncertain. Then he picked up his pace.

A few blocks later, the familiar golden-eyed witch on the Bella Strega's sign came into view. To the average person looking for warmth from the chill of the night or a glass of something to numb the pain of a life lived at the margins, the crowd of the Bella Strega might not have seemed any different from the other saloons and beer halls scattered throughout the city. Legal or illegal, those darkened rooms were a way for the city's poor to escape the disappointment and trials of their lives. But the Strega *was* different.

Or it had been.

Mageus of all types felt safe enough to gather within its walls without fear and without need to hide what they were, because Dolph Saunders had refused to appease the narrow-mindedness bred from fear and igno-rance or to tolerate the usual divisions between the denizens of the Bowery. Going to the Strega meant the promise of welcome—of *safety*— in a dangerous city, even for one such as Jianyu. On any single night, the barroom would be filled with a mixture of languages and people, their common bond the old magic that flowed in their veins.

That was before a single bullet had put Dolph into a cold grave, Jianyu reminded himself as he passed under the witch's watchful gaze. Now that Nibsy Lorcan had control of the Devil's Own, there would be no guar-antee of safety within those walls. Especially not for Jianyu.

According to Esta, Nibsy had the uncanny ability to see connections between events and to predict outcomes. Since Jianyu was determined to end Nibsy's reign, and his life, he couldn't risk returning to the Strega.

Still, Nibsy had not managed to predict how Dolph had changed the plans at Khafre Hall, nor how Jianyu had intended to help Harte Darrigan fake his own death on the bridge just hours before. Perhaps the boy wasn't as powerful as Esta believed, or perhaps his affinity simply had limitations, as all affinities did. Finishing Nibsy might be difficult, but it would not be impossible. Especially since Viola could kill a man without touching him.

That would have to wait for another day, though. Jianyu still had to find Viola and tell her everything. She likely still believed that he had not been on the bridge and that Harte Darrigan had betrayed them all.

The Strega behind him, Jianyu continued on. He could have taken a streetcar or one of the elevated trains, but he preferred to walk so that he could think and plan. Gaining Cela's trust would be a delicate procedure, since Cela Johnson wouldn't be expecting him and few in the city trusted his countrymen. Protecting her and the stone might be even more difficult, since she was Sundren and had no idea what danger the ring posed. But he had promised Darrigan, and he understood all that was at stake. He would not fail.

By the time he reached the South Village, Jianyu detected smoke in the air. As he drew closer to Minetta Lane, where Miss Johnson lived, the scent grew stronger, filling his nostrils with its warning and his stomach with dread.

Jianyu knew somehow, before he was even in sight of the building, that it would be Cela Johnson's home that he found ablaze. Flames licked from windows, and the entire structure glowed from the fire within it. Even from across the street, the heat prickled his skin, making the wool coat he was wearing feel overwarm for the early spring night.

Nearby, the building's tenants watched as their home was devoured by the flames. Huddled together, they tried to protect the meager piles of belongings they'd been able to salvage, while a fire brigade's wagon stood by. The horses pawed at the ground, displaying their unease about the flickering light of the fire and the growing crowd. But the firemen did nothing.

It wasn't surprising.

Jianyu knew the fire brigade's current inaction was intentional. The brigades were mostly Irish, but being at least a generation removed from the boats and famine that had brought them to this land, they considered themselves natives. They looked with distaste on the newer waves of immigrants, from places to the east and the south, and on anyone whose skin wasn't as white as theirs, no matter how long their families had been in this land. When those homes burned, the brigades often moved slower and took fewer risks. Sometimes, if it suited their purposes, they ignored the flames altogether.

If asked, they would say it had been too late. They would tell the people weeping and wringing their hands that the fire had already consumed too much, that it was too dangerous even to try entering the building. Their lives could not be wasted on lost causes.

It didn't matter whether their words were true. The effect was the same. Even now, the men simply leaned against their wagon, their hands crossed over dark uniforms, impassive as the rows of brass buttons lining their chests. Their shining helmets reflected the light of the blaze, as the pale-faced men with long, narrow noses watched a home transform itself into ash. It had happened countless times before, and in the days to come, Jianyu knew that it would happen again.

Still under the cover of his magic, he approached the group of people slowly, listening for some indication that Cela was among them. For years now Jianyu had been Dolph Saunders' eyes and ears in the Bowery. It wasn't only that he was able to evade notice with his affinity. No, he also had a talent for understanding people and reading the words that remained unspoken, a skill he'd picked up when he'd traveled through Gwóng-dūng, before he was caught. He had wanted to start anew and to leave that life behind him, but because he hoped that the Brink could be destroyed, Jianyu had agreed to use his ability for Dolph, to warn him when danger was coming or to find those who needed help but didn't know where to ask.

He used that skill now, listening to the group that had congregated to comfort the family.

". . . saw her take off like the hellhound was on her tail."

"Little Cela?"

"Mmm–hmm."

"No . . ."

"You don't think she started it?"

"She certainly didn't stay around to help, now, did she? Left the Browns upstairs without so much as a warning."

"Always thought there was something strange about that girl . . . Too uppity for her own good, if you ask me."

"Hush. You can't be telling lies about people like that. She was a good girl. A hard worker. She wouldn't burn down her own house."

"Abel wasn't in there, was he?"

"Can't be sure . . ."

"She wouldn't do anything to her brother. Say what you want about her, but Abe doted on that girl."

"Wouldn't be the first time a bitch bit the hand that fed her. Big house like that? She could sell it and go wherever she wanted."

"Abel never would've sold."

"That's what I'm *saying*. . . . They paid the insurance man, same as everyone."

"Carl Brown said there was a gunshot. . . ."

Jianyu turned away from the bitterness and jealousy that dripped like venom from their words. They knew nothing except that Cela was not inside the house.

The gunshot, the burning house. It could have been Cela's doing, but from the way the fire brigade stood silent and watchful rather than putting out the blaze, Jianyu thought otherwise. It was too much like what had happened in other parts of the city. It had the mark of the Order.

Which meant that someone, somehow, might already suspect that Cela had the Order's artifact. As long as she was alone in the city, without protection, she was in danger.

They all were.

THE TRUTH ABOUT POWER

1902—New York

From the table at the back of the Bella Strega, James Lorcan balanced the stiletto knife on its tip as he surveyed the barroom. The knife had once belonged to Viola, but considering that he'd found it lodged in his thigh, he'd decided he'd earned it. He watched the light flash off its deadly blade—a blade capable of slicing through any material—as he contemplated everything that had happened.

He was no longer relegated to a seat off to the side, as he had been when Dolph Saunders was alive. Now James occupied the head of the table—the space reserved for the leader of the Devil's Own—where he had always belonged, and Saunders occupied a small plot of land in a nearby churchyard, where *he* belonged. But it wasn't enough. It wasn't *nearly* enough.

At the table next to him were Mooch and Werner—Bowery toughs who had once taken Dolph Saunders' mark and pledged their loyalty to the Devil's Own. Now they, like the rest of Dolph's gang, looked to James for leadership. They were playing a hand of cards with a few others. From the way the Aether around them wavered and vibrated, one of them was bluffing about the hand he held—probably Mooch—and was about to lose. From what James could read, the others knew and were driving up the pot on purpose.

They hadn't invited James to join in, not that he would have anyway. He had never cared for games—not in that way. Take chess, for instance. Simpleminded people thought it was a challenge, but in reality the game was far too predictable. Every piece on the board had specific limitations, and every move led the player to a limited number of possibilities. Anyone with half a brain between their ears could learn the simple machinations to ensure victory. There was no true challenge there.

Life was so much more interesting a game. The players were more varied and the rules constantly changing. And the challenges those variables presented? They only served to sweeten the victory. Because there was *always* victory, at least for James Lorcan. People, after all, were not capable of untold depths. He didn't need his affinity to understand that at their heart, humans were no more than animals, driven by their hungers and fears.

Easily manipulated.

Predictable.

No, James didn't need his affinity to understand human nature, but it certainly helped. It sharpened and deepened his perceptions, which gave him an advantage over every other player on the board.

It wasn't that he could see the future exactly—he wasn't a fortuneteller. His affinity simply allowed him to recognize the possibilities fate held in a way most people couldn't fathom. After all, the world and everything in it was connected by Aether, just as words were connected on the pages of a book. There was a pattern to it all, like the grammar of a sentence or the structure of a story, and his affinity gave him the ability to read those patterns. But it was his *intelligence* that allowed him to *adjust* those patterns when it suited his needs. Change one word here, and the overall sentence adjusted. Cross out a sentence there, and a new meaning emerged. A new ending was written.

Just the day before, the future he had envisioned and planned for had been within his reach. With the Book's power, he could have restored magic and shown those like him what their *true* destinies were supposed to be—not cowering from ordinary, powerless Sundren, but *ruling* them. *Destroying* those who had tried to steal that power to make the world theirs. And he would have been the one to lead the Mageus into a new era.

But the Book was lost. He'd expected that Darrigan would fight—had even planned for the magician to run—but he hadn't predicted that Darrigan would be willing to *die*.

He hadn't predicted Esta's role either, though perhaps he should have. She'd always been slightly hazy to him, her connections to the Aether wavering and unsettled from the first. In the end, James had been wrong about her. In the end, she'd been as vulnerable and worthless as any of the other sheep that followed Dolph Saunders.

Without the Book, perhaps that particular dream could never be, but James Lorcan wasn't finished. As long as the future still held possibilities for anyone smart enough to take hold of them, his game was not at an end. Perhaps he could not take control of magic, as he'd once dreamed. Perhaps magic would fade from the earth, but there were *so* many other ways for him to win. So many other ways to make those who had taken his family—and his future—pay. So many ways to end up on top of them all.

After all, power wasn't always about obvious strength. Look what happened to James' own father, who had wanted nothing more than fairness for other workers like himself—safe conditions, a good wage. He'd tried to lead, and they'd crushed him. They'd burned James' house, killed his family, and taken everything from them. James had seen too many times what happened when you stepped up to lead.

You made yourself a target.

He didn't have any interest in following Dolph's fate, so he would do what he always did. He would bide his time. He would look to the long game while the small-minded tried to jump from space to space, knocking one another off the board while he watched from afar. It wouldn't take much—a suggestion here, a whisper there, and the leaders in the Bowery would be so focused on snuffing out one another over the scraps the Order left them that they wouldn't bother with James. Which would leave him free to focus on more important matters.

No, he certainly was no fortune-teller, but he could see the future on the horizon. Without the Book, magic would fade and the Brink would become nothing more than an antiquated curiosity. What power would the Order have then, especially without their most treasured possessions?

As their power waned, James would be moving his own pieces, preparing to meet them with a language they understood—the language of money. The language of political influence. Because he understood that without the Book, it would not be those like Dolph Saunders, trying to reclaim some lost past, who would win, but those willing to take hold of a brave and dangerous new future. People like Paul Kelly, who already understood how to use the politicians as his tools. And people like James himself, who knew that power—*true* power—didn't go to those who ruled by force but instead belonged to those who held the strings. True power was the ability to bend others to your will while they thought the bending was their own idea.

Perhaps James could no longer depend on the Book. Perhaps there was no way to save magic, but his game wasn't over. With a tug here and a push there, he would tie up the powers that be so securely, they would never realize where the true danger was coming from. And when the time was right, James Lorcan had a weapon of his own—a secret that Dolph had never known about.

A girl who would become the Order's undoing and the key to James Lorcan's final victory.

SANCTUARY

1902—New York

As she climbed aboard the late-night streetcar, Cela pulled her shawl up around her head to hide her face as she swallowed down a sob. The memory of the gunfire, a sound that had been so stark and clear and unmistakable in the quiet of the night, was still ringing in her ears. She couldn't forget how she'd *felt* the thud of a body slumping to the floor. It had echoed in her chest, and she felt like she would always hear that sound and feel the emptiness that had accompanied it.

Abe. She didn't know how she managed to find a seat when she couldn't hardly draw breath, and as the streetcar rumbled blindly on, it felt like her body would crumble in on itself to fill the gaping hole left in her chest.

She needed to go back. She couldn't leave Abe there, her brother and the closest family that she had left. She had to take care of his body and protect the property that her daddy had worked himself to the bone for . . . but she *couldn't.* Every time she thought about turning around, a wave of such utter fear would rise up in her that she felt physically ill.

As the streetcar rumbled on, she thought of going to her mother's family. They'd moved up to West Fifty-Second Street a few years back, but they'd never liked Cela's father all that much. Her uncles had always looked at him like he was beneath their sister—something the dog dragged in. Now that her grandmother had passed, there wasn't much buffer between the family's judgment and Cela's feelings. She'd end up there eventually—they'd have to be told, after all—but she didn't think she could handle them yet. Not while everything was so raw. Not while it was still too hard to think the words, much less say them out loud.

Especially not to people who would be thinking that Abe's death was his own fault, which was what they'd said about her father. Her uncles didn't know that Cela had been listening when they whispered to each other after the funeral, so they hadn't censored themselves. They'd complained that her father should've stayed inside the house where he belonged, instead of standing watch on the front porch for the angry mobs who had taken to the streets. They believed that her father should have known better than to stand up to them.

Her father had been trying to protect their family, just as Abe had been trying to protect her. Cela knew that she wouldn't be able even to look at her family at that moment without hearing the echoes of those insults. Not now, when her own guilt and grief were vines around her heart, piercing and alive, growing with each passing second.

Besides, as much as her family might have hurt her in the past, they were still her blood. She couldn't risk putting them in danger. Maybe the men who'd come pounding on their door that night weren't after anything more than their property. It wouldn't have been the first time someone thought they had a right to the house just because they wanted it. People had come with pretty promises and drawn up papers plenty of times, and first her father and then her brother had turned them away.

But they'd never come with guns.

And she'd never had a white lady up and die in her cellar before. Maybe those two things weren't at all related, but she had a feeling they were.

She should go to her family.

But it was too late to be waking people up.

But there was no way her uncle would open his door and not ask what the problem was, and there was no way Cela would be able to say the words, the ones that would make what just happened true. Not yet.

She wasn't ready. She wasn't sure if she'd ever really be ready, but she figured it would be a damn sight easier in the light of day. Though she was probably wrong about that, too.

Cela got off the streetcar at her usual stop, letting her body carry her along the streets through a combination of exhaustion and memory. The theater at least was a safe enough space, since it belonged to some rich white man. Nobody was gonna come and burn his property down, and she knew the ins and outs of the world behind the stage to get herself out of there if trouble did happen to find her again.

She let herself in through the back-alley stage door that nobody ever really used, except the people who kept things running from day to day. Inside the theater, it was silent. Even the last janitor would have gone home by now, which was fine. She didn't need to run into anyone anyway.

Her costume shop was in the basement, and since that was her domain, that was where she took herself. She was no stranger to working late to finish a project, but if she didn't want to break her neck on one of the ropes or props, she needed light. She decided on one of the oil lamps that they kept backstage in case of power outages rather than turning on the electric bulbs. The lamp threw a small halo of golden light around her, illuminating a step or two in front of her, but not much more than that. It was all she needed.

Down the stairs she went, counting as she always did so she could skip over the thirteenth riser. It was a habit of hers, but she felt the vines around her heart squeeze a little this time, remembering how Abe had made fun of her for it. She walked through the silent darkness of the cellar, wiping away the wetness on her cheeks before she unlocked the small storage room that had become her costume shop.

Inside, Cela set the lamp on the worktable and sat in the straight-backed chair in front of her heavy sewing machine, the one she spent most of her days in, sewing and cutting and stitching the masterpieces that made the stage come alive. For a moment she didn't feel anything at all—not fear or relief or even emptiness. For a moment she was just a breath in the night surrounded by the warmth of a body. But then the grief crashed into her, and a cry tore free of her throat.

My brother is dead.

She let the pain come, let it take her under into a dark place where not even the light of the lamp could reach her. All she had were the clothes on her back and a ring too fancy to fence without getting herself arrested or worse.

And her job . . .

And herself . . .

She wanted to stay down in that dark place, far below the waves of grief, but those thoughts buoyed her up, up, up . . . until she could feel the wetness on her cheeks again and see the oil lamp glowing softly in the small, cramped workshop room.

Abel would have hated to see her wallowing. After their father had been beaten and shot for trying to protect his own home, hadn't Abe been the one to put his arm around her and make her go on? She'd gone numb from the loss. The city she'd known as hers had become an unrecognizable, ugly place, and the life she'd once dreamed of had been buried with her father's body. But Abe had pulled Cela aside and told her that the choices their father had made needed to be honored with a life well and fully lived. It was the reason she'd gone out to look for work as a seamstress and then had pressed to get a position in one of the white theaters, where the pay was better, even if the respect from the performers was less. She'd *earned* their respect, however begrudgingly, because of her talent with a needle. Abel had pulled those dreams of hers out of the grave and handed them back, forcing her to carry on with them.

She still had that job, the one he'd been so proud of her for getting, and she still had herself. She had family in the city who would take her in if she really needed them, whatever they might think. And she had a ring, a gorgeous golden ring with a jewel as big as a robin's egg and as clear as a teardrop. It wasn't glass, Cela knew. Glass didn't glow like that or shine like a star when the light hit it. And glass wasn't that heavy. Even seated, she could feel the weight of it, tugging on her skirts from the secret pocket she'd stitched to hide it.

But her brother . . .

The vines tightened around her heart until they felt as though they would squeeze it down into nothing. But before she could let grief overtake her again, Cela heard something in the darkness: footsteps coming down the stairs. It was too late for anyone else to be around.

She picked up her shears. They weren't much of a weapon, true, but they were sharp as any blade and could cut just as deep.

"Hello?"

It was a woman's voice, and now that Cela really stopped to listen, she realized they were a woman's footsteps, too. Not that she put down the scissors.

Cela didn't answer. Silently, she willed the woman to go away.

"Hellooo . . . ?" the voice trilled. "Is someone down here?"

She knew that voice, Cela thought with a sinking feeling. She heard it often enough. Every time Evelyn DeMure had an idea for a new way to make her waist look trimmer or her bust look larger, Cela was the one who got to hear about it . . . and *boy* did she hear about it. Evelyn was the type of performer the workers backstage tried their best to avoid. Though she was undeniably talented, Evelyn thought she was more so, and she acted as though the world owed her something for her very presence.

Evelyn DeMure peered around the doorframe and found her. "Well, Cela Johnson . . ." Without her usual lipstick and rouge, Evelyn looked like a corpse in the dim lighting. "What *ever* are you doing here so late at night?"

Cela kept the scissors in her hands but picked up a piece of fabric to go with them. "I had some odds and ends to work on," she told Evelyn.

"At this hour?" Evelyn asked, eyeing her. "I would have expected you'd be home."

Home. Cela fought to keep her expression placid and to keep any trace of pain from her voice when she answered.

She intended to lie and brush Evelyn off, but suddenly Cela couldn't remember why she hadn't liked Evelyn. There was something soothing about the singer, like her very presence was enough to make all the pain and fear that Cela was carrying fade away. Cela hadn't wanted to face her family with all that had happened, but somehow she found herself telling Evelyn *everything.*

She told her about the white lady who'd died on her watch and the brother she would never see again . . . and about the ring, with its perfect, brilliant stone. It all came pouring out of her, and by the time she was done, she felt sleepy. So tired and relaxed now that she'd cried out all the tears left in her body.

"There, there," Evelyn cooed. "Just rest. Everything will be fine. Everything will be *just* fine."

Her eyes felt heavy . . . *so heavy.*

"That's it," Evelyn said, her voice soft and warm. "Just rest your head there. . . ."

Vaguely, Cela felt herself releasing the scissors. Her body, once wrung out with grief, felt soft now. Her chest a moment before had felt cold and empty. Hollow. Now she felt warm. Safe.

Her eyes fluttered shut, and when they opened again, Evelyn was gone. The lamp had long since gone out, and her workroom was as silent as a tomb.

With a groggy moan, Cela pulled herself upright, rubbing at her head, which still felt muddled and fuzzy. Evelyn's visit and the whole night before it felt like a dream. A *very* bad dream. For a moment she allowed herself to believe that it was.

Cela didn't need the light to make her way to the door. She knew her workroom well enough. But when she went to open it, she found it stuck. No. It was *locked.*

Not a dream, then.

Which meant it had happened—all of it had happened. Abe, her home. Evelyn.

Evelyn.

Cela was trapped, and she didn't need to feel her skirts to know that the ring Harte Darrigan had given her was gone.

COMMON RABBLE

1902—New York

Jack Grew smelled like shit. He'd been sitting in a stinking cell, surrounded by the foulest dregs of the city's worst denizens, for who knew how long. Since they'd taken his watch, he certainly didn't. There were no windows, no clock to mark the passing of time. It could have been hours or days for all he knew, and the whole while, he'd been surrounded by flea-bitten filth who were happy to wallow in their own excrement.

Most of them were asleep now, which was better than before. When he had first been tossed into the cell, the five other men had eyed him eagerly, and the largest of them, a tall, bearded man who didn't say much—probably because he didn't even speak English—had crowded him into a corner.

Touching his tongue to the space where a tooth had once been and wincing at the pain in his jaw, Jack told himself that he'd held his own. He'd managed to defend himself, at least. Maybe he hadn't stopped the man from taking his jacket, but he'd put up enough of a fight that the animal had given up and left him alone. They'd all left him alone eventually.

He lifted a hand to scratch at his hair. It had probably become infested with vermin the moment he'd entered the cell, but the movement caused a sharp ache in his shoulder. That damned policeman had nearly jerked it out of its socket on the bridge.

Not one of the idiots had understood what he'd been trying to tell them—that it was Harte Darrigan they should be arresting. That damned magician had been *right there*, and the police had done nothing.

They'd taken in Jack instead. And the worst part? He'd been arrested for *attempted* murder. He'd had a clear shot and was sure the bullet would hit its mark, but then . . . nothing. The bullet hadn't even grazed him. Darrigan was like a damned ghost evading death.

The filth of the cell and the stink of the slop bucket in the corner might have been easier to deal with if Darrigan were dead. The missing tooth and sore arm and hair filled with lice might even have been worth it if Jack had been the one to end the magician's useless life.

The echo of footsteps came from the darkened corridor outside the barred doors of the cell, and the inmates around him started to wake and rustle uncertainly. As the steps approached, men in other cells rattled their bars and called out curses. *Animals, all of them.* When the guard stopped outside the cell where Jack sat, the small barred window of the door was eclipsed by the guard's face, and then Jack heard his name being called as a small window slid open below.

Finally. He hadn't doubted that someone would come for him. He didn't belong there with the common rabble. He placed his hands through the opening, as expected of him.

"Enjoy your stay?" the policeman asked, his voice mocking as he handcuffed Jack through the door. "I s'pose them's not as fancy as the accommodations you're used to."

Jack ignored him. "Where are you taking me?" he asked as the guard pushed him toward the staircase at the end of the corridor.

"You're being arraigned," the guard told him. "Time to answer to the judge."

Once they made their way down the stairs, Jack was led through a heavy set of doors and found himself in a courtroom. A dour-looking judge sat at the high bench, listening to whatever the man in front of him was saying. At the sight of the man's back—the graying hair, the small patch of baldness at his crown, the fine wool of his overcoat—Jack's stomach sank. Not his father or cousin . . . This was worse. *Much worse.*

The man in front of the judge turned, and J. P. Morgan himself stood scowling at Jack as he approached the bench.

When that peasant bitch had caught Jack in her web of lies back in Greece last year, she'd wrapped him up so deeply that he'd practically lost himself. He still didn't remember most of the drunken days and nights he'd spent under her spell, but even then, the family had simply sent his cousin to round him up. If he found himself short of funds at closing time, one of the family's men would show up to pay the bill. His uncle didn't usually bother himself with the minutiae of the family's life, especially not the life of his wife's sister's oldest boy. But there was Morgan himself, in the flesh: his bulbous, cankerous nose, stooped shoulders, and a scowl on his face that meant trouble for Jack.

Shit.

Jack stood in front of the bench, trying to listen to whatever it was the judge was saying, but he couldn't concentrate. Not when his uncle was staring at him like he was something from the gutter.

The judge finished talking. "Do you understand?" he asked.

"Yes, sir," Jack answered, not really caring what he was answering to. He wasn't some damn little boy to be put into a corner. As long as it meant freedom, he would have agreed to anything.

Another officer stepped forward to remove the heavy cuffs, and Jack rubbed at his wrists.

"I expect that I won't have to see you here again," the judge told him. It wasn't a question.

"No, sir," Jack said, silently cursing the judge and his uncle and the whole lot of them put together.

Morgan didn't say anything until they were both in the private carriage, closed away from the prying eyes of the city. Outside, the sky was just beginning to go from the pale light of dawn to full day. He'd spent the whole night in that rotting cell.

After the carriage began to move, his uncle finally spoke. "You're damn lucky Judge Sinclair is up for election this fall, or it wouldn't have been so easy to get you out of there, boy. I don't know what the hell you were thinking, trying to shoot a man in broad daylight."

"I was trying to—"

"You can't possibly think I actually care?" Morgan snapped, his cold eyes silencing Jack as effectively as his words. "You had one job—to meet Darrigan and get the artifacts he stole. All you had to do was to stay out of the way so the Order—not *you*—could dispose of him."

"Darrigan made me look like a fool," Jack said, his temper barely leashed. "I couldn't let what he'd done to me stand."

"You made *yourself* look like a fool," Morgan said. "All that damned magician did was give you enough rope to hang yourself with. None in the Inner Circle wanted you on that bridge, but I convinced the Order to give you another chance, and what happens? You go off half-cocked, as usual. It's bad enough you brought those miscreants into our sanctuary, bad enough that Khafre Hall is in rubble and the Order's most important artifacts are missing. But to go and draw even more attention to the situation? You've embarrassed the entire family. You've embarrassed *me*."

You've embarrassed yourself. Jack, at least, had tried to do something. If the Order had given Jack the access he'd wanted months ago, Harte Darrigan wouldn't have been an issue. "I'll find Darrigan," he told Morgan. "I'll get back the Book and the artifacts."

"Darrigan is dead," Morgan said flatly.

"Dead?" *No. That couldn't be.* Not when Jack had plans to kill the magician himself.

"Jumped from the bridge right after you were taken away. If he had the Order's possessions, he either hid them or gave them to someone else. Not that it matters . . . We'll find the artifacts sooner or later."

"I'll help—"

"No," Morgan said bluntly, cutting him off. "You won't. You're finished. Your membership to the Order has been revoked."

The finality in his uncle's tone told Jack that it wasn't worth it to try explaining or apologizing. Especially not when his uncle had *that* look on his face. He would just have to bide his time, as he had after the fiasco in Greece. Eventually his uncle would cool off, and Jack would make them all understand.

"Further," Morgan continued, "you will be leaving the city *imme-diately*. Your bags have already been packed and are waiting at your mother's house. Once we arrive, you will have exactly thirty minutes to clean yourself up and say your good-byes. When you're presentable, you'll be taken to the train station."

Jack huffed. "You can't force me to leave."

Morgan's eyes narrowed. "Perhaps not. But tell me, how do you plan to live? Your parents have decided they will not be paying any more of your bills until and unless you prove yourself. The town house you leased will need to be paid for. The carousing you do—the drinking and the whoring—will now be yours to deal with. Who do you think will hire you in this town after the embarrassment of yesterday?"

Utter disbelief made Jack's head feel as though it were in a fog. His uncle had ruined him. Morgan had turned Jack's own parents against him, and with nothing more than a word, he could make sure no one in the city would have Jack. The truth of his own impotence burned. "And where will I be going?" he asked, his own voice sounding very far away from himself.

"Where you should have gone yesterday—the job is still waiting for you in Cleveland, just as it was before the fiasco on the bridge."

"And how long will I be working there?" Jack asked flatly.

"Indefinitely." Morgan picked up a newspaper that was sitting on the carriage bench next to him and opened it with a snap. The front-page headline glared darkly at him: THE MAGICIAN'S TRAGIC TUMBLE. Beneath the words was an etching of Darrigan himself, staring from the surface of the newsprint, his half smile mocking Jack.

Indefinitely. "That's it, then? I'm exiled."

"Don't be so damned dramatic," Morgan growled from behind the paper.

Once, Morgan's authority would have made Jack tremble, but now there was something about the sneering quality of J. P. Morgan's voice that made Jack bristle. *They still don't understand.* The Inner Circle of the Order, with their comfortable boardrooms and palatial mansions on Fifth Avenue, saw themselves as kings—as untouchable. They didn't realize that peasants start every revolution, and when the peasants rise up, royal heads are the first to roll.

But Jack knew. He understood.

"You're making a mistake," Jack said coldly. "You have no idea what these maggots are capable of. You have no idea the threats they pose."

With another violent snap, Morgan brought his newspaper down, practically tearing it across his lap, and glared at Jack. "Watch yourself, boy."

"I am *not* a boy," Jack said through gritted teeth. "I've been studying the occult arts, learning everything I can to understand the hermetical sciences and the threats the old magic poses, and still you refuse to recognize the progress I've made or to see me as an equal."

"That's because you are *not* an equal," Morgan said, his voice absolutely cold in its dismissal. "You imagine yourself the hero of some grand drama, but you are not even the fool. Do you honestly believe the Order is not aware of the growing threats? You're not the only one who has seen that Ellis Island has turned out to be a disappointment, that every new arrival threatens the very fabric of our society. Why do you think we've organized the Conclave?" Morgan shook his head, clearly disgusted. "You are nothing more than an insolent pup, too concerned with your own ego to see how little you know. The Inner Circle's work does not concern you, and yet your own arrogance and recklessness have cost more than you can even imagine."

"But the Mageus—"

"The Mageus are *our* concern, not yours. You think yourself somehow more aware, more *intelligent* than men who have years of experience beyond yours?" he scoffed.

"The Order is too focused on Manhattan. It doesn't realize—"

"The work of the Order goes *far* beyond keeping a few ragged immigrants in their place in the Bowery. You imagine me an old man, out of touch with the realities of the world, but *you* are the one who does not understand. The country is at a turning point. Not just our city, but the *country* as a whole, and there are more forces at work than you can comprehend, more forces than you are even *aware* of."

He leaned forward slightly, a movement more menacing than conspiratorial. "The Order has a plan—or we had one before Darrigan mangled it. The Conclave at the end of the year was to be our crowning achievement, a meeting to bring together all the branches of our brotherhood, and the Order was to prove our dominance—our readiness to lead—and once and for all to wipe the dangers of feral magic from our shores. But you brought vipers into our midst. Now, because of you, everything we have worked for is at risk."

"So let me stay," Jack demanded. "I have knowledge that could be useful. Let me help you. My machine—"

"Enough!" Morgan's bulbous nose twitched, as though he smelled something rotten. "You've done more than enough. Go to Cleveland. Keep your head down. Look around and learn a thing or two about how the world *really* works. And perhaps, if you manage not to make an even bigger ass of yourself, we'll let you come back and visit for Christmas."

BLOOD AND WATER

1902—New York

Viola Vaccarelli pretended to examine the produce of one of the Mott Street vendors as she watched the door of the church across the street. The shop's owner, an older man with his long, graying hair plaited neatly down his back, stood at the doorway watching her warily. She wondered if this was what Jianyu would look like as the years passed. But the memory of Jianyu, who Dolph had trusted to be his spy—and who had abandoned them all on the bridge—made Viola's thoughts turn dark.

When the shopkeeper took a step back, Viola realized that she had been scowling. To make amends, she pulled her mouth into a feeble attempt at a smile. The man blinked, his brow creasing even more, as though he knew her for the predator she was.

Basta. Let him be nervous. A tiger didn't apologize for its teeth, and Viola didn't have time to make nice with some stranger. She offered him a few coins for the ripe pear she'd selected, and he reached out tentatively to take them.

Across the street, the side door of the church opened and the first of the worshippers appeared. Viola stepped away from the old man, not bothering to wait for her change, and watched as a stream of women emerged from the side entrance of the church. They were mostly older, though there were a few younger women whose faces were already starting to show the same lines that mapped over their mothers'. They were the unmarried daughters—girls who had been unfortunate in their search for a husband and who still lived under their families' roof and rule. Viola had refused that future. She had turned her back on her family and on every expectation they held for her.

And now she would have to pay for it.

The older women wore the uniform of their generation: sturdy dark skirts, heavy, shapeless cloaks, and a fazzoletto copricapo made from lace or plain linen to cover their heads and preserve their modesty and humility before the lord and everyone else in the neighborhood. Viola had also pulled a scarf over her dark hair for the morning, but she had little interest in modesty. Concealment was her aim.

To anyone else, the line of Italian women might have seemed indistinguishable, but Viola could have picked out her mother in a crowd of a thousand such women. The way her mother's heavy body swayed as she turned west toward the blocks of Mulberry Street had been the rhythm of Viola's childhood.

It had been three years since Viola had spoken to her mother or had even *seen* any of her family, though they lived no more than a few blocks from the Bella Strega. But in the streets of the Bowery, a few blocks were the difference between the safety of home and crossing the wrong gang. Not that Viola worried too much about that . . . She could take care of herself and anyone else who might think to bother her.

Her mother's sturdy hands fluttered like birds as she spoke to the woman who walked beside her. Those hands could strangle a chicken or make the most delicate casarecce. They could wipe away a tear . . . or leave a mark that stung for days.

I should leave her be. She would find another way.

Without thinking, Viola reached for the blade she always kept at her side, the stiletto she'd named Libitina after the Roman goddess of funerals . . . and found it missing. She had launched it at Nibsy Lorcan the day before to protect Esta, the girl she had begrudgingly come to like. But in the confusion of the bridge, Viola had not been able to retrieve it. Now Esta was gone—the girl had disappeared as though she'd never existed—and so was Libitina, into Nibsy Lorcan's keeping. Viola was on her own, without friends or allies, but it was the absence of the knife she felt most acutely, as though she'd lost a part of herself.

She would get back her blade . . . eventually. For the time being, Libitina's replacement was secure in the sheath strapped against her thigh. It wasn't the same, though. The steel of *this* blade didn't speak to her in the same way, and the unfamiliar weight of the knife felt wrong, as though a matter of a few grams could leave Viola herself unbalanced.

But Viola had needed *something* to protect herself. The Bowery was in chaos. The already-corrupt police force had become more emboldened in the past few days. Under the direction of the Order, they'd been ransacking the lower part of Manhattan to find the Mageus who had stolen the Order's treasures from Khafre Hall. Viola had been part of that team. Led by Dolph Saunders, they had been on a mission to take the Ars Arcana, a book with untold power. Dolph had believed the Book could restore magic and free them all from the Order's control—and from the Brink.

Now Dolph was dead, and the thought of him laid out, pale and lifeless, on the bar top of the Strega still had the power to rob Viola of breath. He'd been a true friend to her, and she'd come to trust him—to depend upon his steadiness—even after her life had taught her never to trust. But Dolph was gone, along with the Book and any dream of freedom or a future different from the present's drudgery.

That double-crossing cazzo of a magician, Harte Darrigan, had ruined everything when he'd taken the Book from her in the bowels of Khafre Hall, leaving Viola looking the fool. Because of him, the Devil's Own had viewed her with suspicion shining in their eyes after they'd discovered that the sack she'd carried contained nothing of value. And there was no way to fix her mistakes. Darrigan had taken any hope of recovering the Book with him to his watery grave when he'd jumped from the bridge.

If that wasn't bad enough, on the bridge, Viola had made everything worse. She'd known that Nibsy suspected Esta of being in league with Darrigan. She had specific instructions to make sure *neither* of them got away, but when Nibsy raised a gun to Esta's throat, Viola had acted without thinking. She'd attacked the boy to save Esta—because it was what Tilly would have expected of her. And because it was what her own instincts screamed for her to do.

But her actions meant that she couldn't return to the Strega, not so long as Nibsy Lorcan had the loyalty of Dolph's crew.

Without Dolph, Viola had no one to stand between her and the dangers of the Bowery. Without the Book, she had no leverage with the Devil's Own. She certainly couldn't trust Nibsy to forgive her for skewering him.

Not that she particularly cared. She'd never liked the kid anyway.

But the Strega had been her home. The Devil's Own had been a family for her, one that had respected her skill and accepted her as she was. Perhaps the Book was gone, but she would do what she must to prove that she had not betrayed their trust. Even without the Book, she could finish what Dolph started. She would do everything in her power to destroy the Order.

To do that, she would need help. There was only one person she could think of who could protect her from the patrols—her older brother, Paolo. Going to Paolo had an added benefit: There were whispers in the streets that the Five Pointers were doing the Order's bidding now as well as Tammany's.

Paolo wasn't likely to forgive Viola for abandoning the family, and especially not for escaping his control and working for Dolph, a man he considered an enemy. Still, if her dear brother could help her get closer to the Order, she would suffer what she must. Which was why she had come to this place, to wait for her mother, the one person who might be able to protect her from Paolo's wrath.

Viola handed the pear she'd just purchased to a dirty-looking urchin on the corner and ran to catch up to her mother. "Mamma!" But the title was tossed around the streets of the Bowery so often that her mother didn't react, not until Viola used her first name:

"Pasqualina!"

Her mother turned then, at the sound of her name being shouted over the din of the street. It took a moment before her mother's dark eyes registered understanding, and Viola could read every emotion that flashed across her mother's face: shock, hope, then realization . . . and caution.

After murmuring something to her companion, who gave Viola a brooding, distrustful look before heading on her way alone, Viola's mother frowned at her. But she stopped walking and waited for Viola.

Her throat tight with a tenderness she thought she had long ago killed as surely as any life she'd taken with a blade, Viola approached her mother slowly until the two of them were standing an arm's distance apart.

"Viola?" Her mother lifted a hand as though to caress her daughter's cheek, but she did not finish bridging the distance between them. A moment passed, long and awful, and then her mother's hand dropped, limp at her side.

Viola nodded, unable to speak. For all her family had done, for all the anger Viola still felt, she'd missed her mother. Missed them all. Missed, even, the girl she had once been with them.

Her mother's expression faltered. "What do you want?" Spoken in the Sicilian of Viola's childhood, her mother's words sounded like a home-coming. But her mother's tone was like her eyes—flat and cold.

Viola had expected this. After all, she had committed the cardinal sin—she had abandoned her family. She had betrayed her brother and refused his authority, and maybe worst of all, she'd dared to claim a life that was more than any *good* woman would want for herself.

It didn't matter that Viola had long since considered herself a good woman. Her mother's judgment still stung. She had been on the receiving end of that same expression a hundred times as a girl, but she, who had learned to kill without regret, had never grown immune to it.

Viola dropped her eyes, forced herself to bow her head in the show of the submission expected of her. "I want to come home, Mamma."

"Home?"

Viola glanced up to find her mother's thick brows raised. "I want to come back to the family."

At first her mother didn't speak. She studied Viola instead with the same critical eye she often turned on a piece of bruised fruit at the market right before she haggled for a lower price.

"I was wrong," Viola said softly, keeping her head down, her shoulders bowed. "You were right about me—too headstrong and filled with my own importance. I've learned what it means to be without your family." The words tasted like ash in her mouth, but they were not a lie. Under Dolph's protection, Viola had learned what it meant to be without the expectations, demands, and restrictions her family imposed upon her.

"More like you got yourself in trouble," her mother said flatly, glancing down at Viola's belly. "Who is he?"

Viola frowned. "There is no man."

"I don't believe you."

"You see what's happening, no? The fires, the brawling in the streets? I see now how stupid I was to think I could go without my family—il sangue non é acqua."

Her mother's mouth pinched tight, and her eyes narrowed. "I tell you that your whole life, and now you listen? After it's too late?"

"I'm still your blood," Viola said softly, forcing a meekness into her voice that felt like a betrayal to everything she was.

Viola hadn't understood the truth of that phrase until she'd tried to leave her family behind. No matter the life she'd tried to claim for herself, she was always Paul Kelly's sister—and she always would be.

No, blood wasn't water. Blood left a stain.

"Why do you come to *me*? Why not go to Paolo, as you should? He's head of the family now," her mother said, crossing herself as she looked up to the sky, as though Viola's father might appear sanctified on the clouds above. "You need *his* blessing, not mine."

"I *want* to go to him," Viola said, twisting her hands in her skirts, making a show of nerves, and hating herself for it—not for the lie, but for the display of weakness when she had promised herself to always be strong. "But I'm not sure how to make amends for what I've done. Paolo listens to you, Mamma. You have his ear. If you tell him to forgive me, he will."

Her mother's jaw tightened, her face flushing red. "I see. . . . You come back to me because you need my help? After all you've done to us . . . to *me*—" Her mother's voice broke. "You make me a disgrace." Shaking her head, Viola's mother turned to go, but as she took a step down from the sidewalk into the street, she gasped and nearly tumbled to her knees.

Viola caught her mother before the older woman could hit the ground and pulled her to her feet. Pasqualina Vaccarelli was a stout, sturdy woman, but Viola could feel her mother's fragility, the aging that had taken some of her mother's vitality over the past three years.

It was a risk to use her affinity here, in the open—especially with how dangerous everything had become—but Viola pushed her power into her mother, feeling for the source of the pain and finding it immediately. The gout in her mother's joints had grown so much worse, and without hesitation, Viola directed her affinity toward it, clearing the joints that had gone stiff.

Her mother gasped, the old woman's dark eyes meeting her daughter's as Viola finished and withdrew her hands. Viola's blood felt warm, her skin alive with the flexing of her magic. *This* was what she had been meant for. Her god had given her this gift for life, not for the deaths her brother had forced upon her.

With a look of mingled surprised and relief, her mother raised a hand calloused by years of work and laid it against Viola's cheek. Her mouth was still turned down and her eyes were still stern, but there was gratitude in her mother's expression now as well. "I could have used you these past years."

"I know, Mamma," Viola said, placing her hand atop her mother's as she blinked back the prickling of tears. "I missed you, too."

This, at least, was no lie. She did miss the mother she'd once known, the woman who used to sing as she hung out the wash, who had tried to teach Viola how to knead dough until it became supple, and how to press linen with her bare hands until it was smooth. Those lessons had never stuck. No matter how she tried, Viola hadn't been built for that life. Her hands had been made to hold a blade, to wield magic. Her family had done everything they could to force her into the mold they believed was right. In the end, their expectations had just forced her away.

But now she was back. She would bend to their expectations, but she was older now. Stronger. She would not let them break her.

Her mother withdrew her hand. "I'll talk to your brother."

"Thank you—"

Her mother held up a hand to stop Viola's words. "Don't thank me. I make no guarantee. You'll have to be ready to take whatever penance Paolo gives you . . . *whatever* he demands of you."

Viola bowed her head to hide her disgust. Her mother had no idea what her *darling Paolino* was capable of. Viola's mother knew only that he ran a boxing club called the New Brighton and a restaurant called the Little Naples Cafe. She understood that he knew the big men in the city, but she had no idea that her son was one of the most powerful and dangerous gang bosses on the Lower East Side or what sins Viola's brother had demanded that Viola commit.

Viola wondered if her mother would have cared had she seen the split lip and blackened eyes she wore the first time she found her way into the safe haven of the Strega.

"Come." Without another word, Viola's mother began walking.

"Where are we going?" Viola asked, picturing the cramped rooms she had grown up in. But her mother was not heading in the direction of her childhood tenement.

Her mother turned back to her. "I thought you wanted me to speak with Paolo?"

"We're going now?"

Her mother gave her a dark look tinged with suspicion. "You want we should wait?"

Yes. Viola needed time to prepare, time to ready herself for whatever her sadist of a brother had in store. But it was clear that her mother would offer only once. "No. Of course not, Mamma. Now is perfect." She ducked her head in thanks. *Submissive.* "Thank you, Mamma."

"Don't thank me so quickly," her mother said with a frown. "You still have to talk to Paolo."

MOTHER OF EXILES

The early morning sky was heavy with clouds, and a thick mist coated the water as the ferry slouched through the Upper Bay that separated Brooklyn from New Jersey. At the stern of the ship, Esta Filosik looked like any other passenger. Her long, dark hair had been pulled back in an unremarkable style, and the worn skirt and heavy, faded traveling cloak were the sort of garments that encouraged the eye to glide past without noticing their wearer. She'd torn the hem out of the skirt to lengthen it, but otherwise the pieces fit well enough, considering that she'd liberated them from an unwatched clothesline that morning. But beneath the coarse material and rumpled wool, Esta carried a stone that could change time and a Book that could change the world itself.

She might have appeared at ease, uninterested in the far-off city skyline, now no more than a shadow in the hazy distance behind them, but Esta's attention was sharp, aware of the few other passengers. She had positioned herself so that she could watch for any sign of danger and also so that no one could tell how much she needed the railing behind her for support.

The ship churned through the dark waters, coming up alongside Liberty Island—though it wouldn't be called that for another fifty years—and the lady herself loomed over them, a dark shadow of burnished copper. It was the closest Esta had ever been to the statue, but even this close, it was smaller than she'd expected. Unimpressive, considering how much it was supposed to symbolize. But then, Esta knew better than most that the symbolism was as hollow as the statue. For those like herself—those with the old magic—the lady's bright torch should have served as a warning, not a beacon, for what they'd find on these shores.

She wondered if her disappointment in the statue was an omen of things to come. Maybe the world she'd never thought to see would be equally small and unimpressive once she was finally in it.

Somehow, she doubted it would be that easy. The world was wide and vast and, for Esta, unknown. She knew everything about the city, but beyond it? She'd be working blind.

But she wouldn't be alone.

Standing beside her at the railing was Harte Darrigan, one-time magician and consummate con man. His cap covered his dark hair and shadowed his distinctive storm-gray eyes, making him look ordinary, unassuming . . . like any other traveler. He kept it pulled low over his forehead and turned his back to the other passengers so that no one would recognize him.

Without letting Harte know she was studying him, Esta watched him out of the corner of her eye. When the bottom had fallen out of her world, she'd made the choice to come back because she'd wanted to save him. Yes, she needed an ally, someone who would stand with her in the battles to come. But she'd come back here, to this time and place, because she'd wanted that ally to be *him*. Because of who he was and what he'd done for her. And because of who she was with him.

But his mood was as unreadable now as it had been ever since she'd woken in the early morning to find him watching her. He must have waited up all night, because when she'd finally awoken in that unfamiliar boardinghouse room in Brooklyn, he was sitting in a rickety chair at the end of the narrow bed, his elbows propped on his knees and his eyes ringed by dark circles and filled with worry. How he had managed to get them both through those final few yards of the Brink, she still didn't know.

She wanted to ask him. She wanted to ask so many things—about the darkness she had seen on the bridge, the way the inky black had seemed to bleed into everything. She wanted to know if he'd seen it too. Most of all, she wanted to lean into him and to take what support and warmth she could from his presence. But the way he had been looking at her had made her pause. She'd seen admiration in his eyes and frustration, distrust, and even disgust, but he'd never before looked at her like she was some fragile, broken thing.

At the moment he wasn't looking at her at all, though. As the boat churned onward, Harte's eyes were trained on the receding horizon and on the city that had been their prison for so long. Every lie he told, every con he ran, and every betrayal he'd committed had been to escape that island, yet there was no victory in his expression now that freedom was his. Instead, Harte's jaw was taut, his mouth pulled flat and hard, and his posture was rigid, as though waiting for the next attack.

Without warning, the somber note of the ferry broke the early morning calm, drowning out the noise of the rattling engines and the soft, steadily churning water. Esta flinched at the sound, and she couldn't stop herself from shivering a bit from the brisk wind—or from the memory of that darkness bleeding into the world, obliterating the light. Obliterating *everything*.

"You okay?" Harte asked, turning toward her with worry shadowing his features. His eyes searched over her, as though he was waiting for the moment he would need to catch her again when she collapsed.

But she wouldn't collapse. She wouldn't *allow* herself to be that weak. And she hated his hovering. "I'm just a little jumpy."

She thought Harte was about to reach for her. Before he could, she straightened and pulled back a little. If they were to be partners, they would be equals. She couldn't—*wouldn't*—allow her current weakness to be a liability.

Harte frowned and kept his hands at his sides, but Esta didn't miss the way his fingers curled into fists. Skilled liar that he was, he couldn't hide the hurt that flashed across his features any more than he could completely mask the worry etched into his expression every time he glanced at her.

Esta forced herself to ignore that, too, and focused on staying upright. On making herself appear stronger than she felt. *Confident.*

Harte gave her another long look before finally turning back to watch the land recede into the distance. She did the same, but her concentration was on what waited for them when the ship finally docked.

They had an impossible task ahead of them: to find four stones now scattered across a continent, thanks to Harte. Like Ishtar's Key—the stone Esta wore in a cuff around her upper arm—the stones had once been in the possession of the Order. The Dragon's Eye, the Djinni's Star, the Delphi's Tear, and the Pharaoh's Heart. They had been created when Isaac Newton imbued five ancient artifacts with the power of Mageus whose affinities happened to align with the elements. He'd been trying to control the power in the Book that was currently tucked into Esta's skirt, but he hadn't been able to. After Newton had suffered a nervous breakdown, he'd entrusted the artifacts and the Book to the Order, who later had used them to create the Brink and establish their power in the city—and to keep Mageus trapped on the island and sub-jugated under the Order's control. But Dolph Saunders and his gang had changed that.

Still, even if she and Harte managed to navigate the far-flung world, to find the stones and retrieve them, they still had to figure out how to *use* them to get the Book's power out of Harte and to free the Mageus of the city without destroying the Brink. Because, in the greatest of ironies, the Brink also kept the magic it took. If they destroyed the Brink, they risked destroying magic itself—and all Mageus along with it.

Esta was jarred from her thoughts when the boat lurched as it came up against the dock. Another blast of the horn, and the engines went silent. The few passengers around them began making their way toward the stairs.

"Ready?" Harte asked, his voice too soft, his eyes too concerned.

That worry sealed it for her. She took another moment to look at the skyline in the distance before turning to him. "I was thinking—"

"A dangerous proposition," he drawled. But his eyes weren't smiling. Not like they should have been. He was still too worried about her, and she knew enough to know that fear like that was a luxury they couldn't afford. Especially with all that was on the line.

"I think we should split up," Esta said.

"Split up?" he asked, surprised.

"I can't get us tickets to Chicago with you in the way. You keep looking at me like I'm about to fall over. People will notice."

"Maybe I keep looking at you like that because you look like you're having trouble staying upright."

"I'm fine," she said, not quite meeting his eyes.

"You think I don't know that you've been leaning on that railing like it's some kind of crutch?"

She ignored the truth—and the irritation—in his statement. "I can't lift a couple of tickets with you following me around."

Harte opened his mouth to argue, but she beat him to it.

"Besides, you're supposed to be dead," she reminded him. "The one thing we have going for us is that the Order isn't looking for you. We can't afford for someone to recognize either one of us in there, and that's more likely to happen if we're together."

He studied her for a moment. "You're probably right—"

"I usually am."

"—but I have one condition."

"What's that?" she asked, not at all liking the crafty expression in his eyes.

He held out his hand. "Give me the Book."

"What?" She pulled back. The Book was the reason he'd planned to double-cross Dolph's gang in the first place, and for a moment she wondered if she'd been stupid to think there was something between them.

"You want to split up, fine. We'll split up. But I get to carry the Book."

"You don't trust me," she said, ignoring the flicker of hurt. After all she'd risked for him . . . But what had she expected? He was a con man, a liar. It was part of what she admired in him, wasn't it? She wouldn't have wanted him to be anything else.

"I trust you as much as you trust me," he told her, a non-answer if ever there was one.

"After all I did for you . . ." She pretended to be more irritated than she felt. In truth, she couldn't blame him. She would have done the exact same thing. And there was something comforting in falling back into their old roles, that well-worn distrust that had kept them from falling too easily into each other.

"You have the cuff with the first stone," he told her. "If I'm holding the Book, we'll be even. Plus, if either one of us runs into trouble, we won't be putting both of the things we have at risk."

She could argue. She probably *should*. But Esta understood implicitly that agreeing to his demand would be a step toward solidifying their partnership. Whatever she might feel for Harte paled in comparison to all that they had left to do. Or so she told herself. Besides, if he already had the power of the Book inside of him, he didn't really need the Book itself, did he? What he needed was the stone she wore in the cuff beneath her sleeve, and he wasn't asking for that.

"Fine." She brushed off her disappointment as she slipped the Book from where she'd kept it within her cloak and held it out to him.

A small tome of dark, cracked leather, the Ars Arcana didn't look like much. Even with the strange geometric markings on the cover, there was nothing overtly remarkable about it. Maybe that was because the power of it was no longer held within its pages. Or maybe that was just the way of things—maybe power didn't always appear the way you expected it to.

Harte took it from her, and the moment his long fingers wrapped around the leather binding, she thought she saw the strange colors flash in his eyes again. But if they'd even been there at all, the colors were gone before she could decide.

He tucked the Book into his jacket and then adjusted the brim of his cap again. "You go first. I'll follow in a minute."

"We should decide on a place to meet."

"I'll find you." His eyes met hers, steady. "Get us a couple of tickets and wait for me on the platform of the first train to Chicago."

To keep the artifacts out of the hands of Nibsy Lorcan, Harte had sent most of them out of the city. To keep the Order from finding them, he'd scattered the artifacts. The first stone waited in Chicago, where one of Harte's old vaudeville friends, Julien Eltinge, was performing. They would be one day behind it, and there was a small chance they might even be able to get it before Julien received the package.

But Chicago was only the first of their stops. After Chicago, there was Bill Pickett, a cowboy in a traveling rodeo show who had the dagger. The crown had been sent to some distant family in San Francisco, which was an entire continent away. Worse, she and Harte weren't the only ones after the Order's artifacts or the only ones who needed the secrets of the Book. They would never be able to find them all before Logan appeared in New York in a week, where Esta had left him, and told Nibsy everything—about the future, about who Esta really was, and about every one of her weaknesses.

But they would go as quickly as they could. When they had the four, they would return to the city, where the last stone waited, protected by Jianyu, and then they would fight alongside those they'd left behind.

If there's anyone left.

"I guess I'll see you in a bit, then?" *God,* she hated how the rasp in her voice betrayed every worry that was running through her head and every hope that she was unwilling to admit.

Esta didn't do worry. She didn't do nerves or second-guessing or regrets. And she wasn't about to start, no matter how pretty Harte Darrigan's gray eyes might be or how weak she still felt from whatever had happened to her as she'd crossed the Brink. The only way through was through—and she didn't need anyone to carry her.

Proving that much to herself as well as to him, she started to go, but he caught her wrist gently. She could have pulled away from him if she'd wanted to, but the pressure of his hand gripping hers was reassuring, so she allowed herself the moment of comfort.

"I'm not going anywhere, Esta," he told her, his eyes serious. "Not until we finish this."

And then he'll be gone.

The unexpected sentimentality of the thought startled her. She couldn't allow herself to become so soft. Hadn't Harte just made that much clear? All that could matter now was fixing her mistakes—or the mistakes that she *could* fix, at least. The others—*and there have been so many*—she would just have to learn to live with. She would free the Book before its power could tear Harte apart, and then she would use it to destroy the Order, the rich men who preyed on the vulnerable. Esta would finish the job that Dolph Saunders had begun, even if she had to sacrifice herself to do it.

And before it was over, she would make Nibsy Lorcan pay—for Dakari, the one person who had always been a friend to her. For Dolph, the father she had not been allowed to know, and for Leena, the mother she would *never* know.

The first step was getting the stones back, and they would start in Chicago. *One step at a time. Nothing is more important than the job.*

Esta cringed at how quickly Professor Lachlan's words had come to her. *No,* she corrected herself. *Nibsy's words.* They were the words of a traitor, *not* a mentor and definitely not a father. She didn't have to live by them any longer, and she certainly didn't want them in her head.

Pulling her hand out of Harte's without another word, Esta set off across the upper deck. She kept her head down as she quickened her steps to catch up to the meager stream of early morning passengers making their way from the docks into the larger, busier train terminal. She glanced back just before she stepped through the wide doors, but Harte was nowhere in sight.

THE ARS ARCANA

1902—New York

Harte Darrigan had watched plenty of people walk away from him over the course of his brief life. He'd watched stage managers shut doors in his face and audiences stand up and leave when his act failed to impress them. He'd watched the guys he'd run wild with when he was just a kid turn away and pretend they didn't know him when he'd been forced to take the Five Pointers mark. He'd even watched his mother turn her back on him when he wasn't more than twelve . . . though he wouldn't deny that he'd deserved it. But somehow, watching Esta walk away made him want to howl, to run after her and tell her he'd changed his mind.

It was an impulse he didn't completely trust.

Yes, he admired Esta—for her talent and her determination. For the way she always met his eyes straight on, shoulders back, unafraid of what might come. His equal—his *better*, perhaps—in every way.

Of course, he *liked* her as well—for her sharp sense of humor and the flash in her eyes when she was angry. He liked her steadfastness and loyalty to those she cared about. And he liked that even when she was lying right to his face, she never pretended to be anything other than what she was.

He wouldn't say he loved her. No . . . He had seen what love had done to his mother and to Dolph. To Harte, the very word was a con—a lie that people told themselves and others to cover the truth. When people said love, what they really meant was dependency. Obsession. Weakness.

So no, he would not say he loved Esta, but he could admit that he wanted her. He could maybe, *maybe* even admit that he needed her. But he would only ever admit it to himself.

Now, though, that desire he felt for her—the wanting and needing— was a craving stronger, *darker* than it had ever been. Harte trusted it even less, because it wasn't entirely his own. In the furthest recesses of his mind, he could feel the power that had once been contained in the Book gathering its strength and pressing at his very soul, like some beaked and taloned creature about to hatch.

As Esta walked away from him, Harte's hands gripped the railing of the boat. He had to hold himself steady as he felt that power lash out within him, because it had already discovered the truth—it had already learned that *she* was his weakness.

If he released his hold on the railing, he would follow her, which was what the power trapped within him wanted more than anything. If he followed her as *he* wanted to, it would be that much harder to press the power down, to keep himself whole . . . and to keep Esta safe. Because if the power took hold of him, if he allowed it to reach for her—for all that she was and all that she could be—its razor-tipped claws would claim her. And it would destroy her.

Had Harte known what the Book was, he wouldn't have been so eager to get his hands on it. When Dolph Saunders had tempted him with the prospect of a way out of the city, he hadn't imagined that his own body and mind could become a prison more absolute than the island he'd been born on. He certainly hadn't expected the Book they stole from the Order to be a living thing—no one had. Because if any of the others—Dolph or Nibsy or the rest—had any idea of what the Book *really* contained, they never would have let him near it.

Days ago, everything had seemed clearer, simple even. In the bowels of Khafre Hall, his plan had been straightforward. If he took the Book from Dolph's gang, he would have the freedom he'd wanted for so long, and Nibsy Lorcan—the double-crossing rat—wouldn't be able to use it for his own ends. He'd seen Nibsy's plan, the way he would use the Book to control Mageus and use the Mageus under his control to eradicate Sundren. It would be a world safe for the old magic, but the only one with any freedom in it would be Nibsy himself.

But it hadn't only been Nibsy that Harte had been worried about. Stealing the Book from the Order also meant that Jack Grew would never be able to use it to finish the monstrous machine he was building, the one that could wipe magic from the earth. Too bad that the moment Harte's hands had brushed that crackled leather, all those plans had changed.

He was used to keeping himself away from others. Most people didn't realize how much of themselves they projected, so Harte had long become accustomed to pulling his affinity inward and keeping himself closed off. He hated being caught off guard by the onslaught of jumbled images and feelings and thoughts that most people shoved freely into the world. But he hadn't thought to prepare himself for the Book.

When his skin had made contact with the ancient, cracked cover, he'd realized his mistake. He'd felt a hot, searing energy enter him—a magic with a power like nothing he had ever experienced.

Then the screaming had started.

It had taken only seconds, but those seconds had felt like a never-ending barrage of sound and impressions, an incoherent jumble of languages he should not have been able to understand. But Harte never needed to know the words to understand a person's heart and mind, and touching the Book had been like reading a person.

Actually, it had been far easier. It was as though the power within the Book had been waiting for that moment—waiting for *him* to become its living body. He'd understood almost immediately that the Book was more than any one of them had predicted. It was power. It was wrath. It was the beating heart of magic in the world, and it wanted nothing more and nothing less than to be set free. To become. To *consume*.

And what it wanted most to consume was Esta.

Fortunately, the power he'd unwittingly freed was still weakened by centuries of imprisonment. Harte could still push it down and lock it away when he focused. But the power was growing stronger every day, and he knew that he wouldn't be able to suppress it forever. He hadn't *planned* to.

Harte had planned to die. He hadn't known for sure whether throwing himself from the bridge would silence the clamoring voices, but he'd figured that at least it would mean they couldn't use him as their pawn. But then Jianyu had shown up at the docks the night before the bridge and offered him another way.

By then Harte had already scattered the artifacts, sending most of them away from the city to keep them out of Nibsy's reach. He hadn't realized until it was too late that he could have used them to control the Book's power. He *certainly* hadn't expected Esta to return.

Now stopping Nibsy and the Order and keeping Esta safe depended on controlling it. To do that, they needed the artifacts. But retrieving them meant leaving people behind—his mother, for one. Jianyu, for another. And maybe most worrisome of all, it meant leaving one of the stones.

He'd given one to Cela because he didn't have any other way to repay her for what he'd done when he'd forced his dying mother upon her with his affinity. The ring had been the least obtrusive of the Order's pieces, other than maybe the cuff that he'd given to Esta. Harte had known even then that it wasn't a good enough trade, but now that Esta had returned, he truly understood the danger he'd put Cela in—especially if the boy Esta had brought back with her could find anything. He could only hope that the command he'd planted in her mind with his affinity would be enough to help Cela evade danger until Jianyu could protect her and the stone.

Harte waited a while before he released his hold on the railing, long enough that Esta was out of sight and the crewman on the ferry was beginning to pay more attention to him than was safe.

When he stepped from the boat onto the solidness of the New Jersey soil, he tested himself to make sure that the power within him was still quiet, pushed down deep. It was a new state, but for Harte, who had been trapped on the island of Manhattan his entire life, it might as well have been a new continent.

Around him, people bustled onward, gathering their bags and their children as they moved toward the terminal entrance. He joined them, keeping his cap low, his eyes down, allowing himself to be caught up in the current. He sensed the excitement of some heading off toward new places and the weariness of others making the same trip they'd made countless times before. All of them were oblivious to the miracle it was that they could choose to purchase a ticket, step onto a train, and arrive somewhere else. For Harte, that miracle was one he would never take for granted, however much time he had left.

As he was carried along by the crowd, he almost felt as though the world could be his. Perhaps their mission might actually work and a different future could be possible. But then he heard a whispering begin to grow louder in the recesses of his mind. The dark choir merged into a single voice, one that was speaking in a language he should not have recognized but understood nonetheless. A single word that held untold meaning.

Soon.

THE SIREN

1902—New York

The sun was already climbing into the sky as the streetcar rumbled north through the city. Jianyu kept himself tucked back into a corner, careful not to touch anyone and reveal his presence, until they reached the stop at Broadway, close to Wallack's Theatre, where Harte Darrigan had once performed. Cela's neighbors believed she'd fled from the house because she was guilty of the fire, but Jianyu suspected otherwise. He was not sure where she would go, but he hoped she would eventually return here, to the theater where she worked.

Keeping the light around him was easier now, with the morning sun providing ample threads for him to grasp and open around him. When he reached Wallack's, Jianyu looked up to find familiar eyes watching him from above.

It was only a painting, a large multistoried advertisement for the variety acts to be found inside, but Harte Darrigan's gaze seemed to be steady on Jianyu—though whether it felt like a warning or encouragement, he could not have said.

Still concealed by his affinity, Jianyu surveyed the theater from across the street. He could wait and watch for Cela to arrive, but he decided that inside there might be some hint of where else she would go. Keeping his affinity close, he crossed the street to the stage door. After picking the lock, he slipped into the darkened theater and began searching for some sign of Cela in the area backstage.

Inside, the theater waited, dark and silent. Jianyu had never set foot in Wallack's before, or any of the Broadway houses that advertised their shows on bright electric marquees. He had taken in a show at the Bowery Theatre once, when he had first arrived in the city, but it had been a noisy, raucous affair in a house tattered and broken by the usual crowd. Wallack's was different. It looked like a palace, and Jianyu had a feeling that it would still feel like one, even when the house was full.

He followed the narrow halls back, deeper into the theater, passing dressing room after dressing room. But Cela was not a performer. She would not be given her name on a door. No . . . she would be somewhere else, somewhere quieter. He continued on in the darkness until he came to steps that led down into the belly of the building.

The cellar smelled of dust and mold, of freshly cut wood and the sharpness of paint. It was darker there, but darkness was rarely without some strands of light within it. He took out the bronze mirror disks that helped him focus his affinity and used them to open the meager strands of light, keeping himself concealed as he moved through the cellar.

Jianyu saw the light that flickered behind him before he heard the voice that accompanied it. "Can I help you?"

He turned to find a woman with hair as bright as luck itself staring in his direction.

She cannot possibly see me. . . .

"I know you're there," she said, her eyes steady. Her face was pale as a ghost in the darkness. "I can feel you. You might as well show yourself before I call for someone."

Jianyu stayed still and quiet, barely allowing himself a breath as he considered his options.

"Just so you know, this staircase is the only way out." Her expression never shifted. "I know what you are," she told him, her eyes still not quite finding him. "I can *feel* you."

Without any warning, he felt the tendrils of warmth—of magic— brushing against him. She was Mageus, like him. He could try to escape as he was, but if she had magic, who knew what she was capable of? Better to face her now than to find himself trapped. Perhaps they might even be allies.

He released his hold on the light and watched as her eyes found him in the darkness of the basement.

"There. That wasn't so bad, was it?" she asked with a smile.

"I meant no harm," he told her, keeping his chin tipped down so that the brim of his hat would keep his features shadowed.

"You're here awful early," she said. Her magic was still brushing at him, like warm fingers running down the length of his neck, caressing his cheek and making his blood burn with something that felt suspiciously like desire.

"I am looking for someone," he said, trying to block the temptation of those warm tendrils.

"Well, it looks like you found someone," she said with a too-welcoming smile as she came the rest of the way down the stairs toward him.

He swallowed. Hard. "I am looking for a Miss Johnson . . . a Miss Cela Johnson," he said, fighting the urge to go to the woman. From the looks of it, she was wearing nothing more than a silken robe, and each movement she made threatened to expose more of the creamy flesh beneath.

"Who is it that's looking?" she asked, taking another step toward him.

The warm tendrils of magic were growing stronger now, and in the back of his mind Jianyu registered their danger. "She would not know me," he said, fighting the pull of the woman. "But we have a mutual friend."

The woman took another step toward him, her eyes glittering and her dark lips quirking with something that looked like amusement. He imagined it was the same sort of expression a mouse saw just before a cat pounced. "Does this mutual friend have a name?" she asked, taking yet another step. She was on the same level as he was now.

"I would prefer to keep that between Miss Johnson and myself," he said as she continued to walk toward him.

"Would you?" The woman *tsk*ed at him. "Well, that's a crying shame, seeing as there isn't any Cela Johnson here."

"I see. . . ." It was a lie. He could see it clear as day on the woman's pale face. In another two steps, she would be close enough to touch him, and he knew somehow that he could not let that happen. "Then I suppose I should take my leave—"

She lunged for him, but he pulled the mirrors from his pockets and, in a fluid motion, raised them as he spun away from her. The weak light wrapped around him and he ran, leaving the red-haired woman trying to catch herself as she tumbled to the floor.

If Cela Johnson was not there, the red-haired woman knew something about where she had gone, he thought as he took the steps two by two and sprinted for the theater's exit. He would retreat for the moment, but he would not leave until he searched the theater again. And he would not give up until he found her.

A BRUSH OF MAGIC

1902—New Jersey

Inside the train terminal, the noise of chattering voices was almost deafening under the canopy of glass and steel, but Esta barely noticed the racket. She was too busy bracing herself to do what needed to be done.

Though she had never been out of the city before, the New Jersey train station felt almost familiar. In her own time, she had often gone to Grand Central with Professor Lachlan as part of her training. Together they had studied the passengers as he instructed Esta about human nature. The tourists, overwhelmed by the speed and size of the city, would clutch their bags to them as though the devil himself would try to take their ratty luggage, but the locals had become accustomed to the rush and the noise, and the dangers no longer registered. He'd taught her how to case the commuters, too busy checking their phones to notice a thief watching their every move.

The schedule was displayed on a huge chalkboard over the far wall of the terminal's main hall. There was a train to Chicago departing at half past the hour from platform seven, but she still had to find two tickets. They had decided that buying tickets this close to the city, where they might be recognized, was too risky. The Order was most likely still looking for them—especially for her—and she didn't doubt they would have alerted all the transportation centers. Instead of buying two tickets, she'd have to steal them.

Before, Esta wouldn't have hesitated to pull time slow and slip unseen through the spaces between the seconds as she searched for a mark. But after what had happened on the bridge—after the blackness had bloomed in her vision and the way time felt as though it were dissolving around her—she felt unsure of herself . . . and she felt unsure of her affinity.

It was *not* a comfortable feeling.

But that darkness . . . Even the *memory* of it left her shaken. She didn't want to admit to herself that she was afraid—afraid of what that darkness meant and afraid that if she reached for her affinity now, she might find it missing or mangled in some way by the Brink's power.

So she did what anyone would do in that situation—she *didn't* admit it to herself or to anyone else. Instead, she relied on her bone-deep knowledge that she was a good enough thief to lift a couple of tickets from unsuspecting marks without any magic at all. Even if her legs felt unsteady beneath her.

She was still deciding on the best place to watch for a mark when she felt a shock of energy brush against her, warm and welcoming—the sign of the old magic. Frowning to herself, she searched the crowd for Harte. They had agreed to meet on the platform, but it would be just like him not to follow the plan. She couldn't afford for him to show up and get her caught, but as she scoured the crowd, she didn't find any sign of him. And, though she waited, she didn't feel the warmth of the magic again.

Maybe she'd been wrong. . . .

"There isn't time for breakfast. The train leaves in less than ten minutes, and we still have to find platform seven." The low male voice pulled Esta's attention back to the room around her. *Platform seven . . . the train to Chicago.*

Esta let go of her questions and searched for the source of the voice. Nearby, three men dressed in sharply tailored suits were examining their tickets. One was squinting up at the board, confirming the platform they needed, while another tucked his ticket into the outer pocket of his polished leather satchel. She listened a moment longer, and when she heard one of them say the number of their platform again, she began to walk.

It wouldn't do to follow them—that would be far too obvious. But there seemed to be only one entrance from the main terminal into the train shed. She could cut them off there. At least one ticket would be easy to lift. A second shouldn't be too much harder.

Feeling more like herself with every step, Esta pulled a cloak of confidence around her that was nearly as effective as Jianyu's invisibility. She kept the three men in her peripheral vision as she headed toward the entrance to the platforms. When she was about ten feet ahead of the men, she paused and pretended to read a poster advertising a variety show that had just arrived in town. She kept her expression calm and mildly interested in the sign in front of her, even as she kept her focus on the men. When they passed her, she waited one moment longer before turning to follow them. It would be easier to lift the tickets in the tunnel leading to the trains, where the flow of passengers was naturally constricted and where they wouldn't notice—or think anything of—her proximity to them. Or of being jostled by a fellow traveler.

They were just ahead of her, and she could still see the ticket peeking from the satchel. *Easy.*

As they approached the entrance to the platforms, she picked up her pace. A few steps more and she'd be able to sweep past them. Maybe she could trip and pretend to fall. One of them would probably be polite enough to stop and help her, giving her the opportunity to lift a second ticket. Then she'd be on to the platform and then the train—with Harte—before they even discovered their fare was missing.

Esta was nearly at their heels now—but out of nowhere, she felt another brush of warm energy that made her stumble. She caught herself before she fell and then had to scurry to keep up with the three men, scanning the narrowing passageway as she walked. *No sign of Harte.* And the men were almost to the place where the passage opened onto the platforms. She moved until she was barely an arm's reach away. Closer still . . . She was almost next to them, nearly close enough to slip the first of the tickets out of the satchel, when someone called her name.

"Esta?"

It wasn't the unexpectedness of hearing her name that made her pause, but the familiarity of the voice. Her first thought was *Harte*, but the moment she turned, she realized her error. It was a stupid move, a rookie mistake that she never would have made if she had been more on her game that morning.

Before she could completely register who had spoken, Jack Grew had her by the arm.

THE NEW BRIGHTON

1902—New York

V iola kept quiet as she walked with her mother the seven
blocks to the small athletic club where her brother spent most
of his days. The midmorning air was heavy with the threat
of rain, and the smell of ash and soot mixed with the usual smells of
the neighborhood—the overripe fruit and trash that lined the gutter
and the baking of bread and the thick scent of garlic and spices that
wafted from doorways. When they passed a still-smoldering building,
Viola knew implicitly who was at fault for the tragedy.

She was.

Because she had let the magician outsmart her, she had failed Dolph.
She had failed her kind, and she had failed herself. The Order should
have been destroyed, but instead they had grown more oppressive than
ever, taking revenge on the entire city for the deeds of a few.

She would kill them all if she could. But she needed to stay alive long
enough to do it, and Paolo was her means to that end. First she had to
survive whatever penance Paul had in store for her, and that would be
trial enough, considering how she had betrayed the family by leaving
them for the Devil's Own. Because for all intents and purposes, Paul *was*
the family.

After their father died and the responsibility for the family had fallen
on his shoulders, Paolo had supported them all as a bare-knuckle boxer.
He'd anglicized his name to Paul Kelly because he thought it would pay
better, and it had. But her dear brother hadn't stayed a boxer. Leading the

Five Pointers had turned out to be far more lucrative than getting his teeth knocked in every night. Because he was smart enough to grease the right palms at Tammany Hall, the police looked the other way.

Paul's deals with Tammany ensured the success of his athletic club, which was only a front for less legal activities. Come nightfall, the club hosted bare-knuckle matches, where beer flowed and bets were made—all with Paul taking his cut from the top, of course. Because Paul hid the truth of his work from their mother, she never knew what activities truly put bread on their table.

Unlike The Devil's Own, the boxing club Dolph had run, Paul's place didn't pulse with the warmth of magic. Paul, like their mother, was Sundren, without an affinity, and his gang was populated mostly by neighborhood boys whose childhood roughness had grown into a willing brutality. Viola was the black sheep of the family, an unexpected anomaly when her affinity appeared after generations of nothing. Her parents had seen it as a waste, bestowed as it was on a girl, but her brother had seen Viola's power as an opportunity—one that he felt he had every right to exploit.

Viola, of course, saw things differently, not that it had mattered to Paul or her mother at the time.

It was still too early in the day for Paul's usual crowd, so when her mother knocked at the unremarkable wooden door of the club, it was a boy about Viola's own age who answered and let them pass with barely a word. The main room of the club was mostly empty. A well-muscled man in the far corner pummeled a heavy bag that swung from the ceiling. He was bare-chested, and his left shoulder blade carried the angry red mark of the Five Pointers, an angular brand that was also a map of the neighborhood that gave her brother's gang its name. Another duo of men was sparring in the center of the floor, the heat and sweat from their bodies making the room feel too warm, too close. An older man smoked a thin cigar as he watched nearby.

As Viola and her mother entered, the man with the cigar glanced up, his face flashing with surprise to see her mother and then going flinty when he noticed Viola at her side. His hand went for the gun Viola knew would be hidden beneath his vest. The two men sparring and the other, larger man in the back of the room all paused to see what the interruption was.

"Get my son," her mother said, not paying any mind to the unease filtering through the room.

At first the older man didn't make any move to do as Viola's mother ordered. "What's she doing here?" he asked, nodding toward Viola.

Like Viola herself, Pasqualina Vaccarelli was not more than five feet tall. She might have been a broad, sturdy-looking woman, but her size should have put her at an immediate disadvantage. Viola's mother didn't so much as flinch, though. She gave the man the same look she'd given Viola and every one of her siblings—including Paolo—any time they were *truly* in trouble, the look that was usually accompanied by the sting of her wooden spoon. "Why do you think that is any of your business?"

The man's nostrils flared, but he waved off the two fighters, dismissing them, and then took himself off into the back room to find Paul. Viola's mother took the man's seat. Viola didn't join her. She would meet Paul on her feet.

They waited five minutes, ten, the time kept only by the smack of the other man's fist against the canvas bag. Finally, Paul appeared, dressed in his usual well-cut suit and with his dark hair slicked neatly into place, looking more like a banker than the thug he actually was. He embraced their mother and fawned over her for a minute or two, ignoring Viola completely. She wasn't fooled into thinking he hadn't seen her, though, so she wasn't surprised when he finally turned his attention to her.

Viola saw the attack coming—had expected it—and could have dropped Paul in his tracks to prevent it, but instead, she accepted the blow when the back of his hand collided with her left cheek. She stumbled and saw actual stars as her vision threatened to go black and she struggled to stay upright. But at least she had not so much as yelped at the pain. She wouldn't give him that satisfaction.

The next blow came before she was completely upright again. And then the next, until she felt the warmth of the blood trickling from her nose and tasted its coppery tang in her mouth. Her head spun too much for her to remain standing any longer, and she stumbled to her knees. It felt as though the world had narrowed to the pain her brother's fists had brought to the surface of her body.

Gingerly, Viola touched her mouth where her lip felt split. But she didn't look up at Paolo and she didn't say a word. She simply listened to the dull *thump . . . thump . . . thump* of fists hitting canvas, a sound that matched the beating of her own tired and scarred heart.

Paul pulled her to her feet, and Viola's head swirled as she tried to focus on him. His face was close to hers when she heard her mother's voice saying "basta."

"*I'll* decide what's enough, Mamma," Paul said, tightening his grip on Viola's arm where their mother couldn't see.

Viola could smell his expensive cologne, could feel the heat from his body as he crowded her with his size. He was trying to intimidate her, as he had when they were children. But she wasn't a child anymore. She hadn't been for a very long time.

"She needs to know her place," Paul said.

"You've shown her," their mother said, her tone indicating that nothing more was to be said about this. "Whatever she's done, she's still family."

Paul glared at Viola, who met his eyes without flinching. He held her a moment longer, though, his viselike grip on her arm painful, before he finally released her. Then he walked over and, placing his hands gently on his mother's shoulders, leaned down and gave her a kiss on the cheek. "Don't worry about it, Mamma. I know how to take care of family. I take care of you, don't I?"

Viola didn't have to look to know that her mother's eyes had softened and her stern mouth had tugged up at the corners. She could hear the fondness in her mother's voice. "You're a good boy, Paolo."

It took everything Viola had not to snort at that.

Paul called for one of his boys, and when two arrived, scurrying from the back room like rats, he told them to take his mother home.

Before she left, her mother came over and took Viola's chin with a sure grip. With an almost warm expression, her mother examined Viola's bloodied face. "Listen to your brother, mia figghia. Later we visit Father Lorenzo, and you can confess."

"Yes, Mamma," Viola murmured, lowering her eyes as the bitterness of the words mixed with the blood pooling in her mouth. She ignored the weariness that felt like a weight, the hurt that couldn't be brushed away any more than the tattoo inked between the blades of her shoulders.

After their mother left, Paul came over and looked at her face, disgust—and also jealousy—shining in his eyes. "I know why you're back." His wide mouth curled into a sneer. "Mamma, she thinks you came to your senses, but that's not it, is it?" He gave her still-sore cheek a less-than-friendly pat. "No . . . It's because the damn cripple isn't around to protect you now, isn't it?"

She wanted to spit in his face. She wanted to curse his name and tell him that Dolph Saunders had been more of a man than Paul would ever be. But Viola kept her mouth shut and tried to keep the hate from her eyes.

"What? Nothing to say for yourself?"

"What does it matter why I'm here?" she said, her words thick on her swollen lips. "I came back. I'm yours to use again, aren't I?"

His wide mouth turned down. "You're no good to me if I can't trust you."

"Who else would I be loyal to?" Viola asked. "You're right. Dolph Saunders *is* dead, and I'm not interested in dying or getting caught by some Order patrol. You think I haven't seen your boys working with them? You think I don't know you have friends in high places?" She shook her head. "I'm not an idiota, Paolo. I don't have nowhere else to go. I'll do what you need so long as you keep the Order away from me."

Paul didn't speak at first.

"I know what you want. . . . You want to control the Bowery," she persisted. "Everybody knows what I can do. *Everybody*. You don't think it will be a boon if they know I'm for you now?"

He considered her, his face so much like her late father's and yet so different. It was harder, less forgiving. Much, *much* more determined than her father's had ever been.

Paul stepped toward her, and before she realized what he'd planned, he had her by the throat, his large, meaty hands squeezing her neck so tightly she couldn't draw breath. Tight enough that she would wear the mark of them. "You were smart to go to Mamma, little sister. I'll take you on, for her sake. But if you go against me again, it will be the last time."

With every ounce of strength she had left, Viola pulled her affinity around her and pushed it toward her brother until his eyes went wide and he gasped, releasing her throat and bringing his hands up to his own. The man who had been punching the bag stopped his assault and started to approach them.

"Call him off," Viola told her brother.

Paul's eyes were filled with rage, but his face was turning purplish already from his inability to breathe. Finally, he lifted his hand, and the man halted.

"I didn't come back to hurt you, though the good lord knows I have every reason to, after what you've done. But you touch me again—if you let any of your men touch me—I will *end* you."

She released her hold on him, and he gasped, stumbling forward. "I'll kill you myself," he rasped.

Viola simply stared at him, unimpressed. "The bullet better be quick, Paolo."

He glared at her. "It will be."

"And how will you explain that to Mamma?" Her lips felt tight as she forced her mouth into the semblance of a cold smile. "Don't think

I haven't made arrangements to expose you if anything happens to me. Mamma will know all about your other activities, the whores and the criminals you depend on for your money." It was a lie, of course. If she'd had anyone else to turn to, she wouldn't be standing there, humiliating herself. "I need your protection, and in exchange I'll be your blade, but you and your scagnozzi can keep your damn hands off me."

The siblings studied each other in tense silence until, finally, Paul huffed out a hollow breath that sounded like he was vaguely amused.

Va bene. She needed him to respect her power, even if he didn't respect her.

"Go get yourself cleaned up." He gestured to the blood staining her shirt. "Can't have my blade tarnished, can I? You want my protection? You'll work for it."

"I wouldn't expect anything less." Viola was too tired, too jaded by the violence of her life to feel anything close to relief. But she did feel a certain satisfaction. Paul would have killed her already if he didn't mean to keep her. Until she figured out what she needed to do next, she'd be safe. Or as safe as any Mageus could be in this city.

But before she could go, the bell over the front door rang, signaling that someone else had come into the club.

"James," Paul said, stepping past Viola to greet the new arrival.

She turned to see who had arrived. Silhouetted by the morning light was a familiar face, a boy of no more than sixteen with dirty-blond hair and gold spectacles. *What is he doing here, when he's supposed to be leading the Devil's Own?* He was leaning against a familiar cane, one topped with a silver Medusa head that wore the face of Viola's friend Leena. It had once belonged to Dolph Saunders.

Viola took a step forward, ready to rip the cane from Nibsy's hands. *He has no right.* But the sharp look Paul gave her made her pause. It was too early to cross him. Too early for him to know where her true loyalties lay.

"Thanks for meeting with me, Paul."

"Of course. You know my sister," Paul said, gesturing absently toward Viola. "She's recently come back into the family."

"Has she?" Nibsy Lorcan said as he limped into the room.

She could see the questions in Nibsy's eyes, but she didn't say anything to answer them.

"Hello, Viola. I can't say it's a pleasure to see you again," Nibsy said, gesturing to his injured leg. His eyes glinted behind his glasses. "But it is certainly a surprise."

"I'll give you a surprise," she growled, taking a step toward him.

"You already did." Nibsy's voice was lower and more dangerous than she'd ever heard it. It was enough to make her pause. Then he looked at Paul. "If you can't control your sister, I'm not sure our arrangement will work out. Which would be a shame, since I brought the information you wanted." He pulled a small packet of paper from his coat pocket and held it up, drawing everyone's attention to it.

"Enough," Paul said, barely glancing in Viola's direction. "Go clean yourself up, like I said."

"I'm not leaving until he gives me what's mine." She met her brother's eyes, determined. "You want me to be your blade? It works better when I have a good knife."

Paul's expression barely flickered, but Viola had known her brother long enough to recognize the cold calculation in his eyes. "You forget, little sister, that I know you don't need a knife to kill. As far as I'm concerned, if Mr. Lorcan has something of yours, he can keep it . . . as a gift from me."

"You can't—"

"But I can," Paul said softly. "You're either back with the family or not. You're either loyal to me—*obedient to me*—or we are finished."

Viola glared at him. She thought briefly about ending the entire farce—about ending *Paolo*. But if she did, then what? She would never be able to face her mother, and she would be on her own again. The beating she'd just taken would have been for nothing. And she might never discover what was in the package that Nibsy had offered Paul.

She held Paul's gaze a moment longer, to make sure he understood that she wasn't afraid. This was a choice. She would bide her time and pretend to be dutiful, but when the moment came, she would make sure they regretted what they had done. Death was too easy for her brother. Family or not, first she would make him crawl.

A SERPENT'S SMILE

1902—New Jersey

I *knew* it was you," Jack said, his grip tight on Esta's arm.

He can't be here.

Shock paralyzed Esta for a moment—but only for a moment. Quickly on the heels of shock came the cold sureness of an emotion much darker than fear. *Of course* Jack Grew could be here. The nephew of J. P. Morgan, Jack was practically royalty in New York. His family would have simply paid the right people, whispered in the right ear, and Jack's little *indiscretion* on the bridge would have been brushed away like the morning's ashes. Never mind that the indiscretion was attempted murder.

If it hadn't been for Esta's quick thinking—and her ability to pull time still and move Harte out of the bullet's path—Jack would have killed him. With the terrible machine he'd been trying to build, Jack would have killed every Mageus in the city. Since he still had the same barely leashed wild-eyed look that he'd had the day before, Esta knew he was still dangerous, and she was not about to give him the chance to kill her, too.

Gathering her wits and swallowing down the sharp taste of hatred that had coated her mouth, she drew a serpent's smile across her lips and fell into the fake accent she'd used with Jack before. "Jack, darling," Esta purred, gently testing the strength of the grip he had on her arm. "Is it really you?"

"Surprised?" he asked, his mouth twisting into an answering smile that was all teeth and anticipation. His fingers on her arm just missed the cuff she wore beneath her sleeve.

Esta ignored the fury in his expression and stepped closer. "When the police took you, I was so worried."

Jack blinked, taken off guard by her words, just as she'd hoped. He almost seemed unsure about what to do next, but he did not loosen his hold on her. Then his expression went brittle and cold. "Somehow I doubt that," he said, his eyes narrowed. "You were the one who helped Darrigan make me look like a fool. You *ruined* me."

"No, Jack," she said, her eyes wide with feigned surprise. "You mustn't say such things."

"You think I haven't realized that you and Darrigan were in it together from the beginning?" Jack's fingers were digging into Esta's arm hard enough to leave a mark. "You don't think I know that everything you told me was a lie?"

Esta shook her head. "No . . . Darrigan *used* me," she said, forcing her voice to tremble a little. She had one chance to get this particular performance right. "I didn't know what he had planned that night. Don't you remember? He left me there, alone on that stage, to take the blame. You have to believe me. . . ."

"No. Actually, I don't." Jack glared at her. "If anything you just said was true, the Order would already have you. But you managed *miraculously* to get away—twice."

"I was afraid no one would believe me—"

"Because you don't deserve to be believed," he snapped. "Darrigan got you out of Khafre Hall somehow, and then you managed to get yourself off the bridge, which means you know more than you're saying." He started to yank her along, pulling her away from platform seven.

No. She wasn't going *anywhere* with Jack. Panic was making her pulse race, but Esta drew herself up, and even though fear put an edge to her voice, she leaned into the role she had perfected to hook Jack. "Let me go," she told him, using her most imperious voice as she tried to pull away.

If it weren't for the crowd, Esta would have dropped him in a second. Even with the crowd, a twist of her arm, a shifting of her weight, and Jack would be on his back. The problem was that if that happened, everyone in the terminal would be looking at her.

Any other time she might have risked it, because as soon as she was free, she could have pulled the seconds slow and been gone. But disappearing like that would mean revealing what she was to Jack, and if her affinity was as weak as she felt or if she lost her hold of it—as she had on the bridge—she would be stuck with more witnesses than she wanted. She'd be at the mercy of the crowd . . . and of Jack.

Esta's mind was racing as she stumbled along, doing everything she could to slow Jack's progress. The train nearby let off a hiss of steam, a sign that the boilers in the engines were nearly ready and a reminder that the train to Chicago would also leave soon. Other than the odd whispers of energy earlier, she hadn't seen any sign of Harte. She had to hope that he would still be waiting where they'd agreed, but Jack was dragging her in the wrong direction.

If she didn't show up, would Harte assume the worst and believe she'd betrayed him? It wouldn't be a stretch, considering their history. Would he come looking for her, or would he leave without her?

A cold thought struck her: *He can leave.* She'd given him the Book. She had the stone, true, but she'd given Harte the Book as an assurance that *she* wouldn't run. Why hadn't she considered that *he* might? After all, he was out of the city now. *Free.*

And she was trapped with Jack.

It doesn't matter. Whether Harte was waiting for her, as he'd promised, or had already abandoned her, she needed to focus. If she could just get away from Jack, she might still be able to get out of town. She knew where the first stone was. She could find it—and since she knew where Harte was headed, she could find him, too.

People around them were beginning to stare, so she decided to use that to her advantage and struggled more, putting up a fight to attract even more attention.

"Please, sir," she whimpered at a man in an ill-fitting vest and a scuffed derby hat, whose steps had slowed as he eyed the two of them. "I don't know this man," she pleaded.

But Jack jerked her back, putting himself between her and the person she was appealing to. "She knows *exactly* who I am," Jack told the confused stranger. "She's our maid. Tried to leave town with my mother's necklace."

The man eyed the two of them again, and Esta knew what he was seeing: Jack's expensively cut suit, contrasted with the rumpled skirts she'd lifted from a clothesline that morning. That, along with her fake accent, and the man in the vest paused only a second longer before making up his mind. He gave Jack a nod and kept walking toward the train platform, taking all hope Esta had of a rescue with him.

"Did you really think that would work?" Jack laughed.

Esta glared at him. "Did you really think I wouldn't try?"

"What did you think would happen—that the police would come and take *me* away?" He laughed. "Not likely, and not long after the police took you into custody, the Order would have made you wish you'd ended your life on that bridge with Darrigan."

"Like you aren't going to hand me over to them anyway."

The amusement that lit Jack's eyes made Esta go cold. "Maybe eventually I'll give you to my uncle and his friends . . . after I'm finished with you."

Her skin crawled. "If you think I'd let you touch me—"

"If you think you have a choice, you're not half as smart as you pretend to be," Jack told her. "But I don't want *you*. Women like you are a dime a dozen. I want what Darrigan took from the Order."

"I don't *know* what he took," she pleaded, playing dumb.

Jack gave her a mocking look. "I don't believe that for a second. We both know that Darrigan stole some very important pieces from the Order—a book called the Ars Arcana and the five ancient artifacts. I want them back."

"I'm sure you do, but I can't give you what I don't have," she said, meeting his eyes. "For all I know, the things you're looking for are at the bottom of the river—with him."

"Darrigan might be at the bottom of the river, but I don't believe the things he stole are." He leaned down so that his face was close to hers. With his strong patrician features and his shock of blond hair, he might have been handsome. But there was a detached arrogance in his icy blue eyes that made her skin crawl, and his skin had a sallow, puffy appearance, the effect of the whiskey already scenting his breath that morning. "No . . . I think there's a reason you were on the bridge yesterday. I think Darrigan told you where the Order's things are. Perhaps he even gave them to you."

She shook her head. "He didn't—"

He shook her into silence. "Then he told you *something*. He wouldn't have gone to all that trouble to steal them only to toss himself from a bridge. You know more than you're admitting. But don't worry. . . . I have ways to get the information out of you."

"You're welcome to try," she said, straightening her spine against the threat. He wouldn't get what she *did* have, either. As soon as he had her alone, she would do what she couldn't do here. She would make him regret touching her.

He cocked his head slightly at her boldness. "Do you know what's happening right now, as you stand here pretending innocence? The Order is turning the city inside out to find its lost treasures. And they will destroy anyone who stands in their way. The longer you delay the inevitable, the more who will suffer."

He was right. People were being punished because of her. Because of what she had failed to do. But she wouldn't allow him to use that against her. "To go to that kind of trouble, the Order must be awfully scared. They must know that without their little baubles, they're *nothing*."

His eyes raked over her, too perceptive. "They're the most powerful men in the country."

"They're cowards. Preying on the poor and the weak. I'm glad

Darrigan stole their precious trinkets. I'm glad the Order is afraid."

He did something then that she didn't expect—he *laughed*. "Even without their *trinkets*, they could destroy you." Then the amusement drained from his expression, and he pulled her close, his eyes not quite focused. He traced one finger down the side of her face. "But I could protect you from them. Once I have what Darrigan stole, you won't need to fear the Order any longer."

At first his words made no sense. Then realization struck. "You're not going to give any of it back to them, are you?"

"Why should I?" Jack's voice had gone bitter. "You're right. The Order is nothing more than a bunch of feeble old men. Look how easily trash from the gutter broke through their defenses. If they had only let me consult the Ars Arcana, I could have rid the entire city of the danger. Their precious Khafre Hall would still be standing. I could have *protected* them."

With the machine. Harte had told her everything about the dangerous invention Jack had been working on, a modern solution to expand the Brink's power and wipe out magic—and the people who had an affinity for it. "You would have killed innocent people."

"There are no innocent maggots," Jack sneered. "The old magic corrupts everyone the same." He paused, as though something almost humorous had occurred to him. "I suppose I owe Darrigan a debt of gratitude for liberating the Ars Arcana for me. With it I'll prove to the world who I really am and all that I can do, and the Order will come on their knees, begging."

The nearby train let off another hiss of steam, a reminder that she was running out of time.

"Because you're smarter than them," Esta said softly, infusing a breathiness into her voice as she tried another tactic. "You always have been."

Jack's eyes widened, just a bit, and his breath caught. For a moment he paused, and Esta thought her ploy had worked. But then his grip on her arm tightened again. "Did you really think I would fall for your lies again?"

She shook her head. She'd only hoped. "They weren't lies, Jack."

The flicker of uncertainty passed through Jack's expression.

Ignoring the scent of liquor on his breath, she leaned in closer. "I never lied about my feelings for you, darling." Then, before she could second-guess herself, she tipped her head up and pressed her lips against his.

Jack's mouth went stiff with surprise at first, but then he was kissing her. Or rather, he was mauling her, his lips overeager and without finesse, as though he could claim her simply by bruising her mouth with his. It took everything she had not to pull away or gag.

An eternity later, Jack came up for air, his blue eyes glazed with satisfaction, and she thought he might even loosen his hold on her, as she'd hoped. Instead, his grip only tightened. "If you're lying again—"

"No, Jack . . ." She fought to keep herself calm, but inside she was screaming. It hadn't worked, and now she had the stale taste of Jack coating her mouth. She began to gather her strength to fight him—to do anything she needed to do to get to platform seven before that train pulled away.

"If you betray me, I will kill you myself. And no one will miss you when you're gone. Not the trash in the Bowery and certainly not your con man of a magician." A dark amusement flashed in his cold eyes. "He's too busy feeding the fish in the Hudson."

"You sure about that, Jack?" a voice said, and Esta didn't need to look behind her to know that Harte had finally found her.

A VISION OF
LIGHT AND POWER

1902—New Jersey

Harte Darrigan knew he was a bastard in every sense of the word, but he couldn't stop the wave of possessiveness that flashed through him when he saw Esta tip her chin up and press her lips against Jack Grew's.

The train to Chicago was about to leave, and there had been no sign of her on the platform where they'd agreed to meet, so Harte had gone looking. He'd come around the corner and found her with Jack, and there was no mistaking what he saw—*she* had kissed *him*. On purpose. Even now, pinned against Jack, she wasn't struggling to get away. And if anyone could get away, it was Esta.

For a moment the only thing Harte could bring into focus was the way her fingers were curled around the lapels of Jack's coat. The voice inside of him had roared up, shrieking with a deafening pitch as it clawed at its confines, and by the time he had pushed it away and shoved it back down, Jack was speaking.

". . . con man of a magician . . . too busy feeding fish in the Hudson."

Rage had slammed through Harte, and the voice echoed in approval. "You sure about that, Jack?" he asked, gratified to see the surprise drain Jack's face of color. But in the space of a heartbeat, Jack's expression rearranged itself—surprise transformed to confusion and then to recognition—and he pulled Esta back against him, pinning her to him.

Harte took a step forward, but Esta shook her head.

For an instant the fury within him rose up again, but then he saw how wide her eyes were. There was a fear in them so uncharacteristic that Esta almost looked like a different person. Suddenly the station seemed to fall away, and it felt as though the entire world had narrowed down to the whiskey-colored irises of her eyes.

Her eyes were wide, and her expression was blank with terror. The stones around her glowed, a fiery circle of light and power. One by one the stones went dark, and then the blackness of her pupils seeped into the color, obliterating it, spreading to the whites of her eyes, until all that looked back was darkness. Emptiness. Nothing. And the darkness began to pour out of her. . . .

He stepped forward blindly, not knowing what he could possibly do. Not sure what he was even seeing.

"No!" she told him, the fear in her voice stopping him in his tracks. "Stay back."

All at once, the vision dissipated. They were in the station once more, and Esta's eyes were golden. They were still frightened, but there was none of the yawning blackness he'd seen just moments before. And Jack was smiling as though he'd already won.

"I'd listen to her if I were you," Jack said, his voice calm and level, as if they were discussing something as mundane as the weather or the price of bread. "Or don't listen. It doesn't much matter to me. If we're being honest with one another, I'll probably shoot her either way." Jack's eyes narrowed. "But then, honesty isn't something you're familiar with, is it, Darrigan?"

Honesty? The voice suddenly roared inside of him. *What could he know of honesty?*

Disoriented and filled with a combination of guilt and rage that he didn't quite understand, Harte tried to pull himself together. "Playing with guns again, Jack?" he asked, amazed that he managed to keep any tremor of fear out of his voice. "I'm sure the police over there would be interested in knowing about that."

"She'd have a bullet in her back before you finished calling them," Jack replied lazily.

The other passengers streamed around them like water parting for a rock in a stream, ignoring the tableau they must have made standing there, tense and clearly at odds. But then, wealth like Jack's granted a certain amount of invisibility, Harte thought. No one questioned you when you appeared to own the world.

Harte kept his focus on Jack so he wouldn't have to deal with the fear in Esta's eyes. "You don't really want to hurt her, Jack. Your family might own half the city, but murder is murder. There will be consequences for shooting a girl in the middle of a train station."

"Oh, I think you'll find that you're wrong about that," Jack said, and Harte didn't like the gleam in Jack's eyes. "Even if there are certain *inconveniences*, I think you'll find that I'm willing to deal with quite a lot to get what I want. I'm willing to do whatever it takes."

The determination in Jack's tone was a stone in the pit of Harte's stomach. "I know you are, Jack. But you don't have to—that's what I'm trying to tell you. We can make this easy. You don't *need* to hurt her. She doesn't have what you're looking for."

Jack's eyes narrowed, but Harte could read the anticipation and eagerness in his expression. *Just keep him interested*. Because without Esta . . .

He couldn't let himself think about that.

"And *you* do?" Jack asked.

"No—" Esta started to say, but another jerk from Jack had her gasping instead.

Harte tried to send Esta a silent message, what he hoped was an encouraging look to let her know everything would be fine. They'd get out of this mess. *He* would get them out.

"Of course I do," Harte answered lazily. He knew what Jack wanted. It was the same thing Jack—and everyone else—had wanted from the beginning: the Book. And all the knowledge and power it contained. Well . . . Jack could have one of those things.

"Where is it?" Jack demanded.

Harte didn't know whether the decision he was about to make was the right one or if it was his biggest mistake yet. But from the wild look in Jack's eyes, Harte knew that Jack would do everything he was threatening. After all, to Jack, Esta was expendable. Jack didn't know what she was, couldn't even begin to imagine how useful she might be to him, so Jack wouldn't hesitate to shoot her. And if that happened—if Esta died here and now—Harte would be lost as well.

He shuddered as the voice tried to claw its way to the surface of his mind. Pushing him forward. *Compelling* him.

Harte took the Book from inside his coat.

"You can't—" Esta said when she saw it, but Jack pushed her forward, silencing her with the threat of the gun in her back.

Jack's eyes widened slightly, and a hungry gleam shone within them. "Give it to me," he snapped.

"I know how much you want this, Jack," Harte said, pulling around him the familiar role he'd perfected over the past few years—the even-tempered, ever-confident magician. "How many times did you tell me about how your uncle and his friends kept you from everything you could be by refusing to let you have access to this Book? Well, here it is, Jack. You can have it—the power of the Ars Arcana and all the knowledge it contains. You simply have to release Esta, and it can be yours. *All* of it can be yours."

Jack's icy eyes were determined, and Harte could sense that Jack's desire for the Book burned hot and bright. He wanted to accept. . . .

Then Jack's expression shifted, and his lip curled slightly on one side. "Now I know you're lying. You expect me to believe you would give up all that for *her*? After all you've done to get it?" Jack shook his head. "No girl is worth *that*."

Harte let out a derisive chuckle, even as his stomach threatened to turn itself inside out. "Well, by all means . . . keep her, then—I'd rather have this anyway," he lied, making a show of tucking the Book back into his pocket as he turned to leave.

Ignoring the way Esta's body went tense, Harte shoved down the voice that roared its displeasure at the idea of leaving her behind. All around him, the station seemed to recede. The smell of coal smoke in the air and the noise of the early morning travelers. The hiss of steam from a train nearby and the final call of the conductor. None of the noise or sights of the station touched him, because all his energy was focused on walking away from Esta.

Harte got exactly three steps away before Jack did exactly what he had hoped.

"Wait!" Jack shouted.

Harte turned slowly, pretending to be annoyed at Jack's change of mind. "Yes?"

Jack lifted his chin, a sharp jerk that punctuated the demand in his words. "If it's really the Ars Arcana you have there, you should be able to prove it. Some demonstration of the Book's power will suffice."

Harte kept from showing any bit of the relief he felt at Jack's words. "Of course . . ." He withdrew the Book again. His heart was pounding away in his ears as loudly and as steadily as a train careening down the tracks.

Esta's eyes were determined, frantic to convey a single message that Harte was just as determined to ignore—*no.*

Trust me, he pleaded silently, but he couldn't be sure she understood.

He made a show of examining the Book, of riffling through its uneven pages and admiring it. "Despite its humble appearance, this Book is *quite* amazing. I've learned so much from it already," Harte told Jack, settling deeper into the role and taking comfort in that familiar, reliable part of himself. "I think you would be *very* impressed to see what I can do with it."

Jack only glared at him. "I doubt it. If that book had any *real* power, you wouldn't still be standing here talking."

Harte gave a conceding shrug. "You're right, Jack. So let's not talk any longer." He held the Book out in front of him.

Esta's face was creased in pain, her expression urgent with panic. "No, Harte. You can't—"

But before she could finish, Harte tossed the Book into the air, high over their heads.

THE CHOICE

1902—New Jersey

Esta had stopped worrying about the ache from the gun shoved against her lower back the moment she saw Harte take the Book from his coat and hold it out to Jack like an offering.

"No!" she screamed as Harte launched the Book into the air.

It felt like everything happened all at once: The moment the Book was airborne, Jack loosened his hold on her and leaped for it. In almost the same moment, Harte lunged toward her and took hold of Esta's wrist, urging, *"Now!"*

With a sudden flash of realization, she understood what Harte had intended all along, and with a speed and sureness that came from a combination of instinct and years of training, she drew on her own affinity and pulled time slow . . . just as the Book fell into Jack's outstretched hand.

Esta nearly crumpled in relief as the station around them went eerily silent—steam from the nearby engine hung in the air, an immovable cloud of vapor and dust that cloaked the figures trapped within it, and the people on the platform froze around them. Jack, too, had gone still mid-leap, his face fixed in a wild-eyed look of frenzy, while his fingertips had just barely grasped the small leather volume that was the root of all their problems.

Her affinity felt wobbly, unsure, but it was still there.

Almost immediately, she was being crushed to Harte's chest and surrounded by the familiar scent of him as he wrapped his arms around her.

"Thank god you understood." His breath was warm as he tucked his face into her neck, and she could feel him shaking.

His words barely registered. She hardly noticed the warmth of his body, strong and solid, because every ounce of her concentration was now on the shaky hold she had on the seconds around her.

Without releasing his grip on her, Harte pulled back and searched her face. There was a question in his gray eyes that she couldn't quite discern, and for a moment she thought she saw the flash of strange colors in his irises.

"Are you okay?" he asked finally.

"I've been better," she told him, shrugging off his concern with an instinct that years of training under the stern hand of Professor Lachlan had impressed upon her.

In truth, her legs felt like jelly, and the place where the gun had prodded her—just above her right kidney—still ached from the pressure. She'd have a bruise there later, but she would gladly take the bruise over the bullet that would have certainly been deadly.

All around her, the material net of time seemed to waver and vibrate . . . or maybe that was her own magic. Her power was there, but it felt slippery and too volatile, and she was concentrating harder than she usually had to. The more she focused on not losing hold of time, the more she felt a pain building behind her temples.

Part of her wanted to lean into Harte. He hadn't betrayed her or left her behind, and with the ache in her head and the shaky hold that she had on her affinity, she felt like she *needed* to take whatever comfort and strength she could from the sureness of his body.

But she'd no sooner had the thought than she dismissed it. That kind of need was nothing more than weakness. Instead, she drew on her *own* strength and took a step back, until the two of them were connected only by Harte's gentle grip on her. It was just enough of a connection to keep him linked to her, so he wasn't frozen like the rest of the station around them, and it was enough distance that some of the unsettling yearning she'd felt a heartbeat before eased. But with each second that passed, the struggle with her affinity only worsened.

"We should go," she told him.

Harte studied her a moment longer, his mouth turned down into a thoughtful frown that gave her the strangest urge to kiss him, if only to watch how his expression changed. If only to erase the memory of Jack. But she wouldn't act on her desire, not while her lips still felt fouled by the memory of Jack's punishing, whiskey-laced assault.

Together they approached Jack, who was suspended in the net of time. Harte reached up and easily took the Book from Jack's fingertips, then tucked it into his own coat again. "Ready?"

Jack was still suspended mid-lunge, his arm outstretched and reaching for something that was no longer there. His eyes, though—they burned with a hatred that made Esta hesitate, even as her grasp on time was slipping.

"We can't just leave him here," Esta told Harte, struggling to maintain her hold on the seconds. "He knows you're alive now. He knows you have the Book. When we disappear, he'll guess what we are."

Harte glanced at her, suddenly wary.

"He could tell the Order you're still alive or come after us himself." The pounding behind her temples had increased, and the periphery of her vision began to waver. She felt a darkness beginning to creep into the edges of her sight that mirrored the darkness of her thoughts, and she reached to pry the gun from Jack's hand. "As long as he's alive, he's a danger to us."

"We can't just kill him," Harte said, and his tone scraped against her nerves.

"He would have killed me." She looked down at the pistol she was now holding. Focusing on the weapon, she could almost ignore the way the blackness was teasing at the edges of her vision, growing to match the hate she felt building inside of her as she weighed the gun's solid body in her hands.

She hadn't only been trained to fight with her fists and with knives. A gun wasn't her first choice, but she knew how to use one. She also knew what it meant that the hammer was cocked and ready to fire, so she understood how close she'd come to having a bullet tear through her kidneys and guts—an irreparable wound that would have led to a painful death, especially in this time.

"He wasn't going to let either one of us go," she told Harte.

Harte took her by the wrist gently, as though to stop her, but then he paused. His eyes swirled with the strange colors as they had before, and she felt the beginnings of the same creeping energy that had climbed up her arm when they'd crossed the bridge. She thought he was about to agree, but then he blinked and his eyes cleared as he took the gun from her and eased the hammer back down.

His voice was tight when he finally spoke. "We're not like him, Esta."

"Aren't we?" she asked, thinking of all the people they had both been willing to betray in the weeks before to get the Book—to get what they wanted. She thought, too, of all the people who were innocent but who would suffer because of what she had done, because of the choices she had made. She could end this. She could stop Jack, if nothing else.

At the edges of her vision, the blackness was still growing, bleeding into the silent, still world. She wouldn't be able to hold on to her grasp of time much longer. "If we leave him here, how many more are going to die?"

"If you kill him in cold blood, it will change you," Harte told her firmly. "He isn't worth the price."

"Are you sure about that?" she asked, even as the blackness continued to grow. There was something strangely compelling about it, terrifying as it was. "Because *I'm* not."

She looked again at Jack. It was true that this puppy of a man wasn't the cause of her pain. He hadn't been the one to manipulate her, to murder her family, to strip away everything she thought she was until only the raw wound of a girl was left behind. But he certainly wasn't innocent.

There was so much evil in the world, so much more to come in the future. It might be worth it to trade her soul for a way to stop even a little of it. True, she could walk away and leave Jack here, alive and well—and able to hurt others. Or she could start here, now. She could become the vengeance that burned so hot in the pit of her stomach.

She started to reach for the gun, but Harte held it away from her.

"I *am* sure," he said as he ejected the revolving cylinder, emptied the bullets onto the ground, and placed the gun into Jack's coat pocket.

"Harte—" she started to argue.

"My soul, however, is already plenty stained," he interrupted, drawing back his fist.

The instant Harte's knuckles met Jack's face, the sickening crunch of bone echoed through the silent platform. Her affinity had already felt strained and uncertain with the darkness bleeding into her vision, and the moment Harte's fist made contact, Esta's already wavering affinity was disrupted by the connection between Harte and Jack. Jolted by the addition of another body to the circuit of magic between them, Esta's focus wavered and she lost her grip on time.

The world slammed back into motion at once. All around them the roar of the platform returned. Harte turned to look at her, confused about her failure, but she didn't have the words to explain it—or the time.

Behind Harte, Jack's head snapped back as the world around them lurched into motion, but he didn't go down.

"Come on!" Esta urged, tugging Harte along. She glanced back to see Jack, swaying on his feet as he dabbed at his bloodied nose and blinked in confusion. He was stunned, but he wouldn't be for long. "We need to get to a train."

"What happened?" Harte asked. "Why did you let go?"

"I didn't—" she started to say, but she didn't know how to begin describing the blackness she saw or the emptiness she felt. "Not now," she said, tugging him onward even as she struggled to find the threads of time, to focus enough to pull them slow.

Together they ran, pushing their way through the concerned crowd of people, dodging unaware travelers and carts of luggage as they sprinted toward their only chance at escape.

"I didn't get the tickets," she told him, lifting her skirts to keep up with his long strides.

"It doesn't matter." His hand gripped hers more securely as they ran. "We'll figure it out. We just need to get on a train. *Any* train at this point."

"Platform seven," she insisted, thinking of the stone waiting in Chicago. "We need to get to platform seven."

When they reached the platform, the shrill cry of a whistle split through the rustling commotion of the station. Esta looked over her shoulder to see Jack not far behind them, followed by a station officer. The train was already starting slowly down the track. A plume of its smoke canopied the platform with a heavy cloud of coal and sulfur as the steam hissed from the engines and the train began to pick up its pace.

"Go!" Harte shouted when her steps faltered. Ahead of them, two more policemen were racing toward them, their batons already raised as they shouted for people to get out of the way. He toppled a pile of luggage to create a roadblock for the people following them. But it wouldn't hold them for long. "We need more time," he told her, pulling her around an older man.

Her affinity felt more unsteady than ever, and her magic felt like something separate from her, untouchable. Her heart was pumping, her head was pounding, and time felt like the ragged ends of a scarf that had just been taken out of her reach by the breeze.

"I can't," she told him.

She saw the confusion in his eyes when he looked back at her, but Harte didn't hesitate. Running alongside the already-moving train, he reached the back of one of the cars and pulled her forward, boosting her onto the platform as he jogged alongside the train. He reached for the handle and was about to step up beside her when Esta saw Jack.

"Watch out!" Esta told him, but the warning came too late.

Before Harte could lift himself onto the train, Jack had him by the wrist, yanking him back.

"Harte!" Esta was already preparing to jump from the train when Harte shouted at her not to.

All around them, people had stopped to watch. The entire platform had taken on a strange, hushed atmosphere that had nothing to do with Esta's affinity and everything to do with the curiosity of the other travelers.

Harte jerked away from Jack, pulling his arm out of the coat to get free. Off-balance from losing his grip on Harte, Jack fell back, holding on to the coat. A moment later, Harte had boosted himself up into the train.

"Come on," he said, leading her toward the front of the nearly empty car. "We can't stay here—" he started. But before they could even reach the middle of the car, a station officer had come through the doorway. The moment he saw Harte and Esta, he drew out his billystick and blocked the entrance. The few passengers sitting in the car looked up, curious about what was happening.

Harte stepped in front of her, backing her toward the rear exit slightly. They'd had only a minute to catch their breath when the door of the car opened behind him. Esta turned to see Jack blocking their other means of escape.

"Get us out of this, Esta," Harte murmured as he kept his attention on both ends of the car and the approaching attackers.

"There's nowhere for you to go, Darrigan," Jack said, a satisfied smile sliding across his face.

"He's right, son. Put your hands up and get to your knees, and we can do this easy," the officer said from the front of the car.

They were trapped. Even if she could manage to pull time to a stop, there was nowhere to go—no way to escape.

Except one.

Esta had never tried to slip through time like that before—not in a moving vehicle. Time was connected to place, which meant she could only slip through if that place existed in the time she wanted to reach. But they didn't need to go very far—a day or two, maybe as much as a week—just long enough to be on a different version of this train, away from this danger.

She put all her effort, all her energy into focusing on the seconds around her. Ignoring the pounding in her temples, she drew deeper on her affinity than she ever had before. The stone on her arm, Ishtar's Key, grew uncomfortably warm as Esta focused on the spaces between the seconds and began reaching for the layered moments that make up the reality of a place. She riffled through those moments, hunting desperately to find what she was looking for.

Around them the train began to rattle, vibrating along the track violently enough to have the policeman grabbing at the back of a seat to stay on his feet.

"What's happening?" Harte asked.

But Esta didn't hear anything other than the roaring in her ears, searching and searching until she could see nothing but the multiplicity of moments stacked up around her, solid and real as the present one.

Usually, sifting through time was like riffling through the pages of a book, searching for some word, some detail to key into the right date and time. Usually, she had time to focus and sort through the layers to the precise point she wanted, to a *safe* point. But with the train picking up speed and the heat from the connection between her and Harte tugging at her attention, time itself felt loose and unmoored. Instead of finding a safe place, she found huge gaps where the train they were riding on didn't exist.

To find the same train, in the same place . . . at a different time . . .

She focused everything she had, everything she *was*, pushing against the impossibility of it. Ishtar's Key grew warmer and warmer, until it was nearly burning against her arm. And then, *there*. She saw a flash of possibility.

Even though it felt as though the world was collapsing in on them and the floor was falling out from under them, she didn't stop to be sure. Esta grabbed Harte's hand and dragged them both forward through time.

WALLACK'S THEATRE

Jianyu Lee understood the weight of failure. Its oppressiveness had chased him from his brother's house and later sent him, desperate to prove his worth, to a new land. Like the story of Kua Fu chasing the sun, Jianyu had tried to outrun the disappointments of his boyhood. Instead he'd carried them with him on the endless journey across sea and land, only to find more waiting when he arrived in this city and discovered that the promises of the Six Companies' agent had been lies.

He had tried to make the best of working for Wung Ah Ling, the man who fashioned himself as Tom Lee. With his diamond stickpin and stylish derby hat, the self-proclaimed "mayor" of Chinatown was well known throughout the city. He had been delighted to have a Mageus in his employ and had taken Jianyu under his tutelage. Lee had helped him perfect the English that Jianyu had been taught on his long journey, and Lee had explained that the work of the tong was to aid their brethren in navigating the strange ways of this strange land. To protect them. But the longer Jianyu collected bribe money from poor shopkeepers, living in the same rooms where they worked while Tom Lee lived in the palatial splendor of his three-floor apartment at 20 Mott Street, the more Jianyu realized that Lee was no different from the rich merchants back in Gwóng-dūng who ate well while the poor farmers starved.

The day Jianyu was sent by Lee to collect money from a laundryman whose rasping voice and well-lined skin reminded him of his long-deceased grandfather's was the day Jianyu realized he was still nothing more than a bandit. The new beginning he had hoped for was more of the same. After that, every day that he worked as Tom Lee's lackey, using his affinity against those who could not help themselves, he had added another stone to his burden. But Dolph Saunders had given him a way to lay some of that burden down when he'd offered Jianyu a place in the Devil's Own. The dream of destroying the Brink had given Jianyu hope for a different future—for himself and for each of his countrymen back home who carried an affinity, and who would be threatened if the Order's cancerous power were allowed to spread.

Jianyu had been so busy guarding against the danger of the Order that he had failed to see the danger in their midst. They all had, and Dolph's life had been the cost. In the days following Dolph's death, Jianyu felt the old familiar shame return, creeping in the shadows of too silent rooms, waiting for him to pick up the burden of his failures once again. Perhaps he might have. Perhaps one day he might still, but for now, Jianyu had work to do. Nibsy Lorcan was a danger perhaps even worse than the Order, who seemed focused on their power here in New York. If what Harte Darrigan told him was true, Nibsy's ambitions were much larger. If Nibsy controlled the stones, his power might stretch beyond the seas. Whatever might come, Nibsy Lorcan could not be allowed to win.

Jianyu had made Darrigan a promise to protect Cela Johnson and the stone she carried. It was the first step toward defeating Nibsy, and he would not fail.

First, however, he had to find her before anyone else did.

After the confrontation with the woman in the cellar of the theater, Jianyu knew he could not leave until he had determined whether Cela was inside. Which was why he spent the day watching the theater's doors from an alleyway across the street, wrapped in light, so no one noticed him as he waited. All morning, he passed the time by watching the comings and goings of those who did not have to worry about who or what they were, people who knew they belonged—or those who could pretend they belonged. How many among those who passed by that morning were also Mageus, able to blend in and become invisible within the crowd without using any magic at all? It was a comfort that Jianyu had not had since the day he left his own country.

But then, there magic had been different. There was no Order, no Brink. His affinity had not been a liability as it was here.

He was not sure when the exhaustion of nearly two days finally dragged him under, but it was growing dark by the time he was jolted awake by the toe of a policeman's boot. After producing the required identity papers—falsified documents that served as protection when he could not use his affinity—Jianyu pretended to move along as instructed. When the policeman had moved on, he drew his affinity close and returned to wait until the crowd from the last show had poured out of the front and the performers had finally stopped trickling out of the stage door.

Jianyu waited longer still, until he saw the woman from earlier leave, her hair a bright flame beneath the glow of the evening's marquee. Once she had turned the corner and was out of sight, Jianyu pulled the light around himself again and made his way back into the theater. Inside, he released his affinity, just in case there was anyone else left behind who could sense magic, and allowed his eyes to adjust. Again he began his search for some sign of Cela, hoping all the while that he had not missed her when he had failed to stay awake.

There hadn't been any sign of a costumer's shop backstage, so he went back to the cellar, where the woman had stopped his earlier search. Even if Cela herself wasn't below, perhaps her workroom would give him some clue to where she had gone or where she might be.

It was too dark to search properly without any light, so Jianyu took the chance of using the bronze mirrors in the pocket of his tunic. Focusing his affinity through them, he amplified the minuscule threads of light that surrounded him and wrapped them around the disk until it glowed. The soft halo of light guided him through the dusty space as he searched, looking for some sign that he had been correct—that Cela Johnson was, indeed, there.

Finally, he came to a room at the back of the cellar. The door was closed tight and locked, but he picked the lock cleanly and opened the door to find a workroom. The glow of his mirrors showed it to be a small space, but neat and tidy. Rolls of silks and bolts of fabric were piled all around. He ran his finger along the cool metal of the heavy sewing machine that stood in the corner and it came away clean. No dust had accumulated there or anywhere. It felt as though the room had been used . . . and recently.

"Cela?" he called softly into the emptiness. "Cela Johnson? Are you there?"

He listened, knowing that silence would be the only answer, before he tried once more. "My name is Jianyu Lee, and I've come to help you." He paused again, weighing the risks of divulging too much if someone else were listening, and then he decided to take the chance. "Harte Darrigan sent me to protect you."

He stood for a long time, his ears open and his focus sharp for any sign of life, any indication that Cela was still there. In the corner, he heard a rustling. . . .

But when he lifted his disk, the glowing light revealed the tail of some rodent just before it scurried away.

Cela Johnson had been there not long before. Jianyu was sure of it. But she wasn't there any longer. Only one question loomed larger than all the others—had she left this place of her own free will, or had someone else gotten to her first?

A HEARTFUL OF TROUBLE

1902—New York

Cela hated the darkness. She'd hated it ever since she'd been a little girl and Abel had locked her down in Old Man Robertson's coal cellar to punish her for eating the last of his peppermints. By the time he finally let her out, she'd cried so hard that snot was dripping out of her nose, her face was blotchy, and her voice was ragged. Trying to settle her down, he'd given her an awkward hug, the only kind that on-the-verge-of-manhood boys knew how to give, and he promised her he'd never do it again.

He'd kept that promise for as long as he could.

But Abel is gone.

Again, grief twisted around her heart so tightly that she thought it might stop altogether. She had to pause for a second just to force herself to breathe. But she couldn't stay there. It was up to Cela herself to make do, darkness or not.

She heard the man's voice calling her name again, and then she heard him say that Harte Darrigan had sent him. To protect her, of all things. Well, considering that Harte Darrigan had sent her nothing but a heartful of trouble, whoever was out there could just keep his help. She certainly didn't want anyone else's protection, either. She already had two lives on her conscience who had tried to protect her, and she'd carry those two souls with her for the rest of her days.

Even after she thought he was gone, she waited, just to be sure, before she unlatched the panel of the wall she'd been hiding behind and came out. She'd built herself the little hidey-hole to keep her sewing things safe when she needed to. Didn't matter that everyone at Wallack's got the costumes they needed. One person or another always had sticky fingers, wanting the best bits for themselves.

She'd never intended to hide herself there, but it worked just as well.

Her eyes were already used to the darkness, so she didn't have much trouble navigating the small area of her workroom. She was pleased when she discovered that her visitor had left the door open for her.

Cela didn't bother to gather anything with her but a scrap of fabric to use as a wrap. She closed the door to her workshop and locked that part of her life up behind her—she wasn't coming back. Not ever. Then on quick, sure feet, she followed the soft padding of the man's footsteps, up the steps, through the back halls to the stage door, and out into the night.

EMPTY STREETS

1902—New York

After his failure to find Cela at the theater, Jianyu had reached an impasse. He had no idea where to look for her next, but if the woman at the theater had her—or if someone else did—he would require help. He had to find Viola, which meant that he had to return to the Bowery.

The Bowery, he knew, was in chaos. And with Nibsy Lorcan in control of the Devil's Own, the streets around the Strega would no longer be safe for him, as they once had been.

There was one place in the city where Jianyu's countrymen were welcomed without hesitation—the blocks close to Mott Street known as the Chinese quarter. He might go there, but Jianyu had worn out his welcome more than two years before, when he'd broken his oath of loyalty to Tom Lee and the On Leong Tong by defecting to the Devil's Own.

If Jianyu was caught by the On Leongs now, he would be made to pay for his transgressions. The question was what the price would be. Tom Lee might use simple violence, or he might do more. Jianyu was Lee's nephew only on paper, after all. While Dolph was alive, the secrets he had collected had assured Jianyu's safety from Tom Lee, but the power of those secrets had died with Dolph. If Lee chose, he could alert the authorities to Jianyu's precarious position in the city—and to the falseness of his documents. If Jianyu were deported, it would be tantamount to a death sentence, because being removed from the city would mean passing through the Brink.

It did not seem worth the risk to attempt navigating those dangers in the dead of night, when it would be harder to pull on his affinity for concealment. Instead, he ventured east to Twenty-Fourth Street, just a few blocks from where the newest skyscraper was nearly complete. There, a friend from Jianyu's first days in the city had a small laundry he ran with his wife, a sturdy Irish girl with kind eyes and ruddy cheeks. Since it had been years, Ho Lai Ying was surprised to see him, but understood the reach of the tongs. Though he did not wake his wife or family, Lai Ying gave Jianyu a bowl of the family's leftover meal and a warm place to rest for the night. But Jianyu barely slept, and he was gone before daybreak, so as not to put his old friend in any danger.

As the morning began to warm, Jianyu's path finally brought him to the Bowery. He needed to speak with Viola, but he also needed to find Cela without rousing the interest of anyone else who might be hunting for her or the stone. He was so deep in thought considering his options that he failed to notice the pair of men who had started following him not long after he had crossed Houston. By the time he felt their presence, it was too late to open the light around himself—not without revealing what he was.

Picking up his pace, Jianyu headed down one of the busier thorough-fares. Perhaps they would be less likely to do anything to him if there were enough witnesses. It was a feeble, naive hope. The streets were nearly empty at that early hour, and even if they had been filled, witnesses were more likely to become part of an attack than to prevent one.

In an instant, the men were flanking him, and Jianyu knew that he had little choice. He turned, his hands up, ready for a fight, but the two men only looked at each other and laughed. They were dressed in the familiar uniform of Bowery toughs—brightly colored shirts and waist-coats in stripes or plaids, trim pants, and the ubiquitous bowler hats that they wore cocked over one eye. Their pale, pasty skin looked wan and sickly contrasted against their garish clothes.

"Whaddaya think you're gonna do?" the one said, laughing to the other. "I've seen how they fight . . . like chickens flapping their wings after you chop off their heads." He stepped forward, his narrow-set eyes so heavily hooded, they made him appear half-asleep. "Come on. Gimme the best you got. . . . Go ahead. Your first flap is free."

Jianyu kept his attention split evenly between the two of them as they circled him.

"Come on, you dirty bastard," the other taunted, laughing darkly all the while.

They were expecting something else from him, perhaps. Or maybe their mouths were smarter than they were, but Jianyu took their offer and launched himself at them. The larger of the two was too slow to ward off Jianyu's first blow. He went down easily, splayed in the dirt of the street and groaning with the damage Jianyu's fist had done to his face.

The other goggled for a moment, looking at his friend with a kind of horrified shock that gratified Jianyu to the very marrow of his bones. But Jianyu had spent too much time at The Devil's Own training with the rest of Dolph's crew to miss taking further advantage of the pair's surprise. He whipped around and drove his fist into the other boy's stomach, knocking the air from him, before the boy realized what was happening.

The first was climbing to his feet, his nose dripping with blood and his eyes filled with rage, but a strange calm had settled over Jianyu. With a slow, mocking smile, he raised his hand and motioned for the boy to come closer. He and the boy circled each other, dodging and ducking each other's fists as the second boy came to his feet. Without warning, the second boy ran at Jianyu, tackling him to the ground.

Jianyu's head cracked against the edge of the sidewalk, and for a moment his vision went white. That moment was enough for the two to take advantage. One was on him in an instant, and before Jianyu could protect himself, he felt a fist plow into his side. He lashed out, landing a glancing blow or two, but the other had already made it to his feet again and had joined in.

A vicious kick landed in Jianyu's back, sending a near-blinding pain through his body.

"That'll teach you," one of the boys growled as his fists plowed into Jianyu's stomach again. "Damn dirty—"

Jianyu did not need to hear the rest to know what the boy said. That word—or words like it—had followed him ever since he had stepped off the boat in Mexico. He had heard them as he had ridden the train in silence for days, first crossing the border and then a country that he knew could never be his. Those slurs had been his companion in the dead of night as their ferryman smuggled him into Manhattan. And once he had arrived, he had heard the slur—or some version of the same—every day in the city's streets, tossed about by filthy beggars who were not man enough to look him in the eye when they said it.

He struggled to his knees, but another vicious kick landed in his stomach, and he went over hard again, tasting the coppery blood in his mouth. His ears were ringing. He had to get up, had to get to his feet somehow if he wanted any chance to survive this.

". . . damned dirty . . ."

They had him by the hair. One of them was holding on to the long queue he wore braided down his back. There was a roaring in his ears, but he could not tell whether it was from their punches or from the fact that he knew what they were about to do even before he heard the *snick* of the switchblade opening. His head was pounding, and the sound of a thousand winds howled in his ears. He wanted to scream at them, but his mouth was filled with his own blood.

When it went off, Jianyu felt the gunshot as much as he heard it. It was so close that the echo of it rang through his head and rattled his bones, even though the bullet never touched him.

It took him a moment to realize he was still alive—to realize that he had not been struck by the bullet. He lay with his face pressed to the grime of the street, the sourness of his blood thick in his mouth, but he was still breathing. There was pain in his head, yes, but he was still breathing.

Footsteps came closer until he was looking at the scuffed toes of two brown boots.

"You are lucky I came along when I did," the voice said in the familiar tones of his own language. "They would have killed you once they were done scalping you."

Scalping . . . He knew without reaching for his hair that it was gone, and without it, returning to his own country would be impossible. Without it, the one feeble dream he had carried secretly in his heart for so long crumbled to ash.

"You should have let them kill me," he answered, the words a comfort on his tongue even though his lips were bloodied and swollen so much that they sounded garbled even to him.

"Now, why would I do a thing like that?" the voice said. "I've been waiting so long to talk to you."

IT COULD BE WORSE

New Jersey

Harte came to sprawled on the floor of the moving train car, but the officers were gone. So was Jack.

When he pulled himself up, his head spun so much that he was barely conscious of the soft pile of material he was sitting on or the legs that moved beneath it, but once he was upright, his stomach revolted. Lurching to his feet, he ran toward the door at the back of the train car, barely making it out onto the platform in time to empty his stomach over the railing to the tracks below.

He hung there with his mouth tasting sour, and the warm breeze blew across his clammy skin as the earth sped by beneath him. When the door of the train car slid open behind him not long after, he knew without looking that it was Esta. There was something about the way the air changed whenever she was around him. It had always been like that, but now the voice inside of him whispered *yes* every time she was close. *Soon.*

Harte shoved the voice away, and with what strength he had left, he locked it down tight. The effort it took made his head swim again.

"Are you okay?" Esta asked, coming to stand next to him at the railing.

He nodded, still feeling sick and too warm.

Because the weather *is too warm.*

The sky no longer had the gray heaviness of earlier that morning, and the crisp spring air had been transformed into the balmy heat of a summer's day. "What just happened?" he asked, closing his eyes against the motion of the train.

"You said to get us out. . . ."

Harte turned to her, comprehension already dawning on him, but before he could say anything, the door behind them opened and a uniformed conductor came out.

The man eyed Harte as he clung to the railing, but otherwise he gave no indication that anything was amiss. "Tickets, please."

They didn't have any tickets, but if he could just pull his head together and stay upright long enough to let go of the railing, he could fix this. One touch was all it would take. . . .

But Esta was speaking before he could manage. "I'm so sorry," she said, pulling a dark wallet from within the traveling cloak she wore. "We were in such a rush, and we didn't have time to purchase the tickets before we boarded. Can we pay now?"

"Sure, sure," the man said, pulling out a small booklet and punching two of the tickets with a small silver clamp. "End of the line . . . That'll be three fifty for each."

Harte should have been curious about where the stack of money had come from. He should have been interested to watch this new ritual, the purchasing of a ticket—the validation of his freedom. But it was all he could do to keep his stomach from revolting again and his mind from focusing too much on the reality of what Esta had done.

"Is a Pullman car available?" Esta asked the conductor, taking a couple of bills from the wallet and handing them over. Her voice was light and easy, but Harte could hear the edge in it. "My husband isn't feeling well. I think it might be best if he rested."

"No Pullman," the man said, raising a brow in their direction. "This train's only going as far as Baltimore. You can get a transfer to a Pullman at the next stop, if you're traveling farther."

"Of course. How silly of me," she said with a strained laugh. "Thank you anyway." She'd made her voice into something breathy and light, but she couldn't quite manage to keep a tremor of nervousness out of it.

Harte waited until the man had continued on through the next car before he let himself slide to the floor. His head was still spinning as he leaned back against the railing, and the way the train swayed made his already fragile stomach turn over again. He forced all of that aside too and focused on Esta. "The train on platform seven wasn't going to Baltimore."

She wasn't paying attention to him. Instead, she was trying to reach up her sleeve. Her mouth was a flat line of concentration—or was that pain?

"Esta—"

"Hold on," she said through gritted teeth, and a moment later she pulled the cuff from her arm with a hissing intake of breath. "There . . ." She held it delicately between her fingers, frowning as she examined it.

The cuff itself was a delicate piece of burnished silver, but the metal was less important than what it held—Ishtar's Key. It was one of the artifacts that gave the Order its power, but this particular stone was special because it allowed Esta to travel through time.

Through time . . .

Harte's empty stomach felt as though he'd swallowed a hot stone. "What did you do, Esta? This train was supposed to be going to *Chicago.*"

"You told me to get us out of there, so I did," she told him, but her attention was on the stone in her hand—not on him.

"But this isn't the train we were on, is it?" he asked.

"Of course it is." She finally looked up from her examination of the cuff. "This is the same train—the *exact* same car. . . ." She hesitated, frowning a little. "It's just *slightly* ahead of when we were before."

"How slightly?" he asked, his stomach churning from the motion of the train and the idea of what she'd just done.

"I don't know. A day or two, nothing much mo—" But her words fell away as she glanced at the tickets the conductor had handed her.

"What is it?" he asked, swallowing down another round of nausea that had very little to do with the motion of the train.

She cursed as her face all but drained of color.

He had a very bad feeling that he was not going to like the answer to the question he had to ask: "How far ahead are we?"

"I was just trying to get us away from Jack and the police," she told him, never taking her eyes from the tickets.

"How far, Esta?"

She was practically chewing a hole into her lip. "I was looking for a day or two ahead. I didn't mean . . . I didn't—"

"*Esta.*" He cut her off and took a deep breath—both to calm himself and so he wouldn't be sick again. It could be worse. They could be in police custody right now. They could be at the mercy of Jack and the Order. "How bad is it?"

Silently, she handed him the tickets.

His eyes were still having trouble focusing from the strangely violent push-pulling sensation he'd experienced just moments before. It had felt like the world was collapsing in on him, twisting him about. It had felt awful—*wrong*. As he stared at the ticket, that feeling worsened, because there was no mistaking the date printed there.

"Two *years*?" He was going to be sick again.

Two years ago he was still struggling to climb out of the filth of the Bowery and doing his damnedest to survive. Two years ago he didn't have money in his pocket or a reputation on the stage. Two years ago he didn't even have the name he now wore. Two years was practically a lifetime in a world as capricious and dangerous as his, and she'd taken it from him without a second thought.

"I didn't do it on purpose," she whispered, her expression pained.

"How is that even possible?" he snapped, wincing inwardly at how sharply the words had come out.

But his sharpness was like a flint to a rock, sparking her temper. "Slipping through time isn't exactly easy, you know," she said, snatching the tickets back from him. "On a good day, it takes all my concentration to find the right minute to land, and that's when I'm *not* in a moving train cornered by the police. You're welcome, by the way. Seeing as we aren't currently in jail and all."

"*Two years*, Esta." But then he saw the way her hand holding the tickets was shaking, and his anger receded a little. "I meant for you to"—he waved vaguely—"to slow things down, so we could get off the train and get away."

"We got away, didn't we?" She gestured to the obvious absence of Jack.

He took a breath, trying to hold down the bile in his stomach along with his own temper. "You're right. We were in a tight spot, and you got us out," he told her, trying to mean it. "It'll be fine. You can fix this. You can take us back."

"Harte . . ." Her hesitation made his stomach twist all the more.

"You can *take us back*," he repeated.

Esta's expression was pained. "I have no idea what just happened. I meant to go two days and went two *years* instead."

"Because we were on a train—you said so yourself," he said slowly, trying to keep his composure. "We'll get off at the next station, and then you can—"

"It wasn't just the train," she said, not quite meeting his eyes.

The nausea somehow suddenly didn't seem so important. "What do you mean?"

"My affinity . . . it doesn't feel right. Ever since the Brink, it's felt off. *Unstable.*"

He frowned at her. He'd known that the Brink had done a number on her, but he hadn't realized that it had affected her magic. "Why didn't you tell me? We could have waited another day."

"We needed to go—we have to get the stones," she snapped. "We're running out of time as it is. Soon Logan will be in the city and—" She broke off as though realizing what she was saying. It was already too late. Because of what she'd done, this Logan of hers had already been in the city for two years.

"And *nothing*. You should have *told me*," he said, maybe more forcefully than he'd intended. But his nerves were jangling, and his anger was the only thing that was keeping him from retching over the side of the train again.

"I *know*," she said, biting back at him, but then she closed her eyes and took a breath. "I know," she repeated, her voice softer now. "But everything was happening so fast. We had to find clothes and get out of Brooklyn, and I thought if I could just push through, it would be okay. That *I* would be okay."

"But you're not okay, are you?" he asked, and watched as a series of emotions flashed across her expression—denial, frustration, worry—all mixed together as one.

"You saw what happened at the station. I could barely hold on to time long enough to get us away from Jack," she told him, still staring out at the passing landscape as though she couldn't look at him. "You're right. I never should have tried slipping through time, but we were cornered on a moving train, and I thought, if I could just get us on the next train—if I could just get us to tomorrow—then we would be safe. But once I started to slip through, I couldn't control it. And then with you—"

"Me?" he interjected. "You're saying *I* caused this?"

"Not *you*," Esta said as she shook her head. "But whatever it is that's *inside* you now. I can feel it when you touch me, and when I'm trying to pull on my affinity, it's like trying to hold a live wire."

His stomach turned over again. "You think it's the Book?" At the very mention of it, the voice began to stir deep within him. On the bridge, he'd told her that the power of the Book was inside of him, but he hadn't told her everything. Before, he hadn't been able to find the words to explain what the Book wanted—and especially what it wanted of *her*. Now, with the questions and the *fear* that shone in her eyes, he couldn't make himself say them.

Her hair had come half undone and the dark strands of it were whipping about her face, but her expression was steady now. "I can't be sure. Maybe it wasn't you. Maybe something happened to me when we crossed the Brink."

Maybe he should have consoled her—forgiven her, even. But he was still too upset about the two years of his life that she'd carved away like nothing to give her any reprieve.

Esta sank down next to him, her skirts pooling over his legs. Gently, her hand touched his cheek, turning his head so that he was forced to look at her. "We will fix it," she told him, her eyes bright with determination. "*I* will fix this. But I don't think we should try to go back—not *yet*," she finished, before he could argue. "I don't know why we went so far. I don't know why I couldn't control where we landed. Usually I can. But if I try to take us back now and I miss again, we could be stuck. You saw what happened to the bag of stones I tried to bring back on the bridge."

"They were gone," he remembered. All that had been left were the charred remains of the settings. The stones themselves had turned to ash.

"I don't think the stones can exist at the same time with other versions of themselves. If I can't control my affinity again and we go back too far, Ishtar's Key will cross paths with itself, and it will be gone. We will be stuck whenever we land, with no way out of the city again and no way to stop Nibsy or the Order." She licked her lips. "And I don't know what will happen to *me* if the stone disappears."

"To you?" He shook his head, not understanding.

"Or to you. I told you what Nibsy did before we changed things," she said. "How he sent me forward?"

"When you were a baby . . ."

She nodded. "I think that still needs to happen. If I'm never sent forward, then I can't come back. If that happens, it means I wouldn't have been there to help with the heist at Khafre Hall or to save you—any of it. You'll die. Who knows what that would mean for the Order or Nibsy or magic." A shadow fell across her expression. "If I'm never sent forward as a baby, I'd grow up like I should have . . . in the past. I'm not sure that this version of me would even exist anymore."

Panic spiked inside of him. "You can't just disappear."

"Why not? The stones did, didn't they?" she asked, her gaze steady.

He considered that for a moment, a world without Esta. Everything he'd done to try to send her back to her own time had been to save her—from the past, from the power rollicking inside of him. But she'd come back, and in doing so, she'd given him another chance . . . one he didn't deserve. "Then you're right. We shouldn't chance it. We'll wait."

"You'd be okay with that?"

"The stones we're after still exist, don't they?" he asked. "It's only been two years. They can't have gone that far. We'll find them here . . . *now*."

She was still frowning at him. "And then what? We won't be able to take them back."

"Because they'll still exist in 1902," he realized.

They sat, speechless for a moment, as the *click-clack*ing of the track kept time beneath them.

"It doesn't matter," Esta said finally. "We'll worry about getting the stones back to 1902 when we're sure we *can* get back to 1902. First we get the Book's power under control. We need the stones for that. Maybe once we have them, there will be something in the Book itself to solve the problem. It got us through the Brink, didn't it? If there's not, two years isn't that long."

Two years is a lifetime. "It's not a great plan. . . ." Then he realized—*the Book.*

No.

Harte looked at Esta, unable for a moment to speak. "My coat" was all he could say.

"What about it?"

He saw the moment she understood what he meant, but he said the words anyway, because he had to face them. Because he knew that no amount of silence would make them any less real. "The Book was in the coat. The one I left behind—to get away from Jack."

SOME DISTANT STATION

Y ou should have let me kill him," Esta said, feeling herself go cold as she drew back from Harte. Because one thing was clear: None of this would have happened if he hadn't stopped her from killing Jack. They would still have the Book, for one. And they would still be in 1902, because Jack wouldn't have been chasing them.

She could have done it.

She could have gladly carried that burden with her for the rest of her life. She had no way of knowing what effect her inaction would have, but she knew one thing—nothing good could come from Jack getting ahold of the Book.

Harte was still sitting on the platform at the back of the train when she pulled herself to her feet. He looked pale and unsteady, but Esta was having a hard time finding any more sympathy.

"You shouldn't have stopped me," she continued.

"And then what?" Harte asked. "You would have just walked away, with his blood on your hands?"

"Better his blood than ours."

Harte scrubbed his hand down over his face, expelling a ragged breath as he closed his eyes for a moment. He looked as though he was about to be sick again. "I've done plenty of wrong in my life, but I don't want to be the type of man who can kill someone in cold blood." He opened his eyes to look at her. "Even someone who deserves it as much as Jack does."

There was something about the way his voice changed, the way it seemed to carry to her so clearly on the wind, even with the noise of the train and the tracks, that made Esta pause.

But only for a moment.

This world didn't allow for pausing or second-guessing. It wouldn't permit her to keep whatever delicate sensibilities Harte thought she should have.

All at once the memory of Professor Lachlan's library at the top of his building on Orchard Street arose in her mind. The dimmed lights. The smell of old books that had once meant safety. On her wrists, Esta could still feel the ache of bruises from the ropes that had held her to the chair. She could almost feel the heat of the stones Professor Lachlan had adorned her with, like the sacrifice he'd intended her to be. The man who had raised her would have used her affinity—used *her*—to unite the stones and take control of the Book's power. *You're just the vessel.* He would have killed her.

She lifted her hand to touch the still-healing wound just below her collarbone and closed her eyes against the memory of what had happened. . . . *These things do tend to work better with a little blood.*

That night had been less than twenty-four hours ago and was also still a hundred years to come. In the darkness behind her eyelids, another memory assaulted her—Dakari stepping into the room, unaware of what Professor Lachlan had planned. Unprepared for the bullet that came a few moments later.

The echo of the gun.

The sound of Dakari's body collapsing, deadweight, to the floor.

And the weight of the guilt she bore for his death.

Maybe she'd never had any real softness to start with. Or maybe the last bit of softness had been killed as surely as Dakari that day. Either way, Esta knew that if she could live with the memory of that night, she could bear anything. *Become* anything. Harte might not have believed that she was strong enough, but Esta had already survived the senseless loss of her friends, of her family—of her *father*. A little blood on her hands for the sake of their memory and for the sake of their lives was hardly anything.

Besides, she knew that she wouldn't have to carry any of it for very long. No matter what happened between now and the end, Professor Lachlan had already explained to her how the stones could be used to control the Book. She hadn't yet told Harte. She didn't know how he would react to learning that it would require sacrifice—her affinity and most likely her life—and they didn't have time for him to get all noble again or have second thoughts. But then, she was a girl without a past and without a future. She'd already resigned herself to the fact that she had little hope of walking out of this alive.

Now they would have to live with the consequences of *not* killing Jack when they'd had the chance. Two years had passed, and during that time the world had continued on, history unspooling itself each day. Who knew what had changed in the days and weeks since Jack Grew got his hands on the Book and all the knowledge contained in its pages? Who knew what might wait for them at the station at the end of the line?

Harte looked like he was going to be sick again. Not that Esta blamed him. When she thought of Jack with the Book, she felt like throwing up too.

"It'll be okay," she told him after a few minutes of tense silence, the wind whipping at them as the train sped onward. She wasn't sure that she believed it, but there didn't seem to be anything else to say as the train hurtled down the track, careening toward some distant station she had never thought to see and toward a future that she was determined to meet head-on—the same way she met everything else.

"You know what Jack could do with the Book." Harte turned from her, his eyes unfocused on the passing countryside. "The Order wouldn't let him have access to it because they knew how dangerous it was, and I *gave* it to him. He'll have secrets that even the Order was smart enough to keep away from him."

Every bit of what he'd said was true, but still . . . "If Jack had kept you from getting on the train, it would have been over anyway."

"I could have fought him," Harte said, his jaw tense. "I could have beat him."

"Sure. With the station police on your tail and all those people around *and* the train already leaving. A fistfight is exactly what would have worked." When Harte glanced back at her, irritation shadowing his expression, she continued. "You had to get on this train—*that* train—*whatever*. You made a choice, just like I did. You did what you had to do to get away. Besides, Jack doesn't really have all that much," she reminded him. "The Book's *power* is in you, right?"

Harte's jaw clenched. "There's still the information in its pages. That's more than enough for it to be dangerous."

"So we'll just have get it back." She pulled herself up to her feet again. "I'm a thief, aren't I? I'll steal it."

He looked up at her. "It might be too late for that already."

"If we can get control of my affinity, there is no such thing as too late." Still, there was a part of her that worried Harte was right.

She offered him a hand up. "We can get off at the next station and figure out what to do."

He ignored her offer of help. "We might as well wait until we get to Baltimore. We've already paid for the tickets," he told her. "No sense getting off until we're in a city that's big enough to give us our pick of routes. It's been two years," he said, an answer to her unspoken question. "I don't know where any of the people we need to find are now. I'll have to send out some telegrams, make some inquiries. If Julien is still performing, he shouldn't be that hard to find."

Already, the crowded industrial-looking buildings of the area around the station had given way to more open land. The smell of the coal burning in the train's engine was faint, and the air carried a scent she didn't recognize—something green and fresh and earthy that didn't exist in the city.

"We should probably get some seats," she told him. "It'll be a while before we reach Baltimore."

Harte pulled himself upright without her help but held tight to the railing for a moment to steady himself. "Where did you get the money for the tickets?" he asked as he reached for the door to the car. He held it open for her to enter.

"Compliments of Jack," she told him as she stepped through.

The car was almost entirely empty. In the front, an older man dozed with his head tucked into his own chest. He didn't stir at the sound of the door opening or the noise of the tracks. Still, Harte lowered his voice when he spoke.

"You took Jack's wallet?"

She shrugged. "He's good for it. And he was a little . . . distracted at the time." She slipped into an empty row of seats. When Harte didn't immediately sit next to her, she glanced up at him. He was staring at her with an unreadable expression on his face. "What?"

"That's why you were kissing him."

At first his words didn't make any sense. "Kissing . . . ?" Then she realized what was happening in that pretty little head of his. "You're an idiot. You know that, right?"

Harte had the grace to look a little embarrassed as he slid into the seat next to her. "Yeah," he muttered. "I'm aware."

Esta wanted to say something more, but Harte's attention had been drawn by the landscape speeding by. It was as though sitting on the plat- form of the train car, he hadn't even seen it, but now she could have disappeared altogether and he wouldn't have noticed. All Harte could see was the world outside the windows of the train—a world he had lied and stolen and cheated for.

She decided to let him have it. For now.

Through the seats, Esta could feel the vibrations of the rail, telegraph- ing the shape of the land they were crossing. She'd never thought she would leave the city—had never wanted to—but now she had to admit that the world was wider and more beautifully tempting than she could have expected. Already the towns were giving way to a landscape of fields carpeted with the lush green of summer crops, their stalks rippling in the breeze. The colors were more vibrant somehow. More raw and alive.

She wasn't supposed to be there, beyond the boundaries of the city she had called home for so long.

She should be dead by now, but she had survived Professor Lachlan's attempt to take her power—and her life. She had survived Jack's gun pressed against her back.

For a moment she let herself lean her head against Harte's shoulder and enjoy knowing that until the train pulled into the station, they were safe. Until the train arrived at their next station, it was just the two of them, the green of the landscape, and the steady cadence of the train.

But even as she allowed herself that one stolen moment of peace, Esta knew that her future was waiting. The world outside of that car might have changed in dangerous ways in the years they had skipped. There was only one thing she could be sure of when the train finally pulled into Baltimore: She would survive whatever came next. One step at a time, one moment and then another. Until she righted the wrongs that had been done . . . and made those who had caused them pay.

PART

II

SURFACING

1902—New York

When Jack opened his eyes, the light in the room was lavender. It was like being inside a damn flower. And he felt heavy . . . impossibly heavy, especially his left arm, which had been pinned across his abdomen with some sort of binding. He couldn't seem to move his fingers, but with the lavender light, he couldn't quite bring himself to care. Even if his head felt like it would split in two.

They must have given him something—some drug to dull the pain—because the room around him felt very far away, as though he were seeing it through a tunnel. But how did he get there?

There had been the ambulance. He remembered the bone-aching bumping of the carriage as it carried him to the hospital. . . . But this was not the hospital. Slowly but surely the room started to come more into focus. The walls were covered in a floral brocade, and above, the canopy of the bed dripped with lace.

It came to him then where he was—this was one of the spare guest rooms in his mother's house. Not ideal and yet also not terrible. Considering the temper his uncle had unleashed—how long ago had it been?—his family could just as well have left him alone in a cold, public hospital. Or worse, they could have kept to their word and shipped him westward, injured or not. It seemed that he'd been given a reprieve. A second chance of sorts. He would damn well use it.

Just as soon as he could move . . .

Jack lay there for a long while, his gaze tracing the looping patterns of the lace above his head, his brain feeling thick and heavy. Little by little, the events that had brought him to his mother's spare bedroom began to come back to him.

The train . . . Darrigan and the girl . . .

He remembered suddenly the moment when the medics had given him the coat that was not his and he had realized what was contained within its pocket. *The Book.*

With a start, he tried to sit up, but the smallest movement had his head splitting and his whole arm aching. He groaned and allowed his body to slump back into the softness of the bed. Jack couldn't remember the hospital or whatever had happened to him there, so he couldn't be sure of what had happened to the Book. *Did they find it in the coat? Did they take it?* He needed to know.

The door opened, and a young maid poked her head into the room. She was a bit skinnier than he usually preferred, but her skin was clear and her brown hair would probably float down over her shoulders if he unpinned it from the severe bun she wore.

Considering the state of his head and his arm, that would have to wait, he supposed.

"Mr. Grew?" The girl hesitated before she stepped fully into the room. When he didn't respond, she stepped closer to him. When she called his name again, he allowed his eyelids to flutter open, pretending that he was only just waking. "Are you awake, then? You've got visitors, if you're up for it today?"

"Water?" He was surprised at how hoarse he sounded.

"Of course," she said before she scurried off to get him a cup of water. When she returned, she held the cup out at arm's length, but he didn't bother to reach for it.

"My arm," he rasped. "If you could just . . ."

She regarded him warily, but stepped closer to the bedside to help him with the water. He could tell she was nervous, and it warmed something in him to know that even laid out on the bed as he was, she still understood him to be a threat.

Jack took his time sipping the water and enjoying the girl's nearness. She smelled of the soap they used on the bed linens and of the sweetness of fear. As he sipped, she kept her gaze trained on the glass she held in her slender fingers, refusing to meet his eyes. When he finished the last bit, just before she could pull the glass away, he used his free hand to grasp her wrist and was gratified to hear her sharp intake of breath.

Her wrist was as delicate as the rest of her. It felt temptingly fragile beneath his fingers, and he had the strangest idea that he could crush it as easily as the bones of a bird without much effort at all. But he did not tighten his grip, and she did not try to pull away. Instead, her cheeks flushed an attractive pink as her wide eyes met his.

"You must be feeling better if you're already accosting the help," a voice said from the entrance to the room.

The maid took the opportunity offered by Jack's momentary distraction to free herself from his grasp and scurry back from his bedside. Her movement revealed the source of the voice—it was one of the Barclay boys, the younger one, whom he'd been in school with. Thaddeus or Timothy or Theodore. "Theo . . ."

From Theo's flash of a smile, Jack had guessed right. Yes, it was Theo Barclay who had entered the room like they'd been friends all along, instead of bare acquaintances. And with him was a girl who put the maid completely out of Jack's mind.

"Glad to see that you're not half as bad as everyone made it sound," Theo said, stepping aside so the maid could get by. "You remember I told you about my fiancée?"

Jack didn't, of course, but even with the drugs leaving his mind heavy and dull, he still had enough social graces to lie. "Of course," he murmured, wondering why in the hell any man would bring his fiancée to another man's bedside.

"Theo heard that you'd been hurt, and he simply had to come see you," the girl said, her voice a soft fluttering thing, as utterly female as she was. "I hope you don't mind that I came along." She licked nervously at pink lips. "I know we haven't been formally introduced yet. . . ."

Jack decided that he didn't care *why* Theo had brought his fiancée, because the girl was a sight to behold. The purple light of the room complemented her creamy complexion and fair hair, as though it had been drawn just for her. She was dressed in what might have looked like an ordinary day dress on anyone else, but the high neck was made of a pale lace that looked so delicate, it was nearly sheer.

"I'm not overly interested in formalities," Jack said, wishing like hell he knew what he was wearing under the bedsheets. "I can't offer you any refreshments, since my maid seems to have absconded with the water glass, but feel free to have a seat anywhere you'd like."

"We won't be staying that long," Theo said with another good-humored smile. "We just wanted to check in on you. You had quite the luck, didn't you?"

"Did I?" Jack wondered aloud. Considering that he was stuck in a bed, his arm and head hurting like hell, he didn't feel particularly lucky.

"I'd say," Theo told him with a sure nod. "I've seen the pictures in the papers—the destruction was just incredible. After the stories that have been going around town, I half expected you to be at death's door."

"Stories?" Jack asked, trying to piece together the missing parts of his memory from Theo's words. *There was a train*.

"Rumors," Theo amended. "You know how our mothers can be when they sit around and gossip over tea."

Jack could only imagine what his mother and the other women who sat around clucking over the news of the day might have said about him. "I'm fine," he grumbled, trying to sit up again. But another sharp pain jolted through his arm, and he hissed as he sank back into bed. Like some feeble old man. *Weak*.

The girl took a step forward. "Is there anything we can do—"

"No," he growled, and then, realizing how her eyes had widened at the force of his tone, he softened his voice despite the pain that throbbed through his head. "No. I'm fine. The train derailed?" he asked, trying to remember.

"The authorities aren't entirely sure what happened," Theo said. "But from the pictures, it looked like the earth itself opened up. You're damn lucky—your car was turned on its side, but intact. The car after yours? It looked like the explosion ripped right through it. The tracks and everything else were just . . . *gone*. Some of the papers are calling you a hero for making it out alive."

"And the others?" Jack asked. Because there were always others.

"One of the papers got ahold of the doctor who treated you at the site of the wreckage," the girl told him. "He said that you had been conscious when they pulled you out and that you told him you knew who caused the derailment."

"I did?" Jack asked, trying to recall the moments after the crash. It was a blur of pain and confusion, but he did remember one thing more clearly now. *Darrigan and the girl.* Then it came to him—

"They disappeared," Jack said, talking to himself more than them. Which was impossible. People don't just *disappear*, unless . . .

No. How could he have missed it? But it made sense—a sick sort of sense. How else could Darrigan have duped him so easily? How else could the girl have fooled him with her lies? How could either of them have escaped from Khafre Hall without some sort of feral power? *They're Mageus.*

"Disappeared?" the girl asked. "Who disappeared?"

"Harte Darrigan and the girl," Jack said, his voice rough with the hatred he felt for them. They had taken his free will and used him, just as the witch in Greece had.

"Harte Darrigan . . . the magician?" the girl asked, stepping closer.

"He was on that train," Jack told them. "He was in the car with me before everything happened. I *saw* him. And the girl."

Jack saw the way Theo and his girl traded questioning glances. They didn't even bother to hide their skepticism. It was the same type of look people had traded when he'd been dragged back from Greece. They'd thought he'd simply been a lovesick fool then. He'd tried to explain that he hadn't been lovestruck but bespelled. There had been one night of drinking that he couldn't quite remember, and then . . . he hadn't been able to break apart from her after. Not until his cousin had shown up to remove him.

Jack's embarrassment had burned through any gratitude he might have felt for the rescue. Now his anger at being abused again was the glue holding him together.

"They're con artists and thieves, both of them," Jack told Theo, growing more and more agitated. "They ruined me when they destroyed Khafre Hall and took the Order's most prized treasures, and now they're trying to ruin me again."

"You do know that Darrigan is dead, don't you?" Theo asked, his voice careful. "It was all over the papers—he jumped from the Brooklyn Bridge the day before the accident."

"Did anyone find his body?" Jack asked.

"I'm not sure," Theo said, uncertain.

"Then how can you know he's dead?" Jack asked.

"They didn't find his body in the wreckage, either," Theo pointed out. "If he was in the same car as you, he would have been located." But his tone was too patient, too condescending, and it made Jack bristle.

"I told you," Jack said, his patience fraying. "He *disappeared*. They both did. There wouldn't have been a body to find."

The two traded glances again, and Jack felt fury building.

"I know what I saw—Darrigan and the girl were on the train with me. I'd just cornered them and was about to apprehend them. Ask the station police. . . . There was one of them on the car as well."

Theo frowned. "There was an officer on the same car as you, but he didn't make it."

"You truly think that Darrigan and this girl caused a massive train derailment?" the girl asked. There was less doubt than interest in her voice now. "And then you think he disappeared. The only way that could be true is if he were—"

"Mageus," Jack said, supplying the word.

"But the Brink," she pressed, taking yet another step toward Jack's bed. "There haven't been any verifiable reports of feral magic outside the city borders for years. If Darrigan is Mageus, he wouldn't have been able to pass through it."

"I told you, he stole the Order's artifacts. . . ." Jack considered this, turning the problem over in his mind as his head pounded. "Or the girl did."

"Who, exactly, was this girl?" Theo's fiancée asked.

"A con artist named Esta Filosik . . ." He hesitated. "Or that's what she *said* her name was. She was there the night Khafre Hall burned. She helped Darrigan then, and she helped him on the bridge."

"And the Order allowed the two of them into Khafre Hall?" the girl asked. "They didn't realize what Darrigan and the girl were—"

"No," he snapped, before she could finish her question. He glared at her, daring her to ask anything else. Daring her to judge him.

"We should be going, dear," Theo said to the girl, pulling her back.

"But I have more—"

"*Now,*" Theo said more forcefully. "Can we get you anything before we go, Jack? Anything at all?"

He needed the Book.

"Pardon?" Theo said. "What book is it that you'd like?"

He hadn't intended to speak, and his voice broke as he tried to cover his mistake. "My coat," he corrected. "I meant that I'd like my coat."

"Are you cold?" the girl asked, her expression transforming itself again, this time from avid interest to concern. "I could stoke the fire a bit, or perhaps I could bring you another blank—"

"*No,*" he said, not caring that she flinched. He didn't need her pity. "I don't want any damned blankets, and I'm not cold. I want my *coat.*"

"Hold on there, Jack," Theo told him. "There's a pile of your things over here by the chest. Give me a moment to look."

Jack closed his eyes against the lavender light and the concern in the girl's eyes and the pain that still throbbed through him. But behind the darkness of his eyelids, all he could see was his own failure and impotence. He'd been a fool.

"Is this it?" Theo asked, and Jack opened his eyes to see Theo holding the rough woolen overcoat that Harte Darrigan had been wearing when he escaped.

Yes. Yes. Yes, yes, yes . . .

"Bring it to me," Jack demanded, not caring how he sounded. He didn't know where the sudden force in his voice came from or why he felt such an overwhelming desperation to hold that cracked leather in his hands once more.

Jack had to know if *they* had found it. He was in his mother's home, and there was a chance that someone from the Order would have gone through his things. There was a chance that they could have taken the Book before he had an opportunity to discover all its secrets.

"Would you like us to call someone?" Theo offered as he draped the coat over Jack's torso. "Or maybe I could get you something for the pain. There seem to be some bottles here on the bedside table. . . ."

"No—if I could just rest," Jack said, allowing his eyes to close again. Willing the two of them to leave already.

As the weight of the coat settled over him, Jack felt very far away from himself. He felt so drowsy and tired, and yet at the same time, unbearably alert. It must be the drugs they'd given him, the morphine the doctors must have used to set his arm.

"I'm glad to see that you're okay, Jack," Theo said. "Take care of yourself, now, won't you?"

"It was lovely to meet you," the girlish voice echoed.

Jack never opened his eyes. He pretended sleep until he heard the door latch when they closed it behind them. When he knew they were well and truly gone, he used his free hand to turn the ugly garment over. Ignoring the pain it caused, he searched for the opening to the pocket and then . . . *there.*

He held the Ars Arcana up and examined it in the soft light as victory coursed through his veins. It was difficult to flip through the pages while he was reclined, but sitting upright hurt too much. Grimacing from the effort it took to look, he found the small bottle of medicine that Theo had mentioned being on the table next to his bed. He reached for it, but the pain that shot through his arm was nearly blinding. For a moment he considered calling the maid back, but he couldn't risk her seeing the Book.

Bracing himself, Jack tried again, and this time his fingers brushed the glass bottle, knocking it within reach. He unstoppered it and took out two cubes without bothering to read the instructions. They dissolved into bitterness on his tongue, but the pain didn't immediately subside. He could still feel his heartbeat pounding in his very bones. So he tossed two more of the cubes into his mouth, grinding them between his teeth this time.

Slowly the pain started to recede, and as soon as he could breathe again, he opened the Book. The pages were brittle and not at all uniform. They looked like they had been taken from a number of different sources and then somehow bound seamlessly into the small tome. On their surface, they were filled with faded notes and writing—some in Latin, others in something that looked like Greek. Still others were in languages Jack had never seen.

He let his thumb run over the edges of the pages, and Jack couldn't tell if the warmth he felt was coming from the Book itself or from the morphine settling into his veins. After a moment he found that he didn't care, and he began to read.

A NEW CITY

1904—St. Louis

Compared to the brisk spring they'd left in New York, the St. Louis night felt sultry and close against Esta's skin as she walked next to Harte. None of the people crowding the sidewalks around them seemed to mind, though.

Esta and Harte had crossed the Mississippi and arrived in the city earlier that day. After sending a few telegrams in Baltimore, they discovered that Julien was no longer in Chicago. The vaudeville circuit Julien performed on had taken him to St. Louis, and the two of them had followed on the first overnight train they could find.

It had been something of a shock, arriving in the enormous train station filled with tourists in town for the world's fair, but together they'd managed to find their way to a hotel and to get themselves some clothes. Esta told herself that she and Harte were just partners and nothing more, but a night sharing the close quarters of a Pullman berth had left her feeling unsettled and restless. It had been a relief to get a few hours to herself. Now they were outside the theater where Julien Eltinge was performing, waiting to purchase tickets. The excited murmuring of the people out for the night felt electric.

St. Louis certainly wasn't New York. The streets were wider than in lower Manhattan, and most of them were paved with pounded gravel rather than cobblestones. The air hung thick with the coal smoke coming off the barges and riverboats down on the Mississippi. While the streets were lined with restaurants, their gilded names gracing plateglass windows, the lights seemed dim compared to those that shone on Broadway or even in the Bowery.

Esta wondered what Harte thought of it all. Ever since learning that she'd slipped them forward through time, he'd been keeping everything close to the vest. Even now his storm-gray eyes were steady as the line inched forward. But he was frowning slightly, as though he were weighing and measuring the world he was now a part of against expectations it could never live up to. Still, he looked calm, ready for whatever the evening held.

Actually, considering that he'd spent most of the trip green from motion sickness, he looked damn good, dressed in a sleek black evening suit with his dark hair combed back away from the sharp features of his face. Esta wasn't sure how he could possibly look so fresh, considering all the layers of linen and wool that he was wearing. He barely even looked warm, while she felt like she was wrapped in a blanket beneath the layers of corset and skirts. As a bead of sweat rolled down her back, she started to think that maybe picking the raw silk gown for the evening hadn't been the best idea.

It was too late to change now, though. Behind the walls of the theater in front of them, beyond the crowd with its champagne-tinged murmurs, was the first of the stones—the Djinni's Star.

"What time does Julien go on?" she asked as they stepped forward with the line.

"He'll be late in the show," Harte said, glancing up at the marquee, where Julien Eltinge's name was spelled out in the glow of electric lights. "Maybe around nine?"

"I still think it would be easier to slip into his apartment and take the necklace," she told him. They'd argued about it earlier on the train, but Harte had been insistent.

"Maybe—if we knew for sure that the stone was there. But it's not worth the risk of getting caught breaking in when I can just ask him for it."

"I never get caught," Esta said, cutting a look at him. "And do you really think using your affinity on him is the best idea?"

"It's the simplest way."

But Esta wasn't so sure. If *her* affinity felt off—shaky and unsettled—what must his be, with the Book's power inside of him?

The wind kicked up, providing some relief from the warmth of the night as it gusted between the buildings, rustling Esta's silken gown and taffeta wrap. It had a cool metallic scent to it that promised rain, and the clouds overhead, heavy and gray in the twilight sky, seemed to agree. But it also carried something else—a warm energy that was the unmistakable mark of magic.

"Did you feel that?" she asked, but Harte didn't seem to know what she was talking about. He stepped up to the ticket counter, and she focused her attention on the people around them. At first nothing seemed amiss, but then she saw the girl in blue.

If Esta herself hadn't been a thief, she would have thought nothing of the way the girl tripped or of the way the guy leaning near the lamppost reached out to keep the girl from falling. But Esta *was* a thief, so she didn't miss the flick of the girl's wrist or how the guy palmed the small package in the exchange, using the girl's clumsiness to cover for tucking it into his vest.

It took only a moment. The girl in blue thanked the guy and kept walking onward. The guy continued to lean against the lamppost, his broad-brimmed cowboy hat shielding his eyes and hiding most of his features except for a hard mouth. His shoulders had a slouch to them that Esta suspected couldn't be taught.

She was still trying to figure out what the girl might have given the guy when the shrill trilling of a whistle split the air. A moment later Esta turned to see a trio of men running toward the theater. They were wearing long, knee-length dark coats and had white bands with some sort of insignia wrapped around their right arms. On their lapels, golden medallions flashed in the lamplight. They were a bit smaller than normal police badges, but they had the same official look to them.

The guy with the broad hat glanced up at the commotion, but that stiff mouth of his didn't betray any surprise or fear. Instead, the corner of it kicked up, like he'd been expecting them all along. He pulled out a pocket watch that flashed in the light cast by the lamp when he opened it. Lazily, he twisted the dial of the watch, like he had all the time in the world.

Then he tipped back the wide brim of his hat—and looked straight at Esta. He blinked, and then his eyes widened ever so slightly. The motion pulled the sleeve of his shirt back enough to expose a black circular tattoo that wound around his wrist. If he'd been surprised to see her staring, the moment passed quickly. He gave her a wink as he snapped the watch shut, and a burst of icy-hot energy ricocheted through the air . . . and he was *gone*.

She was still staring at the place where he'd disappeared when Harte pulled her back, knocking her off-balance as the three men burst through the line of people waiting. As they passed, Esta felt another wave of magic in their wake. Instinctively, she pulled her own affinity back as she caught herself against Harte.

She felt his arms tighten around her, and her skin burned from his closeness.

But if Harte noticed the same electric pull between them, he didn't show it. "I felt *that*," he said, frowning as he looked for any evidence of danger. "Come on . . ." He led her toward the entrance to the theater as the trio reached the lamppost and grabbed an unsuspecting man who'd been sitting on a bench near where the cowboy had been.

"But—" She was craning her neck, trying to see what was happening and looking for some sign of where the guy with the watch had disappeared to.

"We don't need to get wrapped up in whatever that is." Harte had his arm around her still as he led her into the lobby of the theater.

"*That* was magic," she said. "How can there be magic here?"

"I don't know," Harte told her, glancing back at the doorway of the theater. "But it didn't exactly feel natural."

"It felt . . . *off*, didn't it?" She should have pulled away from him now that they were inside, but she didn't. Even through the layers of material between them, she could feel the warmth of him, an antidote to the cold, unnatural energy that still sifted through the air. Instinctively, she shifted closer, wanting to dispel the unease the event had left in its wake. As she breathed in the warm scent of him, clean and crisp and so familiar, she leaned into him.

It was a mistake. Harte's posture went rigid, and his expression went carefully blank as he unwrapped his arms from her waist and stepped back. "It reminded me a little of the Brink," he said, his tone neutral and matter-of-fact, like he'd never touched her—or at least as though he hadn't meant anything by it. "But what caused it?"

Esta shook off the sting of his indifference. *If that's how it's going to be . . .* "From what I saw, they seemed to be after some cowboy wannabe with a magical pocket watch." She told him about the girl and the drop, and how the guy had looked right at her before he'd disappeared. "It was like he'd already known that they wouldn't catch him."

"But he saw *you*?" He frowned as though this was a problem.

"Looked right at me," she confirmed, remembering the way his expression had shifted slightly when he'd seen her. "But then, I'd been watching him first. Maybe he noticed."

"Do you think they could have been from the Order?" Harte asked.

"The way they were dressed?" The Order only admitted the richest and most exclusive men in the city—old money. "They didn't look the type."

"Then who were they?" Harte asked, frowning. "And who were the people who seemed to be after them?"

"I don't know. I don't like anything about this," she told him. When they had arrived in Baltimore the day before, nothing had seemed obviously different, and she'd breathed a little easier, hoping maybe it meant that Jack having the Book *hadn't* changed things too dramatically. But the cowboy with the watch and the uniformed men set off alarms. She'd never heard of anything like that before—not outside the Brink. "Let's just go. We can check out Julien's house tonight and come back here tomorrow, if we need to."

Harte looked back at the lobby doors and then at the street beyond like he was considering their options. "We're here already," he said after a moment. "Whatever that was seems to be over now, and no one out there was all that alarmed by it. We'll keep alert, but for now let's just get on with it and get out of this town before we run into anything else."

Esta didn't like it, but Harte was right. They'd come this far, and for her to back out now would mean admitting she was afraid. And she wasn't about to do that, especially when *he* didn't seem to be.

The theater's marbled lobby gave way to crimson carpet and walls dripping with crystal and gold. Compared to the spare brick exterior, the opulence of the theater itself was a surprise. When they made their way into the theater proper, the cavernous domed ceiling was painted with scenes of angels and gods, while crystal chandeliers lit the entire space with a soft, sparkling glow. Although the bill was vaudeville, the audience could have been attending a night at the opera as they sat in their velvet-lined seats draped in silks and furs and ornamented with jewels. Dressed in their finery, no one seemed bothered by the stuffy warmth of the air. Women lazily fanned themselves and men quietly dabbed at the beads of sweat on their foreheads without complaint.

Esta's fingers itched. In the dark, it would be so easy to take one or two of those jewels, especially since she didn't know what else lay ahead for them. The security that one emerald brooch might offer was more than tempting . . . but they still had to find Julien *and* get the necklace from him. Sticking around long enough to be caught was a rookie mistake, and Esta was anything but a rookie.

They'd only just gotten to their seats when the lights went down, leaving the theater in darkness except for the expanse of the crimson velvet curtain over the stage and making it impossible to talk anymore about what had happened. Next to her, Harte leaned forward ever so slightly, waiting for the curtain to rise. She used the cover afforded by the darkness in the theater to study him, his sharp features all shadow and light from the glow of the stage. His eyes were serious as the first act came on and split the silence with song.

For Esta, the next hour felt like it would never end. Stuck in the seat between Harte, who was leaning away from her like he didn't want to even bump her elbow, and an old woman whose furs smelled so strongly of mothballs that Esta's eyes watered, she couldn't manage to work up any interest in the acts. She didn't care about the troupe of dancers who kicked their bare legs to the ceiling or the small, goateed man who performed a monologue that at any other time might have had Esta in stitches. Not even the svelte woman dressed all in black who swallowed swords while telling bawdy jokes. It was more than an hour into the show when an act finally caught her attention—a woman who sang in a sultry contralto.

The woman wasn't classically pretty, but there was something completely compelling about her. She had an interesting face, with pale, milky skin and lightly flushed cheeks. Her wide mouth was painted in a bow, and she was dressed in a glittering aquamarine gown accented with pearls. The woman consumed the stage without moving more than a foot or two in either direction, and her voice . . . It was clear and resonant and contained all the pain and hope and wonder of the lyrics of the song.

"It's time," Harte whispered, leaning forward and gesturing for Esta to go.

"What?" She turned to him, confused. The plan was to leave while Julien was on the stage, so they could beat him to his dressing room.

"It's time," Harte repeated, nodding toward the woman on the stage.

"I thought we were going to wait for Julien's act," she whispered.

"We were." Amusement sparked in his eyes. "*That's* Julien."

INFAMOUS

1904—St. Louis

Harte knew that he should have prepared Esta for Julien's act, but the look of surprise on her face made keeping the secret worth it. The delight in her expression was also an enormous relief. The truth was, Harte hadn't exactly been sure how she would react to learning that Julien Eltinge had made a name for himself by impersonating women on the stage—not everyone accepted Julien's particular talent. But Esta took one more look toward the stage, her full mouth parted in a sort of awe as Julien hit a heartrending and impossibly high note, and she smiled. Then she gave Harte a sure nod and gathered her skirts in preparation to leave.

She was dressed in a gown of cloud gray, one she'd picked because she'd thought it was sedate enough to avoid notice. He didn't have the guts to tell her that it had the exact opposite effect. Made from a silk that looked almost liquid, it rippled against the ground as she walked, making her look like some sort of otherworldly apparition. It had drawn the eyes of men—and women—all the way from the hotel to the theater, and it had taken everything in him not to reach for her, to put a proprietary arm around her, so that every one of those onlookers—and Esta herself—knew who she was with.

But he didn't, because after he'd spent the last twenty-four hours in close quarters with her—first on the train and then as they navigated the unfamiliar city to find a hotel and buy evening clothes—what little self-control he had was fraying.

It had been a mistake to touch her earlier. He'd acted on instinct to pull her out of the way before those men in the dark coats had knocked her over, but the moment his arms had gone around her, he'd sensed her—the energy of her affinity, the heart of who and what she was—even through the thin leather of his gloves and the layers she was wearing. And then she'd settled into his arms as though she belonged there. He could have kissed her right there in the middle of the crowded lobby and damn all the repercussions.

The power inside of him had certainly wanted him to, but the way it had swelled at Esta's nearness had been enough to bring him back to himself, and he'd held it together. He had pushed the power and all of its wanting down and let go of her. He'd managed to keep his hands to himself ever since. He'd just have to *keep* managing.

"Harte?" Esta asked.

"What?" He blinked and realized she was staring at him. She'd been saying something, and he'd missed it.

"I said, which way?" she asked, unaware of the true direction of his thoughts.

Once they were back in the lobby, Harte could hear the rumble of applause within as Julien finished his first song, even through the closed theater doors. They'd have fifteen, maybe twenty minutes before his act was over—not much time considering that Harte hadn't had a chance to case the building.

But theaters were all pretty much the same, and Harte understood the rhythm of life on the stage and the way the world behind the curtain ticked like the gears of a clock, hidden and essential. He went with his instincts and led the way to an unremarkable door at the end of the lobby. Once through it, the lights were dimmer and the familiar energy of backstage enveloped him. He gave his eyes a moment to adjust as he took off his gloves—just in case. He prepared himself, making sure that the power inside of him was locked down tight as he took Esta's hand in his. Ignoring the surge of warmth and wanting that rose up within him, he led her through the maze that was backstage, toward where the dressing rooms were housed.

When they turned a corner, they ran into a woman with dark blond hair and an armful of fabric. From the look of it, she was a costumer, one of the backstage workers who took care of the performers in between acts, and for a moment Harte thought of Cela—of his mother—but when the woman's eyes went wide at the sight of them, Harte knew it meant trouble.

"You're not supposed to be back here," the woman said, her brows drawing together as she looked the two of them up and down, taking in the evening clothes they were wearing.

Esta's hand tightened around his, but Harte simply pasted on his most charming smile—the one that usually got him whatever he wanted. "No wrong turn at all," he said as he dropped Esta's hand and extended his now-free hand toward the woman. "Charlie Walbridge."

The woman only frowned at him as she looked down at his bare, out-stretched hand with brows bunched. Her nose scrunched up as though he were offering her a rotten piece of meat.

"Walbridge, as in the son of Cyrus P. Walbridge . . . the owner of this theater," he added, dropping his hand and infusing his voice with a hint of impatience. "This is my fiancée, Miss Ernestine Francis." It hadn't taken much effort earlier to figure out who the owner of the theater was, along with the names of a couple of the other more important men in town. He had no idea if Councilman Francis even had a daughter, but he knew that names—*certain* names—had power.

The gambit worked. The woman's eyes widened slightly, and she sputtered a hurried apology.

Harte gave her an appraising look. "Yes, well . . . mistakes do happen, don't they? I'll be sure to tell my father how dedicated his employees are to the theater's well-being, especially you, Miss . . ." He paused, waiting for her to supply her name.

"It's Mrs., actually, though my husband's been gone these past three years now. Mrs. Joy Konarske."

"Well, it's been a pleasure to meet you, Mrs. Konarske." He offered his hand again. "I'll be sure to tell my father how dutiful you've been. He'll be pleased to know his theater is being well looked after."

The woman's cheeks went a little pink as she paused to shift her burden of fabric so she could grasp Harte's outstretched hand. Her palm was rough and calloused from the work of laundering the costumes and tending to the performers' wardrobes each night, and Harte felt a flicker of guilt as he focused on pushing his affinity toward her, pulsing it gently—*just a little*—through the delicate boundary of flesh and into the very heart of who and what she was.

Her eyes widened, but she didn't pull away. *They never do,* he thought.

When Harte finally released the woman's hand a moment later, she had a slightly dazed look in her eyes. Giving the two of them a shaky smile, she wandered off, and Harte knew she would leave them be. She would forget having ever seen him—because he had ordered her to. And the moment she heard or saw a description of either Esta or himself, Mrs. Joy Konarske would feel a wave of such revulsion that she would do anything necessary to escape the person asking.

"Did you . . . ?" Esta asked, her voice low.

He met her eyes, expecting judgment but finding instead only worry. Or perhaps that was sadness? "Would you rather she tell someone she saw us here?" he whispered.

"Of course not," she whispered. "It's just . . . do you think it's safe? With the Book's power in you?"

He hadn't considered that. Why *hadn't* he considered that?

"I don't know." It wasn't like he'd had much choice. He'd done the only thing he could do, unless they wanted to be discovered before they even began.

Luckily, they didn't run into anyone else before they found Julien's dressing room and let themselves in. Despite the number of women's wigs and gowns that filled much of the room, it was a masculine space. Which, considering Julien, wasn't surprising. On the dressing table, an ashtray contained the remains of multiple cigars, and the cloying ghost of their smoke still hung thick in the air.

"How long do we have?" Esta asked.

"Maybe another ten minutes or so."

"I'll look here, if you check the dressing table," Esta said, turning to the large upright steamer trunk in the corner.

Harte knew it couldn't hurt to look. If they found the necklace, they could avoid Julien altogether. But he didn't really expect the necklace to be in the dressing room—Julien wasn't stupid. Even if Julien didn't know about the power the stone contained, he would be more careful than to leave it in an unlocked dressing room in a crowded theater. The heavy platinum collar was set with a turquoise-colored stone shot through with glittering veins of some silvery substance that made it look like a sky full of stars. It was singular, and clearly valuable, and Julien would keep something like that somewhere safe . . . *especially* with the note Harte had sent along with it.

But Esta was right. It wouldn't hurt to look while they were there.

Before he'd even managed to sit at the dressing table, Esta had pulled a pin from her hair and popped the lock of the trunk. Harte paused to watch her as she began sorting through the drawers inside of it, and then he turned back to the dressing table.

For a moment he felt the shock of recognition. How many times had he sat at the same sort of table, the glow of the electric light over the mirror illuminating the familiar planes and angles of his own face? There were pots of stage paint and kohl on the tabletop, and their familiar scents came to him even beneath the staleness of the full ashtray, teasing at his memories and inspiring a pang of longing and loss so sharp, it surprised him.

He was never going to sit at a dressing table like this again. He was done with that life.

Even if he managed to get out of this mess alive—even if they could exorcise the power lurking beneath his skin *and* get away from the Order *and* stop Nibsy—Harte was supposed to be dead. He couldn't just resurrect himself. There would be no more applause, no more footlights. He would never again have the quiet solitude of a dressing room to call his own.

Maybe he would find a new name, a new life that he could be happy with, but it wouldn't be on the stage. And he would miss it—the rush of nerves before and the thrill of the applause after. He hadn't realized just how much until that moment.

"Find anything?" Esta asked, still rustling through papers in one of the trunk's drawers. It was enough to shake him out of his maudlin bout of self-pity and get to work.

"Not yet," he told her. He opened the first of the drawers, one filled with small pots of rouge and the powdery smell of talc. He didn't have to search through the items to see that the necklace wasn't there.

"What is all of this?" Esta murmured, and Harte turned to see what she had found.

She was holding a leather box, trimmed in gold and stamped with a gilded filigreed emblem that was inscribed with a stylized monogram of the letters *VP*. Harte came over to look as Esta pulled out a small golden medallion that hung from a green satin ribbon. It was the kind of medallion important dignitaries or generals wear when they dress for a parade. *Odd . . .*

He took the medal from her and examined it. Like the box itself, it was inscribed with an ornate *VP*, but the surface bore the portrait of a long-faced man with a full beard. The figure might have been a crusader or a saint, with his sharp cheekbones and solemn expression, but his face seemed to be partially obscured, as though a piece of fabric was hanging over it. Around the edge of the medallion were markings that could have been simple decorations or an unknown language—it was impossible to tell.

"I don't know," Harte said, frowning at the piece. The Julien he knew hadn't been involved with anything but the theater, and that medallion didn't look or feel like a prop.

"There's more," Esta told him, carefully lifting out a piece of scarlet silk that had been neatly folded into a square. It was a sash of some kind, and it, too, was pinned with another medallion. At the bottom of the box lay a small silver tray, ornately wrought with more of the strange symbols around the edges of an even more elaborate rendering of the same two letters—*VP.*

The light over the dressing table dimmed for a moment before returning to its normal brightness. "Put it away," he told Esta, handing back the medal. "That's the signal for the next act. Julien will be back any second now."

Esta worked to put the trunk back together and relocked it. She was just slipping the pin back into her hair when the dressing room door opened and the painted songstress from the stage entered the small confines of the dressing room.

It was always a shock to see Julien up close when he was dressed for his act. Even without the distance of the audience and the glare of the lights, he had mastered his art. His impersonation didn't rely on any of the camp that other female impersonators used. His stage persona wasn't a caricature of a woman. It wasn't clownish or overdone to get laughs. No, Julien's art—his true talent—was in his ability to become the thing itself. Had Harte passed Julien, dressed as he was now, on the streets, he wouldn't have seen anything other than the woman standing before him.

Not seeming to realize that he wasn't alone, Julien pulled off the perfectly coiffed blond wig and placed it on a wooden mannequin's head. Then he walked over to sit in front of the mirrored dressing table. Before he bothered with the makeup or the dress, Julien took a thick black cigar from a small tabletop humidor and lit it. He took a deep drag, allowing the smoke to wreathe his head as he reached for the decanter next to the ashtray and poured himself two fingers. He took a long drink before he put the cigar back between his teeth and began removing the elbow-length gloves he was wearing.

"You know, Darrigan . . ." Julien looked up and caught Harte's eye in the mirror. His deep, husky voice was completely at odds with the bright crimson paint on his mouth. "You're looking damn good for a dead man."

Harte gave a careless shrug. "I can't say that I feel all that dead."

Julien turned, a half smile curving at his mouth around the cigar as he shook his head. "I can't believe you are standing here. I can't believe you're in my dressing room."

"It's good to see you, Jules," Harte said, stepping forward to extend his hand in greeting.

Julien stood and took Harte's outstretched hand. "It's damn good to see you, too, Darrigan."

"Glad to hear it," Harte told him as he sent a small pulse of his affinity toward Julien.

Harte never saw thoughts clearly, just impressions and feelings. The most immediate of Julien's memories came first—the glare of the lights, the roar of the applause Julien had just received, the hot, sharp satisfaction that Julien had felt. Harte ignored his own yearning for those lights and for the warm rush that applause had always given him and concentrated instead on his purpose—some hint of the stone's fate. It came in an instant, the clear image of the necklace with its fantastical stone, and latching onto that image, Harte focused everything he was and sent another burst of magic toward Julien, transgressing the thin barrier between him and his friend and sending Julien a simple message. A single command.

Julien's expression faltered, his eyes slightly dazed and his brows creasing together momentarily. But then Harte released him, and Julien's expression cleared. Unaware of all that had just transpired, Julien turned back to his mirror and reached for his large jar of cold cream. He ignored Harte and Esta both as he spread the cream over one half of his face and then started wiping away the light base and bright rouge.

Esta had been watching all of this without saying a word, so Harte gestured for her to come forward. "Jules, I want you to meet someone," Harte said.

Julien's eyes lifted to Esta's in the mirror, and Harte knew exactly what his old friend was seeing—the way the silk gown she wore clung to every curve and the way she'd painted her mouth a subtle pink and pinned her hair into a style that looked artful and careless all at once. She looked like she came from money, proper and polished. But with her height and her confidence, she also looked dangerous, like a debutante on the verge of something more exciting.

A look of appreciation flashed over Julien's face as he examined Esta through the reflection of the mirror.

Mine, a voice inside Harte whispered in response, but he couldn't tell if it came from his own thoughts or that other power. Not caring all that much at the moment, he took Esta by the hand, so there was no mistaking who she was with.

"This is—"

"Oh, I know exactly who this is," Julien interrupted, turning Janus-faced to look at them both once again.

"You do?" Esta asked, glancing at Harte with a wary expression.

"Of course, Miss Filosik." Julien picked up the stub of the cigar again and gestured toward them before raising one brow in their direction. "I knew who you were the moment I walked into this room. After all . . . you're *infamous.*"

THE ANTIDOTE FOR GOSSIP

1902—New York

Jack could hear the commotion in his mother's parlor long before he made it to the bottom of the staircase. By the time he reached the lower steps, a cold sweat had broken out on his forehead and he wanted nothing more than to sit down, but the rumble of his uncle's voice told him that he should keep moving.

Thank god the mousy little maid had gotten over her initial fear of him. Without her mentioning his uncle's sudden arrival, Jack might have slept through the visit, completely unaware of how his family was arranging his future. It didn't matter if his head was swirling with the morphine he'd just taken or that his body still felt like . . . Well, it felt like he'd been hit by a train, didn't it? He would walk into the parlor under his own power and take the reins of his own fate.

". . . someone got to him," his uncle was roaring, waving a crumpled handful of newsprint at his mother.

"No one has been here," his mother said, her voice shaking as it often did when she was overwrought. "I think I would know if a newspaperman came into my home."

"How else would they know any of this?" Morgan waved the paper at her again.

"Pierpont, dear—" His aunt Fanny was sitting next to Jack's mother, and her tone had a warning in it, not that his uncle seemed to care.

Jack's cousin was there as well, standing off to the side with his arms crossed and the same scowl on his face that he had worn the entire voyage back from Greece last year. It truly was a family affair, which always meant trouble for Jack.

It took a moment before any of them realized that he'd arrived. His mother saw him first, and she leaped to her feet at the sight of him. "Darling, what are you doing out of bed?" She wasn't three steps toward him before his uncle stepped in her path and waved the newspaper he'd been brandishing in Jack's face.

"What is the meaning of this, boy?"

The room was spinning a little, but Jack forced himself to stay upright. "The meaning of what? I've been abed for—" He looked to his mother. The days had all run together. "How long have I been up there?"

"Three days, dear," she said, a small, sad smile on her face as she beamed at him. "You should sit down. You're not well." She went over to the tufted chair closest to him and began arranging the pillows.

He couldn't stand her constant fussing, like he was still a child. It was how they all saw him, he knew. And they were all wrong. "I'm fine," he said, waving her off.

He wasn't fine, but he damned sure wasn't going to admit it in front of his uncle and his cousin. The last thing he would be was weak in front of them. "I've no idea what you're referring to," he told Morgan, meeting the old man's gaze. "Perhaps if you'd stop shouting and explained it, I could offer a response."

Morgan glared at him. "Who did you talk to?"

"Recently?" Jack asked. "No one but my mother and the ever-present parade of doctors and maids who insist on constantly intruding on my rest and recovery."

Most of the maids were pretty enough, but all the doctors had been a nuisance, constantly checking on him and telling him to rest, when all he wanted to do was study the Book he'd hidden beneath the mountain of pillows and blankets the maids piled onto the bed. Day and night, he wanted only to pore over the pages and unlock its secrets.

"Then how did the *Herald* manage to publish this story?" Morgan thrust the paper at him.

Jack swayed a little on his feet, but he opened the crumpled page to find a headline about himself. He let his eyes skim over it. "What of it?" he asked. Nothing seemed amiss. "None of this is untrue. Darrigan and the girl were on the train before it derailed. The authorities said that there wasn't a bomb, so it might well have been magic that caused the accident."

"None of that matters," Morgan said. "I don't care about some damn train derailment. I care about the fact that this reporter knows what happened at Khafre Hall—that the fire wasn't an accident of faulty wiring. Do you know what lengths the Inner Circle undertook to ensure that the truth of the Khafre Hall disaster did not become public? It was a delicate thing, to steer the press away from the real cause of the fire, and yet here it is, a full-page spread that reveals not only that we were robbed of our most important artifacts, but that we were robbed by common *trash*. This article knows everything. Who did you talk to?"

The past few days were a haze of pain and morphine . . . and the thrall of the Book. Jack could have talked to Roosevelt himself, and he wouldn't necessarily have remembered. Not that he would admit that now. "No one," he said instead. "I've no idea how this . . . Reynolds, whoever he is, knows any of this."

"Well, he does, and it's made a damn mess of things," Morgan said, ripping the paper from Jack's hands. "Do you know how *weak* this makes the Order look? We're already getting word from the other Brotherhoods that they're concerned about the state of the Conclave—about the Order's ability to host it. After all, if I can't control my own family, how can we possibly think to arrange an event as important as the Conclave?" He tossed the paper aside.

"I don't know why you assume it was my fault," Jack said, bristling at his uncle's tone.

"Because it usually *is* your fault," his cousin said. "It's one scheme after another with you, Jack, and none of them are reasonable. You don't think things through. Are you sure you didn't give this interview?"

Jack clenched his jaw to keep from railing at the snideness in his cousin's tone. Across the room, his mother was still looking at him with a sadness in her eyes that made him want to smash his fist into her precious collection of figurines. When he spoke, it took effort to make his words measured and calm. "This is the first I've even been out of bed."

But his cousin wasn't listening. "Maybe we should give Jack something of a holiday, to recuperate," his cousin suggested to his uncle. "Until this all blows over."

"It's not going to blow over," Morgan spat. "This isn't a private family matter, like the problem in Greece last year. That damn article is everywhere, and the other papers are picking up the story as well. If we send him off now, it's going to look like we have something to hide. That's the last thing we want—it would give credence to the story."

"What else can we do with him?" his cousin asked.

"I'm standing right here," Jack said darkly. He felt out of breath just standing there, but thankfully, the morphine he'd taken before he came down had eased the pain in his arm and in his head.

"As though that matters in the slightest," his uncle sneered. Then he turned back to his son, Jack's cousin. "We'll demand a retraction."

"From the *Herald*?" His cousin shook his head. "It's not much more than a gossip rag these days. They don't care whether the story's accurate, so long as it sells. It might be better to meet them on their own terms. Get another story out there, one that sheds some doubt on this one. I can talk to Sam Watson, if you want. You remember, I introduced you at the Metropolitan. He's been a great friend to the Order, first with the theft at the Met and then in the past few weeks with his editorials about the dangers of a certain criminal element. I'm sure he could do an interview with Jack and reframe the story."

"I don't want to do any damn interview," Jack said, but no one was listening.

"Do that," his uncle said, pacing. "It's a start, but it's not enough. Retracting the story doesn't change the fact that this Reynolds has made the Order look like old fools."

Which you are, Jack thought. But even with the morphine loosening his mind, he managed to keep his mouth shut tight. He didn't need to worry about his uncle or the Order any longer now that he had the Book.

"It sounds to me like what you need is an engagement," his aunt Fanny ventured.

Morgan turned to her, impatient. "Thank you, dearest, but this matter doesn't concern you."

His aunt ignored the dismissal. "If you're trying to neutralize unwanted gossip, you need something more exciting for the press to focus on than an interview, Pierpont. Trust me. The world of gossip is one I am intimately familiar with, and I have far more experience at controlling it than you do. When a girl's reputation is soiled, the best thing her family can do is to get her engaged, and quickly. There's nothing like a big society wedding to distract the gossips. Isn't that right, Mary?" she asked, turning to Jack's mother.

His mother, a small, weak woman who'd become even more so with age, looked troubled. "I don't think Jack's in any condition to court anyone," she said tentatively, "though I suppose the Stewart girl might be interested since she had such a dismal season."

"I am not being shackled to some failed debutante," Jack said. He certainly wasn't going to allow his mother and aunt to arrange a marriage to save his reputation, like they might for some ruined girl.

"No, dear," his aunt told his mother. "I would never do that to some poor girl."

Jack opened his mouth to argue, but he couldn't figure out what to say. He didn't want to be married off, but his aunt's flippant dismissal was insulting.

"We don't need an *actual* wedding. If you want to stop gossip, you give them something else to talk about. It must simply be an event. A *spectacular* event." His aunt turned to Morgan. "A party or a gala of some sort. The Order could host it, which would make it a show of your continued strength."

"It's hardly the time for a party, Fanny."

His aunt *tsk*ed. "One does not hide from the world when tongues begin to wag, Pierpont. One shows up at the opera wearing the finest gown one can find."

"It is also no time to think about shopping," Morgan growled.

"Mother has a point," Jack's cousin said, rubbing at his chin thoughtfully. "The Order could host a gala—something large and elaborate. Even better if it's an exclusive event. That would get the papers interested in covering it."

"And where would we host it?" Morgan asked darkly. "Khafre Hall is a pile of rubble and ash, if you remember correctly."

"Use our ballroom," his aunt said. "But you can't simply throw a ball. You need something more original than that." She considered the problem for a moment. "What about a tableau vivant?"

"Aren't they a bit risqué?" his mother asked.

"They're perfectly appropriate, if they're depicting great art," his aunt said primly. "But yes. They're often considered quite risqué, which is the entire point. News of it would cause a stir. There would be speculation for weeks about which artworks would be selected and who would be posing for each of the scenes."

"Not simply art," his cousin said, shaking his head. "Scenes from some flouncy rococo paintings won't do. If we're to restore the Order's reputation, we need to present great works that show the Order's strength and importance. Scenes of the dangers of feral magic and the power of science and enlightenment to protect the people. It could work."

"Possibly," Morgan said darkly, considering the proposition. "But we would have to make sure this one doesn't muck everything up again," he added, nodding toward Jack. "We'll have to make sure he's well out of sight."

"*This one* is standing right here," Jack muttered again. And again they ignored him. He'd had enough, he thought, and began to retreat to the relative sanity of his room. They could figure out whatever they wanted to do as long as it didn't include parading him around as a bridegroom. He had other, more important matters to attend to.

"Oh, no," his aunt said. "You can't hide him away."

"Why the hell not?" Morgan asked.

"Every society wedding needs a bride, Pierpont. That's the entire point," his aunt said.

Jack stopped in his tracks and turned back to the room.

"Everyone shows up to the church to see the chit dressed in white and redeemed," his aunt continued. "Everyone wants to know if it was truly a love match, or if the groom looks ready to dash. If you want to discredit this article, you need to show you've nothing to hide."

"I am not marrying some girl," Jack said again, his voice clipped and barely containing his frustration.

"I'm not talking about you taking a bride, dear. I'm talking about you *being* the bride," his aunt said with a dreamy smile.

"Like hell—" Jack started to say, but his aunt was still talking.

"You must make Jack the focus," she told his uncle.

"Absolutely not," Morgan growled, his nose twitching with disgust at the idea.

"It's the only way," his aunt said, looking at Jack with a dangerously thoughtful expression. Nothing good ever came of meddling women when they started to think. "Yes. I can see it now," she told Morgan. "You make Jack the man of the hour, the celebrant of the night. The event will show that the Order isn't afraid or weak or even laid low, and you can use this story to your advantage. You can't retract what's been written any more than a girl can reclaim her virginity, but you can use it to help your cause. Recast Jack as a hero who discovered the danger on the train, a danger that reveals the continued necessity of the Order."

"I don't like it," Morgan said.

"That's not the point, dear," his aunt told Morgan. "What poor girl likes being forced into marriage because of one little indiscretion when men get to have as many as they like? The point is in the necessity. You must take the story and make it your own. It's the surest way, and it will shore up the Order's power at the same time."

"I'm not some pawn to be used," Jack growled. His head felt light and heavy all at once from the morphine in his veins, but his anger felt like something pure. How dare they try to arrange his life. How *dare* they treat him like some stupid little chit being traded between men. "I deserve to have a say in this."

Morgan turned to him. "From the evidence in this article, you've already had your say. Now your choice is to listen or to leave. Do I make myself clear?"

He was clenching his teeth so tightly that he suspected they would crack at any moment, but Jack gave his uncle a tight nod. "Crystal."

They turned back to their planning as though he were no more than a misbehaving child, scolded and dismissed. *Fine.* Let them think that. Let them believe that he would bow and scrape to win their favor again. They didn't realize that already they were becoming unnecessary. The world was spinning on without them, and so would Jack. While they fussed like women over linens and china patterns, he would be learning and planning, and when the moment was right, he would step into their place and make the old men who thought they ruled the city obsolete.

But until then Morgan wasn't the only one who had contacts and people who could do him favors. Jack would use one of his to find this R. A. Reynolds. He'd met Paul Kelly a few weeks back, and from all he'd heard, Kelly wouldn't have a problem with delivering a message for him. He would make sure that damn newspaperman was sorry he ever crossed Jack Grew.

CONSEQUENCES

1904—St. Louis

Had Esta not been trained since she was a child to suppress every flicker of emotion when faced with some sudden danger, her jaw might have dropped at Julien Eltinge's words. Instead, she kept her features placid, the combination of boredom and cool poise that never failed to evade attention. As much as she now loathed the man who had raised her, she was grateful in that moment for her ability to hide her reaction so completely. But inside, her instincts were on high alert, and her stomach felt like she'd just been sucker punched.

"Infamous?" Esta asked. "I'm not sure what you've heard about me, but surely infamous is overstating things, Mr. Eltinge."

Julien's mouth hitched up around his cigar again. "Oh, I don't think it's overstating things at all," he replied, his dark eyes glittering. They were too sharp. Too perceptive—and she had a feeling that so was he. Setting the cigar back in the ashtray, Julien turned back to the mirror and began removing the makeup on the other side of his face. "After all, you can't destroy a train and not expect to get a reputation, you know," he said as calmly and easily as someone talking about the weather.

Destroy a train?

The dressing room seemed to fall away, and all at once Esta felt as though she were back on the train out of New Jersey. The stone that she was wearing against her arm almost felt warm at the memory of how hard it had been to grasp the seconds, to find the right moment to pull them through to get away from Jack. Though she was on solid ground, Esta's legs felt suddenly unsteady, just as they had when the ground beneath the train had seemed to quake, like the train was about to run itself off the rails. And even in the warmly lit dressing room, the darkness that had tugged at her vision and her consciousness haunted her.

No . . . that's impossible.

"But please, let's not stand on ceremony. You must call me Julien." He glanced up at Esta in the mirror, smiling slightly as he wiped more of the makeup from his face. "After all, a friend of Darrigan's is a friend of mine."

"What are you going on about, Julien?" Harte asked. "She didn't destroy anything—certainly not a train."

"I suppose it would be the sort of thing one *would* remember. . . ." Julien gave her another of those too-perceptive looks. "It's what all the papers claimed, though."

"And you believed them?" Harte asked, scorn coloring his tone. "You of all people should know not to trust those muckrakers."

Julien's affable expression flickered slightly, but he didn't immediately respond. Esta noticed that he was still watching her, and he continued to study her for a few moments longer, before turning back to the dressing table. He took his time wiping the rest of the cold cream and makeup from his face, erasing the woman who had commanded the stage until all that was left was the man beneath, a man who was no less compelling.

There was nothing remotely feminine about Julien's features without the light base or the brightness of the rouge on his cheeks and lips. Instead, he had a rugged, almost Mediterranean look to him, with olive-toned skin, sweat-damp black hair that held the hint of a curl, and coal-dark eyes that were as perceptive as a raven's. He picked up the cigar again—an affectation, Esta realized—wielding the thick stump of it like a sword.

Julien turned to face the two of them then, and his voice was serious when he spoke. "To be honest, Darrigan, I didn't pay attention to the story when it first happened. There's always some accident or another the papers are going on about. But then that one fellow claimed it *wasn't* an accident. The only reason I even noticed it really is because he claimed *you* were there."

"What fellow was that?" Harte asked.

"What's his name—the one who always runs with Roosevelt these days," Julien said, wagging the cigar in the air as he tried to think. "Grew, I think it is. Gerald or James . . ."

Esta's stomach went tight. "Jack."

"That's it." Julien pointed the cigar at her. "Jack Grew—one of the Morgans, isn't he?"

"J. P. Morgan's nephew," Harte supplied, but his voice sounded as hollow as Esta suddenly felt.

Julien nodded, apparently not noticing either of their reactions. "Yes, that one. He got caught up in the mess. A few days after it happened, one of the papers came out with this whole story about how the derailment wasn't an accident. Jack Grew claimed that the two of you were the ones who set some fire and burned down the headquarters of the Order of Ortus Aurea in New York to cover a theft and that he'd tracked you to the train and had almost apprehended you when you attacked him—"

"*I* attacked *him*?" Esta didn't even try to hide the disgust in her voice.

"And blew up half the train to escape," Julien finished. "A lot of people died in the crash, you know. After Grew claimed it wasn't an accident, the powers that be started paying attention—oh, don't look so offended, Darrigan. I'm just telling you what the papers said."

"You're accusing us of destroying a train, Jules," Harte said, his voice lower and more dangerous now. "Of killing innocent people."

"I'm not accusing *you* of anything. You're supposed to be dead, after all. Nasty fall off a bridge, from what I heard."

"So you're accusing me?" Esta asked, still trying to make sense of the strange person that was Julien Eltinge.

She knew men like him, men who used their good looks and easy confidence to get their way. Men like Logan, who she'd thought was a friend and a partner until he'd turned against her. Men like Harte, too, if she were honest with herself. Julien's charm was a warning of sorts—a sign that she had to be on alert. But there was something else beneath the charm, and that part of him was still a puzzle.

"I'm not accusing anyone," Julien said.

Harte let out an impatient breath. "You're trying my patience, Jules."

Julien gave Esta a wry look out of the corner of his eye. "You know, he can be a jackass sometimes." He paused to consider what he'd just said. "Actually, he's a jackass more often than not, isn't he? But I never knew him for a murderer. You, on the other hand . . ." He looked at Esta full on now, a question in his darkly perceptive eyes. "I don't know *you* at all."

"She's with me." Harte stepped forward, slightly in front of her, to assert himself physically as he spoke. "That's all you need to know."

Esta barely stopped herself from rolling her eyes in exasperation. Harte had pretty much ignored her since they'd left New York, and *now* he was suddenly interested? Typical. But in front of Julien, she let him have his little moment.

Jules gave Harte an inquiring look. "I see," he said, amusement brightening his expression when he finally looked at Esta again. Then he let out a soft chuckle. "Harte Darrigan . . . I never thought to see the day. . . ." He laughed again.

Esta lifted her chin slightly and affected what she hoped was a look of utter disinterest, even as she was still trying to process everything Julien had just told them. Something had happened to the train they were on after they had slipped through time—something that had never happened before.

"Tell me about the train," Esta demanded.

Julien held Esta's gaze a few moments longer before he began to speak. "There was a big derailment a couple of years ago. The accident tore a gaping hole into a section of track just outside the station in New Jersey. From the reports in the papers, the track was gone. Utterly *demolished*, and half the train with it. The inspectors said that damage like that could have only been the result of an explosion. At first they thought it was one of the anarchist groups that are always blowing things up when they don't get their way, but then a couple days after, the *Herald* broke the story about this Jack Grew character. Apparently, he claimed that the two of you were responsible. Of course, most people thought he was cracked, seeing as how Darrigan here was supposed to *already* be dead— no offense—"

"None taken," Harte said, but his jaw was tight, and Esta had a feeling he didn't like to be reminded.

"And then there was his claim that it wasn't a bomb. He said you used magic."

"Magic?" Esta asked, pretending to be surprised.

"Claimed that you were Mageus," Julien said, implying the unspoken question.

"We've known each other for ages, Jules. If I were Mageus, don't you think you would know?" Harte asked, bringing Julien's attention back to him. "If either one of us were Mageus, how would we have gotten out of the city?"

Esta tried not to hold her breath as she waited for Julien's answer.

"That was the question everyone was asking," Julien said finally. "Dangerous magic outside the protection of the Brink? It should have been impossible. But they never found your bodies in the wreckage, and Grew continued to swear you had both been there.

"Of course, his people used the whole thing as proof that the Order's work was still important. The Order denied that magic could escape the confines of the Brink, just as they denied that the fire at their headquarters had been anything but an accident—faulty wiring or some such thing. Nothing could have been stolen from them because only the devil's own thief could have broken into the Order of Ortus Aurea's vaults. As you can imagine, the public *loved* that. The Devil's Thief."

"The Devil's Thief?" Esta asked.

"That's what they started calling you," Julien said, stubbing out the cigar for good this time. "You were in all the papers for a while. Everyone was trying to figure out who you were and where you'd gone. Every reporter was trying to unmask the Devil's Thief."

"Damn stupid name," Harte muttered.

Julien laughed. "Maybe, but it made a helluva headline, if you ask me."

"I didn't," Harte said flatly.

Julien ignored him. "It has the right . . . je ne sais *something*. Really grabs attention." He glanced more directly at Esta. "It would play great onstage, if you're ever interested in the theater business?"

Harte spoke before she could answer. "She's not."

Esta shot Harte a look, but he didn't even see it. His focus was on Julien, and his impatience felt like a living, breathing thing.

Julien didn't seem to notice. Or maybe he didn't care. With a shrug, he continued. "Damn shame. Tall girl like you? I bet you've got a great set of legs under those skirts—"

"Julien . . . ," Harte ground out.

"I can't believe you really don't know *any* of this," Julien said, confusion replacing the amusement in his expression. "I figured that was why you'd gone to ground—that you were either dead or hiding out somewhere. Either way, I didn't ever expect to see you back here."

"We were . . ." Harte paused as though unsure of how to explain.

"Out of the country," Esta supplied easily.

Julien frowned, considering the two of them. "Still, you'd think that news like that would have reached—"

A knock sounded at the door, cutting Julien's words off midsentence.

The sudden alertness in Harte's posture mirrored Esta's own feeling of unease. There was only one entrance—and, therefore, only one exit—to the dressing room. If Julien was right about them being wanted and if *he* had recognized her so easily, it was possible that someone else had too. They couldn't be caught there. Not after how far they'd come, and not with all they still had left to do.

"You didn't—" Harte started, but Julien held up a hand to silence him.

"Who is it?" Julien shouted, not bothering to move to open the door. He, too, seemed suddenly on edge.

"It's Sal."

"The stage manager," he whispered to Harte.

"Well, what do you want?" he boomed. "I'm a little busy at the moment."

"There's some of the Jefferson Guard here. They're doing a sweep of the whole theater," the manager shouted through the closed door. "Thought I'd warn you in case you were . . . uh . . . indisposed."

"Well, I am." Julien's gaze moved between Harte and Esta. "Can you hold them off for a few minutes?"

"I can probably get you five," the voice called from the other side of the door.

"Do that and I'll owe you a bottle of something better than your usual swill."

The three of them waited in silence for Sal's footsteps to retreat. The moment they could no longer be heard, Julien was on his feet. "Come on. You two need to get out of here." He pushed aside a rack of beaded evening gowns that glimmered in the light as they moved.

"What's going on?" Esta asked Julien. "What's he talking about—the guards?"

"The Jefferson Guard. They're a private militia here in St. Louis." Julien began to work on loosening a panel on the back wall. "Their main job is to hunt down illegal magic, but they've been on higher alert than usual with the Exposition going on this year—especially since the Antistasi attacks that happened last October."

"Antistasi?" Harte asked at the same time Esta said, "What attacks?"

"The Antistasi are a group of anarchists, but instead of the usual dynamite and bullets, the Antistasi use magic to make trouble. They started cropping up after the Defense Against Magic Act went into effect last year, but you probably don't know about that, either." When they shook their heads, he continued. "Basically, it made all forms of unregulated, natural magic officially illegal," Julien explained as he continued to loosen the panel in the wall.

"The Antistasi . . . they're Mageus?" Esta asked.

"That's what they claim," Julien said. "Once the Act went into effect, they suddenly seemed to be *everywhere*, making all kinds of trouble. Actually, you and the train became something of an inspiration for them."

Harte's eyes met Esta's, and she knew he was thinking the same thing she was.

Mageus living outside the city—outside the Brink? The old magic wasn't supposed to exist anywhere else in the country. Wasn't that what she'd always been taught? It was what she'd been brought up to believe. But she'd felt it herself outside the theater. There was magic in the streets of St. Louis. Strange magic, but power just the same. Had something changed because of what they'd done back in New York when they stole from the Order and let Jack get the Book? Or had everything she'd known been a lie?

Once, Esta had been grateful for the education she'd been given. Her deep knowledge of New York allowed her to be a master of its streets no matter when she landed, but now she was even more aware of the holes in that education. Had Professor Lachlan withheld the information about Mageus outside the city from her on purpose to keep her blind? Or was this some new future she couldn't have been prepared for?

One thing *was* certain—in her own time, there hadn't been any Defense Against Magic Act.

"Don't worry, sweetheart," Julien said softly, misreading her concern. "We'll get you out of here." He worked at pulling the panel aside, to open a hole into the wall. "The Jefferson Guard might not be looking for you specifically, but I'm willing to bet the bounty on your pretty little head is a lot bigger than their usual price."

"There's a bounty?" Esta asked.

"Christ," Julien said, half-disgusted and half-astounded. "You really have been away for a while. *Of course* there's a bounty. J. P. Morgan himself offered it. You can't just go blowing up trains without consequences, you know."

"I told you, she didn't do anything to that train," Harte ground out.

"And I've already said I'm inclined to believe you, but it will be harder to convince the Guard if they find you here. They're not known for fighting fair, so you'd have a hell of a time getting away."

"But—" Harte started to argue.

"He's right," Esta interrupted before he could delay them any more. "Let's go while we can." She sent him a silent look that she hoped he understood.

"Smart girl," Julien said.

She didn't bother to acknowledge the compliment. Her mind was swirling with the implications of everything they'd just learned: She was a wanted criminal and there was magic—maybe even Mageus—outside the confines of the Brink.

By then Julien had completely removed the panel of the wall, exposing a passageway behind it. "I've used this in the past when I wanted to slip out without dealing with the stage-door crowd." His expression faltered, and Esta couldn't help but wonder what that meant. "Follow this passage to the left," Julien instructed. "It'll bring you to the boiler room. From there you should be able to find your way out easily enough."

"About that bounty, Jules . . ." Harte's expression was as sharp as the part that split his dark hair. "You sure you don't have any interest in claiming it for yourself?"

Julien looked legitimately taken aback. His voice held a warning when he finally spoke. "I would have thought you knew me better than that, Darrigan."

"Like you said, it *has* been a long time," Harte said, and there was something unspoken, charged between them. "A lot seems to have changed while I was gone. I just need to know whether you have too."

"I don't want their blood money," Julien said flatly as he nodded toward the opening. From the look in his eyes, Esta could even believe that he meant it. "Go on. When the Jefferson Guard comes through, I'll make sure they're distracted for a while so you can get well away from the theater."

"We still need to talk, Julien," Harte pressed.

"Sure, sure," Julien said, waving them onward. "I'll meet you at King's in a couple of hours."

"Where's King's?" Harte asked.

"It's a saloon down on Del Mar—a hole in the wall where nobody should recognize you, or care even if they do." Julien stepped back to allow them entrance to the tunnel behind the wall. "Go on, then. Before they come back."

A SKY DARK AND STARLESS

1904—St. Louis

Harte hesitated only a second longer, searching Julien's face for any indication that the opening in front of them was some kind of trick or a trap, but he found none. Julien's eyes were steady, his expression seemingly sincere. Still, it wasn't worth taking any unnecessary chances.

Harte extended his hand. "Thanks, Jules."

Julien grasped Harte's hand without hesitation and gave the most fleeting squeeze of pressure before he drew it away. But skin to skin, it was enough. A pulse of power, and they'd be safe—from Julien, at least. Considering all they'd just learned, though, Harte wasn't sure how far that safety would extend.

Without another word, Harte followed Esta into the dark tunnel, which got even darker when Julien replaced the panel behind him. They waited in the gloom, listening to the scrape of the rack of dresses, as Julien hid the panel and their eyes accustomed themselves to the lack of light. Even without seeing her, Harte could sense Esta nearby. The warmth of her—and of her affinity—called to him, and to the power within him. For the moment that power was quiet, but he knew it was only watching and waiting for him to let down his guard.

"Come on," Harte whispered to Esta when he could almost see the shape of the passageway. "We should go while we can."

Eventually they came to the boiler room, a larger chamber that smelled faintly of coal and dust. Since it was summer, the room was silent and empty, the fires long since gone cold. The large steel tanks that heated the water before it was pumped to radiators throughout the theater loomed over them, shadowy shapes that made it impossible to see if anyone waited on the other side of the room. They moved carefully, as silently as they could, and soon enough they found the workman's entrance on the far side of the chamber.

"Are we sure this isn't a trap?" she asked as she looked at the window-less exit door.

"Not one that Julien set," he assured her. "I took care of it."

"We should still be careful. I've never heard anything about these patrols. I don't know if they're something new or . . ." She seemed lost for words. "I don't remember learning anything about them or the law against magic he was talking about. None of this existed in the future I knew."

Harte thought he understood the emotion in her voice. Back in Manhattan, there had been Mageus willing to sell out their own kind for a handful of coin, but the Jefferson Guard and whatever this act was that made magic illegal were dangers they hadn't expected.

"Even if these patrols are Mageus, they shouldn't be able to find us unless we're using our affinities. We don't need to use any magic to get back to the hotel," he told her, answering her unspoken worry that they would be discovered. "This isn't any different from Corey's boys back at the Haymarket. If we keep our heads down and our affinities cold, we'll be fine." He hoped.

Esta seemed to believe his false bravado—or she pretended to. She gave him a sure nod, and they eased themselves silently out into the back alley behind the theater, but as they went, Harte kept himself alert, just in case someone was waiting. The way seemed to be clear, and they walked toward the end of the alley as thunder rumbled in the distance.

"Slow down," Esta hissed. He opened his mouth to argue—to tell her that the faster they were away from those Guardsmen, the better—but she explained before he got out a single word. "You start scurrying and it'll draw more attention. You'll look guilty."

She was right. Even though every instinct in him wanted to run, Harte forced himself to slow his pace as they approached the mouth of the alley.

To the right, a Black Maria waited in front of the theater. Next to the windowless carriages stood more of the men dressed in dark coats. They must be the Jefferson Guard, from what Julien had said, which explained why they had been after the cowboy Esta had seen earlier. Stationed at the theater doors were four more similarly dressed men, all facing the theater and waiting for the audience to depart. Their posture was alert and clearly watchful.

"We can go back around the block," Harte suggested. "It's a bit farther, but at least we won't have to pass them."

"I thought you said they wouldn't be able to sense us."

He frowned, remembering the burst of cool energy that had accompanied the three Guardsmen when they'd rushed past outside the theater. It hadn't been completely natural magic, which would have felt only warm. "I don't think they'd be able to, but with the Book's power inside me and with what happened earlier . . ."

She nodded, her golden eyes serious. "You're right. It's not worth chancing it."

The theater was only a handful of blocks from the hotel they'd found, the Jefferson, which was close to the Mississippi River and nestled near the heart of downtown. The building was thirteen stories tall and capped with an ornate decorative cornice that sat like a crown on the top. It was clearly a new building, built for the crowds who would travel to the fair. Even in the overcrowded city, the dirt and grime of horse carts and the soot from the smokestacks of nearby riverboats hadn't yet marred the building.

Maybe they should have gone with something more inconspicuous, but it had been two years since they'd left New York. They'd assumed two years would be enough time and St. Louis would be enough distance that no one would be looking for them. Besides, the Jefferson featured private baths, and the promise of soaking away the grime of the previous days and the long train ride in his own room—away from Esta and the way she provoked the power inside of him—had proven too great a temptation to resist.

Now, with the clouds hanging even heavier in the sky, flickering with the warning of the storm to come, the hotel looked like a sanctuary. In their rooms, they'd be safe. They had a couple of hours before they were supposed to meet Julien, when he'd bring them the stone, as Harte had silently demanded before they parted ways. He needed that time to fortify himself. It took so much energy to keep the voice inside of him locked down, to keep a handle on the power that constantly threatened to bubble up—especially when Esta was so close.

When they entered the peacefulness of the lobby, it was a marked difference from the bustling and cramped city outside the front doors. The moment he was inside, Harte felt some of the evening's tension drain from him as he was enveloped in the hush of the hotel. A mezzanine balcony ran along all four sides of the lobby, and marble columns ringed the room, supporting an arched ceiling that was painted with the verdant green of lifelike palm trees, while crystal chandeliers threw their soft light through the fronds of *real* palm trees throughout the room. From somewhere far off—maybe the ballroom upstairs—music was playing, but despite the small groups of people still milling about, there was a sense of safety in the cavernous, two-story atrium.

They were barely across the lobby, heading for the bank of elevators, each encased in an ornate brass cage, when Harte caught a bit of motion out of the corner of his eye. When he turned, it looked as though the palm trees that were planted in small, private groves around the room were moving, as if blown by some invisible breeze. As he watched, puzzled, the music went silent so that all he could hear was the wind, and the lobby around him seemed to shift—to fade into a different place . . . a different time. . . .

It was night, the ceiling above had turned into a sky dark and starless, and the wind that rustled the palms carried upon its back the scent of betrayal, thick and metallic like old blood. . . . A friend turned foe who would destroy the heart of magic if he held it in his hands. He was coming. . . .

Harte blinked, and the vision faded.

Who is coming?

When he looked again, the palms were still, and he was surrounded once more by the opulence of the lobby, and in the air, there was only the tinkling of music from far off and the quiet murmur of conversation. But the power *inside* of him was rioting.

Esta's arm had tightened around his.

"What is it?" he asked, thinking that maybe she had just seen the same dark night and felt the same unsettling awareness that something awful was on its way.

"To your left, there by the large palm. Gray pants and a light-colored jacket," she said, and he knew in that instant that she wasn't talking about whatever it was he'd just seen.

"There's one leaning against the front desk—*no!* Don't actually look at them," she hissed.

"Who?" he asked, fighting the urge to crane his neck around and trying to ignore the way the voice inside of him was rumbling, its power churning and building.

"I don't know, but they're definitely not guests. I've known how to case a place since I was eight. I know what a cop looks like even when he's not in a uniform," she told him. "They just have this way of standing and a watchfulness about their eyes that isn't quite easy, no matter how good they are at being undercover." She finally glanced over at him. "You're *sure* Julien wouldn't go after the bounty?"

"I made sure," he said, bristling at her doubt. The memory of the vision had put him on edge, and Esta's questioning only made it worse.

"Well, maybe it didn't work—"

Before she could finish, he pulled her to the side, backing her against one of the large marble columns and positioning them both behind one of the palms, so she would have a view of the room behind him. Wrapping his arms around her, he leaned in, so his face was close to her neck. He was gratified to feel the hitch in her breath.

But the voice was seething with anticipation.

Her voice came soft and breathy. "What are you—"

"See how many there are," he whispered close to her ear, testing his self-control even as the power inside of him surged at her nearness.

He felt the moment she realized what he was doing. Her body went pliant against his and her arms reached up to wrap around his neck, joining in on the ruse. *It's just an act,* he told himself, ignoring the fact that he didn't care if it was.

She must have used the French-milled soap she'd found in a shop earlier that afternoon, when they'd purchased the evening wear, because she smelled different than she usually did. The scent was something darkly floral, but beneath the heady, flowery scent was still Esta, clean and real and so familiar that it took all of Harte's strength to not move closer.

The voice within him purred its encouragement, and he could feel the unnatural heat of it gathering and shifting, ready for the moment when he would be at his weakest. The moment he would forget to hold its power in check.

He wouldn't let that happen.

He thought of the vision he'd had at the train station—Esta with her eyes replaced by an endless darkness—and he vowed that he would never be that weak. If the power inside of him grew too strong, he'd leave. He would protect her, even if it meant losing all hope of reclaiming himself. He'd been willing to destroy himself once to quiet the Book. He would be willing to do it again, if it came to that.

But with Esta in his arms and the soft music in the distance and the scent of her surrounding him, thoughts of death faded. He couldn't quite stop himself from brushing his lips lightly against the warm column of her neck.

Her breath hitched again, and Harte felt the voice urging him on. So he pulled back, refusing both himself and the power any measure of real satisfaction.

"There are six, maybe seven in the lobby," she told him, sounding steady and sure. But this close, he could feel the rise and fall of her chest, and if nothing else, he knew she wasn't as unaffected as she pretended—he wasn't alone in how he felt.

"You're *sure* it's the police?" he asked.

"I'm pretty sure," she told him, her voice a low rasp. "The Jefferson Guards who were at the theater were all wearing armbands—they weren't hiding what they were."

"Maybe, whoever these men are, they aren't here for us," Harte said hopefully, pushing his luck and his self-control as he nuzzled his nose gently into her hair. The strands felt cool against his skin, like silk, and the voice hummed in anticipation. Instead, he pulled back again, proving to the power inside of him—and to himself—that he could. That he was in control—not his desire and certainly not the voice that was now ever-present in the recesses of his mind.

"Oh, they're here for us," Esta assured him. "Or maybe they're just here for me. . . . The one by the fern keeps throwing glances our way." She let out a sigh, her breath warm against his neck. "I can't believe how stupid I was to let you talk me into this place. Even with false names, it was too much of a risk. It's too big, too central."

"I know," he told her, feeling the guilt tug at him. She'd suggested somewhere more out of the way, but after the flea-ridden room in Brooklyn, he'd wanted hot running water and a bed without anything crawling in it. "But it's too late to go back. We need a way out of here now."

"Well, it's not going to be the way we came in," she said, leaning into him even more.

He couldn't tell if she was doing it on instinct or if it was part of the ruse, but he held himself back just the same. He could feel the power within him preparing itself, anticipating the moment he would cease to hold it back, and he could not let it win.

"There are too many of them," she said.

He wondered if she realized how perfectly they fit together, her softness against his own lean lines, or if she knew what it did to him to have her so close and not be able to let himself go any further. His heart pounded in his ears, but he kept himself composed. "Maybe there's a service exit?"

"Probably," she murmured, pulling back a bit. "But they'll be watching it, too."

He felt her shift in his arms. "What is it?" he asked.

"We have to go," she whispered. "They're starting to move. Just . . . act natural. We'll have at least some advantage if they don't know we've realized they're here."

Esta let out an airy laugh that he wouldn't have expected she had in her. Then she ducked her head away, a show of coyness that was all a display for those watching, before tucking her arm through his and starting to lead him away from their spot among the palms.

Harte saw immediately that it was hopeless. If the men hadn't looked like police before, they did now, arranged as they were across the room. There was no mistaking what they were doing—covering the exit, so the two of them had nowhere to go. "Now what?"

"I have an idea," she told him. "The elevator."

Again they started walking in the direction of the bronze cages, but now Harte was even more aware of how the men in the lobby were able to track them without so much as moving their heads. "Are you mad?" he said, slowing his steps and pulling her back. "If we get into an elevator, we'll be trapped."

"We'll also be out of their sight," she said. "That will buy us some time. . . . Unless you have a better plan?"

The elevator bank was only a few yards away. "We could run for it. If you think you can control your affinity, you could slow things down and give us a chance to slip out of here."

"Maybe . . ." Her focus was on the elevators just ahead of them. "But if I can't control it, we could be in worse trouble."

Before Harte was ready, they'd arrived at the elevator bank, and before he could stop her, Esta had reached out and pressed the button to call the elevator. Above them, the hand of the elevator's dial moved steadily toward the bottom, like a clock winding down their time as the men in the lobby began their approach.

THE POCKET WATCH

1904—St. Louis

Jericho Northwood—North to most people who knew him—startled a couple of pigeons when he reappeared against the lamppost a few hours past when the Guard had come tearing in after him, but it was late enough that no one much was around to notice. His eyes were still looking in the direction where the girl had been, but she was long gone.

He still couldn't quite believe she'd been there. She'd just been standing in line for tickets to the theater, like any of the other nobs in town. Like she wasn't one of the most wanted Antistasi in the country.

The sketches the newspapers had published back when the first train accident happened made her look like a wild harridan, an avenging demon set to destroy all Sundren who offended her. The girl he'd seen was every bit as tall as the reports claimed, but she was younger than any of the pictures made her seem, and softer looking too. North had recognized her just the same, though. There was no mistaking it. Esta Filosik—the Devil's Thief—was in St. Louis.

North looked at his pocket watch again, the one his daddy had given him when he'd turned eleven. Who knew where his daddy had gotten it from—he'd always known, somehow, that he wasn't supposed to ask. It was dangerous enough living with a secret like magic, even back before they passed the Defense Against Magic Act right after the Great Conclave of aught-two. But the trade in objects that could bolster a dying affinity? Well, asking questions about that could be damn near deadly if the wrong person caught wind of it. Even as a boy he'd known that.

The watch was a scratched-up bronze piece that might have once looked like gold, but the years had worn away the lie. The glass that covered its simple face had already been cracked when he'd received it, but seeing as how he didn't use it to *tell* time, that hadn't ever worried him none. He'd had it for near seven years now, and he hadn't bothered to fix it. Why should he, when it worked just fine? When he used it, he thought of his daddy, and for all the other moments, he kept his thoughts about his father and everything that had happened put away, where they belonged.

North tucked the watch back into his vest pocket—and the memories along with it—next to the package Maggie had given him a few minutes before. He didn't have to examine it to know what it was—a key to the chemist's down the block. He'd cursed Mother Ruth three times over for sending Maggie in to do such a dangerous job. The girl didn't have any business stealing keys when Ruth had plenty of others who could do it just as easily and with less risk. But North always had the suspicion that Ruth liked to test her baby sister—to make sure of where Maggie's loyalties lay and to keep her sharp.

From North's perspective, Maggie was more than sharp enough. The girl was a miracle of a genius when it came to creating serums and devices, and he would have thought Ruth would want to keep her out of harm's way, considering how important she was for their next deed.

They'd borrowed the idea of "propaganda of the deed"—using direct actions to inspire others—from the anarchists, but the Antistasi weren't sloppy enough to use bombs. They used magic instead. In the year since North had come into town and found Ruth, he'd helped with plenty of the Antistasi's deeds—including the one last October—but the one they were currently planning was different. It was more than a statement for attention; it was a demand for recognition. A deed so monumental, so dramatic, that it would transform the country.

It was also coming too soon. From North's view, there were still too many variables and too many unanswered questions. They had only a few more weeks to get them answered, because they would have only one chance to hit the biggest target of all.

But North was just a foot soldier. He wasn't the general. He didn't particularly want to be the general either.

Taking the packet from his pocket, North unwrapped the key it contained. The slip of paper had a list of items in Maggie's crooked scrawl. He knew Maggie needed the materials for her tests, but he also knew that Ruth would want to know about what he'd seen. He wasn't sure if having Esta Filosik in town was a good omen or not. Maybe she could help them. . . . But then, if anyone else knew of her appearance, it could mean trouble. The Guard would be more alert, and the whole town would be on edge.

Well, there wasn't a reason he had to do a thing about it right then. Maggie had a list of items for him to obtain, and he wasn't about to disappoint her.

North pulled his hat down low over his eyes as he turned into the alley next to the chemist's shop, making sure no one saw as he used the key to slip inside. When he was done, he'd have plenty of time to tell Ruth everything. He had his watch, after all.

DUST AND METAL

1904—St. Louis

While Harte watched the dial of the elevator creep steadily downward, he had the clear sense that their time was running out. Each second that ticked by was one closer to the moment when the police in the lobby would reach them. But after a string of seconds, nothing had happened.

"They're not coming," he said, when he realized the plainclothes officers had stopped approaching.

"If they already knew we were here, they probably have people stationed in our rooms," she told him, sounding far calmer than he was feeling. "There's no reason to create a public scene if they can get to us there."

Which didn't make him feel one bit better. "If we can't go to our rooms, where are we going?"

She glanced at him. "We're in a hotel, Harte. It's *filled* with rooms. We don't need our own."

Inside, the power of the Book felt unsettled, as though it were a caged animal pacing. "They'll be able to see which floor we stop at," he argued, his chest feeling tight as the hand of the dial reached the bottom and the elevator groaned to a stop.

"That's the idea," she said, leaning forward to press a soft kiss against his lips.

It was over before he'd realized what had just happened. He barely registered the shocking warmth and the softness of her mouth against his. If it weren't for the absolute torment of the voice's realization that he'd let her slip away again, he might have thought he'd imagined the whole thing.

The elevator doors opened, revealing an interior empty except for the operator. "What's the plan?" he murmured as they stepped inside the close quarters of the elevator.

Earlier that day, he'd admired the polished wood and gleaming mirrors of the interior. When they'd first checked in, Harte had thought the elevators were sleek and modern, a marvel of the age, but now the mirrored cage felt as airless and constricting as a prison cell. Once the doors closed and the elevator started moving, they would be even farther from any chance of escape.

"Seven, please," Esta told the operator, an older man with deep brown skin who was dressed in the pristine uniform of the hotel porters.

Harte realized that she had spoken loudly enough for the men in the lobby to hear.

"Yes, ma'am," the operator said as he set to closing the gate.

The moment the doors were closed and the operator had pressed the lever forward, causing the elevator to rise, Esta leaned over and whispered in his ear, "It would probably be better if he doesn't remember any of this, but we need the elevator to keep moving. Maybe a little more slowly." She nodded toward the operator. "Have him stop at seven . . . *nicely.*"

Harte gave her a small nod to let her know that he understood, even if he had no idea how she planned to get them out of the mess they were in once they reached the seventh floor.

The operator perched on a small stool, silent and stoic, facing the switch and monitoring the elevator's rise, ignoring the passengers in the car, as he'd presumably been trained to. If he'd heard any of their exchange, he pretended not to. If he sensed that anything was amiss, he didn't show it. But his uniform presented a problem. The operator was buttoned up to his neck, his hands and wrists covered with white gloves. Because Harte's affinity needed skin-to-skin contact, the only option he had was the strip of exposed skin between the high collar of the man's jacket and the straight edge of his hairline, a gap caused by the way his shoulders were hunched, probably the effect of the long hours he spent on shift.

Harte felt guilty for taking advantage of him, but he couldn't see any other way out of the mess they were in. He took a deep breath, focusing his affinity and preparing himself—he'd have only one chance to pull this off without having to resort to other, more violent measures. As the elevator passed the second floor, the bell in the car rang and the car itself vibrated slightly. Harte took the opportunity to reach forward and gently touch two fingers against the nape of the man's neck, pushing his affinity toward the boundary between flesh and soul all at once.

The operator went stiff for a moment, but he kept his hand on the lever, releasing the pressure only a little so the path of the elevator slowed slightly. Harte withdrew his fingers a moment later, and the operator didn't so much as flinch. The elevator kept climbing, though now more sluggishly, and the operator kept staring at the dial. He and Esta might have been two ghosts for all the poor man knew or cared.

"Boost me up," Esta said, staring at the wood paneling on the ceiling.

He realized then her intention—above them, the soft light thrown by the glass globe exposed a panel. "You can't be serious," he muttered, but he didn't bother to argue. It wasn't as though he had a better plan.

Girding himself against the usual rumbling excitement of the voice, he offered his hands so Esta could step into them and then lifted her toward the low ceiling. It took her only a moment to swing the panel open and pull herself up through it.

"Come on," she said, reaching her hand back for him.

The elevator was still progressing slowly and steadily upward. The bell dinged again as they passed the fourth floor.

"I can get it myself," he told her, and with a short leap, his fingertips grasped the edge of the opening. As the elevator continued to move, he pulled himself up into the darkness of the shaft. It smelled of dust and metal, and the moment Esta replaced the ceiling hatch, the only light they had to see by were the narrow beams that came through the brass grates marking each floor. The hotel had a bank of three elevators, and together the sound of the machinery driving the cables echoed around them as the individual cars stopped at the various floors.

"Now what?" he asked, reaching out to hold the cable of the still-moving lift to steady himself. The movement of the elevator reminded him too much of the swaying of the train. He took a deep breath and held on more tightly.

Esta didn't seem bothered by the movement, since she wasn't holding on to one of the cables. "With any luck, those guys from the lobby are running toward the seventh floor right now. But we won't be in the elevator when it stops."

"We can't stay here, either," he said. "Even if that operator can't tell them where we went, they'll figure it out eventually."

"*Eventually,*" Esta agreed, speaking loudly enough that he could hear her over the mechanical clicks and groans. "I'm betting on that, too. They'll waste manpower and time stopping the elevators and looking for us. But we won't be here by then, either." She was peering over the edge of the car, far enough that he wanted to pull her back. "Give me your hand." She reached back without looking to see if he'd comply.

"What?" he hesitated.

"Your hand. Now!" She looked back at him then, determination flashing in her eyes. "Trust me, Harte."

Before he could think of all the reasons he shouldn't, Harte slipped his hand into hers.

Satisfied, she turned back to the edge. "Ready?" she asked, not looking back at him. "One . . ."

"No, Esta—"

"Two . . ." She wasn't listening.

The contents of his stomach were quickly working their way up his throat. "Don't—"

"Three!"

A TURNING OF THE TIDES

1902—New York

James Lorcan felt his view of the future rearrange itself as he laid the paper onto the worn desk in front of him. Once, it had been Dolph's desk, just as the apartment he was sitting in had belonged to Dolph as well.

The apartment was much better outfitted than the pair of cramped rooms above that James had called home before. But the comforts of the rooms were unimportant compared to what else James now had at his fingertips—all Dolph's notes, all his books, and all his *knowledge*.

And my, my . . . what Dolph had been hiding. James had used some of Dolph's secrets already to secure Paul Kelly's alliance. He would use more of them in the days to come to position the players in the Bowery exactly where he wanted them.

On the wall hung a portrait of Newton beneath a tree, a spoil from a heist Dolph's team had done at the Metropolitan. To the average viewer, the painting depicted nothing more than the most astounding revelation of the modern age—Newton's discovery of gravity. At the man's feet lay an apple, red and round, and above him the sun and moon shone, a pair of guardians in the sky.

But to someone more astute, the painting showed something more. The book Newton held in his hand was rumored to be the Book of Mysteries. The portrait depicted the point in history where Newton's two lives converged—Newton the magician who had nearly gone mad from his experiments with alchemy and Newton the scientist. Both were in search of eternal truth and untold knowledge, and in the portrait, both found it within the pages of the Ars Arcana.

Across the centuries there had been stories and myths about the fabled Book. Some said it was rumored to contain the very source of magic. Others thought it was the Book of Thoth, an ancient manuscript buried in the Nile River that held the knowledge of the gods, knowledge unfit for the feeble minds of men. Still others thought it was a fantastical grimoire, a book of the most powerful ritual magic ever developed. Many had hunted for it—James himself had hunted for it. Two days ago he had thought the Book gone, forever beyond his reach, but now . . .

James let his eyes scan over the newsprint once again, allowing his affinity to flare out, searching for new connections in the Aether as he considered this development.

He almost hadn't noticed. The papers were always filled with the trivial—stories meant to grab attention with lurid details of death and tragedy. James hadn't cared to read the story about the train and the carnage of its derailment. In fact, he'd already tossed the paper aside when Kelly told him about the reporter that he was sending Viola to kill.

Now his eyes caught on the name of a dead man.

Harte Darrigan.

If the papers could be believed—and, in truth, often they *couldn't*—Harte Darrigan wasn't dead. And neither was Esta. If the two had made it through the Brink, it meant that not only was the Book still out there and attainable, but that they were *using* it.

James took Viola's knife and balanced its point on the tabletop as he considered the possibilities. Two days ago he had believed that the fate of the world had already been inscribed: Magic would die. It would fade away until it was nothing but a memory and a superstition. The future would belong not to Mageus with their innate connections to the world, but to the Sundren. In the days following the mess on the bridge, James had accepted this fate. He'd considered his options and made adjustments to shore up his power, but this new information changed things again.

After all, the pages of a book could be torn out. A story could be rewritten. His affinity wasn't perfect, of course—or it wasn't perfect *yet*. But if this new information meant anything at all, it meant there was a very good possibility that he would get everything he wanted in the end.

James allowed the tip of the knife to sink into the page, carving out the names as one might carve out a heart. He tucked them into his vest pocket, talismans for the future, as he made his way down to the bar-room to hold court over his new kingdom. He had a sense that something was coming, some change in the Aether that could mean a turning of the tides for him. There was much to consider, but Harte Darrigan and Esta Filosik would not escape him again. They would pay for their perfidy. James would make sure of it.

MOCK DUCK

1902—New York

Jianyu looked up from where he lay in the filth of the street, his head throbbing and his vision blurred, to find Sai Wing Mock, the leader of the Hip Sings and Tom Lee's rival in the Chinese quarter, standing over him. If Tom Lee and his On Leongs might occasionally take advantage, the Hip Sings were ruthless, and none was more so than the man who went by the name of Mock Duck.

Mock dressed like a dandy, his Western-style suit cut close and his queue tucked up under a slate-gray porkpie hat, but it was rumored that he wore chain mail beneath his clothes—a defense against the enemies he had made in the years since he had started the war between the On Leongs and the Hip Sings. His hand still held the gun he had used to scare off Jianyu's attackers, and his fingers were sharply tipped with long, polished nails—an overt sign of his wealth and position. No common laborer had fingertips as deadly as that.

At first the leader of the Hip Sings simply stared at Jianyu lying on the ground. His dark eyes were thoughtful. "I've heard stories about you, Mr. Lee," he said finally, again using the Cantonese they shared.

"Lee isn't my name," Jianyu told him, speaking before he had fully considered his words. It was stupid of him to provoke Mock, especially here, where he was alone and unarmed and at the mercy of a man who was rumored to have ordered any number of murders. But here, at the mercy of Tom Lee's rival, it seemed important to make it clear that he had no side in their bloody war.

Mock Duck's wide, full mouth twitched. "I have heard that, too."

Jianyu wanted to know why Mock Duck had been looking for him and what the tong leader might want of him, but he understood implicitly that silence was safer. When staring down a viper, surviving often meant not giving the snake a reason to strike. Instead, Jianyu focused on his affinity and tried to find the threads of light. But his head swirled from where it had cracked against the street. He was struggling to remain conscious, and he couldn't focus enough to keep the light from slipping through his fingers.

"Pick him up," Mock commanded, "and bring him."

Mock was not alone. *Of course not.* The boys who had jumped him would not have been scared off by a single man, gun or not.

Jianyu felt himself being roughly hoisted, and his head swam again with the movement. In response, his stomach, empty as it was, heaved, and it was all he could do to keep from retching, which would be taken as a further sign of weakness. Jerking away from their support, he forced himself to stay upright. He would walk under his own power, if he did nothing else.

Mock led the way as the group traveled through one of the tunnels that connected the various blocks around the Chinese quarter. The air underground was thick and stale, and the echoes of their footsteps were the only sounds. When they emerged, they were close to the Bowery, far from the Hip Sings' usual territory.

Jianyu knew where they were headed before he saw the golden-eyed witch on the sign over the Strega, so he was not exactly surprised when Mock Duck went through the saloon's front doors as though he owned the place, his highbinders escorting Jianyu behind him.

The barroom was mostly empty, since it was so early in the day, but Jianyu recognized a couple of Dolph's boys—Mooch and Werner were in the back, and Sylvan was wiping down the bar under the watchful eye of one who could only be a Five Pointer. They looked up when Mock Duck entered, but their expressions showed little more than curious interest.

There was no sign of Viola.

Once the Strega had been Jianyu's home, a sanctuary from the dangers of the city streets. Stepping into the familiar barroom as a prisoner felt somehow worse than all his injuries. His head felt like it would split open from where it had struck the pavement and his gut throbbed where it had taken a boot, but being treated like a stranger in this place that had once been a home made him feel lost in a way he had never felt before. With everything else, it was nearly too much, and the only thing that kept him steady was the sight of the traitor who had murdered Dolph.

At the back of the barroom, sitting in the seat that he had killed for, Nibsy Lorcan lifted his eyes to see what the commotion was. His spectacles flashed in the light, the blank lenses giving him the appearance of a button-eyed automaton Jianyu had once seen at a dime museum. Soulless. Driven by some mechanism within that Jianyu did not comprehend.

The two highbinders holding Jianyu shoved him forward as Mock Duck presented him.

"You found him," Nibsy said, and Jianyu could not decide if it was satisfaction or simple anticipation that colored the boy's voice.

"And you can have him as soon as I receive my fee," Mock said.

Nibsy shouted to the barkeep, and the boy brought a stack of bills wrapped in paper and a ledger. Mock Duck counted the money carefully and then flipped through the notebook, murmuring appreciatively. "This is all on Tom Lee?"

"And a few others who might cause you problems," Nibsy said.

Mock Dock gave Nibsy a small, satisfied nod as he closed the booklet. "I trust we will do business again, Mr. Lorcan." He held out his hand, and Nibsy took it.

"Likewise." Nibsy directed two men—Five Pointers, if Jianyu wasn't mistaken—to take hold of Jianyu. Then he waited until Mock Duck and his men left before he looked at Jianyu. "So . . . ," he drawled, bringing himself to his feet and using the cane that had once belonged to Dolph to make his way to where Jianyu stood. "The traitor returns."

With Jianyu's vision swirling, there were two of Nibsy, but Jianyu sneered at both of them. "You dare to call *me* the traitor?"

"We were all on the bridge, weren't we?" Nibsy asked, and Jianyu realized that his words were meant for the people watching warily throughout the Strega. "We were there for Dolph—for the Devil's Own—and *you* weren't. Your cowardice doomed us all."

His head was spinning and the edges of his vision were starting to dim. It was a struggle to stay conscious, but Jianyu forced himself to focus and allowed the corner of his mouth to curve. "Are you so certain that I was absent?"

He saw the realization flash behind the lenses of Nibsy's spectacles, but the boy's expression never so much as flickered. "If you were there, you didn't help us. You let the magician get away, and with it, our chances of defeating the Order. You betrayed everyone here."

The people in the barroom were murmuring now, an uneasy buzzing like a hive about to erupt. Jianyu understood what drama was playing out too well. Nibsy would use the Devil's Own against him. He would convince them of Jianyu's treachery, and in turn they would do Nibsy's dirty work. It would take very little. . . . It had been only Dolph who had held them back when Tilly was hurt, after all.

"I am not the traitor in this room," Jianyu said, his voice rough from a combination of pain and anger. "It was not my gun that ended Dolph's life. It was yours."

The barroom went still.

"The lies of a traitor." Nibsy laughed, but Jianyu could feel the questions still hanging in the air around them. "A feeble attempt to cover your own guilt," he said, stepping even closer. He pulled from his jacket a familiar knife—Viola's—and held it to Jianyu's face.

Where did he get Viola's knife? She prized it above all others and would not have willingly given it to anyone—even if she had believed them to be a friend. She could not be dead. Not Viola. Not when he needed her.

"Do you know what we do to traitors, Jianyu?"

The knife flashed in the light of the barroom, but Jianyu did not so much as flinch. "Traitors deserve death," Jianyu said, struggling to keep his voice even despite the pain of simply breathing. They must have broken a rib, maybe two. "Are you prepared to die, Nibsy?"

"My name is James," Nibsy said, bringing the knife closer until the tip of it was poised against the skin under Jianyu's chin. "And it's not me who is going to die today."

The air in the room was electric. Everyone was focused on Jianyu, Nibsy, and the point of the impossible blade held between them. But Jianyu simply stared at Nibsy, refusing to back down. Refusing to take back his accusations.

After a long, fraught moment, Nibsy smiled and pulled back. "I think a quick death is too easy for this one, don't you?" he asked the room, but the barroom returned nothing except uneasy silence. "I think he should tell us everything he knows—about where Darrigan is and what he's done with the Order's treasures. But not here. No, we wouldn't want to make a mess before the afternoon rush. Take him up to my rooms, would you, Mooch? I think we can continue our little conversation there."

Perhaps Jianyu should have fought once they were out of the main barroom and making their way up the familiar staircase. He didn't suspect it would take much. Though Mooch had trained under Dolph's watchful eye in the ring of the boxing club, the same as Jianyu, Mooch hadn't trained for nearly as long. But Jianyu was still too unsteady from the beating to risk it. One more hit to the head and he doubted he would remain conscious.

More important, he didn't think he would convince Mooch of anything by attacking him. Nibsy was playing a long game, and so must he.

MOTHER RUTH

1904—St. Louis

They called her Mother Ruth, but she was no one's mother. At least not by blood. Her arms had never held a babe of her own, nor had they ever yearned to, because she knew a simple truth—giving yourself over in that way was a weakness. She would never allow a man to take that freedom from her, because she'd had enough of her freedom taken already. Hadn't she watched her parents scrape by with barely enough to feed their family? Hadn't she seen with her own two eyes how her mother wasted away, babe after babe, until finally, her fourteenth had taken the last she had to give?

Or perhaps her own mother had wasted away for another reason. Ruth often wondered—was it truly the babes? Or was it that her mother had given away the part of herself that made her whole? Because Ruth had to imagine that what made her mother whole was the very thing that made Ruth herself whole—magic.

Ruth's father had been a small-minded man. Only heaven knew why her mother had made herself small to get a ring on her finger. But when her father had learned that his wife had the old magic, he'd done what he could to beat it out of her until she'd found ways to keep it hidden from him. But something like magic can't be pressed down forever.

Her mother had only kitchen magic, a kind of power she could weave into the food she made or the ale she brewed, but Ruth herself knew the power that something so seemingly simple could bestow because her own power was the same. She'd never understood it, a woman like her mother, cowering in fear of a man such as her father. But even as a small child, Ruth had been old enough and wise enough to know that some things in the world weren't meant to be comprehended. Ruth's mother had hidden her magic, and before she'd died giving birth to her fourteenth child, she'd taught the rest of her children who'd been born with affinities—Ruth included—how to hide theirs.

On the day they'd buried her mother, Ruth's father had told her in no uncertain terms that, as the oldest, the children were her responsibility now. Ruth might not have had a choice in the what, but she decided that day that she would chose the how. She taught her brothers and sisters how to stand on their own and how to cultivate their magic so that they couldn't ever be pressed small by anyone.

Maybe she could have run off. Maybe she should've.

After all, she was already more than twenty when her mother died, and in those days, she was still young and pretty enough that there were plenty of boys whose heads turned when she walked by. She could have picked any one of them, thick-skulled and easygoing as they were, but why trade one duty for another? Better the devil you knew, she reasoned.

So she'd managed to raise all her brothers and sisters to adulthood. Mother Ruth, they called her, even when she told them she wasn't their mother. Most of them took themselves far from the meagerness of their childhood, which was fine by Ruth. Fewer for her to worry about. They could do what they would with the world, and she would do the same.

Her whole life, Ruth had exactly one hour to herself each week—the hour she took to go to Mass. But on a fateful Sunday, she never made it. That Sunday she chanced to dart under the cover of a random livery stable for shelter from the rain on the way to St. Alban's. In addition to the soft rustling of horseflesh, she'd found herself interrupting a meeting, and it surprised even her that she'd stayed to listen to what was being said instead of continuing on. But there had been magic in the air, a warmth that she'd missed from her own mother's arms—a warmth that called to her in a way that nothing else ever had. And there was something else: a righteous anger that she felt an answering call to deep in her bones.

Instead of praying, she learned to shout. Instead of kneeling, she learned to rise. And she hadn't stopped since.

The Antistasi had been a new beginning for her. When she found the group that day, they were little more than a ragtag bunch hoping for companionship and an escape from their hard-scratched lives. They were disorganized and undisciplined, taking their name from bedtime stories about another time, when Mageus had fought fiercely against their annihilation during the Disenchantment.

But since the Great Conclave two years before, since the Defense Against Magic Act had made the very thing she was illegal, something had changed in the organization. And Ruth had changed right along with it.

She had given the movement everything she had, everything that she was. She used money from the brewery she had built for herself and her siblings, and she used the Feltz Brewery building in support of the Antistasi's cause as well. Now she walked through the rows of women cleaning and filling bottles, and she knew that she'd been put on this earth for a purpose. Not only to save the girls who worked for her from a lifetime of servitude for a moment's indiscretion, but for something much larger—a demonstration of the power those who lived in the shadows held. A demonstration that could change *everything* for those who still had a link to the old magic.

Her eyes were sharp on her workers as she walked toward the nursery, which was housed in the back of the brewery. The nursery was Maggie's doing. Ruth's youngest sister—and the one who had taken their mother's life—Maggie was already seventeen and was the last to remain with Ruth. They had no pictures, so Maggie couldn't have known that she was the image of their mother, with her ash-brown hair curling about her temples and the small pair of silver-rimmed spectacles perched on the end of her upturned nose. And her eyes . . . For Ruth, looking at Maggie was like seeing her mother peer at her from the beyond. Or it would have been, except that Maggie's eyes had a strength in them that Ruth had no memory of her mother ever possessing.

When Ruth entered the small nursery, Maggie was tending to the newest little one, a bundle of energy who had been abandoned by parents who either couldn't take care of him or didn't want to. It happened too often, Mageus born to parents after generations of affinities gone cold. Many of those children were seen as anomalies. Freaks. Abominations.

Some parents accepted their children as they were—but that was rare. Most of the time, when the parents' efforts to curtail their children's powers didn't work, they discarded them. Asylums or orphanages across the countryside were filled with these castoffs, strange children who didn't understand who or what they were. Those sent to the asylums rarely left whole—if they left at all—and at the orphanage, the rod wasn't spared. Those children left mean as junkyard dogs, dangerous and volatile, easy marks for the police or the Jefferson Guard.

The other children in the nursery were the victims of the Act. Their parents had been rounded up and imprisoned or sent away. The children who were left behind might be taken in by friends or neighbors, hidden away so that the Guard couldn't find them, but not everyone had someone. Those who didn't were often brought to the brewery until they could be placed in homes where they would be safe.

It had been Maggie's idea to start taking in the urchins—to steal them from the children's homes and asylums when necessary—and to raise them with an understanding of what they were so they could be placed with families who would appreciate them. So they could thrive the way Ruth had allowed *her* to thrive, Maggie reasoned.

The girl was too innocent for her own good. She'd meet a hard end if she didn't look past that rosy tint she saw the world through. Ruth permitted the nursery because it seemed like good business. More children with magic meant that the Antistasi could grow rather than die. The Society and other organizations like them could do what they would to snuff out the old magic, but another generation was waiting to rise up behind.

Maggie glanced up from the child, who had just managed to set fire to the blanket he was holding, and gave Ruth a look of utter exasperation.

"I see this one is still causing you problems."

"He doesn't mean to," Maggie said, stomping out the last of the flames.

"If he burns down my brewery, it won't matter if he meant it or not," Ruth said.

"We're working on it," Maggie said, but her pale cheeks flushed with embarrassment, her emotions clear as day on her porcelain skin.

"Use the Nitewein if you need to."

"He's a baby," Maggie protested.

"He's a menace if he can't control his affinity. See that he's taken care of, or I'll do it for you. We're running too far behind schedule to have anything go wrong now."

"Yes, Mother Ruth," Maggie murmured, her eyes downcast.

Ruth sighed. This wasn't what she'd come for. "North just returned."

"Jericho's back already?" Maggie said, and Ruth could see the interest in her sister's expression.

Even as hardened as she was, Ruth understood the power of roguish eyes set into a lean face. North had the same appeal as a raggedy stray cat—you believed you could tame it and then it would love you forever. But Ruth didn't doubt that, like any stray, Jericho Northwood had claws.

From the way her sister's expression brightened, it was clear Maggie's interest in the boy hadn't faded. She'd deal with Maggie's little infatuation later, but for now . . . "He's brought the supplies you asked for."

But Maggie didn't pay her any mind. She was still fussing with the baby. "I'll get to them soon enough." Her tone offered no excuses.

The spine of steel her baby sister hid beneath her soft outer shell always did manage to surprise her. "You know how important the serum is," Ruth insisted.

Maggie nodded. "But it can wait until the little ones are in bed."

"Maybe it can, but the news North brought with him can't. You'll need to come."

The boy Maggie was tending picked up a small carved wooden horse, his fingertips flaring to a brilliant orange that caused the toy horse to smolder.

Ruth gave Maggie a warning look before she took her leave. There was an unexpected visitor in her city. Tonight the Antistasi had more important business to attend to than someone else's children.

THE RISK OF MAGIC

1904—St. Louis

In the dim light of the elevator shaft, Esta felt Harte's fear as clearly as the vibrations of the machine beneath their feet, but she didn't have time to explain.

As the car next to them descended, it created a rush of air warm with the scent of dust and axle grease that rustled the silk of her skirts and whipped at the hair coming loose around her face. Harte's hand was gripping hers tightly enough that she could feel the sizzle of energy between them creeping against her skin.

Not for the first time, she had the feeling that it wasn't him she was sensing. The energy wasn't the same brush of warmth she'd felt from him when he'd manipulated her in the theater weeks ago or tried to read her thoughts in the carriage on the way to Khafre Hall. This energy felt different. More potent. More *compelling*, which was a sure sign of danger if she ever felt one.

She didn't have time to worry too much about it at that moment, though. She would have one shot at this, one chance to get it right. And she might be making a huge mistake.

The moment the two elevator cars drew even with each other, Esta focused on her affinity and pulled time still. The vibrations beneath her feet stopped, and the noise in the shaft went silent. At the same time, she pulled Harte forward onto the roof of the next car and let go of her hold on time.

The elevators lurched back into motion as she released Harte's hand.

Relief flooded through her as Harte grabbed for the cable to steady himself. *It worked.* She hadn't known for sure what would happen when she used her affinity. She hadn't known if she'd even be able to. She'd thought about taking the jump without slowing the elevators, but the risk of using her magic for the briefest moment seemed preferable to falling to their deaths.

Her gamble had paid off. Together they watched the elevator they had just been on continue to rise above them as the car they now were on top of descended. She'd used her affinity and nothing odd had happened. It had worked, just as it always had worked—easy. *Right.* But it wasn't enough. They couldn't keep standing there, because every second brought them closer to the ground floor, where more police waited.

When the car they were riding on lurched to a stop at the fourth floor, Harte seemed to gather his wits about him. "We can't stay here," he said, echoing her thoughts.

She listened for the sound of the doors opening and felt the slight bounce as people entered the elevator. "We're not going to," she told him. "We're getting off."

"Esta, there are too many people in there." He gestured to the car below their feet.

The sound of the doors closing told her that they were about to move again. "We aren't leaving that way. Hold on," she said, just before the cables lurched back into motion.

Harte frowned at her, shadows thrown by the dim light of the shaft flickering across his face. "What's the plan?"

"The doors to the shaft," she said, pointing to the fourth-floor opening they were descending away from. "When we get to the second floor, I'm going to slow things down again long enough for us to open them. If anyone's watching in the lobby, the elevator won't look like it stopped."

"You really think you can?" he asked.

"It worked a minute ago. We'll just have to hope our luck holds." The second floor was quickly approaching, and any moment now, the police who were probably waiting for them on the seventh floor would discover the empty elevator car. "Give me your hand," she commanded, and this time he didn't argue.

When the car was halfway past the third floor's ornate brass grate, she focused on the seconds around her. Against her skin, she could feel the stirrings of the power simmering within Harte, but she ignored it and focused instead on the way time hung in the spaces around them, as real and as material as the cables that held the cars and the dust that tickled her nose. It would take longer than a few seconds to climb out of the elevator, and she wasn't completely sure what would happen—not with Harte and the Book's power making her own affinity feel so unstable again. But she didn't have any other ideas.

She found the spaces between the seconds, those moments that held within them reality and its opposite, and she pulled them apart until the elevator slowed and the world around her went silent. But with the heat of the Book's power prodding at her, it wasn't easy to keep her hold on time.

"Help me," she told him, grasping the metal grates with her free hand.

Understanding, Harte took the other side, and together they began to pull the doors apart. Once they were wide enough, Esta checked to make sure the way was clear. Standing a few feet away, at the opening to the stairs, was a man who could only be one of the plainclothes officers. He stood, staring sightlessly in their direction.

"Can you hold it?" Harte asked.

The tendrils of heat and power that had vibrated against her skin when she took Harte's hand were climbing her arm. The more they twisted themselves around her, the more slippery the spaces between the seconds felt. A moment ago those spaces had felt solid and real, but with every passing heartbeat, her hold on time—her hold on magic itself— grew murky, indistinct. As though neither the seconds nor her magic really even existed.

"Not much longer," she told him through gritted teeth as she fought to keep hold of her affinity.

"Then we'd better hurry." Harte climbed down from the roof of the elevator and into the hallway and then turned to help her.

Esta's feet had no sooner touched the ground than she realized the darkness of the elevator shaft had followed her into the well-lit hallway. It hung in the edges of her vision, threatening.

From inside the shaft, she heard a groaning of cables, a sound starkly out of place in the silent hush of the timeless moment. "Did you hear that?"

Harte frowned. "What?"

The groaning came again, louder this time. *"That,"* she told him. There shouldn't have been any sound, not now when she had slowed the seconds to a near stop and the rest of the world had gone still and silent. Fear pooling within her, Esta tried to pull away from Harte, but he held her tight. "I can't . . ."

"Esta?" He tightened his grip on her, his eyes stormy with confusion.

There were people in those elevators, people who had nothing to do with the officers chasing her. People who might die if the cables broke and the elevator plummeted to the ground below, just as people had died on the train. She didn't understand what was happening, but she knew she had to stop it.

Esta wrenched herself away from Harte, away from the unsettling energy that felt like it was trying to claim her, and allowed time to slam back into motion. Suddenly, the gears of the elevator began to churn and she could hear music coming from somewhere nearby.

"What—" Harte started, but before he could question her any further, the man at the stairway shouted.

"Hey!" He pointed at them, his eyes wide with disbelief that he hadn't noticed them standing there before. Lifting a whistle to his mouth, he reached for the golden medallion he wore on his lapel, but before he could touch it, Harte attacked, tackling the man and then knocking him out before he could do anything else.

"We have to get out of this hallway," he told her as he rubbed at the knuckles of his right hand. "Before someone comes."

Esta had already realized they'd need a hiding place. By the time Harte had pulled himself to his feet, she had one of the nearby rooms unlocked. "Bring him in here," she said, stepping aside. "If we leave him out there, they'll know."

The room was exactly like the one she had checked into earlier that day. The walls were papered in the same elegant chintz, the bed had been covered in the same fine linens, and the furniture had the same burnished wood and brass fixtures as hers. This room, though, clearly belonged to a man. There were trousers and socks strewn about the floor, and even with the window open, the smell of stale smoke and old sweat hung in the air.

"What are we supposed to do with him?" Harte asked as he locked the door behind him.

"Take him into the bathroom," Esta told him as she propped her leg up on the bed and hitched up her skirts.

Instead of moving, Harte was looking at her exposed leg.

She ignored the heated look he was giving her—and the answering warmth she felt stirring inside of her—as she unfastened the silk stocking she was wearing and pulled it down her leg. "Snap out of it, would you? Here," she said, tossing the stocking to Harte, who still looked stunned as he caught the scrap of fabric. "Tie him up with that." She rolled off the other stocking and tossed it to him as well.

If they weren't in such a bind, the way his ears went pink as he caught the bit of silk might almost have been adorable, but they needed to get out of the room and the hotel as fast as they could. The longer it took, the more likely they'd be caught. After all, it was only a matter of time before the police figured out what she and Harte had done and started searching rooms.

While Harte was in the bathroom tying up the watchman, Esta began stripping out of the gown she was wearing. The second she had slipped it on at the department store, she'd known it was perfect. She'd never been one to care all that much for clothes, but she'd loved the dress, despite knowing that she was in no position to be admiring silly, pretty things. She sighed a little as it tumbled to the floor in a puddle of silk the color of quicksilver. *The exact color of Harte's eyes.*

Esta shoved that unwanted thought aside as she stepped out of the pile of fabric and balled the gown up, the physical action reinforcing how unimportant the garment was. She kicked it under the bed.

"What are you *doing?*"

Esta turned to find Harte, his eyes wide and his cheeks pink.

"Getting rid of the dress," she told him.

"I see that," he said, and she didn't miss the way his hand clenched into a fist or the tightness in his voice. "But *why* are you getting rid of the dress?"

"It's too noticeable," she said, frowning. "And I'm too noticeable in it."

"You don't think *this* is going to be even more noticeable?" he asked as he gestured stiffly toward her, standing as she was in nothing more than a corset and a pair of drawers.

In her own time she saw people wearing less than this on the city streets. Not that Harte would understand. So often, she forgot how different they were—how much a product of his own time he was. Moments like this reminded her . . . but he was just going to have to get over it.

"I wasn't planning on going out there like this," she said, heading to the wardrobe. "There has to be something in here," she told him.

She gathered some of the men's clothing that was hanging clean and freshly pressed inside the wardrobe. When she saw the doubt in his expression, she ignored it.

"That is never going to work," he muttered, more to himself than to her.

"Look at how easily Julien recognized me, and he wasn't even looking for me—I'm too tall not to stand out," she told him. "At least for a woman."

He looked unconvinced. "You really think you look *anything* like a man?"

"I think people usually only see what they *expect* to see," she said as she slipped a stiffly pressed shirt on. It smelled of fresh linen and starch, scents that brought to mind memories of Professor Lachlan, of a childhood spent trying to please him, the days she'd spent studying next to him in the library that took up the top floor of the building.

But now the memory of that library brought with it a different image. *Dakari.* And the smell of linen and starch only served to remind her that lies often hid behind the faces you trusted.

Pushing aside the past, she buttoned the shirt, but not before she loosened the ties of her corset a little, so it didn't press her into such an hourglass shape. Finally able to breathe, she finished fastening the buttons.

"Let's hope they're all blind," Harte muttered. "Every single one of them." But he left her to finish getting dressed while he went and checked on the man in the bathroom one last time.

She tried not to be too pleased with his response as she found a top hat in the wardrobe and, smoothing out the stray strands around her face as best she could, tucked her hair up into it. Frowning at herself in the ornately beveled mirror, she wondered if Harte was right. Her face was still too soft looking, and she didn't have time to do much more than try to rub away the powder she'd put on earlier that night.

It will work. She'd dressed like a man before—when she'd helped Dolph Saunders rob Morgan's exhibit at the Metropolitan Museum of Art a few weeks back. She'd walked into a room filled with members of the Order—including J. P. Morgan himself—and no one had noticed that she was a woman. Of course, it might have only worked then because people never pay any attention to the servants.

"Ready?" she asked, giving her lapels one final tug to cover what evidence there was of the shape of her corset beneath the suit.

Harte turned and gave her a good long, appraising look. "We should just use your affinity and slip out without all"—he gestured toward her new outfit—"*this.*"

"Didn't you see what happened in the hallway?" she asked, shuddering a little at the memory of the darkness. There was something about it that felt both empty and all-consuming at the same time, like if she stared at it straight on, she might lose herself in it. And then there were the sounds of the cables groaning. She didn't trust her affinity right now—at least not when it was linked to Harte.

"If you're still feeling weak, we can go in small spurts. You don't have to hold time for so long." The desire she'd seen in his eyes earlier was gone now. Instead, Harte was looking at her with the soft pity that made her skin crawl.

"I feel fine," she told him. It was a lie—she felt shaken and unsure of her affinity, but the darkness wasn't her fault . . . or was it? Had she brought something through the Brink—something dangerous and unexpected? She didn't know, and they didn't have time to figure it out. All she knew for sure was that she hated the worried emotion in his eyes. "There's no reason to push our luck. Let's just do this my way, okay?"

She didn't leave him much choice; she was in the hallway before he could argue.

Once again the sounds of an orchestra and the distant murmuring of a party came to them through the quiet. "If we can get to the ballroom, we can use the crowd to hide," Esta said, pointing in the direction of the music. "If there's a ballroom, there has to be a way to get to the kitchen—a service hall or something. From there maybe we can find a delivery entrance for the hotel."

"They'll be watching those doors too," Harte said, checking behind them as they continued onward down the hall.

"Probably." They paused only a moment before crossing in front of the stairwell the man in the bathroom had been guarding. "But if I have to chance using my magic, I'd rather wait until then," she said.

"*If* we get that far," he muttered under his breath.

She shot him a hard look. "They'll have discovered the empty elevator by now, and if they figure out that the guard on this floor is missing . . ."

"I'm not planning on standing here, waiting for them to find us,"

Harte finished, sweeping his arm to indicate that she should lead the way.

They followed the sound of the music to the mezzanine entrance of the ballroom, a narrow balcony that ringed the dance floor below on three sides. Inside, the glittering chandeliers were dimly lit, giving the ballroom a soft glow. On one end, a stage held a small orchestra that was playing a waltz, but no one on the dance floor below was dancing. Probably, Esta realized, because the room was filled with men. Even the servers, all dressed in white jackets and dark pants, were men. There wasn't a woman in sight.

Esta leaned close to Harte so she could speak in a low voice. "Feel free to admit I was right any time you'd like."

THE HANDS OF JUSTICE

1904—St. Louis

Thunder crackled in the sky as Jack Grew's carriage made its way through the streets of St. Louis. He'd come to this shithole of a city as part of the president's entourage to visit the world's fair, and also as the Order's representative for the meeting of the Brotherhoods that the Society was hosting in a couple of weeks. For the past two days, he'd been annoyed at being away from New York for so long, but now it seemed the trip had suddenly become more promising. Word had come only moments before. *They found her.*

Two years. Two years without a trace of her, and now Esta Filosik would be his.

Jack had been waiting for this moment long enough that he'd already run through many possibilities for their first reunion. He'd considered a quick sneer and a cold laugh as he watched her dragged away to rot in prison. But he'd also considered doing something she wouldn't expect— perhaps he would *thank* her for what she'd done, for what he'd become.

Of course, she hadn't been the one to give him the Book—Darrigan had done that. But the train accident that had left his arm broken had, ironically enough, created a new future for him. The girl had been a very convenient scapegoat, a target for the public's anger and evidence of the continued need for the Order and their like.

Once, the Order had been seen as a curiosity, unimportant to the average person. Since the day on the train, though, the tide had turned. If magic had once been a distant fairy tale, the train accident and all the attacks that followed had made it an immediate danger. The entire country was afraid, which worked just fine for Jack. With every new Antistasi attack, with every new tragedy committed in the name of the Devil's Thief, the Order's power—and Jack's along with it—had grown.

As the carriage rumbled along the final few blocks to the hotel, Jack couldn't help but chuckle to himself. Yes. When he finally came face-to-face with her, she would be in handcuffs, and he would *thank* her. In his mind's eye, he imagined her full mouth parting in confusion. She would, most likely, plead with him. Miss Filosik—if that was even her name—wasn't stupid. She would understand immediately that her life was, for all intents and purposes, *finished*. Over. But before she met with some untimely accident in the women's prison, Jack would take the opportunity to thank her for all her treachery. It had, after all, made him a star.

How could his family send him away when he was a hero who had tried to stop a madwoman? *They couldn't.* So they had publicly lauded his bravery, the whole lot of them. But despite all his success—all the power he'd attained and all he'd done to ensure the Order remained relevant enough that he could use it to his own ends—they whispered to one another about him. They still wondered if he'd imagined the events on the train or made them up.

But Jack had known he wasn't mad. He'd known that not only had Esta been on the train, but that she had *survived*.

He reached into his vest and let his fingers brush against the Book that he carried with him everywhere. He'd had all his clothes altered to conceal it, and he kept it on his person at all times. He would not leave it behind, no matter the event. Nor would he trust servants or safes, not when the Book had opened doors to a consciousness he had only dreamed of.

Unable to resist its call, he took the Book from its home close to his chest and thumbed through the pages. Greek and Latin he could read, thanks to the interminable schooling he'd had as a boy, but there were other, less comprehensible languages mixed with strange symbols that graced many of the pages. Those pages should have been impossible for him to understand, and yet he'd woken in his mother's house after being dosed with morphine that first time to discover that he'd somehow translated them just the same.

Now his own small, neat hand filled the pages with notes and translations, but looking at the writing in the jarring carriage caused his head to ache. He took a small vial from his waistcoat pocket and placed one of the cubes it contained on his tongue. It took only a moment for the bitterness to erupt, familiar and satisfying, in his mouth, and then only a few moments more before he felt the tension behind his eyes ease.

The notations came into focus as he searched for the page he wanted. A protection charm of sorts, or so he believed it to be. Alone in the carriage, he let the strange words roll from his mouth, filling the cramped space with the cool resonance of the power that would forevermore be his.

He had known the girl was alive all along. And now he would prove it to everyone else.

The carriage pulled up in front of the Jefferson, and Jack tucked the Book back into the safety of his waistcoat as he prepared himself. He would thank Miss Filosik, and if she wanted to beg for her life, he would accept whatever she offered. Then he would toss her back to the hands of justice—hands that were controlled, of course, by his family and others like them.

Jack's personal servant and bodyguard, Miles, opened the door for him and waited silently with an umbrella in hand. When he stepped from the carriage, Jack noticed the line of dark wagons manned by uniformed officers and smiled. *There will be no getting away this time.*

"Wait here," he commanded, brushing past Miles without bothering with the umbrella. What did a bit of dampness matter when Jack was so close to victory? He would have satisfaction. He knew it as surely as he felt the Book in his jacket, its familiar weight reminding him that he held all the cards.

THE TRAITOR

1902—New York

Jianyu did not fight Mooch as he was led up the familiar steps of the Strega.

"I am not a traitor," he said softly as he forced his legs to move through the pain of lifting himself one step at a time.

But if Mooch heard what Jianyu said, he didn't respond.

When they reached the second floor, Mooch opened a familiar door and pushed Jianyu through. Then he shoved him into one of the chairs Jianyu had sat in countless times before during conversations with Dolph.

"I am not a traitor," he repeated as Mooch tied Jianyu's arms behind him and his ankles to the chair legs. "The traitor is the one who has taken a fallen man's home, just as he took his life. The traitor is the one who carries Dolph's cane and commands his holdings as though he has any right."

Mooch eyed him. "You can't really expect me to believe that little Nibsy was the one to put a bullet in Dolph's back? He don't have it in him."

"Then why do you follow his orders?" Jianyu asked softly.

"Maybe Nibs ain't tough, but he's smart," Mooch said after a minute. "And anyway, who else am I gonna follow, you?"

"He will discard you the moment you're not of use to him," Jianyu said. "Look at what is already happening."

"Nothing is happening," Mooch said.

"Then why are there Five Pointers in the Strega?" Jianyu asked. When

Dolph was alive, it would have never happened. Every one of the Devil's Own knew what Paul Kelly's men were capable of. Every one of them had been furious when the Five Pointers attacked two of the Devil's Own not even a week before.

"We have an understanding now," Mooch said, but the edge in his tone told Jianyu that not everyone was happy with this understanding.

"Do you?" he asked softly. Every breath he took was a pain, but he continued. "Because Nibsy trusts Kelly?"

"Don't nobody here trust Kelly. We all know he's a snake, but Nibsy's explained it—Kelly's got connections we need. He's kept the Strega from burning, hasn't he?"

"So he has." Jianyu kept his voice low and as steady as he could. "But catching a snake by the tail will not keep him from striking you."

"You know what? Just shut your yap, okay?" Mooch told him, more agitated now. "If you didn't betray us, where was you on the bridge while we was getting our asses handed to us?"

"I was following Dolph's orders," Jianyu told him. It was nothing more or less than the truth.

"Dolph Saunders is *dead*," Mooch said, his voice breaking with something that sounded like pain and frustration all rolled into a single emotion. "He was already laid out and cold before we went to the bridge."

"His death did not invalidate the task he gave me," Jianyu said carefully. "*Me*. Not the traitor you follow now."

Mooch took a step back and began pacing. He wasn't the smartest of the Devil's Own, and what Jianyu had said was clearly having an effect on him.

Mooch was shaking his head as though the action might jar loose an errant thought. Then he stopped and glared at Jianyu. "No. I'm done listening to you and your lies right now. Just . . . You just keep your damned ugly mouth shut, you hear me?"

Jianyu didn't respond to the slur. He watched the boy who had once been loyal to Dolph pace with a nervous energy that told Jianyu that his words had struck a nerve. The boy's cheeks had gone blotchy with his consternation. If Jianyu could just keep himself upright and conscious for long enough, perhaps he could continue to pick at Mooch's doubt.

But there wasn't time. Before he could say anything else, Werner burst through the door.

Mooch turned in surprise, his fists already up like he was expecting an attack.

"You gotta come—"

"What the hell are you doing, bursting in here like—"

"The Strega's on fire." The other boy grabbed Mooch by the sleeve. "We gotta help."

The color drained from Mooch's face, but he didn't hesitate to follow Werner.

"You cannot leave me here!" Jianyu called, but they were already gone.

The Strega took up the first floor of the building. If the saloon was on fire, the building could go quickly, and Jianyu was stuck two stories above and tied to a chair. He jerked at the ropes binding his wrists and found that they were too tight to slip free of. The same with his feet.

Faintly, he could smell the evidence of the fire as the breeze blew in through the opened window. Perhaps if he could scoot the chair close enough, he could call for help.

With all the strength he had left, he swung his body forward, moving the chair inches in the direction he wanted to go. The motion made his head swirl again, and his stomach threatened to expel its contents, but he tried again. His skin felt clammy, damp with the exertion as he struggled to move the chair closer to the window, but when the door behind him swung open, Jianyu went still.

"There you are."

He turned to see a girl entering the room. She was about his age—perhaps seventeen—and of average height. Though her figure was trim, there was a softness in the curve of her hips and the swell of her bosom. Her heart-shaped face held expressive, deep-set eyes that were upturned at the corners, and her thick, dark hair had been parted in the middle and smoothed back into a chignon at the nape of her neck, a style recently fashionable in the city. But around her temples, fine wisps of hair had started to curl out of their style. The dress she was wearing was a sage green that complemented the deep burnt umber of her skin. Even as rumpled as it was and as dirty as the hem had become, the gown was so perfectly tailored that it might have come from the finest dressmaker's shop on Fifth Avenue, which told him who this must be.

"Cela Johnson?" he asked, sure that he could not be right. It was not possible that the girl he had been searching for was *here*, in the Strega.

Cela gave him a small nod, the only affirmation he would have for now, it seemed.

"What are you doing here?" he asked, trying to focus on her. His head ached so badly that it looked as though there were two of her.

"Saving you," she said with a tone that told him he should have figured that much out on his own. "Or can't you tell?" She was already working at the ropes around his wrist with her nimble fingers.

"But how did you find me?" he asked, wincing at the way she tugged at the ropes, jarring him.

"I followed you from the theater."

His wrists were free and she started on the ropes at his ankles. He should have helped her, but the very thought of movement made the room spin.

"But why—"

"Look, Mr. Lee—"

"Jianyu," he said, not wanting her to use a name that wasn't truly his.

"Mr. Jianyu—"

"Simply Jianyu. No mister."

She made an exasperated noise in the back of her throat. "We don't have time for this. They're going to figure out pretty quick that the fire I started isn't any real threat. We need to be gone by then."

Even through his pain, that surprised him. "*You* started the fire?"

"You have a lot of questions," she muttered as the last of the ropes came untied. "That's fine, because I have some of my own. But all that is gonna have to wait. We need to move. Can you walk okay?"

Jianyu gave her a sure nod, hoping it was not a lie as he got to his feet, using the table to steady himself. His eyes caught on a piece of newsprint sitting there. It had been cut unevenly, and when his eyes caught on the headline, he understood why. Crumpling the paper, he stuffed it into his tunic pockets.

"Come on," Cela urged, already at the door.

On unsteady feet, he followed, but the specter of smoke that signaled the burning of the Strega hung heavy in the air.

INTO THE FIRE

1902—New York

The moment Jianyu Lee told Cela that Harte Darrigan had sent him, she'd had a feeling that he would be trouble. Watching him try to keep himself upright as they made their escape from the building, she knew she'd been right.

She never should have followed him. Once she was freed from her workroom, she should have turned north and gone straight to her family, but curiosity had gotten the better of her when she'd watched him walking away from the theater late the night before, his long braid swinging down his back.

She hadn't known that Darrigan was friends with any Chinese men. She didn't know *anyone* who even knew any of the Chinese people, who mostly kept to themselves as they held on to their strange dress and stranger customs. So she couldn't help but wonder if Darrigan really had sent the man to help her, and if he had, why? Did he know who was responsible for her brother's murder?

If he knew anything about what had happened to Abe, it seemed worth the risk, so she'd followed him, keeping herself back a ways as he headed first to a Chinese laundry on Twenty-Fourth Street, at the southern edge of the area some called the Tenderloin and others called Satan's Circus. She probably should have left him there, but she'd felt almost safe hiding in the quiet side alley near the laundry. She'd only meant to rest for a little while, but she'd fallen asleep without meaning to and only woke when she heard the door of the laundry close sometime around dawn. Rousing herself, she'd followed him as he walked south, toward the Bowery.

She had seen the boys following before he did—stupid, rangy things who barely had hair sprouting on their pale, pimpled chins, and mean as rats. There wasn't even time to warn him before they had him cornered and on the ground, and she wasn't big enough or strong enough—or stupid enough—to jump into a fight she couldn't win. She'd thought to wait until they'd left to help him, but then that other one came.

Mock Duck, they called him, and everyone in the city had read about what he was capable of. The papers had been covering the war between the tongs on Mott Street and Pell Street the same way they covered the gossip of the people who lived in the mansions on Fifth Avenue—like it was some kind of sport. But while the people in the fancy mansions wore the wrong hats or went out dancing with people who might not be their own wives, the violence stirred up by Mock Duck and his highbinders killed innocent people.

Cela had almost left then, because she'd figured the guy she'd been following must've been one of Mock Duck's highbinders himself. They'd take care of their own, even if they wouldn't be able to put his hair back onto his head. But it was clear soon enough that Mock Duck wasn't saving him so much as taking him prisoner.

A smarter woman would have called it quits right then and there, maybe. A woman with some brains in her head wouldn't have followed them deeper into the Bowery. But she was a woman without much more to lose. Jianyu Lee had claimed that Darrigan had sent him to protect her. Her brother had already died doing that—just as her father had—and she would carry that knowledge with her all her days. She wasn't about to add another life to her load.

Out of the frying pan, she thought as she pulled the scrap of fabric she'd taken up over her head. She kept her distance as she followed them to some saloon on the Bowery. And then, when she needed a distraction to get Jianyu on his own, she made one.

She was in the fire now—literally, if they didn't get out of there, and fast. But from the way Jianyu was moving, it didn't seem like fast was an option.

They were nearly to the ground floor, nearly free, when they heard voices—angry voices—coming their way.

She looked back up at Jianyu, who was standing on the step above her, to see if he'd heard them. From the expression on his face, it was clear that he had. Maybe they could go back up. . . . But if the fire was still burning—she didn't think it would be, but if it *was*—she wasn't ready to die quite yet.

The boy didn't look half as concerned as Cela felt. With a smooth, practiced motion, he withdrew two dark disks from the inside pocket of his tunic.

"Step up here and hold on to me," he told her.

"Hold on to you?" she repeated, sure she must have misheard him.

"You're right. It would be better if you climbed onto my back." He maneuvered past her and then stooped slightly, waiting.

"I'm *not* climbing up onto you. I don't know you from Adam," she said, thinking that maybe she should take her chances with the fire. "You can barely walk as it is."

"I'm fine," he said, clipping out the words through clenched teeth.

She saw the way he was masking the hurt with the fire in his eyes. She'd done the same thing many times herself.

"It's nothing personal. I just—"

"Unless you would like to explain to the men coming up the steps who you are and what you're doing here, you would be wise to do as I say and climb onto my back."

The voices were getting closer.

"Fine," she said, hoping with every bit of her being that her mother wasn't watching from the hereafter as she used his shoulders to pull herself up and wrapped her legs around him.

The first thing she thought, and it was maybe the least sensible thing she could have picked to think, was that the guy beneath her was all muscle. He looked half-dead from the beating he'd gotten, but with her legs secure around his midsection and her arms around his neck, she could feel the strength beneath his loose clothes.

The second thing she thought, once she got over the idiotic first thought, was that the papers were wrong. But then, she should have known that the papers would be wrong. Weren't they usually when it came to anyone who wasn't white? She'd read all sorts of things about the Chinese men who made their home in the city—about their strange habits and the filthy conditions in which they lived, refusing to become good, solid Americans like everyone else. But this boy smelled like the earth, like something green and pleasant.

She was still thinking the second thought when Jianyu made a subtle movement of his hands, and she felt the world tilt.

"Hold on," he said, and started down the steps.

When they reached the landing below, he paused, listening. She could feel his labored breathing. "Stay still and be quiet," he commanded, as though he had some right to command *her* when she was the one who was doing the rescuing. But seeing how she was the one who'd climbed up onto him, however unwillingly, maybe he wasn't too far off the mark.

Men were coming up the steps—the same swarthy-skinned Italians who'd been standing around at the saloon. They were dressed in dark pants and coats and there was a meanness to the air around them, but the guy carrying her didn't do more than pull back against the wall.

And just like that, those men walked past them like they weren't even standing there. Like she wasn't nothing but a haint walking in the world.

The men were still too close and Cela was too unnerved to ask what had happened. She decided instead to take the blessings as they came and to hope that their luck held.

As the men continued up, Jianyu began to descend again, and a moment later they were out the back of the building and into the busy traffic of Elizabeth Street.

"Don't let go," he told her just as she started to release his neck.

She probably shouldn't have listened, but there was something about the way he said it—more desperate than commanding—that made her comply.

"They can't see us," he whispered, answering her unspoken question.

"None of them?"

"Not as long as you stay where you are," he said, hitching her up higher on his back and walking away from the building she'd rescued him from.

She understood then. "You're one of *them*," she said. But though his jaw went tight, he didn't answer.

He didn't put her down until they were two blocks away. In the distance, she could hear the clanging of a fire brigade's wagons as he released her. His face was turned, solemn and serious, toward the direction of the sound.

"What is it?" she asked.

"Dolph built the Strega from nothing. To see it burn . . ." His voice fell away.

"The bar, you mean? It won't burn," she assured him. "I only set a small fire in a waste can—one that would make a lot of smoke and look worse than it is. Besides," she said, pausing to listen to the approaching sirens, "it sounds like someone there has friends in high places if the brigades are already coming."

He turned to her. "Thank you for rescuing me, Miss Johnson." His straight, dark hair was hanging lank and uneven around his face from where it had been so unceremoniously chopped. It should have looked a mess, but instead it served to accent the sharp angles of him—his razor-blade cheekbones and sharp chin, the wide, strong nose, and the finely knit brows over too-knowing eyes.

"You might as well call me Cela. Everyone else does."

"Cela," he repeated, swaying a bit on his feet.

"Whoa, there," she said, catching him up under the arm before he toppled over. "They messed you up good, didn't they?"

"I'm fine," Jianyu said, grimacing even as he said it.

"Sure you are." She helped him over to a shuttered doorway, where he could lean and rest.

"Come," he said. "We're still too close."

He led the way to a streetcar stop another block over, and he didn't speak again until they were heading uptown and away from the Bowery. "Is there somewhere you can go?" he asked her, still clutching his stomach as the car rattled along, like he was trying to hold it in. "Somewhere you would feel safe?"

"Safe?" Cela wanted to laugh from the sheer absurdity of the idea. "I'm not sure what safe even is anymore."

BEWARE THE DEVIL'S THIEF

1904—St. Louis

Harte Darrigan was probably more likely to put on a dress himself than ever admit to Esta that her decision to wear the clothing she'd found in the hotel room was a good idea, even if the ballroom below *was* filled with nothing but men. For one thing, admitting that she had been right would only embolden her, but more important, maybe, it was taking everything he had not to be distracted by the shape of her legs in the trousers she was wearing. So he shot her a dark look instead and focused on the problem at hand—getting them out of the hotel before they were found.

"The kitchen entrance must be there," Harte said, ignoring her remark as he pointed toward the far end of the room, where a door periodically swung open as white-coated servers came and went at regular intervals. "There are steps in the corner there, by the stage. Then we'll keep to the edge of the room until we have to cut across. Stick close, but not too close," he said, "and try not to sway your hips so much."

"I do *not* sway my hips." She glared at him.

"You *do*," he told her flatly. He should know, since he'd just followed her down a hallway. She opened her mouth as if to argue, but he cut her off. "You walk like a woman." He took a moment to look her over for any other flaw that might give her away. "Pull your hat down lower," he told her as she stared at him. "Your eyes—they're too soft. Christ," he swore, his stomach twisting. There was no way she was going to make it through a room full of men without them noticing what she really was.

She might as well have worn just the corset. "We're dead."

"We'll be fine," she told him. "I've been around men my whole life."

"Yeah, well, in case you haven't noticed, I've actually *been* one," he grumbled.

"It would have been kind of hard for me to miss." Her mouth twitched, and he thought he saw something warmer than mere amusement flicker in her whiskey-colored eyes. At the sight of it, the power inside of him flared with anticipation. He was too busy pushing it back down to return her banter, and she let out a tired breath at his silence. "Oh, come on, Harte. Most of the people in here are drunk. They're not going to notice me."

"Let's hope not." But he didn't have a lot of confidence.

Once they'd descended to the main ballroom, the sounds of glasses clinking and the rumble of men amused at their own jokes surrounded them. As they skirted the edges of the ballroom, something in Harte's periphery drew his attention, and he glanced up to see that there were now a few men standing at the edge of the mezzanine, searching the crowd below. They were wearing the same dark coats and white armbands as the Guard outside the theater.

"Don't look up," he told Esta. He nodded to a bleary-eyed old man as he lifted a bowl of champagne from a passing tray.

"What—"

"I said, *don't look*," he said through clenched teeth as he raised the glass to his lips. He didn't drink, but instead used the motion to cover his survey of the room. "There are two men up on the mezzanine now—maybe more."

"Police?" she asked.

"The Guard." His gaze slid to her. "We're running out of time if they're already looking for us here."

"For me," Esta corrected. "They're looking for the Devil's Thief." Her eyes were steady and her jaw tight.

"Well, they're not going to find her." Harte glanced at Esta over the rim of the glass. "You could get us out of here right now."

She shook her head. "You saw what happened in the hallway. I could barely hold on to the seconds. We don't know what the Guard is capable of. And if they can track magic . . ."

She was probably right. If the Brink or the power of the Book inside of him had done something to her magic—or to his—it was better not to chance it until they knew more. "Let's go."

They left behind the relative safety of the mezzanine's overhang to cut a line across the ballroom floor. Directly across the room, the double doors to the kitchens swung loosely on their hinges every time a waiter appeared with another tray of champagne or canapés. Behind the doors, the light of the service hallway was a beacon, urging them on.

If Harte could have made a beeline to those doors, he would have, but too fast or too direct and it might draw the attention of the men watching from above. As much as everything in him was screaming to *Run. Go. Get out*, he forced himself to keep the interminable pace as he meandered through the crowded floor, stopping at random intervals to pretend to watch the orchestra or take one of the hors d'oeuvres from the white-coated servers circulating through the crowd.

It felt like they would never reach the other side . . . and then, all at once, they were there, nearly to the edges of the ballroom. Only a few feet more and they could duck into the safety of the back of the house. But just before they could slip through the doors, the orchestra abruptly went silent. All around them, there was a delayed reaction, a ripple of awareness that filtered through the crowd as the men in the room, drunk as they might have been, realized something had happened.

Harte turned too, just long enough to see that one of the plainclothes officers had taken the stage and was lifting his hands, telling the crowd to be patient as the lights on the chandeliers suddenly grew brighter.

"If I could have your attention, gentlemen," the officer shouted. "I'm Detective Sheehan of the St. Louis Police, and I'm sorry to interrupt your evening, but there's a wanted criminal on the loose. She was spotted entering the hotel a few minutes ago, and we believe she may still be in the building."

The rustling around them increased as the men craned their necks, searching for a woman among them. Next to him, Esta pulled the hat lower over her brow.

The officer continued. "We just need a moment of your time as my men secure the room and do a quick sweep."

"I'm here, Officer," a voice called over the din of the crowd.

Esta—and everyone else in the room—turned to look up at the balcony, where a figure stood dressed in a crimson gown. Her face was half covered by a red porcelain mask tipped with horns, and she stood on the edge of the railing with her arms lifted, as though she were about to dive into the crowd. The Guardsmen started charging around the mezzanine to where she stood. With a swirl of her arms, she took a sweeping bow, and in a sudden plume of scarlet smoke, the figure was gone.

"You'll have to be quicker than that if you want to catch me," another voice called from the other side of the ballroom. Again the heads in the room swiveled to find the source of the sound. This figure was wearing the same devilish mask, but she was dressed in a gown of midnight, and standing on the railing above, she looked like a shadow against the gilded walls.

"Or me," a voice bellowed. This one was dressed in ghostly white, her face masked as well.

"Or me." Another voice, again from a different corner of the mezzanine.

"Or me." The woman in red was back.

Their voices echoed off the walls as the sound of thunder rumbled through the ballroom, and the air seemed suddenly charged and electric. A strange, impossible wind began to swirl through the room, eliciting more nervous rustling from the men who'd been having fun only a moment before. A single word circulated through the ballroom, as quickly as a wildfire fed by the air: *Antistasi*.

The men in the ballroom were already running toward the door, but the police had blocked the exits.

"Who are they?" Esta whispered, her hand on Harte's arm.

"I don't know," he said, looking up at the women. Each was balanced precipitously on the balcony. "From the sound of it, we've found the Antistasi that Julien told us about."

"Beware the Devil's Thief," they chanted in unison as more smoke billowed from beneath them. "Her enemies, beware her wrath." With a flash of light, the figures were gone, but the trailing smoke was still moving steadily toward the ballroom floor, like something alive.

"They're incredible," Esta whispered, her voice filled with something like wonder.

But Harte didn't feel the awe that was clear in Esta's expression. There was something eerie about the apparitions. Something more than unsettling. And it didn't help that the masked women were using that damned name, the one the papers had pinned on Esta, which could only mean trouble for them as long as they stayed in this town.

Then Harte felt the icy heat of magic in the air and knew it had something to do with the fog of smoke hanging over their heads. He wasn't about to wait and see what that fog contained. "Let's go." He took Esta's hand and moved in the opposite direction of the rest of the now-panicking crowd.

He didn't bother to check if anyone noticed them crossing the final few feet toward the service doors. Once they were in the hallway beyond, they began to run.

"This way." Esta pointed at a narrow staircase that led down toward the first floor.

They took the steps at a sprint, and at the bottom they found themselves in another hall of linoleum floors and cream-colored walls. Harte could already hear noise coming from the stairs behind them. To the right, other voices seemed to be drawing closer. He didn't know whether it was more police or just the kitchen staff, but they couldn't stay to find out.

Harte tugged Esta down the hall in the opposite direction and through a doorway.

"It's a dead end," she said, looking around for some other exit.

It was a storage room. One wall was lined with gleaming silver serving ware, soup tureens, and domed platters. In the corner, two large wheeled carts were filled with clean linens.

From just outside the door came the sound of voices, and Harte went to lean against it, cracking it open so he could listen. "There's someone out there," he told her as he tried to make out what they were saying. "I think they're looking for whoever those women in the ballroom were. We need to get out of here."

"What about that?" she asked, pointing out a smaller door on the far wall. It was square, about halfway up the wall, and when she opened it, he could see it was some kind of chute. The space was just large enough for a person to fit through. "Looks like it goes down to the basement. Maybe it's the laundry?" she offered, indicating the carts filled with linens.

"It could just as easily be a trash chute leading to an incinerator." He walked over and poked his head into the dark opening for a moment.

Outside the door, the voices were growing louder. "I think we should risk it," she said, already lifting a leg to wedge herself into the chute. "If we get down to the basement, there has to be a way out."

"Esta, no," Harte said, pulling her back as they heard another door in the hallway bang open. "We don't know how far the drop might be or what's down there."

"But—" He scooped her up before she could finish her protest.

"We can't risk breaking a leg or something," he said as he carried her, squirming, over to the laundry bins.

He saw her eyes widen as she understood what he was about to do. "Harte, don't you even think about—"

But he was already dumping her into the rolling bin. "Cover up."

Esta struggled to right herself amid the slippery piles of fabric. "But—"

"We don't have time to argue," he said, pulling extra linens from one of the other bins. Whoever those women in the ballroom were, they'd bought Harte and Esta some time with their distraction. At least Harte hoped they had. "I trusted you in the elevator. Now it's your turn."

"Harte—"

"Get down and *stay* down," he snapped, and then piled another load of linens on top of her before she could argue any more.

Harte tied one of the white tablecloths around his waist, approximating the aprons he'd seen the servers wearing earlier. He wasn't dressed in one of the white jackets the other hotel workers wore, but he had to hope it was like Esta had said: No one ever noticed the help.

"Ready?" he asked the cart, and he got a string of muffled curses in reply. He figured that was as good as a yes.

Carefully, he backed out of the room, pulling the cart behind him. Turning away from the voices and trying to figure out where he was, Harte tried to look natural as he maneuvered the cart down the hall. He was nearly to the first turn when he heard someone calling out behind him.

"Hey! You there!"

Pretending that he hadn't heard them, Harte kept his pace brisk but steady as he headed for where the hall branched into a T.

"Hey!" The shout came again. "Stop!"

He took the first right and then broke into a run. He didn't bother to slow down for the set of swinging doors ahead, but instead took them at full speed and plunged into the kitchen. Surprised chefs raised their heads, pausing their work to watch him rush through. On the other side of the kitchen was an empty service hall. He didn't look back to see how close their pursuers were, but tore down the hallway and then out another set of doors that led to the lobby.

The front door of the hotel was ahead of them—just a few more yards and they would be out into the night—when the shrill screech of a whistle split the air, causing the tinkling of the piano to cut short and people all throughout the lobby to stare. And in front of him, blocking the one exit he had left, two uniformed policemen stepped into his path to stop him.

In that moment Harte knew they were done. There would be more police outside, and even if he got them through the front doors, they'd have no place to go. Not that he would go easily.

"Hold on," he told Esta as he picked up his speed.

"Harte, what are you—"

He'd expected the two men to move out of the way, but they held their ground, bracing for impact, so when the cart plowed into them, they all went over. Esta tumbled out of the cart, disoriented and with her hair falling from her hat, but Harte was already on his feet, taking her by the hand.

"Run!" he shouted, half dragging her as he sprinted toward the exit, but suddenly there were three more men blocking their way. He pulled up short as he realized there was no way to get through them—not without magic.

"Esta—" Her name was a question and demand all at once.

She tightened her hold on his hand as though she understood, but at first nothing happened.

"Any time now," he said as the men started to close in on them.

She blinked over at him. "Right—"

Harte almost stumbled when the men chasing them seemed to halt in midstride, and Esta let out a shaking breath. Together they wove through the men and out the front doors of the hotel. He'd been right: There were police wagons and a row of dark-suited police standing along the front of the hotel, waiting for them.

The storm that had threatened all evening had started, and the cold drops of rain, suspended midfall, felt needle-sharp against Harte's face as he and Esta continued to run from the hotel. Above, the sky glowed from a flash of lightning, the bright forks of the electric bolts frozen like cracks in an iced pond. They lit the night with their brilliance.

Next to him, Esta's breath hitched as she stumbled, nearly pulling him down with her. But he caught the two of them in time. "Esta?"

"I can't—" she said through gritted teeth. "It's too much." She was trying to pull away from him.

He realized then that where their hands were clasped, ribbons of energy, like miniatures of the lightning bolts that hung in the sky, were winding about, binding them together. These weren't frozen in time, though, like everything else around them. This energy was alive—hot and dangerous and creeping up her arm. The voice inside of him was howling in victory.

"We're too close," he said, looking at what was happening with a numb sort of horror. The hotel was still in sight. The police were still a danger. Everything they'd risked, everything they'd done to escape, would have been for nothing if they didn't get away. "I need you to hold on for just a few more minutes."

Esta's face was twisted with the effort of what she was doing. "It feels like fire." But she nodded, and without pausing or asking for permission, Harte scooped her over his shoulders, in a fireman's carry, and threaded his way through the now-still traffic. He ignored the needlelike cold of the raindrops. The power inside of him surged again, pulsing with satisfaction, but he gathered all his strength and pushed it down.

He was barely across the street, just out of view of the hotel, when Esta gasped and the world around them righted itself. Above, the sky went dark, and a moment later thunder crashed over the steady patter of raindrops. He ran for the cover of a doorway and lowered Esta to the ground.

"Did we make it?" she whispered.

"Yeah," he said, brushing back the hair from her face. "We made it. We have to keep going, though. I need you to help me here. You're going to have to walk."

She wasn't listening. Her gaze was glassy and unfocused as she stared up at the night sky. "Can you see that? It's like the darkness is eating the world."

Harte didn't bother to look. His attention was on Esta as her eyes fluttered closed and her limbs went limp.

AN UNEXPECTED CHALLENGE

1904—St. Louis

Ruth waited beneath the cover of the brewery's wagon, across from the Jefferson Hotel, watching for some sign of what was happening within. Along the street near the front entrance, the dark bodies of police wagons blocked her view of the front door. She had more Antistasi stationed at the other entrances, just in case.

She wasn't sure what she was expecting. Ever since the legend of the Devil's Thief was born after the train accident two years before, Ruth had always assumed it was a lie perpetrated by the Order and the other Occult Brotherhoods to stir up anger against her kind. Ruth had never really believed that a girl, a simple *girl*, could have done what the reports claimed she had. Which had not stopped Ruth and the other Antistasi leaders from claiming the Devil's Thief as their own, or from using her name to unify their cause.

All across the country, there were pockets of Mageus who lived quiet lives, but something changed after the Defense Against Magic Act was passed. Ordinary people who were happy living ordinary lives suddenly realized they had never been safe. They began to look to the Thief for the promise of a different future, and groups like Ruth's had been more than happy to provide them with hope.

When other deeds—small and large, across the country—were done by people claiming to be the Devil's Thief, Ruth had always assumed that it was simply a group of Antistasi like her own. She'd never thought that the same girl could have been involved. The Devil's Thief was nothing but a myth, a folk hero like Paul Bunyan or John Henry. Maybe she'd been a real girl at some point, but the Thief had become something so much larger than any single person. She'd become an ideal. A calling.

But then, earlier that night, North had seen the girl, the one whose face had been in papers across the land, and Ruth had to accept the possibility that she'd been wrong. She also had to face the possibility of a challenge to her own power in St. Louis. After all, stories are often easier to tame than actual hearts.

Ruth had no idea who this girl was or what she wanted. She didn't even know if the girl *was* the Thief, though the police and the Guard certainly were treating her as such. At best, the girl's appearance was a minor distraction. At worst, the girl might have come to the city to take control of it. Ruth had worked too hard, had far too much planned, to allow that.

Still, it wouldn't do for the girl to be caught now. If she was, the specter of the Devil's Thief would be useless as a shield against any retaliation that Ruth's Antistasi might incur. There was too much at stake, so she'd brought her people to the Jefferson. They would provide a distraction for the girl to escape, and if possible, they would bring the girl to Ruth. As a competitor, the girl could be a problem, but as an ally—or better, a *subordinate* . . . Well, that idea held a certain attraction.

It had been too long. With North and his watch, time was flexible, but waiting was still interminable. As long as her people were inside, Ruth would worry.

She didn't have to worry for much longer, though. Lightning flashed in a brilliant arc overhead, illuminating the street and the facade of the hotel, and before the thunder could break, a pair appeared out of nowhere. Ruth squinted through the rain as the taller of the two scooped the other up and ran. And she felt the crash of warm magic sift through the air, unusually strong. Impossibly pure. Ruth hadn't felt power like *that* in her entire life.

A moment later four masked figures dressed in gowns appeared just out of the beam of the streetlamp nearby. They ran toward the wagon and were inside before anyone could see them. The back door of the wagon closed, and a window slid open near the driver's perch.

"Did you run into any problems?" Ruth asked, peering back into the darkness of the wagon's covered bed. North had already taken the mask from his face and was stripping out of the dark gown.

"Not one," North told her. "Maggie's devices worked like a charm."

"They usually do," Ruth said, a spark of pride for her youngest sister glowing within her.

"We didn't find the Thief inside. Do you think she got out?" Maggie asked, pulling her own mask from her face. It was always a moment of shock to see Maggie dressed in scarlet, when Ruth was used to the girl wearing more sedate colors. From the look on North's face—the open longing—Ruth suspected that he felt the same.

She looked back in the direction where the two people had appeared in the rain. "I think she did," Ruth told them. "But North was right. She's not alone."

"Do you want me to follow them?" North asked.

Ruth considered his offer—and the way her sister's expression filled with worry at the mention of it. With the power the Thief clearly had, having her on their side might be a boon, but she knew that if Maggie was worried about North, she would not be able to focus on the work necessary to complete the serum. Thief or no Thief, they were running out of time. "We have eyes enough in the city. If they surface again or cause any problems, we'll know. For now, I need you close."

RESPONSIBILITIES

1902—New York

As the streetcar rattled north toward Fifty-Second Street, where her uncle and his family lived, Cela couldn't stop her voice from cracking as she told Jianyu about how Abe had been killed in their own house. Tears fell down her cheeks as she explained how the theater workroom that had been her pride—her sanctuary—had been turned into her prison.

"I *knew* you were there," he said.

She nodded. "I heard you, but I didn't know who you were. With the night I'd had . . . Then you went on about Darrigan, and I didn't think it was smart to reveal myself, not after everything else."

"It is understandable after what happened to your brother and your house," Jianyu said simply, an acknowledgment that Cela didn't quite understand.

"I didn't say anything about my house," she told him, her stomach suddenly feeling like she'd swallowed molten lead.

"You do not know?" His expression faltered. "When I came to find you, it was burning."

Even sitting down as she was, it was her turn to sway and his turn to steady her. That house had been her daddy's pride and joy. It was his mark in the world, and if Jianyu was right, it was gone. Just like her brother. Just like everything she'd loved. All in a single night.

The vines around her heart grew thorns, and her breath felt like it was being pressed from her.

Has it already been two days?

Cela pulled away from the comfort of Jianyu's hand over hers.

He let her go, but his eyes narrowed thoughtfully.

"What?" she demanded, her very soul raw and weeping from the losses that had been piled one on another.

"Harte Darrigan lied about many things, but he did not lie about you," he told her softly. "He chose well."

"Well, he should've chosen somebody else," she told him, unable to keep the bitterness out of her voice.

Jianyu let out a ragged breath, a sigh that Cela took for agreement. They rode in silence for a while longer, but eventually he turned to her again. "Darrigan's mother?" he asked gently. "He told me that he left her with you. She was not in the house?"

"She died before I left," she assured him. *Before it burned.*

"Who was it that killed your brother?"

"I hoped that you would know," she said. "I was in the cellar when it happened. I heard the gunshot, and I ran. I don't even know *why* I ran. It's like I couldn't stop myself. I left Abe there. I left him like some coward."

Her voice hitched, and the memory of Abe—his laughing eyes and his strong features that were so much like their father's—threatened to overwhelm her. Threatened to pull her down so she'd never get back up.

"You are far from a coward, Cela Johnson." Jianyu reached over and gently wiped the tears from her cheeks. It was a strangely intimate gesture, a liberty that he didn't have any right to take with her. But she didn't stop him. She simply accepted his comfort as the gift she knew he'd intended.

"It's because of Darrigan, isn't it? Everything that happened to me— to Abe—it's all because I took his mother in and accepted that damn ring as payment."

"I cannot be sure, but . . ." He inclined his head, wincing a little at the movement.

"It's why Evelyn locked me in my workshop. She wanted the ring Darrigan left me," she told him. Cela still didn't understand how the stupid wench had managed to get it out of the seam of her skirt, or why she had given it up without so much as a fight.

"Do you still have it?" Jianyu asked, his eyes cutting to her and his voice suddenly urgent. "Did Evelyn get the ring?"

"She must've taken it," Cela said.

"No—"

"Good riddance to it, too. Evil old thing didn't bring me anything but bad luck."

Jianyu was looking paler than he had before. His skin had golden undertones before, but now the color all but drained from his face. "It'll bring worse luck if we do not retrieve it."

"We. There isn't gonna be any 'we,'" she told him. The streetcar was pulling to the curb and she wasn't going to continue on this ride. "This is my stop. I'm going to go to my family, heaven help them, and you can go wherever you'd like, but I don't want anything to do with that ring, or Harte Darrigan, or anything else. Now, I freed you, and you freed me, so I think we'd better call things even and part ways right here and now."

Jianyu frowned, but he didn't argue.

"I can't exactly say it was a pleasure, but it was interesting." She held out her hand. "God go with you, because lord knows that if you go after that ring, you're gonna need every bit of his protection."

He reached for her hand, but Jianyu's skin barely touched hers before she registered how cool it felt—too cool—and then he was collapsing as though the life had gone right out of him. It was only her quick reflexes that kept him from hitting his head a second time.

She hadn't realized he was in such bad shape. He'd seemed fine a moment before. Well, he wasn't her responsibility. Cela propped Jianyu back up onto the seat and then started to go. But she got only about four steps away before she turned back.

She couldn't leave him there. She *should*, but she couldn't.

With a sigh, she jostled Jianyu until he was conscious again, just enough to get himself up. Even then she had to support his weight—his arm draped over her shoulder—to get him down the aisle and off the streetcar, apologizing to the folks who were watching her with clear disapproval as she went. Once outside, Cela took a moment to get her bearings. Jianyu was barely conscious, but he was at least on his feet.

"Come on," she told him, heading deeper into the neighborhood. "Let's get you somewhere before you go and pass out again."

She hadn't been relishing the idea of going to her family to start with. If her uncle Desmond and his brood looked disapprovingly at her before, she could only imagine what he would do when she showed up on his doorstep, homeless, grieving, and with a half-dead Chinese man in tow.

MISSED OPPORTUNITIES

1904—St. Louis

I t was madness inside the Jefferson Hotel. Jack stopped short not three steps into the lobby. Dark-suited police were everywhere. Some were talking to groups of people clad in evening finery—women in satin dripping with jewels and men in sharply cut tuxedoes that would have made even a Vanderbilt green with envy—while others had created a border around the room and watched any new arrivals with suspicious eyes.

"You can't come in here now," one of the officers barked at Jack, but the man's voice was enough to bring him back to attention. And the morphine he'd just ingested was enough to make him not care. He stepped past the man without bothering to argue.

The man took him by the arm and whipped him around. "I said you can't—"

"I was told to come," Jack said, cutting him off.

"By who?" the officer blustered, narrowing his eyes.

"By me," a voice said from behind the officer.

"Chief Matson, I presume?" Jack said, jerking free of the other officer's grasp. He held out his hand in greeting.

The chief was a short man, stout and sturdy with the eyes of a hawk. "It's good to finally meet you, Mr. Grew," the man said as he shook Jack's hand. "But I'm afraid it's been a waste of your time."

The man's words cooled some of the easy warmth the morphine had spread through Jack's veins. "You said they were here," Jack said, his voice clipped.

"They were, but they're gone now," the police chief said.

"Gone." The impossibility of the word was a punch in the stomach. "They can't be gone. Didn't you have men at all the exits?"

"Every one, regular and service alike. They didn't get out any of the exits."

"Then they have to be here," Jack said, trying to keep his tone level. "Have you searched the whole hotel?"

"We don't need to," Matson told him.

Jack could practically feel the vein in his neck throbbing. Even with the morphine to dampen the noise and confusion of the lobby, the chief's words sparked his temper. "Why the hell not?"

"What's the point? We saw them disappear," the chief said. "Hell, half the force saw it. Just about five minutes ago." The chief pointed to a spot not twenty yards from the front door. "We had them surrounded, all their escapes blocked. They were there one minute and then—boom—they were gone, just like that. Like they were ghosts."

I was right. They laughed behind my back and called me a fool, but I was right.

"'Course, I don't believe in ghosts," the chief of police said. "So I called the Guard."

"The Guard?" Jack felt like the world had narrowed until he could concentrate on only one thing.

"The Jefferson Guard. They take care of any problems we have round these parts with illegal magic."

"They didn't take care of this one," Jack said darkly. "This is unacceptable, Chief Matson. You assured me that you could secure the area for Roosevelt's arrival."

The chief bristled, his heavy jowls wobbling as his cheeks turned red. "I have the utmost faith in our people to make sure everything is secure when the president arrives. Hey, Hendricks, come on over here," the chief called.

Across the room, a ruddy-faced man with a high forehead and a mop of honey-colored hair lifted his head. "I'll be done in a second."

"You'll be done now," the chief snapped forcefully enough to draw the attention of everyone in the room. He turned back to Jack and huffed in annoyance. "The Guard thinks that because the city council has given them free rein, they've got some standing, but they're still just amateurs."

"Hendricks, meet Mr. Jack Grew," the chief said once the other man had come over. "He's here to help prepare for the president's visit at the gala. I was just assuring him that we have everything under control."

Hendricks kept his hands tucked behind his back and his chin lifted. Up close, the man was younger than Jack had expected. He couldn't have been more than twenty, but he had the kind of broad shoulders and lean, strong features that made Jack puff out his own chest a little more.

"Hendricks here is a colonel with the Guard," the chief explained. "He can explain everything we have set up. I'll leave Mr. Grew with you, Colonel?"

"Yes, sir," the guy said, his expression never flickering.

"Right, then. You'll be in good hands." He gave Jack a rough pat on the arm before he walked off to find another of his officers.

"You have questions about our security measures?" Hendricks asked.

"This Guard . . . What is it?" Jack asked.

"The Jefferson Guard is tasked with protecting St. Louis from illegal magic," Hendricks said, reciting the words as though from memory.

"What does that entail, exactly?" Jack asked, eyeing the man.

"We do what the normal police can't." The colonel's eyes were emotionless when they met his. "We use a specific set of skills and tools to hunt Mageus who refuse to assimilate themselves as productive members of society."

Even with the haze of morphine dulling the brightness and noise around him, Jack felt his attention peak. "Really? You hunt Mageus?"

Hendricks nodded. "We show them back to the gutters and the prisons where they belong. We eliminate the danger they pose to proper society."

"Excellent," Jack said, reaching for the vial of morphine cubes. "Absolutely outstanding."

PART

III

DELMONICO'S

1902—New York

The boning of the new corset was digging into the soft flesh of Viola's hip, but there wasn't a thing she could do to adjust it, not so long as her brother's scagnozzo had her by the arm. And also not so long as she was supposed to be playing the part of a lady. It had been four days since Viola had accepted her brother's beating as the cost of using his protection. In four days, the split in her lip had healed itself enough for her to be presentable in public. In those four days, she'd bided her time and done everything her brother had asked of her, no matter how insulting. She'd played the part of the dutiful, penitent sister, but she'd kept her eyes and ears opened and she'd started to plan.

The maître d' was checking over his ledger, searching for their reservation. Occasionally, he'd glance up at Viola and her escort with a questioning look, as though he knew that neither of them belonged. The longer they stood there, the more Viola felt the eyes of other people on them. She wished the stuffed-shirt fool would hurry up. She was more than ready to have a table between her and her escort for the night. Already he'd been too free with his eyes . . . and his hands.

Paul didn't fool her one bit, arranging all of this just so she could dispose of one stupid journalist for an *important friend*. There were a hundred ways to kill a man, maybe more, and not one of them required a fancy dress, with her tette pushed up to her chin and her breath pressed out of her lungs. Nor did they require her to have dinner at a fancy restaurant with John Torrio, the man all the Five Pointers called the Fox. No, her brother had set this up because he didn't trust her yet. Torrio, or John, as he'd introduced himself, was nothing more than a nursemaid—though she doubted he'd appreciate being thought of as such. He was only there to keep an eye on her and to make sure she did what Paul had asked of her.

So what if a lady needed an escort to dine at a restaurant like Delmonico's? Killing a man in the middle of a crowded restaurant was a fool's errand. She could have killed him in the streets just as easily.

But Paul didn't want this Reynolds killed easily. Her brother was making a point. With so many witnesses, Viola would be forced to use her affinity—and in doing so, she would have to break the vow she had made to herself years ago. As long as she could get a clear view of this man, it would be easy enough to make it look like he'd died naturally, and with no obvious attack, it would be impossible for anyone to see the man's death as anything but a tragic misfortune. In the blink of an eye, Paul's friend would be rid of his little problem and Viola's soul would bear another black mark that could never be erased.

Even so, the act didn't require a fancy restaurant. Viola knew *exactly* what Paul was up to. It was no accident that he'd sent Torrio with her— her brother was matchmaking. His plan to marry her off had been the last straw to drive her away before. Now that she was back in the bosom of the family's control, he was testing her. The old goat he'd tried to tie her to the last time was probably dead by now, so it only made sense for Paul to try shackling her to the man he was grooming to be his second—all the better to keep them *both* under his control.

Out of the corner of her eye, Viola studied Torrio as they were shown to their table. He wasn't bad looking—a tall, striking boy from just outside Napoli with dark eyes and dark hair combed straight back from his face. He didn't have the characteristic crook in his nose that most who ran in the gangs wore as a badge of honor, but even dressed in a fancy dinner jacket, he didn't have Paul's polish. Torrio still looked like the streets.

And like all men, he walked through the world as though what he had in his pants was enough to make him a king. *But then,* she thought, watching Torrio snap out orders to the waitstaff, who all jumped to meet his demands, *maybe it is.*

Dinner was interminable. Viola tried to keep her mouth drawn into what she hoped was more smile than snarl as her escort droned on about all his accomplishments, but the task wore on her. He didn't stop his bragging to eat the first two courses. Instead he talked around the food in his mouth. When the steaks came, huge slices of meat that were dressed with herbed butter and creamed spinach, Torrio finally—thankfully—shut up.

Better he focus on his steak than continue to imagine that he had a chance with her. Men never took that news well, and she couldn't afford to maim or kill the guy when she was trying to convince Paul she could be trusted. He and Nibsy were planning something, and gaining Paul's trust was the first step in finding out what it was.

Viola shifted in her seat as she picked at her bloody steak and the gelatinous oysters, hating the entire situation she'd found herself in. The food was too rich for her, right along with everything else in the restaurant. Her whole life, she'd stuck close to what she knew—first her mother's kitchen and then the Strega, where she worked behind the bar, serving people of her own class and station. She had never really gone much farther than the streets of the Bowery, even when she left her family. But all around her, the dining room was filled with brilliantly white linen and gleaming crystal, candlelight and brightly polished silver. Delmonico's, with its gilded opulence, was evidence of how big the divide was between what she was and what the rest of the world held.

And the people . . . The men who could signal a waiter with a look instead of the roughly barked orders Torrio used and the ladies with their pretty manners and their tinkling, girlish voices all served to remind Viola of exactly *who* she was—and who she would never be. She hated them all almost as much as she hated the full corset biting into her skin and the ruffled flounce at her shoulders that pinned her arms down at her sides.

Worst of all, the longer they sat, the more she began to think that the entire evening had been pointless. Paul had been confident in the intelligence he had from his network of busboys and cooks that R. A. Reynolds dined at Delmonico's on Thursday nights at seven thirty. Reynolds always sat at the same table, a private corner booth, and Paul had arranged for Viola and Torrio to be seated at a table across the room with a clear view of the booth.

But seven thirty had come and gone, and there had been no sign of R. A. Reynolds or anyone else. The whole fiasco had been an absolute waste of time. As Torrio downed another glass of the expensive scotch that Paul was paying for and cut large pieces of beefsteak to shovel into his mouth, Viola picked at her food and counted the moments until she could go home and take off the ridiculous dress.

It was close to eight when a flurry of commotion erupted behind them. Viola turned to look and saw that a young couple had just arrived. They weren't much older than Viola herself, but they were clearly favorites. The girl, especially, seemed to know almost everyone, because she stopped and chatted at nearly every table they passed.

In a sea of lavish gowns, the girl stood out like a peacock among pigeons. She was dressed in a gown that looked, even to Viola, who knew very little about such trivial things, *expensive*. It was perfectly tailored to the girl's lithe body, and its color—a light blush that matched the flush of the girl's cheeks—would have looked ridiculously frivolous on anyone with less confidence. Instead, the pink hue only served to accent the glow of the girl's creamy skin and the dark fringe of lashes around her eyes.

She was as slender and delicate looking as a reed, with polished fingertips that had clearly never seen a day's worth of work. Her blond hair had just a touch of copper when the candlelight hit it, and the long, graceful column of her neck was ringed with a simple strand of pearls that lay against the fragile notch at the base of her throat.

Her skin would be soft there, fragile and fragrant with whatever scent she wears. Lilies, maybe . . . or roses . . . something floral and as pink as she is.

Viola's cheeks felt warm suddenly, as she realized the direction her thoughts had gone. She'd been staring openly. She glanced at Torrio to make sure he hadn't noticed, but he was still busy shoveling the last of his potatoes into his mouth. Confident he wasn't paying her any attention, she allowed herself one more peek at the girl. At the very moment Viola looked up, the girl's eyes met hers. Dark blue, the color the sea had been in the middle of the Atlantic, and just as dangerous.

Viola looked away as a wave of shame crashed over her—it had been only a few weeks since she had lost Tilly, and there she was, so easily distracted by a girl whose every breath screamed of wealth that Viola could never begin to dream of. And to be distracted *here*, of all places, when she was clearly being watched by her brother's escort?

Merda. If Paul heard of it . . .

She knew exactly what would happen if Paul heard of it. He'd make sure Viola was either married or dead, because everyone knew her soul was already too blackened for the convent.

But Torrio hadn't noticed the entrance of the couple or the direction of Viola's thoughts. As he signaled the waiter for yet another drink, Viola couldn't help herself. She chanced one more peek at the girl just in time to see the maître d' pull back the curtain to open a private booth—the Reynolds booth—and let the couple in. The girl had already disappeared behind the velvet curtains, but her escort had stopped to speak with the maître d'.

Viola didn't allow herself to wonder about the way her heart sank the moment the girl was out of sight. Her focus was on the girl's escort, R. A. Reynolds. The man she was supposed to kill.

Viola pulled on her affinity and sent it outward, searching for the link to this R. A. Reynolds across the room. She found him easily, his heartbeat steady like the ticking of a clock, pulsing nearly in time with her own.

She could do this. It would be so easy to simply slow the flow of blood, to call to that living part of him and command it, to *stop* it.

Why should she care that Reynolds was so young?

Why should she care that he looked the maître d' in the eye when he spoke to him—as though they were old friends? Or that the girl in the booth would have to witness her escort crumpling into a lifeless heap?

She shouldn't care. She *didn't*.

Who was this Reynolds to her? Un pezzo grosso. A rich boy living off his father's money and name who had never worked—had never *slaved*—a day in his life. His hands would not have calluses beneath the gloves he wore. His stomach had never known the carving pain of true hunger. There were a hundred more like him, each less important than the one before. The world wouldn't miss this one.

Still, Viola hesitated.

She'd killed many times before, and her soul was, surely, already stained beyond reckoning with the blood of her victims. It *shouldn't* have mattered.

Viola was still staring at the velvet curtain of the booth long after the man had disappeared behind it and the tether she'd had to the steady beating of his heart went slack.

Torrio's foot nudged hers beneath the table. "That's them, ain't it?" Torrio asked. "Why didn't you . . . ?" He waggled his fingers at her.

Yes . . . why didn't I? Viola realized that Torrio was looking at her, his dark eyes sharp and far too suspicious. She'd just done exactly what Paul had been afraid of—she'd missed her opportunity to take out Reynolds when she could have. Now he was behind the velvet curtain, hidden from her sight and out of reach of her affinity.

"Paul didn't tell me Reynolds dined with other people," she told him, trying to pull herself back together. It was a feeble excuse, and the look on Torrio's face told her that he suspected what had happened. "I was thrown off by the other one."

"The girl?" Torrio's brows drew together.

"She's a witness," Viola said, knowing that the excuse was ridiculous. A witness to what? It wasn't like her magic could be seen.

"So take her out too," Torrio said with a shrug. "What do you care?"

"I don't," she lied. "But Paul might. We don't know who she is. What if she's the daughter of someone important? It could cause a lot of problems for Paul, killing the wrong person."

"It'll cause more problems if you don't take care of the *right* person. You had a clear shot there."

"It's not so simple."

He frowned as though he could see straight through the lie to the truth of her, and for a moment Viola wondered if he knew what she'd been thinking—if he understood the real reason for her hesitation.

Torrio leaned forward, his elbows on the table and his expression menacing. "Well, what are we supposed to do now?"

"We wait?" she offered, even though the last thing she wanted to do was spend another minute sitting across from Torrio in that oppressive restaurant. "Maybe the girl will leave. Or maybe it would be better to go."

"You want to go?" Torrio's brows flew up. "That ain't happening. This gets done tonight. We can do it your way and make your brother happy, or we can do it mine, and you can deal with Paul later," he told Viola, his tone sharp.

"No," she said, backtracking. She knew full well what was at risk if Paul was unhappy. "I only meant that we could wait and catch them outside. We don't know when they'll come out of there, and if we stay too much longer, we're gonna draw attention."

Torrio frowned. "We'll wait a little while longer." Then he barked at a passing waiter to get him another drink, and as he waited for it, he studied her from across the table. For most of the dinner, he'd ignored her, but now Viola felt the full weight of his perceptiveness. She could see exactly why Paul had selected Torrio and why Paul was also stupid for trusting him. It didn't matter that fancy ladies uptown prized the soft fur of the fox—Viola knew well enough that foxes were just overgrown rats.

"It must sting," Torrio said, leaning back in his chair.

Viola didn't take the bait his comment was intended to be.

"Being back under your brother's thumb, I mean."

"I know what you meant," she said, leveling her gaze at him so he would know she didn't care.

Amusement flickered across his expression, but on Torrio it only made him look like he was up to something. "What was it like working for the zoppo?"

Viola's skin felt hot, and she was struggling to keep her temper from erupting. But Torrio kept pushing.

"I hear Dolph let you lead him around like a dog on a chain."

"You mean like Paul leads you?" she retorted, keeping her voice flat, bored.

Her words hit their mark. Torrio's mouth twisted with a look of utter disgust.

"At least I wouldn't let a boy get the best of me."

"What boy?" Viola said.

"You didn't know?" Torrio laughed. "The one with the occhiali."

"Nibsy?" she said, and the moment the boy's name was past her lips, it felt like the first time she'd cut herself on Libitina's blade. At first she'd felt nothing at all, and then the bite of pain began to throb and ache. It was like that now. Numbness followed by a sharp, cutting pain.

But it made sense—the way Nibsy had taken over the Strega when the rest of them had been too shocked, too broken, to do more than make it through the next day. The way he'd attacked Esta on the bridge. Of *course* it had been Nibsy.

Dolph couldn't have known, and yet Viola didn't doubt that he had suspected. He'd been even more guarded in the weeks before the Khafre Hall job. He'd pulled away from her, but she hadn't been the one to betray him. If Torrio spoke the truth, it had been Nibsy.

"Face it, Viola. You chose the wrong man to follow. Dolph was as weak as his leg. Or maybe it wasn't only his leg that was weak, eh?" He leaned toward her as he laughed.

Her temper snapping, Viola reached for her steak knife, but Torrio didn't notice. His attention had been drawn by something else, and he jerked his chin, signaling her to look. "She's leaving."

The girl in the blush-colored gown had just exited the booth. "Where's she going?" Viola asked, balling her hand into a fist so she wouldn't take the knife and teach him the lesson he deserved.

"How should I know? But this is your chance," Torrio told her.

"My chance for what? Reynolds is still behind the curtains," she told him.

"Then you should get your pretty little ass behind the curtains too," he said, the impatience clear in his voice.

"You think nobody's gonna notice if I just walk into a private booth and leave a dead man when I walk out? You're pazzo, Johnny. Stupid and crazy."

Torrio ignored her use of the nickname. "I've been called worse, cara. Too bad I'm also the one in charge right now. I'll create a diversion," he told her. "I'll make sure nobody in this room is looking at you when you get close to Reynolds' booth."

"That is a terrible idea," Viola said through clenched teeth.

"It's not an idea. It's an order." John Torrio leaned over the table again. "Unless you want me to tell Paul that you aren't going to work out, you don't really have a choice in the matter. Now *go*."

Viola wanted nothing more than to spit at him. But she was dressed as a lady, so she decided to act the part. Letting her affinity unfurl, she found the slow beating of his heart, and she tugged—just a little. Torrio gasped, and Viola answered his strangled breath with a sharp-toothed smile.

"We need to get something clear, Johnny." She lowered her voice until it was the throaty purr that she knew men liked. "I *always* have a choice. For instance, I could choose to take your life right now, you miserable excuse for a man, but I won't because I promised my brother, and I've chosen my family. Now, I'm gonna do what you say, but not because I have to. Not because you talk to me like I'm no better than some dog.

I'm gonna go take care of Reynolds because right now I don't want to look at your ugly face no more. And once I'm done, I'm gonna tell my brother to keep you the hell away from me."

With a swish of her silken skirts, she released her hold on Torrio's life and started to walk toward the booth. It was a risk, she knew, turning her back on a rat like Torrio, especially after she'd embarrassed him. She wasn't so stupid as to think that he wasn't carrying a gun or to believe that he wasn't crazy enough to shoot her here, in front of the entire world and the reporter they were supposed to kill, just to prove what a man he was. But even if she had to lower herself to wallow in the muck of her brother's dealings, she wasn't ever going to crawl. Not for someone as pathetic as Johnny the Fox.

She took her time making her way past the white-topped tables glowing with candlelight and filled with the stomach-turning scents of roasted meat. But the sight of the rare beefsteaks only reminded her of flesh and of the life she was about to take. Of the promise to herself she was about to break.

REASONABLE

1904—St. Louis

Esta clawed her way back to consciousness, scrabbling up through the murky darkness that had pulled her under. Slowly, she became aware of the rattling movement of her seat. Vaguely, she realized that she wasn't alone. Her head was cushioned by a warm lap, and someone's fingers were gently stroking the hair at her temples. *Harte.*

Not again . . .

Swatting away his hand, she struggled to sit up.

"Careful," Harte said when she bobbled. His hands caught her before she could tumble over onto him, but she pulled away. She could damn well sit up on her own.

"What happened?" she asked as she rubbed at her eyes, blinking away the last of the darkness as she willed her vision to clear. She remembered the strange events in the ballroom and escaping the hotel, but the last thing she recalled was her vision fading behind a heavy fog of inky black and a sense that the world itself was flying apart. And then . . . nothing.

"You fainted," he told her. "Again. Don't worry, though. I managed to get us away safely while you took your little nap." But the lightness of his words didn't mask the worry in his voice. "You can show your appreciation later."

She bristled. She didn't need his worry. Didn't want it either. "In your dreams," she said, shooting him a dark look.

But he didn't throw back a reply, as she'd expected him to. Outside the carriage, lightning flickered, illuminating the planes of his face and exposing the concern in his eyes. A few moments later, farther off now, thunder rumbled, echoing in the distance. When the sound faded, the carriage descended into an uneasy silence.

"For a minute back there, I thought I'd lost you," Harte said softly.

"I'm fine," she said, brushing aside the emotion in his voice. She did not tell him that for a minute she had felt lost. That there was something about the darkness—the absoluteness of it—that made her think that if it gained too much ground, there wouldn't be any going back.

His eyes were steady. "You're lying."

The certainty in his voice struck a nerve. "I'll stop when you do."

Esta made sure that Harte was the first one to look away.

"Those people in the ballroom," she said, testing the silence that had grown between them.

"The Antistasi?" Harte said, frowning. "If that's who they were . . ."

"I've never seen anything like that," she told him. When she'd seen the first figure appear, the one dressed in red, she'd been shocked, but as more appeared, she'd felt a thrill coursing through her blood that she'd only ever felt before she lifted a diamond or cleaned out a safe.

"They're a damn menace," Harte said darkly.

"What?" She turned to look at him, confused. "They were *amazing*. The way they stood up to the police and the Guard."

"They were performing," he said, his tone skeptical. "That was a show."

She shrugged. "Well, at least they weren't cowering or hiding what they were."

"They were using *your* name," he said.

She crossed her arms and tried to figure out what his problem was. "I thought you didn't even like the name."

"I don't. But whether I like it isn't the point," he said, clearly frustrated. "Look at how easily Julien recognized you, Esta. What if other people recognize you as this Devil's Thief too? If these Antistasi are using your name, it means that more people will be looking for you. It makes everything we have to do more dangerous."

He was right. She knew he was right, and yet the sight of those four women, strong and powerful and *unafraid*? They'd sparked some small fire in Esta. She'd been running and hiding for so long—her whole life, covering up who and what she was. To have that kind of freedom? She would gladly take the danger that went along with it.

"Well, I think these Antistasi, whoever they might be, are admirable," Esta said. "If magic's illegal, like Julien told us, they're at least trying to do something."

"That's what I'm afraid of." Harte looked like he was about to say something more, but the carriage was slowing. "We can argue later," he said, peering out of the window as the cab rattled to a stop. "We're here, and I don't have any money to pay for this taxi. We're going to have to run for it—if you're feeling up to it?"

Esta gave him a scornful look. "*Thief*, remember?" She slipped a wallet from the inside pocket of her stolen jacket.

"In the ballroom?" he asked.

"I figured we'd need it eventually," she told him, giving him a couple of damp bills.

While Harte handed over the money and made sure that the driver forgot them, Esta dashed for an overhang to get out of the rain, and to prove to him—and to herself—that she could.

The lightning was more sporadic now, and the rain itself seemed to be slowing, but Harte was still damp by the time he made it to where she had propped herself against a wall to catch her breath. As he approached, she straightened a little to hide just how unsteady her legs actually felt, but from the expression on his face, she knew he understood.

Her hair had fallen, wet and lank, around her face, and Harte reached to brush one of the sodden clumps back. He let his hand cup her cheek, and for a second she forgot how annoyed she'd been with him and marveled at the warmth of his fingertips. She considered closing the distance between them to prove just how okay she was.

A step closer and it would be so easy to press her mouth against his, to let herself go. So much had happened in the last two days. So much had changed in the last two years. Esta only wanted one moment in the stretch of their past and future to put aside all that lay ahead—to forget the sacrifice she would make to ensure that *this* future, the one where magic was illegal and Guardsmen hunted Mageus, wouldn't be the one that lasted.

Harte pulled back from her, and the possibility that had been between them evaporated into the humid air of the summer night.

"We need to find somewhere to get dry," he told her, tucking his hands back into his pockets and making it clear that he hadn't felt the same as she had. "Your skin is like ice."

They found a boardinghouse a few blocks farther into the neighborhood. It was a run-down, semi-attached building about three blocks from King's Saloon. The matron who answered the door was dressed in a clean, plain shift, and her gray hair was tucked away under a dark kerchief. At first she eyed them suspiciously, her gaze lingering on Esta's disheveled hair and the suit she was wearing, but when Esta produced a stack of bills from the stolen wallet, the woman's eyes lit. She waved them inside and didn't ask any questions or bother with their names.

There was only one room left, the woman told them, leading them up the dark, narrow staircase and opening a door at the top. It was small, with a narrow bed and a desk with a rickety chair. A second chair stood near a squat stove in the corner. It certainly wasn't the plush luxury they'd had at the Jefferson, but at least it seemed clean. *Sort of.* The coverlet on the bed was stained, but the linens seemed to be freshly washed and the furniture was free from dust and grime.

The woman lit a small fire in the stove before she left them alone, closing the door behind her.

"We need to get you warmed up," Harte said.

"I'm fine," she said, trying to hold herself still so he wouldn't see her shivering.

"You're *not* fine, and it's only going to get worse if you don't get those wet clothes off." He went to her and helped slip the wet dinner jacket from her shoulders before she could argue. Turning his back to give her some privacy, he draped her jacket over the edge of the second chair and moved it so the warmth of the meager fire could dry it out. "Give me the rest."

"Harte," she warned.

"I won't look," he told her before she could argue any more.

She didn't really care, but it was clear he wasn't going to give in, so she unbuttoned the shirt she was wearing and took it off. She rolled it in a ball and threw it at the back of his head. "There."

"The pants, too, and then get into bed," he told her.

"We're supposed to be meeting Julien soon," she argued. But he was right about her clothes. They felt clammy and uncomfortable, so she stepped out of the soaked pants.

"*We're* not doing anything. You're going to stay here and warm yourself up before you end up sick. I'll go meet Julien alone."

His words chilled her faster than the rain had. "Excuse me?"

He turned then. "You heard me, Esta."

"You are *not* going without me," she said, but as she took a step toward him, her legs went out from under her.

He rushed to catch her before she hit the ground. "How are you planning to meet Julien when you can barely keep yourself upright?"

"Get off," she said, and he let her go willingly and watched her stagger back from him. "I'm fine. I'm going with you."

"Esta, please. You have to be reasonable."

"*Reasonable?*" she said, not caring about the edge in her tone.

He didn't move any closer. "You need to rest."

"I should be there too," she argued. She took a step toward him and then another, testing her own strength. "I *need* to be there."

"Why?" he asked. "Unless you still don't trust me."

She wasn't sure how to answer that. She did—or she wanted to.

He pulled away from her. "There are people looking for you," he reminded her. "Those people in the ballroom didn't help with that."

"They think the Devil's Thief is a *girl*," she reminded him.

"A pair of trousers doesn't make you look any less like a girl." Harte let out a ragged breath when she glared at him. "Look at you," he said, pointing at her. "Your hair is . . ." His voice faltered. He started again. "And your eyes . . ."

"What about my eyes?" she asked, narrowing them at him.

"They're *pretty*!" he gasped in exasperation.

"They're just eyes, Harte."

"And you . . . your . . ." He waved his hand in the general direction of her whole body.

"My what?" She glared at him.

He groaned with frustration, his cheeks and the tips of his ears pink. "Look. *Please.* Just let me do this. I can run over to King's and wait for Julien. He should be bringing the stone with him," he said, and before she could interrupt, he added, "You can be here, warm. *Resting.* Getting stronger, so we can leave town before anything else happens."

"For the last time, I don't need to re—"

"Please," he said softly before she could finish. "*I* need you to. You saw what the Antistasi are capable of tonight. You saw the police and the Guard. We have no idea what might be waiting for us out there, and I can't keep you safe when you can hardly stay on your feet right now."

Esta flinched at the emotion behind his words. "It's not your job to keep me safe. I'm not some liability, Harte."

"I never said you were."

"You just did," she told him, not bothering to disguise the hurt and anger in her voice. "We're supposed to be in this together."

"We *are*." He picked up the pants she'd left on the floor. "But this time, for once, just stay put and let me handle it." And without another word, he scooped up the rest of the damp garments she'd taken off—the only clothing that she had—and walked out the door.

KING'S SALOON

1904—St. Louis

Harte was nearly a block away from the boardinghouse when he realized what he'd just done. Esta was going to murder him—or worse—and he would deserve every bit of it.

When they'd first arrived at the boardinghouse, he hadn't intended to leave her there, but she looked so miserable and tired that he thought it would be better for her to rest. When he turned and saw her half-dressed, though, he had to get away. With her hair falling around her face like some sea nymph come to the surface to tempt him, the power inside of him urged him to go to her.

Or maybe he couldn't blame that impulse *entirely* on the Book. It had felt a little like the first time he'd seen her, that night at the Haymarket, when he'd found himself walking toward her even before he understood what he was doing. *That* particular decision had earned him a sore tongue, so he didn't trust his instincts one bit where Esta was concerned.

Nor would he let himself become some puppet for whatever was living inside of him. Not as long as he could fight it. If the voice was telling him to go to Esta, to let himself have her, then he would do the opposite.

But in truth, he'd left her there because he was a coward. And he probably could have used her at King's. After all, he hadn't been the one to notice the police at the hotel, and he doubted he'd be able to pick any out at King's, should they be waiting.

When Harte stepped into the saloon, there was no sign of Julien. He ordered a drink at the bar and found a table in the corner to wait—and to watch.

King's was about half the size of the Bella Strega, the bar Dolph Saunders had owned back in the Bowery. Like the Strega, smoke hung thick in the overwarm air and the customers crowded at the bar or around tables, hunched over their glasses as though the whiskey they had ordered would run off if they didn't stay watchful. But the Strega was always filled with the comforting warmth of magic, and that energy had marked Dolph's bar as a safe space for Mageus like Harte.

There was a different sort of magic floating through the air in King's Saloon—a jolt of energy that had nothing to do with the old magic Harte had an affinity for. This magic came from the notes of an upright piano in the corner, where a man wore a porkpie hat pushed back to reveal a wide forehead and a face completely enthralled by the song he was playing. Harte had heard the bouncing melodies of ragtime tunes before, but this man's fingers flew over the ivory keys with a trembling intensity like nothing Harte had ever experienced. When the man hit the song's minor chords, Harte felt their dissonance vibrate down into the very core of himself, stirring something he hadn't known was there. He wasn't the only one affected—on the tiny dance floor, couples swayed close together, driven by the moody chords and compelling rhythm, their bodies intimately intertwined.

Twenty minutes passed, maybe more, but each time the saloon's front door banged open, it wasn't Julien. The meager chunk of ice in Harte's drink had long since melted. Esta would be waiting, and she'd be mad enough as it was without Harte spending even more time. Maybe something had gone wrong—maybe Julien had gotten himself caught up with the Jefferson Guard or maybe Harte hadn't given the right suggestion.

Or maybe the Book interfered with my affinity, just as it did with Esta's.

But he shook off that thought. He felt fine, and in some ways his affinity felt even clearer and stronger than ever. Still, as the moments ticked by, Harte started to think that if Julien were coming, he would have arrived already.

Nearly an hour past the time when Julien should have arrived, Harte gave up and drank the now-warm whiskey, wincing as it burned down his throat. As a rule, he hated hard liquor—hated the way it made his head foggy and his reflexes sluggish—but he had a feeling he'd need some fortification for whatever Esta dished out when he went back to the boardinghouse. He was already on his feet, gathering his still-damp coat to leave, when the door opened once more and Julien appeared, silhouetted by the streetlight behind him.

Julien Eltinge entered the barroom the same way he'd entered the stage earlier that night—like someone who knew he was born to command attention. It wasn't that he made any fuss—the door didn't slam, and he didn't do anything obvious to draw attention to his arrival—but the energy in the air seemed to shift, and the entire barroom felt it.

Though he probably saw Harte immediately, Julien didn't come over right away. Instead, he took his time circulating through the room, shaking every hand that reached out to greet him, and then accepted a drink from the barkeeper, downing it in a single swallow. It wasn't an accident, Harte knew. Julien was making it clear whose turf they were on and who was going to take the lead.

Which was fine with Harte. He could just feel the whiskey starting to soften the world, and he needed a moment to gather his wits. When Julien finally decided to approach Harte's table, Harte got to his feet just long enough to greet him with a handshake.

Julien took the chair across from him without being asked and called for the bartender to bring another round of drinks. "I still can't believe you're here. Harte Darrigan, back from the dead and come to haunt me," he said, chuckling.

"Like I said, Jules, I was in Europe, not dead."

"You were gone an awfully long time." Though Julien's words were neutral, his expression held an unspoken question and, more worrisome, doubt.

"The tour was going well, and we found we liked European sensibilities," Harte told him, trying to keep his tone easy and carefree. "You know how it is when you find an audience. You milk them while you can. But eventually the money dried up, like it always does. I got tired of the scenery, so here we are."

"I'm surprised you came back at all." Julien eyed him. "It was a risk, considering who you're traveling with—the Devil's Thief."

"Don't start with that again," he said testily. After the strange women who'd appeared in the ballroom, he'd had enough of the Devil's Thief nonsense. "She has a name, you know."

"Yes," Julien said, studying Harte as though trying to determine the truth of his story. "There are plenty of people who are aware of her name."

Despite the way the whiskey was making him feel loose, Harte met Julien's gaze steadily. After a moment Julien seemed to relent. He pulled a case of cigars from his inside pocket and offered one to Harte. When Harte waved him off with a polite refusal, Julien shrugged.

"Your loss." He cupped his hand around the end of the thick cigar, inhaling as he held a match to its end to light it. Taking a couple of deep puffs, Julien leaned back in his chair, the picture of confidence as the bartender delivered their drinks. But there was still a question in his eyes. "We both know you're not really here to talk about your European holiday," Julien said.

Harte's unease grew, but he put on a mask of outward calm. "Not really, Jules."

"I didn't think so. From the company you're keeping these days, I'd be surprised if you weren't wrapped up in something big." He let his words trail off, allowing Harte an opening.

Harte didn't take it. *Just give me the stone, already.* "Look, Jules, I'd rather not have to lie to an old friend—"

Julien shrugged. "It wouldn't be the first time."

"Maybe I've turned over a new leaf," Harte said, with a calmness meant to mask his nerves.

Julien huffed out his contempt at that sentiment. "Like hell you have,

Darrigan. I know you too well to believe *you* could change."

"Maybe you knew me," Harte said gently. "But it's been an awful long time." It had been even longer for Julien, who hadn't had two years pass by in a matter of seconds. "Can we just leave it that there are some things you're better off not knowing?"

Julien studied him a moment longer, puffing out acrid clouds of yellowish smoke from the cigar clamped between his teeth. After a long, thoughtful moment, the corners of his mouth hitched up, and he let out a rusty-sounding laugh. "It's always something with you, isn't it, Darrigan? All the times I tried to take you under my wing and show you how *not* to get yourself in trouble, and here we are again."

"Did you really expect anything less from me, Jules?"

"Tell me this much, at least—is it the girl?" Julien asked.

"It usually is a girl, isn't it?" Harte said, trying to make light of Julien's question.

Julien's mouth kicked up at the joke. Then he leaned forward, his gaze darting around the room, as though concerned that someone might overhear. But his eyes glinted with mischief, and for a moment Harte could see in them the Julien he'd once known—the old friend who smiled his way through a fistfight and then walked into a barroom with his shoulders back and his head up just to prove no one could keep him down.

"Tell me straight, Darrigan," Julien said in low tones. "Did she do it? The train, I mean . . ."

Any warmth he might have felt drained away, and Harte was suddenly aware of the cold dampness of his clothes and the danger of the situation. "Esta had nothing to do with attacking any train. And if you ever knew me at all, you'll know I'm telling you the truth about that."

Julien stared at him as though considering what he'd just said. Finally, he sat up straight, a knowing look in his eyes as he clamped the cigar between his teeth again. "Because we were friends once, I'm willing to believe you . . . for now. But I'll tell you this—as a friend—if she *is* planning on causing some kind of problem here, especially at the Exposition, you'd best steer clear. The mood in the city right now? It's not good. With all the outsiders, there's been rumblings about Antistasi causing problems."

"What's the deal with them, anyway?" Harte asked. "I've never heard of them before."

"They're a fairly recent phenomenon," Julien explained. "Until the Act passed last year, Mageus hadn't been much of a problem outside New York. Everyone assumed that the Brink had taken care of them, but once the Act went into effect, the Antistasi started causing trouble *outside* the city. It got bad here in St. Louis when they were trying to build the grounds of the Exposition. A lot of people died."

"The Antistasi killed people?" Harte asked, his stomach twisting. It was one thing to dress up and set off smoke packets, but murder was something else entirely.

Julien nodded. "Last fall was the worst. Back in October, not long after the Act went into full effect, there was a major attack on the building crews of the Exposition. They used some kind of fog that ate up a good part of Lafayette Park. People who saw it from the outside said it was like a living thing—you could *feel* the evil coming off it—and the people who got trapped in it lost their minds. Masons destroyed walls they'd just built, electricians set fire to half a block of buildings, and fights—*nasty*, deadly fights—broke out between people who were friends. When the fog finally lifted, the whole area was covered in ice. People had frostbite— they lost fingers and toes—and water mains all over the site had burst. It set everything back months and nearly caused the Exposition to delay opening. The Antistasi claimed credit for it."

Harte's awareness was prickling. The people in the Jefferson had used the same sort of thing for their little performance in the ballroom. He hadn't stuck around long enough to see what the effect of it would be, but he'd felt the cold magic in that room. From what Julien was saying, they might have escaped more than they'd realized.

Harte had met plenty of Mageus in New York, but he'd never heard of anyone using a fog. Magic—true magic—didn't need any trick to make it work. It was just a connection with the very essence of the world itself. Now, ritual magic—*corrupt* magic—that was something different. Ritual magic was about separation. It was a breaking apart of the elements of existence in order to control them instead of working within their connections.

Ritual magic—like what the Order did when they'd created the Brink and what Dolph had done when he'd created the marks worn by the Devil's Own—always came with a price.

"Did they ever catch the people who did it—these Antistasi?" Harte asked.

Julien shook his head. "No. The Antistasi are damn good at evading capture. But ever since the attack last October, the Jefferson Guard was given as much authority as the actual police to stop them," he said. "If your girl is here to cause problems, she's going to have a hell of a time trying to get away after. The police and the Jefferson Guard both . . . none of them are taking any chances. Not with the world watching the Exposition."

"Esta's not here to cause any trouble," Harte told him, which was nearly the truth. Esta certainly wasn't an Antistasi or any other kind of anarchist. They just needed the necklace, and once they had it, they'd be gone.

"I guess I'll have to take your word for it," Julien said. "Where is the minx anyway?"

"I left her behind at our hotel. Told her to stay put," Harte said gruffly, inwardly glad that Esta wasn't there to hear him. But it was easier this way, to speak Julien's language—and to pretend that he had some actual control over the situation. In reality, the idea of anyone being able to control Esta was laughable. "I thought we could handle this between the two of us old friends."

"Ah," Julien said, stubbing out his cigar in the ashtray. "So we come to it at last . . . *old friend*."

Harte shrugged. "You said yourself that I wasn't here to talk about my European vacation."

"I know this is about the package you sent me a couple years back," Julien said darkly. "That necklace."

Something about Julien's tone put Harte on edge. "So it is," he said carefully.

"When I got the damn thing, I told myself that it would come back to bite me." Julien leaned his elbows on the table. "The second I got the package and that ridiculous note of yours, I told myself, 'This is going to be trouble.' I wanted to send it back, but by then, I'd already heard about your leap from the bridge. I thought about just tossing it, but I couldn't bring myself to do that, either."

"I can solve that problem right now by taking it off your hands once and for all," Harte said easily.

"Don't I wish," Julien told him, more agitated now. "I'd like nothing better than to give the blasted thing back to you, but I can't."

"Of course you can," Harte said, urging him on.

But Julien was shaking his head, and Harte had the sinking feeling that he wasn't going to like what Julien had to say next.

"I don't have it," Julien told him, and at least he had the grace to look embarrassed.

Before Harte could say another word, a voice broke through the music and noise of the barroom. "What do you mean, you *don't have it*?"

Harte looked up, knowing already who would be standing there, knowing before his eyes took in the rumpled, dirty coat and the wide-brimmed hat that Esta would be glaring down at him. But he wasn't ready for how she looked or what she'd done to herself.

"Well, well," Julien said as he took her in, head to toe. He tossed a sardonic look Harte's way, and he knew Julien was laughing at him. "So much for telling her to stay put."

UNEXPECTED

1902—New York

Viola made her way across the restaurant toward the private booth where R. A. Reynolds waited, shoring up her resolve for what she was about to do. It wasn't that she was squeamish. She'd taken lives before and had still found a way to live with herself, but the men she had killed in the past had deserved their deaths, as much as anyone could deserve such a thing. At the very least, those men had each had a fighting chance, because she'd used skill, not magic. She hadn't taken a life with her affinity since she was just a child, back when she'd believed that duty to family was more important than her own soul. Before she'd understood that she was more than the blood that ran in her veins.

She knew what those in the Bowery believed about her—that she could kill without touching them. It was true enough, but she'd used their fear of her and her affinity as armor. She killed, yes, but only those who preyed on the weak. And she killed not with what she was—what her god had made her to be—but from choice and practiced skill. She killed with a blade.

But her favorite blade was in the hands of a traitor. All she had left was herself.

Her own heartbeat felt unsteady as she drew closer to the booth. She didn't know what Torrio would ultimately do—whether he would create a diversion, as he'd said, or whether he would attack her for what she'd done to him. But when she was only a few steps away from the velvet draperies that hid Reynolds from the prying eyes of the other diners, she heard Torrio erupt behind her.

"I asked for scotch, damn you!" he shouted.

Viola glanced over her shoulder just in time to see him throw a glass of scotch into the face of one of the waiters. With the eyes of the restaurant on the scene he was making, Viola took her chance and slipped behind the curtain of the booth.

The man in the small private dining room looked up from his soup, and Viola saw the moment when expectation became confusion.

"Yes?" he asked. "Can I help you?"

He has a nice face.

It was a ridiculous thought. She could see from across the room that Reynolds was a handsome man, but here in the muffled intimacy of the private dining booth, she saw that he had the kind of face that would grow old well.

"Are you Reynolds?"

"Excuse me?" The brows drew together, but there was no threat in his expression. Only interest.

"Are you R. A. Reynolds?" she repeated more slowly.

The man's face went blank, and he leaned forward in his seat. "Who is it that's asking?"

His confidence told the story of who he was. From his fine suit jacket to the look of boredom on his face, it was clear that this Reynolds came from money. He was no better than the rest of them, no better than the people in the dining room whose lives were so far above Viola's that she could barely imagine them.

She *could* kill him, she realized. It wouldn't really be so hard to let her affinity find the blood pumping in his veins again and stop it. Just as she'd healed her mother's gout, she could fell him in an instant, and no one would know. One less rich boy to grow into a rich man. One less danger for her kind in the future. She was already damned—what would one more mark on her soul matter in the end?

But there was a warmth in the way he was looking at her that made her hesitate.

"Is there something I can help you with?" he asked, and his expression didn't at all have the cool disinterest that most of his class carried.

"I come with a message," she said, stalking toward him.

"I see," he said, eyeing her as she approached. If he sensed the danger she posed to him, he didn't show it. "And who, exactly, is this message from?"

"Unimportant." She reached for the knife tucked into the folds of her gown even as she moved closer to him. "But he's a dangerous man. An important man in this city."

"Ah," the man said, and now a spark of humor glinted in his eyes. "I suppose you've come to warn me off."

Viola frowned, thrown by his response. He was not reacting the way he should. Perhaps because he didn't realize that Death could wear a woman's skirts.

"I imagine this is about the column in the *Herald*," he said, sounding more bored than concerned. "Let me guess. If I don't stop looking for trouble, trouble will find me, or some such thing?" He smiled at her, and she knew she had been right. The way his eyes crinkled at the corners, the dimple that softened his left cheek—as an old man, he would wear the traces of his happiness.

But he would not make it that far.

In a flash, Viola closed the distance between them and had her blade out at his throat. But he didn't so much as flinch. "I don't think you understand," she told him.

"Oh, I understand perfectly." The man's eyes met hers calmly. He was pazzo, this one, with a knife to his throat and not a worry on his face. "You intend to kill me to keep me from writing more columns that anger your employer, whoever that may be."

"You don't believe I'll kill you right here and now?" She pressed the tip of the knife in until it dented the skin just above the large vein that runs down the neck. Any more pressure and he'd be dead before anyone could help him.

He glanced at the blade poised at his throat and then back at her. "On the contrary," he said softly, "I'm quite convinced you could kill me. Though I'm a little surprised at the knife, to be honest. A gun would do the job just as easily, and there would be less chance of a mistake."

Viola glared at him. "With a knife, I never make a mistake."

The man seemed even more amused at this. "Still, I would advise against killing me right now. It wouldn't have the effect you're intending."

Confused, Viola pulled back. "And why is that?"

She heard the click of a pistol's hammer at the same time a woman's voice spoke: "Because he's not R. A. Reynolds."

Viola drew in a sharp breath and, keeping her knife pointed at the man's throat, she turned to find the girl in pink leveling a pistol steadily at her. The way the girl stood, confident and sure of the weapon in her hand, Viola knew she wasn't bluffing.

"I suppose that's who you've come looking for?" the girl asked, keeping the gun trained on Viola as she stepped closer.

"Yes," Viola said, considering her options. With the gun aimed at her, the hammer already back and ready to fire, she was trapped. She was accurate and deadly with a knife, but she wasn't faster than the bullet would be.

She could still kill them. A flare of magic and her affinity could snuff their lives as easily as a candle. "I have a message for R. A. Reynolds."

"They always do," the girl said, her airy tone more bored than truly annoyed. "I'm surprised your employer didn't do his homework—I'm assuming it's a him. Men with fewer brains than balls usually do underestimate me."

The girl's brash words didn't match the flounce of silk or delicate air she had about her. "You?" Viola asked, trying to make sense of the girl's meaning as she let her affinity flare out into the room. She found the man easily, his familiar heartbeat steady and slow, and then the girl's, which was just as steady. But even as steady as it was, Viola could sense the satisfaction—and excitement—coursing through the girl's blood.

She'd assumed that the girl was nothing more than a bit of fluff, a pretty thing to amuse Reynolds, but she'd been wrong. *This one, she's more than she seems.*

"Yes," the girl said. "You see, he's not R. A. Reynolds. *I* am."

"You are the newspaperman?" Viola asked, forgetting her focus and letting her affinity go cold again.

"Do I look like a man?" the girl asked, her pink lips curving into a mocking smile.

Viola glanced between the man and the girl in frustration.

"I'm afraid she's telling the truth," the man said cheerfully, the point of the knife still pressed against his throat.

"Who are you?" the girl asked, leveling the gun in Viola's direction. "Who sent you?"

Viola could only stare, awed at the girl's confidence and shamed by her own shortsightedness. She had assumed that R. A. Reynolds was a man. She who knew well enough what it meant to do a man's work in a man's world, and all the while to do it better than most. She'd been a fool. And now she was trapped, because she knew then that she would never be able to take this particular girl's life.

"I asked you a question," the girl said, her eyes steady and her expression serious. "Let's see. It's usually Tammany and their goons making threats, but with my most recent column, I suspect it might be someone from the Order. I can't imagine they would have enjoyed that piece, and I can't see why anyone from Tammany would care about the train."

"The Order?" Viola spoke before she could stop herself. She wanted to destroy the Order, not to do its dirty work.

"You don't even know why you're here, do you?" the girl asked.

"I know enough," Viola said. "I know you should stop before something happens. Before you can't take it back."

"The one thing you should know about me, especially if you're so set on doing me harm, is that I never take anything back," the girl said, stepping forward. "Do I, darling?" she asked the man.

"Unfortunately for the rest of us, no, you never do. Even when you're wrong."

"Which is why I try never to be wrong." The girl took another step toward Viola. "I must not have been wrong about the train for your employer, whoever it is, to send you after me. The Order knows it was magic that destroyed those tracks, don't they? They're well aware that the people who stole their treasures are still out there, and they don't want anyone else to know. They're afraid of being seen as weak and ineffective. I'm right, aren't I?"

This one, she knew too much, but not so much as she thought. She didn't know that one of the people who stole the Order's treasures was standing in front of her. "Enough with the talking," Viola said.

"But you haven't answered my question." The girl's aim was as steady as her gaze. "And considering that you are currently threatening the life of my fiancé, I think the least you could do is provide me with some answers."

Her fiancé?

Before Viola could begin to think about why her chest had gone tight at the girl's words, there was a rustling of the curtains, and a moment later, Torrio appeared.

"Ah, more guests, darling," the still-seated man said lazily as Torrio took aim.

He definitely was pazzo, that one, acting as though her knife couldn't spill his blood before he could blink and as though Torrio's gun wasn't a threat at all.

But the girl—Reynolds—seemed to realize what her escort hadn't about the danger Torrio posed them. She took an instinctive step back. Her small silver pistol was still raised, but now she swiveled it to aim toward the newcomer.

"I know who you are," the girl said, her expression lighting with something suspiciously close to excitement. "John Torrio. You work for Kelly's gang."

They were both pazza, and the girl's mouth was going to get her killed.

Torrio's dark eyes met Viola's with a silent threat that was unmistakable—her way or his. It didn't matter that Torrio would assume that the guy at the tip of her blade was Reynolds; he would kill the girl in pink just for being there. One way or another, the couple would die.

So Viola did the only thing she could do. Allowing her affinity to unfurl, she found the now-familiar heartbeats of the man with a face that could have aged into kindness and the girl who looked no older or more serious than a debutante until she opened her smart mouth. Viola let her magic flare, pulling at the blood in their veins until the girl's eyes went wide a heartbeat before she crumpled to the floor. The man gasped, grabbing his chest before slumping over into his soup.

But even after the two were completely still, Torrio didn't lower his gun. Instead, he took a step forward and nudged the girl's body with his toe. His finger was still on the trigger of his revolver.

"Leave it," Viola hissed, putting her knife back in its sheath beneath her skirts.

"Just to be sure," Torrio said flatly as he took aim.

Viola came around the table and stepped between Torrio's gun and the girl's body. "If you shoot their bodies now, it can be traced back to you—and then back to Paul. Leave them be, and no one can prove anything," she said.

Torrio considered the two bodies, as though trying to decide if it was worth the risk.

"Let's just go before someone comes," Viola pleaded, taking a step closer to Torrio. "Before we're found."

He didn't answer immediately, probably just to make it clear that he was the one in charge of the situation. "Fine," he said as he eased the hammer back down and tucked the gun into the holster he wore beneath his jacket.

Viola didn't look back as Torrio dragged her from the privacy of the curtained booth. The dining room was still in chaos. The whole restaurant had erupted into a near brawl. Those who hadn't already fled were huddled in the corners of the restaurant, trapped by men in once-crisply pressed tuxedos who had turned the palatial dining room into a bare-knuckled ring.

"What did you do?" Viola asked. She pulled away from him as he headed toward the back of the room.

He didn't answer.

In the kitchens, the white-coated staff watched them silently pass into the alley behind the restaurant. It smelled of rotting trash, and the ground was coated with a layer of grease that had Viola slipping in her ridiculous heeled shoes, but Torrio held her firmly by the hand and practically shoved her into the carriage waiting at the end of the alleyway.

They were moving before Torrio had even latched the door, but he settled into the seat across from her with an unreadable look on his face.

"You weren't going to do it," he accused.

She met his dark, emotionless eyes and lifted her chin. "I don't know what you mean. They're dead, aren't they?"

"You hesitated," he told her flatly. "I could see it in your eyes. You were going soft."

"And you were going to make a mess of things," she told him, putting as much scorn into her tone as she could muster. "Men." She gave a disgusted harrumph. "Always thinking their *leetle* guns are the answer to everything. Going off half-cocked without thinking. *Too early.*" She held his gaze a moment longer to be sure he understood her meaning, and just as his cheeks started to turn red, she dismissed him by turning to look out the window of the carriage.

But Viola couldn't dismiss the memory of the girl—Reynolds—or how she'd had so much fire in her eyes . . . until Viola had snuffed it out.

A FINE SPECIMEN OF MANHOOD

1904—St. Louis

Esta looked down at Harte, savoring the way his eyes had gone wide and the color had drained from his cheeks. "Is that what he told you?" she asked, giving the two boys a smile that was all teeth. "That I was supposed to *stay put*?"

Harte's mouth was still hanging open in shock, and he had "guilty" written all over him. But really, it served him right, leaving her like he had.

Julien, on the other hand, didn't looked surprised at all by her appearance. Instead, there was the glint of appreciation in his expression. "He might have said something to that effect." He nodded in her direction. "This getup—it's a good look on you. Join us?" he said, gesturing to the empty chair at the table.

Esta sent one more glare in Harte's direction before taking the offered seat. She removed her hat and faced him straight on, daring him to speak.

He closed his gaping mouth and then opened it again, as though he wanted to say something, but all he did was sputter.

"What is it, Harte?" she asked in a dangerously sweet voice. "You're not choking on your drink, are you?" She batted her eyes coyly. "Such a shame," she drawled, pausing for a beat. "Maybe next time."

Finally, he seemed to find his voice.

He could have asked any number of things—how she'd managed to get clothes when he'd left her half-naked in the room, or how she'd found King's on her own, for starters—but the first question he asked was the one that probably mattered least of all:

"What did you do to your hair?"

"Do you like it?" Esta asked, blinking mildly at him as she ran her hand down the nape of her bare neck.

"I . . ." Harte was trying to speak, but while his mouth was moving, no words were coming out.

She decided to take that maybe not as approval but as a success. Anyway, she didn't care much whether he approved or not—it was her head, her hair.

Maybe it *had* been a moment of madness on her part. At least, that was certainly how it started. When Harte had walked out on her—like he had any right to tell her what to do—weak as she'd felt, all she could do was rage. She *might* have knocked over the chair, and she'd definitely slammed her fist against the scarred surface of the desk . . . which had hurt more than she'd predicted. It had also jarred the drawer open and revealed a pair of old, rusted shears.

Maybe she hadn't really been thinking, and maybe she hadn't *really* considered the permanence of her actions when she took that first fistful of her hair and hacked through it with the dull blades. But she certainly didn't regret it.

She'd stood there for a moment with a handful of hair, shocked by her own impulsiveness. In a daze, she'd let the severed strands fall to the floor, and her stomach had fallen right along with them. But then she'd pulled herself together and finished the job—because, really, what else was there to do? She had resolutely ignored the twinge of fear that *maybe* she was making a mistake. Instead, she'd embraced the racing bite of adrenaline every time another clump of her dark hair fell at her feet.

It was a terrible haircut, ragged and uneven and slightly shorter than a bob, but the more hair that fell, the more weight she felt lifting from her and the more she'd hacked away. After all, it had been the Professor who'd made her keep it long. Growing up, it would have been so much easier to deal with a shorter style on a daily basis as she trained with Dakari or learned her way around the city. But Professor Lachlan didn't want her in wigs when she slipped through time. Too much of a risk, he'd said. Not authentic enough.

But there wasn't any Professor Lachlan. There was only Nibsy and the lies he'd built up like a prison around her childhood, hiding the truth of what he was. Of who *she* was. With every lock she snipped, she'd cut away the weight of her past, freeing herself more and more from those lies.

Then she'd found herself some clothes.

It had been a risk to use her affinity after all that had happened that night, but Harte had left her trapped in the room with nothing but a corset and a pair of lacy drawers. It was either take the risk to venture out or admit that he'd won. She'd been too livid to allow him to win, so she'd used her affinity to sneak out to a neighboring room. She'd waited for the blackness to appear again, but it never did. Which meant that it wasn't *her* who was the problem—it was *Harte*. Or maybe it was the power of the Book, but considering how irritated she was with him, it amounted to the same thing.

"How about you, Julien? Do you like it? I think it suits me." Esta raised her chin and dared Julien to disagree as the piano player in the corner crescendoed into a run of notes that filled the air with a feverish emotion. The song he was playing sounded the way wanting felt, and it stroked something inside of her, something dark and secret that had yearned for freedom without knowing what freedom truly was.

"It's a daring choice," Julien said, smiling into his glass as he took a drink and watching the two of them with obvious amusement.

In reply, Esta shot him a scathing look. She hadn't cut her hair and bound her breasts and found her own way to King's for Julien's entertainment. She was there because she was *supposed* to be there. Because it was her *right* to be there. She wasn't about to allow Harte to discard her like some kind of helpless damsel while he took care of the business that they were supposed to be attending to together. After all, it wasn't Harte who'd recognized the danger at the hotel earlier. It wasn't Harte who'd thought fast enough to evade the police waiting for them.

So what if she'd fainted a little after? She'd gotten them out of the Jefferson when Harte had miscalculated in the laundry room. Even with whatever was happening to her affinity, she wasn't weak. Harte should know that much about her by now. And she shouldn't have to prove herself—*especially* not to him.

Yet there she was, sitting in some run-down saloon doing just that. Because she had to send Harte—both of them, really—the message that she wasn't someone they could just push aside when the boys wanted to play.

Harte leaned over the table toward her and lowered his voice to where she could just barely hear it over the notes of the piano. "You can't really think this is going to work."

"I'm fairly certain it already has," she told him, reaching across to take the glass of amber liquid sitting in front of him. "You're the only one who seems to be bothered." Leaning back in her chair, she brought the glass to her lips, satisfied with the flash of irritation that crossed Harte's face. She took a sip of the tepid liquor, trying not to react as it burned down her throat, searing her resolve.

"She certainly has the bone structure to carry it off," Julien said, appraising her openly. "And the nerve, apparently."

"Don't," Harte warned Julien. "The last thing I need is for you to encourage this."

"It doesn't look like she needs any encouragement," Julien told Harte, sending a wink in Esta's direction.

She lifted her glass—a silent salute—in reply.

"If you need some pointers?" Julien said, offering Esta one of the thick black cigars from his inside jacket pocket. "I'd be happy to oblige."

She waved off the offer of the cigar—the sting of the whiskey was enough for one night. "Pointers?"

"Don't—" Harte warned again, but they both ignored him this time.

"If you're going to go through with this little impersonation, I could be of some assistance. You know, I'm something of an expert." Julien struck a match and let it flare for a second before he lit the cigar she'd just refused, puffing at it until smoke filled the air. He waved his hand to extinguish the flame and tossed the spent match carelessly into the ashtray on the table between them. "For instance, your legs."

"What's wrong with my legs?" Esta asked, frowning as she looked down at the dark trousers she'd lifted from the neighboring room. They fit well enough, she thought, examining them critically. They certainly were a lot more comfortable than the skirts she'd been wearing for the past few weeks.

"Men don't sit like that," Julien said, exhaling a cloud of smoke that had Esta's eyes watering. "Women make themselves small. It's pressed into them, I think. But little boys are taught from birth that the world is theirs. Spread your knees a bit more."

Esta raised her brows, doubtful. She didn't need *that* kind of help.

Understanding her point, he smiled. "Not like that. Like you deserve the space." He leaned forward, a spark of amusement in those raven's eyes of his. "Like it's *already* yours."

Julien was right. Even in her own time, the men she'd encountered on buses and in the subway claimed space around them like they had every right to it. That understanding—plus the expression on Harte's face that warned her not to—had her sliding her knees apart a little. "Like this?"

"Exactly," Julien said. "Better already."

"Julien, this is ridiculous," Harte said, his voice tight.

She had the feeling that if she looked, Harte's ears would be pink again, but Julien was still watching Esta, and she wasn't about to be the first one to look away. After a long moment, he turned to Harte. "She'll be fine. If I could turn *you* into"—he gestured vaguely in Harte's direction—"*this*, then I can teach her just as well."

"What do you mean?" Esta asked, not missing how Harte's lips were pressed in a flat line.

"He doesn't mean anything. Just ignore him," Harte said, eyeing what was left of the glass of whiskey in her hand like he wanted it.

Julien acted as though Harte hadn't spoken. "What I mean is that I taught Darrigan everything he knows about becoming the fine specimen of manhood that you see before you today. I even gave him his name."

"Did you really?" Esta asked, more than a little amused at the silent fury—and embarrassment—etched into Harte's expression. She tossed back the last of the liquor, just to irritate him.

"Where else do you think he learned it from? You should have seen him the first time he auditioned at the Lyceum. It wasn't even one of the better houses, you know. Catered mostly to the riffraff who could afford a step above the theaters in the Bowery, but not much more. I'd been working on my own act for a while then and was having a fair amount of success. I happened to be around for auditions one day, and I saw him—"

"Julien," Harte said under his breath.

"He wasn't any good?" she asked, leaning forward.

"Oh, the act itself was fine." Julien looked to Harte. "What was it you did, some sleight of hand or something?"

Harte didn't answer at first, but realizing that Julien wasn't going to let it go, he mumbled, "Sands of the Nile."

"That's right!" Julien said, snapping his fingers to punctuate his excitement. "He didn't get to finish, though. The stage manager let him have maybe a minute thirty before he got the hook. You couldn't blame the guy—anyone could tell what Darrigan was within a second or two of meeting him. You should have heard him then. His *Bow'ry bo-hoy* twang was as thick as the muck of a city sewer—I could hardly understand him. And it didn't help that he looked as rough as he sounded . . . like he'd punch the first person who looked sideways at him."

Esta glanced at Harte, who was quietly seething across the table. "He still looks like that if you know which buttons to push," she said. *Actually, he looks like that right now.* Which was fine with her.

"So you helped him?" she asked Julien. "Why?"

"That's the question, isn't it?" Julien took another long drag on the cigar, spouting smoke through his nose like some mischievous demon.

Esta suspected that he wasn't really thinking through the answer. The pauses were too purposeful. It was a fairly ingenious ploy, she had to admit, and one Julien was damn good at—pulling the listener along, making them want to hang on his every word. By the time he finally spoke, even she was aching for his answer.

"I could say that I'm just the sort of kind, benevolent soul that likes to help others—"

Harte huffed out a derisive laugh, but Julien paused long enough so that nothing distracted from the rest of his statement.

"I *could* say that, but I'll tell you the truth instead," he finished, his gaze darting momentarily to Harte. "That day I saw something in him that you can't teach—I saw *presence*. Even as untrained and uncouth as he was then, when Darrigan got up on that stage, he commanded it like he was born to walk the boards. There was something unmolded about his talent—something I wanted to have a hand in shaping."

"That's bullshit and you know it, Jules," Harte said, apparently unable to take any more. "You only helped me because you needed someone to take care of the Delancey brothers." Harte glanced at Esta. "They were a couple of wannabe gangsters in the neighborhood who didn't understand that Jules' act was just an act. They'd taken to stalking him after shows, trying to intimidate him to prove what big men they were."

"I held my own with them," Julien said stiffly.

"Sure you did, but the rules of the gentleman's boxing club don't exactly hold water in the Bowery, and swollen eyes are hard to cover up, even with all the face paint in the world." Harte shrugged. "So yeah, Jules here taught me how to not look and act like trash from the gutter, and I taught him how to fight dirty so he could get rid of the Delanceys. It's as simple as that."

Julien's expression was drawn. "You know how to ruin a good story, you know that, Darrigan?"

"I'm not here to tell stories," Harte told him, and then glared at Esta. "And neither is she. We're here for the necklace."

Julien frowned, and Esta didn't miss how he'd blanched a little. "I already told you, I don't have it."

"How could you get rid of it after that letter I sent you?" Harte said, his voice low. "Did you miss the part where I asked you to hold on to it for me? To keep it *safe*?"

"No," Julien said, his voice going tight. "I understood, but I also believed you'd jumped off a bridge and were supposed to be dead."

"So you decided to ignore my dying request?" Harte asked.

Julien looked slightly uncomfortable. "I held on to it for so long, and it's not like I thought you were ever coming back—"

"Enough drama, Jules. Just tell us where it is already," Harte demanded, a threat coloring his voice.

"Harte," Esta murmured. "Let him talk."

Julien sent her an appraising look, less grateful than interested. "Like I said, I *did* hold on to it. I kept it under lock and key, just like you told me to. But then last winter, Mrs. Konarske, the costume mistress at the theater, created a gown that was practically made for it."

Harte groaned. "You didn't."

"I figured you were dead and gone, and I couldn't resist." Julien snubbed what was left of the cigar into the ashtray. "I wore it for less than a week before someone offered to purchase it."

"You sold it?" Esta asked, her instincts prickling. If Julien had simply sold the necklace, it meant that it wasn't lost. She was a thief; she'd just steal it back.

"I didn't really have a choice." From Julien's uneasy expression, Esta knew there was something more he wasn't saying. "Anyway, if it makes you feel any better, I haven't worn the gown since." He sounded almost disappointed.

"I don't care about your costume, Jules. I need to know who you sold the necklace to." Harte's eyes were sharp and determined.

"That's the thing." Julien looked up at Harte, waiting a beat before he spoke again. "I have no idea."

Harte swore at him until Esta kicked him under the table. As frustrated as she was with Julien, they needed him on their side, and at the rate Harte was going, he was going to say something he wouldn't be able to take back.

"You must have some idea of who purchased it," she said more gently. "Even if you don't know who the buyer was, someone had to have given you the money and taken the stone."

"Oh, of course there was an exchange," Jules agreed. "But that doesn't mean I know who it was that made it."

Esta could practically feel Harte's impatience. "Stop talking nonsense, Jules."

"I didn't sell the necklace to a *person*." Julien's voice was calm and even, and he paused to take a long swallow of whiskey.

"I'm not getting any younger," Harte said through clenched teeth.

But Julien refused to be rushed. It was a master class of a confidence game. He leaned forward, his dark eyes ringed with the reflection of the lamp on the table between them. "If you're thinking of getting it back, you might as well forget it," he said softly, pausing to draw the moment out. "Because I sold it to the Veiled Prophet."

THE SOCIETY

1904—St. Louis

Harte felt the ends of his patience fraying as the power of the Book churned inside of him. It had started the moment he'd looked up and found Esta standing there, her hair shorn and her eyes bright with anger. He wasn't ready for her unexpected appearance, hadn't prepared himself to hold the power back, and when he felt the fury radiating from her, the voice reared up, pushing toward the feeble boundaries he'd erected in his mind.

He could feel the sweat at his temples from the exertion of keeping that power in check. He wanted to throttle Julien just for looking at Esta, and doubly for the meandering explanation, but Harte managed to keep his voice somewhat calm when he spoke. "Who, *exactly*, is the Veiled Prophet?"

Julien considered the question. "The Veiled Prophet isn't so much a who as a *what*."

"If you don't stop talking in riddles—" Harte started to growl, but he felt another sharp kick under the table. Across from him, Esta shot a warning look that had the power inside of him purring. It liked her anger—and it liked his even more so, because it distracted him. Made him weak. So he buttoned his temper back up the best he could.

"What Harte *means* to say," Esta cut in, shooting him another look, "is that we're in a bit of a bind. As you might have surmised from my new look, the police know I'm here in the city. We only took the risk of meeting you because we need the necklace. And since you don't have it, we need to find it and get out of town—and out of your hair—before they find me. If there's anything you can do to help, we'd be grateful."

"See, Darrigan, *this* is how you deal with a friend." Julien's mouth curved up before he turned back to Esta. "The Veiled Prophet isn't just a person. He's an institution in this town—a figurehead of sorts—and the person who plays him changes," he explained. "Each year the Society selects someone new to fill the role, but the identity of the Prophet himself is never revealed. So you see, the person I sold the necklace to could have been any number of people. I never saw his face."

"What's the Society?" Esta asked.

"The Veiled Prophet Society," Julien explained.

"Never heard of them," Harte told him, trying to keep his voice even.

"You're new in town, so that's not surprising," Julien said with a shrug. "But you know how it is—the rich always have their little clubs. The Society's not so different from the Order. Mostly, it's a bunch of bankers and politicians who see themselves as a sort of group of the city fathers, and just like the Order back in New York, they model themselves as a philanthropic organization. Each Independence Day, they put on a big parade and throw a fancy ball to crown a debutante. Nothing—and I mean *nothing*—happens in this city without the Society knowing or having a hand in it."

"Which is why you had to sell the necklace when they offered to buy it," Esta said.

She was right. With the kind of act Julien did, he'd be a target. He'd need the Society behind him, not against him.

Julien nodded. His jaw was tight as he took another long swig of the whiskey in front of him. "It wasn't just money they were offering," he told her. "The Veiled Prophet himself came to me after one of my shows— showed up in the dressing room without an invitation, a lot like you two," he said, but there was no real humor in his voice. "Said he'd pay a king's ransom for the necklace, and when I refused—because honest to god, Darrigan, I never intended to part with the stupid thing—when I didn't accept his offer right away, he made it clear that if I didn't sell, I wouldn't work in this town, maybe not in any other, ever again. But if I sold . . ."

"They offered you protection," Harte finished.

Julien nodded tightly. "I'm *this* close to making it big, Darrigan. I've had people from the Orpheum Circuit checking out my act multiple times now, and I've even been talking to this bigwig in New York about developing a whole show for me, maybe even opening back on Broadway. But they aren't completely sold on the idea yet. You know how it is. They're waiting to see how the rest of this run goes. With the Exposition and all the visitors in town, it could go pretty well, but if the Society decided to make things hard, I could lose everything I've worked for. You understand?"

Harte nodded. He *did* understand. He knew what it was like to be on the edge of success, one step away from the grime of your past. Sometimes you did what you had to do. How often had Harte himself ignored the coincidence of a lucky break that came not long after a "favor" he'd done for Paul Kelly? Too many. So yes, Harte understood, but . . .

"It doesn't change anything," he told Julien. "We still need the necklace."

"You have to understand, Darrigan. As much as I'd like to, I can't help you. Not if the Society's involved," Julien said. "There's too much at stake for me right now."

Harte almost felt sorry for him. He definitely felt the twinges of guilt for his own part in the mess Julien was in, and he probably would have felt more than just twinges had Julien not gone against his explicit directions. "I'm afraid, Jules, that you don't really have a choice."

Julien's brow furrowed. "You can't force me to help you."

He was wrong about that, of course. A simple handshake or tap, and Harte could force Julien to do whatever he wanted him to. From the tentative expression on Esta's face, that was what she expected to happen. But he didn't want to do things that way if he could help it. He didn't want to treat an old friend like a common mark.

Harte leaned over the table and lowered his voice. "Let me ask you a question—do you really think that J. P. Morgan gives a fig about some dead people on a train?"

Suddenly Julien looked wary and unsure. "What are you talking about?"

"The bounty on Esta's head," Harte told him. "It isn't because of any train derailment. It's because of what we took from the Order."

"The Order denied that anything was stolen," Julien said, but his voice wavered.

"They lied," Esta said. "They couldn't let anyone know what we did. It would have made them look like weak fools if word got out that they'd been taken so easily."

"Their headquarters at Khafre Hall was basically a fortress," Harte added, "and we still managed to relieve the Order of their most prized possessions, including the necklace."

"No," Julien said, his voice rising.

"Settle down, Jules," Harte told him gently. His frustration had given way to pity—and to guilt. "People are starting to look."

"You *wouldn't* have put me at risk like that," Julien said, his voice shaking. "Not after all I did for you."

"I needed someone I could trust to keep the necklace safe for me," Harte said. *I needed someone good at keeping secrets.* "And if you remember, I gave you specific instructions to keep it hidden unless you needed it for an emergency. An *emergency*—as in life or death. I didn't tell you to go parading it out onstage because you got a new outfit."

Julien's hand trembled as he went for the cigars in his coat pocket. "I still don't see how any of that's my problem." He tried to light one, but after fumbling for a moment with the matches, he gave up.

"Oh, come on, Jules. Don't make me spell it out for you," Harte said. "These rich men are all alike—and they talk. You don't think eventually the Order is going to find out this Prophet has the necklace?"

"And if the Order finds out, they're going to wonder if you know where the other things are," Esta added. "They're going to come after you."

Julien's face had gone ashen. "I knew it. I knew the second you appeared in my dressing room that you were going to bring me nothing but trouble. I should have let the Jefferson Guard have you last night, friends or not."

"Maybe," Harte agreed. "But be glad that you didn't."

"I can't imagine why," Julien said with narrowed eyes. "I wouldn't be in this mess right now."

"You made this mess when you wore the necklace onstage, but if you want to get out of it, you're going to need to help us," Harte said, remembering the strange items Esta had found in Julien's dressing room. "We need someone on the inside, someone who knows the Society. You're going to help us figure out where this Prophet of yours has the necklace, and then you're going to help get us in so we can take it back before anyone else finds out."

THE SECRETS OF THE BOOK

1904—St. Louis

J ack Grew let himself into his suite and locked the door behind him. Once he turned on the lamp, he was welcomed by the sight of rich mahogany and silk, plush Persian carpets, and the glint of brass, but it was the silence that soothed him. *Finally*, blessed silence.

The past few hours at the Jefferson Hotel had been a mess of noise and confusion, but in the end only one thing mattered: Esta had escaped. The police and the Guard had both had her cornered, trapped, and she had still managed to slip past them.

After checking the lock once more, just to be sure, and pulling the curtains closed, Jack loosened his tie and took the Book from the secret pocket of his waistcoat. Sitting in the wingback chair by the fireplace, he ran his fingers over the now-familiar design on the crackled cover. The Sigil of Ameth—the seal of truth. He took a moment, as he always did, to trace the lines carved into the leather. There was something mesmerizing about the design. The figures seemed distinct and separate—rhomboids and triangles laid one on top of another. Tracing them, however, revealed a different reality—the shapes were not separate, as they appeared, but infinitely interlocking. Much like the pages of the Book itself, there was no beginning or end to the lines, simply the endless circuit that drew him deeper and deeper into the truth.

Calmed by this ritual, he took the vial of morphine cubes from his pocket and placed two on his tongue, welcoming their bitterness like an old friend. He could already feel their effects as he opened the small tome. Little by little he felt the tension of the day drift away as the morphine pushed back the ache pounding in his temples. Little by little, his senses came to life, and he felt more aware than he had all evening.

For two years he'd studied the pages of the Ars Arcana, and still he had not unlocked all its secrets. Some days it seemed like he could turn the pages endlessly, never reaching the back cover. Other days the Book seemed smaller and more compact. It was never the same volume twice, and the surprise of what would greet him each evening when he opened it was his favorite part of the day.

Tonight the Book's pages numbered only thirty or so, and they were pages he'd seen many times before. His own handwriting annotated the incomprehensible markings on page after page, evidence of his devotion to the Book. Of his devotion to the craft and the *science* of magic. It didn't matter that he shouldn't have been able to read most of them. He never worried when he came out of the haze of morphine and scotch and found a new page deciphered, a new secret unlocked. It was simply part of the Book's power, a signal of his own worthiness as the Book revealed truth to him when his mind was clear and open and ready to receive it.

He crushed one more morphine cube between his teeth as he searched for the passage he had been working on a few days before, but his mind kept drifting away from the Book and back to the fact that Esta Filosik and Harte Darrigan were here, in this city.

It wasn't a surprise somehow. Almost from the moment he'd stepped off the train, he'd sensed that this trip wouldn't be like the others. He'd sensed the promise in the air, but he'd assumed it was a political victory on the horizon.

Two years had passed without any sign of her or Darrigan. Of course there had been claims that she was responsible for any number of tragedies. The Antistasi were keen to claim the so-called Devil's Thief as one of their own and to use her to further their aims. Which was just fine with Jack. The more the Antistasi tried to resist the march of history, the more they made themselves a target for the hatred and fear of the ordinary citizen. Every attack, no matter how small, had surely and steadily built support that allowed them to pass the Act. Every death the Antistasi caused had been another example of why the country couldn't allow magic to go unchecked. Yes, two years had gone by without Esta Filosik, but they had been two very fruitful years for Jack Grew.

Ever since the train derailment, Jack had used the publicity it had garnered to work his way up the rungs of power. He'd started with the Order, using the Book to obtain a place on their council at the Conclave, where he'd spoken of the dangers of feral magic outside the city. That oration had caught the ear of a senator, who had asked for Jack's help to accrue enough votes to pass an act outlawing magic. The president hadn't paid attention until the Antistasi had started their attacks, but considering that Roosevelt himself was in office because of the act of the anarchist who assassinated McKinley, he had a keen desire to see any additional threats quashed. Once Jack had Roosevelt's ear, he'd used it wisely, and it wasn't long before he was an advisor the president turned to often.

After all, who better to fight the outbreak of magic, the destruction of national unity, than someone who had been so hurt by it?

For nearly six months he'd been traveling as an attaché for President Roosevelt, combing the country to collect intelligence about what remained of the illegal magic and the maggots that continued to cling to it. It wasn't an official cabinet position—not yet at least—but Jack had hopes. No. Jack had *ambitions*. And he would not stop until they were met.

Flipping through the familiar pages, Jack relaxed into the clarity of the morphine and let his mind open to the possibility of the Book. He found the page he wanted—one that didn't always appear. It was a sign, he knew, that this was what he was meant to do. His fingers ran down the notes he'd made in the margins, but when he read the words on the page, it wasn't English he spoke but a language far more ancient.

Jack wasn't an idiot. He knew there was a reason Esta and Darrigan had surfaced here and now, and he knew that their appearance in St. Louis had everything to do with the Society's most recent acquisition: a necklace that they touted as an ancient treasure—a necklace that Jack had every intention of taking for himself. With it he would be one step closer to claiming the power within the Book as his own and wiping even the *memory* of the maggots who would try to stand against him from the face of the earth.

UNEXPLAINED DARKNESS

1904—St. Louis

Esta watched Julien's back as he made his way through the crowded barroom and then out into the night. "You're sure he won't just run to this Society of his and rat us out?" she asked Harte, turning back to him.

His brows drew together. "He won't tell anyone he's seen us."

"But that stuff in his dressing room—the medallions and the sashes," she pressed. "They were all inscribed with the letters *VP*. He's one of them."

"I know, but Julien's not stupid," he said. "He might not like it, but he'll give us the information we need to protect himself and his career."

Esta frowned as Harte called for another glass of whiskey, and when it arrived, he drank it down in a single long swallow. He didn't say anything else at first. He simply sat, staring sightlessly for a moment, his cheeks flushed from the drink as the piano's music wrapped the room in its hypnotic rhythm. It was a ragtime tune, a syncopated run of grace notes and black keys. It had been in the background all night, but now with the silence hanging between her and Harte, she couldn't help but listen. And as she did, she could practically hear the future in the rhythms and chords—the lazy, laid-back, just-behind-the-beat attitude that would eventually become the blues and jazz and then rollick through the twentieth century with chimerical transformations.

For now, though, it was simply a ragtime tune on the verge of something more, but it seemed to be a promise—or maybe a warning—that they, too, while safe for the moment, were on the verge of something they couldn't predict.

"So Julien is . . ." She wasn't sure what she wanted to say, not with the way Harte was looking at her, eyes stormy and unreadable.

"He's a damn genius," Harte said flatly. It did not sound like a compliment. "You saw him onstage earlier, and you saw him here tonight."

She had. Everything about Julien, from the sharp part dividing his dark hair to the way he used the thick cigars as props to punctuate his words, was the portrait of male confidence. If Esta hadn't seen Julien remove the blond wig and stage makeup with her own eyes in the dressing room earlier, she would have had trouble believing he was the same *woman* who had captivated the entire auditorium with her throaty, heartrending song.

"Which Julien is the real Julien?" she asked. "And which is the act?"

Harte frowned. "Honestly, I'm not sure it matters."

"No?"

He shook his head. "A long time ago I reached a point where I decided that Julien is whatever he wants to be. He *is* the woman who captivates audiences onstage *and* he's also the man he appears to be off the stage." Harte paused, like he was choosing his words carefully. "They're the same person, and that ability he has—to switch between the two without losing any of himself—he taught me how important it is not to lose the heart of who you are when you're becoming someone else."

Esta realized then what Julien had meant when he'd said he'd taught Harte everything he knew. She'd seen in Julien the echo of the same male swagger that Harte carried himself with. Or rather, she supposed, she saw the origin of it. But she couldn't help wondering who Harte became when he was with her.

"Look, don't worry about Julien," he said darkly. "*I'll* take care of him."

She narrowed her eyes at him. "You're not cutting me out of this, Harte."

"I'm not trying to cut you out," he told her. "I'm trying to keep you safe."

"Well, stop trying. I've been just fine on my own up until now. I don't need some knight in shining armor."

"I never said I wanted to be one." His voice was clipped. "We're supposed to be in this together, but you don't want me to worry about you or do anything to help you. What *do* you need, Esta?"

I need you to stop pulling away from me.

The unexpectedness of the thought surprised her. "I need you to back off and trust that I know my own limits," she said instead. She saw the hurt flicker across his features, but she didn't apologize. "I need you to trust *me*."

"You mean like you trust me?" He stared at her for a moment, shaking his head. "I left you alone for an hour and you cut off your hair."

"It's *my* hair, Harte. I can do what I want with it."

He frowned, his gaze sweeping over her face, down the nape of her neck, and taking in the too-large coat and the rumpled shirt beneath it. As much as she hated to admit it—even to herself—she couldn't have felt warmer if he'd used his hands instead.

"I would have brought you with me if I'd known you were going to do something so drastic," he said finally.

"You shouldn't have left me at all."

His eyes met hers, and she swore that they were filled with everything he wasn't saying. Then he blinked and glanced away as though he couldn't bear to look at her any longer.

She sighed, annoyed at his dramatics. "You're giving yourself way too much credit, Darrigan," she told him. When he didn't acknowledge her words, she rapped on the table between them to get his attention. "Did you hear me? This was *my* choice."

He still wouldn't look at her. "If I hadn't left you and made you angry—"

"I would have done it anyway," she said, interrupting him before he said anything even more stupid. "It was a *necessity*. I'm taller than most women. I stand out. But as a man, I'm average. Easy to overlook. And you saw what happened back at the Jefferson. A hat can fall off or hairpins can come loose. We can't risk that happening again—*I couldn't risk it.* It's just hair."

He frowned at her as though he didn't believe her—or maybe he just didn't want to believe her.

"Besides, I like it," she told him, lifting her chin in defiance. "Julien's right—I have the bones to pull it off . . . *and* the confidence."

His expression told her that he didn't agree, but there was some other emotion in his eyes. Something almost hungry. For a moment she felt caught by the intensity there.

"You're dangerous enough on your own without Julien's help."

Her cheeks felt suddenly warm. "You think I'm dangerous?" she said, fighting to keep her lips from curling into a smile. She liked the idea of him seeing her that way, liked the idea of keeping him on his toes even better.

"From the moment I saw you in the Haymarket. But you don't need me to tell you that." The stormy gray of his irises seemed somehow darker than it had been a moment before. Again she thought she saw the flash of unnamed colors in their depths. "You already *know* you're dangerous."

He was right. She'd trained her whole life to be a weapon, but him acknowledging it didn't delight her any less.

"This will work." She felt the truth of it now, deep inside. "Julien will help us get the necklace, and then we'll move on to the next stone. After all," she said with a self-satisfied smirk, "I am the Devil's Thief, aren't I?"

Something shifted in his expression. "I'm not sure that's a title you want to be claiming."

"You're not still worried about the people in the ballroom, are you?" she asked, remembering the thrill she'd felt at the sight of them—their masked faces and billowing skirts. Most of all, she remembered the way the mood in the ballroom had transformed from festive to fearful as the men surrounding them scurried like roaches to escape.

"If those were the Antistasi, we need to steer clear of them," Harte said. Then he told her what Julien had relayed to him, about the attacks on the Exposition and other places around town.

"They've hurt people?" Esta asked, feeling a tremor of unease—and, oddly, disappointment.

"And they've done it using the name of the Devil's Thief," Harte said darkly.

"Because of the train," she said, her mood falling. "Because I started this."

Harte's brows drew together. "You didn't blow up that train, Esta."

"Maybe not intentionally," she said. "But something happened to it. I slipped through time, and people died."

"Maybe. Or maybe you had nothing to do with it," Harte argued.

She shook her head. "You don't really believe that. Look what happened in the hotel, and in the station. Even on the bridge, when we were crossing the Brink. Something happens to me when I use my affinity around you. There's something about the power of the Book that changes it. Whenever I try to hold on to time, I see this darkness I can't explain."

"Darkness?" Harte asked. He'd gone very still.

"When I use my affinity, I can see the spaces between time, but when I'm touching you, it's like those spaces become nothing. Like time itself is disappearing. Didn't you hear those elevator cables? It sounded like they were about to snap." She licked her lips, forcing herself to go on. "What if that's what happened to the train?"

He was frowning at her again, and when he finally spoke, it sounded as though he was choosing his words carefully. "You don't know that. What we do know is that you didn't *intend* to do anything to that train. If these Antistasi are using whatever happened for their own benefit, they're nothing but opportunists."

"Or maybe they're just trying to make some good come of a tragedy," she argued. "You heard Julien. Jack used the derailment to drive fear and anger against Mageus. Maybe the Antistasi are just answering those lies."

Because *someone* had to. "These Antistasi might be opportunists, but they helped us escape tonight. Maybe that makes them our allies."

"We don't need allies," Harte argued. "We need to get the necklace and get out of town as quickly as possible. The sooner we get the necklace, the sooner we can collect the rest of the artifacts and get back to the city to help Jianyu."

"Fast might not be possible. We had a whole team going into Khafre Hall," she told him. "If there are a group of Mageus here in St. Louis who are actively working against the Guard, maybe we could use them."

"To do that we'd have to find them and convince them to trust us. And we'd have to figure out if *we* could trust *them*," Harte told her. "The police and the Guard already know you're here. The Order will know soon too. The faster we're out of this town, the better."

Esta couldn't disagree with that. Even though she was less recognizable with her new haircut and wearing a man's suit, the longer they stayed, the more dangerous it became. Finding the Antistasi *would* take time, but she wasn't sure that Harte was right about his reluctance to at least look into them.

By then the pianist was playing the final chords of his song and the people on the dance floor had started to thin. "We should go," he said, but she didn't miss the tightness in his voice or the way the muscle in his jaw ticked with frustration.

Fine. He could sulk all he wanted as far as she was concerned. What he couldn't do anymore was leave her out.

POPPIES

1902—New York

After Delmonico's, Viola knew she was being watched even more closely than before. She had not exactly failed Paul's little test, but her hesitation to kill the reporter had made her suspect. Her brother still didn't fully trust her—rightfully so, since her submissiveness was nothing more than a ploy. But his suspicions made things uncomfortable and inconvenient. Especially since he seemed to be working with Nibsy Lorcan, the rat.

She would have killed Nibsy already for his treachery, but she couldn't risk crossing her brother. Not until she discovered what he was doing with the boy. Paul was powerful enough and his Five Pointers were vicious enough that they could have crushed Nibsy and the remaining Devil's Own before now. Which meant that Nibsy had something Paul needed. Perhaps Nibsy was simply holding Paul at bay with the secrets Dolph had collected about the Five Pointers over the years, but from what Viola had seen, their interactions were more cordial than blackmail would suggest.

Staying under her brother's watchful eye meant subjecting herself to Nibsy *and* to the Order. Both were repugnant. Unthinkable. But staying where she was meant that neither Nibsy nor the Order were likely to touch her. She would bide her time and learn their weaknesses. She would use Paul against Nibsy, and she would get her knife back.

And when the moment was right, she would destroy the Order from the inside.

Unfortunately, biding her time meant pretending a meekness that was contrary to everything she was. In the days after Delmonico's, her hands had become dried and pruned from scrubbing dishes, and the only blade she'd been able to get close to was the small paring knife that she had tucked in her skirts. It was a pathetic thing—only about four inches long, made of flimsy steel that had long ago bent at the tip. In a fight, it would be of little use at all, but then, she had no opportunity to fight. She'd offered to be his weapon, but he'd made her into nothing more than a kitchen maid. Already, she could feel herself dulling, like a knife tossed into a drawer and forgotten, and she worried that the razor edge of what she had once been was starting to wear away.

The kitchen door of the Little Naples Cafe opened behind her, and Viola turned, her hand already reaching for her insignificant knife. But it was only her mother, coming to look over the pot that Viola was tending.

"'Giorno, Mamma," Viola said, her eyes cast down at the floor as she stepped back to give her mother access.

Her mother's expression was serious, her eyes appraising, as she took the spoon from Viola and gave the pot of lentils a stir. She made a non-committal sound as she brought the spoon to her mouth and tasted, but then her mouth turned down. "Not enough salt. Did you use the guanciale, like I told you?"

"Yes, Mamma," Viola answered, her eyes still trained on the floor so that her mother would not see the frustration in them. "Sliced thin, like you said."

"And you rendered it enough before you put in the beans?"

"Yes, Mamma." She clenched her teeth to keep from saying more.

"Well, I guess it will have to do, then," her mother said with a sigh. It was the same sigh Viola had heard nearly every day of her childhood. "For today . . . You'll do better tomorrow."

"Yes, Mamma." Viola tried to relax her jaw and glanced up at her mother, who was already picking at the potatoes Viola had sliced for the greens.

"Too thick," her mother was muttering as she examined Viola's work.

It didn't matter that the potatoes were perfectly cubed, uniform and even—Viola knew how to use a blade, after all—it was always the same. Too thick or too thin, too salty or not enough. Every day her mother came to inspect Viola's work, and nothing was ever good enough for her *Paolino*.

But for Viola?

She was too brazen, too prideful. *You want too much.*

Viola shook off the ghosts of the past. "Will you be eating with Paolo today, Mamma?" She asked, a feeble attempt to get her mother out of the kitchen before Viola said or did something she couldn't take back.

"Sì," her mother told her, and lifted a dish to examine its cleanness. "Bring me some of the bread, too."

Viola made up two dishes of the lentils and paired them with slices of bread. That, at least, her mother could find no fault with, because Viola had learned to make bread from a master. She'd watched Tilly day in and day out in the Strega's kitchen, as her friend transformed a pile of ingredients into the warm loaves that kept Dolph's people filled and happy. Viola had memorized the movement of Tilly's hands as she'd measured and stirred and kneaded—the way her nimble fingers had worked over the lump of flour and yeast until it turned smooth and supple as flesh. She'd been happy there, content to simply watch the girl she'd fallen in love with, the friend who had no idea what she meant to Viola.

Tilly had been brave. She'd died because she'd rushed in to help without thought of herself or of the danger she might have been in. Even after her magic had been stripped from her, Tilly had fought until the end. And so would Viola.

Viola wiped the dampness from her cheeks and picked up the two plates. She pasted on the smile that her brother liked to see her wear. As she pushed through the doorway, into the main room, she felt the eyes of Paul's boys on her, but she ignored their heated looks. She wasn't interested, and she knew that none would touch her so long as Paul acted as though she were his property. Her mother and her brother were sitting at a table in a corner, and she served them their lunch with a bowed head and a hardened heart, knowing that sometimes bravery must be soft and secret, just as Tilly's was.

She left the two of them to eat, and needing some air, she carried a bowl of scraps out to the rubbish pile in the back. The string of curses she muttered as she walked would have made even the most hardened Bowery Boy blush if any of them could've made out the Italian she used. Though she didn't use her mother tongue to save anyone's delicate sensibilities. She didn't care if a lady would know the words she was using—she'd stopped being a lady the first day her brother forced her to kill a man.

She'd just placed her scrap bowl on a bench outside the building when she realized she wasn't alone. Pretending to wipe her hands on her raggedy apron, she pulled the small knife from her skirts and continued to move toward the outhouses. When she sensed movement out of the corner of her eye, she didn't hesitate. With a single fluid motion, she whipped around and sent the knife flying at her target.

It hit true, as it always did, pinning the intruder by the edge of her sleeve to the wooden fence.

Her sleeve?

The girl's eyes had gone wide with fear—or was it simply surprise? But then fear gave way to pleasure, and her entire countenance lit. "Oh, bravo!"

It took a moment for the truth of what Viola was seeing to register. It was the girl from Delmonico's, but instead of the flouncy pink confection she'd been wearing before, she had on a dark skirt and what appeared to be a man's waistcoat. A cravat was tied neatly at the neck of her crisp white shirt, and she was wearing a gentleman's cap on her head. She looked ridiculous, like a child playing dress-up with her papà's clothes.

She looks perfect.

"What are you doing here?" Viola hissed, ignoring the warmth that had washed over her as she tossed a glance back toward the kitchen door. After all Viola had done to keep her alive, the girl had just walked straight into the den of the lion.

"Right now I'm trying to get myself free," the girl said as she tried to wiggle the knife out of the wood.

Viola stalked toward her, and with a jerk that made the girl flinch, she withdrew the knife and held it at the girl's throat. "You should not be here."

She heard the click of the pistol's hammer before she realized they were not alone. "And you shouldn't be threatening her again, Miss Vaccarelli."

He knows who I am. Viola glared at him to show that she didn't care, and she did not drop the knife.

"Yes, well, if you'll be so kind as to come along?" He motioned with the gun, which looked about as comfortable in his hand as a live fish would have.

Americani and their guns. They all thought they were cowboys. Too bad cows had more brains than half of them. "I'm not going with you," Viola said.

The girl frowned at her accomplice. "Theo, stop being an idiot and put that thing down." Then her midnight-blue eyes met Viola's and her cheeks went pink. "We've no intention of hurting you, whatever Theo might want you to believe. We simply want to talk."

Viola glanced back at the man—the same one from the restaurant. "I don't have nothing to say to you."

The girl sighed. "As you can see, we know who you are—Viola Vaccarelli, sister of Paul Vaccarelli, the owner of this fine establishment and also the leader of the gang of ruffians known as the Five Pointers, who have been terrorizing the Bowery ever since the elections last summer. Of course, with his alleged connections to Tammany—"

"*Shhh,*" Viola hissed, looking back over her shoulder again.

"She could go on for days like this," the man said jauntily. "I've found the best way to shut her up is to let her have her say."

"He's probably right about that," the girl said with a smile that wrinkled her nose.

It was the sort of simpering smile Viola should have wanted to smack off the girl's face, but for some reason it shot a bolt of heat straight to Viola's middle.

"Viola?" Torrio called from the kitchen. "You still out there?"

Viola froze. She had thought she'd made it clear she wanted nothing to do with Torrio, but since his courtship was being encouraged by Paul and since Torrio saw in Viola a way to solidify his influence in the Five Pointers, he kept coming back. Day after day. Like a rash.

She pushed the girl around the side of the building. "You have to go. *Now.*"

"Well, we're certainly not leaving after we've come all this way to talk with you," the girl said primly.

"Hey, V," Torrio called again. "You need some help or something?" His voice had an edge to it. Like he thought he had some claim over her.

"I'm fine," she called back, trying to make her voice nice. She sent the two a silent warning to keep quiet.

"What're you doing out there?" His voice was closer now.

Panic crept up Viola's spine. If Torrio saw the two here—alive and well—he would know that she hadn't killed them. Worse, he'd know that when she stopped him from shooting their bodies, she'd stood in the way of direct orders. She had to get rid of him. "I'll be there in a minute," she called. "I have to take a piss, all right? You can't help with that."

There was a moment of horrified silence. *Men. So delicate about simple things.*

Torrio's voice came a second later, gruffer and more demanding: "Your mother's leaving, so hurry up about it, eh?"

Viola let out another string of muttered curses as she waited to make sure that Torrio went back inside. When she turned back to her intruders, the girl was smirking at her.

"What's so funny?" Viola demanded, her hands on her hips.

The girl didn't look embarrassed. Instead she gave Viola a long, amused look, taking her in from head to toe and landing finally on Viola's face. Something in the girl's expression shifted, but Viola couldn't tell what it was. "Nothing," the girl told her, more serious now. "Nothing at all."

"If the two of you are ready, perhaps we should take our discussion elsewhere?" Theo suggested.

"Yes," the girl said. "Let's. We have so much to talk about."

Viola tossed another glance over her shoulder to make sure no one was looking for her. "Fine," she said, knowing it would be easier to get rid of the girl once and for all if she simply gave in now.

"Perhaps you'd fancy going on a short drive with us?" the man offered. "We've a carriage waiting just down the road."

"Fine, fine," Viola said. Anything to get them away from Torrio and her brother.

But as she walked next to the girl, away from Paul's building and toward a gleaming carriage at the end of the block, she realized the girl smelled not like the sweetness of lilies or the simpering softness of roses, as Viola had expected. Instead, she smelled of something far more earthy, like poppies. The moment that scent hit her nose and wrapped around her senses, Viola knew she was in bigger trouble than she'd bargained for.

CLOSE QUARTERS

1902—New York

Ruby Aurelea Reynolds knew she was in trouble the moment the carriage door shut, closing her and Theo in with the small Italian girl who took up all the air in the space. Ruby was rarely the type to feel out of her depth. She was the youngest of five girls and had survived a childhood of teacups and pinafores to become what she wanted to become—a published journalist who had carved out a career for herself despite her mother's protests and society's dismay. And if she'd caused a few scandals here or there? Well, scandal was an excellent way of dispensing with the nuisance of unwanted suitors, who were really only after the fortune her father had left behind.

She'd braved the slums of the city and the matrons of society, but sitting across from Viola Vaccarelli, their knees almost touching as the carriage jostled along, Ruby suddenly felt nervous. It wasn't because Ruby had been naive enough to believe that Viola wasn't dangerous. Of course she was. After all, the girl was the sister of a nefarious gang leader and had been holding poor Theo at knifepoint the first time they'd met. That, coupled with the deadly little trick Viola had just accomplished with an ordinary kitchen knife . . . No, Ruby had expected danger.

She just hadn't realized . . . not really.

It had all seemed so simple when she and Theo had set out that morning—they would find Viola, and then Ruby would charm her into giving up whatever information she might have that would bring the Order to its knees.

People in the city thought so highly of the Order of Ortus Aurea because they didn't know the truth. The Order pretended to be above the fray, blameless protectors of the city against an unenlightened horde. Maybe once they had been, but they certainly weren't any longer. Her sources revealed them to be in league now with the corrupt politicians at Tammany, and her recent experiences proved that they weren't above using common criminals like Paul Kelly to do their dirty work. All to shore up their power and protect their reputation. And for what? The city was no safer. And whatever story her family might have spread about her father's death, Ruby knew it was the Order's fault that he'd left his wife to raise five girls on her own.

But now that Viola was scowling at her in silence, Ruby was beginning to doubt her plan. Viola did not look as though she would be easily charmed. Still, there was so much at stake, so much good that Ruby could do if she were just brave enough to take the first step.

After a long silence accompanied only by the rumble of the wheels against the uneven streets, Ruby decided that she was hesitating, and she never hesitated.

"Perhaps we should begin with introductions," she said, mimicking her mother's brightest hostess voice. Her words came out too high, too false sounding. "I'm R. A. Reynolds, as you know. The R stands for Ruby. And this is my fiancé, Theodore Barclay."

"Please, call me Theo," he volunteered, the dear.

Viola didn't speak. She just continued to glower at them, and Ruby realized that her narrowed eyes were the most startling shade of violet, like the irises Ruby's mother grew in the greenhouse on their roof.

"Well, we already know who you are," Ruby said, chewing nervously on her lips. This wasn't going well at all. "Theo, darling, you need to put that thing away. How can anyone relax with you pointing a gun at them?"

Viola glanced at the weapon, but she didn't seem bothered by it. Nor did she seem any more relaxed when Theo finally tucked the pistol back under his coat.

"Truly . . ." Ruby's voice was low as a whisper. "Despite the little . . . um . . . *event* at Delmonico's, we don't mean you any harm. I know you didn't want to hurt us."

"You do?" Viola asked, her dark brows winging up in surprise.

The girl nodded. "Of course. It was the other one—John Torrio— who made you do it. I've been doing some investigating, and I've learned all about him and his more . . . *inventive* tactics. But I hadn't realized until the night at Delmonico's what he *is*."

Viola continued to frown, but otherwise she didn't react. She certainly didn't volunteer any information.

"You *know*," Ruby said expectantly, hoping that Viola would pick up her meaning. "One. Of. *Them*."

"Torrio, he's bad news, and that's all I know about him," Viola said, eyeing Ruby as though she were the worst sort of fool. Ruby understood that look—it was the same look everyone gave her when she tried to speak up about anything important. It was the look that meant she should go back to the sitting room and pick up some needlepoint and have babies and forget about any sort of real life.

"He's a Five Pointer, same as your brother, but that's not all that John Torrio is, is it?"

Viola gave her a look of disgust. "Look, Miss Reynolds—"

"Ruby—"

"*Miss Reynolds*," Viola insisted, keeping a clear boundary between them even as their knees bumped. "I don't know what you're playing at, but you don't want to mess with John Torrio or my brother. They're not nice people. They don't play by any rules you would understand, and they won't think twice about getting rid of anyone who causes them a problem."

"I'm not afraid of them," Ruby said, lifting her chin. They couldn't possibly be worse than half of her sisters' friends, the jealous harpies who wouldn't hesitate to cut your reputation to shreds with a whisper just for looking at them the wrong way.

"Then you're an idiot. This isn't a game. My brother, Torrio, they *kill* people," Viola said, and there was something in the way her voice broke that made Ruby's heart clench. "They make people disappear."

"And Tammany Hall protects them," Ruby said, knowing even more surely that the path she was on was the right one. "The very people elected to serve everyone are protecting the . . . the . . . *criminals* that they're supposed to be stopping."

Theo patted Ruby on the knee, making her realize just how animated she'd become.

"She gets a bit overwrought sometimes," he told Viola.

"I am not overwrought," Ruby said tartly, pushing his hand away. She felt her cheeks flame and cursed her mother for giving her skin so fair it showed every emotion in the same color—pink.

"Of course you're not," he told her, but she knew that tone of voice. As much as she adored Theo, she couldn't stand it when he got all paternal.

Ruby cut him a sharp look, and he was smart enough to raise his hands in mock surrender. She turned back to Viola. "I'm *not* overwrought," she repeated. "I'm simply passionate about the causes I believe in. You see, I'm a journalist."

"This one, he's your fiancé?" Viola asked.

"Guilty, I'm afraid," Theo said with his usual lopsided smile.

"And you allow her to do this?" Viola asked, her expression incredulous. "You're an idiot too."

He laughed as the carriage bumped along.

"He doesn't *let* me do anything," Ruby cut in, her cheeks feeling even warmer than before.

"True," Theo agreed. "I merely follow along, cleaning up the chaos that ensues in her wake," he said cheerfully. "The things we do for love."

Enough. She tried to give him what she hoped was a scathing glare, but he just continued to grin at her. Probably because he knew exactly how much it would annoy her.

"I'd prefer not to be caught up in anybody's wake," Viola said. "I have troubles enough of my own. I don't need any of yours. If you could just let me out—"

"But we haven't even had a chance to talk," Ruby said with a sudden burst of panic. She reached over and clasped Viola's bare hand.

It didn't matter that she was wearing gloves—Ruby felt the warmth of Viola's skin even through the delicate leather. She wondered if Viola felt that same jolt of energy, because the moment after their hands met, Viola pulled away like she'd been burned.

"So talk," Viola said, her voice rougher than it had been a moment before. Her violet eyes seemed darker somehow.

"Talk . . ." It took Ruby a second to remember what she'd wanted to talk about. "Right." She pulled her small notebook and pencil from inside of her handbag to allow herself a moment to gather her wits again.

She flipped through the pages, each filled with her own familiar looping scrawl. Glancing over them, she focused, centering herself on the job at hand. Viola Vaccarelli was not some silly missish debutante, like most of the girls Ruby had grown up around. Her spine was too straight, her gaze too direct. It was as though she could see through all Ruby's posturing to every one of the doubts that lurked beneath.

Taking a steadying breath, Ruby set her own shoulders and began. "I'm working on a story about the corruption at the very heart of the city. I know the Five Pointers are in league with Tammany—"

"Everybody knows that," Viola said, crossing her arms over the fullness of her bosom.

She isn't wearing stays. It was an absurd thought, but the moment it occurred to Ruby, she couldn't dismiss it. There was nothing lascivious about Viola's dress, though. Nothing at all provocative. She simply looked . . . comfortable. Free.

Focus, Reynolds.

"As I was saying, people know about their connection to Tammany, but after our encounter at Delmonico's, I realized that your brother must also be working with the Order of Ortus Aurea."

"Why would anyone care about that?" Viola challenged, but her expression closed up so tightly that Ruby knew she was onto something.

"People might care that the organization that claims to be protecting the city is working with violent gang leaders like Paul Kelly, but I think they would care even more if they knew the Order was working with the very people they were trying to protect us *from*. I want to expose them, Miss Vaccarelli. I want everyone in the city to know that the Order isn't the benevolent force they believe but are instead harboring dangerous criminals."

"You can't," Viola said, shaking her head.

"Of course I can," Ruby said. "It's what I *do*."

"Not if you want to make it to your wedding day," Viola told her, and there was an odd tremor to her voice. "My brother and the Five Pointers, they won't want you messing in their business. That's what I was trying to tell you at the restaurant. You need to stop before they stop you."

"They can try, but it won't matter if I can expose them first," Ruby said, trying to imbue her words with the conviction that she felt so firmly. "But I need your help."

"What could you possibly think I can do for you?"

"Don't pretend that you don't know Paul Kelly has Mageus in his ranks."

Viola's face had gone pale, and she looked as though she wanted to leap from the rolling carriage. *Maybe she doesn't know.*

"John Torrio is Mageus," Ruby said in a hushed voice. Although why she bothered to lower her voice, she couldn't have said. It was only the three of them in the carriage.

"Torrio?" Viola's expression bunched in confusion.

"You must have known," Ruby insisted. "I knew it the second I woke up from whatever that was he did to us back at Delmonico's. For both of us to faint with no provocation whatever? And . . ." She lowered her voice. "It *felt* like magic, didn't it, Theo?"

Theo gave Ruby a long-suffering expression. "It felt like my head hit the table, darling."

Ruby shot him another annoyed look before she went back to ignoring him. "It felt positively *electric*."

"You think John Torrio has the old magic?" Viola said, her voice hollow with what could only be disbelief.

She didn't know, the poor dear.

"Yes. Oh, I realize this is all coming as a shock to you, but you see now why the story I'm working on is so important. If I can prove that Kelly's gang uses Mageus and that the Order is protecting the Five Pointers, then I can prove the Order is protecting the very thing they say they want to destroy. Can't you see?" She leaned forward and, without meaning to, took Viola's hand again. This time she ignored the bolt of heat she felt. It was adrenaline. Excitement. *Surely* Viola felt that as well. "With your help, I could end the Order."

UNEXPECTED BENEFITS

1902—New York

Viola was speechless. She took in the girl, this Ruby Reynolds, with her expression expectant and her eyes shining, and all Viola could do was gape. The girl thought *Torrio* was the Mageus?

"You understand how important this is, don't you?" Ruby asked. "You'll help me?"

"Why?" was all Viola could manage at first.

Ruby frowned. "Why what?"

"Why would you want to destroy the Order?" Viola asked. "They're like you—rich and white, native born. You have the world at your feet. Why do this?"

Ruby looked as though someone had struck her. "Maybe *I* don't want to be like *them*, Miss Vaccarelli."

Viola had not known that an expression could go quiet until that moment, but it wasn't an easy silence brought on by fear. It was a fierce stillness that she understood too well. In that instant, the painted bird turned into a tiger, silent and deadly.

"Yes," Ruby told her in a voice that was as brittle as broken glass, "I do have the world at my feet. I have a *wonderful* life filled with all the best people at all the best parties in the best city in the world." She leaned forward, her expression serious. "But I'm tired of pretending that everything about my life is as it should be. I'd rather be dead."

Viola refused to let herself be moved by the rich girl's pretty words. "You poke around Paul Kelly and you will be."

"Then at least I'll know I've lived well, won't I?"

The man, Theo, patted Ruby's leg gently, as though to comfort her, but even Viola could see that Ruby didn't need comfort. Her skin was flushed and her eyes were clear and determined. She was a strange creature—not half so fragile as Viola had first suspected. But perhaps every bit as spoiled if her people allowed her to flit about the city, chasing after every idea that entered her head.

"The Order is a menace to the city," Ruby said, her voice softer now, grave and serious. "They've grown weak, and they're afraid of that weakness. They're afraid of their own irrelevance in this new, modern age, so they've turned to Tammany to help shore up the power they've lost, and now they've turned to your brother. They've become the very thing they're supposed to be protecting the city from. Look at what they did, sending you and Torrio to scare me, all because I wrote a *story*. A story that was the truth. But it was a story that showed them to be weak and ineffective. They don't want anyone to know about what really happened at Khafre Hall. They don't want anyone to understand how pointless they are, so they will use any means—corrupt politicians and criminals, even Mageus—to protect themselves. To prop up their dying institution. And people will die."

"People already have," Viola said darkly.

"Then you understand?" Ruby asked, her voice tinged with hope.

The three of them sat in an uneasy silence for a long while before Theo finally spoke. "We can provide you with compensation for your testimony, of course. We can get you out of the city, if you're worried about your safety."

We. Because they were together. Because they would be married. And once they were, the girl would be like every other girl who gathered a bouquet and pledged herself to a man. Viola wondered what would happen to the girl's fire then. Would it sputter out, or would it explode, destroying the pretty picture of their lives together?

"I don't worry about my safety," Viola said, shaking her head. The girl was a menace to herself, to Mageus everywhere, and now, to Viola. And there was only one way to make sure that danger didn't go unchecked. And if it also helped Viola chip away at the Order's power? Then that was an unexpected benefit. They would make strange allies, these two. But they seemed sincere. "Fine," Viola told Ruby. "I'll help you."

"Thank you—" Ruby started to say, but Viola held up a hand to silence her.

"I have a condition."

"What type of condition?" Theo asked, looking at her now as though she were a roach that had just crawled out of the cupboard.

"You don't write no more articles until our arrangement is done. Not a one," she said, when the girl was about to argue.

"But I have to write," Ruby said. "It's my *profession*."

Viola shook her head. If the girl published anything else, everyone would know that Viola hadn't actually killed Reynolds.

"Can she write under a different name?" Theo asked.

"But, Theo—"

"It's only until you get the information you need," he said, and then glanced at Viola. "How long will that take?"

"It depends on what she wants from me."

"I need information," Ruby said. "From what I can tell, the Order is looking for the people who destroyed Khafre Hall. I need to know what they took. I need names, evidence of the Order's connection to your brother and the Five Pointers. I need incontrovertible proof that the Order isn't what it appears to be. That it is a danger to the city."

"You ask for a lot—too much maybe. It will take time," Viola said before Ruby could even open her smart mouth. "Paul, he doesn't trust me. To get the information will be a delicate thing." But it wouldn't be impossible. And if Viola could implicate Nibsy as well? She could take out two birds at once. "If you write more of your stories, it will make it harder for me to find what you're asking for. It will make it dangerous for me, too," she finished, playing on the girl's emotions.

"Well, she can't go on without writing indefinitely," Theo said. "There has to be some sort of limitation."

Until Libitina is in my hands again, Viola thought, but that wasn't anything she could say out loud. "Until I say so. That's my offer. Take it or figure out how to get access to the Five Pointers some other way."

Viola waited, half-convinced that her bluff would be called and that Ruby would reject the offer and continue on her reckless course alone and half hoping she wouldn't.

Finally, Ruby nodded. "Deal," she said, extending her hand.

Viola examined it for a moment, cursing herself for getting mixed up in all of this. She should walk away and wash her hands of everything. But if the girl helped her to destroy the Order and put her brother in his place all while making Nibsy a target? It was an opportunity she couldn't refuse.

She didn't like this Ruby Reynolds. She didn't like her perfectly white teeth or her pert nose or the way her cheeks turned pink every time someone spoke to her. Maybe Ruby wasn't so fragile as Viola had expected, but the girl was still too delicate for Viola's world. Whatever happened, Viola had tried to warn her.

Viola took Ruby's hand and shook, ignoring the warmth that washed through her body when her skin slid against the smooth, soft leather of Ruby's gloves. Their eyes met, and for some reason, Viola could only see Tilly looking back at her. And she hated Ruby Reynolds that much more.

The carriage had come to a stop without Viola even noticing it. Once she finally did, she pulled her hand away.

"When should we meet next?" Theo asked, breaking the silence.

Viola shook her head. "I'm not sure."

"That won't do—" he started, but Ruby stopped him.

"I'm sure she has responsibilities to tend to," Ruby told him, but her eyes didn't leave Viola's. "She'll send word when she has something. . . . Won't you?"

Just days ago she'd been stuck in the Bowery, where she would live and die. She'd been mourning Tilly, but she'd been content with her lot in life, with knowing what it was—what it would be. Now everything was uncertain. Now she didn't know where she would land. But she was determined that it would be on her feet. "I'll send word when I can."

Theo pulled a creamy white card from his jacket pocket and handed it to her. "You can contact us here," he said.

As she took it from him, she noticed his perfectly manicured nails, the smooth skin of his fingertips, and the Madison Avenue address. She had killed men far more dangerous than Theo Barclay, but for the first time in a long time, Viola felt the uneasy stirrings of a different type of fear.

Theo opened the door and let her alight from the carriage. She realized she was back where she'd started—all that had just happened, and they'd only circled a couple of blocks.

"We'll talk again soon," Ruby told her before the carriage door closed.

Viola watched the carriage drive away until it turned the corner, leaving the filth and the poverty of the Bowery behind without any evidence that it had ever been there.

Shaking off her foul mood, Viola started back toward Paul's building. Whatever she pretended to be, Ruby Reynolds was nothing but a poor little rich girl, having a good time as she played her little games. She was everything that Viola had grown to hate—privileged, careless, and ignorant of the realities of the world.

Or she was supposed to be. But Viola had seen the way her expression changed when she spoke of a different sort of life. Yes, Ruby Reynolds was everything that Viola was supposed to hate, but Viola knew without a doubt that she would do whatever she must to make sure that pretty, delicate Ruby Reynolds survived long enough to see the error of her ways.

FURIOUS

1904—St. Louis

Outside King's, the night air was damp and still held the coolness of the storm that had passed earlier. Esta pulled her cap down low over her eyes, but she kept her shoulders squared and her strides purposeful, remembering what Julien had told her. She was still annoyed with Harte, still thinking about the train and the Antistasi and about what all of it might mean, but as they walked, her annoyance eased.

Around her, the unfamiliar city felt strangely comfortable. Maybe it was that the energy of the city—the feeling of so many people living and breathing and fighting and loving all in a small parcel of land—was the same. Crowded. Eminently alive, even in the dead of night.

When they reached the boardinghouse, Harte hesitated. The sky had cleared and now moonlight cast its pall over his features.

"What is it?" Esta asked.

"Nothing. I just . . ." But he shook his head instead of finishing the sentence and led the way up the front porch steps and then up the narrow staircase to the room they'd rented a few hours before.

Once she'd unlocked their door, all she could think about was getting out of the stale-smelling clothes she was wearing. Everything reeked of the cigars Julien insisted on constantly smoking and the body odor of the clothes' previous owner. She stripped off the jacket and tossed it aside, then started unbuttoning the shirt before she realized that Harte still hadn't moved any farther into the room than just inside the doorway. He had his hands tucked into his pockets and a look on his face that made her pause.

"Aren't you coming in?" she asked, shrugging off the shirt.

His eyes drifted down to the strips of bedsheet that she'd torn to wrap around her torso, binding down her breasts to better hide her natural shape. "This isn't going to work," he said.

Not this again. "Julien thinks it'll work just fine. No one in that saloon even looked twice at me, and you know it." But he was shaking his head, disagreeing with her. He was always disagreeing with her. "You're just angry you didn't think of it first," she told him.

"You think I'm *angry*?" he said as he took a step toward her. There was something oddly hollow in his voice, something unreadable in his eyes.

"Aren't you?"

He took another step, then another, until he was close enough that she could feel the heat of his skin. "Furious." But he didn't sound it, not even a little.

There was an odd light in his eyes, but it wasn't the strange colors she'd seen in them before. Instead, it was a question, a spark of wanting and hope and need so fierce that she couldn't do more than simply tilt her chin up in an answer and invitation all at once.

Then his lips were on hers, firm and confident, without any space between them for more questions. She could have stopped him, could have stopped *herself* from wrapping her arms around his neck and pulling him closer, but she didn't want to. All the fear and frustration and worry of the night was still there, but suddenly it simply didn't matter. All that mattered at that moment was the feel of his lips against hers and the reality of Harte, solid and warm and wanting, as he deepened the kiss, pulling her into it. Losing himself as well.

And then all at once he backed away, breaking the connection between them. His eyes were brighter now, and she could see the unnameable colors shimmering there as his chest rose and fell with the effort of his breathing. She wanted to draw him back and kiss him again, but she waited, because she sensed that any movement would break the fragile hope spun out of the moment.

Slowly, tentatively, he reached out to brush the fringe of hair back from her face. "I can't believe you did this to your hair."

"It's just hair, Harte," she said, the warmth that had blossomed inside of her cooling a bit at his words. But his fingers sifting through her short locks were making it hard to stay angry at him. "I don't really care if you like it or not."

He frowned at her. "I never said I didn't like it," he told her softly.

"At the bar, I thought . . ." He was running his hand down the bare nape of her neck. "You looked so upset."

"Can you blame me?" he whispered, and then he leaned in until his forehead rested against hers. "You surprised me. I thought you were safe, and then you appeared . . . like this—"

She pulled back, about to snap at him again, but she stopped when she saw the expression on his face. The desire and *need* that matched her own.

He ran his hand down the side of her neck, and in its wake, she felt her affinity ripple and warm, felt herself warm as well. "You might as well have arrived completely naked, with your neck so exposed and the shape of your legs in those pants where every person in the bar could see them."

"No one was looking." She was frustrated and amused all at once at his prudishness.

"*I* was looking," he told her, and he drew her in to him again, kissing her with a desperation that made her lose her breath.

She was only partially aware that the door was still open behind him because all of her senses were taken up with the kiss. His hands ran down her neck, over her shoulders and her arms, smoothing away the anger and fear of the day, pressing aside the emptiness she'd felt when her affinity had slipped from her grasp and sparking something else—something warmer and brighter than she'd felt before. Then he was tugging at the bindings around her chest until they fell away completely and her bare skin brushed against the rough fabric of his coat. She could have stopped him at any moment, but she didn't *want* to. Instead, she threaded her fingers through his hair, drawing him closer, urging him on. Meeting him will for will, want for want.

It wasn't until the back of her legs hit the low bed that she realized they had been moving across the room, but then they toppled together onto the thin mattress, Harte's weight pressing down onto her and boxing her in. *Yes,* she wanted to say, but the second they were horizontal, Harte went completely still. He pulled back from her, and she watched his expression close up like a house before a storm, while the strange colors bloomed within his irises.

"Harte?" she whispered, touching his face when he didn't move other than the ragged rise and fall of his chest as he caught his breath. But even though his eyes were open, staring straight into hers, Esta had the sense that Harte wasn't really there.

THE WOMAN

1904—St. Louis

Harte was a breath away from Esta. He could feel her skin hot against his, the softness of her body against the firmness of his own, but it wasn't her he was seeing. The dingy room had fallen away as well, and he felt the oppressiveness of summer—a dry, baking heat that licked along his skin.

There was a woman dressed in white linen robes that draped the floor, and the woman was screaming. She was Esta and she was another woman all at the same time, and she was—*they* were—screaming. The sound echoed in his ears so loudly that he couldn't hear anything but the terror and agony and *rage* in her voice. The woman was looking at him, her face superimposed over Esta's, and though there was a part of Harte that dimly realized none of this was real—that this was some sort of vision or waking nightmare—he could not shake himself free of it.

He wanted to scream at Esta to get away. He needed to break the connection between them, but it was too late. The voice had swelled within him, blotting out Esta's face completely.

And then there was only darkness and it was as though he was the woman. As though he was seeing what she saw, feeling what she felt.

Ahead there was a light, and she went toward it until it grew brighter and brighter and became a chamber that was lined with scrolls and parchments piled high upon the shelves. Knowledge and power and all the secrets of the world.

She'd done this.

She'd created it all, but none of it had worked. There was still more to do, or the power in the world would fade as surely as moonlight in the brightness of dawn.

In the center of the room stood a long, low table, and upon its surface gleamed five gemstones—stones not hewed from the earth but made.

The power she wielded was dying. Magic had been fading for some time, growing weaker with each division, with each breaking apart. She had tried to stop its slow death. She had created something to suspend power, pure and whole. To preserve it. So she had created the word and the page. But it had not worked. It had been stolen from her, perverted and abused.

She had meant to save them all, and instead she had created magic's undoing. But she would stop that. Now. Here.

She ran her fingers over the stones that she had created, and he could feel the way they called to her. He could feel the pull of them, strong and sure and clear.

And then the vision tilted and changed again. The world tipped and there was a woman—or perhaps it was Esta? Her dark hair was wild around her face. Her eyes had gone black and empty and she was screaming. The stones were aglow, and she was trapped within their power. Pain and rage and fury whipped about the chamber. And fear. There was a fear thick in the air—fear, and the pain of betrayal.

"Harte?" He felt cool fingers touch his face, drawing him up from the depths, and he flinched away, surfacing from the nightmare that had intruded into his waking.

"Don't touch me," he said, his voice strained and sharp. He pulled back. Scuttled away from her with an awkward jerking step, falling out of the bed to get away. "Just—stay over there. Stay away."

The vision still haunted him. The woman and Esta, their faces alternating as he tried to shake the image of the woman screaming from his mind.

Esta turned on her side to look at him. "What is it?" she asked. "What's gotten into you?"

"I *want you*—" But he clapped his hands over his own mouth, because it wasn't him who'd spoken. The voice had taken advantage of his weakness and had forced itself up from within him, taking his body and using it as if he were nothing more than a puppet.

Her mouth curved and her golden eyes went dark. "Well, I think what just happened proves that you can have me," she said impishly.

"No!" he roared. And the word was his own. He was *himself*. Harte Darrigan, not whatever lived inside of him.

Esta flinched, and he saw hurt flash across her face. "Harte, what's wrong?" She was reaching for him and looking so beautiful and fragile and utterly breakable.

He knew what the vision meant—*he* would break her. The Book—the power inside of him, whatever it was—would break her and use her and it would be his fault. *All my fault.* He would break her like he broke his mother, but this time there would be nothing left afterward, nothing but the blackness that still haunted him long after the vision had faded.

The blackness, just like the darkness that Esta had told him she saw when their affinities connected.

Swallowing hard, he forced himself to look at her—to make sure that the blackness in her eyes wasn't real. Her hair was a mess, the short strands chopped in uneven lengths and falling around her face like some sort of fairy creature, but her eyes were her own. There was concern and pain and a question in their whiskey-colored depths. "I can't hold it back," he told her. He saw the flash of pleasure in her expression before he killed it with the words he said next. "It's the Book. . . ."

"The *Book*?" she asked.

"The power of whatever it is inside of me. I—" He stopped, corrected himself. "*It* wants you. It wants to use you, and if it does . . ." *The blackness was so empty, like nothing at all. Like it will bleed into the world and no one will be safe.*

"What are you saying?" she asked slowly, her tone cooling now. "Are you telling me that you didn't *want* to kiss me?"

"Yes," he said, shaking his head. But it didn't feel like the truth. "I don't know."

Esta sat up the rest of the way, frowning at him. She pulled the sheets around her, but not before he saw the flash of brownish pink and the smooth expanse of skin that had almost been his.

Yes . . . Mine . . .

"No!" he said. His voice was like the report of a gun in the tiny room, and she flinched again. But he would not let it have her. "I don't know what this is inside of me," he told her, his voice rough. "I don't know what this is between us. I don't know if I want you or if it's the power that does, but *this* can't happen. This can't *ever* happen."

"Harte . . ." There was an ache in her voice that pierced him.

"I've seen things," he whispered, the memory of the visions crashing over him again.

"What are you talking about?" she asked.

"Visions. At the station, at the hotel, just now . . ." He looked at her, willed her to understand as he told her what he'd seen. "I'm going to hurt you. If I touch you, if I let myself go with you, I'll destroy you."

"You won't—"

He let out a ragged breath. "You can't know that."

"I'm not some fragile flower, Harte. We'll figure this out. We'll do it *together.*"

She reached for him, but he drew back, avoiding her touch. The voice was too near to the surface of him. Then he turned away, because he knew that if he looked at her now, saw the hurt in her eyes and her body bared to him as it was, his control would crumble. "I apologize," he said stiffly, his voice brittle and clipped.

"There's nothing to apologize for." She was on her feet now. He could hear her wrapping the blanket around herself. "In case you missed it, I was right there with you."

But he was already grabbing his coat, heading for the door, which was still open. *We didn't even close the door.* So much for control.

"You're seriously leaving?" she asked.

"I'm going to walk for a bit." He did turn back to her then, and her hair was rumpled and her lips were bruised red from their kissing. "I need some air."

"Harte—"

"And some space," he finished, striding out the open door. Once he was through it, he closed it behind him with an unmistakable finality.

His legs were shaking as he ran down the steps of the boardinghouse and out into the night. It was still warm, the air was damp from the rain, and the clouds had parted above to show the stars, but Harte didn't notice any of that. He didn't even notice which way he was going. He simply walked, as quickly and as doggedly as his feet would go.

He'd kissed her. He'd kissed her, touched her, and it had been *everything*—*more* than everything. More than he could have imagined.

He could have had her. She would have given herself to him, and he could have taken her there, on that narrow, dirty bed in that narrow, worn-out room. *And she would have hated him for it later.*

Onward he walked until the power inside of him receded and the soles of his feet felt as ragged as he did, as he vowed with every step he took that he would never let that happen.

THE REMAINS OF
WHAT HAD BEEN

1904—St. Louis

Esta looked at the crackled paint on the back of the closed door as the realization of what Harte had just done settled in her blood. She was holding the blanket up over her bare chest, and through the open window she could hear the sounds of dogs barking and the occasional rattle of a carriage in the distance. Her heart was galloping, and her skin felt flushed and warm from Harte's kisses, even as her fury mounted.

His words echoed in her mind: *I'm going to hurt you.*

At least he hadn't been lying about *that*.

She had known all along that uniting the stones and taking control of the Book might mean the end of her. Professor Lachlan had told her as much when he'd tried to take the power of the Book himself. *You're just the vessel.* Wasn't that what he'd said?

She had hoped that the Book would hold some key to changing that fate, but the Book was in the hands of Jack Grew, and who knew where he was? The only way to get back to the time and place where they lost it was to get Harte under control. But when she touched Harte, she could barely slow down the seconds. She wasn't about to trust slipping through time until they figured out how to control the power he had in him.

Power that, apparently, wanted her.

She shuddered at the thought of it. Suddenly the room felt too close—and at the same time, unbearably empty. Esta pulled on the chemise she'd worn earlier beneath her corset. For a moment she just stood in the silence, taking in the narrow, sagging bed with its stained cover rumpled and askew, the faded curtains looking so tired and worn that they would fall at any moment, and the pile of hair she'd left on the floor earlier.

She'd almost slept with Harte Darrigan. A few minutes ago she'd trusted him enough to lay down all her defenses. And he hadn't even been there. He hadn't even been the one—the *thing*—in control. Everything that had just happened—he wasn't even sure it had been him.

A coldness settled over her as she reached up to push what was left of her hair out of her eyes. Her fingers still remembered what it had felt like just hours before to run through the long strands, to tuck the locks that had fallen back behind her ears, but now her own hair felt foreign to her. Tentatively, she brushed at the nape of her neck, where the ragged ends of her hair felt coarse and sharp, but it only reminded her of the way Harte had touched her.

Across the room, she caught her reflection in the scarred mirror, and without thinking, she stepped closer. She barely recognized herself—the dark rings beneath her eyes, the way her short hair made her jaw seem sharper and her mouth harder, even as her mouth was still rouged from the friction of Harte's kisses. Her eyes were no longer softened by the makeup she'd used to darken her lashes. It was more than the haircut that had changed her. It was the fire in her eyes kindled by heartache and senseless tragedy. It was the determination in the hard set of her mouth.

For a moment she examined this new version of herself and realized the overwhelming reality of what she had done—to her hair, with Harte—of where they were and what was at stake. And of what might still lie ahead.

She didn't yet know the person looking back at her, but she liked what she saw. Or she would learn to. She would do what she must to make sure that Nibsy could never have the stones. She would make sure that the Book and its power were protected from the Order and others who might use them to harm those like her. But she would harden herself against Harte Darrigan. She would be his partner, would even save him if she could, but she would not allow herself to open her heart to him.

She would not make the same mistake again.

At her feet, the remains of what had once been her hair littered the floor. She considered it, the long strands soft beneath the leather soles of the men's shoes she still wore. That hair had belonged to a different girl. Esta could no more go back to being that girl than she could reattach the hair to her head. No more than she could wipe the memory of Harte's kisses from her lips. Gathering the pile of hair from the floor, Esta tossed it into the stove, but the fire had already gone cold and dead.

TOO LATE

1902—New York

T he fog that had descended upon the Bowery was thick and
murky as the night itself. The soft halo of the streetlamps barely
cut through the gloom. The streets, wet with the day's rain,
shone like the water that flooded the rice paddies around his village. For
a moment Jianyu almost felt like he was there, standing on a hillside and
looking over the endless sweep of fields around his family's home, the
water-soaked ground drowning the weeds that would otherwise choke
the life from the rice. But then the image flickered, and it was only the
city he saw—the grimness of the streets, the sloshing puddles that would
never be enough to wash away the filth and poverty that choked the life
from the Bowery.

He was late. He had already failed Cela, and now he would fail again.

Picking up his pace, he did not bother with magic. His affinity would
be of no help, not with the way his footsteps could be traced from puddle
to puddle, but he kept to the shadows and moved faster. He could not be
late. If the boy reached Nibsy, the results could be devastating. With the
boy, Nibsy would hold knowledge of what was to come. It could make
him unstoppable.

The streets were empty, a spot of luck in an otherwise dismal string of
days. Lonely and silent, they offered no comfort. To be taken off guard, to
have been beaten so soundly, and then to be handed over by Mock Duck
for a handful of secrets? Perhaps he should have been grateful that he was
alive. Certainly he should be grateful that Cela had been following him

and had risked her own life to rescue him. But it galled him to know that he had required *her* protection. He had failed her—just as he had failed Dolph—but he would not fail again. He would not allow the boy from another time to win. If that happened, if Nibsy became as powerful as Harte and Esta predicted, the impact would be felt far beyond the reaches of the city, perhaps even far across the seas.

A shadow on the other side of the street moved, drawing Jianyu's attention. As he turned, a man stepped from the darkness into the gloom of the lamplight.

Mock Duck. The silver buttons of his waistcoat glinted like eyes in the night.

Jianyu kept his head down and picked up his pace. He reached for his bronze mirrors but found his pockets empty. *No matter.* He called to his affinity and opened the light around him as he began to run, cutting down an alley to the next block. He did not turn to see if Mock's high-binders were following. Instead, he focused on avoiding the puddles that would expose his exact path.

Two more blocks and then another half a block west, and he would be where Esta said the boy would arrive . . . if he had not already missed him.

He turned onto Essex Street and pulled up short. Ahead, a group of men were surrounding another.

Too late.

Jianyu kept the light close to him as he edged nearer, careful to avoid the telltale ripples his shoes would cause in the puddles at his feet. When he was close enough to see, his stomach tightened. Tom Lee and a trio of On Leongs were standing over someone—a man or a boy—and the person on the ground was deathly still.

He should go. Tom Lee would not forgive Jianyu for abandoning his oath to the On Leongs. Perhaps Lee was not as violent as Mock Duck, but Jianyu knew that if Lee found him there, Lee would not hesitate to attack. But Jianyu needed to know—was the man they stood over the boy he was looking for? He edged closer, keeping his affinity tightly around him.

One of the On Leongs kicked the man with such violence that Jianyu felt an answering ache in his own gut. The man moaned in pain and rolled onto his back.

Jianyu's blood ran cold.

The person on the ground was not the blond boy Esta had described on the bridge. In the wan glow of the lamplight, Jianyu saw *himself* on the ground—it was not the boy's face but his own contorted in agony as Tom Lee's men prepared to attack again.

He stumbled back in stunned disbelief, splashing into stagnant water. In the shock of the moment, his affinity slipped.

Tom Lee and his men turned at the noise, and their eyes widened to see him there. Their expressions were a mixture of surprise and horror as they looked between Jianyu, standing as he was in the weak, flickering lamplight, and the body on the ground, barely moving. But Tom Lee showed no such fear. He stepped toward Jianyu, a gleam of anticipation in his expression as he pulled a pistol from inside his coat and raised it.

Jianyu turned to run, but the echo of the gun's explosion drowned out his footsteps. He felt the pain of the bullet tear through him, and then he was falling.

Falling toward the muck and wetness of the rain-slicked streets. Falling through them—on and on—as though death were nothing but a constant descent. Falling as though he would never stop, as though he would never land.

Until his body hit hard, and he jolted upright, struggling to get to his feet. He had to run—

"Just settle down there," a voice said, and it was not the Cantonese that he expected. It was in English, soft and rolling like none he had heard before. "Cela! Get in here, girl."

Jianyu's eyes opened, and the street melted away, leaving a small but comfortable room. The glow of a small lamp lit the space, and the air felt close and warm, smelling of sweat and stale bodies.

No, not the room. It was *he* who smelled of stale sweat. His clothes were damp with it, and he suddenly felt unbearably hot and cold all at once.

"What is it?" Cela was there in the doorway.

"He's waking up," a male voice said. It was the person holding him down, an older man with tawny-brown skin, his hair gray at the temples of his broad forehead. "Deal with him."

The hands were gone, and a moment later the bed dipped and Cela sat next to him. Her graceful hands felt cool against the skin of his forehead when she touched him.

"How long?" he asked, his voice coming out as a dry rasp as he struggled to sit up. His side still ached and his head pounded.

"Hold on," Cela said, reaching for a cup of water. She tried to put it in his hands, but he pushed it away.

"How long have I been here?" he asked again, his heart still racing from the dream of death.

"You've been in and out for nearly five days," Cela said.

No. He was late. *Too late.* He tried to swing his legs off the bed, but the motion made him dizzy.

"You have to sit down," Cela told him, holding him by the arm as he swayed.

"I have to go," he said, shaking her off.

"Go?" Vaguely he realized that her voice sounded very far away. "You can barely sit up. Where do you think you're going?"

He struggled to his feet. *Too late.* But his vision swam, and he stumbled backward.

"You're not going anywhere," Cela said. She pushed him gently back into bed, and his limbs felt so weak that he could not fight her. "You're going to drink this water, and if you keep that down, you can have some broth."

"I am too late," he told her, taking the cup. His hands were trembling from the weight of the water, and he could not seem to make them stop.

"You had the life half beaten out of you. Whatever it is can wait," she said, indicating that he should drink.

She was wrong. The boy would not wait to arrive, would not wait to find Nibsy. Jianyu drank the water reluctantly, but he was surprised at the coolness of it, at how parched he suddenly felt. It was gone before it even began to touch his thirst. "More," he asked, his voice a plea more than a command. *Five days.*

He took the second glass and drank, as much to prove that he could as for his thirst. *Five days.* He had lost five days. Which meant that he was already too late.

DISCARDED

1902—New York

For Logan Sullivan, traveling through time wasn't the romantic adventure the movies made it out to be. For one thing, he didn't get to sail along in a floating car or a magical police box. It wasn't an easy jump. It hurt. And another thing—it made his head spin, his guts feel like they were about to fall out, and his very *self* feel like it was about to shatter. There was always a moment just as Esta dragged Logan from one time to another when he swore that there was a chance they wouldn't make it at all, a point where it felt like he didn't even exist. In short, time travel was a difficult, dangerous, and frustrating pain in the ass.

But then again, so was Esta.

She was the one who had always been able to see right through him, and that was damn inconvenient for Logan Sullivan, considering he'd discovered a long time ago that it was easier to move through the world if you let your pretty face do the talking.

Still, pain in the ass or not, he'd felt bad about the gun he'd pressed to her side and even worse about the bullets Professor Lachlan had loaded into it. It wasn't that he didn't believe the Professor when he'd told Logan that Esta had turned on them and couldn't be trusted. It was that Logan might have been a lot of things, but he'd never thought of himself as a murderer. He didn't like the idea of having to put a bullet in her back. Even if she had done the same to Dakari.

So he'd been glad when she hadn't fought him as they'd walked to the departure point. He'd been relieved when he'd had to nudge her only once to get her moving, but he should have known it couldn't be that easy. Nothing with her ever was. One minute he felt like the whole world was being ripped apart, like his very soul was collapsing in on itself, and then he felt the solidness of the pavement beneath him again.

Before he could even pull himself upright, he'd felt a pain tear through his shoulder joint, and his hand had gone numb as Esta slid away from him. He'd stumbled, trying to get to his feet, but his vision was only *just* clear enough to see Esta scoop up the bag he'd been carrying and disappear.

Logan was trying to get his eyes to focus, when the reality of his situation hit him. The dampness of the cobbled street, the smell of coal smoke and soot in the air. The strange slant of light coming down through the overcast day, and the bustle of voices around him in languages he didn't understand. Professor Lachlan had tried to teach him, but he never had the head for words the way Esta had.

Esta. Who was always good at everything. Esta, who had definitely abandoned him.

In the past.

There was a scent in the air with the sootiness—a ripeness that indicated something alive. Or something that had once been alive. Animals or rotten food or shit. Yeah, definitely shit. In the cool morning air, the stench was muted, but Logan could imagine the smell would be thick enough to choke when the heat of the summer swept over the city.

He wasn't supposed to be there during the summer. Professor Lachlan had promised. Once Logan had delivered the bag and the notes, Esta was supposed to bring him back to his own time—*their* own time.

Where. He. Belonged.

The bag he'd been carrying was long gone, but at least he still had the notes, he thought as he patted the pocket of his jacket. *Yeah. Still there.*

Logan finally managed to sit up. His pants were damp from the puddle he'd landed in. *Rainwater . . . Let it be rainwater. . . .* Rubbing at his head where it had hit the concrete, he realized he was being watched. Two broad-shouldered guys with dark coats and hats tipped low over their eyes were stalking toward him. One had a stick of some sort—a club, but with a wicked spike at the end.

Scrambling to his feet, Logan put his hands up as he tried to back away, but he backed up instead into someone else.

"Whoa," he said, his head still swirling as he struggled to stay up.

"What do we have here?" the largest of the guys asked, taking another step toward Logan and penning him in. The guy smiled, a ruthless sort of grin that made Logan feel like he'd just swallowed a stone. He wasn't the fighter—that was Esta. He was more of a talk-your-way-out-of-the-situation type. But these guys didn't look like they were interested in listening.

"Where'd the girl go?" the other one said, his expression as flat as his broken nose. "She was just here and then—"

"Stuff it," the larger one said, jabbing at Logan with his stick. "She's one of them." He pinned Logan with a look. "Wasn't she? Does that mean you're one of them too?"

"Look, I don't want any problems," Logan told them.

"Too late for that now, ain't it?" the large one said as the man Logan had backed into took him by the arms. The other one picked up the gun Logan had been holding just moments earlier, his insurance against Esta's probable attempt at escape, and pocketed it. "I think you'd better come with us. The boss is going to want to see you."

Jerked and pressed along, there was no choice but to walk—walk and curse Esta and her damn treachery the whole way.

THE SIREN

1902—New York

Jack Grew had had enough of the constant coddling and fussing of his mother after two days. After five, he was finished completely, so he moved himself back into his own set of rooms. It had given him some peace, not having a constant parade of maids and doctors checking on him, and also some space from the rest of his family, who seemed always to be showing up to remind him about the next interview or appointment they'd arranged.

They were always doing the arranging. Never asking. Never consulting. Only demanding, and he was damn well sick of it. Now, at least, he had time to pour himself into deciphering the Ars Arcana.

When the clock struck eight, its long, sonorous chimes dragged Jack from his stupor. He blinked a few times, trying to remember where he was or what he had been doing. On the table in front of him, the Book was lying open, the page filled with symbols and markings in a language he didn't recognize.

Right. He'd been reading. Or he'd been trying to.

He rubbed at his eyes. He'd sat down not long after five to wade through a page of Greek and must have fallen asleep at some point. That was the thing he'd discovered about the Book—when he was studying it, time seemed to have no real meaning. He'd often wake in the morning, still dressed in the clothes he had been wearing the night before, his neck aching from sleeping upright in a chair, and the Book open in front of him.

Or perhaps that was simply an effect of the morphine, he thought dully, even as the ache in his head made him grimace. Taking the vial from his pocket, he removed a cube of the morphine and popped it into his mouth, cringing at the bitterness of it. But a few moments later the pain started to fade.

Not quickly enough, he thought, placing two more of the bitter cubes into his mouth. A little while longer, maybe, and he'd stop using the painkiller. He wasn't some damn soldier who couldn't give it up. It hadn't been *that* long, he thought, his mind already softening and growing clearer. It simply took time, he told himself as he turned back to the Book.

It wasn't the ringing of the clock that brought him out of his stupor the second time. *No.* That was a different bell altogether.

He blinked, his head still swirling pleasantly and the pain in his head feeling very far away. He went to rub his eyes only to discover that his hand held a pen. The Book was still open, but now the page that had been completely incomprehensible before was filled with notations . . . and they were in his own hand.

Not just notations. Translations. And he didn't recall writing any of it.

The bell was still ringing.

The doorbell. Sam Watson. He'd almost completely forgotten about the appointment his uncle had made for another interview. The first one had been a complete waste of time, but apparently the Order felt that they needed to put a word in the ear of the press about the gala, and they were using Sam—and Jack—to do it.

Jack groaned as he closed the Book with a violent snap. The pages rippled, bouncing with the force of it. *The bell—and Watson—could damned well wait,* he thought as he took the Book into his bedroom and secured it in the safe. He took two more cubes of morphine to dampen the pain that was already shooting through his head from the incessant ringing of the bell. Then he went to the door.

It wasn't Watson.

"Miss DeMure," Jack said, surprised to see her standing in his doorway.

She was wearing a silk gown of the deepest emerald green, which contrasted with the red of her hair and lips.

She'd come with Sam before, to the first interview he'd had with the reporter. From the looks she'd given Jack during that interview, she'd been interested in Jack—*more* than interested. He'd hoped to see her again, but he hadn't expected her to arrive at his town house, unannounced and alone.

He looked past her, for some sign that Sam Watson was with her.

"Sam couldn't come," she said, stepping past him. "Regrettably, he was detained by something at the office. I thought you might enjoy my company instead." She tossed a smile over her shoulder, and Jack, who was not one to overlook a gift like this, shut the door behind her.

"Your company?" he asked expectantly, turning back to her.

She was running her gloved fingertips over the smooth, dark wood of the entry table. "Was I wrong?"

"No," he said, feeling a flush of warmth and satisfaction. "Not at all. Please, come in. Something to drink?"

The went into the parlor, and he poured them both glasses of sherry. She took the offered drink with a coy smile, but then she turned from him to examine one of the figurines on the sideboard.

He understood immediately the dance that she'd just started, and his gut went tight at the thought of what was to come—the give and take as they circled each other. The tease and the promise of it. And the moment he would triumph.

After a moment Evelyn turned to him, her eyes glittering in the soft light. "I knew Harte Darrigan, you know. . . ."

"Darrigan?" Irritation coursed through Jack as his mood went icy. The last thing he wanted to think about when he was entertaining a willing woman was that damned magician.

Evelyn nodded. "Some might say that I knew him *intimately*."

"Did you?" he asked, not bothering to hide the disgust in his voice.

"Oh, don't be jealous, Jack," she said, and then she laughed, deep and throaty.

Despite his irritation, the sound tugged at his gut again, but the morphine was still in his blood, making his mind clear and his thoughts direct. She was toying with him.

But he was no mouse.

He stalked over to her slowly, so she wouldn't be afraid. So she wouldn't realize that it wasn't he who was the prey. "I wouldn't waste my time being jealous of trash like Darrigan," he told her.

Her red mouth drew up into a smile. "I didn't think you would. I knew from the moment I heard you speak to Sam the other day that you were too smart, too shrewd for an emotion as petty as jealousy. Which is why I thought you might be interested in information I have about him."

He took another step closer, until he could smell the cloying perfume that hung around her like a cloud, brash and loud—just like she was. "What information?"

"I was there that night, you know," she told him, sipping her sherry and never once breaking eye contact. *A challenge if ever there was one.* "I was at Khafre Hall the night everything happened. I know the Order is trying to cover the truth, that they're using you to distract the public from what actually happened. If you say Darrigan was on the train, I believe you."

"You do?" Jack asked, coming closer yet and placing his glass on the sideboard.

"Of course, Jack. I knew Darrigan, and I knew that bitch of an assistant he found. She's the one to blame for all of this, you know."

He took her by the arm and was gratified to see the flash of fear in her eyes. "I'm not interested in games. If you know where Darrigan or the girl are, you will tell me."

"I don't know where he is. I don't know if he even made it off the train—" He tightened his grip on her arm, and her eyes went wide. "But I do know that he might have left something behind . . . something that might interest you."

"Did he?" Jack asked, releasing his hold on her a little and then releasing her completely. The morphine had finally bloomed in his veins, softening everything and making him feel very present, like he was everywhere in the room at once. "What did he leave behind?"

"Information like that I could only share with my friends. My very *close* friends," she purred. "Are we friends, Jack?"

"Of course," he murmured.

His mouth curved up of its own accord as she stepped toward him, her eyes lighting with victory, clearly believing that she had won.

But oh, how very, very wrong she was.

THE EXPOSITION

1904—St. Louis

Harte waited with Esta at the corner of Lindell and Plaza, across from one of the main entrances to the world's fair. She hadn't spoken to him all morning, but it wasn't as though he had been willing to bring up what had happened between them the night before. They were both cowards, it seemed, but Harte didn't miss the way she had been careful not to touch him, not even allowing her arm to brush against his as the streetcar carried them through the town.

Standing outside the gates and watching the steady stream of visitors, Harte began to realize just how large the world's fair actually was. Lafayette Park, where the Exposition was being housed, stretched for miles in each direction. The scope of the event was astounding. In the distance, he could hear the roar of the crowds and the din of music coming from inside the gates, and every so often, the boom of a cannon or the sharp report of a gun echoed through the air.

"You need to relax," Esta said, her voice finally breaking through his thoughts. "Looking like that, you're going to draw attention."

"Like what?" he asked, risking a glance at her. It was, of course, a mistake. Her eyes were alert and her cheeks pink with the excitement of the day—or maybe it was just the heat—and at the sight of her, something clenched inside of him, something that had nothing to do with the power that had been rumbling ever since he'd kissed her the night before.

"Like you're about to attack someone," she said, cutting him an unreadable look out of the corner of her eye.

"I do not look like—" But he saw a familiar face approaching. "He's coming."

Despite being more than twenty minutes late, Julien strutted over to them as though nothing were amiss. "You're late," Harte told Julien, reaching out to shake hands in greeting.

"Unavoidable," Julien said with an affable shrug. But the expression in his eyes didn't match the ease of his words.

When Julien took Harte's hand in greeting, Harte thought briefly about using his affinity, just to be sure. But across the street, a troop of what was clearly the Jefferson Guard stood at attention near the gates. If Julien was right about them being able to sense magic, it wasn't worth the risk.

Esta held out her hand as well. "Good to see you again, Jules," she said, her voice pitched lower than usual.

"Well, well," Julien said, taking the greeting in stride.

Harte let out a muttered curse. "This is madness," he said. "There's no way someone isn't going to notice what she actually is."

"No one's going to be paying her any attention," Julien said, nodding toward the entrance across the street. "Not with the wonders that await them within."

"What wonders are those?" Esta asked, apparently enjoying herself. If she was mad about the night before, she hadn't said anything. Which meant she was definitely mad about it, and eventually he would have to face the consequences.

Not that he blamed her. He'd taken advantage of her and then he'd walked out on her. He deserved whatever she meted out.

Julien tucked his thumbs into his waistcoat pockets and rocked on his heels. "In there? Only the largest and most impressive fair the world has ever seen," he said. "Within those walls lie the evidence of our civilization's brilliance and the wonders of the wide world—all the innovations and discoveries this age has to offer."

"You can cut the drama any time now, Jules," Harte said, bristling at the way Esta's eyes were laughing at Julien's words. *She won't even look at me.* "All we want is the necklace. You said it was here?"

Julien shot Esta a conspiratorial look. "Patience, Darrigan." Then he started across the street, leaving them to follow.

"He's a little insufferable, isn't he?" Esta asked, making sure to keep her voice low enough that Julien wouldn't hear.

"More than a little," Harte said dryly.

"But I still like him."

Harte glanced at her. "Most people have that reaction. Try not to fall for it. Okay, Slim?"

"Slim?"

"Just trying it out," he told her with a shrug. "I need something to call you if you're going to insist on this getup."

She glared at him, and he felt almost relieved. "Well, it's not going to be Slim."

It was the way her cheeks flushed that sealed the deal for him. "I don't know," he said, his mouth twitching. "I think the name's already growing on me."

She started to argue, but he simply picked up his pace to walk next to Julien, leaving her to catch up with them.

They paid their entry fees and followed the crush of people through the ornate arches that acted as gateways into the fair. The crowd around them moved slowly, in part because directly in front of them was a bandstand where a full brass band was playing a bouncing march. As the three of them pushed their way through the crowd that had gathered to listen, Esta pointed to the big bass drum painted with the band's name.

"It's Sousa?" Esta asked Julien.

The band's conductor was dressed in military blue and his baton snapped out a pattern with almost mechanical precision to keep time for the music. Harte had heard of John Philip Sousa, of course—*who hadn't?*—but he wondered what it was about the bandleader that put a look of such serious concentration on Esta's face.

"I told you, they have the most famous performers, the most astounding displays from countries all over the world, and the most magnificent grounds ever built," Julien said. "The Society wants this Exposition to put St. Louis on the map—make it as important as Chicago, maybe even as important as Manhattan."

Esta glanced at Harte, and the look she gave him indicated that it wasn't going to happen. But the moment their eyes met, her expression faltered.

Harte's stomach sank as she turned away from him again. "I just want the necklace, Jules. Can we get to it?"

They had to push their way through the crowd around the bandstand. To their left, a tree-lined alley led deeper into the park, and Harte could see the sun glinting off a body of water. Julien continued to follow the path past administrative buildings and then onto an area with signage declaring it THE PIKE.

"Here we are," he said, gesturing toward the brick-paved path before them.

The wide boulevard led into a kind of surreal fantasy world. At the entrance, mountains at least ten stories high dwarfed a small alpine village, which sprouted up next to the replica of a castle that could have come from the stories of King Arthur. As far as the eye could see, the street was lined with a jumble of buildings painted in colors too bright to be real. In the distance, Harte heard the echo of gunfire again.

"What is that?" Esta asked.

"Probably the reenactment of the Second Boer War they stage twice a day," Julien said, checking his pocket watch. "Ah, yes. Nearly ten thirty, when the cavalry is usually set to attack."

"The cavalry?" Harte asked, wondering where the hell they were.

"Actors, mostly, but some were actually in the real fighting." Julien gave him a wink. "Welcome to the Pike. There's nothing that's ever been built like it. Here, you can take voyages anywhere in the world without ever leaving the city. You can travel to Hades or into the heavens. You can meet a geisha or ride to the North Pole and back. Amazing, isn't it?"

"It's something," Harte said doubtfully as he studied the wide boulevard in front of him.

He'd dreamed his whole life of escaping the city, and now it seemed that he had an opportunity to do more than escape—he could be transported—but somehow none of it felt right. Harte had never been anywhere but the island of Manhattan, but he knew at a glance that nothing they were about to see was real. Every building was too brightly painted and too perfect. With the electric signs and lampposts—lit even though the sun was overhead—and the noise of the barkers, each shouting to entice the fairgoers into paying another twenty-five cents to experience some new wonder, the Pike had a carnivalesque feel to it that he knew meant it was a poor approximation of the real wonders the world held.

Actually, the exhibitions of the Pike felt a little like the dime museums in the Bowery. The popularity of those tawdry little storefronts had always made Harte uncomfortable with the way they paraded people as oddities, as nothing more than objects to be viewed for a couple of coins.

From the half-horrified look on Esta's face, Harte could tell she must have felt the same.

The Pike was lined with *strangest* combination of buildings. A Japanese pagoda was the neighbor of a building meant to represent ancient Rome. A large man-made cavern with the words CLIFF DWELLERS stood butted up against a building that could have been something from St. Mark's Square in Venice.

"Those aren't actually Native Americans?" Esta asked Julien as they passed the Cliff Dwellers building and she noticed a pair of dark-haired women standing silently and offering beaded bracelets for sale.

"They're Indians, if that's what you mean," Julien said, giving her a strange look. "What else would they be?"

"Actors?" she asked, but Harte couldn't tell if it was hope or fear he heard in her tone.

"What would the point of that be?" Julien asked, and from the look of surprise on his face, he seemed legitimately confused.

"I don't know," Esta said vaguely. "Do they live here, on the grounds?"

"Who knows," Julien said dismissively. "They seem happy enough, don't they?"

But from the look on Esta's face, Harte could tell that she wasn't convinced. Her brows were furrowed, and there was concern—maybe even dismay—coloring her expression. "Do they force them to be here?" she asked.

"How should I know?" Julien said with a shrug. "But I'm sure they're compensated."

He didn't care, Harte realized, because it wasn't his problem. Julien had been born free to make his own choices, to pick his own paths—to go *wherever* he wanted, *whenever* he wanted. He couldn't understand what it might be like to live a different life.

One of the women caught Harte's eye and lifted her arm to offer him a bracelet. He shook his head in a gentle refusal, but not before he realized that Esta was right. Behind the placid expression the woman wore was something Harte recognized too easily—a frustration and disappointment with the world that she hadn't been able to hide, at least not from him. Because he felt it too keenly himself.

He pulled out a couple of coins and traded them for one of the bracelets. The woman showed no sign of pleasure as she pocketed the money and selected an item for him. Not even bothering to look at the bracelet, he ran his thumb over the smooth beads as he tucked it into the pocket of his waistcoat—a reminder that the world was wider than he had realized and there was no end to the troubles it contained.

The three of them made their way through the parade of grotesquely beautiful sights. The architecture might not be authentic, but it was still astounding. All along the brick-lined boulevard, average citizens mixed with people dressed in fanciful costumes. Whether they were authentic, Harte didn't know, but the embroidery and beading and detail of each costume had a certain beauty nonetheless.

Music poured out of the buildings, the different styles blending and clashing with the noise of the street. The fair's organizers had created a world where fantasies of far-off lands and exotic people could come to life for anyone willing to pay twenty-five cents. Maybe it wasn't real, but Harte understood implicitly that veracity didn't matter—to the fair or to the people who attended. Those who handed over their coins here were no different from the ones who had sat in the seats watching his act night after night. They didn't want reality, with all its messy complications and unpleasant truths; they wanted the fantasy—the possibility of escape. And even Harte, who knew better, couldn't help but be a little drawn in by the spectacle of it all.

"Here we are," Julien said, when they arrived at an enormous archway emblazoned with the words THE STREETS OF CAIRO.

Beyond the opening, the street led through a veritable city of sand-colored buildings, all with Arabic flourishes—a series of arches and minarets accented the flat-sided buildings. Above, domed rooftops blocked out the blue summer sky, and in the streets, men dressed in flowing robes called out, advertising camel and donkey rides through the streets of the reproduced city. It was clearly supposed to be Egypt, but it was a fanciful, stylized version of Egypt that was meant for those who would never travel there.

"This had better have something to do with the necklace, Jules," Harte told him.

"This is the Society's special offering for the fair," Julien told them, his voice barely audible above the noisy streets. "The centerpiece, from what I've been told, is a mystical artifact from the ancient world—a necklace with a stone that contains stars within it."

"It's here?" Esta asked.

"Not that it'll do you any good," Julien said. "The security is top-notch, and with the recent activity of the Antistasi, everyone is on high alert."

"We'll worry about that later," Harte said. "Let's make sure it's the necklace we're looking for."

Together they followed the maze of buildings past a makeshift bazaar, with stands selling reams of brightly woven material and small trinkets that looked like items that could have been taken from a pharaoh's tomb. There was an enormous restaurant that spilled the scent of roasting meats and heady spices out into the streets, tempting the people who passed. Finally, in the deepest heart of the attraction, they came to a building carved to look as though it had come directly from ancient Egypt.

A large, deep portico was flanked with striped sandstone columns, each painted with something that looked like hieroglyphics. It reminded Harte of Khafre Hall, with its gilded flourishes and bright cerulean accents. From the way Esta had gone very still, as though every cell in her body had come alert, he figured she thought the same.

"Are you ready to take a trip down the Nile?" Julien asked.

But Harte didn't have the patience for Julien's games. The heat of the day was getting to him, making his head pound and his vision swim, and suddenly he couldn't hear anything but a roaring in his mind.

The sun was high enough that the temple threw no shadow. It would be cool inside, welcoming and safe within the shade of its thick walls.

Just as quickly as the vision had submerged him in a different time and place, it drained away, leaving Harte's ears ringing and a cold sweat coating his skin.

"Harte?" Esta was saying his name, and when he met her eyes, he saw the worry in them. It should have felt better than the indifference she'd shown him all day, but the vision had left him shaken.

Pull yourself together.

"I'm fine, Slim," he told her with a wink.

Her eyes flashed with annoyance. "But you just—"

"Let it go," he told her. Then he directed his attention to Julien, who was watching him with a serious expression. "Let's get this done and see what we're dealing with."

Apparently, Julien wasn't being overly dramatic—inside the building they found a line of people waiting to board actual boats that were shaped like long, flat-bottomed canoes with upturned ends, meant to look like boats that had once sailed down the Nile. When it was their turn to board, Julien slipped the line attendant a few coins and managed to get them a boat to themselves.

"After you," he said to Esta, allowing her to step into the small craft first.

She took a bench in the middle, and Julien began to follow, but Harte grabbed his arm, to stop him.

"Youth before beauty," he told Julien as he took the opportunity to slide into the seat next to her. He ignored the knowing smirk playing at Julien's mouth and pretended that he didn't notice Esta's annoyance.

At the rear of the ship, an oarsman was dressed in a linen robe shot through with gold and the worst wig Harte had ever seen. The black coiled braids were ratty and matted, and they hung around the man's lean face, framing bright blue eyes that had been ringed with kohl. It looked like his skin had been turned tan with makeup as well—it was too russet colored to be natural. He probably was supposed to look like an Egyptian painting come to life, but unlike Julien's impersonation of a woman, the oarsman's costume was a caricature. Like the white vaudeville performers who blackened their faces with burnt cork for minstrel numbers, it was a mockery of the very people it was trying to depict.

The oarsman remained silent as the boat started moving. Slowly and steadily, he pushed the craft away from the loading dock and down a narrow channel of unnaturally blue water. Next to Harte, Esta was straight-backed and alert, taking in everything as the boat approached a darkened tunnel.

"Here we go," Julien murmured, tossing a mischievous look back to the two of them just as the boat glided into the tunnel.

The farther they went, the darker it became, until the boat was traveling through an artificial night, and the only noise was the soft lapping of the water as they moved onward.

"In the beginning there was only the sea, dark and infinite. . . ." The oarsman's voice came to them, deep and overly dramatic. "This primeval sea was made only of chaos. . . ."

The oarsman's voice fell silent again, leaving them to float along in the murky darkness, but Harte couldn't relax—not with Esta so close and not with the power inside of him stirring in the darkness.

Though they were out of the heat of the midmorning sun, the attraction felt close and muggy, almost like breathing through a blanket of dampness. The air tasted of mold and dust, like it might in an ancient tomb. Harte wondered if that effect was intentional as he swallowed against the tightness that had risen in his throat and fought the urge to loosen his collar.

He didn't need to see Esta to know how close she was, and neither did the voice inside of him. The darkness seemed to embolden it, and he struggled to ignore its echoing and unintelligible chorus, which was damn difficult when the oarsman was droning on about something behind him.

"The chaos was endless and it held no life until the waters split and the sun god Ra emerged to bring forth order and to create the world."

Ahead, a pinpoint of light appeared, which seemed to grow as they approached, until their boat passed into another room. The next chamber was painted in gold so that, with the light reflecting off the domed surface, it looked as though they were within the sun itself. The voice retreated, just a little, but it was enough that he felt like he could breathe again. Next to him, Esta's face was turned away. She was taking in the sights of the chamber they were passing through—or maybe she was still avoiding him, he couldn't tell.

Harte regretted ever touching her, and yet he couldn't regret it completely. Even now, even hours away from those stolen seconds when he could feel every inch of her body, strong and capable and *soft* beneath him, even in the bright, cleansing light of day, his lips still remembered the taste of her and his fingertips still held the memory of her skin's heat. If all he ever had of her was that memory, he would gladly take it.

He couldn't help but use the opportunity to study her: the graceful line of her neck where it met her shorn hair, the lips that were too pink and too soft to belong to any boy, and the shape of her legs—long and lithe and strong—outlined by the trousers she'd insisted on wearing. The oarsman was going on again, this time about the adventures of Ra and Osiris, Isis and Horus, and other deities Harte had learned of when he was preparing his old act, but he wasn't listening. Not really. He knew these stories already—had learned them as part of his so-called training in the occult arts. Instead, he ignored the oarsman and let his mind replay the handful of minutes from the night before when his world had felt unmoored and dangerous and perfect all at once.

As if responding to the memory of it, the power inside of him seemed to rouse itself, swelling until Harte could barely hear the soft swish of the water, and the oarsman's narrative was a sound coming from far off in the distance. Considering he hadn't slept more than a couple of hours the night before—and in an uncomfortable straight-backed chair, no less—it took every bit of his strength to press it back and keep it from growing. He was barely aware of the rooms they passed because his attention was focused on the power threatening to erupt within him. And on Esta, less than an arm's reach away.

After the boat passed through the third chamber—one filled with a makeshift temple—they entered a chamber lined with shelves filled with different tablets and piles of rolled parchments. All at once the voice inside of him went quiet. But it wasn't an easy quiet. The power that had been bunching and flexing within him seemed to fade until all he felt was a silent emptiness.

MAPPING THE FAIR

1904—St. Louis

N orth was watching the gondolas glide across the lagoon toward the Festival Hall, making notes about their timing, when he saw the guy. At first North couldn't figure out why he looked so darn familiar, but then it came to him. It was the same guy who'd been standing outside the theater the night before—and he'd been with the Thief.

Curious, he tucked away his notebook and started following from a distance.

Since he'd left Maggie at her building an hour before, he'd been doing what he did most days as he waited for her—learning everything he could about the Exposition. It was an enormous place, filled with people and passageways that could mean trouble, and they were running out of time to make sure they knew everything they could. So far he'd mapped out the entire eastern side: the display of the villages from the Philippines and most of the agriculture and forestry exhibits. He'd been slowly working his way westward, through the offering from Morocco and the replica of Jerusalem. He knew where the entrances and exits were, where the Guard often congregated when they were supposed to be watching the crowd, and when they changed shifts. He knew all the places where they could be exposed and all the places where someone could lie low if need be. Little by little he'd accounted for all the dangers, because Ruth wanted him to determine everything that might cause them trouble. North figured that this guy certainly counted—especially since he wasn't alone.

When the guy and his two companions turned onto the Pike, North used the noise and confusion around him to get a little closer. There was a pretty big crowd of people waiting to get into the Hereafter, which was a damn idiotic thing to want as far as North was concerned, but he used the cover they provided to maneuver around and get ahead of the three he'd been following. He cut across the boulevard to the deep overhand of Creation, where he could wait without being seen. A moment later they came through the crowd, and North barked out a laugh of surprise that startled a woman standing next to him.

One of the other guys wasn't a guy, after all. It was the Thief. She looked different in the suit and cap, and her hair had been chopped to just above her collar, but anyone with two eyes in their head—or at least anyone who was paying attention—would have known who it was.

But what's she doing here?

It was one thing to have the girl that all the papers called the Devil's Thief appear in town at the same time Ruth was close to the biggest—and most dangerous—deed the Antistasi had ever planned. Maybe it was just a coincidence. But having her appear at the fair—the same venue that Ruth had been eyeing for months? And just when everything was about to come together?

North didn't like it.

With his hat pulled low over his forehead, he kept as close as he could and followed the three down the Pike, until they came to the Streets of Cairo. He didn't like how they'd gone directly to the Society's attraction, passing everything else with barely a look.

Maybe he should have followed them in, but he'd already mapped it out—there was one way in and one way out—and he'd been through the darn boat ride enough already. There wasn't any reason to take the risk of being seen or recognized, because the last thing the Antistasi needed was for the Guard to start paying attention to North. He still had about a third of the fair left to map out, after all. Instead of following them into the attraction, he found a place under the Chinese archway across from Cairo to wait instead, watching for the three to exit.

Most of the fair didn't bother him, but North didn't much like the Pike. Everything about it was too big and too loud and too brash. Though, he had to admit, the horse they called Beautiful Jim Key had been a sight, all right. Smartest damn animal North had ever heard of, much less seen with his own eyes. But that was the fair for you—unbelievable. Above him, the arch was something to see too, painted in a red brighter than blood and gleaming with gold. Strange symbols in black and bright blue covered the surface, and at the tip of every roofline was a fanciful curli-cued dragon, looking down upon the crowd like guardians.

But not even those guardians could stop what Ruth and the Antistasi had planned.

At the end of the month, the top representatives from all the Brotherhoods would be in the city. For one night they would be in one place, together. The perfect target.

If all went well, they wouldn't just make a statement to the Society; they would make a statement about magic and the world and what the future could be. The deed Ruth was planning was impossible and yet it was so obvious. If it worked, it would change everything—*absolutely everything*. The Society would crumble, the Brotherhoods would be left without their leaders, and magic itself would be free. *Restored*.

Legend or not, North wasn't about to let the Devil's Thief get in the Antistasi's way.

THE DJINNI'S STAR

1904—St. Louis

The oarsman was still talking, but all Esta could think about was how close Harte was and how he was pretending to ignore her. His silence grated on her. She hadn't slept all night because she'd been thinking about what had happened between them. He hadn't returned until it was almost morning, and by then she'd been too angry and frustrated—with him and with herself—to talk, so she'd turned away and pretended to be asleep.

But even once they'd gotten the message from Julien to meet at the Exposition, Harte had been sullen and silent. Since she wasn't the one who had stormed off, she wasn't about to be the first to offer an olive branch.

She could almost still feel him on her lips. She would probably always remember the weight of his body as it pressed her into the mattress. How could he sit there acting as though *nothing* had happened between them?

Unless it really *was* only the power of the Book that wanted her and not Harte. Which meant that she'd made a fool of herself over him for no reason at all.

Esta shoved those thoughts aside and turned farther away from Harte, pretending to concentrate on the ride. Each room the boat passed through was elaborately decorated to simulate some scene in ancient Egypt—or at least what people in the early twentieth century imagined ancient Egypt might look like—but Esta barely saw them. Her focus was constantly being drawn back to Harte—the stiff set of his spine and the way he smelled clean, like soap and linen, despite the heat of the day.

"Finally, we come to the House of Books," the oarsman said as they came to a chamber lined with shelves, each filled with different tablets and piles of rolled parchments. "Here the god Thoth, master of the Library of Life, invented the art of writing and gave it to the people."

Harte had held himself away from her, still and watchful for the entire ride, but when the oarsman spoke about Thoth, something changed. It felt like the moment before it rains, when the air has a specific quality that feels like a storm is coming. When Esta glanced over at Harte, he had the strangest look on his face.

"Is that what they say?" Harte asked, his words dripping with a scorn that seemed out of proportion to the moment. "Thoth, the *master* of the Library?" A dark laugh bubbled up from his chest.

He was acting so strangely that Esta forgot her irritation for a moment. "Harte?" She reached out to touch him, and the moment their skin met, he whipped his head around to face her. His hand snaked up to latch on to her wrist, and she felt a burst of heat that had nothing to do with Harte's magic. Still, she couldn't pull away, not without causing the boat to rock or tip.

"Thoth didn't invent anything," Harte told her. But his voice sounded off, and his eyes were all wrong. Like the night before, he was looking at her without seeing her, but now his pupils were enormous, dilated enough to obscure the color of his irises. Something peered out from within him, a darkness that reminded her of the inky blackness that had seeped into her vision at the train station and the hotel.

"Harte," she said softly, trying to call him back to himself. "What are you talking about?"

"Thoth was nothing but a *thief.*" Harte practically spit the word with disgust. "He took knowledge that wasn't his, and when that didn't satisfy him, he took more." Again came that strange, deep, mirthless laugh, which had Julien sending a questioning look in Esta's direction.

She shook her head just slightly, to indicate that she didn't know what Harte was up to. "Shhh," she hissed, when his laughter didn't stop.

Before Esta could say anything more, the oarsman started up again, explaining how the ancients believed that whatever was written in the library in Cairo would be transcribed and made real in the world of the gods. "Thoth was one of the ancient civilization's most important gods. He gave the world not only writing, but science and magic," the oarsman continued. "He carved order from the chaos of the cosmos through the creation of the written word, and through the inscription of spells, he eliminated the wild danger of magic and made its power safe."

"Lies," Harte muttered. "All lies . . ."

"What is *wrong* with you?" Esta whispered, jabbing at him with her elbow.

Harte blinked. "What?" Frowning, he pulled back from her. His eyes were still wrong, but she could see the gray halo around the black returning. Maybe he'd been wrong to kiss her the night before. Maybe she'd been wrong in wanting him to. But looking at his strange, half-dazed expression, some of her anger cooled.

The oarsman was still going on and on with his sonorous narration. "Because he was a benevolent god, Thoth contained the cosmic dangers of that chaos within a book. He buried the Book of Thoth in the Nile, protected by serpents, and those who attempted to retrieve it paid a steep price, for the knowledge of the gods was never meant for mere mortals."

The Book of Thoth? Esta glanced at Harte. Whatever had come over him a moment before seemed to have passed. He was still tense, but he was listening to the oarsman now. Or if he wasn't, he was focused on something, since his expression was one of concentration rather than disgust.

They passed out of the library chamber and made their way into a brilliantly blue room that contained a large diorama. On a hill far off in the distance stood a white temple, shining under an artificial sun.

"As time passed and civilizations transformed into new empires," the oarsman explained, "Thoth became known as Hermes, but he continued in his quest for knowledge and his commitment to man. Myth tells us he stole knowledge from Olympus for humans, and so he became the patron of thieves. Later, he would become Hermes Trismegistus, inventor of the Emerald Tablets, which held the secrets of the philosopher's stone, the very foundation of alchemy.

"Through the secrets of the Emerald Tablets, the power to transform the very essence of the world was revealed to man," the oarsman told them as he navigated past what was obviously supposed to be Mount Olympus. "Through the careful study of the hermetical arts, we have learned to control the power that once posed a danger. And through alchemy and the occult arts, those who perfect themselves, like the Veiled Prophet himself, can stand against the wild dangers of uncontrolled power."

They glided into the darkness of another tunnel in silence, and on the other side, they found the end of the ride.

"And now," the oarsman said, "if you'll proceed along the Path of Righteousness to the Temple of Khorassan, the Veiled Prophet offers a view of one of his most prized treasures, a collar forged in the ancient world that contains a stone rumored to have been created by Thoth himself."

The hairs on the back of Esta's neck rose at his words. From the look on Harte's face, he'd shaken off whatever had happened back in the House of Books. But his expression didn't hold the same anticipation she felt. His eyes were still glassy and distant, his jaw was tight, and there was a sheen of sweat on his temples. It was like he hadn't even heard the oarsman.

The path was painted to look like it was paved in silver, but it was as fake as everything else on the Pike. As they walked along it with the other, completely oblivious tourists, the music changed to a softly driving melody that sounded vaguely Eastern. The path emptied into a smaller chamber that was already filled with people. In the center of the room, blocked from view, a glass case was illuminated from above.

Esta didn't need to see the case to know that it would contain the Djinni's Star. She could feel it calling to her, just as it had called to her in a posh Upper East Side jewelry store not long after the turn of the millennium—the last time she stole it.

If she could just slow time, perhaps she'd be able to take it here and now, but the closer she got to the case in the center of the room, the more she knew that using her affinity would be impossible. It wasn't only that they'd walked past a pair of Jefferson Guards to enter the chamber but also that there was something sickly sweet scenting the air.

"Opium," Harte whispered to her, his expression still distant, but more serious now as well.

"It's just a bit of fragrance," Julien told him, brushing aside Harte's concerns. "They wanted to give the whole sensory experience."

But Esta didn't doubt that Harte was right. She'd smelled that scent before and had experienced the numbing effects of the drug as it took her ability to pull time slow when she'd been captured at the Haymarket, back when she'd first arrived in Old New York. Even now her magic felt dulled, softened by the drug. It wasn't enough to harm anyone, but it was enough to make an affinity weaker.

Soon the three of them were standing in front of the glass case, and there, laid against midnight velvet, was the Djinni's Star. Set into the platinum collar, the stone was polished to a brilliant shine, and within its depths, it looked as though it contained galaxies.

"I hope you can see how impossible getting your necklace back is going to be," Julien said, leaning in close so no one else would hear. "The Streets of Cairo is the Veiled Prophet Society's offering at the fair, and that necklace is the centerpiece. They're never going to sell it back to you."

They hadn't exactly been planning to pay for it.

"Then I suppose we'll have to take it," Esta said with a shrug.

"Take it?" Julien's mouth fell open. He looked to Harte, who was staring at the stone with a thoughtful expression. "From the Society? You're completely mad."

"No," she whispered, giving Julien a smug smile. "I'm a thief."

THE STREETS OF CAIRO

1904—St. Louis

Harte's skin felt like it was on fire, even as the blood in his veins felt like ice. In front of him was the Djinni's Star, and the power inside of him was churning, but whether it was in approval or fear, he couldn't tell. Dimly, he realized that Esta and Julien were talking about the necklace, but he hadn't been following their conversation . . . until Esta said that she was a thief.

"Not here," he told her in a hushed voice. They were in a room filled with people, surrounded by Jefferson Guards. There was confidence, and then there was idiocy.

She gave him a scowl, but she closed her mouth.

"Come on," he said, needing air. There was only so long even he could hold his breath, and he was already feeling light-headed from whatever had happened on the boat ride. Without waiting to see if they were following, he pushed through the overcrowded room and out into the street so he could finally take a breath of air that wasn't filled with the cloying, dulling power of opium and could collect himself enough to push back the power that was rumbling excitedly inside of him.

Once he was outside, it took a moment for Harte's eyes to adjust to the brightness. He inhaled to clear his head, but his pulse was still pounding in his temples. Instead of exiting where they had entered the attraction, they had been dumped back out onto the main thoroughfare of the Pike. The noise was deafening, and the crowd all seemed to be surging in the same direction.

Harte turned to find Esta and Julien in the crowd and was relieved to see them there, right behind him.

Julien tugged at Harte's sleeve. "Come on," he said, trying to lead Harte in the direction everyone else seemed to be heading. "You can't just stand here in the middle of this mess. We'll get trampled."

As Julien pulled him back, a large flat-bedded wagon pulled by a team of matching gray horses passed by. A small hut made of what looked like dried palm fronds and lashed-together branches had been built at the back of the wagon's bed. In front of the hut, an older man with darkly tanned skin who was wearing nothing more than a swath of fabric around his waist sat on a stool, looking completely uninterested in any of the people who were staring or yelling around him. Other men who were similarly dressed stood at attention, while a gaggle of children sat in the center. They might have been singing or shouting—Harte couldn't tell because of the noise of the crowd.

"What is all of this, anyway?" Harte asked, following Julien and Esta closer to the shelter of the buildings, where the crowd wasn't as thick.

"It's a parade," Julien told him.

"I can see that, but *why*?" Harte asked, feeling unaccountably irritated. The power inside of him was still churning, and the heat of the day was starting to creep against his skin. "Isn't the fair itself enough?"

"It's all part of the fun, Darrigan," Julien told him. "How else will you know what exhibits to visit? That one that just passed, it's for the Igorot Village—fascinating stuff. They wear hardly anything. . . . Anyway, it'll be over soon enough. The parades never last very long, since they have at least two a day. This one's the midday offering. There will be another later, when the lights come on."

The three of them stood in the shade of the building for a few minutes, penned in by the crowd as the parade went by. After the wagon came a group of women dressed in silken robes, their faces painted white like geisha. Around them, the Jefferson Guard marched in straight lines, creating a boundary of protection so that the eager crowd couldn't get too close. Whenever someone—usually a man—tried to approach, the closest of the Guards would push him back with a kind of bored violence.

"Are you okay?" Esta asked, eyeing Harte with a worried frown.

"I'm fine," he said, shrugging off her concern.

"Because you look—"

A loud wailing split the air, and the parade erupted into chaos as three figures dressed in rumpled gowns and wearing odd, misshapen masks descended on the parade, attacking the Jefferson Guard. A sharp *pop* sounded, cutting through the noise and the confusion of the crowd, and colored smoke suddenly began streaming from one of the figures' fingertips.

The Guardsmen who had been surrounding the geisha sprang into action, countering the attack.

"The Antistasi," Julien said, and his voice contained a note of true fear. But Harte wasn't so sure. There was no trace of magic in the air, no indication that the smoke was anything but a distraction.

Other Guardsmen came out of the Nile exhibit and barreled through the crowd, pushing over anyone who happened to be in their way as they rushed toward the masked figures. A woman screamed as they knocked her aside, causing her to drop the child she'd been holding up for a better view of the passing floats. The child started to wail, but the Guardsmen didn't stop to help. With an urgency that bordered on violence, they began grabbing anyone trying to escape the fog. Man or woman, even children—it didn't seem to matter.

One of the figures had been caught by a group of the Guard, who'd already ripped the mask away. Beneath it was a boy who couldn't have been more than fourteen. He spit at the Guardsmen and shouted, "Forever reign the Antistasi!"

"Long live the Devil's Thief!" cried another in reply.

In response, one of the Guardsmen buried his fist in the boy's stomach.

Esta took a step toward them, but Harte caught her wrist. She turned to look at him, her eyes bright with fury. "They're *children*," she said, her voice breaking on the word.

"We can't help them," Harte told her.

"*I* can—"

"No," he said, cutting her off. If she used her affinity here, now, in the middle of this mess? There was no telling what might happen, especially considering the clear threat posed by the gates behind them.

"We can't just leave them," she told him, starting to pull away.

"If they catch us, things are going to get worse. We need to *go*."

But Esta was staring at him like he was her enemy, like she would tear the sun from the sky to stop what was happening. For a moment Harte thought he would have to carry her—or worse, betray everything they'd built between them by *forcing her*. But he couldn't risk it. Not only because it would be the worst kind of treachery, but also because he was already having enough trouble keeping the power inside of him in check while he held her arm.

He could feel it pressing at the most fragile parts of him—the parts that wanted Esta, the parts that *agreed* with her. Together they could destroy the Guard. They could help the boys, who clearly were no more Antistasi than anyone else in the crowd. He could see it, how easy it would be to make a different choice. A single touch, and he could make the Guardsman who was beating the child destroy *himself*.

The violence of the image, the sharpness of it, startled Harte enough that he gasped. Then he shook it off and focused on what was real. On what was *true*.

The power was still struggling to get closer to Esta—as though it craved her fury. He would not let it have her.

"Come on," Harte said, jerking her back and following Julien as his friend led them in the opposite direction of the parade, away from the noise of the Pike and toward one of the smaller side routes that led back into the main part of the fair.

Esta eventually came, looking back toward the Pike every few steps, until they came to where the entrance of the Pike met the regular walk-ways of the fair. The noise of the crowd was a low murmur here, and

Harte could barely hear the confusion of the Pike. Manicured pathways led to large, palatial buildings, and well-dressed people came and went from their entrances.

"We need to get out of here," Harte said, releasing Esta's arm and feeling the power inside of him rage.

"You might want to wait," Julien suggested. "With an Antistasi attack, they'll be checking all the exits."

"They weren't Antistasi," Esta said, her voice hollow as she looked back toward the Pike. From there they couldn't see anything but the outlines of the buildings. There was no way to know what was happening.

"It doesn't matter who they were," Julien said. "You saw how the Guard reacted. They'll be looking for anyone involved, and you don't want to get caught up in it."

"Jules is right," Harte said, needing that time to gather his wits and his strength. "We'll wait for a while—play the tourist until we're sure things have died down."

"I, unfortunately, cannot," Julien told them. "This, I believe, is where I say my good-byes."

"You're leaving?" Esta asked, turning back to them.

"*I'm* not a wanted fugitive," Julien told her. "I have nothing to fear from the Guard, and I also have a matinee today."

"We're not done," Harte said, trying to keep his voice level even as the power inside of him was still unsettled over his refusal to accommodate its wishes. He took another step back from Esta, just to be sure.

Julien frowned at them. "I've done what you asked—I've shown you the necklace."

"We don't *have* the necklace yet, though," Harte pointed out. "As long as it's on display like that, you're at risk."

Julien visibly bristled. "Then take care of it, Darrigan. She might be a thief, but I'm not."

"You want us to take care of it? We need information—about the security or any events that might be happening. We need to know whether the necklace is always there or if they move it at night."

"Why would you think I could get you that information?" Julien asked, clearly annoyed, and if Harte wasn't mistaken, more than a little uneasy.

"Because you're in the Society," Harte pressed, not caring when Julien blanched. "Did you think we didn't know, Jules?"

"It's just a courtesy membership," he said. "I'm no one to them. A *joke*."

Harte didn't miss the bitterness in his friend's voice, but he couldn't do anything about it. "You're closer to the Society than either of us," Harte told him. "You want to get rid of us? You'll get us the information."

"Fine," Julien said. "But it'll take time."

"The sooner we can get the necklace, the sooner we're out of your hair," Harte told him. "And the sooner you can go on with your life like none of this ever happened."

Julien let out a frustrated breath. "If I never had to see your face again, it wouldn't be soon enough, Darrigan."

Harte watched Julien walk off, keeping his eyes on his friend until he'd lost sight of him in the crowds.

"We could have helped those kids," Esta said, her voice low and angry.

He let out a tired breath and reluctantly turned back to her. "I know," he told her.

"Then why—"

"Because we have more important things to do," he said.

"They were kids, Harte. Those were smoke bombs and costumes," she said, her voice shaking. "They were dressed up as Antistasi—as *me*. The skirts and the masks. You saw it, didn't you? They were playing the Devil's Thief. And those Guardsmen were *vicious*. They had to see they were just kids, and it didn't matter."

"You're not responsible for that," he told her, and the moment he said the words, he knew that it had been the wrong thing to say. Her eyes flashed with fury, and the power inside of him warmed.

Her voice was cool and detached when she spoke again. "Aren't I? Maybe *you* can separate what you want from what everyone else is suffering through. God knows you have before. But I can't. I *won't*."

Her words hit their mark, in part because of how true they were. The mess they were in was his doing, all because he'd wanted to be free of the city. Because he'd been willing to sacrifice almost *anything* for that one dream. But that didn't change the fact that they were on a mission, and if they didn't succeed, Mageus would have a lot more to worry about than the Guard.

"We have to find the stones, Esta," he said softly. "We need the necklace, and then we need to find Bill to get the dagger, and then we have the rest of the continent to cross for the crown, and we can't do that if we're in jail or *dead*." He paused, gathering himself, pushing away the power that was poking at his weaknesses. Esta's eyes were still blazing at him, but he went on. "If we don't get the stones, Nibsy wins. Jack wins. I wanted to help those kids, but doing that would have put a great big target on our backs. You want to help those kids and countless others like them? We have to *win*. We have to find the stones and get the Book back." *I'm running out of time. And so are you.*

The thought came to him so clearly that he knew it was true.

Esta frowned at him, but some of the heat in her expression drained. "I hate them," she told him, her voice hollow. "I hate the Guard and I hate the Society—all of them."

"So do I," Harte said, meaning every word. "So let's not just beat up a few Guardsmen here and there. Let's bring them to their knees. We steal the necklace, we humiliate them, and then we move on and do it again until we have what we need. Until we can go back before any of this happened—before the Act, before the Guard—and stop it. *That's* how we're going to save those boys."

She let out a heavy breath and scrubbed her hand over her mouth. It was an utterly guileless gesture, and one that made her look every bit the man she was dressed as. "You're probably right," she said. "But that doesn't change how angry with you I am right now."

"Be as angry as you want," he said. "As long as you're angry here, and not in some jail."

"There isn't a jail that can hold me," she told him, cutting her eyes in his direction.

"I don't know. . . . Those bars on the Nile exhibit might do the trick."

Her expression faltered at the mention of them. "Speaking of the Nile, you want to tell me what happened on that boat?" she asked.

He took a breath. "I don't know," he said. "I was there, and then I wasn't."

"You were talking about Thoth like you knew him," she said, a question in her eyes. "You called him a liar."

Vaguely he remembered saying those words, but they felt like they were someone else's memories, someone else's words. "I think it's whatever—or whoever—was trapped in the Book. Every day it gets stronger. Every day it gains a little more control." *And being around you is making it worse.*

"Well, whatever it is, it sure doesn't like Thoth," she said, looking away from him.

"It's old," he told her, not sure where the words came from. "I get this sense that it's been waiting a very long time to be freed. . . . It's not going to wait much longer."

Esta glanced up at him, and for a moment the anger in her eyes was replaced by worry. "Well, it's gonna have to," she told him. "We're close. The necklace is right there." She pointed toward the Pike. "And opium or the Guard or whatever, that building isn't Khafre Hall. We can do this." She paused, thoughtful. "What if we used a parade as a distraction?"

A couple passed close by, the man eyeing the two of them with a serious frown. "Maybe, but let's not talk about it here," he said. "We don't know who might be listening."

"Fine," she said. "What do you want to do, then?"

"We need to waste a little time, but standing around like this is drawing attention. You want to go in there and see what's inside?" he asked, pointing to a nearby building. "It might be cooler, since we'll be out of the sun."

The building turned out to be the Palace of Transportation. The enormous hall was filled with all manner of machinery—sleek steam engines and automobiles that gleamed under the electric lights. As they walked through, pretending to be tourists until they could safely leave, Esta had a far-off, almost sad look in her eyes.

"Someday, everyone will have one of these," she told him as she ran her finger along the curved metal of an automobile. "No one really stays in one place unless they have to. You could get onto an airplane and fly anywhere you want. . . ."

"*Fly?*" It seemed impossible. "Like in an airship?"

She shook her head. "Faster. And higher. You can be across the country in a handful of hours." Her expression faltered. "Or some people can." She glanced over at him, a spark of hope in her eye. "When we get the stones and the Book—because we *will*—we have to do something with them. We have to figure out what to do about the Brink—fix it or destroy it. There's an entire future coming, and Mageus won't survive by being trapped in the city. Maybe they'd have a chance if things were different. Maybe that's why we ended up here, so we could see what might be. So we could understand that things *can* be changed. That *we* can change them, only this time, we can change them for the better. Even if we can't go back. We can start now."

He couldn't feel an answering hope. Standing in the Palace of Transportation, he was surrounded by machines built for speed, all ways for ordinary people to escape from their lives and travel wherever their hearts desired. They were machines of the future, machines that one day would be. But Harte Darrigan knew that they were not for him. He was a man without a future, and not one of those wondrous machines could move fast enough or go far enough to help him escape from the danger he carried within.

NEVER ENOUGH

1904—St. Louis

N orth had been trying to see past the spectacle of the parade to the Cairo exhibit when everything erupted. As soon as the Jefferson Guard went charging in, he gave up his attempt to follow the Thief and made his exit, working his way through the crowds that were all trying to flee in the same direction. They were Sundren, so they couldn't tell that the eruption was nothing more than smoke set off by some stupid kids trying to play Antistasi.

He didn't exactly blame them for trying. He'd spent his whole childhood hiding the bit of magic that flowed in his veins. His daddy had taught him how to keep it still, so that no one would know. But hiding away their magic hadn't improved their lives any. It certainly hadn't saved his father.

North had been seventeen and already two years on his own when that train derailed in New Jersey and the newspapers began spreading the fear that Mageus were beyond the Brink. Until then, most Sundren thought magic was something that the Brink had dealt with. They went through their ordinary lives not thinking that Mageus could be among them.

Until then, hiding had to be enough for people like him—a quiet life, a quiet death.

It had never really been enough. And sometimes death wasn't quiet or easy.

It had not been enough for his father, who'd withered away because of it. He'd done his best to raise North after his mother had run off, but by

the time he died in the Chicago slaughterhouses where he worked, he'd become a small man, tired and far older than his years. The day North buried his father, he didn't have enough money even for the plainest of tombstones, and there was less than a week left before his landlord would knock on the door, demanding the rent. He could have gone to the same plant where his father had worked and died, and they would have taken him on, tall and strong as he was even then. But he'd decided to go west instead, hoping that in the wide-open spaces of the country, he could find some kind of life for himself.

He'd traveled to the endless sweeping plains and realized that no matter how far he went, no matter how big the sky above him, there wasn't really any way to live free. Not for someone like him.

The first time he'd heard of the Devil's Thief, North was working at a stockyard in Kansas. He'd looked at the picture of the girl staring up from a crumpled piece of newsprint and had felt a spark of hope that had set him off to search for others who were also tired of never having enough. He'd ended up in St. Louis before he finally found the Antistasi, and once he saw Maggie, that was about it for him.

If he'd been a little younger, he probably would have done something just as stupid as those kids. Had his daddy not been around to keep him in line for so long, he probably would have done something that stupid even *without* hearing about the Thief.

He wondered for a second if those kids had fathers who would tan their hides for getting caught up by the Guard, or if they were on their own, like so many kids were these days. North supposed he'd have to take care of them later—get them out of the holding cell the Guard were bound to put them in and either get them back to their parents or find them a safe place to go. But before he worried about those kids, he needed to get to Maggie.

Her building was a monstrosity of a thing, flanked by two enormous towers. Inside, a row of some mechanical contraptions helped to keep tiny infants alive. Ruth hadn't wanted Maggie to bother with working

at the fair. They had plenty of people to do reconnaissance, and Ruth thought she would have been better served to keep working on the serum. But small and delicate as Maggie might look, his girl had a spine of steel when she wanted something. In the end, Maggie had won . . . mostly. North still escorted her to and from work, but she tended to the children and watched for any with an affinity all the while.

North moved along with the crowds until he came to the railing and could catch her attention. She looked up from her work and frowned when she saw him. They didn't need words. From just a look, he understood her point, and he maneuvered his way through the crowd of mostly women to the side hall. A moment later, Maggie was there.

"What is it?" she asked, clearly irritated that he'd interrupted her.

"We might have a problem." He told her about what he'd seen, about the Thief and the other guys she was with. "There's only one thing they could want in there."

"The necklace," she agreed.

North remembered the first time he'd gone through the Cairo exhibit and had seen the necklace. He'd thought the five artifacts were nothing but myth, just as he'd doubted the Thief's existence before he saw her, but there one was, real as anything else. He'd known it wasn't a fake because he'd felt its power. Like the watch he had tucked in his pocket, there was an energy around it—an energy that was eminently compelling. But unlike his watch, the necklace had felt like so much more. He figured that every Sundren in that room felt it, even if they didn't know why they were all enthralled by the display.

There was no way the Society or any of the Brotherhoods could be allowed to have power like that. Ruth had planned to take the necklace in the confusion of the deed, but maybe that couldn't wait. "Everything depends upon us having that necklace when the smoke clears," North said. Without it, there would be little chance of uniting the Antistasi and leading them. Without the necklace and the power it could impart, the deed wouldn't change who was in control—the members of the

Brotherhoods were all rich men, living in a country where money could buy anything at all, especially power. No, the Antistasi needed the necklace so they could stand above the rest with power of their own. "We can't let her get it first."

"No . . ." But Maggie was still frowning, her gaze distant like she was thinking through all the implications of this most recent development. Then she blinked and looked up at him. "Or maybe we just can't let her *keep* it."

INVISIBLE ENERGY
ALL AROUND

1904—St. Louis

T he heat of the day had waned some by the time Jack Grew finally
pulled himself out of bed, popped two more morphine cubes
into his mouth, and made his way to the Exposition. St. Louis
was a dump compared to the grandeur of New York, no matter how
glorious the Society believed their little fair was. They'd never reach the
status of the Order, now that he had transformed it, and their city would
always be a backwater town wishing it were something more.

Still, begrudgingly, he had to admit that the lights were something to
behold. They covered every surface of the fair, reflecting in the enormous
lagoon and shining brightly, late into the night. The crowds had started
to dwindle, and the Streets of Cairo were nearly empty. They were also
nothing more than a second-rate attempt at resurrecting the splendor of
a long-lost civilization. It was nothing compared to what Khafre Hall had
been, or what the Order's new headquarters would be when they were
complete. They didn't even have an authentic obelisk, he thought with
some disdain, not like Manhattan, where one was planted in Central Park
for everyone to see.

But none of that stopped Corwin Spenser and David Francis from
preening about their Society's offering at the fair—a singular stone set
into an exquisite collar of platinum and polished so that it seemed to
gleam from within.

An artifact that had once belonged in the Order's vaults.

Do they know what they have? Jack wondered as he stared at the necklace in the velvet-lined case before him. Could these two men—and the rest of their ridiculous Society—know that the stone was one of the treasures taken from Khafre Hall? Were they gloating because they thought he cared about the Order's power? Or did they truly believe they'd discovered some new object of power? He couldn't be sure.

He didn't actually care. The Order and its business only interested Jack insomuch as he could use them. He had already proven how easily the Inner Circle's leadership could be made inconsequential back at the Conclave nearly two years ago. Impotent old men, all of them.

What Spenser and Francis didn't realize while they boasted about the Society's power was that the Order was simply a means to an end, a convenient tool for gaining Jack access to the right people and the right places. Places like this chamber, which had been closed for the night to the public but which Jack now had free access to, without the worry of being watched.

"Where did you say you found this piece?" he asked, keeping his voice casual and easy.

"Oh, we couldn't reveal our contacts," Spenser said, sheer satisfaction on his face.

"With the number of people coming through, it must be difficult making sure that you secure a treasure like this," Jack mused. "Quite the feat, really."

They took the bait. "Not difficult at all," Francis boasted. "This chamber is fitted with the most modern security conveniences around. The walls are two feet of steel-reinforced concrete, impervious to bombs or bullets, and should anyone try to disturb the case, the doors seal over with vaults thicker than the bank downtown."

Inconvenient, but not impossible.

"We've also protected against any . . . less desirable elements," Francis added, his chest puffed out. "The ventilation system in this chamber is equipped with a machine that distributes a low level of suppressant for anyone who might think to use illegal powers to access it. Any disturbance and it increases the dosage tenfold, incapacitating the miscreant before they can cause any trouble."

"And the Antistasi?" Jack asked. "I hear your city has had trouble controlling that element of late."

Spenser bristled at that. "The Antistasi are not a threat to this city. The Society and their Guard have dealt with that problem, and should any other troubles arise, they too will be dealt with, swiftly and judiciously."

"Perhaps, but you failed to deal with the Devil's Thief, did you not?" Jack asked, keeping his tone mild and enjoying the way their faces flushed in consternation.

"We have it under control," Francis insisted.

"Do you?" Jack asked. "Because she *will* come for this piece, gentlemen. You must know that?" He paused, letting his implication sink in. "But you must have everything in hand, because it would be quite the embarrassment to have her take it from you before the ball, especially after all you've promised. I know my brothers at the Order are well familiar with the sting of *that* particular humiliation," he said, clearly implying that they'd enjoy witnessing the same thing happening to others. "And they're eager to see if the necklace is all that you've promised."

Spenser looked uneasy. "I'm sure you'll be able to tell them that it is," he said.

"Of course," Jack said. "Most definitely. Congratulations, gentlemen." He offered his hand to Spenser first. "You've outdone even the Order, I think."

Spenser still looked somewhat uneasy as he took Jack's hand. *Perfect.* Let them worry. It would keep the necklace safe from Darrigan and the girl until Jack could get his hands on it.

Across the room, Hendricks—the Guardsman from the hotel—was watching the group. Jack said his good-byes and motioned for Hendricks to follow him as he headed for the exit.

Outside, the Pike was as overcrowded as it was gauche. Jack led Hendricks away from the scene until they came to the building that housed displays of electricity. Inside the templelike structure, the De Forest Wireless Telegraphy Tower was sending messages through the air to Chicago and back. From what he understood, a similar technology combined with the hermetical arts was responsible for the Jefferson Guard's ability to communicate so effectively and efficiently. According to Hendricks, the Guardsmen each wore a small medallion that could be activated to alert the others when a danger was spotted. It was, he reluctantly admitted, ingenious.

It was also a development that had captured Jack's attention, since it wasn't all that long ago that he himself had been interested in building his own machine. He'd nearly forgotten about how close he'd been those years ago, but this exhibit made him want to revisit the idea. The Book, after all, held answers he could only imagine, and a secret within its pages that might make his machine finally possible.

"Is there something you needed, sir?" Hendricks said. If he had any concerns about their excursion, he didn't show it.

"I want to know where the Society found the piece they've displayed in the Streets of Cairo," he said. "The necklace that everyone comes to gawk at."

Hendricks' brows went up, a question in his eyes.

"I'm hoping they might help me find another," Jack said easily. "I'm a bit of a collector myself." He slipped the Guardsman a large bill.

"I'm sure I could look into it," Hendricks said, tucking the bill into his dark-coated uniform.

"There's much more where that came from if you do. I want to know everything about the necklace—where they store it, when it will be moved, *everything*. I need a good man to help me, Hendricks. I'm hoping that good man will be you."

"Of course, sir," Hendricks said, his eyes shining with avarice. "Happy to be of service."

"Excellent, Hendricks," Jack said, thumping him roughly on the back and leaving him there, with invisible energy all around.

THE VEILED PROPHET

1904—St. Louis

Julien Eltinge was trying to catch his breath from the exertion of his final number as he walked to his dressing room, his heart still pounding from the excitement of the ovation he'd just received. It had almost been enough to erase the stress of earlier that day. When Darrigan and Esta had announced their plans to steal the necklace, Julien had seen his future crumbling. All his work, all his careful plans, destroyed on a whim. As though anyone could steal something from a place like the Exposition or from an organization as powerful as the Society. But his performance had recentered him, and the roar of the applause had eased the tension that had been building behind his eyes and the worry he'd been carrying in his limbs, just as it always did.

He still remembered the first time he'd understood what applause meant to him. Not the sound of it or even the way people looked standing and cheering, but the way it *felt*. How it had hit some essential part of him, deep down in the very marrow of who he was. That first round of applause had broken open something in him, and it had sent him on a chase to find more. For a long time, he chased it high and low, as eager and determined as a terrier after a rat. Now he knew better. Now he let the applause come to him.

All that he'd worked for, the success he'd dreamed of for so long, was almost within his reach. Every night he took the stage, the applause was louder. Every night, more and more people came to see his act, his *artistry*. And they understood.

His parents had scoffed at him when he'd tried to explain it, but they hadn't stopped him when he'd gotten on the train, his dreams packed in his suitcase next to the costumes he'd made for his act. They probably thought he would fail so miserably that he would be forced to crawl back to them and admit they were right.

He had vowed that would never happen, and he'd kept that vow. He'd fought tooth and nail—and often with his fists—but in the end, he'd won. St. Louis wasn't New York, but he was a star here, and that star was rising, and rising fast. Why, just that night he'd caught sight of Mr. Albee in the box to the left of the stage. It was a good sign that he'd come all this way to take in Julien's act. He was one of the most powerful vaudeville promoters around, and Julien had a feeling he'd come to make good on his promise.

An entire show of his own—a musical revue starring him, Julien Eltinge—in one of the biggest and most luxurious houses on Broadway. That could still come to pass, he told himself. Darrigan would keep his promise and retrieve that damned necklace before anyone realized Julien's connection to it. Things would work out. He and his career would be *fine*.

Julien closed the dressing room door soundly behind him and took the wig from his head, relishing the coolness of the air as it hit his sweat-damp hair and the solitude. Carefully, he arranged the curls on the dummy, making sure not to rumple any of them—it was more of a pain to fix them later than to take the time now. Then he grabbed his customary cigar from the dressing table and lit it, letting the richness of the tobacco coat his mouth and fill his senses. A reward for a job well done, as always.

In the mirror, the sight of the thick cigar held between his painted lips made him chuckle to himself. With her dark lashes and brightly painted lips, her blushing cheeks and the way he'd used makeup to sculpt her features into something more delicate, a woman looked back at him. It was the transformation—not the femininity—that gratified him, not the corset that was currently cutting into his rib cage or the gowns with their heavy beading and ruffles that scratched at his skin or even the way women would cut their eyes in his direction, their jealousy proof of his success. No. It was the performance itself. It was the artistry of making one thing into something else entirely. The impossible magic of it.

A sharp knock came at his dressing room door, and Julien called to see who it was.

"You got visitors," Sal said, poking his head into the dressing room.

After the day he'd had, Julien simply wasn't in the mood. "Tell them I'm not available."

The stage manager shook his head. "Not these visitors,"

"Then tell them I've already gone," Julien said, turning back to his reflection in the mirror.

"I'm afraid it's too late for that," a voice behind Sal said.

In the mirror, Julien watched as the door opened wider to reveal a tall figure, its face shielded by a white veil of lace. The stage manager gave Julien a half shrug and moved out of the way to allow the Veiled Prophet to enter the dressing room. The figure closed the door behind him, and the sound of the latch engaging was as loud and resolute as a gunshot.

"Mr. Eltinge," the figure said.

"Mr. . . ." Julien trailed off, unsure of how to address the man who was taking up all the air in what had been a sanctuary moments before. He was suddenly aware of his in-between state. Without his wig, he wasn't completely one version of himself or another, and without either role to fall back on, he was at a loss.

The night that the Veiled Prophet had come to demand the necklace, he'd made it clear that the Society had kept careful tabs on Julien from the moment he'd arrived in town. They'd believed his act to be a danger at first, a corruption of the true values of the esteemed people of the city. They didn't need any of the tawdriness of the East, and if he mis-stepped, if he thought to bring any depravity to their town, they would act. They would end his career.

He knew then that they hadn't understood the first thing about him, and because of that, Julien had given in to their demands. He'd sold them the necklace for a song and everything had been fine—at least until Harte Darrigan and the girl had shown up and dragged him into this mess.

The Veiled Prophet, whoever it was behind the screen of lace, didn't bother to answer. "We have a proposition for you, Mr. Eltinge."

"A proposition?" Julien said, hating the way his voice cracked.

They can't know. . . .

"A job," the figure said. "One that would make good use of your talents."

Julien didn't miss the scorn in the Prophet's voice, but he wasn't a clown to be paraded out and made fun of. "And if I'm too busy for any extra employment at the moment?" he asked, taking another puff of the cigar, just to prove he couldn't be bullied.

The figure inclined its head, making the heavy lace in front of his face wave. "You know how far our influence reaches, Mr. Eltinge. We saw that Mr. Albee was at the theater this evening. He is a *particular* friend of ours."

Julien's stomach clenched. They could destroy all that he'd worked for if they had the ear of Mr. Albee. His show, his dreams, his future—all gone. "I suppose I could make a little time to hear you out," he said. "I've got a busy schedule with the show. Tomorrow evening, maybe? We're dark then."

"Tonight, Mr. Eltinge. Now, in fact."

"Now?" he asked, looking down at the gown he was still wearing.

"We'll give you time to make yourself more . . . presentable." His tone rang with distaste. "Our carriage will be waiting," the Prophet said before he took his leave.

Julien had a very bad feeling about this whole situation. He looked at himself in the mirror, but it was Darrigan and the girl he cursed. If the necklace was so dangerous, Harte should never have sent it to him in the first place. At the very least, Darrigan should have had the courtesy to stay dead.

PART

IV

THE MEMORY OF HER NAME

1904—St. Louis

The late-June day was warm, and the sky was a bright, clear blue. All around Esta, the pristine white buildings of the fair were a marked contrast to the dirt and grime of the rest of the city. The couples who walked arm in arm and the families who held tightly to the small hands of their children could not have imagined that the well-dressed gentleman waiting at the water's edge was actually a woman, or that she was about to commit a crime.

There was something about the moments before a job began that made Esta's skin tingle—not with dread or apprehension, but anticipation and the sheer satisfaction of doing what she was born to do. Maybe it was just adrenaline, but Esta always felt like it had to be more than some random chemical reaction that made her body feel like it was singing, that made her mind feel clear and ready. It had to be a sign—a good omen of sorts. There had been very few moments in her life when everything felt completely right—when the pieces fell into their places—and most of them had been in the moments before a job. As she waited next to the railing near the large lagoon that anchored the Exposition, Esta was fairly certain that *this* was another of those times.

Maybe nighttime would have been a more expected choice, but after a few days of planning and after the information Julien had given them, she and Harte had decided that it would be easier to lift the necklace during the day rather than waiting until the fair closed. For one, they could use the crowds to their advantage, but more important, they knew what the Exposition was like during its open hours. They'd spent the last few days walking the grounds and pretending to be tourists as they cased the areas around the Streets of Cairo and the Pike. They knew how many Guardsmen were stationed there and when their shifts changed.

On the other hand, night was a black box. They didn't know what kind of security there might be or even how the necklace was housed at night. But during the day? The fine folks who ran the fair were even kind enough to draw them up a schedule so they knew when everything was happening—and what the best times were to create distractions.

According to the schedule, there were always at least two parades—one at midday and one later in the evening. They'd considered using the evening parade, since the darkness could give them some cover, but in the end they had decided that the safest and easiest plan required exposure.

Esta saw Harte approaching before he noticed her, and she allowed herself to take a moment to watch him as he walked through the crowd. In the last few days, they'd settled into a steady, if not completely comfortable, equilibrium. It was as though, without uttering a word, they'd come to the agreement that they wouldn't speak about the night they'd arrived—the kiss or the argument. It didn't mean that she felt any less hurt, but after what had happened during the boat ride, she didn't press. He would tell her everything eventually or he wouldn't—she couldn't force him to trust her or to see her as someone to depend on any more than she could stop the way her heart clenched a little each time she saw him—each time she remembered what it had felt like to have his lips against hers.

He was dressed in trim, olive-green pants paired with a matching waistcoat and lighter-colored jacket. With the straw boater shading his face and the easy way his arms swung relaxed at his sides, he looked fresh and crisp, like the portrait of a summer day. She knew the moment he saw her waiting—his mouth flattened and his eyes went tight, like he was preparing himself for something. But then his expression relaxed, and it was as though the tightness from a moment before had never existed.

As he approached, she had the oddest vision of his face lighting with a smile and him offering her the crook of his arm. She could almost see them, walking arm in arm, taking in the sights and sounds like anyone else. For a moment she wished they could let go of everything hanging over them and make that vision come to life. For a moment she wished that they could forget what they were about to do and pretend that they were just two people enjoying a sunny day at the fair.

But wishes were for suckers, and Esta didn't plan on being one of those, not ever again. Especially not when it came to Harte Darrigan.

"I don't think I'll ever get over this place," Harte said, pausing long enough to look at the water. The lagoon itself extended into the heart of the fair, and at the far end stood a pristinely white domed building—the Festival Hall. It glimmered with lights, even at noon. All along the tree-lined edges of the water, fountains sent cascading arcs of water into the air, while the cool white marble statuary stood as silent guards.

"The world isn't really like this," she said, her mood suddenly darker. She leaned against the railing and pretended to take in the scenery, but her attention was elsewhere. The stone beneath her hand looked like carved marble, but it was just painted concrete. *Fake, just like everything else in this place.* "Half these buildings are just shells. They'll come down in a few months, and it'll be like none of this had ever been here."

"I know . . ." His voice was wistful, and she glanced over to see him watching the gondolas gliding across the smooth, clear surface of the water. "Still. They put on a damn good show."

He wasn't wrong. The fairground itself was a marvel, even to Esta's jaded eyes. The buildings flanking the wide lagoon looked like they were made from marble and granite. They reminded Esta of buildings she'd seen in pictures of the great cities of Europe. But even with all the grandeur of the Exposition, compared to New York, St. Louis itself looked half-formed. Outside the walls of the fairground, the city was still a city on the edge of the frontier and worlds away from the crowded streets of New York. Beyond the city, the world waited.

"Did you take care of it?" he asked.

"Of course," she told him, pretending to look at the scenery while she made sure that no one was watching them. It hadn't been very difficult to pick the lock on one of the maintenance gates not far from the Pike. She'd left it closed, so it looked secure, but it would provide them an easy exit once everything happened. "You?"

He nodded. "No one was watching the armory. I replaced all the bullets I could find, but I'm not sure if it'll be enough."

"It'll have to be," she told him. "This will work." *It has to.*

But it wouldn't be easy.

The trickiest part about the entire job wasn't that it would happen in the bright light of day or in the midst of a crowded midway. It wasn't even that it was just the two of them. Julien wouldn't be there—they'd picked a day with a matinee show to ensure that he had an airtight alibi. He'd done what he could to help them, and now they would do what they could to keep him out of the rest. No, the trickiest part was that they would have to do almost everything without magic. With the Jefferson Guard on high alert, they couldn't chance using either one of their affinities—not unless they absolutely had to. They'd have to go in straight and use sheer skill. And, thanks to both Harte and Julien, a bit of showmanship.

"The parade starts in about fifteen minutes. We need to both be in Cairo by that time. You'll have to move fast. You have the charges?"

"I've got it, Harte," she said, annoyed with how quickly he'd shifted from enjoying the day to fussing at her. It reminded her a little of the way Logan used to, and suddenly she couldn't help but wonder what had happened to him. Had Jianyu found him? Or had Logan been able to reach Nibsy? But there would be time to consider that later. For now, she had to focus.

Theirs wasn't an elegant plan, but it was workable. They had smoke charges that they'd placed on fuses at various places along the Pike, and she would set them off right before she and Harte went into the Nile ride—just before the parade arrived at the area in front of the Streets of Cairo.

There was only one way in and out of the chamber where the necklace was displayed, and if they'd timed the fuses right, the charges should go off, flooding the Pike with strange-colored smoke that would, hopefully, be taken as an Antistasi attack. They were betting on the Guard rushing to the area and leaving the stone less guarded than it otherwise might have been.

If the schedule was accurate—and so far, it had been—before the smoke completely dissipated and the crowd realized there was no danger, the veterans of the Boer War, who reenacted their skirmishes twice a day, would be starting their first assault. Since Harte had replaced the blanks they usually used with more smoke charges, all hell should break loose again as soon as they fired their first volley of shots.

Between the people flooding out of the Boer War demonstration and the confusion on the Pike, the Guard should be nicely tied up. She and Harte should be able to slip the necklace out of its case and be on their way.

"If anything is off by even a few minutes, we could be stuck," Harte reminded her as he checked the pocket watches they each had to make sure the times were the same.

"I *know*." She was itching to get started. "We've gone over this a million times."

She snatched one of the watches from his hand as a family came up to the railing to look at the water. The parents were young—about the same age that Dolph had been. The father had by the hand a small golden-haired boy who looked like his miniature. When the boy started to cry, the father lifted him up gently so the boy could see the fountains just beyond the railing, while the mother fussed with the little boy's hair.

Esta didn't even realize she was watching them until Harte cleared his throat next to her, drawing her attention back to him.

"You need to focus." His voice was gentle, but the reprimand stung nonetheless.

"I *am* focused," she said, trying to ignore the way the little boy squealed in delight at the view of the water.

"You know that everything has to go perfectly for this to work, and we aren't even in control of most of the pieces. It isn't going to be easy."

"It never is." She glanced one last time at the family.

Maybe it was the brightness of the day or the sweetness of the vanilla and caramel wafting through the air, but as she watched the family go about their day—their lives—without a care in the world, Esta's hands curled into fists. She let her nails dig into her palms, accepting the flash of pain so that she could hold back the spike of anger that had caused her blood to go hot. *They have everything, and they have no idea.* And she would fight and scrabble and scheme . . . and in the end, she would get nothing at all. *And no one would even know.*

Or maybe they would, she thought with a spark of hope. Maybe these Antistasi, whoever they were, would keep the memory of her name and what she had done—or tried to do—alive, just as they had for the past two years.

"Hey, Slim." Harte's voice came to her from a distance. "Did you hear what I said? Are you okay there?"

"Yeah." She blinked, confused for a moment by the direction of her thoughts. "I'm fine."

It was the truth.

Who cared if she couldn't have everything? Who cared if the man who had been a father to her was a lie and her actual father was lost to her before she ever knew? Whatever pain lay in her past could just stay there. Her past had given her skills and talents she might not have otherwise had, and whatever the lies that had forged her, they didn't determine her future. She would be what she had chosen to become. And if she didn't make it through? Perhaps she would live on in some other way.

She straightened her spine and gave Harte the cockiest smile she could dredge up. "Let's go steal us the fair."

ON THE EDGE OF THE WEST

1904—St. Louis

Harte would have paid almost any price to be able to reach across the distance between them, pull Esta close, and kiss the smile off her face. But he didn't trust himself—or the power inside of him—to be able to stop. Instead, he stood with his hands tucked into his pockets so he wouldn't do any of the idiotic things running through his head.

As quickly as she gave him the smile, Esta was turning away, heading toward the Pike to set their plan in motion. His gaze followed her trim silhouette until she disappeared into the crowd. Inside his mind, the voice shifted and rumbled, clearly frustrated with his decision to let her walk away from him—again. He was getting fairly good at ignoring it, probably in the same way a person learns to ignore a chronic cough or a bad knee. You simply lived around it. But he couldn't ignore the fact that the power was getting stronger and the voice that spoke through it was getting clearer every day.

Still, despite the warmth of the afternoon, ice inched down his spine. A premonition. Or perhaps it was simply rational, levelheaded fear. They were about to steal a well-guarded necklace from the middle of a crowded fair in broad daylight.

This is never going to work.

Too bad that it had to. Julien's best chance of evading the Order's notice was for them to get the Djinni's Star and get out of town fast.

Harte pulled his cap down and checked his watch for the umpteenth time before he started walking. He didn't go in the direction of the Pike, as Esta had. Instead, he followed the waterways east, past the ornate palace-like buildings that held the exhibitions on electricity and industry, and then farther, past the Palace of Transportation, with its six identical sculptures bearing shields to guard the high arched entrance.

Everything is a palace, he thought. Even here, on the edge of the West, where the whole country was possible, Americans still wanted to be royalty. It was why people like Jack Grew and the rest of the Order could do what they did—the ordinary person allowed it. The average citizen liked the idea of a future where they might be as rich as a king or as powerful as an emperor. They might have talked about democracy, but what they wanted was the spectacle of royalty.

He continued past the building and entered the Pike close to Cairo, checking his watch again as he found a place near the Cliff Dwellers exhibition. *Perfect.* Already, he could hear the noise of the parade approaching.

But there was no sign of Esta.

A NEW ERA IN THE BOWERY

J ames Lorcan would have paid handsomely to have just one answer to any of his questions. There were too many variables at play, too much at risk. It had been five days since Mock Duck had brought Jianyu to the Strega and traded him for a handful of dollars and a notebook of secrets he could use against Tom Lee. Five days since James had had Jianyu in his hands, and five days since the damnable turncoat had somehow managed to escape.

At least the fire had been minor, and Paul Kelly's connections with Tammany meant that the brigades did more than just watch the building burn. Because of their help, James was able to sit at the back of the barroom and survey his domain.

At least Viola was taken care of. The image of Dolph's favorite assassin, bruised and bleeding from her brother's fists, still served to comfort— and amuse—him. As far as James was concerned, it proved that Dolph had always thought too highly of her. Viola had always been moody and temperamental—a liability. She'd never liked James, that much he knew. From the look of pure hate in her eyes the other day, she still didn't, but at least she wouldn't be a problem. She'd overplayed her hand when she'd gone back to her brother's protection, and all evidence so far indicated that Kelly would be able to control her. That much, at least, was a comfort. It made for one less thing to worry about.

The future was still too unsettled for his liking, though. James could not make heads or tails of the variables that seemed to waver in the

Aether, the paths rising up and then disappearing like ghosts. But he knew one thing for sure. Something was coming. Something that promised to change *everything*.

At the front of the Strega, the door opened, letting in a burst of cool air that James could feel even from the back of the room. It seemed that his thoughts of Paul Kelly had summoned the devil himself. All at once the atmosphere in the barroom changed as the people realized that the notorious leader of the Five Pointers had just arrived.

A few weeks ago Kelly's appearance there in the saloon that Dolph Saunders had ruled his empire from would have been unheard of. Before Dolph's death Kelly never would have dared to confront the Devil's Own on their own turf. But this was a new city, a new world. And all James could think was *Finally*.

Kelly was followed by two of his Five Pointers, broad men with the same ruthless expression that Kelly himself wore. Between them, they held a towheaded fellow James didn't recognize. The unlucky captive looked to be slightly older than James, but he had a softness to his features that almost made him seem younger. His left eye had been blackened and was already swollen shut, no doubt the effect of tangling with Kelly's men.

Sensing trouble, the patrons in the barroom murmured uneasily as Kelly and his men stopped just inside the doorway and surveyed the saloon. Most kept their eyes down, studying their cups as though the liquid within them might burst into flames at any moment. A few drained their glasses and left, giving Kelly and his men a wide berth as they departed.

Seemingly pleased with the reaction his entrance had caused, Paul Kelly made his way through the unusually quiet room. As he approached, James rubbed his thumb along the silver topper of his cane—a gorgon head with the face of an angel. *Leena's face.* The silver snakes that coiled beneath his thumb felt unnaturally cool, a reminder that whatever strength the Five Pointers might have in the streets, James and those he now controlled had power that Paul Kelly could only dream of.

But the coolness was also a reminder of how much was at stake. There was power locked within the silver gorgon head—the part of her affinity that Dolph had taken from Leena and used to ensure his control over the Devil's Own. But that power was useless to James, who didn't have the affinity to reach it . . . not until he had the Book to unlock it.

Kelly was nearly across the barroom, and James was still sitting. He refused to be seen as weak—not there on his turf and in front of his own people—so, ignoring the pain in his wounded leg, he stood up and steadied himself with the cane.

Sundren as he was, Paul Kelly could not have felt the way the magic in the room flared as he walked through the saloon. The air filled with the nervous warmth of affinities on the verge of becoming, as each Mageus present watched, wary and ready, for whatever would happen. To James Lorcan, it felt in that moment as though the whole world was no bigger than that particular smoky barroom and the people within it, each of them holding their breath and waiting.

"Paul," James said, greeting Kelly like they were old friends. "What brings you to the Strega tonight?" He glanced beyond Paul Kelly to the boy the Five Pointers was holding. "Or maybe I should ask what you've brought me?"

Kelly smirked. "My guys picked him up down on Broome Street. He's got a pretty enough face," he said, giving the blond a couple of sharp smacks on the cheek that had the boy wincing. "But not too many brains. He demanded I bring him to you."

"Did he?" James asked, ignoring the unsettled energy that permeated the barroom as he examined the blond.

"He did," Kelly said. "Which causes a problem for me. We need to get something clear, Lorcan—whatever mutually beneficial understanding we might have between us, I don't take orders from you or yours. Got it?"

"He's not one of mine," James said, turning his attention back to Kelly and assessing the danger in the air.

"He says otherwise."

The blond was breathing heavily, as though he were in pain, and staring at James from his one good eye. James ignored his face and focused on the Aether around him. It was hazy, indistinct, but it didn't seem to indicate that the stranger posed any threat. If anything, the way it was already fusing with the set patterns was a positive sign. He stepped toward the trio, the tap of his cane punctuating the uneasy silence in the bar.

"Who are you?" James asked the blond when they were face-to-face. There was definitely something to the boy—the warmth of magic hung around him, clear to anyone who shared it.

"Logan," the boy told him, never once flinching under James' steady stare. "Logan Sullivan."

"Who sent you, Logan Sullivan?" James asked.

The guy's expression never flickered. The Aether around him never wavered. "You did."

"*I* did?" James said, studying the stranger for some sign of deception.

"That's what he kept telling my guys," Kelly said.

"He's lying," James told Kelly as he continued to eye this new entity. "I don't know any Logan Sullivan, and I certainly don't know him."

"You do, and I can prove it," the boy said.

James got the sense this Logan Sullivan, whoever he was, wasn't lying. At least *he* didn't believe he was lying. Which wasn't going to help James' position with Kelly. He had to neutralize this danger quickly, before everything he'd so carefully positioned started to fall apart.

"I'm not interested in listening to your lies," James said, starting to turn away.

"Maybe you'd be interested in the Delphi's Tear," Logan said. "It's here, you know. In the city . . ."

James turned back to Logan. "What are you talking about?"

"You know exactly what I'm talking about," Logan told him, his expression never wavering. "You want the ring? I can find it for you. It's not far from here, but it's moving even as we speak."

"What's this?" Kelly asked, his voice dark and suspicious.

It was a delicate thing, to lead Kelly on without giving him too much. Information was power, and knowledge was the noose that could be slipped around a neck. But James didn't hesitate in his answer.

"It's one of the jewels I told you about—the ones that Darrigan and the girl made off with."

"The ones I sent my guys after?" Kelly narrowed his eyes in suspicion. "You'd better not have sent me on a chase, Lorcan."

"I didn't," James said, ignoring the threat. "Darrigan and the girl are out there, and when you find them and the things they stole, the Order will reward you handsomely."

Or they would if I wasn't planning on taking them first.

James considered Logan. "Where's this proof you claim to have?"

"Left inside jacket pocket," Logan told him.

Again James was struck by the stranger's steadiness, but he didn't read any danger here . . . quite the opposite.

James approached Logan again. "If I may?" The Five Pointers looked to Kelly, who gave them a subtle nod, and then James reached into Logan's jacket and fished out a small, paper-wrapped package. "What is it?" he asked.

"Open it," Logan said, his gaze calm and sure.

Too sure.

James tucked the cane under his arm and made quick work of the wrapping. His eyes told him what he was holding before his brain could accept it. "Where did you get this?" he asked.

"Like I said, you gave it to me."

It wasn't possible. The small notebook he was holding in his hand was instantly recognizable. After all, he had an identical one in his own jacket pocket.

"I didn't give you any—" His words were lost as he flipped through the book to find his own cramped, familiar handwriting on its pages. He stopped and went back to the beginning. . . . It was *definitely* his notes.

And his own notebook was *definitely* still in his pocket. Even now he felt the comforting weight of it.

Flipping forward, James stopped at the page he'd written earlier that morning. But *this* notebook continued on, still all in his own hand.

"What is it?" Kelly asked, clearly impatient to know what James saw in the notebook.

"It's nothing," James said, closing the notebook. "He's lying. This doesn't tell me anything at all."

Kelly frowned at James as though considering whether to believe him. Finally, he seemed to relent. "What should we do with him, then? I can have my guys take care of it if you want."

"Leave him to me," James told him.

"You?" Kelly seemed surprised, and more than a little disappointed.

"He's dragging my name through the mud. I think I should be the one to deal with him," James told him. Kelly wouldn't have respected him otherwise. "He won't bother you or yours again."

Kelly studied James for a long moment, and the unease permeating the room around them seemed to swell in the silence. But then he gave his two men another nod, and they dropped the boy, who crumpled to his knees, clearly injured.

"Mooch," James said. "Would you escort our guest to the cellar? Tie him up and make sure he's quiet until I get there. With force, if need be."

"No—" Logan tried to scramble to his feet, but Mooch and one of the other boys were on him before he could get far. With his soft features, he didn't stand much of a chance.

James waited until they were gone before he gestured to the table he'd been sitting at a few minutes before. "Have a drink with me? I owe you for bringing that bit of trouble to my attention."

Kelly studied him for another long moment before agreeing. "What could it hurt?" he said with a shrug. "Let's see what kind of swill Saunders stocked this place with."

"Better than you might imagine," he told Kelly, well aware of the nervous energy around them as he thumped the other man on the back.

James knew that every person in that barroom feared Kelly and the damage his Five Pointers could do. Even Dolph hadn't been able to protect them from the Five Pointers' viciousness in those final days.

Let them see, James thought. *Let them all see and understand exactly who I am and what influence I have.*

He poured two fingers of the house's best whiskey for each of them and raised his glass in a salute. Kelly watched him toss back the liquid before drinking his own.

"So," James said as he poured another glass for each of them. "How is your delightful sister these days . . . still raising hell?"

Kelly smirked. "Viola?" He laughed softly into his glass. "She doesn't raise anything unless I tell her to."

Perfect, James thought. *Exactly what I wanted to hear.*

A LAND SOAKED IN BLOOD

1902—New York

Barefoot and wearing nightclothes that were too large for him, Jianyu took a moment to test his balance while he had the bedpost to hold on to. The movement still made his vision waver, like he was looking through a fog, but he took a deep breath and forced himself to stay upright. It had been too long. *Far too long.*

By now, certainly, the boy Esta had warned him about would have arrived. By now the boy would have made contact with Nibsy. Which meant that he'd failed. *Again.*

He was not completely sure where he was, and he could not be sure how long he had been there. The times he had woken, he found that he could barely hold on to consciousness before the ground fell out from beneath him and he drifted back into the heavy darkness. But finally he had managed to claw free. The sun was slanting in through the thin curtains covering the single window in the room, and the air was warm and heavy with the smell of something laden with spices that were unfamiliar to his nose. But then he realized that he could pick out the sweetness of clove and the pungency of garlic, scents that reminded him of a home he would not see again.

Spurred on by that thought, he forced himself to take a step, pausing to make sure that the earth remained steady beneath him, unlike a day— or was it two?—before. Then, his desperation to find the boy Esta had warned him about had been so urgent, he had pushed too far and instead collapsed to the floor, jarring his already tender head again.

He took slow, tentative steps at first, testing himself, and when he was satisfied that his legs were steady, he followed the sound of voices through the door of the small bedroom and down a short hallway to a narrow living area, where he found three women sitting and stitching piles of men's pants. Cela was one of the three, but where the other two were engrossed in conversation with each other, she was working with her head bowed, concentrating on the task in front of her. She seemed separate from them somehow. Where the other two wore simple dark skirts and faded shirtwaists, Cela was wearing a gown the same shade of pink as a tea flower. It was a simple day dress, like any might wear, but again he was struck by the cut of it, the sharp tailoring that made it seem like something more. Her nimble fingers finished the cuff of one leg and moved on to the next, but her expression seemed far away—more sad than thoughtful.

He had spent only a few moments in her workshop at the theater, but that space had been neat and organized, the bolts of fabric stacked in straight lines and the bowls of beads and crystals arranged without even a spangle out of place. But nothing in this room sparkled. There was no silk or satin, and Cela herself looked tired.

The older of the other two glanced up and noticed Jianyu standing there, leaning against the doorway to keep himself upright. She cleared her throat, causing Cela to look up as well.

"You're awake," Cela said, the low tones of her voice making it sound like an accusation. "You shouldn't be up."

She was right, of course. The words were no sooner spoken than Jianyu felt himself swaying, and Cela was on her feet in an instant, helping him to the chair she had just been sitting in.

He thanked her, but along with gratitude, he felt the burn of shame. To be so weak here in front of these women. To be unable to fulfill his promises . . .

"You okay?" Cela asked, settling herself on the floor and taking up the pants she had been working on a moment ago.

He nodded rather than speaking, but the movement of his head caused his newly shorn hair to brush against his cheek, reminding him of all that had happened.

The older woman was watching him as she stitched, while the other one, a woman just a few years older than Cela, kept sliding glances his way as well. But it was the older woman who was the first to speak. "So, Mr. Jianyu . . . how long will you be staying with us, now that you're up?"

"Auntie—" Cela said, a note of warning in her voice. But the words that came next, Jianyu could not follow. They seemed to be in English, or some of them did, but Jianyu had trouble making sense of them. His head, perhaps . . .

But Cela's aunt seemed to understand. She answered back using the same unfamiliar tongue. The two women spoke for a minute, trading words, and Jianyu did not need to know the language they were speaking to discern their meaning, especially when the older woman's eyes kept cutting to Jianyu as the two spoke. After a moment, the older woman put down her sewing and motioned for the other to come with her, leaving Jianyu and Cela alone in the suddenly quiet apartment.

Cela made a few more stitches, but then her hands went still and she let out a long breath. Jianyu could see the tears turning her dark eyes glassy, but he had nothing to offer her.

"If I have caused you trouble with your family—"

Cela shook her head and wiped her eyes with the back of her hands. "My auntie is just like that sometimes. My cousin Neola is a bit easier to abide."

"The other girl?" Jianyu asked.

Cela nodded. Then she put aside the sewing she'd been doing. "How are you?"

"Well," he said, feeling that it was not a lie so long as he remained sitting.

"You look better," she told him. "That knock to the head you took was something awful. For a couple of days, I wasn't sure that you'd wake up."

There was something in her voice that sounded broken and brittle, but Jianyu felt he had no right to ask. "Thank you," he told her, his voice stiff. "You did not need to trouble yourself for me."

She gave him a doubtful look. "You're right about that, but seeing as how you got me out of the theater and away from Evelyn, I couldn't just leave you half-dead on the streetcar. And don't worry about my family," she said.

"Your aunt . . . she seemed angry," he told her.

"She usually is, around me," Cela said, waving away his concerns, but at his questioning look, she let out a sigh and began to explain. "My mama's family came from the Windward Islands. They always did think they were better than the people who've lived here for generations— definitely thought they were better than my daddy, who came from down South and whose parents weren't even born free. She's probably happy to see me sitting here stitching pants. They all told me I was a fool for trying to find a job in the white theaters. Said I didn't know my place, and if I just listened to Mr. Washington, I'd know I need to cast down my bucket where I was, not go looking for other oceans." She shrugged. "I always thought they were jealous because they didn't make half as much money as I did. Maybe my mama didn't give me her light skin, but she did give me her skill with a needle and her backbone. . . ." She hesitated, her gaze sliding away. "But maybe they were right all along."

Her words stoked something inside of him, some small ember of frustration he had carried over an ocean. He didn't understand her situation, but he understood the note of disappointment in her voice. "I doubt that," he told her, hoping that it was true for him as well.

"I don't know," she said with another deep sigh. Her eyes were shining again with the wetness of unshed tears. "Maybe I should have just been happy with the lot I'd been given rather than searching out greener fields. I got that from my daddy, though. He was never happy with good enough—and neither am I. But all his wanting cost him his life in the end, and all mine cost me everything I had. My home. My brother." Her voice broke, and she paused for a second as though trying to collect herself. "Now I'm back here, stitching some old pants, just like they said I would be. And the one person who understood me no matter what is gone."

"It seems, then, that I am doubly in your debt," he told her.

She shook her head. "We're even now, as far as I'm concerned."

"Darrigan sent me to protect you and the ring," Jianyu told her. "I have done neither."

"I didn't ask for no protecting," she told him, her expression tight.

"That matters little," Jianyu said. "It was not well done of him to give you the burden of the ring, to put you in such danger without warning you of what might come. But it was I who failed to protect you."

"That stupid ring," Cela said, pulling herself from the floor. "I wish I'd never laid eyes on it, or Harte Darrigan."

"I'm sure there are more than a few people who feel that way about the magician," Jianyu said dryly.

She looked at him, a question in her eyes. "Does that include you?"

He inclined his head. "Most definitely. Although, if I had not known him, I would also not have met you, and it seems to me more than a fair trade to know that someone with your strength and kindness is a part of this world."

She looked away, her cheeks flushing with what could have been embarrassment or pleasure, but at least the sadness in her expression had eased, if only a little. "You know," she said after an almost comfortable moment of silence between them, "I could help you with that hair of yours."

His hands went to the shorn strands that hung around his face. *There cannot be any help for this.*

"I'm pretty good with a pair of shears, and I used to cut my brother, Abel's—" She lifted her fist to her mouth, as though she was trying to keep the pain inside instead of letting it out. After a moment, she spoke again, her voice softer this time. "I used to cut Abel's hair all the time after our mother died. I can't put things back the way they were, but I can clean up the edges for you."

This was an offering he had not expected. It was also a gift he did not deserve, but somehow he could not stop himself from accepting it.

They sat in the small kitchen, a worn towel around Jianyu's shoulders to catch the clippings. At first, Cela was tentative, as though she was afraid even to touch him. But eventually the shyness and reluctance between them dissolved, and her fingers were strong and sure. The scissors whispered their steady tale as she worked.

"So, tell me about this ring," she said, letting her voice trail off, giving him the space to speak.

He told her what he could of the ring and of the rest of the artifacts, and once he started speaking, he found that he could not stop. He had often sat with Dolph in the evenings, speaking of any number of things—news of the city and hopes for the future and even thoughts about power and magic and its role in the world. But in the days before Khafre Hall, Dolph had been too busy plugging leaks on the bursting dam that was the Devil's Own to sit and visit, and after Khafre Hall they had all been alone in their grief—Jianyu, maybe, most of all. He had been so silent for days now that just having Cela's ear felt like a balm.

Cela listened without interrupting, her fingers and the scissors moving steadily over his head.

"So I must find the ring and keep it from those who would do harm with it," he finished.

She was silent for a moment as she worked, snipping at the hair along the nape of his neck. "You know, all this fuss over magic. People are so busy trying to keep it and control it that they're willing to do all sorts of evil for it." Her hands went still, and she stepped back to look him over. "But maybe nobody's meant to have it. Maybe it's just meant to fade away." She tilted her head to the side and then trimmed another piece of his hair.

"If you ask me," she continued, "it's because there's something wrong with this land. The people who were here first—the ones who truly belong here—got killed off or pushed aside, and that does something to a place, all that death and violence. Magic can't take root in blood-soaked earth. If you ask me, maybe it's a good thing. Maybe nobody should have that kind of power over anyone else." She brushed off his shoulders. "Go on. See what you think."

There was a small square mirror hanging on the other side of the room. Jianyu stepped toward it tentatively, in part because he was already unsteady on his feet, and in part because he was afraid to see the person who would greet him in the cloudy glass.

He didn't really look like himself. The hair that he'd once worn pulled back now framed his face. It wasn't his father's son that looked back, but some new version of himself. American and unrecognizable. He felt a thrill of something that might have been fear . . . or maybe it was simple readiness.

Cela was safe. He would find the ring. He had not yet failed, and he would not allow himself to.

THE MAP OF THE WORLD

1902—New York

J ames felt the map of the world shift as he finished reading the final
page in the notebook he'd taken from Logan Sullivan. He wanted to
believe that it was a hoax because the alternative was too impossible. He
wanted it to be a fabrication meant to lead him astray, but his senses told
him that the notebook and all that it held was nothing short of the truth.

He placed the notebook on the worn desk in front of him, next to
its twin.

Taking his glasses from his nose, he polished the lenses and considered
the possibilities. Every victory and every mistake he would ever make
were contained in the book Logan had brought him. With the strength
of his affinity and the knowledge in those notebooks, he could remake
his future. He could rewrite his own history—and more.

But first James had to be sure—*absolutely* sure—of who this Logan
Sullivan was. He'd spoken of the Delphi's Tear, and so James would give
him an opportunity to retrieve it. If Logan proved unable to do what he'd
promised, James doubted it would be much of a loss to dispose of him.

He considered the identical notebooks before finally taking up the
one Logan had brought him and tucking it into his pocket. Until he
knew for sure whether to trust the stranger, he would keep it close. After
all, since it possibly held a record of his life, it wouldn't do for anyone
else to find it. Then he grabbed his jacket and pulled on his cap, locking the door securely behind him as he left, and he went to talk to the
newcomer—the boy who would change his future.

THE PIKE

1904—St. Louis

The Pike was its usual circus of noise and confusion as Esta entered it, prepared to carry out her part of the plan. She had about ten minutes to get from the entrance, next to the huge monstrosity that was the fake Alps, to where she would meet Harte just outside Cairo. He'd take a different path—around the back of the Pike and entering from the east side of the boulevard—so that there was no chance of them being seen together.

In her pocket she had packets of smoking powder rigged with fuses. They were nothing more than some harmless stage props that Harte and Julien had made in preparation for the day, but it would take a while for the people who saw the smoke to realize that.

She passed the concessions for Asia and Japan and continued toward the enormous domed building that was the Creation attraction. Like the Nile boats in Cairo, it was also a ride. Like everything else, it was brash and too bright and overdone. She stopped near a vendor selling huge salted pretzels and checked the pocket watch she'd taken from Harte. Five minutes to go. She had at least two more to wait. In the distance, faintly, she heard the stirrings of the parade, the rumble of drums that told her the time was close.

She checked her watch again, and as she did, she had the strangest feeling she was being watched. Glancing up, she realized her instincts were right. Across the street, close to the entrance of the Incubator building, was the cowboy she'd seen disappear that first day at the theater. And he was looking straight at her.

There was no way she could do what she needed to do as long as he was watching her. Taking a breath, she pushed aside the panic and used a play from the cowboy's own book. She gave him a wink, and then she darted into the crowds of the Creation attraction, making herself as unnoticeable as she could while she pushed her way deeper into them. She looked back only once and saw that the cowboy was following her, so she shoved on until she found a small alcove to the right of the ticket window, where she pulled time slow.

Releasing a breath, she relaxed a little as the world went silent around her. Only a couple of days had passed since she'd tested her affinity when Harte left her at the boardinghouse, but during those days they'd been extra careful not to use their magic, just in case the Guard was nearby. It felt like it had been *so long* since she'd been able to flex her affinity, and now the sureness of her magic gave her the impetus to get on with it. She dodged through the crowd, until she was face-to-face with the cowboy who'd been following her. This close, she saw that he had eyes as green as a cat's, but one was flecked with brown enough that it looked like they were two different colors.

This should keep him busy. Lighting the fuse on the first packet, she tucked it into the outer pocket of his coat. Then she darted away, releasing time as she went.

She let her feet carry her toward Cairo, watching for marks. Pausing next to a trash bin, she pulled on time just long enough to light another fuse and place the packet into the bin. Then she moved on, releasing time once she was safely away. She had eight packets, which meant she needed to place six more before she reached Cairo. Working her way up the Pike, she found an empty baby carriage here, a half-drunken man there. Each time she approached, she used her affinity just long enough to place the packet.

It was working. Already she could see the Guards, who were stationed at odd intervals around the Pike, coming to attention as they sensed the magic in the air, but she was always far away from the location by the time they detected it.

When she reached the Cliff Dwellers attraction, where she and Harte were to meet, Esta knew she was later than they'd planned. The parade was too close, and she could tell by the thin set of Harte's mouth that he was trying not to be too obvious as his eyes searched the crowd for her. But his features relaxed and his mouth parted slightly in relief when he saw her.

"You're late," he said by way of greeting.

"I had a little trouble."

His brows went up. "What kind of trouble?"

"The cowboy from the other day? He saw me."

Harte frowned. "Maybe we shouldn't—"

"It's fine," she told him before he could finish his statement. "I took care of it—made sure that he didn't see me. And I left him a little surprise."

"I see," Harte said, but he still had that nervous, worried expression on his face.

"Let's go," she told him. "The parade's almost here."

She didn't give him time to argue before she started across the wide boulevard, toward Cairo and the necklace.

THE WEIGHT OF BELONGING

1902—New York

L eaving under the cover of darkness without so much as a good-bye was hardly any way to repay the kindness Cela's family had shown him over the past six days as he had healed, but Jianyu had already allowed too much time to pass since the ring had gone missing from her possession. He had been delaying the inevitable, but now he had another promise to keep. A wider world to protect.

Jianyu told himself that Cela would be fine, even if the tension in the house was thick enough for him to swim through. He saw the way they looked at her, but they were her family. She would be safe now that the stone was no longer in her possession, and they would take care of her until she was on her feet.

Perhaps he was a coward for not telling Cela that he was leaving, but if anyone came looking for him, she would be *safer* for not knowing.

He could have used his affinity to conceal himself, but his head still ached occasionally, and using the bronze disks would be too much of an effort. Besides, he was still unsteady, and he needed to save his strength for what was to come.

When he reached the corner of Amsterdam Avenue, a familiar figure stepped from the entrance of one of the saloons. He could have opened the light to hide himself, but it was too late. She had seen him. To run now would be disrespectful and insulting.

"I had a feeling you'd leave tonight," Cela said when he finally came to where she was waiting for him, her hands crossed over her chest. "That's it, then? You were just gonna go without so much as a good-bye?"

He did not respond. What was there to say? She was correct in her words and in the anger stirring behind them.

"After all I did for you? After I made my family take you in?"

"I owe you all a debt of gratitude—" he started, but Cela's temper snapped.

"This don't look anything like gratitude." She glared at him. "Where are you going, anyway?"

"It is better that you do not know," he said softly, hating the emotion in her eyes. Suspicion. Disgust. It was the emotion he regularly saw mirrored back to him in the eyes of those he met, the eyes of those who looked at him and saw not the person he was or the heart he carried, but the skin he wore. "You will be safer," he tried to explain.

"*Safer?*" she asked, a bark of ridicule in her tone. Then her brows beaded together. "You're going after that ring, aren't you?"

He did not respond, but from the way her expression shifted, she understood.

"Why? After all the trouble it's caused for everyone, why not just leave the blasted thing be?"

He gave her the only answer he could: "Because I have to."

"Why?" she pressed.

"I made a promise," he told her. "I gave Darrigan my word that I would see you safe and protect the ring. I have done the first, and now I must turn to the other."

"You don't owe Darrigan anything," she said, more softly now, a frown tugging at her full lips. "Neither of us owe him a single thing more."

"Perhaps," he conceded. "But I explained to you what the ring could do, did I not? In unworthy hands, it could have devastating effects. I cannot allow that to happen. I cannot allow the Order or anyone else who might do harm with the stone to obtain it."

Cela stared at him for a moment, her dark eyes sharp in their intensity as she considered his words. Then she let out a jagged breath that was as much frustration as it was understanding. "I'm coming with you, then."

"No—"

"I'm the one who lost that ring, so I'll help you find it."

"This is not your fight." Jianyu shook his head. "You will stay here, with your family, where you belong."

She gave him an exasperated look. "Were you in that house with me? I don't *belong* there."

He had seen, had felt the tension between them, but . . . "They are family. Your *blood*."

"They might be my mama's people, but they've never *really* been mine, blood or not." Her jaw was set and determined. "My grandparents didn't ever approve of the choice my mama made when she married my daddy for lots of reasons, but mostly it boiled down to his skin being too dark. Didn't matter that he worked his knuckles to the bone to give us a good life: a roof over our heads and shoes on our feet. According to them, he was low class, and when we came out with skin every bit as dark as his, so were we," she told him. "They never said it outright, but we knew."

Her shoulders seemed to sag with the weight of her confession. "My mama's people put up with us for her sake, but they never were any sort of safe harbor, even when she was alive. They blamed my daddy when she died a few years back from consumption, and now they're blaming me for Abel's death. I can see it in their eyes. They heard the whispers about how I ran from the house, and maybe they don't say it outright, but they're sure as hell thinking I had something to do with it. So no, I don't belong there. If you're leaving, I'm coming with you."

Jianyu understood the expression Cela wore as she lifted her chin, daring him to contradict her. It was the same as the mask he often wore himself, the steely armor that served as protection from the never-ending menace of a world that did not welcome him. But because he recognized it, he also knew what was beneath—the soft, essential parts of the soul that could be damaged beyond repair.

He frowned. "This is my burden to carry."

She let out a long sigh, and she looked suddenly fragile. "That's where you're wrong. The moment they came and took my brother, it became mine, too."

"But—"

She cut him off. "Tell me, did you have a plan for finding Evelyn?" She paused for his answer, and when it did not come, she shook her head. "What were you gonna do, wander around until you ran into her? It's a big city. At least I know where she lives."

NOT AS PLANNED

Nothing had gone the way Logan Sullivan had expected. When he'd left Professor Lachlan's building that morning, he hadn't planned to end the day tied up in the dark, dank cellar of some rotting building, guarded by two guys who looked like they'd started shaving when they were eight.

The redheaded one was especially worrisome. He kept rubbing his fingertips together, causing flames to dance at the tips of them, all the while leering at Logan. It was like he was just waiting for Logan to make a wrong move.

Which wasn't going to happen.

Maybe things hadn't gone that smoothly. Maybe Professor Lachlan had been wrong about how easy it would be—about how his younger self would *certainly* be able to tell that everything Logan said was the truth. It would have been a hell of a lot easier if those big goons hadn't caught him first, and it *definitely* would have been better if Esta hadn't made off with the package Professor Lachlan had entrusted Logan to deliver; the Book and the stones would have gone a long way toward smoothing things over.

But he'd still had the notebook, Logan reminded himself. Once the Professor read about himself, he'd know that Logan was telling the truth. He'd know exactly how helpful Logan had been to his future self, and he would believe him now. Maybe he'd even be able to help him get back to his own time. Although Logan had a sinking feeling that without Esta, that was going to be impossible.

Shit.

Footsteps echoed on the staircase that descended steeply into the cellar, an uneven gait that Logan recognized immediately. *There.* He'd been right all along.

Logan gave the redheaded guy—Firebug McGee, or whatever his name was—a smug look. It was only a matter of moments before Logan would be vindicated.

It was still a shock to see just how young the Professor was here, in this time. He couldn't be more than fifteen, close to the age Logan himself had been when he'd received a ticket and an invitation to fly across an ocean and start a new life. His uncle, a low-level fencer of stolen goods, had been one of the Professor's contacts in England, and he hadn't given Logan a choice in the matter. To the thirteen-year-old Logan, the whole thing had seemed almost too good to be true: He got out from under the constant threat of his uncle's fists, and the professor paid for his mother to have the house in the country, like she'd always wanted. And if Logan had to deal with a life behind the Brink or the headache of traveling through time or Esta's smart-ass tendencies, it had been worth it for the comfortable life and for the respect the Professor had given him.

But this boy wasn't yet the man the Professor would become. The Professor's younger face didn't even have a shadow of hair on it, and the eyes behind his gold-rimmed glasses, while familiar, were clear of the cloudy cataracts that would haunt him in the future. Still, there was the same uncanny knowledge in his eyes, the spark of intelligence that had let Logan know the very first time they'd met that the old man wasn't to be messed with.

It will be fine.

"Leave us." The boy who would one day become the Professor made it to the bottom of the stairs and stood in front of Logan, eyeing him with a familiar expression.

"You sure, Nibs?" the redhead asked, snapping the fire between his fingers as he watched Logan uneasily. "I can stay, just in case."

The Professor turned on the redhead. "You think I can't handle myself?" he asked in a voice like acid.

The fire on the redhead's fingertips went out. "I just thought—"

"We'd be in trouble if I depended on you to do the thinking, Mooch. But I don't. I depend on you to do what I ask, when I ask it. And I'm asking you to leave me with our prisoner. I'll deal with him myself."

"Right, Nibs. Sorry." Mooch cut Logan another threatening look, but he took himself up the steps, leaving Logan with the younger version of his friend and mentor.

"So," Logan said after a long beat of uneasy silence. He was unsure of where to start. The man this boy would become had been like a father to Logan. He'd taken Logan under his wing and taught him everything he knew, but the boy in front of him was a stranger. "They call you Nibs?"

"Only those who don't know better." The Professor's nostrils flared slightly, just as they had every time Logan or Esta had managed to do something to piss him off. It was eerie to see the action on this younger boy's face. "You can call me James, since I assume we know each other."

"Then you read the notebook," Logan asked, still too nervous to feel relief.

"I did." The Professor—James—leaned on the silver-topped cane. "It's quite an object you brought me. Too fantastical to be true, really."

"You don't believe it?" Logan asked. Unease prickled at the nape of his neck. *He has to believe.* Logan was royally screwed if he didn't.

"I don't believe anything without proof," James said, pushing his glasses farther up his nose. "You spoke of the Delphi's Tear?"

"It's here, in the city," Logan told him. Apparently, the notebook hadn't informed him about the package of other stones. Probably a good thing.

"You know this how?"

"It's what I do," Logan said, and when James narrowed his eyes, he explained further. "I mean, I can find things. Or, I guess I should say that

I can find things that are imbued with magic. I can find other things too," he said quickly, when James frowned at him, "but I'm most accurate when there's some kind of power involved."

"What about the rest of the artifacts? The stones and the Book?"

Logan felt his chest go tight. "The rest of them?" he hedged.

"You were supposed to deliver them to me, according to the notebooks. If the notes in those pages are to be believed, you should have a package for me. If you don't have the package . . ."

"I had it," Logan pleaded. "I swear I did."

"But you don't now," James said, looking more than ever like the disappointed professor Logan had known.

"Esta took them," he explained. "She knows how I am right after we slip through time, and she took advantage of it."

"Esta?" James had gone very, very still. When he spoke again, his voice was urgent. "*She* has the Book and the artifacts. You're sure of this?"

Logan nodded. "She left me here without them, and then those big guys picked me up before I could get to you."

"Kelly's boys," James murmured, but he wasn't looking at Logan. He was staring into the dark corner of the cellar, clearly thinking through something. Then, all at once, he seemed to come to a decision. "It's an interesting story."

"It's the *truth*."

"So you say. And I'm inclined to believe you, but I have no way of knowing for sure. You could have used the Book to deceive me."

"I didn't," Logan said, feeling again the itch of panic. "You have to believe me."

"Actually, I don't. Which presents a problem—for you, at least." He adjusted his grip on the head of his cane, a movement that was as much a threat as his words.

"Let me prove it to you," Logan begged.

"How?" James asked. "What more proof could you possibly offer?"

"Let me find the Delphi's Tear—the ring. It's close. I *know* it is. I'll find it and give it to you, and then you'll know I'm not hiding anything."

The boy's expression didn't betray even a flicker of interest. "You're sure that you know where it is?"

"Not exactly," Logan said. "But I could take you to it."

James considered the offer. "Mooch!" he shouted, his voice bellowing louder than Logan would have expected from such a slightly built boy.

"Yeah, Nibs?" The redhead appeared at the top of the steps with a speed that told Logan he'd been waiting.

"Bring Jacob and Werner and come down here."

That wasn't the reaction Logan wanted. While James watched the steps expectantly, Logan tested the ropes on his hands. If he could loosen them, maybe he could wiggle free. But the ropes were as tight now as they had been when Mooch first tied them, and before he could do anything, the three larger boys had come down the steps and were waiting for further orders.

"You wanted our help?" the sandy-haired one asked, and Logan gasped as he felt the air pressed from his chest.

"Not yet, Werner," James said, his gaze on Logan. "We need him alive . . . for now."

BREAKING AND ENTERING

1902—New York

When they finally arrived at the building, Jianyu looked up and found the darkened windows of the apartment where Cela said Evelyn lived and wondered—not for the first time—if the path he had placed himself on was the right one. As a child, he had never intended to become a thief. And now, because of the choices he'd made, he was without country or home, far from his family and in a situation beyond his imagining or his control. For a moment he looked up at the darkened sky above him, the sweep of stars that were the same constellations of his youth.

He found the stars that were the Cowherd and the Weaver Girl, as he often did on clear nights. In the tale, the two were banished from each other, divided by the band of the Silver River, just as he was divided by a continent and a sea from his boyhood home. But Jianyu's own choices had led him from his first home, and there would be no magpies to carry him magically back, and even if there were, he couldn't go. Not without the queue that was prescribed by Manchu law.

The future to come was unknown. His path was surely here now, in this land, but what might he do with it? Where might he go or what might he become if he were not bound by the Brink, now that he could not return to his homeland? And if the Brink was to remain, how would he choose to live in this world, where he was?

But the questions were premature. No future would be possible if the stone fell into the wrong hands. So he would make the choice to become a bandit—a thief—once more, to have a chance at some other future.

"You're sure she lives here?" Jianyu asked.

Cela nodded. "I had to fit her wardrobe a few months back when she was too busy or lazy to come in when the theater was dark. We should have plenty of time."

"*We?*" Jianyu said, turning to her as panic inched up his spine. He couldn't get the stone and keep her safe. "You're not coming," he said, his tone more clipped and short than he had intended.

"Like hell—"

"I need you *here*," he told Cela, trying to calm her temper before it erupted. There was not time for an argument. "To watch for any trouble."

"And just what am I supposed to do if I see some?" Cela asked doubtfully.

"Warn me." Before she could argue further, Jianyu added, "Can you make a birdcall of some sort? The window is open." He pointed to the way the curtain fluttered from the open window.

He knew she was angry, but he could not linger. Before she could stop him, he had opened the strands of light, pulled them around himself, and started for the building.

It was a simple thing to find Evelyn's rooms, but when he let himself in, the apartment was not what Jianyu had expected. The woman herself was like the ostentatious kingfisher in her dress and adornments, but the rooms were cold and barely furnished, with clothes heaped about in haphazard piles. It was the kind of place someone came to sleep off the effects of too much Nitewein or because they had no other option—not because it bore any resemblance at all to a home. Jianyu almost pitied her for living in such a place, but then he reminded himself that her actions did not lend themselves to pity. Evelyn had made her choices, and now she would bear the consequences of them.

There was enough moonlight coming through the open window that he could navigate easily enough, searching through boxes and under beds. He worked methodically, lifting silken stockings and then replacing them as carefully as he could, so it would appear that no one had been there. Better not to warn her.

He was sorting through the piles on her bed when he heard the sound of an owl.

Not an owl, he realized when the sound came a second time . . . and then a third. *Cela.*

Placing the piles of clothing back the way he had found them, Jianyu was already heading toward the door when he heard the click of the lock releasing. With nowhere to go, he pulled the bronze disks from his pocket and used them to open the wan moonlight and wrap it around himself. Certainly, Evelyn would be able to sense him, but if he was quick, she would not be able to catch him.

Positioning himself next to the door, he waited. But the person who came through was not Evelyn after all.

SESHAT

1904—St. Louis

The excitement of the parade had done its job, pulling people out into the wide boulevard and leaving the winding streets of Cairo nearly empty. Harte followed Esta as they made their way through the various bazaars selling their cheap trinkets and past the restaurant that left the air perfumed with the scent of heavy spices and roasting meats. His stomach rumbled at they passed, but he kept his focus on the back of Esta's narrow shoulders and the constant hum of energy from the power inside of him.

When they came to the replica of the Egyptian temple that housed the boat ride, Harte nearly stumbled from the way the power inside of him lurched, letting its presence be known. There was something about this particular attraction that agitated the voice, but there was only one way in and out of the chamber that held the necklace, and that was through the Nile River. He did his best to ignore the power as he slipped the attendant a few extra coins for a private boat and then followed Esta into it.

A moment later their oarsman pushed off, and they were entering the darkness of the first tunnel. The world of the fair fell away, and there was only the gentle sound of the water being parted by the oar and the stale mustiness of the canal. Harte didn't need to see Esta to know exactly where she was in the darkness. Even with the odor of the water, he could sense her next to him. Since she'd decided on the ridiculous ploy to dress like a boy, she'd given up the soft floral soap she'd used before. Instead, she had been using something simple and clean, and when the scent of it came to him in the darkness, the image of her in the morning, damp from washing and freshly scrubbed, rose in his mind.

It was a mistake—the power vibrated against the shell of who he was, pressing at the delicate barrier. Harte was intimately familiar with that boundary, because he often breached it himself when he let his affinity reach into a person to read their thoughts or shape their actions. Having his own threatened like this was an uncomfortable reminder of just how dangerous his affinity could be.

The oarsman was reciting his script in a monotone, but Harte could barely pay attention—all his focus was on keeping the power inside of him from bursting out. They passed through scenes depicting life in ancient Egypt—the building of the pyramids and the flooding of the Nile, with its resulting harvest. Faintly, the names of gods and goddesses registered, but as the boat progressed, the power grew stronger, and it became harder and harder to hold it back.

Esta was sitting next to him, her back straight and her attention forward—preparing, probably, for what they needed to do—but Harte could barely see straight. His hands felt clammy. His head swirled and the edges of his vision wavered as the voice echoed in his ears, screaming words he didn't understand in a language he did not know.

When they neared the end of the ride, the voice went silent and the power stilled, both falling away and leaving only a hollowed-out emptiness behind. Panting now, Harte forced himself to take a deep, steadying breath. They were nearly there. Two more chambers and then they would disembark and walk the so-called Path of Righteousness to the Temple of Khorassan, where the Djinni's Star waited. But the moment the boat began to enter the chamber filled with parchments and scrolls, the power lurched once again.

If Harte had thought it strong, or if he had thought himself able to control it, he realized that he'd been wrong. *So wrong.* Everything he'd experienced before had been nothing but a shadow of its true power. It had been hiding itself, perhaps waiting for this moment.

The boat, the false Nile, and the room of scrolls transformed itself into a different time, another place. The walls were rounded up to a ceiling that had been painted gold, and in the center of the room stood an altarlike table that held a book. A woman stood over it, her coiled hair hung around her lean face. Her kohl-rimmed eyes were focused on the parchment in front of her, and the very air seemed to tremble with the urgency she felt. There was magic here, warm and thick and stronger than Harte had ever felt before.

The woman's mouth was forming words that he could not hear, but he understood their meaning because he could feel their power vibrating through the air, brushing against him with an unmistakable threat. It reminded him of what it had felt like when Esta pulled him through time, awful and dangerous and *wrong*. As though the world were collapsing and breaking apart all at once. He watched with dread as she took a knife and sliced open her fingertip, dripping the dark blood into a small cup.

She picked up a reed and dipped it into the cup, mixing it before she touched it to the parchment. With each stroke, the energy in the air increased, whipping about with an impossible fury. Hot. Angry. Pure. Her face was a mask of concentration, her darkly ringed eyes tight and her jaw clenched as the power in the air began to stir the hair framing her face. She made another stroke with her reed and then another, until finally, her hand trembling, she finished.

The woman looked up at him as though she could see to the very heart of what he was. Every mistake he'd made. Every regret he bore day in and day out. Every fear. Every want. She looked into him and she knew them all.

And then, without warning, the woman dropped the reed and screamed as though she were being torn apart. The power swirling through the room swelled until there was only a furious roaring that felt as though it were bubbling up from the very heart of who Harte was. As though he had become her.

As she made the final stroke, the screaming was coming from deep within her and it was coming from outside of her as well. The world was roaring its warning, but she could not listen. She *would* not listen. She would finish what she had started, even as she felt herself flying apart, a sacrifice and an offering to the power that was the heart of all magic.

An offering that would transform her into something so much more.

Even as she felt the very core of who and what she was shattering, even as she felt the spaces within her swelling and splintering, she screamed again, clinging to the table as the power of the spell—her greatest and most awful creation—coursed through her.

He was coming. But it did not matter. He was too late.

Too late to stop her.

Too late to take the power that was held within the parchment and ink, the skins and blood that she had created. He had tried to steal this magic and make it his own, tried to dole it out for favor and power, to give it to those who had no right to touch it.

He was coming, and she would destroy him. She would rip the very stars from the sky if need be, but he would not triumph.

Traitor. Thief. He would die this night, and her masterwork would be safe.

But first . . . She took up one of the polished gems on the altar in front of her—a lapis lazuli—and focused her magic, pushing a part of herself into the stone. And then she took up another—malachite—and another, breaking herself apart so that she could become something more.

She took up the last of the five and felt herself splinter once more, divided and broken for some greater goal. As the stones began to glow, all at once the pain she had felt—the horror of unbecoming—ceased. She slumped over, catching herself on the table in front of her.

There was no time to rest. She moved quickly on unsteady legs as she placed the stones on the floor around the table. One by one, she positioned them around the outline of a perfect circle that had been drawn, even and balanced, to ring the table that held the Book.

She heard the sound of footsteps approaching and she turned. There was someone waiting in the shadows.

A man. An unseen face.

"Thoth," she said, her vision red with hatred.

The man stepped from the darkness and into the light. His head was bare, the brown skin of his scalp shaved clean of any hair.

"I knew you would come." Her voice was brittle in its accusation.

"Ah, Seshat . . ." He shook his head sadly. "Of course I came. I came to stop you from making a terrible mistake."

Her lip curled. "Do you think you can? You're nothing but a man."

"They call me a god now," he said with a soft smile.

"They'll see the error in their judgment soon enough," she said, coming around the table so that she was between the altar and the man.

"You can't destroy the pages you've created, Seshat. You would be damning all of us."

Her eyes were bright with anticipation. The fear, if it had been there to start with, was gone now. "Who said I want to destroy them?"

The air, hot and dry from the arid desert day, began to move, swirling around the altar, and the stones began to glow.

"Stop," Thoth commanded.

But she wasn't listening. The stones had become bright points of light, like stars that had fallen to the ground, and between them, the threads of being—the parts of the world that held chaos at bay—began to glow in strange, eerie colors.

"You tried to take what was not yours to have," she said, laughing a high, strange laugh. She sounded manic, unhinged, even to her own ears. Hysterical in her glee, she walked toward him. "You thought that you could wield power, you who were not born to it? You will never again touch the heart of magic. And your followers will turn on you. They will tear you to shreds. And I will dance over your bones as they dry in the sun."

The man, who had been wearing a look of horror, lunged for her, his face contorted now in rage.

She wasn't ready for his attack. She clawed at him, her nails raking red trails across his face, but he was stronger, and in the end she tumbled back, through the swirling colors and glowing threads that formed a boundary line around the altar, screaming as she went.

"Demon bitch," Thoth said, sneering at her as he wiped the blood dripping from his cheek. He looked at it with disgust and then he stepped toward her, approaching the line of glowing air but not coming close enough to touch it.

Inside the circle, her eyes were wide with panic. She was trapped, just as she'd intended to trap the secrets of magic. "What have you done?"

"I've used your own evil against you," he said. "You thought you could take all the power in that book for yourself?" He shook his head as he took the sword from his back, its blade curved like a scythe.

Inside the circle, Seshat raged and shrieked like the demon he'd called her.

"You know my weapon, Seshat, don't you? A knife made from the stars. Iron that fell from the sky." He walked over to the first of the stones and lifted the blade. "Capable of severing anything."

"No," she screeched, her voice ripping through the chamber.

But there was nothing she could do. Thoth brought the curved blade down and the stone split in two, its separate halves going dark. In response, Seshat released a keening wail that contained all the pain—the fear—that she felt.

Thoth walked to the next stone. "You won't be able to cause any more trouble," he told her, bringing the blade down again. "You won't be able to collect power for yourself any longer," he said, destroying the third stone.

By now she'd crumpled to the floor and was trying to pull herself to the altar where the book waited. When she looked up, her vision was going black. The darkness seemed to be consuming her, consuming the world.

Thoth walked to the fourth stone, and when he destroyed it, her spine arched and she fell backward onto the floor. It was darkness now pouring from her mouth, filling the room along with her wailing. But she pulled herself up again and looked at Thoth, the darkness in her eyes a living thing.

"There is nowhere you can hide from me," she told him. "I will find you, and I will tear apart the world to make you pay."

When Thoth drove the blade into the fifth and final stone, Seshat screamed one last time, the darkness pouring out of her until there was nothing left. No body. No blood. No bones. Only the empty echo of her screams.

THE UNMAKING

1904—St. Louis

Even as he came back to himself, Harte still felt like he was flying apart. He was haunted by the memory of the woman giving way to nothingness, could still feel the woman's panic and her dread and frustration at being bested. At being *unmade*. In a flash of understanding, he felt her longing and fury. An eternity of being trapped within the pages of the Book, waiting and planning and growing more and more angry.

The power inside of him had a name.

Seshat. A demon who would destroy the world to take her revenge.

She had lived and walked and tried to take magic for herself, had tried to keep it from the world. She had been stopped. She had been destroyed . . . except that she hadn't. A part of her had lived on in the very essence of the words she'd inscribed using her own blood. That part of her, the only part left after the rest had been destroyed with the stones, had waited in the pages of the Book, weak and broken and angry—*so angry*. But now it was ready—*she* was ready—to be reborn. To rip the world apart in retribution.

Harte was shaking with residual pain and trembling from the anger seething within him. Even as he surfaced from the vision, the shadows of a different time still hung around him, a haze through which his own world lay. He felt the dull smack of a hand across his cheek, and the shadows began to melt until only reality was left.

"What the hell, Harte?" Esta asked, and though her voice sounded angry, he was vaguely aware that there was a very different emotion in her whiskey-colored eyes. *Fear.*

He didn't want her to be afraid. Without thinking, he raised his head and pressed his lips against hers, but she didn't kiss him back. Instead she jerked away, with a look of absolute horror on her face. Her movement set the floor swaying.

Not the floor . . .

They were still in the boat, on the fake Nile in the heart of a fake Cairo, and they were supposed to be stealing a necklace. Behind him, he heard the oarsman make a shocked and disapproving sound. *And Esta's still dressed like a boy.*

"We need to go," she whispered through clenched teeth. "*Now.* Before he calls someone."

Harte wasn't sure if he could stand, but there wasn't really a choice. Using the railing to steady himself as he disembarked, he forced his legs to move, even as his head pounded dully and his vision was still wavering.

"We need to call this off," he told Esta as they joined the stream of other riders moving toward the exit. His legs felt unsteady beneath him as they started down the silvery path toward the chamber.

"It's too late for that. And we're too close," she hissed. "What is wrong with you, anyway?"

"I think it's more of a who than a what," he said, remembering the heat and the pain and the feeling of himself bursting apart. *And the betrayal.* The ache of it was still so real, so palpable, it had left him reeling.

She cut him a frustrated look. "You *are* going to explain to me what that was back there—if we manage to get out of here, that is. For right now you are going to pull yourself together. You have the packet, right?" she asked.

He patted his coat and felt the final smoke packet beneath his hand. "Yeah . . ."

They were already nearing the end of the silver path, where it opened into the larger chamber. All that was left to do was set off this final packet and use the smoke as a way to clear the room of other people and as a cover to escape with the necklace. It wasn't elegant, but it was workable.

But something wasn't right. Unlike the previous days, when the crowd in the room was five or six people deep to take a look at the necklace, the chamber was empty except for the handful of other riders who had disembarked with them. There were so few people that they had a clear view to where the glass cabinet stood, holding the Djinni's Star.

"No . . ." Esta's voice came to him the same instant Harte saw it. "It can't be gone," she said, walking toward the clearly empty display case in the center of the room.

The power inside of him lurched, and for a moment Harte felt as though the entire world was spinning on, very far away from her, and he was stuck, unable to reach it. The necklace was gone.

"It can't be—" he started, but on the far end of the room, a pair of Jefferson Guardsmen were watching the two of them. The other people had continued on through the chamber, because there wasn't anything to see or draw their attention, so the Guardsmen had noticed Esta and Harte's hesitation. But it was already too late. The Guardsmen traded glances, and one touched the gold medallion pinned to his lapel.

"It's a trap," he whispered, and the tone of his voice was enough to have her eyes going wide with understanding. "Come on."

They ran for the exit, but Guardsmen were already moving as well. Ahead of them, the door to the Pike was a bright beacon, urging them onward, but even as they closed the distance, Harte heard the metallic scraping of the gate starting to close. The exit was only a few feet away, but they would never make it. Already, the bars were descending over the door, and he could feel the cold warning of corrupted magic, a power that felt too much like the Brink.

The power inside of him churned as it realized they would be trapped, and Harte stumbled from the intensity of its anger—*her* anger. But Esta was there, catching him before he could fall. All at once, the room went silent and the bars paused. He turned to her and could see the concentration on

Esta's face. Around them, the dust swirled in the air and the light slanted toward them from the Pike, calling to them, urging them to run. Faster. The power inside of him—Seshat—roared in triumph and pushed toward the surface, pressing at the already weak barriers he'd tried to keep up between her and the world.

In an instant, he saw what she saw, understood what she understood— the terrible power that was the beating heart of magic, the threat of chaos overtaking the world.

Magic lived in the spaces between all things, but if it ever escaped, it could destroy the very bonds that held the world together. In that instant he could *see* it, the dark emptiness that lived in the spaces—the same emptiness he'd seen in the woman's eyes when she'd been consumed by it . . . The emptiness that had bled out of *Esta's* eyes like a horrible nightmare of what was to come. It stretched and grew, tearing apart the pieces of the world. It wasn't just destruction. It was an *unmaking*.

His new understanding was sharp and vivid and *so* real. If Seshat took Esta, if she used Esta's power, she could destroy the world. He could see it—the world dissolving into nothing—but the clarity didn't last for long. The moment they slipped through the gates, Esta released his hand and the world spun back into motion.

Outside the exhibit, the sun was blindingly bright and the Pike was in chaos, just as they'd planned it to be, but the Guardsmen from inside the exhibit were on their heels. Even before the two from inside could get out of the building, others were coming, pushing through the crowd to rush toward Cairo. Harte's head was still pounding and his legs felt as though they would give way with every step, but he grabbed Esta's hand, not caring how it might look, and pulled her onward.

The power inside of him surged toward her, but Harte didn't bother to shove it back down. All his strength was focused on pulling Esta through the frantic crowd and escaping from the Guard. He found the passageway that led back into the rest of the Exposition, just as they'd planned, and as soon as they were free from the confusion of the Pike, they ran.

DISCOVERED

1902—New York

Jianyu pulled himself far back in the corner as he watched the stranger enter the apartment. The man was young—tall, but more of a boy, really—with blond hair and a worried expression on his face. He closed the door behind him softly as he stepped into the apartment, and then Jianyu felt magic fill the room. The tendrils that brushed against him were warm, familiar, and the guy turned to stare into the corner with a confused expression.

Jianyu held his breath, certain that the boy had found him when the blond took a step toward the place Jianyu was standing. The boy's eyes narrowed, as though he were squinting to see through Jianyu's concealment, and took another step toward him, his hand raised.

But then, suddenly, the guy turned back toward the darkened room. He waited, silent, as though he were listening for something. Then he went to the window and knelt beside it.

Jianyu considered his options: If he left, the door would open and the blond would know someone else had been there. If he stayed, it might be just as dangerous—the blond was clearly Mageus, and the more Jianyu pulled on his own affinity, the more likely he would be found. Either way, he chanced being discovered, and caught.

Then the blond did something that made Jianyu's mind up for him— the boy began to tug at the windowsill. A moment later, the wooden trim came loose and he set it aside.

Again Jianyu heard the owl crying outside the window.

Too late.

But the boy was already pulling something from the space behind the window frame—a small package wrapped in cloth. Jianyu didn't need to see what was inside the package to know that it was the ring. He could feel it, somehow, its energy sifting through the air, cool and hot all at once. Strange and yet also compelling.

Logan. With his light hair and the decisiveness with which he found the ring, it could be no one else. Why Logan had come here was a question that would need to be answered, but Jianyu set aside that question for the time being and focused on the opportunity the boy's appearance afforded. This was more than a second chance—the ring and the boy here, together. The blond had located the ring, and now Jianyu would relieve him of it. And then, he would keep this Logan from causing any more trouble.

Slowly, he stepped closer as the boy began replacing the loosened piece of wood on the window. Carefully, so as not to make a sound, Jianyu moved toward the boy. A few feet more and the ring would be his.

Behind him, the door opened and the bare overhead bulb flickered on. Jianyu turned to see Evelyn in the doorway, her mouth as red as her hair and her eyes filled with fury.

"Well, what do we have here?" she asked with a smile that looked sharp enough to cut.

Jianyu backed out of Evelyn's path as she sauntered toward Logan, who looked even younger and more unseasoned than he had appeared when the room was dark. The boy's light eyes widened at the sight of her, and he tucked the package he had found in the windowsill behind his back.

"Now, now," she said softly. "What do you have there, handsome?"

Jianyu felt Evelyn's affinity flood the room. It was a soft, enticing magic that made him want to lean in and be seduced, and he could see that Logan felt the same when the boy's eyes went glassy. He brought the package out and showed it to her.

"That's better, isn't it?" Evelyn's mouth curved up as she took it from him and unwrapped it. Then she slid the ring onto her finger, and when she did, Jianyu felt her affinity swell. She reached out to caress the boy's cheek, running her fingers through his light hair. He leaned into her hand, like a cat purring with contentment, but just as his eyes closed in satisfaction, she grabbed a handful of hair and, without warning, wrenched the boy to his knees. His eyes were still soft, submissive, as they stared sightlessly into the room, the effect of whatever Evelyn had done to him.

"Come out, come out, wherever you are," she trilled in her singsong voice. Her eyes were bright with power and her teeth were bared beneath her bloodred lips. "I know he's not alone. I can *feel* you here."

Jianyu went still, glancing toward the open door as he felt the warmth of her affinity increase, the tendrils of it curling under his chin like fingers caressing him. He struggled to resist it.

He could run now, but to run meant leaving the ring behind and leaving Logan to her mercy. Jianyu knew he could do neither.

"Let's make this easy," Evelyn said to the apparently empty room. It was clear from the way her eyes tracked without focusing on him that she had not yet found him. "You show yourself, and I'll let this one go. Or leave now if you'd like. You'll never get the ring, and I'll keep this handsome boy here as a pet." She stroked the boy's cheek with her free hand, then slapped his cheek sharply to punctuate her point.

Evelyn's magic was filling the room, already teasing at Jianyu's will. He could stay. He could give himself over to Evelyn and—

No. Jianyu gave himself a mental shake and wrapped his affinity around himself more tightly, like armor against her onslaught. Perhaps he could still retrieve the ring. If he moved quickly, it could be his, but he would not be able to save the boy. Not with the magic floating through the air, calling to him even now.

He took a step toward them, but he could not tell whether he was stepping toward the ring or Evelyn's call. He could not have stopped himself either way.

"That's it," Evelyn purred. "Why bother to fight?"

ONLY EMPTINESS

1904—St. Louis

Even as she ran, her lungs burning and her heart pumping, Esta could feel the heat from the power of the Book creeping along her skin where her hand was clasped in Harte's. It felt as though it were testing her, a snakelike thing slithering alongside her own power, licking at her to probe for a weakness in her armor, for a way in. It was so much worse than back at the train station in New Jersey. Stronger. More dangerous—and also more enticing in a way it hadn't been before.

But her mind was too full with the crushing disappointment of not getting the Djinni's Star to really be tempted. The necklace wasn't there. *It was a trap.* Which meant that someone knew they wanted it. Someone knew they would try to steal it. And if the Guard caught them now, they might never have another chance to find it.

Esta refused to let that happen.

Together, she and Harte ran past the transportation building and then cut deeper into the fair, where the paths were narrower and the landscaping provided more cover. They dodged a cluster of families watching a puppet show and then weaved through a group of young men who were taking in the sights. All the while, the Guard was gaining on them, but when she heard hoofbeats, she knew that they couldn't outrun a horse.

Harte glanced back over his shoulder. "We need to get out of here," he told her. "*You* need to get us out of here. We need time."

He was right, but she was still reeling from a few minutes before when she'd gotten them out of the chamber. The darkness had been so immediate, so *strong* when she'd pulled the seconds apart to stop the gate from closing.

"I'll control it," he told her as though he understood her hesitation. "You have to—"

The riders were gaining on them. She could practically feel the thunderous pace of the horses telescoping each hoofbeat through the ground beneath her feet, like the earth had a heartbeat all its own. They rounded a bend and past the clock made of flowers that was the size of a carriage before they headed toward a smaller lagoon, but the horses were gaining on them. Their hoofbeats were like thunder, and she could practically smell the sweat of horseflesh and angry human.

"Now, Esta . . . *Now!*"

Never slowing, she clenched her jaw and found the spaces between the seconds, pushing her magic into them, pulling them apart so that the noise of the fair died away. They didn't stop running as the birds in the trees went silent and everyone around them went still, suspended in the moment. She glanced over her shoulder to find the horses frozen in an impossible tableau, like the statues that dotted the fairgrounds. Their mouths were open, pulled back violently by the bits between their teeth, and their manes looked like fingertips grasping at the air. And above the whole scene, a darkness was seeping into the world like a trail of black ink splattered across the page of reality, following them.

Following *her*.

The power sliding against her skin went hot as a brand, and the darkness lurched, growing until it blotted out everything. For a moment there was only the darkness, only emptiness, and at the sight of it—the *feel* of it—she ripped her hand from Harte's. The world slammed back into motion without warning, and the darkness that had threatened to obliterate everything just a second before faded, like a fog burned off by the sun.

"Esta?" Harte was reaching back for her, but his eyes lifted to something behind her, and from the fear in his expression, she felt suddenly wary.

She turned back, expecting to see the Guard, but instead she saw madness. A deep chasm had opened in the ground, like an enormous sinkhole. It almost looked as though the path they'd just come down had been ripped in two. The horses stopped short at the gaping wound in the earth, tossing the riders from their backs.

Esta let out a strangled sound and her feet started to slow, but Harte took her hand again and tugged her onward. She ran blindly, until she realized they'd stopped because they'd made it to the wall of the fair, where the exit she'd unlocked earlier waited. Her mind raced with the implications of what had just happened. It was the Book—there was no question of that. When Harte touched her, she could feel it as clear and true as she could feel the warmth of his skin. But what was it doing to her? To her affinity? The train and the elevator at the hotel, and now this gaping hole she'd—*they'd*—somehow created here at the fair . . . Her affinity was for time, not for the inert, so why was the Book having such an effect?

She was dazed from the reality of what had happened as she stumbled through the doorway, so she didn't see the people waiting on the other side until it was too late. Harte came through a moment later, and at the sight of them, his eyes met hers, and she thought she saw the colors flash in them.

The cowboy from before stepped out of the shadow of a waiting wagon and pushed his broad-brimmed hat back a bit as he came toward them. He had a gun in one hand, and the click of its hammer was clear as the peal of a bell, even over the distant noise of the fair.

Together Esta and Harte lifted their hands in surrender. If it had just been her, she could have pulled time still and ran, but Harte and the number of their opponents complicated things.

"Well, well . . . We meet at last," the cowboy said with a self-satisfied expression. "The Devil's Thief, in the flesh."

He knew. "Who are you?" Esta asked, lifting her chin as though *she* had cornered them and not the other way around.

"You can think of us as the cavalry," the cowboy said, touching the brim of his hat. "Unless you'd rather take your chances with the Guard."

Esta exchanged a silent, questioning look with Harte, but he only gave a small shake of his head.

"What do you want with us?" Harte asked.

"Me? I personally don't want anything at all," the cowboy said. "But there's someone who does want to make your acquaintance, and it's my job to make that happen. We can do this the easy way or the hard way, but either way, it's gonna happen. So what will it be?"

"You're not exactly giving us much of a choice," Harte said.

"There's always a choice to make," the cowboy drawled. "There's always a side to take. At the moment we're taking yours." He shrugged. "We could have just as easily not have. Give us a reason, and we're liable to change our mind."

Esta glanced at Harte, whose expression had gone flinty, but whose skin still had an unhealthy-looking pallor from whatever had happened in the Nile. Behind them the noise of the fair was growing closer. They had to get out of there. *Now.*

When she looked back to the cowboy, she straightened her spine and cocked her head to one side, making a show of confidence. "I suppose we could use a ride if you're offering."

"That's what I thought." The cowboy's mouth twitched as he lowered the gun and stepped aside to open the back of the wagon. As she approached to climb in, he held out a limp burlap sack. "I'm sure you'll understand that we need to take certain precautions?"

"I thought you were taking our side," Harte challenged. "We're not a threat to you."

"With all due respect, I have a hole in my pocket from one of your smoke devices that says otherwise," the cowboy told him. "If you're not a threat, then you shouldn't mind proving it."

They were wasting time. Without waiting for Harte's reply, Esta took the sack from the cowboy and shot Harte a determined look before she put it over her own head. A moment later her hands were being secured, and she felt herself being lifted as strong hands tossed her into the wagon. Not long after she heard Harte land next to her—he gave a small groan as the air went out of him—and then the door slammed shut.

The wagon lurched, and they were moving.

"Are you okay?" Harte asked, the hood over his head muffling his voice. She could hear him moving, probably already maneuvering his wrists and working at the ropes like this situation wasn't anything more than one of his magic tricks.

"I think so," she said, relieved that he'd made the choice to follow her without a fight.

"I'll be out of this in a second," Harte told her as the wagon lurched around a bend. "I can't imagine what you were thinking."

"I was thinking we needed a quick getaway, and they were offering. They're Antistasi," she added, as though that wasn't painfully obvious.

"Clearly. And they knew who you were," he said, his voice a combination of frustration and smugness.

"I know. I figured we can use that to our advantage," she said, hoping that she was right.

"They've certainly used you enough," he muttered. She could hear Harte still struggling against his own restraints. "Almost got it . . ."

Suddenly she heard the pop and the hiss of something close by.

"What was that?" Harte asked just as she began to smell something musty and sweet.

Esta didn't even have time to answer him before everything went dark.

THE PRESIDENT'S MAN

1904—St. Louis

Jack choked down the bland, overcooked chicken and sipped at a watery cocktail as he pretended to be interested in the plans Francis and Spenser were detailing about the ball that would occur at the end of the month. It was to be the first meeting of the Brotherhoods since the Conclave of 1902, an event that had gone a long way to solidifying the Order's power among its brethren and to coalescing Jack's own power as well. He would have gladly left before the second course had even been served, but he wasn't there on his own behalf. He was there on behalf of Roosevelt, so he called for another glass of scotch and pretended to be interested in the plans their committee was making for the president's visit.

Francis and Spenser were still tripping over themselves to impress Jack. It was pointless, really, considering that their suits were at least a season out of date and the food they'd selected had been out of fashion in Manhattan since before Jack left for his grand tour. But Jack understood. The men who populated the Veiled Prophet Society, including these two, believed that their little parade and subsequent ball would change things for their city. They thought that if they kissed Roosevelt's ass, they could bend his ear and accumulate the same power and influence the Order enjoyed.

What they didn't seem to understand was that Roosevelt was a New Yorker first and foremost, and the men of St. Louis would always be nothing more than merchant stock in fancy shoes. And they couldn't comprehend the future that was flying down the tracks to greet them at the speed of a steam train. What would matter in the years to come wasn't the squabbles among regions, but the country as a whole, and Jack would put himself in position to elicit any advantage he could when that time came.

He was finishing his drink when the door of their private dining room opened and a figure appeared in the doorway wearing a white lace veil over its face. Jack nearly snorted scotch through his nose at the sight of it, but the other men at the table went silent and stood in a respectful welcome, so he choked back the laugh that had almost erupted and followed suit.

The veiled figure—it must have been this Prophet the Society was always going on about—had another man with him, a dark-haired fellow who didn't look any happier to be there than Jack himself felt. Behind them came two Guardsmen, one of whom was Hendricks.

"Good evening, gentlemen," the Prophet said, directing them all to take their seats. "I'd like to introduce you to Mr. Julien Eltinge. Some of you might be aware that he's been gracing the stage down at the Hippodrome for a few months now. He's graciously agreed to help us with the parade by wearing the necklace until it arrives at the ball."

Jack set the glass he was holding back onto the table, his interest piqued. He'd been considering the easiest way to get to the necklace, and this presented a possibility. Whatever the men from the Society thought of this Julien Eltinge, the man didn't look all that impressive. In fact, he looked damn uncomfortable about the whole situation, which was just fine with Jack. Discomfort was something he could certainly exploit.

THE RETURN

1902—New York

Cela called again from her hiding place in the alleyway across from Evelyn's building, hooting into the night like some sort of deranged owl to warn Jianyu about the boy who'd gone into the building looking like all kinds of trouble. But the building across the street was dark and quiet. There was still no sign of Jianyu.

Maybe the boy was simply going home. Maybe he wasn't a danger after all. But Cela had been around long enough to know that her feeling about him was probably right. He was with a small group of other boys, a ragtag bunch that looked like they belonged on the streets of the Bowery—their brightly colored outfits and cocky strutting were out of place in the neighborhood where Evelyn lived.

Cela waited a moment longer and then made up her mind. She didn't want to return to her uncle's apartment with its cramped rooms and the family in it looking at her as though Abel's death had been her fault. Just the thought of the way they traded glances when they didn't think she was looking made her chest feel hollow, but it was nothing compared to the twisting vines of grief around her heart. If that boy was trouble, as she suspected, it might mean danger for Jianyu. She wasn't going to let the people who killed Abe have even one more victory.

Resolute, she took a breath and started out from her hiding place, but she hadn't even made it to the halo of the streetlight's glow before she was grabbed from behind and pulled back into the shadows.

Cela tried to scream, but a broad hand was clamped over her mouth, just as tight and unyielding as the one that was wrapped around her waist.

"*Shhhhh,*" a voice hissed, close to her ear. "It's me."

If she hadn't been supported by the strength of the arm that held her, Cela would have been on the ground. Her legs went liquid beneath her, because she *recognized* that voice. And it was impossible.

"I'm gonna let you go now, but keep quiet, okay?"

She nodded, tears pricking her eyes. A moment later, the hand came away from her mouth and she spun to find her brother, Abel, standing there behind her, alive and whole and every bit as real as he'd ever been. For the first time in days, it felt like she could actually breathe.

Her arms were around his neck in an instant, and she couldn't stop the sob that welled up from inside of her.

"Shhhh," he repeated, his strong hands patting her back. "I told you, you have to keep quiet."

She pulled back and looked at him again, just to be sure he wasn't some terrible trick her mind was playing on her. Her hands cupped his cheeks. "Abe. You're dead."

"Do I look dead?" he asked, giving her the same doubtful look he'd given her a hundred times before when she'd tried to follow him and his friends through the city, nothing but a tiny girl tagging after boys who didn't want her.

"But *how?*" Her head was spinning and the vines around her heart were trading thorns for blooms. "They shot you."

Abe gave her a look like she should have known better. "Nobody shot me, Rabbit."

Her heart nearly broke to hear that stupid nickname on his lips again. "But I heard them," she said, her voice cracking without her permission. "I heard the gunshot, and then your body hit the floor."

"They tried awful hard, but I wasn't the one who got himself killed," he said, his expression going dark.

Abe isn't dead. Which meant . . . for the last week, he *hadn't* been dead. "Then where have you *been?*" she asked, realization hitting her. She'd been at her uncle's for nearly a week, and he'd never once come for her. He'd left her to think the worst. He'd left her to deal with their family on her own. He'd left *her*. She smacked at his chest. "I thought you were *dead*. I've been crying myself to sleep every night over you." She slapped his chest again. "And every morning I woke up not remembering for a second, and every morning I had to *re-remember*," she said, her voice breaking. And then, because it hadn't felt half as good as she'd wanted it to, she raised her hand to slap him again.

He caught her wrist gently. "I'm sorry I couldn't come, but I didn't want to lead the people who were after me to Desmond's place," he said, taking her by the hand. "I've been watching, though. Waiting for you to get far enough away for me to talk to."

"What do you mean, the people after *you*?" she asked, hesitating. "They were after *me*. Because of Darrigan's mother." *And the ring.*

Abe shook his head. "They were from the railroad."

"Why would the railroad come after you?" she asked.

"They were just trying to scare me off. A few of us guys have been talking with the Knights of Labor about unionizing the Pullman porters so they'd have to pay us a better wage and give us better shifts. That's about the last thing the company wants, so they thought they could convince me to stop, but their convincing looked an awful lot like forcing."

"So you *shot* them?" she asked, not understanding how the person in front of her could also be the brother she knew would never have hurt anyone intentionally.

"Things got heated, and they threatened you," he told her, his voice as dark as the shadows around them. "Look, I have a safe place uptown to stay with some guys from the *Freeman*. It'll be okay. We can talk about all the rest later."

"Abe—"

"I promise I'll tell you everything, but right now we have to go," he said, starting to tug her back toward the alley.

She took three steps before she stopped and pulled her hand out of his. "But Jianyu is still in there."

Abe nodded. "Which is why we need to go now, before he comes back."

He reached for her again, but she held her hand out of reach. "You don't understand. He's a friend of mine, and—"

A carriage had just rattled to a stop across from the alley, and with a sinking weight in her stomach, Cela recognized the woman who got out of it. She walked to the mouth of the alley as Evelyn started toward the building.

No. As soon as Evelyn had closed the entry door behind her, Cela stepped out of the alleyway and started hooting again. Abe tried to pull her back, but she shrugged him off.

"What are you doing?" he asked, looking at her like she had lost her mind.

"If that woman who just got out of the carriage finds him, there's gonna be trouble. I'm not going to just leave him."

"His trouble doesn't concern us," Abe said, putting his arm around her.

"It concerns *me*," she said, allowing herself a moment to enjoy her brother's warmth and strength. *Abe. Alive.* "Jianyu saved my life when you were off hiding without sending me so much as a word," she told him, her voice clipped and her nerves feeling like live wires. *Abe is alive.* He was into more than she'd understood, but he was alive.

He was quiet a moment before he let out a long-suffering sigh. "Then I guess we'd better go in after him."

Cela let Abe take the lead, since she knew they'd waste time arguing about it otherwise. They didn't run into anyone or any trouble in the building, but they stopped just down the hallway from Cela's open apartment door. She could hear someone talking, but she couldn't make out what was being said. From the voices, she knew that Evelyn and Jianyu were still in there, and that Evelyn wasn't happy.

"Let me go first," Cela whispered.

"No——" Her brother was adamant.

"Evelyn *knows* me," Cela explained. She didn't tell Abe how the bitch had also locked her in a room and stolen the one thing of value Cela had left. "I can distract her long enough to get an advantage."

"I'm not letting you——"

But Cela was already walking away from him. She didn't really have a plan, except that she'd lost her brother once that week. She'd lived through that pain, that horrible knowledge that he was gone, and she'd do whatever she could to make sure she never had to feel that again—even if it meant putting herself between Abe and that red-haired she-devil.

She didn't bother to knock or make any sound to introduce herself— the bigger the distraction, the better as far as Cela was concerned—but when she stepped into the open doorway and took in the scene unfolding, she realized she was in over her head. Evelyn's eyes were lit with some unholy light and she was holding a handful of the blond boy's hair as he knelt next to her, but across from her Jianyu had a knife to his own neck. The strain on his face was clear and his hands were shaking, like he was fighting to keep himself from pressing the blade into the soft skin of his throat.

Magic, she realized. Evelyn was one of them too. Her whole life she'd lived in the city and thought that the old magic had never touched her. She'd known it to be a dangerous force, a fearsome thing that the ordinary person had to be protected from, so it had come as an unsettling realization to know that she'd been living side by side with it all along. First Jianyu and Darrigan and now Evelyn. And while Evelyn was a dangerous hussy, Cela didn't figure it was the magic that made her that way.

Evelyn glanced up and saw Cela standing in the doorway, and her expression turned dark and thunderous. "Ah, Cela, I'd wondered where you'd scurried off to, and here you are." The corners of Evelyn's painted mouth curled up to reveal her teeth. "What an unpleasant surprise. But since you're here, do come in."

Cela felt herself softening, wanting to move into the room even though she knew it was a bad idea. She took a step toward them without meaning to, and then she fought against taking another.

"I was just entertaining a couple of unexpected guests," Evelyn told her. "Or rather, I should say, I was just teaching a couple of thieves a lesson. Perhaps you'd like to join us?"

"I'm just here for my friend. And what you took from me," Cela said, gritting her teeth against the strange pull she felt. Even though she knew what Evelyn was, what the woman was capable of, Cela felt drawn to her, enticed by her.

"You mean this?" Evelyn lifted her hand, and the ring that Darrigan had gifted Cela flashed in the light. "You're welcome to try to take it from me." She laughed. "Though I doubt a Sundren like you could manage."

Cela's feet were inching toward Evelyn. One and then the other, no matter how she fought. *Abe. I need Abe.*

She got the burst of a gunshot in answer.

The sound echoed through the cramped room as Evelyn crumpled to the floor with a gasp, grabbing her right arm. At the same moment, Jianyu dropped the knife he'd been holding and collapsed to his knees, his breathing heavy, and the boy Evelyn had been holding by the hair fell to the floor. He seemed too dazed to get himself up.

Abe was standing in the doorway, a pistol sure in his hand. "Let's go," he said.

"You *shot* her," Cela said, the shock of it still fresh and numbing as she watched Evelyn grab her arm, writhing in pain. The brother she'd known wouldn't have hurt a fly. *Who is this man who looks so much like him?*

She'd been content to see him through little-girl eyes for so long that she hadn't realized how strong and certain he'd become. But she *should* have. For two years Abel had taken care of her and protected her after their father had been killed. For two years he'd been her rock. She should have known that he would have had their father's sureness and their mother's stubborn strength inside of him, just as she did.

Cela turned back to the scene behind her. The blond boy lay there, not moving, as Jianyu climbed to his feet and went to Evelyn. He took her hand and tried to pull the ring from it, but even with her injured arm, she lashed out at him. He drew back, out of her reach.

"We have to go," Cela told him.

Jianyu glanced at her, his expression still slightly dazed and his forehead damp with the exertion of what he'd been through. "We can't leave without the ring."

"Then you'd better get it fast," Abel said. "Somebody will have heard the shot." He had Cela by the hand, but if her feet had moved on their own a moment before, it seemed like she couldn't move them at all now.

Evelyn was struggling up from the floor, her eyes glowing again with that strange, unholy light. "Come and get it," she purred, taunting Jianyu. "If you can . . ."

But Jianyu's face had gone slack, and his body was suddenly deathly still.

"Jianyu?" Cela asked, ignoring how her brother was trying to pull her from the room.

Jianyu was on his feet and his eyes were open, but he didn't seem to hear her.

Even as blood pooled beneath her, Evelyn was laughing, a deeply maniacal cackling that twisted into the pit of Cela's stomach. She took a step back.

"That's right," Evelyn said to Cela. "Run away. Run far, far away, little Cela." She laughed again, her face pale and her voice ragged. "The boys are mine."

"We can't leave them here." She ripped herself away from Abel and went to Jianyu, whose gaze was on some unseen thing in the distance. He wasn't listening to her, but she could tug him along. "Get the other one."

With a ragged grumble, Abe released Cela's hand long enough to scoop up the blond boy from the floor. "*Now* can we go?" he asked. "Or is there anyone else you want me to collect and carry for you?"

Evelyn was on the floor, trying to pull herself up as she grabbed her bleeding arm, and everything was chaos, but Cela felt a laugh bubbling up. With all the mess they were in, Abe was alive. As long as she had him, the rest didn't matter.

By the time they were in the stairwell, Jianyu had come back to himself and was walking under his own power. "The ring," he said, when they reached the bottom of the steps. He started to turn back.

"No." Cela tugged at him.

"We can't let her have it," he argued, trying to break loose from her grip, but she could feel how gently he treated her.

"You go back there now, you're going to be arrested for trying to kill a white woman," Abe told him.

From the expression on Jianyu's face, he wanted to argue.

"Can you get back in without her knowing?" Cela asked.

Jianyu met her gaze, and she saw the calculations play out in his mind. Finally he shook his head. "Even if she can't see me, she could sense me."

"Then you can't go back," she told him. "Not now."

"But the ring—"

"It won't do anyone any good if you're dead," Cela said. "We'll come back for it. I promise."

"Don't make promises you can't keep," Abe snapped. "We can't be here when the police arrive."

The blond didn't stir, so Abe didn't put him down. They ran into the night, leaving Evelyn howling behind them.

THE BREWERY

1904—St. Louis

Esta came to slowly, reaching toward consciousness like a swimmer struggling up to the surface of a cold, deep lake. Her head pounded as she lay in the darkness and breathed in the dusty scent of the burlap sack still over her head. She didn't know where she was or how long she'd been out, but she remembered who had taken her.

The Antistasi.

Her breath hitched at the memory of everything that had happened at the fair—the missing necklace, the way the darkness had descended stark and empty and absolute when her affinity touched the power of the Book. The ground splitting open . . . *The ground* split *open.*

She pulled herself upright, but nearly toppled over again from the dizziness brought on by whatever they'd used to knock her out. Opium, maybe, from the way her affinity felt dull and numb, but not *only* opium. This was different from anything she'd experienced before—there was something about whatever they'd given her that made her feel untethered, like she wasn't quite attached to the earth but was floating free, even as she could feel the solid floor beneath her.

She called for Harte, but there was no answer.

After a while she thought she heard voices, and moments later the door opened. "Come on," a voice said. Since she didn't recognize it, she figured it must not be the cowboy. Rough hands grabbed her by the arms and dragged her from where she was lying. The moment they took her by the arms, she realized that her cuff was missing. Panic seized her as she realized what that meant, but she kept that emotion locked down. She would have a better chance of getting it back if they didn't know how important it was to her.

Once she was outside the wagon, Esta could hear buzzing insects and the soft rustling of trees. *Not the city.* She wobbled at first but recovered before anyone had to support her. Whatever was about to happen, she'd walk on her own two feet. But her head ached worse now that she was upright.

"Where are we?" she asked. Her tongue still felt clumsy and thick in her dry mouth, but her voice sounded strong. At least she *thought* it did.

"You'll see soon enough, but I'm going to warn you before we go in." It was the cowboy this time. "I'll give you the same warning I gave to your friend. If either of you even thinks about causing a lick of trouble, there ain't a person here what would think twice about taking care of you for good—no matter who you think you are. You got that?"

"Understood," she told him, even as she was already considering all the possible options for freeing herself and Harte if things went downhill.

"That's fine. Come on, now. This way . . ."

With her head pounding from the drug and her whole body feeling like her joints had come loose, it was a challenge to stay on her feet as she was led blindly through what felt like an obstacle course of ramps and steps. Finally, they entered a building—she knew, because the insects went quiet. From the way their footsteps echoed, it had to be a larger room, and from the other voices, they weren't alone. There were two, maybe three others already there.

They pushed her into a chair, and she felt them secure her to it with more rope. Then, without any warning, the sack they'd put over her head to blind her was pulled off. She blinked. Dim as the lighting was, it caused even more pain to shoot through her already throbbing head.

Esta ignored the pain as she squinted, trying to get her eyes to adjust. She'd been right. They were standing in something that looked like a large warehouse. On one side of the room, enormous silver tanks lined the wall. On the other side, a series of long tables held wooden crates filled with glass bottles. The stools in front of the tables stood empty. *A factory of some sort.* The people were gathered in a smaller, open space between the tanks and the tables. In addition to the cowboy, there was a handful of people—men and women of various ages. They seemed to be waiting for something.

Across from where Esta was sitting, two other guys in workman's clothes flanked a chair that held one last person—Harte. He still had the burlap sack covering his face, but that didn't seem to matter. Even with his face covered, she knew that he understood she was there—his head turned in her direction, and his entire body seemed to come to attention, straining against the ropes that held him to the chair.

"Is that you, Slim?" he asked. "They didn't hurt you, did they?"

"I'm fine," she told him, keeping her voice low and clipped. "You okay?"

"I'd be better if I could see something," he said, shaking his head a little, as if to shake off the bag.

"You'll see soon enough, when Ruth decides what to do with you," the cowboy told him. He frowned at Esta, but before he could say anything else, they heard a door opening from somewhere deep within the factory. The group turned toward the sound of the approaching footsteps, making it clear that someone important was arriving.

A moment later a woman appeared on the walkway above. She looked over the gathering below for a moment, before descending the steps to the factory floor. She was maybe in her early forties, but her hair was already shot through with gray, and she wore an expression that labeled her as the person in charge.

The woman—clearly the Ruth the cowboy had mentioned—gave a silent nod, and at her order, one of the men flanking Harte drew the sack off. He'd lost the hat he'd been wearing earlier, and his dark hair was a mess, sticking up in all directions. His eyes found hers, but they were too wide, too wild, and she narrowed hers at him in warning. If he wasn't careful, he was going to give away too much.

Stop it, she tried to tell him silently. But she wasn't sure if he understood. The cords of his neck were tense, and they didn't relax at the sight of her.

Without any introduction, Ruth turned to Esta, her voice unyielding as she asked a single question: "Where is it?"

Esta blinked. "Where is what?"

"The necklace," Ruth said, stalking toward the chair where Esta was tied.

"I don't have any necklace," Esta said, well aware of *exactly* what necklace Ruth was referring to. And if they knew about the necklace, it was possible they'd also realized what her cuff was.

Ruth pursed her lips, clearly not believing her. "There is only one thing you could have wanted in the Streets of Cairo—it's the same thing we want. We know you intended to steal the necklace, and we know that you went to the Exposition today to do just that. I allowed this particular farce to run to its conclusion because it suited my purposes, but the time has come. I'm out of patience." She leaned down until she was close enough that Esta could see the fine lines that had already started to carve themselves into her face. "I'll ask you this question only one more time: What have you done with the necklace?"

"We couldn't steal what wasn't there," Esta told her. "It was a trap. When we got to the chamber, there was nothing in the case, and the Guard was ready for us."

Ruth's expression faltered. "You're sure of this?" When Esta nodded, Ruth turned to the cowboy, but he only shrugged and gave a slight shake of his head. "I knew this would never work," she told him. "We should have stopped them days ago and gone after the necklace ourselves."

"Days ago?" Esta asked.

"A haircut and a suit might be enough to fool the Guard, but I'm not half so simple," Ruth said. "Esta Filosik. The Devil's Thief. I've had people watching you ever since North here saw you outside the theater."

Esta kept her expression from betraying even a flicker of the anxiety she felt at the woman's words. The fact that Harte had been right about her disguise barely even registered over the sudden and unpleasant realization that they'd been watched for days, and Esta hadn't even suspected. She was either getting rusty, or these people—these Antistasi—were more formidable than she'd expected.

"If you knew who I was, I can't imagine why you'd waste your time having me followed," she said, trying to affect a haughty indifference. "You'd know already that we're on the same side."

"Are we?" Ruth said.

"Of course," Esta insisted, refusing to show even a hint of her apprehension. She'd bluffed her way out of more difficult spots than this. If they thought she was the Devil's Thief, then she would use every bit of that title to her advantage. "That *is* that why you use my name so freely, isn't it?"

The woman's nostrils flared in irritation, but she didn't deny it.

"Yes, I know all about that," Esta said, going on the offensive. "I've seen the masks and gowns. I know how your little group pretends to be the Devil's Thief—to be *me*." She watches Ruth's expression go dark. "I know all about the Antistasi."

The woman let out a hollow laugh. "We are no more the Antistasi than a drop of water is the sea."

"But you're part of them," Esta pressed, testing the mood in the room as she spoke. Whatever doubts Ruth might have about her, the rest of the Antistasi in the room felt more tentative, supportive even—except maybe for the guy they called North. It seemed that even if Ruth didn't much care whether Esta was the Devil's Thief, the others in the room *did*. If she could use that to keep Harte safe, she would. "Or did you steal their name as well?"

"I've stolen nothing. We have *earned* the right to call ourselves Antistasi," Ruth admitted, her tone dripping with acid.

"So I've heard," Esta said, keeping her tone detached, aloof. She kept her eyes focused on Ruth, even as she wanted to look at Harte.

Ruth considered her. "Have you?"

Esta nodded. "You have quite the reputation in this town. It's impressive what you've accomplished," she said, playing to the woman's ego.

But the ploy didn't work. Ruth's eyes narrowed. "Then you know already that we are not to be trifled with. If you knew anything at all about us, you would know that we don't hesitate to destroy those we consider enemies."

"Of course," Esta said easily. "But I'm not your enemy. From what I hear? Seems like I'm more like your muse."

"You?" Ruth laughed again before her mouth drew into a flat, mocking line. "You're just a *girl*. The Devil's Thief is bigger than any single person—she's certainly bigger than *you*. You're unnecessary at best. At worst, you are a problem that needs to be dealt with."

"I'm not a problem," Esta told her. But then she considered her words and gave Ruth a careless shrug, refusing to be intimidated. "Then again, maybe I am, but I'm definitely not *your* problem."

"No?" Ruth mused. "From where I stand, you are a liability to myself and to the Antistasi."

Esta gave a cold laugh, using the motion to glance at Harte, who was watching the conversation with a tense expression of concentration. "How do you figure?"

Ruth stepped toward her. "The police and the Guard have been looking for you ever since the night we helped you slipped past them at the Jefferson Hotel. For a week they've been on high alert, searching everywhere for some sign of you, which has been more than a simple inconvenience for me. Your presence in my town has made it nearly impossible for my people to do their jobs and has put every one of us in danger of being discovered. All because the authorities believe you to be something special, something *dangerous*. The Devil's Thief," she said, but there was a hint of scorn in her voice. "But here you sit, at my mercy. Barely a woman and too soft for anyone with eyes in their head to mistake you for a man. You are nothing but a liability."

Esta let her mouth curve. "If you really believed that, you wouldn't have tied us up and drugged us just to have this little conversation."

"I don't take unnecessary risks," Ruth said, visibly bristling. "Not when the safety of my people is at stake."

"I haven't done anything to your people," Esta countered. "There's no reason to think I would."

Ruth tipped her head to the side. "You didn't plant a smoking device on my man?"

"He was following me," Esta said, unapologetic. "And it's not like he bothered to introduce himself. I didn't know who he was or that he was one of yours at the time, and I had to distract him. Besides, he seems to be just fine."

Ruth's brows drew together. "While I'll admit that I'm inclined to be impressed by anyone who's able to get the better of North, I'm *less* inclined to be forgiving of your attempt to incriminate us with your reckless display at the fair."

North. That must be the cowboy, Esta thought, and the way he was glaring at her only confirmed it.

"Do you know what would have happened if you were caught today?" Ruth continued. "Do you realize what it would have done to us?"

"I can't see how me being caught would have affected you in the least," Esta said.

"Which only shows how foolish you are," Ruth said. "I don't know who you really are, and I don't know if you have done even one of the many things that have been attributed to you, but I do know this— the Guard catching you would have been a victory for the Society and the other Brotherhoods. It would have been a fatal blow to the Antistasi movement *everywhere*. To catch you would have meant an end to the legend of the Thief. That legend is what keeps us safe even as it inspires fear in our enemies. Without it, we'd be exposed."

She hadn't even considered that. Esta had seen the women in the ballroom, she'd heard Julien talk about the exploits of the Antistasi, and she had admired them. She hadn't realized that she might be putting them in danger just by *actually* existing.

"It wasn't my intention to put any of you in danger," Esta said, trying to make her voice sound contrite. "I don't want to be a liability. I'd much rather be an asset."

"But you're not an asset, and without the necklace, what can you offer me?"

"Besides my name?" Esta asked, trying to come up with something that would be convincing enough to assuage Ruth's doubts.

"We already have that," Ruth told her. "Even without you, we can continue to use it."

"But you don't have a way into the Society," Harte said from across the room.

Ruth's brows drew together and she turned away from Esta to focus on Harte. His expression was strained, but he had a look of sheer determination in his eyes.

"Why would you imagine we need that?"

"Because we know that you have big plans," Harte said, drawing Ruth's attention toward him. "And we know what you're still missing."

BENEDICT O'DOHERTY

1904—St. Louis

Harte's head was still pounding from whatever they'd used on him in the wagon, and inside, the power of the Book was churning uneasily. It didn't like whatever that drug had been—and, to be fair, neither did Harte. His affinity felt hazy and indistinct, like the magic that was his usual companion was too far for him to reach.

Fine, then. Harte might be a magician by trade, but he was a con man at heart.

"If you know so much, perhaps we should dispose of you now," Ruth said, stalking toward him. She had a combination of fear and fury in her eyes—a combination that might prove dangerous—but at least she wasn't so focused on Esta any longer.

"That would be a mistake."

"Unlike you," Ruth said, "we do not make mistakes."

"Maybe not yet," Harte said, not so much as blinking. "But not taking advantage of what we can offer you? *Definitely* a mistake."

"Why do you think we need entry into the Society?" Ruth asked.

"The necklace wasn't at the fair. If you don't have it, that means the Society has moved it. How are you planning to get the necklace if you don't even know where it is?" He paused, letting his question hang in the air before he spoke again. "You're already running short on time."

Ruth straightened, and Harte could tell from the way her expression shifted that her actions were a show for everyone in the room. "You don't know what you're talking about."

"No?" Harte asked easily, relying on the impressions he'd gotten from when his captors had touched him without realizing the danger. "Your guys are spooked because they know you're not quite ready. They're thinking that maybe it's too big a risk, especially that one." Harte nodded toward the one who had held his hands behind his back—the one he'd managed to read just before he was tossed into the wagon. "Frank, right? He's got a sister up in Chicago. Figures that he could take off and go live with her instead of getting himself killed."

Ruth turned to the guy, whose face had gone pale. "Is this true? You doubt our undertaking?"

The guy shook his head dumbly for a second or two before he found words. "He's lying, Ruth. He's just trying to confuse us." But the fear in the guy's expression told a different story.

"Cowardice will kill you, Frank. Not my plans." Ruth nodded to one of the others. "Take him downstairs and make sure he's secured. There isn't room for misgivings and fear. Not now." Then she turned on Harte. "I know who she is, but who are you?"

"Someone just like you," he said simply. "I hate the Society and every-thing it stands for. We heard about what you did last fall—the attack on the construction of the Exposition. It was brilliant. Masterful, even."

Ruth considered him. "What is your name?"

"Benedict O'Doherty," Harte told her, the name slipping from his lips before he could consider it. "I'm called Ben for short." *Or I was, once.* It seemed he'd been resurrected twice now, he thought darkly.

"I don't trust either one of you," Ruth told him.

"That only proves you're not stupid," he said simply. "But not accept-ing our help—that *would* be stupid. Especially when we could help you be more successful than you've even dreamed. Give us a chance to prove ourselves. The one you just had taken away was worried about a job you had for him. Let us do it instead."

Her eyes narrowed as she thought it over. Then her expression cleared. "Fine," she said, her lips curling. "I'll give you this one chance to prove yourselves." She glanced at the cowboy. "Take him away and make sure he doesn't cause any problems."

"But the job—" Harte said.

"I think we'll let the Thief do it. If she's so powerful and so anxious to work with us, she shouldn't have a problem. And if she does anything at all to betray us, you'll be the one to pay."

JUST A GIRL

Maggie watched as her sister's people led the Thief and her companion away. They went calmly, though clearly reluctantly, and the way that the guy—Benedict—looked at the Thief, as though he would do anything at all to keep what was about to happen from occurring, nudged at something deep inside of her.

"Was that really necessary?" she asked Ruth, who was standing, impassive as always, watching as well.

Her oldest sister, the only mother she'd ever known, glanced over at her with impatience shimmering in her gaze. "Are you questioning my judgment?"

Maggie shook her head. "No, Mother Ruth. Just wondering . . ." But secretly, she *was* questioning her sister. She'd been questioning Ruth and her tactics for some time, but right now, she knew this was where she had to be. "If Lipscomb's people catch her—"

"Then they take care of a problem for me," Ruth said in a tone that brooked no argument. "She's not the Devil's Thief, Maggie. She's just a girl, same as you. Same as I once was. The Devil's Thief is bigger—it's something *we* created through our actions. If she's so stupid as to get herself caught by Caleb Lipscomb and his half-witted socialists, then it's what she'll deserve."

"And if she doesn't?"

Her sister's expression brightened. "Then she'll already be part of this. Think of it, Margaret. If she delivers the device, there won't be any way for her to change her mind. She'll be responsible for the explosion and for everything that happens after. If it goes well, as you've assured me it will, that means that she will have a hand in the effects of the serum. Not only will she understand the power it contains, but she will have the pride of knowing that she was part of it. She'll understand and be one of us for good. More important, everyone who might stand against us will know she's *ours*. When the other Antistasi groups know that the Thief chose *us*, it will go that much further toward solidifying our leadership."

Maggie couldn't help but frown. "You don't think you should tell her what we're doing?"

"Why should I?" Ruth asked. "This will be a test of her resolve—of her *loyalty* to our cause . . . and to me. If she's truly for us, she'll be willing to kill for us. And if she's not, we'll know now, before she has the chance to harm more important plans."

OUTMATCHED

1902—New York

Jack hadn't been backstage at Wallack's Theatre for weeks, not since he'd visited Darrigan, believing the magician to be an ally instead of an enemy. He would have gladly avoided the theater for the rest of his days, except that he was more certain Evelyn had something he wanted—and something that someone else was willing to kill her for.

It galled him that he still didn't know what it was.

The day after she'd come to his town house, ready and willing, he'd awoken to find her gone and his head pounding from all the sherry they'd had together. Because he'd overindulged, the memory of that night was still hazy and indistinct. Clearly, she hadn't been all that memorable, so he'd dismissed her. But then he'd read in the *Herald* about how she had been attacked. Intruders had broken into her home to rob her and shot her instead. Of course, she was using the attack for publicity, but that didn't change the fact that she must have had something of value. Which had reminded him of her earlier teasing.

The promise of discovering what she had was worth overcoming his disgust and the anger he felt simply walking through the maze that lurked behind the stage. No one stopped him months ago, and they didn't bother to now, either. Tucking the bouquet of roses beneath his arm, he knocked twice on Evelyn's dressing room door and entered when he heard her voice answer.

Her dressing room was nothing like Darrigan's. It was slightly larger, and the walls were draped with swaths of silks and satins, giving it a feeling of being both exotic and sensual. But Jack wasn't taken in by it. This time he would remain in control of the evening's progress.

Evelyn was draped across a chaise lounge, arranged like a painting in her silken robe. He couldn't see her injury, but clearly it hadn't been life threatening. Her red mouth curved up when she saw him. "Hello, darling," she purred. "Are those for me?" She lifted herself from the couch to accept the flowers from him, and when she did, he noticed the glint of gold on her finger.

The ring was enormous. Its golden filigreed setting held a stone far too large for a common trollop like Evelyn, and he knew in that moment that it was what the thieves had been after and what he'd come for.

"What is it, Jack?" Evelyn asked, arranging the flowers in the vase on her dressing table. "You look like you've seen a ghost."

"Not a ghost," he told her, his voice heavy with anticipation. "An *angel*."

Her eyes glowed, and she went to him, willing and warm and ready.

Later, when he was riding in the carriage back to his town house, he came out of the fog of desire and realized that he'd forgotten completely about the ring—*again*. He'd been right there, and he'd never even touched it. And he couldn't remember why. He couldn't even remember what had happened between them.

His hands clenched into fists. This time he couldn't blame it on the drink.

He should have known better. Something like this had happened to him before, in Greece, when he would wake without any idea of what had transpired in the hours before morning. He'd joked then that the girl he'd fallen for was a siren, tempting him to the rocks that would be his death, but he hadn't known how right he'd been. How devious the girl had actually been.

With sudden understanding, he realized that Evelyn was the same. Like the girl in Greece who had nearly ruined him, Evelyn was a witch—maggot scum who thought she could best him at his own game. But Jack wasn't the green youth he'd been then. Greece had changed him, and the Book that he had locked away safely in his rooms had made him into something new. Evelyn might have feral magic, she might even have a ring that amplified her powers, but she didn't have the Book. She couldn't begin to predict how outmatched she was.

THE SECRET ON
ORCHARD STREET

1902—New York

James Lorcan had a feeling that things would become more interesting not long after he'd watched Logan Sullivan enter the apartment building and heard the hoot of something that wasn't an owl nearby. He sent the others back to the Strega, except for Mooch, whom he kept nearby. He didn't need the muscle; whatever was about to happen, tonight wasn't the place for a fight. That would come later.

He kept to the shadows and watched the entrance of the building, until he saw the group of people appear. A sturdy-looking man with deep brown skin had Logan looped over his shoulder, and a girl James didn't recognize kept close by Jianyu. An unexpected development, to be sure, but it answered one question. And at least his companions were Sundren. Uninteresting, except for the way they now had two people who should have been his prisoners.

Mooch took a step toward the group of them already scurrying down the sidewalk, putting distance between themselves and the building, but James caught his arm.

"Just follow them. Find out where they're going, but don't do anything else. Then come back to the Strega."

Mooch looked like he wanted to argue, but James narrowed his eyes at the boy, and he seemed to decide against it.

Jianyu had Logan, but really, it didn't matter. The boy was as much a liability as he was an asset. Besides, James still had all the secrets he needed on the shelves of Dolph's bookcases, and now in the notebook tucked into his coat.

Jianyu's appearance here, at this apartment where he had no real cause to be, told James one very important thing—Logan hadn't been lying about who he was or what he could do. Which meant that the notebook he'd delivered wasn't a trap or a trick. It was nothing more or less than the truth.

It was late—nearly midnight—but there was another stop James needed to make now that he knew he could trust the words tucked near his chest, the words he would himself someday write.

The lights in the building on Orchard Street were out when he finally arrived, but that didn't concern him. He paid the woman on the third floor more than enough for the inconvenience of waking her.

She wasn't happy, but she didn't complain as she let James in and led the way down the narrow hall to the small room where the girl slept. He dismissed the woman and went to the girl's bedside, kneeling beside it so that he could wake her. The small face scrunched at the interruption, but eventually she reluctantly opened her sleep-crusted eyes to squint at him.

It used to be hard to look at the girl without seeing Leena looking back at him, judging him for the choices he'd made and the path he'd chosen. It had gotten easier, in time, to see past Leena's features—the golden eyes, the wide mouth that the girl would someday grow into—to the child beneath them. The promise in her.

Once he had thought that he could save her from Leena's faults. Dolph's partner, his wife, really, in everything but name, had been too soft when she should have been steel, too generous when she should have kept her cards close to her chest. It had been a surprise—a delightful one, but a surprise nonetheless—when Leena had decided to hide the child from Dolph. But in the end it had been her undoing.

He had hoped to mold the girl, to use her for his own bidding. Now James knew that in the end it would never work. He was raising a viper who would one day threaten everything he'd built, everything he was destined to become.

He could kill the girl now, but time was a funny thing, tangled as a knot and woven into a pattern that even he could not yet see. If he killed her, what might that change? What might he lose that her appearance had helped him to gain?

He couldn't kill her. Not yet. But he could use her to send a message.

He took Viola's blade from his jacket.

"Come, Carina, we're going to play a little game." He would send Esta a message through time and space and the impossible world. He would tell her he was waiting.

Using the blade named for the goddess of funerals, he began to cut.

THE DROP

1904—St. Louis

The carriage rattled onward through the night, carrying Esta toward some unknown destination. On the bench across from her, sprawled with a lazy confidence, North took up too much room. He had a revolver in his hand, a clear threat that she shouldn't try anything.

"Best not jostle that too much," he said, when she shifted the notebook that was resting on her lap. It looked like an average-size leather-bound notebook that anyone might carry with them, but it weighed more than an ordinary book should. Whatever was between the pages was dense and heavy—and dangerous. "We don't want it going off before you deliver it."

His warning made her sit a little straighter. "Where are we going, anyway?"

"You'll see," North said.

"I think I have a right to know who I'm going to kill," she told him, trying to affect a bored indifference. In reality, her hands were damp with nervous sweat as she tried to keep the book as still as she could while the carriage bumped along. Considering the roughness of the roads that led from the edges of town, where the brewery was, into the center of St. Louis, it had been a challenge.

"Who said anything about killing anyone?" North asked. His eyes were shadowed by the brim of his hat, but his thin mouth hitched up in the moonlight that shone through the carriage's window.

"It's a bomb, isn't it?" she asked, not yet allowing herself to feel any relief.

North's lips flattened, a thin scar at the edge of them flashing white with his annoyance. "Bombs are for Sundren. They're messy and sloppy. Nobody's gonna die tonight," he told her. "Except maybe you, if that package doesn't get to where it needs to be. And definitely your friend, back at Mother Ruth's, if you do anything to cause a problem."

Esta frowned, ignoring his bluster. If the Antistasi wanted her and Harte dead, they would have already tried to kill them. "If it's not a bomb, what is it?"

"It's a gift," he told her. Then he turned to watch out the window, signaling the end of the conversation.

A gift? Like hell.

The woman she'd heard the others call Mother Ruth had made it clear that whatever was in the parcel was dangerous. None of the Antistasi wanted to be anywhere near it when she handed it over to Esta with the warning not to open it until she was ready to make the drop. Ruth's instructions had been simple: Don't leave it anywhere but the center of the building, as close to the target as she could. And don't do anything to betray the mission, or Harte will die.

If Esta got caught? Well, that wasn't Ruth's problem. The people she was delivering the book to wouldn't take kindly to an intruder. Esta would be on her own and at their mercy, but no one had told her who the target was.

"At least tell me who I'm up against," she said, trying to draw North's attention back to her. The open road had given way to the stacked buildings of the outskirts of town, the factories and warehouses that lined the river.

"Does it matter?" he asked with a mocking smile. "You're the Devil's Thief, aren't you?"

"I like to be prepared," she said with a shrug in her tone. "And I like to be the one who decides whether the risk to my life is really worth the cost of theirs."

North looked at her, his odd, uneven-colored eyes piercing her unease.

"Who are *you* to make that judgment?" he said softly. "This isn't the first deed done in your name, and it certainly won't be the last. Now's not exactly the time to be getting all high and mighty about things."

His words rattled something inside of her. He was right. The Antistasi had used her name who knew how many times before. It didn't matter that she hadn't been the one to perpetrate any of the attacks; a choice she had made had set all of this into motion.

"That's what I thought." North turned to the window, scratching at the scruff on his jawline as he watched the passing city. Eventually, the carriage rumbled to a stop and North checked the window to see where they were. "We're here." He pushed his hat back so he could look her dead in the eye. "Unless you've changed your mind?"

Esta considered the options before her. She didn't doubt that the notebook she was carrying, whatever North said, was something dangerous. She could still say no. She could drop the notebook here, pull time around her, and run.

But then what?

Mother Ruth and the rest of the Antistasi back at the brewery still had Harte. They'd taken him away not long after he'd opened his big mouth, and Esta had no idea where they'd put him. By the time she figured it out, he might already be dead—she couldn't hold on to time *that* long, especially lately.

And even if she found Harte before they hurt him, she had no idea what they'd done with Ishtar's Key. She hadn't asked, because she didn't want to alert them to its importance if they hadn't already realized. But if they *had* already realized what kind of power the stone had . . .

She couldn't worry about that. For now she had a job to do. And if her choice was between Harte and the person this delivery was set for, there wasn't really a choice. Dakari, Dolph . . . Esta had lost too many people to lose another.

But there was one other thing, a point that kept niggling at her like an itch she couldn't reach. She knew she was being used. Esta's name had been thrown around for nearly two years now without her ever knowing, and if Ruth had her way, the Antistasi would continue to use it. But she'd had enough of being a pawn in someone else's game. She'd been led like a marionette on a string her entire life by Professor Lachlan. She wasn't about to allow Ruth the same power over her now.

No, Esta had seen the mood in the building when Ruth talked, and she'd heard the fear in Frank's voice when Ruth accused him of cowardice. The Antistasi might follow Ruth, but that didn't mean that they liked her or trusted her. Which gave Esta an opening. But to gain their trust, she had to start by proving that she was one of them—beginning with North. Which meant that she had to go through with this.

"I'm not going to change my mind," she told North. "Who's my mark?"

He studied her for a second or two, as if trying to figure out whether this was just another trick. "Just remember, you're not the only one who can pull a disappearing act. If you try anything, your friend dies."

"I'm aware." She gave him a bored look. "Are we going to sit here all night," she asked when he continued to stare at her, "or are you going to tell me who this package is meant for?"

"Just making sure we're clear," he said. "You're looking for Caleb Lipscomb. You can find him at number four thirty-two. It's just down this row of warehouses and then to the right. Once you're inside, go up to the second floor."

Caleb Lipscomb. She'd never heard of him, but that didn't necessarily mean much. "How will I find him?"

North's strange eyes flashed with amusement. "You'll know him when you see him. He likes to be in the center of things. Off you go now," he said, unlatching the door.

Outside the carriage, the air was cooler, but it carried the scent of the river, a muddy, earthy smell layered over with the heaviness of machine oil and coal from the factories that lined its banks. Esta readjusted the parcel under her arm, making sure to keep it steady and the pages tightly closed. They'd told her that the fuse inside would activate when she pulled a loose sheet out of the center, and she didn't need that happening before she found the person it was intended for.

Her chest felt tight. She didn't believe North's claim that it wasn't a bomb, and even as she walked toward her destination, she had her doubts about whether she could go through with it. It was one thing in theory, but it was another when her feet were steadily moving her toward the moment she'd have to decide.

True, she's been ready to kill Jack back at the station. She'd had the gun in her hands and the resolve to end him—because he'd *deserved* it. Because she knew that he would hurt countless people if she'd let him live. And she'd been right. From what she'd learned, Jack had been one of the proponents of the Act. He was the reason that magic was now illegal and that Mageus could be hunted openly, oppressed legally. But this felt different somehow. Esta didn't know this Caleb Lipscomb, whoever he was. He was a faceless name, an unknown who had done nothing to her.

Still, she couldn't see a way out of the situation, not unless she wanted the Antistasi as another enemy. And not unless she was willing to risk Harte's life.

The building labeled 432 was a long warehouse that ran the length of a block—a factory or machine shop of some sort. A single dull yellow bulb lit the door. Everything about it felt like a trap. She looked back, considering her options, and saw that North was still watching her.

He gave a nod. *Go on,* the motion seemed to say, and she took the final steps into the sallow light of the bulb. Opening the door of the building as silently as she could, she stepped inside.

THE BETHESDA FOUNTAIN

1902—New York

Viola pulled the shawl up over her head and tucked it around her chin, keeping her face turned away from the other people riding the streetcar as it traveled north, toward Central Park. Paul thought she was going to the fish market over on Fulton Street, so she'd have to be sure to stop there—or somewhere—before she returned. She couldn't chance him becoming any more suspicious than he already was. Not when she was getting so close to the information she needed.

She got off the streetcar near Madison Avenue and walked along East Drive through the park until she came to the large open piazza where the enormous fountain stood, topped by a winged angel. She didn't come to the park much on her own—there wasn't really a need to. Most days, seeing people lounging about in the grass and enjoying a stroll through the wooded pathways only served to remind her of what she would never have. But on the occasions that she did pass through it, she made sure to take a path that would bring her past this fountain. It depicted the story in the Bible of an angel healing people with the waters of Bethesda.

In a family of Sundren, Viola had been an anomaly. The magic she'd been born with had felt like a mark that meant her life had been damned from the very beginning. So the story of the angel who healed with nothing but some water had always struck something inside of her, as though there were a chance her own soul might be cleaned someday, just the same.

But Viola was not a dreamer. She'd learned long ago that fairy tales were for other people. She lived in the body she'd been given and was gratified with the life she'd made for herself. She didn't imagine other lives, and she didn't yearn for impossible things, so it was doubly troubling when her chest felt tight at the sight of the pink muslin and ivory lace on the girl sitting by the fountain.

Ruby was waiting where her note had promised she would be. Next to her was a pile of packages all tied up with string and her fiancé, Theo. He was leaning back on the bench, his hands cradling his head as though he owned the world, and Ruby was writing in a small tablet, her face bunched in concentration. Gone were the sleek dark skirt and high-buttoned shirt finished with a tie, as she'd worn the day Viola had taken the pointless ride in their carriage. Today Ruby's gown looked like something designed for an innocent debutante. It was the palest pink, with softly puffed sleeves and a delicate flounce of lace at her throat. She looked like a picture, sitting there by the water. She looked untouchable. *Impossible.*

Some days it seemed as though the pearls Ruby had been wearing the night of Delmonico's—the delicate strand of ivory beads, and the way they had lain perfectly against the dip at the base of her throat—were seared into Viola's memory. She had a feeling that this moment would join that memory.

Bah! She shook off the thought and the heat she felt. The weather was changing—that was all. The sun was high and bright, and the warmth she felt brushing against the skin beneath her blouse had nothing to do with the stupid, *stupid* little rich girl who had been brainless enough to send a note by messenger to the New Brighton—right under Paul's nose. Ruby was going to get them both killed, but then, what did the rich care about a little thing like dying? They probably thought they could give the angel of death a few dollars and send a servant instead.

Theo saw Viola first and nudged Ruby, who looked up from her writing and squinted across the piazza. The girl's entire expression brightened the moment she saw Viola coming toward them, and she put the tablet of paper and pencil back into the embroidered clutch hanging from her wrist.

"You came!" Ruby said, and before Viola knew what was happening, she found herself enveloped in the rich girl's arms and in a cloud of flowers and amber and warmth.

When Ruby released her, Viola's legs felt weak, and she stumbled backward, her shawl falling from her head as she caught herself. At the sound of Ruby's gasp, she pulled the fabric back up, covering her head and the side of her face. But Ruby wouldn't let well enough alone. Silently, her delicate features twisting in concern, she reached up to move it away from Viola's face.

"Who did this?" Ruby asked, her voice so soft that Viola could barely hear it over the rushing of the fountain's water.

"No one. It's nothing," Viola said, hitching the shawl back up. She knew what Ruby was seeing—the purple-green bruise on the side of her jaw, the cost of slipping out to take the carriage ride without telling Paul where she was going. She'd missed saying good-bye to her mother, and he'd decided to beat some manners into her.

She could have killed him, but instead she'd taken the punishment without fighting. It had seemed to appease him well enough. What else could she do? She couldn't very well have told him where she'd been. But every time she spoke or took a bite of food, the bruise throbbed, and every time it ached, she promised herself that she'd pay him back tenfold.

Still, Viola felt somehow wrong for being here, with these people. They would hurt Paul if they could—especially the girl. They would break him, destroy him. She should want that—she *did* want that—and yet, he was still family. Still her blood. She didn't know anymore if that word meant anything, or if it was just another lie, like happiness and freedom.

"That is *not* nothing," Ruby said, reaching for her. "Someone hurt you."

"It doesn't matter," Viola said, brushing away her concern. People hurt other people all the time. Why should she be exempt?

Ruby's manicured fingertips reached to touch her cheek. "We can help you, you know. You don't have to—"

"Basta!" She pushed away Ruby's hand again. "What are you going to do? Take me home like some stray dog?"

Ruby blinked, clearly surprised at the tone of Viola's voice. Probably because no one else had ever dared talk to her in such a way. Ruby Reynolds was the type of girl who'd grown up without hearing the word "no," and Viola had been born with the taste of it in her mouth.

"Don't pretend you understand my life," Viola said, a warning and a plea. "Don't pretend you can do a thing to change it. And don't imagine that I want you to." She raised her chin. "I'll take care of it myself." It was a declaration and a promise all at once. "I don't need some little rich girl's charity."

She saw Ruby flinch, but the girl didn't back down. "I didn't mean it that way. I just wanted to help."

"I came like you asked," Viola said, ignoring the hurt in Ruby's voice. "Now, what is it that you wanted?"

"I thought we could talk." Ruby worried her pink lower lip with the edge of one of her straight white teeth.

"So talk," Viola told her.

"Maybe we could go somewhere more private," Ruby said, glancing around as though she were worried someone might see her talking to a woman as common as Viola.

Viola's chest felt tight, like when she'd been trussed up in stays that night at Delmonico's. She shouldn't have come.

She could still leave. She should, before she allowed this bit of rich fluff to make her start doubting herself or the life she'd chosen. But leaving would mean that Ruby had won, and Viola couldn't have that, either.

"Fine," she said, the word coming out even sharper than she'd intended. "Where do you want to go?"

"Perhaps we could take out one of the boats?" Theo said. "It's a pleasant enough day, and I could use the exercise."

Viola swallowed the sigh that had been building inside of her. She couldn't imagine a life so easy, so filled with luxury, that Theo needed to find work. Pointless work, rowing in circles and getting nowhere at all. *Ridiculous.* But the sooner they were done with it, the better. "Fine," she said, not quite looking at Ruby. "Let's go."

A BIDDABLE GIRL

Viola was mad at her for sending the note. Viola hadn't said anything specifically, but Ruby knew that the fire in the other girl's eyes had everything to do with being summoned. It wasn't what Ruby had intended to do, and yet now she could see that it was what she'd done just the same. She'd summoned Viola, the way she might call for her maid or ring for the cook to make her some tea. And somehow Theo had just made it worse by suggesting that they take one of the rowboats out onto the lake.

But Ruby found that no matter how quick her brain or how smart her tongue might be in any other situation, whenever she was around Viola, they both failed her. With Viola's violet eyes glaring at her, she hadn't been able to do much more than nod weakly.

"This is a terrible idea," she whispered as she walked next to Theo, with Viola trailing behind them.

"Why's that?" Theo asked, glancing over at her.

"Because she hates me," Ruby said, soft enough that Viola couldn't hear.

"She's a source, Ruby. Treat her like any other source. She doesn't need to like you. She needs to *help* you."

He was right, of course, but it certainly didn't *feel* that way.

Things didn't improve when the attendant who prepared the rowboat for them suggested that their servant could wait on the bench near the boat shed.

"No," Ruby said, her cheeks heating with absolute mortification. "She's coming with us." From the corner of her eye, she saw Viola's head whip around at her. "I mean to say, she's not my servant—our servant. She's our . . ." What, exactly, was Viola?

"Our friend will be coming along," Theo said, breaking in to rescue her.

Not that it stopped the heat that had already climbed up Ruby's neck and into her cheeks. Her skin would be blotchy and red. It was mortifying. Really, it was.

Viola was silent as they clambered into the boat and the attendant pushed them off into the water. Theo began rowing in long, slow pulls, causing the boat to glide away from the shore and into the center of the lake.

It *was* a beautiful day, just as Theo had said. Any other time, Ruby might have enjoyed the outing, floating on the water far from the worries and responsibilities that she usually carried with her. Weightless and serene. When she was just a girl, she had positively loved it when her father would bring her and her sisters down to the park, especially on early spring days like this one, when it seemed like the city would be in bloom at any moment.

But that was before everything happened. Theo had brought her a couple of times last summer, trying to cheer her up, but nothing worked for that better than work itself.

This *was* work, she reminded herself. But with Viola glaring at her, Ruby found it decidedly uncomfortable.

Viola was just so . . . *much*. It wasn't that she was large. She was even shorter than Ruby herself, and she certainly wasn't fat or even plump. But Viola's body had the curves and softness that Ruby's did not. She wasn't any older than Ruby, but somehow she looked like a woman rather than a girl. There was experience in her eyes. Knowledge.

Oh, but her poor face.

Viola noticed Ruby staring again and hitched her shawl up farther to cover her bruise.

Someone had hit her. Someone had *hurt* her, and it made Ruby want to destroy them in return.

Theo was whistling some unnameable melody as he moved them in slow, looping circles around the lake.

"Yes, well . . ." It was an inane thing to say. "We should talk."

Viola didn't reply. She simply waited expectantly, and Ruby, who always knew what to say, didn't know where to begin. It was vexing the way Viola stared at her as though she could see right through her, down to the parts that she hid from everyone except Theo—to the parts she hid *even* from Theo. In all the ballrooms she'd been in, swirled about in the arms of countless beaus, Ruby had never felt half as unsure of herself as she did with Viola's eyes on her.

Ruby took out her small tablet and pencil. It was a simple enough action, but it helped to center her a bit. "What do you know of your brother's association with John Torrio, Miss Vaccarelli?"

"Torrio is one of his guys," Viola said. "Paolo, he's grooming Torrio to take a stake in his businesses. He likes him," she said with no little disgust. Her nose wrinkled, a clear indication that she thought differently.

"And your brother," Ruby said, focusing the notes she was writing so she wouldn't have to look into Viola's eyes again. "What can you tell me about his businesses?"

"He has the New Brighton and the Little Naples Cafe, which are the ones our mother knows of, and then he has the Five Pointers." She listed out a few more things, a couple of brothels and other connections that Paul Kelly had, but they weren't anything Ruby didn't already know. "My brother is un coglione . . . how do you say? He's not a nice man. A bastard not by birth, but by choice."

Ruby believed every word of what Viola was telling her, but other newspapers had already dealt with Paul Kelly's connections to the underbelly of the city. It wasn't what Ruby was interested in.

"He sent John Torrio to kill me, didn't he?" Ruby asked, finally looking up from her paper. But this time it was Viola who wouldn't look at her. "It's okay," she told Viola. "I know you were there, but I know you didn't want to hurt me." She laid her hand on the other girl's knee.

Viola's eyes flashed up to meet hers, and, embarrassed and suddenly too warm, Ruby drew her hand away.

"Do you know why Torrio was sent to kill me, Miss Vaccarelli?"

Viola shook her head. "You wrote something they didn't like so much."

"Exactly. I wrote a story about a train accident, and it had nothing at all to do with Paul Kelly or any of his Five Pointers." Viola's brows had drawn together, but she didn't speak. Her eyes instead seemed to urge Ruby on. "The story was about a derailment outside the city, nine days ago. There was a man on that train, a friend of Theo's from school—"

"I wouldn't exactly call him a friend," Theo said dryly. "Especially not now . . ."

"They were acquaintances," Ruby corrected, trying to keep her own temper from erupting. "He told the medics who rescued him that he saw a man on the train who should have already been dead. When they pulled him out, he'd hit his head pretty badly, but he was talking about Mageus—about a magician named Harte Darrigan and a girl."

Viola's eyes widened slightly. "Harte Darrigan?"

Viola knows that name. But Ruby didn't know what that meant. "And a girl," she repeated. "I talked Theo into getting me access to this man, Jack Grew. He either didn't know who I was or he didn't care, because he told me everything that happened. It was a *monumental* scoop. And the Order did everything they could to kill it, up to and including trying to have me killed. So you see, I have a very personal stake in all of this. I will not be silenced, Miss Vaccarelli. I will not go be the good, biddable girl that they want me to be. I will expose them, and I will do everything I can to destroy the Order's power in this city." She paused, forcing her anger and impatience back down. "But this is bigger than the Order."

"It is?" Viola asked, her expression thoughtful and serious.

Ruby nodded. "If Jack Grew was right—and I think he was, considering the lengths the Order has gone to, all to shut me up—that train derailment wasn't an accident. It was an *attack*. And it was done with magic."

THE SWP

1904—St. Louis

W hen Esta went inside the building, it was dark, but she could see a light coming from a hallway to the right. In the distance she heard something like the murmuring of a crowd. Because Harte wasn't there, she took the risk of pulling her affinity around her and followed the source of the light until she found that it was coming from a set of stairs.

Keeping her hold on time, she went up the steps slowly, careful to keep the notebook balanced under her arm. At the top, there was another hallway, but at the far end of it, she saw a glow coming from beneath a door. As she walked toward it, the sound of her footsteps echoed into the silence that had been created by her magic. She found it unlocked, and with time still motionless, she slipped through.

On the other side was a large room filled with people. The high-ceilinged space stretched the entire width of the building, and the men and women within it were caught in the web of time gone slow, their mouths open and their expressions rapt as they listened to a speaker standing in the center. Though some sat on benches at the edges of the room, most were on their feet, crowded around the man elevated on the small platform of a stage. The speaker was dressed in shirtsleeves, which had been pulled back to reveal the broad forearms of a workman, but it was clear that his working days were behind him. His balding hair was nearly white, and his face was partially obscured by a full beard. His hand was raised, and his face was rapturous, his mouth opened and his eyes wild.

Esta had a sense that this man in the middle of the crowd was Lipscomb. She could leave the device here and go, but if she was wrong, it could mean trouble. She needed to make sure she had the right target.

Making her way through the crowd, Esta was careful not to touch anyone or bobble the parcel under her arm. She found a spot in the back corner, far from anyone who might notice her sudden appearance, and then she let go of her hold on time. The room spun back into life. The noise of the crowd was deafening, and the air suddenly held an electricity that had nothing to do with magic.

In the center of the room, the man's voice boomed over the crowd. "The bourgeois care nothing for the workers," he shouted. "They would print their money with the blood of our children. While our families work themselves to death in factories, the rich men of this city plan parties and balls. They feast while we starve! Look at the excesses of the Exposition," he shouted, pounding his fist against his hand to punctuate his words. "Instead of celebrating the worker—the true spirit of this country—the Exposition celebrates a feudal past that can*not* be allowed to rise again. They've built palaces and temples in our city, a city where native-born sons die without a roof over their heads.

"Look at the Society, with its heathenish ways. They look to magic, to the *occult*, because they understand that the workers of this country will not be silenced. They know that only the heathen power can subdue the power of the workers when they unite. But we will show them that not even their sorcery will be enough to extinguish the fire lit here, in this place, tonight." He paused, looking around the room with satisfaction. "The Society has planned a parade—"

The room rumbled with disgusted murmurs, punctuated by low boos. The man's voice didn't carry with it any hint of magic, but there was power there nonetheless. Esta could feel him stirring the souls in the room all around her with nothing more than his words. The people around him were leaning in toward the platform on which he stood, their minds open and willing to accept what he was saying.

"Yes. Their parade is an abomination. Their prophet is a false one, an idol of profit and power created to suppress the voice of the proletariat. You all know this. You have seen it for yourselves every year since the brave porters stood up and demanded a living wage and were crushed by the powers of the bourgeois pigs. Every year the bourgeoisie remind us that they hold our lives in their hands—hands that have never known the weight of a hammer or the sting of labor—but not this year.

"This year we will rise up. This year, with the world watching, with the president himself viewing the spectacle, we *must* rise up and say *enough*. We must demand what is ours—with force, if necessary."

The crowd erupted around Esta, and she lifted her hands in half-hearted applause, so she wouldn't be noticed. But his words, along with the anger and hatred in his tone, made her uneasy. The room felt like a powder keg about to ignite.

"This your first meeting?" A girl had come up next to her and was examining her with an appraising look in her eyes.

"What?" Esta asked, unnerved at how easily she'd missed the girl's approach. She was wearing a dress of slate gray that was buttoned up to her chin. The color seemed too severe for how young she was, but the plain cut of it seemed to suit the girl's stern expression.

"You're a new face," the girl said, a question in her eyes.

Esta's mind raced. "I heard about this . . . this meeting," she said, improvising as she went. "And thought I'd see for myself what it was all about."

"Who'd you hear from?" the girl asked. Her voice was soft but determined. And her eyes were suspicious.

"Oh, one of the guys at the brewery told me. Said I might find it interesting."

The girl studied Esta a long moment more, like she wasn't sure if she believed the story, but then she relented. "I'm Greta, and you are?"

"John," Esta said, picking the plainest, most forgettable name she could think of.

"We're glad to have you, John," Greta told her as she handed Esta a sheet of paper. "Our movement needs more able bodies willing to stand firm."

Keeping the notebook clamped steadily beneath her arm, she accepted it without reading it. "Thanks," she said. "Who's that speaking now?"

The girl's eyes narrowed a little. "Your friend, the one at the brewery, he didn't tell you?"

Esta's throat felt tight. "He just said I'd be interested . . . didn't say much else."

"Where is he?" the girl asked. "This friend of yours?"

"Who knows?" Esta said, and when she sensed that it wasn't the right answer, she added, "Probably working overtime." She gave a shrug that she hoped looked tired and frustrated. "You know how it is—when the foreman says stay, you stay."

The girl's expression relaxed slightly. "Yes. We all know how it is." She looked to the speaker and then back at Esta. "That's Caleb Lipscomb. He's the current secretary of the SWP. He's brilliant."

"What's this parade he's talking about?"

"The Veiled Prophet Parade?" the girl asked, and the suspicion was back in her eyes. "They have it every year. . . ." Her voice trailed off like this was something Esta should have known.

"I'm new in town," Esta told her. "Came because my cousin said there was work, what with the Exposition and all. Only been here about two months."

The girl's expression didn't relax. "Where did you say you worked again?"

Esta felt as though the stiff collar of her shirt were strangling her, but she'd been in tighter situations than this. "The Feltz Brewery," she said, giving the name of Ruth's place, since it was the only place she knew of.

The girl made a sound in the back of her throat. "He's talking about the Veiled Prophet Parade that's set for Independence Day."

"This parade . . . It's a big deal?" Esta asked, trying to get a sense of what the girl thought of it.

"That depends on who you are. A lot of people in town like the spectacle of it, but there's plenty of us who know the truth." Greta shrugged. "It's just a show of power. The Society started the parade back in seventy-eight, after a railroad strike threatened to shut down the city. They couldn't let a bunch of simple workmen get away with an action like that, especially not ones with skin darker than their own, so they invented the Prophet and the Parade. They use the threat of magic to keep the workers in their places all the year through, and the parade is a reminder of their power—a reminder of who is truly free in this country." The girl's expression lit with determination. "We never make it easy for them, and this year's parade won't be any exception."

"I see," Esta said, glancing at the sheet in her hand. The bold, dark type only accented the anger in the words printed on the page.

"Well, enjoy the rest of the evening," the girl said. "If you have any questions at all, any of us with the broadsheets can answer them."

"Thanks," Esta told her, and turned her eyes back to the man speaking in the center of the room.

Go away, she thought as she felt the girl's eyes on her.

She pretended to pay attention to what Lipscomb was saying. After a few minutes, she glanced over her shoulder to find the girl still watching her. Inwardly she cursed. As long as the girl was there, Esta was stuck— she couldn't disappear, and she couldn't drop the package, not without giving away either what she was or what she was doing. Magic would make what she had to do easier, but with the girl, she couldn't risk it.

An opening parted in the crowd in front of her, and Esta took the opportunity it presented to slip through, little by little making her way closer to the small platform that Caleb Lipscomb was standing on. Every so often she paused, as though considering his words, and then would take the opportunity some shifting in the crowd offered to slip closer yet. She didn't doubt that the girl was still watching her, but there wasn't anything she could do about that.

When she was standing right in front of him, she stopped, keeping the notebook in her hands secure. She'd give it a minute or two before she made her move.

"But we must be vigilant," Lipscomb was bellowing. "We know there are those who would corrupt our purpose. Undesirable elements that bring with them the feudal superstitions of the old countries: the Catholics with their papist loyalty and those who refuse to set aside their feral magic to join the true proletariat. You know what I speak of," he shouted, his voice rising in a feverish pitch.

"Maggots!" shouted someone deep in the crowd.

Esta saw the curve of Lipscomb's mouth at the sound of the slur. "Yes. Why do they come here? Why do they seek to take the jobs we've worked so hard for? To disrupt the country we are trying to build with their dangerous ways?" Lipscomb shook his head dramatically. "We must guard against those who would pervert the true proletariat with their shadowy powers."

She pretended interest, hiding her disgust beneath a placid expression. *No honor among thieves, and no solidarity among the downtrodden, apparently.* Maybe she didn't know this Caleb Lipscomb, but she knew those like him and felt some of the guilt she'd been carrying about what she was supposed to do lift from her.

He would do the same to me, she thought as she pressed even closer to the platform. *He would do worse.*

When someone bumped into her, Esta let the sheet of paper the girl had given her drop to the floor. She waited until it landed at her feet before she stooped to retrieve it, and in a subtle movement perfected during her years of training, she placed the parcel on the floor and held on to the edge of the loose sheet within it. Then she slid the notebook forward, until the loose sheet came free and the device was directly under the platform.

The Antistasi had explained that she had less than five minutes once she removed the fuse, but when she got back up to her feet, she realized that she was penned in, trapped by the crowd that was on its feet, shouting with the fervor of true converts. There was no opening, so Esta made one, throwing an elbow sharply into the stomach of the man behind her. The man groaned and tumbled backward into the people behind him, and the crowd, already whipped into an excited frenzy, responded by pushing him back. In a matter of seconds, someone threw a punch, and the room erupted into chaos.

Esta ducked, keeping herself low as she shoved her way to the edges of the madness, and when she reached the other side, she pulled time around her and ran.

She didn't let go of time until she was outside the building and at the carriage where North was waiting. The sounds of the night returned as she opened the door and climbed in.

"Go!" she told him, looking back out the window.

He didn't look up from picking at his fingernails with the blade of a knife.

"Go!" she said again. "We need to get out of here."

"Let's just give it a minute or two to be sure."

He's insane.

Her breathing was still ragged from running out of the building and down the block, and her heart felt as though it would pound its way straight out of her chest. When you did a job, you didn't just wait around to get caught. "We need to get out of here before the police come."

"We have time," he said again, putting the knife away in his back pocket. He took out the pocket watch from inside his vest and considered it. "I'd say we got at least two more minutes to go."

Because she'd used her affinity to escape, it took nearly four.

North had just picked up the revolver when they heard the echo of a small explosion.

Esta's stomach dropped. "You said it wasn't a bomb," she told him, her mouth dry as she thought of all the people who had been in that room—workers, laborers, all who had come to listen because they needed hope. She'd been so angered by Lipscomb's words that she hadn't considered the other people when she set the device for him.

"No," he said, meeting her eyes. "I said nobody was going to die, and they won't. The explosives in that package won't do more than take a leg or an arm—just enough to put Lipscomb into the hospital and keep him out of our way." He twisted the knob on the side of his watch as the first of the people began to pour from the doorway of the building. With them came a dense, cloudlike fog, and even from more than a block away, Esta could feel the strange, icy-hot magic in the air.

"What did you do to them?" she asked.

"It's not what we did *to* them," he told her, glancing up from the watch. "It's what *you* did *for* them."

He clicked the watch closed, and Esta didn't have time to contemplate the meaning of his words before she felt her veins turn to ice and the world went white.

THE LAKE

V iola felt as though she couldn't breathe. "What do you mean, it was done with magic?" she asked Ruby. The girl's skin had gone from the palest cream to a high pink as she spoke, moved by the furor of her convictions. It didn't make her any less attractive.

"Jack was clear. The train didn't just derail. There wasn't a bomb. The two of them—Harte Darrigan, who was supposed to have died on the Brooklyn Bridge the day before the accident, and this Esta Filosik— used magic to destroy the train." Ruby leaned forward. "They used magic *beyond* the Brink."

"That isn't possible," she told Ruby. Not unless Darrigan had the Book. And for Esta to be with him? *No.*

"If it wasn't true, why would the Order go to such lengths to stop me from telling people?" Ruby asked.

But all Viola could do was shake her head numbly.

"The very fact that they were willing to hire your brother to kill me shows just how true it is. There are Mageus outside the city, and there's more," Ruby added. "Jack told me what really happened at Khafre Hall the night it burned."

Viola's stomach suddenly felt like it was filled with molten lead. "He did?" she said, trying to keep her voice steady, even as she wondered how deep the water around her might be. Had this all been a trap?

"They were robbed," Ruby told her, satisfaction shining in her eyes.

"A group of Mageus walked into their headquarters and took all their precious treasures."

"Oh?" Viola's voice sounded weak, even to herself.

Ruby nodded, her midnight eyes shining. "Yes, but the Order is still trying to cover it up. No one has let anything slip about who the thieves were or what they stole. As long as the people in this city believe that the Order is all powerful, they'll keep supporting them. That's why I need you. I need to know what happened in Khafre Hall."

"I don't know anything about what you're talking about," Viola said, forgetting where she was for a second. She almost lurched to her feet, but the rocking of the boat reminded her. "Take me back," she told Theo. "I'm done with this. With all of this."

"What is it?" Ruby asked, legitimately confused. "If you're worried about being attacked, we can protect you."

"You?" Viola laughed at the ridiculousness of the girl's statement. "*You* are going to protect *me*?"

"We can make sure you're safe from Paul Kelly when the story comes out—"

"Paul?" Viola asked, surprised.

"Don't you see?" Ruby said, lowering her voice. "It all makes sense. Kelly has Torrio—a Mageus—working for him at the same time that Khafre Hall is robbed? Paul Kelly, who is already known to be a notorious criminal—no offense," she added, her cheeks going pinker still.

Viola waved away her apology. "You think my *brother* is the one who broke into Khafre Hall?" she asked, astounded. It was better than Ruby knowing about Viola's own involvement, but not much better.

"I don't know for sure, but that's how you could help me. If we could prove that he did it, we could take down a crime boss and the Order all at once. Tammany would have to turn against Kelly, because they're interested in the Order's favor, and everyone would know that the Order is weak and pointless. And if we can find out what Kelly's guys took from them, maybe we could even track the objects down and make sure they don't fall into the wrong hands."

Ruby's mind was a marvel, but it was a dangerous marvel. If the girl insisted on investigating this, it was more than possible that she'd eventually discover the connection to Dolph, and to Viola herself. But if Ruby depended upon Viola for the information, Viola could direct it the way that she wanted. And if she was very smart, she could destroy Nibsy Lorcan in the process.

She'd been wavering about what she would do, but the idea of seeing Nibsy brought low made up her mind. Yes, her brother might be her own blood, but he'd chosen his path. Viola took a packet from the basket she was carrying and held it out to Ruby.

"What is this?" Ruby's eyes widened as she held out her hands.

Viola hesitated. "Receipts for the last few months," she told her. "I don't know what's in it, or if it will even help, but Paul, he has big plans. In the last week alone, he's already sent four of his Five Pointers out of the city."

"For what?" Ruby asked.

Viola shrugged. "I'm not sure, but he wants a bigger piece of the world than the streets of this city can offer, and I know my brother. The wide world doesn't need him meddling in it."

Ruby's brows drew together as she flipped through the receipts, studying them. "Is there anything more?"

"There's more, but Paul keeps them close. I haven't been able to get to them." Viola frowned at the thought of how closely her brother and his boys watched her. "But I will."

"When?" Ruby pressed, holding the package close to her.

"When I can," Viola said, irritated at the note of insistence in Ruby's tone.

"That isn't good enough," Ruby told Viola, her voice rising in volume as she hugged the parcel of documents even closer. "I need to know a date."

"Ruby," Theo said gently. He'd been rowing them steadily back to the edge of the lake.

"I'm not your servant," Viola huffed. "You don't get to tell me what to do or when."

"I never said you were," Ruby said, her pale cheeks flaming red. "I just meant—"

"You meant *nothing*, principessa," Viola snapped. The stress of being trapped so close to Ruby, of being cornered in so many ways, broke over the dams she'd built and poured out of her in a fiery tirade. "That is your problem. The risks you take, the dangers you put yourself in, all while dragging this one along with you like a puppy to heel—"

"Hey," Theo interjected, but Viola ignored him and continued.

"In your pretty little world, you're too safe to know what danger is. You give your commands, and you don't even bother to watch people jump. But you can't make me jump."

"I never—" Ruby started. "That is . . . You're just—" And then she sputtered a bit more before she made an exasperated sound and turned away.

Viola pretended that she hadn't seen the way Ruby's eyes had gone glassy or the way her voice shook. Instead, she too turned away, ignoring both of them.

For the next few minutes, Theo continued to row them back. The moment they docked, Ruby was on her feet, being helped out of the boat by the attendant. She stomped off without another word, spoiled rich girl that she was.

Theo hopped out first and then helped Viola, who hated the feeling of the boat lurching beneath her, onto the dock. For a moment they stood in an uneasy silence, as though neither of them wanted to be the first to leave.

"I'm not going to apologize, if that's what you're waiting for," she said to Theo, who was watching her with too-steady eyes.

His mouth curved up, but his expression was sad. "I wasn't waiting for anything of the sort."

She glared at him. "Then why are you still here?"

"I'm thinking. . . ." He tapped his chin, his eyes squinting against the sun. "She means well, you know."

Viola just glared at him.

"I know what she looks like to you, but I've known Ruby since we were both knee-high. She's had a rough time of it, first with her father and then with everything that's happened to her family since. She really does want to help. In her own way, she's trying to do something worthy." But when Viola continued to glare at him, he let out a sigh. "This isn't going to end well, is it?"

The sincerity in his eyes had the fight draining right out of her. "Paul Kelly, he's not one to mess with—"

"That's not what I meant," he said, shaking his head. "But you're probably right about that, too. It was good seeing you again, Viola."

She reached out and caught him by his sleeve. "Is there any way to talk her out of this crazy plan?" she asked, somehow unable to keep an unintended urgency from her voice.

He laughed. "I've yet to be able to talk Ruby out of anything. She has more lives than the proverbial cat." Then his face softened. "Be careful with her, won't you?"

Viola frowned. "I don't know what you mean. . . ."

"I imagine you do," he said, giving her the funny, wobbly grin that would have looked half-drunken on anyone else. On Theo, it simply looked innocent and . . . well, too damn *nice*. "I think you know, and despite your bluster—which I quite enjoy, by the way—you will take care with her. If not, you'll answer to me."

He tipped his hat at her, and then he turned to gather Ruby's parcels before he ran to catch up with Ruby, leaving Viola alone at the edge of the lake with her mouth hanging open in confusion and feeling like somehow she'd just lost an argument she hadn't known she was having.

THE DIFFERENCE BETWEEN

1904—St. Louis

Harte didn't have any idea where the Antistasi had put him, but it had the subterranean feel of a coal cellar or a basement. They hadn't taken any chances, because not long after they'd dumped him on the floor, he'd heard the same *pop-hiss* he'd heard earlier, in the back of the wagon. A moment later he smelled the same thick odor that made his head feel like it was floating and his affinity go dull. Whatever it was had evaporated some time ago, but his affinity still felt like it was miles away.

The ropes on his wrist were too tight for him to wriggle out of, so he just sat there in the darkness they'd forced upon him and waited. The only positive development was that whatever the drug was, it shut the voice up inside of him. He figured it had to be something more than opium for it to have that kind of effect.

By the time he heard a door open, his arms had gone completely numb from being tied behind him. He scrambled to his feet, ready. If Esta had failed, they wouldn't be coming to celebrate.

"Come on, then," a familiar voice said. It was the cowboy—North.

The hands that took him by the arm weren't exactly gentle, but they didn't do anything more than lead him along.

Finally, they stopped, and when the sack was removed from his head again, he blinked past the sudden brightness to see that he was in a small office. And he wasn't alone. The woman was there—Mother Ruth, North, another girl with silver spectacles perched on her nose, who'd been there earlier, and Esta. She had a tired, worried look on her face, and even once she saw him, it didn't change. But they didn't have her tied up, and he wasn't dead yet, so he figured that meant something.

Even in that ridiculous suit with her hair chopped close around her face, she looked damned near perfect.

His eyes met hers. *You okay?*

She gave him the smallest of nods, but then her gaze shot to Ruth. "I did what you wanted, just like I promised. You can untie him now," Esta said. There was something in her voice that bothered him, but she looked unharmed.

"We'll untie him when we're ready," the cowboy said, his mouth hitching a bit on one side.

"She did everything you asked, North." It was the girl this time. She was a mousy-looking thing, especially with those glasses, but he didn't let that sway him. The last time he'd underestimated a person wearing glasses it had been a mistake.

"Maggie's right," Ruth said. "The girl has proven herself . . . for now. You can untie him."

In a single, fluid movement, the cowboy took out a thin knife and flicked it open. *Show-off.* But Harte kept his feelings to himself and masked his irritation with a look of utter boredom.

"Considering what you had me do, I think we've earned your trust, period," Esta told the woman.

"You delivered a package," Ruth said. "That's hardly grounds for you to make demands."

"I nearly killed a man," Esta said, her voice steady. "I set off some sort of magical bomb that did who knows what to all those people—people who never did anything to me."

The power inside Harte lurched at her words, stirred up with something that felt too close to pleasure for his liking. He must have made a sound, because North glanced at him. But Harte gritted his teeth and forced himself to remain composed.

Ruth gave Esta a pitying look. "Any one of those people would have done the same to you had they been given the opportunity."

"You don't know that," Esta said, but she didn't sound convinced.

"Do you know what the SWP is?" Ruth asked.

"They're socialists," Esta answered. "Workers who want a better life." But there was something unsettled in her voice. Something that made the power inside Harte pause and take notice.

"They do, but at what cost?" Ruth asked, stepping toward Esta. "I know those workers as well as I know the Society. They're the people who look up and dream of one day being tapped by the Veiled Prophet himself. Year after year they elect those who would erase magic from these shores. Year after year they buy into the fears of rich men; they lift up those fears and carry them on their shoulders, all because it's not they who will be harmed. The Act, the Guard, even the Society itself—none of it affects them.

"Perhaps they *were* innocents," Ruth continued. "Perhaps they simply wanted a better wage and more food on the table for their families. But Caleb Lipscomb knows exactly what he's doing. He uses them for his own advantage. Who do you think those workers are truly angry at? The capitalists who live in the fancy houses on McPherson Avenue?" She let out a derisive laugh. "*No.* Every man in that warehouse listening to Lipscomb speak wants to *become* those men. They picture themselves in those same fine houses, their children in silken pinafores and their wives dripping with jewels bought with the blood of the common worker. The people who follow SWP aren't really angry at the men who run this city. They're angry at those beneath them—the freshly arrived immigrants who are willing to work for a fraction of the wages they themselves demand. And they're angry at Mageus, who did nothing at all to achieve power they can't even begin to imagine."

She gave a shrug that also managed to broadcast her irritation. "Lipscomb knows that. His people were the cause of a riot three weeks ago over in Dutchtown. Three people died because Lipscomb started a rumor that the people who lived there were harboring Mageus who would use their power to take food from the mouths of the ordinary worker. He sees our kind as a threat because he knows that our power means we have a loyalty to something bigger than his group of angry men. He uses the people's anger because he can, because they fear what they don't know and won't understand. Do you know what Caleb Lipscomb is planning?"

"Something with the Veiled Prophet Parade," Esta told her.

"He was planning to place bombs on the parade route. You did the world a favor by putting him in the hospital, where he won't be able to stir up his followers."

"Why would you care about saving the Veiled Prophet Parade?" Harte asked.

Ruth turned to him. "I *don't* care about the parade, but every time there's an action by some group like the SWP, the Society turns the people's hatred toward the old magic. It helps them shore up their power, preying on the people's fears and prejudices. The loss of innocent lives would have been blamed on *us*."

"Then why the attack last night?" Esta asked. "It wasn't just a bomb that went off. I know there was magic involved. Won't those people blame you too?"

"Blame us?" Ruth laughed. "They'll *thank* us. But you're right. That wasn't a bomb. It was something infinitely more powerful—a gift of sorts that Maggie created." Ruth walked over and tipped the girl's chin up affectionately. "The Society and those like them might think they understand alchemy, but my sister has a talent for it they can only dream of."

"It's what you used in the attack last fall," Harte realized. And in the fog that they used to keep him and Esta subdued. It wasn't just opium and it wasn't simple magic. It was some combination of the two, some new thing altogether. At this realization, the power inside of him swelled, and he heard a voice echoing in his mind. *See?* It seemed to whisper. *See what they are capable of? The damage they will continue to do?*

But he shoved the voice aside, even as part of him realized that it was right. It was bad enough that men like those in the Order would pervert magic to claim power, but for Mageus to do it as well . . . ?

"No," Ruth said, releasing Maggie's chin. "Not *quite* like last fall."

Maggie turned to them. "Then, we were simply trying to slow down their progress," she told them. "My serum wasn't ready quite yet, and we needed more time."

"Serum?" Esta asked. She met Harte's eyes, but he didn't have an answer to the question.

A knock sounded at the door, and Ruth called for the person to enter. It was one of the guys from before—one who had been close to the wagon.

"You have news?" Ruth asked, her expression rapt.

"It worked," the guy said, beaming at Ruth. "They just brought in the first case to City Hospital. A girl who causes flowers to sprout from everything she touches."

Ruth let out a small breath, and Harte could see the relief—the victory—flash across her features. "Good. Have Marcus keep track of them and let me know if anything changes." Then she turned to Maggie. "*You did it.* This time, you finally did it."

"Did what?" Harte asked, frustration getting the best of him.

"She solved the problem that has been plaguing our kind for centuries." Ruth's eyes were practically glowing with satisfaction.

Harte shook his head, not understanding.

"Why do the Sundren hate what we are? Why do they cut us off and round us up and force us to suppress what we are until we become shells of ourselves? Until generations pass and the power in our veins passes with it?"

"Because we have an affinity for the old magic," Esta said, her voice oddly hollow. "Because we're different, and they know we have power they can't ever equal."

"Yes. Because they've *forgotten*," Ruth said fervently. "There was once magic throughout the world. Everyone had the ability to call to old magic. But through the ages, people have moved from where their power took root, and they left their memories behind them. Those who had forgotten what they might have been began to fear and to hunt those who kept the old magic close. Do you know what it means to be Sundren?" she asked. "It means to be broken apart, to be split from. Those who have let the magic in their bloodlines die are separated from an essential part of themselves. They're wounded and broken, and they have no idea what lies dormant deep inside. It's why they claw at the world, destroying anything in their path to get some relief from the ache they cannot name, the hollow inside themselves." Ruth paused. "But what if we could awaken that magic? What if we could heal that break? What if we were no longer different, because *everyone* had the magic that they fear in us?"

"The fog—" Esta's brows drew together.

"Don't you see?" Maggie asked, her expression hopeful. "We *cured* them."

But Harte wasn't so sure. He knew the difference between the warm, welcoming natural power that Mageus could touch and the cool warning of ritual magic. Everything he'd seen and experienced in his short life had told him that unnatural magic was a corruption. A danger. Dolph had believed he could use it, and he'd died instead. He'd taken Leena along with him.

"You mean you infected them," Harte said. "You didn't ask their permission or give them a chance to refuse." He couldn't see how that would turn out well.

North took a step toward him, but Ruth held up her hand. "What we did goes far beyond the individual people in that building tonight." Her voice carried the tremulous surety of a true believer. "We proved tonight that those ancient connections to the old magic are still there, waiting and latent. We simply woke them up and reminded them of what this world was supposed to be."

"According to whom?" he wondered. Harte had known people like Ruth, people who were so certain of the path before them. Dolph Saunders, with all his plotting and planning, willing to hurt even those he loved for what he thought was best. Nibsy Lorcan, who saw a different vision but believed it to be no less valid. Even the Order and men like Jack, who thought they knew exactly what the world should be. It was clear to him that Ruth and her Antistasi weren't so very different.

The mood in the room shifted as Ruth's eyes went cold. "You think this is my plight alone?" she asked. "The Antistasi are as old as the fear and hatred of magic. Their mission is one that has come down through the centuries. The Thief has proven herself admirably tonight as an ally to that cause. I wonder . . . will you?"

Esta's expression was pleading with him to keep quiet, but with the unsettled power inside of him, he couldn't help himself. "I make my own choices. I'm not a pawn, and I won't be used," he said, and the moment the words were out. Esta's jaw went tight, and her gaze dropped to the floor.

Ruth's mouth curved, but her expression was devoid of any amusement. "Well, then, if I were you, I'd choose quickly, Mr. O'Doherty."

THE OPPORTUNE MOMENT

1904—St. Louis

J ack had been standing at Roosevelt's side earlier that evening when word came of the attack. The president had just arrived on the morning train, and they'd gone straight to the fair, where he was presiding over an event in the Agricultural Building of the Exposition. Roosevelt had been examining a bust of his own likeness carved entirely out of butter, of all things, and as he posed for a photograph with his buttery image, Hendricks had come up next to Jack.

"There was an event last night," the Guardsman whispered into Jack's ear. "We have it under control now, but I thought you—and the president—would want to know right away."

"What happened?" Jack asked, leading Hendricks away from where anyone could hear. This could be exactly what he'd been waiting for. He'd known all along that sooner or later, the maggots would go too far and he would be able to use their mistakes against them.

"One of the factories down by the river, sir," the Guardsman told him. "A group of socialists were having a meeting. Lipscomb was injured in the explosion."

"Lipscomb?" Jack asked, not really that interested.

"He's one of ours, from here in St. Louis. A socialist rabble-rouser who works for the SWP. From the evidence we found, it looks as though his group was planning an attack on the parade next week."

"Did the explosion kill them?"

Hendricks shook his head. "No, sir. But there were . . . other injuries."

Roosevelt was already looking over at Jack and indicating that it was time to go. "What do I care about the injuries of a few damn socialists?" he asked, impatient at the apparent pointlessness of the interruption.

The Guardsman lowered his voice. "The attack used magic, sir, and the people who were injured, they have very . . . *peculiar* ailments."

"Peculiar how?" Jack asked.

"They've isolated the ones who've been brought into the hospital, but they're exhibiting some strange symptoms. One keeps setting fire to his bedclothes with nothing but his fingertips. Another makes it rain every time she cries. They reported a cloud of mist after the bomb went off, and the ones who've come in so far have said that they started experiencing their symptoms after it touched them." He hesitated. "They seem to be infected, sir."

Jack searched Hendricks' expression for any sign that he might be exaggerating. "Infected?"

The Guardsman's expression was grave, but there was a look of distaste in his features, like he'd just smelled something rotten. "By magic."

Roosevelt and his party had left the Exposition immediately, of course. No one was willing to take the chance of another attack until the perpetrators were rounded up and dealt with. Jack had overseen that, too. Roosevelt had left it to him, as he usually did. The president didn't understand, not really. His politics were nearly as popular as he was. He'd supported the Defense Against Magic Act in private, but he never made a fuss about it publicly. There were still too many who thought the old magic was nothing but a superstition, those who saw the maggots as ordinary people just trying to get by.

But Jack could already sense that the wind was shifting. These attacks were new, different, and infinitely more dangerous. If things kept up like this, the maggots would dig their own graves. And Jack would be there to bury them.

THE CUFF

1904—St. Louis

Ruth looked out over the floor of her brewery and watched the final few women clean up for the night. A total of fifteen had been brought to the hospital showing signs of magic. Fifteen Sundren whose affinities had been awakened—it should have felt like more of a victory, but there certainly had been far more than fifteen people present at Lipscomb's meeting.

Perhaps others would appear tomorrow. Perhaps even now some were keeping themselves concealed because they knew what their symptoms meant. Because they knew what the world thought of the powers that were growing within them. If not, the serum would need to be adjusted further, and they were running out of time to get it right.

On the Fourth, dignitaries from all over the country would pour into the city for the Veiled Prophet Parade and Annual Ball, and her Antistasi needed to be ready. This year marked an opportunity unlike any other— with the Exposition, the Society was hosting more than their usual ball for the rich men of St. Louis. Instead, this year's ball was an attempt by the Society to wrest control of the country from the Order. A desperate bid to move the center of power from the east to the west. The list of attendees included not only the members of the Society and the usual dignitaries, who made an impressive enough target on their own, but also representatives from the various Brotherhoods across the country. Everyone of any importance would be there—politicians and titans of industry, oil barons and railroad tycoons—and most important of all, Roosevelt himself.

The boyish president was popular, but Ruth knew the truth: He was a friend only to those who could help him consolidate his power, which meant he cared nothing at all for those like her. He'd allowed the Defense Against Magic Act to pass without so much as a word against it, and now he would know the cost of that decision. If the Antistasi could unlock within him the magic that others feared, *everything* would change. A new civilization would be born, with the old magic as the equalizer between them all. But if the serum didn't work, or if it did not affect the most important targets, they would not have another chance.

Maggie was a smart girl—this early evidence of their success was proof of that. If need be, she would make the adjustments and her serum would work as it was intended. Ruth would accept no other alternative.

She turned away from her workers and went back into the solitude of her office, closing the door against the sounds of the storeroom below. In the top drawer of her desk, wrapped in a piece of flannel, was the bracelet they'd taken from the Thief when her men had searched the girl for weapons. It was an elegant silver cuff with an enormous dark gemstone that seemed to hold the colors of the rainbow within its depths.

The stone was too heavy for something so small. And it stank of magic. . . .

It wasn't the old magic, not completely. But it also wasn't the same as the objects she'd run across before, pieces like North's watch, which had been infused with freely given power to augment an affinity. The trade in those objects was cutthroat, but this piece was different. Older and more powerful.

Objects like the cuff she was holding took more than a simple ritual to create. Objects with power so deep and heavy took a life sacrifice, and they took a very special, a very rare sort of affinity.

Ruth knew that all Mageus had a unique connection to the very essence of existence. Most had an affinity that aligned with either the living, the inert, or the spirit. Affinities were as unique as people and might show up as strong or weak, as highly specialized or relatively vague.

Over time and across distance, they tended to wane. All Mageus knew that.

Once, though, there had been another kind.

Mageus with the power to affect the bonds of magic itself had always been rare. Most thought that such an affinity was nothing but a myth, like the tales of gods and goddesses of old. But every story held a kernel of truth deep within its heart, and the fear that this particular kernel would find root had been enough to spark the violent frenzy that was the Disenchantment. Those with an affinity for the very essence of magic had been eradicated, and thousands of others had become collateral damage as well.

Magic had suffered in those dark years, but it had not died, as its enemies had hoped. And it would not die now. Instead, with Ruth's plan and the help of Maggie's serum, it would flourish once more. But the appearance of this cuff was an unexpected windfall. Both the necklace and this cuff were powerful objects, capable of giving their holders power beyond the pale. Both would be essential in consolidating the Antistasi's power once magic was awoken, or at least they would once she had the necklace, too.

North appeared in the doorway of her office. "We got the two new ones set up. The girl's in with Maggie, and I locked the other one in a separate bunk. He won't be any trouble until morning, at least."

"Make sure the others know to watch him," she told him. "I want to know if there's any sign he's going to prove troublesome."

"Will do," he said, going off again into the darkened building.

Ruth wrapped the stone back in the flannel and then, for good measure, she locked it in her safe. She would keep it close, but she would keep the girl who had carried it closer. It wouldn't take much—the right words, a gentle push, and Ruth could mold the Thief into a weapon for her own use. And if the other one caused trouble? She would take care of it, just as she took care of all the problems that crossed her path.

PART

V

IT'S QUIET UPTOWN

1902—New York

There were too many men around, taking up the air in the place, Cela thought as she watched her brother and Jianyu eye each other from across the room. At the rate they were going, someone was going to draw first blood before morning. If the boys kept up their preening and posturing, it was going to be her.

"Would you two quit it already?" she said as she handed Abel a cup of the strong coffee she'd just brewed.

"I'm not doing anything," her brother said, still giving Jianyu an appraising glance.

"You're trying to lay him low with nothing but a look," she told him, her heart easing a bit at the very idea that he could give such a look. *Abel is alive.* "I should know, since you've tried to do it to me often enough."

"I just want to make sure we haven't made a mistake by bringing them here," her brother told her, gesturing to Jianyu and the boy they'd taken from Evelyn's apartment. "I didn't exactly ask Mr. Fortune's permission to have any more."

Abel had brought them to the house he'd been staying at ever since the fire, a nondescript building on 112th Street, in a part of town called Harlem. The building belonged to one of the publishers of the *New York Freeman*, the most important newspaper for the black community in the city. They'd apparently taken a recent interest in the labor issues that Abel had gotten wrapped up in.

"Jianyu is fine," Cela told him. "I told you already, he's a friend."

"Maybe he is, but what about that other one?" Abe asked, nodding to the white boy. He'd still been unconscious when they'd arrived uptown and was lying on his side, dead to the world.

"He's my responsibility," Jianyu said. He'd been quiet and watchful ever since they'd arrived at the building, cramped full of too many people. "I am in your debt for all that you have done for me tonight, and I will not impose on that generosity any further. I will take the boy and go."

"That's fine," Abe said, but Cela was shaking her head.

She knew what it was like to walk into Wallack's every day, the only brown face in a sea of white. It didn't matter that they wanted her there for her talent and skill. She was always separate from the rest, from the basement workroom they gave her to the way the performers acted around her. She wondered if Jianyu felt that way as well when he walked through the streets of this city that would always see him as an outsider, and whether he felt that way now, in a too-tight room filled with people he didn't know. But her brother's friends were all huddled together, turned away from the newcomers and talking among themselves.

"No," she told them. "You don't need to leave. Tell him, Abe. Tell him he's welcome to stay."

Her brother hesitated, and her irritation spiked.

"*Tell* him," she demanded. "You left me alone for nearly a week, Abel Johnson. I was at Uncle Desmond's most of that time, and you never once came for me, but Jianyu did. He got me out of that theater where that harpy actress had locked me up, so I'd say we're about equal in owing debts, wouldn't you?"

Abel frowned. "This isn't our fight, Cela," he said softly. "We have our own worries right now, our own battles to wage."

"Maybe it's not," she told him, "but have you ever considered *why* it's not?"

"Because we have enough problems without worrying about Mageus, too."

"That's what they want us to do, isn't it, though?" She was pacing now. "You don't see what Tammany is doing, offering black saloons their protection so long as we vote their way? They're not helping us. They're *using* us, same as politicians have ever done. You're fighting for better wages, aren't you? But who are you fighting? Who owns the railroads?" she asked, but she didn't give him time to answer. "I'll tell you who—they're all in the Order."

Her brother was considering her words, but he wasn't looking at her. He was staring at Jianyu like he was trying to make up his mind.

"You don't think that there are Mageus who look like us?" she asked. "Don't you remember the stories Daddy used to tell us? There were Africans who could *fly*, Abel."

"Those were just tales."

"Were they?" she asked softly. "Because he told those tales like they were the truth."

"Cela—"

"No," she said, shaking her head before he could use that condescending older-brother tone with her. "When I thought you were dead, when I was alone this last week, it changed me. I can't go back now. Maybe this isn't *your* fight, but Jianyu's my friend, so it's become *my* fight."

Jianyu was watching them, his expression unreadable. "You do not have to take on my fight," he told her. "You never should have been brought into this. Darrigan never should have involved you."

"But he did," she told him. Then she looked back at Abe. "If he goes, I go with him. I can't just hide forever, Abel. Not when I know that Evelyn has the stone, and not when I know how powerful it is. If the wrong people get that ring, who do you think they'll come after next? We won't be safe just because we don't have any magic."

Abel looked like he wanted to argue, but he was just silent for a long, heavy minute. When she saw his mouth hitch upward, she knew she'd won.

"You're worse than Mama, you know that?"

She smiled full-on then, her eyes damp with tears that she'd been holding back. "Why, Abel Johnson, that may be the nicest thing you've ever said to me."

"Don't let it go to your head, Rabbit." Then her brother's expression faltered. "What do we do with the other one?"

Cela glanced over to where the white boy had been lying. Her stomach sank. "Well, we'd have to find him before we can do anything with him," she said. Because the white boy was gone.

NIGHT WALKING

1904—St. Louis

The room Ruth had assigned to Esta was still draped in darkness when she finally gave up trying to sleep. Too much had happened—the missing necklace, being taken in by the Antistasi, and the choice she'd made in that warehouse. Her thoughts felt like birds taking flight, but she couldn't tell if they were flying toward some new freedom or away from some unseen danger.

When Esta had dropped the package at the warehouse, she'd been acting out of anger and desperation. Lipscomb's words had stroked that part of her that still hurt from everything she'd lost and that craved retribution. But the moment she'd heard the explosion, she'd realized how far she'd gone. It was only when news had come of what the bomb really was—what the Antistasi had truly done—that she felt as though she could breathe again.

Ruth had awakened magic in Sundren. The idea was almost too fantastical to be true.

Except that it made a certain sense. Hadn't Professor Lachlan revealed to her how the Order had once been Mageus? Rich men, they had come to a new land, hiding what they were in plain sight and hoping to start anew, without the threat of the Disenchantment and the fear of who they were. As their magic began to fade over time, they worried that the newer arrivals would be stronger and more powerful, so they'd built the Brink to protect their own power. But they'd made a mistake—the Brink had become a trap instead of a shield, and as their magic continued to fade through the following generations, the Order themselves had eventually forgotten who they once were. Or maybe they simply refused to remember.

It was logical to think that those lost affinities could still be there, waiting below the surface to be awoken. And if that was possible, it meant that a different future was possible as well—one without the threat of divisions or the death of magic. In the version of the future that Esta had grown up in, a hundred years to come, most people believed magic was a fiction and Mageus were all but extinct. But if the Antistasi could resuscitate magic for everyone now, the future could be different. Maybe even better.

Clearly, Harte hadn't felt the same promise that Esta had at hearing the news. It wasn't long after he made his opinion known that North had escorted him from the room. Esta hadn't been able to go after him—not without losing the ground she'd gained with Ruth—but she needed to see him. Something had happened to him in the Nile, and she had a feeling it had something to do with the way he'd acted in Ruth's office.

She wasn't surprised to find the door to the room they'd put her in locked, especially after Harte's little display. She didn't blame Ruth and the rest of the Antistasi for not trusting her, despite what she'd done for them—she probably would have done the same. But a locked door had never been a problem for her, so she pulled her affinity around her and made quick work of picking the lock. She stepped over the Antistasi who'd fallen asleep at his post in the hall outside and started her search for where they'd put Harte.

She found him on the floor below, and she slipped inside the small, closet-like room before releasing her hold on time. There was a canister on the floor like the one from the wagon, probably used to make sure that he didn't cause any trouble.

Harte was sleeping on a narrow pallet, his breathing soft and even. She knelt next to him and pushed his hair back from his forehead as she whispered his name. When he didn't respond, she gave him a gentle shake until his eyes opened.

He blinked and turned toward her, finding her in the darkness of the room. "Esta?" he whispered, her name soft with sleep on his lips. His hands lifted to cup her face, his thumb brushing across her cheek and sending jolts of warmth through her.

"Are you okay?" she whispered, keeping her voice low so they wouldn't alert the guard outside his room.

He nodded as he pulled her toward him, slow and tentative, testing the moment. Lifting his head, he touched his lips against hers, so softly that her throat went tight. She felt another jolt of heat against her skin and an answering desire, and she didn't pull away. For the first time since that night they'd kissed at the boardinghouse, she felt like she could finally breathe.

Esta barely had time to register that the warmth she felt against her mouth wasn't brought on by the heat in their kiss. Just as she realized that it was the power inside Harte seeping into her, his entire body went suddenly rigid, as though all his muscles were contracting, and he jerked away from her. Scrambling upright, he retreated.

"You've come," Harte said, but it wasn't his voice she heard. There was something else to it, some other power layered over it. Impossible colors flashed in the depths of his eyes, and it wasn't completely Harte she saw looking out at her.

"What—" Her voice broke in a combination of fear and betrayal.

"I knew you would," the voice that was not Harte purred. The colors in his eyes faded, and the darkness that replaced them was pure in its emptiness, devastatingly cold and impossibly ancient. "You see the world as it is, fractured and terrible, and you have come to me, just as I predicted. I feel your anger, the rage that pulses clean and true. I can be the blade that lets you cleave the world in two."

Harte gasped, a horrible clutching sound, and then doubled over.

"Harte?" She wanted to reach for him and to back away all at the same time.

"Stay there," he rasped, breathing heavily. His jaw clenched as he fought whatever was inside of him.

She couldn't do anything more than watch and wait until, eventually, his breathing slowed and his body relaxed. When he looked at her again, it was only Harte she saw.

"What were you thinking?" he asked. "You can't just sneak up on me like that."

The sharpness in his voice cut straight through the already frayed leash that was holding her temper at bay. "What the hell, Harte? Were you there for *any* of that?" she asked, afraid to know the answer.

"You mean, do I remember kissing you?" he asked shakily. He raked his hand through his hair and looked miserable enough that she could almost forgive him for snapping at her. "I thought I was dreaming, and by the time I realized I wasn't, she'd already taken hold."

Her instincts prickled. "She?"

He let out an exhausted-sounding breath. "This *thing* inside me. I think it's a she." Then he told her everything that he'd seen when he'd lost it in the Nile—about the woman and the Book, about Thoth and the circle of stones. "Her name's Seshat. I think she's some kind of demon or something. Thoth was trying to stop her, but he didn't. And she didn't die. Part of her was trapped in the Book."

"You saw all of that?" she asked.

"More like I felt it. Like I was there, experiencing what she experienced," he said, shuddering a little at the memory. "She had stones—not the ones that the Order had, but ones like them. When Thoth destroyed them, it damaged her. I think it's what we need to do to contain her again. If we can connect the stones, we could trap that power again. We just have to figure out how to connect them."

But Esta already knew the answer to that. *She* could connect them. It was what Professor Lachlan had tried to do to her, and it was what she'd already known she would have to do if she wanted to end this madness once and for all. "We have to connect the stones through the Aether," she told him. "We'll need the Book, but once we have that, I can do it."

She reminded Harte about what had happened when she'd returned to her own time, and now she saw the moment when he realized what she meant. "No." He was shaking his head. "Absolutely not."

"It's the only way," she told him.

"I refuse to believe that," he said. "We will find another way. We'll get the Book back and there *will be* another way."

He looked so horrified and determined and ridiculously stubborn that she just nodded. "Sure," she said. Because what was the use of arguing? She wasn't there to save her own life. She was there to make sure that Nibsy couldn't win, to make sure that the Order and others like them couldn't destroy even one more future. And maybe, even to make sure that Harte could someday be free, like he'd dreamed.

"We need to go," he said, pulling himself to his feet. "We've already lost time, but if we can get back to Julien, we can figure out what the Society did with the necklace and get out of this town, just like we planned."

She was already shaking her head as he spoke. "We can't."

"We *can*," he told her, his eyes shadowed.

"The Antistasi—"

"The Antistasi aren't our problem," he said, dismissing her words before he even heard them. "The sooner we can find the Book, the sooner we can find a solution to how to control whatever this is inside me, and the sooner we can go back and stop Nibsy."

She was still shaking her head. "They have Ishtar's Key."

A CHOICE IN THE MATTER

Harte went very still. "They have your cuff?"

Esta nodded, her expression tight. "I think they took it while we were unconscious in the wagon."

"Why didn't you say something?" he asked, feeling a bolt of panic. Without the cuff, they were stuck in 1904. Without the cuff, they couldn't control the Book, and if it got into the wrong hands . . .

"When was I supposed to tell you—while I was unconscious, or in the middle of the room while everyone was listening?" she asked, narrowing her eyes at him.

She was right. Between being captured and being separated while the Antistasi forced her to run their errands, there hadn't been any time to talk. "It's fine," he said, but he felt like he was trying to convince himself as much as her. "We'll get it back."

At first she only frowned, as though she were considering another option.

"You can steal it back," he insisted, because that much should have been readily apparent.

"I don't know if we should," she told him. "Not yet, at least."

"Of *course* we should. You're a thief, and a damn good one at that," he said, trying to figure out what she was thinking. "Why wouldn't you want to take it back?"

"I do," she insisted. "I'm just thinking . . . maybe we should wait. Hear me out," she protested, before he could argue. "We don't know where the necklace is right now."

"Julien can get that information," he reminded her. But they couldn't get to Julien as long as they were stuck here with the Antistasi.

"Sure. But what if we need more than the two of us to get it? Ruth and the Antistasi want the necklace, right? Why not use them like they're using us?"

He gave her a doubtful look. "They don't exactly seem like easy marks."

"Neither was Dolph," she argued. "But that didn't stop you from trying. Why not keep them as allies? Once they get the necklace, I can take both, and we can be gone."

Harte shook his head. "This plan of theirs—to infect people with magic—I don't like it. People should have a choice in the matter. Besides, it's dangerous, and if we get caught up in their mess, we might not get the opportunity to find the other stones."

But Esta brushed off his concern. "We won't have to get caught if we *help* them," she said.

"They're *attacking* people, Esta."

"They're *giving* them magic," she argued. "They're trying to make a difference."

Harte shook his head. *How can she not see it?* "Those people in the meeting didn't do anything to deserve what happened to them. What if they didn't *want* magic? What if they were happy with their lives as they were?"

Esta crossed her arms. "You heard what Ruth said about them—"

"Yeah," he told her before she could go on. "I heard what *Ruth* said. But we don't know those people. We don't know anything about who they are or what they've done. You're taking her word for it, when she's basically kidnapped us?"

Even in the dim light, he could see the determination in her expression, and at the sight of it, the power inside of him lurched with excitement.

"I heard the socialists talking," Esta told him. "I heard what they said about us."

Harte let out a breath. "You don't think that Ruth's attack might have just proven them right?"

Esta lifted her chin, her eyes blazing. "Maybe it was worth it if it changes things," she said.

"Esta—"

"No, Harte. Listen, we don't know where Jack or the Book are. We don't have *any* of the artifacts at this point. We are worse off than when we started," she pointed out. "The only way we know of to stop the power inside you from taking over is if I use my affinity. If it takes over—"

"It *won't*," he said, his voice hard. He would *not* allow her to sacrifice herself for him.

"*If that happens*," she repeated, "I won't be able to take you back. You'll be stuck here in 1904. If that's the case, the Antistasi might be the only chance we have left to fix the things we've changed. If their plan works, if they can really restore magic, you'll have a future. Every Mageus will. And neither Nibsy nor the Order will be in control of that future."

He shook his head, refusing to agree. "I can't believe that is our only option."

"Maybe it's not, but we have to at least consider that it might be."

"No—"

"Let's just give it a day or two," she pleaded. "We still don't know where the necklace is, and until we figure that out, we don't know if we'll need the Antistasi to get it. There's no sense burning bridges. Not until we have to."

He didn't like it. He didn't like this Mother Ruth or her Antistasi. And he didn't like how the power purred at seeing Esta so set on this path. There was something about its approval that told him this path wasn't the right choice.

But he knew Esta, and he knew that with her jaw set as stubbornly as it was now, there was no sense in arguing any further with her. Not at that moment, at least.

"Fine," Harte told her. "But at the first sign of a problem, at the first indication that things are going too far or spinning out of control, we are *gone*. We leave and we don't look back. Promise me that much, at least."

But before she could, the door to his closet-like room swung open, and North stood eyeing the two of them, his expression like flint. He stared at them for a moment, suspicion clear on his face.

How much did he overhear?

"Come on," North said, his voice as cool and flat as a penny. "The both of you."

Every one of his instincts told Harte that they should run. Now. Take the cuff and get the hell out before they were any more entangled with these Antistasi. Their fight wasn't his fight. The future they saw wasn't one he needed. But Esta gave him a pleading look, and he found himself unable to refuse.

THE AFTERMATH

1904—St. Louis

Esta glanced back to make sure that Harte was coming with her as she followed North. Somewhere deeper in the building, she heard a noise that she couldn't place until they came to a large, brightly lit room. Inside, Maggie and a couple of other women were trying to settle nearly a dozen children, most of whom were crying inconsolably.

"Thank god for more hands," Maggie said, handing the baby she was holding to Esta, who was too shocked by the whole situation to refuse the armful of squalling infant. Her arms tightened around the squirming baby, which only made the thing scream more, but at least she didn't drop it.

"Where did they all come from?" Esta asked as Maggie walked over to a toddler huddled in the corner and crouched down to brush the small girl's hair from her eyes.

At hearing footsteps behind her, Esta turned to see Ruth darkening the doorway they'd just come through.

"It seems our attack on Lipscomb struck an unexpected nerve," Ruth said. "The Guard just raided Dutchtown, probably looking for whoever carried out the attack. One of ours brought the children here. They know Maggie has a soft spot for little ones."

"But why the raid?" Maggie said as she scooped the girl into her arms. "The meeting was for the SWP. The Society should have been glad to be rid of that lot."

"I'm not sure why they retaliated," Ruth said, "but this is the effect."

"What happened to their parents?" Esta asked, adjusting the warm—maybe wet?—bundle in her arms. *Definitely wet.*

"Arrested," Ruth said. "They'll be charged and probably found guilty, which means either jail or deportation."

"But they didn't do anything," Maggie said, rocking the girl until her cries died to whimpering.

The one in Esta's arms didn't seem interested in being consoled.

"When has that ever mattered?" Ruth asked.

Esta looked around the room at the cheeks and red eyes of so many children. They should have been in the arms of their mothers or fathers, and she knew that they would always remember this moment, when the people who were supposed to protect them were torn away.

She remembered the day Dolph had taken her around the tenements of the Bowery. There she'd seen children no older than these kept indoors and away from sight so their powers wouldn't be exposed. He'd wanted to make a better life for them by destroying the Order and bringing down the Brink. He'd wanted a new future, and instead all he'd gotten was a bullet in the back. She wondered what had happened to the children he'd once protected in the two years since his death.

One thing was clear: The Society was no better than the Order. They used their Jefferson Guard to rule the city, the same as the Order used their power. It didn't matter that they were outside the Brink, on the far side of the Mississippi and on the edge of the West. Even away from the prison that was Manhattan, there wasn't any freedom here, not for Mageus. Not when the very magic that ran in their veins—the magic that was an intrinsic part of who they were—was despised and feared and hunted. Nothing would change. *Not until it was forced to.*

"North?" Ruth turned to him. "I want you to take some of our men and go round up the injured at the hospital."

"The socialists?" North asked, clearly surprised.

"The Society's retaliation was unexpected. I don't trust the Guard to look after the injured. Better to have the newly woken on our side than to have them against us," she said. Then she gave Harte and Esta appraising looks. "Take Ben with you. We'll need to get them out before dawn, and he can help you with any who prove difficult."

Harte met Esta's eyes from across the room, and she understood what he was thinking. This was exactly the type of danger he'd been worried about them getting caught up in, but standing there with an armful of squirming, screaming child, she felt even more strongly that she had to stay.

She had seen the terrible thing that lived inside Harte, and she knew now, more than ever, that she would give up herself to keep that power from breaking free. If she didn't make it, she needed to do whatever she could now to make a better future for him. She would help to ensure that neither the Order nor the Society could use the old magic against any Mageus ever again.

FERRARA'S

1902—New York

It was late morning when Viola made her excuses and left New Brighton to head south, toward the streets of the Bowery she'd once called home. Already the sidewalks were teeming with vendors selling their carts full of wares and the shoppers who were haggling for the best price. Groups of children littered the streets, playing with whatever they could find and minding themselves, since most of their parents would be working at one of the factories or sweatshops in the neighborhood. Viola remembered those days, when she'd just arrived and the streets of the city seemed like a strange and dangerous new world. She'd learned her English on those street corners, and she'd learned how different she was as well.

Putting those memories aside, Viola turned onto Grand Street, toward the gleaming glass windows and gilded sign of Ferrara's. When she stepped through the swinging door, the toasted bitterness of coffee and the sweetness of anise tickled her nose as she was enveloped in the warmth of the bakery. It smelled like her mother's kitchen at Christmas, when, even though her parents had hardly enough to pay for the roof over their heads, her mother would spend the days baking biscotti to gift to their neighbors. She'd picked this place because of the familiarity of it, because it was on her turf rather than theirs. But she'd forgotten what a powerful poison nostalgia could be. With a pang, it pulled her under and she was there again, a small girl with wild hair and a wilder heart, who had no idea how the world would try to press her small and demand things that she did not have to give.

But she wasn't that girl anymore. She understood too well now the dangers of the world, the hardness of hearts that learned early to hate.

In the back of the bakery, Ruby and Theo were already waiting for her. Ruby was dressed in another frock that made her look like a rose about to bloom, but her eyes were wide as she took everything in. On the table in front of them, a plate of pastries and three small cups of espresso sat untouched.

Viola was nearly to their table when Ruby finally saw her. Theo stood in greeting, but Viola waved him off as she slid into the seat. She was here on business, not pleasure.

"This place is a marvel," Ruby told Viola, giving her a stiff sort of smile that looked like she was trying too hard. "Thank you for sending the note," she said, taking one of the sfogliatelle from the plate of pastries. "You have news?" She took a bite of the pastry as she waited for Viola's answer.

Viola had barely opened her mouth to get to business when her words left her at the sight of the sudden rapture on Ruby's face as she ate the pastry. Her pink tongue darted out to catch the flakes of the delicate sfogliatella as she made a sound of pure satisfaction. And all Viola could do was watch, frozen with a strange combination of desire and hopelessness, as Ruby took another bite.

"Well?" Ruby glanced up at Viola, and as their eyes met, Ruby's widened just slightly and her cheeks turned a pink to outshine even the ridiculously feminine dress she was wearing.

"I think what she means to say," Theo interjected as he slid the plate closer to Viola, "is that you should try one, please, while you tell us your news."

"I know what they taste like," Viola told him, her mouth too dry to eat anyway. She gave herself a mental shake and focused on Theo, who was easier to look at. "I can tell you what they stole from the Order," she said, forging onward.

Ruby set the pastry down and leaned forward. "You can?"

Viola nodded. She still wasn't completely sure that she should reveal everything, but giving Ruby this much would be evidence that the Order's attempt to cover up the robbery was a lie. It would be one step closer in chipping away at their power. And it was that thought that spurred her into telling them about the Book and the five artifacts. "I don't know what they were," she lied, "but they were part of the Order's power."

Ruby's eyes shone. "Do you have proof?"

Only my memories, she thought as she remembered the strange chamber, the bodies they'd found there, and Darrigan's betrayal. "No, but I brought you some papers." Taking the packet from the pocket of her skirts, she slid it across the table. Within the package was evidence that connected her brother to Nibsy and the Five Pointers to the Devil's Own. "It's not enough," she told them. "But it's a start."

She almost didn't want to let the package go. It felt like the worst sort of betrayal of Dolph to point attention to the Devil's Own and the Strega. But he wasn't there anymore, she reminded herself, and if she could turn the Order on Nibsy and her brother both, they could help with the work of destroying them.

Ruby tucked the packet of papers away without so much as looking at them. "Thank you for this," she told Viola, reaching across the table and taking her hand. Ruby's cheeks went pink the moment that her gloved hand rested upon Viola's bare one, and she pulled back.

Viola glanced at Theo, and she saw him watching, his usually playful eyes serious. Which was a problem. That one, he looked like a puppy, but he saw too much, and Viola had been around long enough to know that she couldn't underestimate him.

"I think Paul has more," she told them. "There's something he's planning, something big that he keeps sending people out of the city for. I think it's connected to the Order and the items that were stolen." She frowned. Family or not, she couldn't imagine allowing her brother to ever have access to the power that the Order once had.

At the front of the bakery someone had come in and was talking in excited tones, loudly enough that it drew Theo's attention.

Ruby, realizing that he was listening, put down her pastry. "What is it?" she asked. "What are they saying?"

"Something about a fire," Viola said, translating the Italian for them. "One of the engine companies seems to be burning."

"An engine company?" Theo asked, frowning. "That's odd."

Viola listened again, following the conversation and understanding the fear in the voices. "Not so odd," she told them. "Do you know how many buildings have burned in the last week alone, all while the fire-fighters do nothing at all?"

"Why wouldn't they stop the flames?" Ruby asked, frowning at her.

"The Order has a point to make," Viola said with a shrug. She hadn't wanted to touch the offered food, because she didn't need them to buy her a thing, but Ruby still had a dusting of sugar at the corner of her mouth and Viola had to do *something* to distract herself. So she took the tazza of espresso sitting on the table in front of her and downed it in a single swallow, letting the hot bitterness of it steel her against her own stupidity.

"I don't understand," Theo said.

"Tammany controls most of the police and fire departments in this part of town," Viola explained. "The Order has been using Tammany's influence in the Bowery for revenge against what they lost for almost two weeks now."

"They're looking for the artifacts?" Ruby asked.

"And sending a message." Viola frowned as she listened to the man's voice rise in volume.

"Now what's he saying?" Ruby asked, leaning forward.

Viola wanted to reach across the table and brush the sugar from the corner of the other girl's mouth, but she wrapped her fingers in her skirts and held herself back instead. "It seems that things are turning," Viola said. Ruby was watching her again with those eyes the color of the ocean. They would pull her under if she wasn't careful.

"What do you mean?"

She didn't need to tell them any more. They didn't have to know. But there was something about the way Ruby was looking at her, so earnestly—as though maybe she saw Viola as a friend, as an equal—and Viola spoke before she could stop herself. "According to those men, water isn't even touching the fire," she told them. "The flames are being fed by magic."

THE NEWLY WOKEN

1904—St. Louis

N orth didn't really care what Maggie said about giving the new guy a chance, and he didn't care that the Thief had managed to deliver the device like she was supposed to. He'd found them too late to hear much of what they'd been talking about. But he still didn't trust either one of them, even if Ruth was starting to. Which was why he found himself sitting next to the one who called himself Ben as they drove the brewery's wagon toward the hospital to collect their new brothers-in-arms before the Guard could get to them. After the rounding up of the Mageus over in Dutchtown, Mother Ruth wasn't taking any chances. Considering that Ben looked like a born liar, North wasn't taking any chances either.

The hospital was on the north end of town, far from the excitement of the Exposition. It was still the dead of night, so they didn't pass more than one or two other travelers on the road. Rescuing the newly awoken should be an easy enough job, considering that they had one of their own on the inside working as a night charge.

He gave the horses another gentle flick of the reins to urge them on. Easy or not, the faster it was over with, the better. Next to him, Ben was silent, but North could feel the weight of his stare as he drove. After a couple of miles, he'd had about enough.

"You have a problem?" he asked, glaring at Ben. "Something you want to say?"

At first North didn't think he would answer, but then he spoke.

"Your tattoo . . . ," Ben said, and there was something funny about his voice.

North had heard enough about the mark he chose to wear on his arm in the years since he'd gotten it, which was why he usually kept the tattoo covered. But he hadn't bothered to button the sleeves of the shirt he'd tossed on when he'd been woken about the kids, and as he'd driven the horses, his sleeves had fallen back to reveal the dark circle that ringed his left wrist.

"What about it?" North asked, lifting his chin and daring him to say something.

"I knew someone who had a tattoo something like that," Ben said.

"I doubt that." He rotated his wrist to reveal the bracelet of ink formed by a skeletal snake eating its own tail. "Not unless he was Antistasi."

"It was *something* like that," Ben said, frowning down at it. "Is that what the symbol is—the mark of the Antistasi?"

"This symbol?" North said. "It's an ouroboros, which goes back way before the Antistasi. But, yeah, the Antistasi adopted it, probably some-time during the Disenchantment. They used it as a sign so they could identify each other," he said, pulling his sleeve back down. This time he fastened the cuff to hide the mark from view.

"You had to accept it, then, to be part of Ruth's organization?" Ben asked. North could tell he was trying to keep his tone light, but he was failing miserably.

"I didn't *have* to do anything," North said. He'd had the tattoo since he was sixteen, a promise to himself and to the father he'd lost. It was sheer luck that he'd run into Mother Ruth and her people not long after that, and even better luck that she'd taken him in. "Nobody is forced to take the sign. It's not the Middle Ages anymore."

"But you *did* take it."

"Because I liked what it stood for," North explained, answering the implied question. "The snake eating its own tail is an ancient symbol for eternity. Infinity." *Rebirth*. He'd been a different person before, and the serpent on his wrist reminded him he'd be a different person yet again someday.

"The serpent separates the world from the chaos and disorder it was formed from," Ben said, as if he knew something about it. "Life and death, two sides to the same coin, as my friend used to say. You can't have one without the other."

North frowned, not sure what to make of Ben's statement. He'd never thought of it like that, and he wasn't sure he cared to. "The Antistasi use it because it represents magic itself. Because everything in the world—the sun and the stars and even time itself—it all begins and ends with magic."

"And if magic ends," Ben said, his voice low and solemn, "so does the world."

North huffed out his disagreement. "Magic can't end," he said. "That's what the symbol shows. Magic has no beginning and no end. Since the Disenchantment, they've tried to snuff us out and kill us off, but they haven't been able to. We learn and bend, and then we change."

"You believe that?" Ben asked, looking at North with curious eyes.

"You don't?" North tossed back.

But Ben didn't answer, and it was too late anyway, because they'd arrived.

North pulled the wagon around back, just like they'd agreed to, and gave the signal—a couple of sharp whistles that were returned in kind. A few minutes later the back gates of the hospital opened and their work started in truth.

There were about a dozen people to move. One had his hands wrapped in gauze, and they all had a sleepy, docile quality to them.

"What's wrong with them?" Ben asked. "Did the serum do this?"

North shook his head. "This isn't the serum. The hospital doped them up to make sure they can't do anything. Morphine, probably." He understood why the nurses had drugged them. The newly made Mageus had caused too many problems because they didn't know how to control their powers.

He'd understood what Ruth's goal was in giving these people magic, but seeing it up close like this—it wasn't what he'd expected. Ruth had talked about freeing something inside these people, but they didn't look free. They looked worn and tired and like they'd been dragged through the mud and back. And they looked scared.

The last one out was a young woman who couldn't have been more than eighteen. Her blond hair hung limp around her face, and the smattering of freckles across her nose gave her the look of someone much younger. Like the rest, she had a stunned look to her, but unlike the others, she stopped to speak to North.

"Who are you?" she asked. "Where are you taking us?"

"We're friends," North assured her. "And we're here to take you somewhere safe."

She frowned at him, her eyes still glassy from the drug. "The hospital isn't safe?"

North sighed, feeling every minute of the sleep he was missing. He didn't have time to explain the reality of the girl's new world to her. "What's your name?" he asked instead.

"Greta," the girl said, frowning sleepily at him.

"Do you know what's happening to you, Greta?"

She shook her head. Her eyes shone with unshed tears. "I don't mean to do it, but I can't stop it. . . ."

"It's okay, sweetheart. Something inside you's woken up, that's all. The old magic is yours now." He tried to infuse his voice with the same reverence that Ruth used, but it didn't come out right, and the girl only frowned at him more.

"Mr. Lipscomb—Caleb. There was an explosion. Is he—"

"He'll be just fine," North assured her.

"They wouldn't tell us anything. They kept us locked up but wouldn't tell us what was going on."

Of course. Now that these poor souls had the old magic, they'd be treated like the pariahs they'd become. "We're here to free you," he said gently.

But her chin trembled, and the next thing North knew, the girl's cheeks were wet. He thought it was from tears, but a moment later North realized his cheeks were wet too.

"It's raining," Ben said, looking up. "There's not a cloud in the sky, and it's raining."

"I'm sorry." Greta sniffed. "I don't know why that keeps happening. I don't know how to make it stop."

North didn't know what to tell her. He'd imagined the people they'd given magic to as reborn, but these poor souls looked more like they were ready to curl up and die. He didn't have the words to comfort that kind of sorrow, and he wondered if he had any right, considering what his part in it had been. Without another word, he helped Greta into the back of the wagon. Before closing the door, he popped the fuse on a bottle of Maggie's Quellant and tossed it in with them.

"Is that really necessary?" Ben asked. "They could barely walk as it is. I doubt they're going to cause any trouble."

"They're like children," North explained. "They don't know how to control what they have. We got one in there who sets fire to his own hands because he can't stop it and another one who leaves a trail of growing vines on everything she touches. It's a long ride back to the brewery, and we can't risk them not being able to hold themselves together until they're safely back and we can show them how to control it." He glanced over at Ben. "You remember what it was like, don't you? When you were just a kid and you didn't realize everything you could do?"

"Yeah . . ." Ben's voice held the ghost of some past regret in it. "I remember."

"There you go," North said, climbing up into the driver's seat of the wagon and knowing without a doubt that he wasn't the only one with ghosts following his footsteps through life.

Bringing up his childhood apparently was enough to shut Ben up good and tight, which was fine by North. He didn't care to deal with any talking when he had thinking to do.

They rode in silence back through town to the brewery, with the first light of dawn setting the horizon aglow. But it was Ben who saw the smoke first.

"What's that?" he asked, pointing in the direction of a glowing place on the horizon, where a plume of black rose up like a nightmare, blocking the stars in the sky.

The brewery was on fire.

LIBITINA

1902—New York

By the time Viola made sure that Theo and Ruby were headed toward the safety of their own part of town and she made her way back to the New Brighton, Paul had already heard about the fire. He was pacing and shouting at his men, while the one they called Razor stood nervous and waiting nearby.

"Where have you been?" Paul asked, turning on her the second she was through the door. His face was mottled an ugly, angry red.

"Out," she told him, pretending that she didn't notice his agitation.

"Out?"

She shrugged. "I needed air." After the meeting with Ruby, she *still* felt like she needed air, not that Paul had to know about that.

"I needed you here," he snapped. "Station thirty-three, she's on fire, and it isn't any normal fire." He glared at her as though it were somehow her fault.

"You think *I* did this?" She glared at him in return.

"You were, as you said, *out*."

She frowned, realizing that all of the Five Pointers were now watching her with a question in their eyes. "Fire is not my style, Paolo. You know that."

"If that station burns, Tammany is not gonna be happy," Razor said. "We have to do something."

Paul let out a frustrated growl and took Viola by the arm. "These are your people, so you're going to help me."

By the time they got over to the station, the air was heavy with smoke. Flames were tearing from the arching windows, and the front of the brick building was black with soot as the fire brigade pumped water toward the blaze. The steady stream from the pump truck didn't seem to be doing anything to stop the fire, probably because the heat of the flames wasn't the only warmth in the air.

Someone with an affinity for fire had to be nearby, feeding the flames, but where? She scanned the crowd, searching for some sign. The old magic was about connecting with the larger world, so it required focus and often needed contact—a sight line or direct touch. Whoever was at fault would be close.

"Find the maggot doing this or don't bother coming back to the New Brighton," Paul said.

Viola shrugged off the slur on her brother's lips. He'd called her worse. "And what am I supposed to do when I find him?"

"You're my blade, aren't you?" Paul glared at her.

"I don't have a knife," she told him. "You made sure of that."

"How many times do I have to tell you, you don't need one?" he said, his meaning clear. "Go on. Before it's too late."

She thought about arguing, but before she could, she heard the shattering of glass as a window cracked and flames poured out of it. If this station was destroyed by someone with the old magic, Tammany would retaliate. Innocent people would be at risk of being caught in the cross fire.

Without much choice, Viola ducked into the crowd, her eyes sharp for some sign of the perpetrator as she focused the warm energy that had nothing to do with the flames. She was halfway through the crowd when she saw a familiar figure standing on the steps of a building about half a block away. *Nibsy Lorcan.*

The boy's gold-rimmed spectacles flashed in the light from the blaze, and next to him was a boy with hair the color of flame focusing all his attention on the burning fire station.

She sent her affinity out, searching for the heat of the boy's affinity, the beating of his heart, and when she founded it, she tugged, just a little. Not enough to kill him, but more than enough to make him collapse to the ground.

Nibsy watched him go down, and then he began to scan the crowd. A moment later he found her, and his mouth curved up, as though he knew exactly how useless she'd become.

Too soft, an assassin who couldn't properly kill.

But that boy—he'd been one of Dolph's once. What was his name? She couldn't remember, but she knew that he wasn't the one who needed killing. That honor belonged to Nibsy, who was smiling at her as though he knew what she was thinking—and didn't care.

What she would give to wipe that smile from his face.

Viola let her affinity find the steady pulsing of the blood in his veins and reveled in the understanding that she held Nibsy's life. It would be so easy to end him. She could trade what was left of her soul for vengeance for Dolph's murder. Her soul, tarnished as it was, was hardly a worthy trade, but in that moment she felt as though it might do.

Better. She would kill him with her own hands.

Around her the street was in chaos. The crowd, who had gathered to watch a fire that could not be quenched, jeered their disappointment as the water began to have an effect on the flames. But Viola barely heard the noise, and though her eyes watered from the smoke, she didn't care as she walked toward Nibsy.

He started down from his perch, to meet her halfway. The nearer she came, the more amusement shone in his eyes.

"I hope you've made peace with your god, Nibsy," she said as she approached him. "I've come for you."

He didn't so much as flinch. "If I believed in a god, I would have lost faith in him years ago. You don't scare me, Viola. If you wanted to kill me, I've no doubt I would already be dead."

She curled her mouth into a deadly smile. "Perhaps, in your case, I prefer to play with my prey."

"I see that spending time with your family has only improved your delightful personality," Nibsy said, rocking back on his heels a bit.

"Bastardo," she spat. She would wipe the smugness from his face, and she would do it with her bare hands.

"I'm not your enemy, Viola," he said softly.

"Funny," she said. "You look just like him. I know what you did, how you betrayed Dolph. How you betrayed all of us."

"I never betrayed you. Dolph Saunders was a danger to himself and to our kind. He would have started a war that we couldn't have won. I protected the Devil's Own—and all of those like us," he said, sounding like he actually believed it.

"I never needed your protection," she sneered.

"No?" he asked, his tone mocking. "You're enjoying your time with your brother, then?" When she only glared at him, he spoke again. "You were meant for more than being Paul Kelly's scullery maid, Viola. Yes, I know how he uses you. He brags about it to me. *His blade.* His sister, who has learned her place." Nibsy shook his head. "Some blade—sharp enough to cut his potatoes and not much else these days, from what I hear."

"I could cut *you*," she told him.

"With what?" he asked, taunting her. "You miss her, don't you?" he asked, the glint in his eyes mocking her as much as his words.

Libitina. "You aren't man enough to wield her. But don't worry. I'll take her from you soon, and then I'll cut your heart out and leave it on Dolph's grave as a tribute."

"So bloodthirsty," he said, a laugh in his eyes. Then his face grew serious. "You're welcome to try to take your knife, but I'd rather *give* her to you."

She narrowed her eyes. It was a trick. This one, he was slippery as an eel, and just as treacherous. "Why would you? A boy as smart as you pretend to be should know I would only turn around and sink her into your heart."

"Because, despite everything that's passed between us, I think we could be friends."

A FINAL GAMBIT

1902—New York

James Lorcan watched the disbelief flash in Viola's eyes and then harden into hatred.

"Never," she said, practically spitting the word.

It was no more than he'd expected, but it wasn't enough to dissuade him. He inclined his head, conceding her point. "Then allies, perhaps."

She shook her head, and he knew she wanted to argue—she *always* wanted to argue—but he continued before she could deny it.

"We want the same thing, don't we?" he asked, measuring her mood. True, she could kill him in a blink, knife or no, but he knew her weakness, the secret that Dolph had hidden from everyone else—a misplaced sense of morality that kept her from killing with her affinity. Besides, if there had been any indication that she might strike, he would have known long before she did. So he pressed on. "We both want the end of the Order. Freedom for our kind."

"Dolph wanted those things as well, but you killed him," she pointed out.

"*Is* that what he wanted? Truly?" James paused, letting his words penetrate. He'd watched Dolph and Viola in the days before everything fell apart. Dolph's preoccupations had made this particular play more than easy for him. "Did Dolph tell you that himself? I don't think he did. He never told any of us the entirety of his plans. He didn't tell you what might happen at Khafre Hall, did he? He let you walk into a trap set by Darrigan without bothering to warn you."

He watched as her jaw tensed, but she didn't deny it—she couldn't.

"I would wager the Strega itself that he didn't tell you how he drove Leena to her grave."

"Lies," she hissed. "He did no such thing. He would never have hurt her."

James forced himself to keep his expression doleful and to hide every ounce of satisfaction this conversation was giving him. "You wear his mark, don't you, Viola? How do you think he found the power to make them into weapons against us?" he asked. "He took it from her. Why else would she have been taken so easily by the Order?"

She shook her head, as though refusing these truths, but he could tell that his words were worming their way beneath her skin, wriggling into her thoughts. Eating away at her sureness.

"You don't have to take my word for it," James said, pulling a package from his coat. "Here—" He offered it to her.

The moment she took the paper-wrapped parcel in her hands, he could tell she knew what it was. Her eyes narrowed at him, as though waiting for the trick. She wasn't stupid, after all. But that didn't mean that she was any match for *his* cunning.

"It's just a little gift, to show that I mean you no harm. You'll find everything you need to know within it," he told her. Thanks to the note-books in the apartment, he could offer her proof in Dolph's own hand that everything he'd told her was true . . . or at least it would appear so. "Unlike Dolph, I don't keep secrets from my friends."

"We are *not* friends, and I don't need your tricks," she told him, but he didn't miss the way she held the package close to her. "But I will keep my knife."

"No tricks, Viola." He took a step back and started to go. He took three steps toward where Mooch was still lying unconscious—but not dead—on the ground. He gave her those three steps to think about all that had just happened, to let her doubts start to grow, before he turned back to her. "One thing, though. Why are you so sure that *I'm* the traitor?

What of Jianyu? He wasn't with us on the bridge. He's never returned to the Strega. I'm convinced he was working with Darrigan."

"Why would he?" she asked.

"Why not?" James said. "He wasn't ever really one of us, was he? I always told Dolph he was too soft for trusting one of them. But if you don't believe me, perhaps you can ask Jianyu yourself. I'd put good odds on him being at the Order's big gala. Word is that one of the artifacts might turn up there—a ring that has the power to amplify an affinity. Jianyu has already tried to get it for himself once. I imagine he'll try again."

And when the two of them faced off against each other, James would be the one left standing.

A BLIND RUSH OF FEAR

1904—St. Louis

In the driver's seat beside Harte, North urged the horses on as they raced toward the burning brewery, but the tired team barely picked up any speed. Or at least that was how it felt to Harte, who watched the flames grow in ferocity as they approached.

By the time they pulled into the driveway, at least half the brewery's warehouse—where the kegs of prepared ale and lager were stored—was completely in flames. The main building, with the offices and bunk rooms, wasn't burning, but Harte wouldn't feel better until he saw Esta for himself, safe and whole.

At the thought of losing Esta, it wasn't only Harte who felt the blind rush of fear. The demon inside of him, Seshat, was also afraid. He could feel her pawing and clawing at him, urging him on with a desperation that let him know exactly how important Esta was to both of them.

He jumped from the moving wagon as North slowed and ran toward Ruth, who was standing in a small clutch of people with her hands on her hips and murder in her eyes.

"What happened?" North gasped.

The flickering light of the flames only served to highlight the furious expression on Ruth's face. "We've been accused of aiding criminals," Ruth said, her voice jagged with anger. Her eyes darted to a line of men in dark coats with familiar armbands. *The Guard.*

"Criminals?" Harte asked.

"It doesn't matter," Ruth told him. "They've drummed up some false charge, and now they're making their point because we dared to help the children."

"The Guard started the fire?" Harte asked.

"Not that there'll be any proof of it," Ruth told him. "They have people who can start fires without touching a match, same as us. They've just chosen the other side."

"Where's Esta?" Harte asked, looking around the group that had gathered and not finding her.

"She's with Maggie and a couple of the others," Ruth said. "They're getting the children out the back, so the Guard doesn't notice."

"I'll help," Harte said, and took off toward the building.

"They won't let you through," Ruth called, but Harte wasn't listening. All he could think about was finding Esta and making sure that she was safe.

He had just reached the line of Guardsmen when an explosion erupted, and windows on one side of the main building shattered as flames burst from them. Harte picked up his pace, but Ruth had been right. He hadn't taken more than a few steps before the Guards were on him, roughly wrestling him back.

"No one crosses," the tallest of them said. His mouth hitched up. "For safety reasons."

"There could be people in there," Harte said, lunging toward them again in an attempt to get past, but there were five of them, and it was easy enough for them to push him back.

There was dark smoke pouring from the doors of the main building, where the large vats of lager were fermenting. Flames had already started eating the roof, but in front of them, a line of Guards was preventing anyone from doing anything to stop the fire.

A moment later, North was at his side.

"Maggie's in there," North told him, and Harte heard his own fear echoed in North's voice.

"Ruth said there was a back entrance?" The fire hadn't reached the end of the building that housed the living quarters, but the smoke would be a problem. "Maybe they're already out."

"There is a back entrance, but there's also a dozen babies to get out of there." North looked at the burning warehouse, where the flames had grown to consume even more of the building. "If that fire starts to spread—"

"Is there a way around back?" Harte asked.

North gave him a tense nod. "But if we go now, we might draw their attention. They'd have Maggie and the kids."

"So we split up," Harte told him. "I'll distract them, and you go around back."

North's brows drew together, and Harte knew North was considering how much to trust him.

"Go on," Harte said. "You can hate me later."

He didn't wait for North's agreement but went charging into the line of Guards, pulling at his affinity as he went. He had time to land one punch before the others were on him, but one punch was enough—fist to face—to change the Guardsman's intent. The Guardsman turned on his brothers and attacked. In the confusion, Harte managed to get his hands on two of the others, and in moments, they were fighting each other instead of him. He took the opportunity the confusion offered and slipped past, running as fast as he could toward the now-burning main building.

The front doors were open, and Harte could already feel the heat coming from inside the building, but he didn't stop to think about that. All he could think was that without Esta, he was lost. But what that meant—whether it was him or the power that spurred him on—he didn't bother to analyze too closely.

The fire seemed contained to the east side of the building. If he hurried, he could make sure Esta and the kids got out the back. He darted inside, pulling his shirt up over his mouth and nose to ward off the smoke that already hung heavy in the air. The main brewing chamber was a mess. The heat from the flames had already caused one of the giant vats of beer to explode, and Harte didn't want to be around if another one blew. He took the steps up to the offices quickly, breathing only sporadically, to avoid the smoke. The bunk rooms were empty, so he moved on to the nursery, calling Esta's name and not caring who heard him.

When he got to the nursery, the room was—thankfully—empty. *They must have gotten out.* Which meant that he had to get himself out.

Harte was halfway down the hall when another explosion hit, throwing him from his feet and knocking him into the wall. He staggered to his knees, steadying himself as he heard a crackling and another explosion. And then the ceiling broke open above him.

INTO THE FIRE

1904—St. Louis

Esta was helping lift one of the children into a wagon that had been waiting in the yard behind the warehouse when she heard the explosion and turned to see the main building go up in flames behind her.

We were just in there. A matter of a few moments and they would have *still* been in there.

Maggie gasped, her hand to her mouth as she adjusted the toddler on her hip. "No," she whispered. "No, no, no . . ."

Esta set the child she was holding into the wagon and turned to take the one from Maggie, who let go of it reluctantly. Her eyes were wide and glassy as she watched her family's business burn.

"We're safe," she told Maggie. "The kids are safe too. You can rebuild anything else."

But Maggie was shaking her head, and Esta couldn't tell if she was disagreeing or if she simply couldn't even hear her from the shock of it. North was there a moment later, taking Maggie in his arms like he didn't care who saw. His face relaxed in relief as he held on to her, whispering into her hair.

The last child had just been loaded into the wagon along with the dozen or so patients they'd rescued from the hospital when Mother Ruth came around the side of the building with a small group of people.

"Where's Har—Ben?" Esta said, correcting herself before she uttered the wrong name. He wasn't with the rest of the group.

"He's not with you?" North said, turning to Ruth.

Another explosion echoed from within the building.

Ruth shook her head. "Last I saw him, the crazy fool was running into the building."

"He thought you all might still be in there," North said, his voice sounding as hollow and shocked as Esta felt at the idea of Harte being inside of that building.

"He's inside?" Esta asked, the words clawing themselves free from the tightness in her throat. Above them, the roof of the main building crackled and shifted. As if reading her mind, Maggie grabbed her wrist.

"You can't—"

Esta tore her arm away and started running.

As soon as she was close, she pulled time slow and stepped through the doorway of the burning building without looking back.

She had no idea where Harte would be, but she'd start at the nursery. If he'd come in looking for her, that was where he would have gone.

The heat of the fire radiated in the passageways around her, but the flames themselves had gone still, like brilliant flowers blooming on the walls and ceilings. She couldn't stop time completely, so she couldn't stop the process of oxygen consumed by the fire. The heat was a constant, and the air hung heavy with deadly smoke, but she wouldn't stop. She *couldn't*. Not until she found Harte.

Esta's chest clenched when she turned into the hallway where the nursery waited and saw the pile of burning rubble. She nearly lost her hold on her affinity when she saw the shoe peeking out of it.

She didn't waste any time in starting to move the pieces of ceiling that had fallen on Harte, but it was taking too long. She uncovered his face and saw that his eyes were open—he wasn't dead, but he also wasn't any help, nearly frozen as he was. Considering her options, she let go of the seconds. The flames crackled to life in a roaring blaze, and Harte gasped as more pieces of the ceiling fell.

His eyes met hers, his face blanching when he saw her standing there above him.

"Help me," she said, trying to pull more of the rubble off him.

She could hear the building creaking as they worked, until finally he was free of the large piece that had pinned his legs down. "Can you walk?" she asked, coughing from the heat and the smoke.

"I think so," he told her, getting to his feet but tottering a little. She caught him before he could fall.

"Can't you . . . ?" He meant that he wanted her to stop time.

"No," she said. "Not with you. The building's too unstable." She could tell he wanted to argue, but she didn't give him the chance. With her shirt up over her nose and mouth, they moved as fast as they could through the hallway, toward the back of the building.

They were almost out when Esta stopped.

"What are you doing?" Harte asked, pushing her onward.

"My cuff. Ishtar's Key is in here," she said.

"Do you know for sure?" He coughed.

She shook her head. "But if it is . . ." The fire had started unexpectedly, and Ruth had been too busy arguing with the Guard—distracting them, so Maggie could get the children out—to do anything else. Maybe it wasn't in here, but she couldn't take that chance. "I can't leave without it," she said, turning back into the fire. Without it, they would be trapped there with no way back. And no way to set things right.

"No, Esta—" He grabbed at her hand.

"Let go," she told him, trying to shake him loose. But he was too stubborn, and already she could feel the heat of the power within him creeping against her skin, as stark and real as the fire.

"I'm not leaving you here. It's not worth dying for."

But hadn't she already made that decision? "I'm dead either way."

He shook his head and was about to argue with her, but she cut him off.

"I need that stone, but I can't do this with you, Harte. Not with whatever is inside you. Let me go, and I can at least try. I got *you* out, didn't

I?" She could tell he wanted to disagree, but he couldn't argue with that point. "I'll be back outside before you even notice."

"No, Esta," he said, tightening his hold on her arm until his fingers were digging painfully into her skin. There was something dark in his expression, a desperation that was stark and pure. In that moment, she couldn't tell what it was moving behind his eyes—whether it was he himself who cared that desperately or if it was something else. Seshat. The demon-like power inside of him—did Seshat know that the stones would be her undoing?

That thought made up her mind for her. "I'm sorry," she said, as she wrenched his arm to the side and laid him flat on his back. The moment his hand released her, she pulled time slow and dodged back into the flames once more.

A PEONY IN A TOMATO PATCH

1902—New York

*L*ies. Viola knew that the words coming from Nibsy's mouth were as foul and polluted as the muck that flowed in the sewer, and now that she had Libitina in her hands once more, she would show him what she thought of his lies. She began to unwrap the comforting weight of the knife when, from the corner of her eye, she saw a flash of pink that was utterly out of place in the dreary, sooty air of the Bowery.

She should have known that the girl wasn't going to listen to her and go back uptown, where she belonged. She shouldn't have been surprised to find Ruby there, craning her neck to see what was happening with the fire and looking every bit like a peony in a tomato patch.

Ruby was too engrossed in trying to see what was happening, but from the look of concentration and worry on Theo's face, he had realized that the crowd's mood was turning now that the steady stream of water was beginning to extinguish the blaze. With their source of entertainment dying, they were beginning to grow restless and rowdy.

Viola's instinct was to go to them. Neither of them belonged in the rough world of lower Manhattan, not like she did. But there was Nibsy to think of, and her revenge was so close she could taste the sweetness of it in the back of her throat.

Torn, Viola turned back to Nibsy, only to find that the rat was no longer there. She saw him, already a ways off, disappearing into the crowd and leaving the red-haired boy prone on the ground. *Dolph would never have done such a thing.*

But the boy wasn't her concern. He'd cast his lot when he'd started the fire.

Instead of going for him, she headed toward where Ruby and Theo were being jostled by the increasingly restless crowd. She was nearly to them when she saw that just beyond Ruby, her brother was heading in her direction. And he had John Torrio with him.

Viola could see what would happen—Torrio would catch sight of Theo, thinking he was Reynolds, and he would know that she had not killed the reporter. It would not matter that Theo hadn't ever been the target. All that would matter was that he would be proof that Viola had betrayed her charge, and more, she'd stopped Torrio from completing the job. If Torrio saw Theo and Ruby, if he realized what Viola had—or rather, had *not*—done, she'd be dead. And what's more, Theo and Ruby would both be dead, as well.

Waving her arms, Viola ran toward her brother and Torrio, trying to draw their attention so they would not turn slightly to the left and notice Ruby, pink and petaled as a flower. Because they would not fail to see her, not with how polished and delicate she looked amid the toughs of the Bowery.

"Paolo!" she called, desperate to reach him, but they were both searching the crowd, not hearing her. She shouted again, her voice clawing from her throat as he moved closer to where Ruby and Theo stood watching the fire.

Finally, Paul noticed her, and then Torrio did as well. When they saw Viola, they turned away from their original path—the one that would have taken them to Ruby—and came toward Viola instead.

"What is it?" Paul asked, his expression conveying his disappointment that she didn't have the culprit in hand.

"The one who did this, he's there, on the ground," she told him, pointing to the spot where the boy still lay, unconscious from her magic. "A red-haired boy, maybe fifteen years old. One of Nibsy Lorcan's boys."

"One of Lorcan's?" Paul asked, his expression filled with suspicion. "Are you sure?"

Viola nodded, keeping her expression steady even as she let her affinity unfurl to find Ruby's now-familiar heartbeat in the crowd. When she found it, steady and calm, she knew the girl was still safe—for the moment, at least.

Paul glanced at Torrio, sharing some unspoken communication between them before he turned back to her. "Did you take care of him?"

"Better," she told Paul. "I left him for you. A gift for Tammany," she explained.

"That wasn't what you were told to do," Paul said. "I told you to kill him."

"Killing him is no good. Think of it," she argued, before he could interrupt again. "If I killed him, what proof do you have that you've caught the one responsible? You can't tell if a dead man is Mageus. You can't ask him why he attacked or who he worked for. This way, you have the boy—you have *evidence*," she said. *Which means that you have proof that Nibsy is not to be trusted*. "Take him to Tammany and give them the favor of dealing with him themselves. They'll thank you for it."

Torrio was eyeing her suspiciously, but she didn't give him so much as a glance. Whatever Paul might want for the two of them, Viola wasn't interested.

Before Paul could agree or argue, Viola sensed the fluttering of Ruby's heart. The steady rhythm gave way to a more rapid beat, and Viola knew something was happening. "Quickly!" she shouted, pointing in the direction she'd left the boy.

Her actions had their intended effect. Paul and Torrio turned, almost as one, and the second their attention was diverted, she darted into the crowd to look for the birdbrained girl who was about to get herself killed.

DRAGGED UNDER

1902—New York

E ven from her place far back in the crowd, Ruby Reynolds could
feel the heat of the strange flames that were consuming the engine
house. Now that she was standing amid the rabble and the crowd,
she could tell for herself that what was happening had everything to do
with magic. A moment before something had changed, and the water that
had been streaming from the hoses began to have an effect on the flames.

The crowd had not liked that, not *at all*.

"We need to go," Theo said, using his body as a shield against the rest-
lessness of the crowd.

"Just a minute more," she pleaded. "If we could only get a little
closer . . ."

"We're *not* going any closer," he told her in a tone he rarely used on her.

"But, Theo—"

She barely had his name on her tongue when the crowd surged and she
stumbled with it to the left. Suddenly, she was aware that what had been
avid interest colored by excitement when she and Theo arrived had quickly
turned to frustration, maybe even anger. Once, when she was younger, her
father had taken her and her sisters to Coney Island to play in the surf, and
she had ventured too far into the waves and had been dragged under. Being
caught up in the suddenly raucous crowd reminded her of that moment,
and she felt the same pang of betrayal she'd felt as a child when the water
had turned against her.

At the time, her father had caught her up under the arms and set her back on her feet as though nothing had happened. Now Theo did what he could to shield her from the other bodies that were pressing and shoving against them, the dear, but it was all she could do to stay on her feet.

It was unbearably exciting.

From the look on his face, Theo didn't feel the same. *The poor dear.* He always had been so buttoned up and careful. But he'd also been her truest friend, through everything—her father's breakdown and the embarrassment it had caused her family and her mother's meddling to get all her daughters married off after his death. And then there was society's constant judgment. Not that she cared a fig for their judgment, but society made things so much harder than they needed to be. And through all of it, Theo had been there.

She was the worst sort of person to put him through this, and yet, if she could just figure out how the fire started—

"Ruby!" The voice cut through the noise around them. "Theo!"

Ruby turned and realized it was Viola, her violet eyes blazing with something that looked incredibly like fear. "Viola?"

She barely had time to recognize a warmth flush through her that had nothing to do with the fire before the crowd surged, pushing them to the left. Ruby staggered away from Theo, losing her balance, and fell into Viola. She had a moment to appreciate the other girl's strength. Viola was shorter than Ruby herself, but beneath the softness of her curves, her body was sturdy and strong enough to keep Ruby on her feet.

For a moment the connection between them felt absolutely undeniable. Her stomach fluttered as her chest went tight, and she felt the entire world narrow down to the piercing violet of Viola's darkly lashed eyes.

Viola froze, her arms going rigid around Ruby, and in that moment, the crowd fell away and there was a roaring in her ears as she was sure, *sure* that Viola had felt the same energy between them. But Viola simply set Ruby upright again and stepped back.

"Come on," Viola told them, taking hold of Ruby's wrist. "You need to get out of here. This way."

The warmth that had coursed through Ruby just a moment before cooled, but her skin was still hot where Viola's fingers circled her wrist. She tried to jerk away, but Viola held firm and turned to her.

"We need to go. *Now*," Viola commanded, glancing to Theo for support.

"She's right," he told her, his expression apologetic. "It's not safe here."

Safe? What was safety but a cage? Her whole life had been designed to keep her safe—away from trouble, away from harm—away from anything real or important. *No.* She'd made the decision that she wasn't interested in "safe" the day they found her father in his study, driven mad by his own obsession with safety. He'd tried to master magic, just as the men in the Order had instructed, and it had mastered him instead. No, not just mastered him, *destroyed* him—and it had nearly destroyed her entire family along with him.

Now Ruby was interested only in *truth*, and the truth was that no male journalist in her position would run because of a little scuffle.

"I can't leave now," she told her. "I need to find out what happened. The story—"

"It's not safe here for you," Viola said, pulling at her arm.

"I don't care," Ruby said, her face creased in frustration.

"Ruby—" Theo tried.

"No, Theo. We came to see the fire, and I'm going to see the fire." She turned to Viola, her veins warming with her determination. "If the flames weren't natural, I need to know. Don't you see how important this is?"

"It won't be important if you're dead," Viola said, struggling to stay upright in the tumultuous crowd.

There were worse things than dying, Ruby thought, thinking of her father in the sanitarium upstate before he died finally and her sisters, who sometimes loved their husbands but often did not. And of herself, forced to live stuck in a narrow slice of a life that should be so much bigger, so much *wider*.

"I think we should listen to Miss Vaccarelli," Theo told her. *The traitor.*

But Ruby shook her head and pushed her way farther into the crowd.

She hadn't gone more than three steps when a man nearby threw a punch that transformed the crowd into a cascading wave of violence. The people around her shoved, some diving into the fray and others desperately trying to retreat, and in that moment, she had the first inkling of fear. She stumbled back, and Theo was there, just as he always was.

Please, his familiar eyes pleaded, and as much as she wanted to be stronger, as much as she wanted to stand firm, she couldn't deny him. She gave him a nod, and together they followed the path that Viola was cutting through the crowd.

They were nearly there, nearly to the edge of the madness. A few steps more, Ruby thought, and they would be safe. But they'd barely reached the edge of the crush of bodies when the sound of sirens erupted through the air—the police were coming. In response, the crowd surged again, and as Ruby tried to regain her balance, a gunshot exploded over the noise and Theo's hand let go of hers.

She looked back in time to see him falling, the brightness of his blood blooming like a carnation tucked into his lapel.

HELPLESS

1902—New York

The sound of Ruby's scream cut through the noise and hit Viola like a dagger to the gut. She turned in time to see Ruby trying to catch Theo as he fell to the ground.

The crowd was scattering now, no longer bothering to fight each other as they tried to get away from the threat. Another gunshot erupted, and then another, as the street descended into madness.

Viola looked around, searching for her brother and Torrio even as she lunged back into the mess of the crowd for Ruby and Theo, but instead of finding the Five Pointers, she realized that the gunshots had come from a different source—two groups of the Chinese tongs were facing off in the midst of the madness. It was as though the entire Bowery had completely lost its mind.

Theo was on the ground, the fine wool of his suit already marred by the dirt of the streets and the blood that was seeping from his chest, and Ruby was there with him, cradling him. The girl's rosy complexion had gone an almost ghostly white, and her mouth was moving without any words coming out. But Theo was still breathing. His eyes were open, and he looked at Viola. "Get her out of here," he said, his voice racked with pain.

"No." Ruby glared at Viola. "I'm not leaving without him."

All around them was violence, but from the seriousness in Ruby's expression, Viola knew it would be pointless to argue. "Then you'd best help me get him up," she told Ruby.

With a sure nod, Ruby helped Viola hoist Theo upright as he groaned in agony. If Viola had expected the willowy-looking girl to falter beneath the weight of him, she was wrong. Ruby's face was creased with the effort of supporting Theo's weight as he dropped an arm over each of their shoulders, but Viola admired the girl all the more for her determination.

Even as her heart clenched to see the way Ruby looked at Theo.

By the time they moved him far enough away from the fighting to be safe, Theo was all but deadweight. Still, Viola urged them to go a little farther, until they found the relative safety of a doorway to a tenement that she recognized. Once, the people inside had been loyal to Dolph. She could only hope that they would recognize her as a friend instead of a traitor.

They pulled Theo inside, where the noise of the street was blocked out by the door. One tenant opened his door long enough to determine he wanted nothing to do with whatever was happening in the hallway.

Ruby cradled Theo against herself, patting his cheek softly, but Theo was fading. His eyes were half-open, but Viola could tell by their glassiness that he wasn't focusing on either one of them. His skin had gone pale as death, and his lips were already tinged with blue.

"No," Ruby said, her voice nearly breaking when he didn't respond. "You stay with me, Theodore Barclay. Do you hear me?" There were already tears on her cheeks. "Don't you dare leave me here alone."

But Theo didn't respond. His breathing was shallow, and there was a rattling sound coming from his chest that Viola knew too well. All at once she was in Tilly's apartment again, helpless to do anything as she watched her friend die.

Except she wasn't helpless this time.

"Please," Ruby said, leaning her forehead against Theo's. Over and over she pleaded, her voice trembling. But Theo didn't respond.

"Move," Viola said. Her voice sounded as empty and hopeless as she felt inside, but she could do this one thing, even if it meant exposing what she was. *"Move,"* she repeated, pushing gently at Ruby.

Ruby looked up at Viola, her eyes filled with tears, and opened her mouth to refuse, but Viola cut her off.

"I can help him," she said more gently. "But you need to let me."

Reluctantly, Ruby backed away from Theo, who was still bleeding. He was alive, though. Viola could tell from the blood that continued to flow from the wound in his chest.

She didn't want to touch him. She didn't need to touch him, but she knew it would be easier and would work faster if she did, so she placed her hand on his chest, over the wetness of the fabric. His blood was hot and slick beneath her fingers, but she ignored how clearly it spoke to her of dying as she pressed her affinity into him.

Little by little, she found the source of the damage and used her magic to knit him back together, until his body forced the bullet from the wound and into her hand. She didn't stop or allow herself to look up at Ruby, but continued to direct her affinity toward him, into him, pulling together the spaces that had been ripped apart by the violence of the bullet.

Pulling the life back into him.

He gasped suddenly, and she waited until he opened his eyes to back away. Her hands were sticky with his blood and holding what was left of the bullet. But he would live. He would be *fine*. And so would Ruby.

Viola looked up, drained but satisfied with what she had managed, only to find shock and horror in Ruby's eyes.

"It was *you*," Ruby whispered before Viola could so much as explain. "It was never John Torrio who was Mageus, was it?"

Viola's head was shaking of its own accord, even as she wanted to explain, to tell Ruby everything—how she had been ordered to kill her and how she had refused. But something in Ruby's tone stopped her, a coolness that Viola hadn't expected.

"You lied to me," Ruby said. "All this time, you were lying to me." There was something new in Ruby's eyes now. "You're *one of them*."

Confusion swamped her. "I—" She didn't know what she was supposed

to say. "But you told me you wanted to destroy the Order," Viola pleaded.

"Because they depend on magic for their power." Ruby's expression was a well of disgust. "Because this city will never be safe as long as unnatural power remains a threat. It destroyed my father—my entire family was nearly destroyed as well because of it," she said.

"I thought—"

"I can't believe I didn't see what you were." Ruby's eyes were filled with angry tears. "I should have known, but I let you get close to us. I actually *begged* you for help," she said, her words crumbling into a fit of hysterical laughter that broke into a sob. "And look what happened."

Something about the accusation in Ruby's voice had Viola's temper snapping. "I never asked you to come after me. I told you to stay away. I tried to warn you, didn't I?"

But Ruby wasn't backing down. "Theo nearly died because of *you*."

Theo made a soft sound, but Ruby couldn't see that he was already improving, not through the haze of hate that shone in her eyes.

Viola staggered to her feet. "I'm not the one who dragged him into that mess today. I'm not the one who refused to leave." She lashed out at Ruby with all the hurt and anger she felt burning inside of her. It was a flame that would consume her. "That was *you*, Miss Reynolds. You can blame me all you want. You can hate me for what I am, for something I had no choice in and no ability to refuse, but while you're telling yourself stories about who and what is evil, you should remember that Theo getting shot is *your fault*," Viola said, her voice breaking. "I'm the one who *saved* him."

"Get away from me," Ruby told her, shielding Theo with her body. "From both of us."

The look in Ruby's eyes was one Viola had seen too many times before. The combination of loathing and fear struck her clear to the bone. She had spent too long trying to be what she wasn't, so this time she didn't fight. She honored Ruby's demand, and without another word, she turned and left. And she didn't look back.

DENIAL

1902—New York

Ruby could barely see from the tears in her eyes, but she wasn't sorry to see the back of Viola Vaccarelli. She *wasn't.*

She barely noticed that Theo was moving in her arms until he was already pulling himself upright, rubbing at the place on his chest that was still damp with blood.

"Theo?" His name came out in a rushing gasp as she threw her arms around him.

But he shook her off. "I'm fine," he told her, his voice still weak. "That was rather harsh, though, don't you think?" He cocked one brow in her direction, and her heart flipped to see the familiar, endearing look.

"What was?" she asked, already knowing exactly what he was talking about.

He only stared at her.

"She's one of them, Theo. What did you want me to do?"

"You could have thanked her," he said gently.

He was right, of course. *But she's one of* them.

"She lied to us," she said instead. She brushed his hair back from his face. "Are you truly all right?"

Taking a deep breath, as though testing out his lungs, he nodded. "I think I am, actually. Are you?" he said, his voice softening.

"I'm fine," she told him. "I'm not the one who was shot."

"That isn't what I mean. You *liked* her," he pressed.

"I didn't—"

"Don't," he said gently. "You lie to the whole world, but you've never needed to lie to me."

Ruby felt the burn of tears threatening again, but she shook her head, trying to will them away. "It doesn't matter," she told him. "She is one of them, and you *know* how I feel about magic. You know what it did to my family."

Theo didn't speak for a moment, but then he took her chin and turned her toward him. "Ruby . . ."

"*Don't*, Theo." She shook her head again, not wanting to think about any of it.

"No," he said, cupping her face. "You are my dearest friend, and because I love you as well as I've ever loved anyone, I'm going to tell you something that I should have told you months ago—before you started this quest of yours: Your father made his own choices, love."

She started to argue, but he stopped her with a single look. They'd been friends since they were both babes in leading strings. No one understood her as he did because no one had ever felt as safe as he had. But now he didn't look safe. Now he looked like the truth staring at her and forcing her to accept it.

"Yes, the Order might have driven your father deeper into an already unhealthy obsession, but he knew what he was doing when he started, and it had nothing to do with the good of your family or the good of the city. Magic didn't drive him to his breaking point. Perhaps it helped, but he did that on his own."

She was shaking her head and wishing that she could block his words, but in her heart—in that place where she had always understood unspoken things—she'd known this all along. She had been so young when her father had lost his mind and tried to attack a friend over some supposed magical object. He'd nearly murdered someone over a *trinket*, and it had been so much easier for her—for *all of them*—to blame the magic itself, that thing outside and apart from him. It had been so much more satisfying to hate and fight against *that* than to accept that her father had been the cause of her family's misfortunes.

Perhaps he'd dabbled in alchemy and other occult studies because of the Order. But Ruby knew the truth. Her father had always been the sort of man who wanted to be bigger and more important than he was. His membership in the Order wasn't separate from that. When she was a girl, his boasting and posturing had made it seem as though he were some paragon of manliness . . . like he was untouchable.

But she wasn't a girl any longer.

"She's never going to forgive me," Ruby whispered, remembering every awful word she'd spoken to Viola.

"Do you want her to?" Theo asked gently.

"I don't know," Ruby said, knowing the words were a lie even as she spoke them. But she was still so angry and felt so betrayed that she would never, *ever* admit it.

CLOSE TO THE SURFACE

1904—St. Louis

Harte hit the ground before he knew what was happening, the force of Esta's blow and his fall knocking the air from his chest. By the time he shook himself off and sat up, Esta was already running into the burning building again. He saw her silhouetted by the fire, and then she was gone.

At the sight of her disappearing, the power inside Harte rose up with a violence he wasn't ready for. All at once he was pulled under into darkness, where all he could feel was the pain of being torn apart, the rage at being betrayed, and the unbearable longing that had built over centuries of being imprisoned.

He didn't realize that he was trying to run toward the fire himself until he came to with North and one of the other brewery workers holding him back as he tried to tear himself away from them. *I will rip them apart to find her.*

But in a blink, his vision focused and he saw Esta appear again, walking toward them whole and unharmed. She met his eyes with a frown, and he could tell that she hadn't found the cuff.

He was grateful in that moment that the two guys had hold of his arms. Seshat was so close to the surface that he couldn't have stopped himself from going to Esta. He couldn't have stopped Seshat from taking her.

And Esta wouldn't have been prepared. She wouldn't have known until it was too late.

As his body started to relax, North and the other guy slowly released him. Concern was etched across Esta's features, but he didn't go to her. The power was still pressing itself at his boundaries, testing him.

He didn't trust himself to even be near Esta, let alone touch her, so he shook his head, warning her off.

Hurt flickered in her eyes, but he turned away from it, knowing that if he went to her now, the demon-like power inside of him would win.

"We need to go, before the Guard decides to do anything more," Ruth told the group.

Harte wanted to go to Esta, to wrap her in his arms and convince himself that she was still safe and whole, to convince her to leave these Antistasi and all the danger they presented, but Esta's hurt had turned to hardness. She was already walking away from him, helping Ruth and Maggie and the rest climb into the remaining wagon. And all Harte could do was follow.

THREATS AND PROMISES

1904—St. Louis

It was close to midnight by the time Julien Eltinge let himself out through the stage door and cut back through the alley behind the theater. The humid warmth of the night felt oppressive without so much as a breeze to cut through it. Still, it was quiet, a more than adequate respite from the exhausting day he'd had.

The morning had started with a meeting with Corwin Spenser, who had wanted to go over the plans the Society had been making to ensure security at the parade. Not everyone in town appreciated the Veiled Prophet's celebrations. The Society always expected trouble, rabble who would do anything to disrupt what should have been an evening of entertainment, but with the president in town, nothing could be allowed to go wrong—especially when it came to the necklace. Julien had assured the old man yet again that he was more than capable of taking care of anyone who might try anything during the parade. That meeting had been followed by back-to-back shows, where the house had been full but lackluster. The heat was affecting everyone.

He'd just turned the corner toward his own apartment when he realized that the carriage on the street behind him seemed to be following him. Slowing his steps, Julien waited for it to pass, but instead it pulled up alongside him and the door opened. Inside was a man he'd seen before—at a dinner the Veiled Prophet had required him to attend earlier that week. He wasn't one of the Society, but was a representative from one of the other Brotherhoods. Which had it been?

"Mr. Eltinge?" the man called. "Could I offer you a ride?"

New York, he thought suddenly, recognizing the clipped accent of the man's speech. Which meant he was from the Order.

"Thanks," Julien called, too aware of the sweat that was dripping down his back. "But I think I'll walk. It's a lovely night for it." He waved and continued on, hoping that would be the end of it.

It wasn't, of course. The carriage pulled up alongside him again.

"Oh, I think you'll want to come for a ride with me, Julien." He leaned forward so the streetlamp lit the planes of his face. "Unless you want me to explain to the Order where you *really* found that necklace."

The night felt sultry against his skin, but Julien's veins had turned to ice. "I'm not sure what you're referring to." He considered his options, but he doubted outrunning a horse was one of the better ones.

"I think you do," the man told him. "So I'm going to give you a choice—you can get into this carriage, and tell me everything you know about the Society's plans for the necklace on the night of the parade. If you do, I can protect you. I can make sure the Order never knows about your connection to Harte Darrigan or the theft of their most precious treasures. Or you can keep walking and count me as one of your enemies."

The man wasn't old, but he was soft, bloated from too much drinking and too little exercise. In a ring, Julien could flatten him, but life wasn't a boxing ring. Life was more of a chess game, and Julien was not about to find himself in check because of Harte Darrigan. "You know," Julien said, trying to keep his tone easy, "I think I could use a ride after all."

DISILLUSIONED

1902—New York

Viola didn't even know where she was walking. She was blocks away, nearly to the edge of the island, when her feet finally slowed and the haze that she was blindly walking through lifted. Suddenly exhausted, she stepped into the safe cover of a recessed doorway and sank to the ground, her legs collapsing beneath her. Realizing that the bullet was still in her hand, she tossed it away in disgust.

Then she took the package that Nibsy had given her from the pocket of her skirt. Viola paused a moment to allow the comforting weight to rest in her hands before she began to open the wrappings. Finally, she felt balanced. Grounded. *Ready.*

To hell with all her plans. Why should she wait for some future retribution? Why should she allow the Order to destroy Nibsy Lorcan when she could have the honor herself? She would carve him from the world, and then she would go for her brother. And when she had finished with them, she would go for the Order. The silvery blade flashed as soon as she tore the paper away, and she held it up, examining it. Reveling in its power.

She pulled herself up, letting the wrapping fall to the ground, but the markings on the paper caught her eye as it fell. Leaning over, she picked it up and examined the clear, familiar hand. She knew that writing, the way the letters slanted precisely to the right and the bold, confident stroke of the pen.

Dolph.

Her chest ached at the memory of her friend and at the loss of him, but as she let her eyes scan over the lines of writing, the ache turned into something else. Disbelief. Denial.

It can't be. Dolph wouldn't have written these words. He couldn't have harmed Leena this way. But there, stark as the letters on the page, was every step he'd taken and every intention he'd had—to take her power, to *use* her. The woman he'd claimed to love.

It must be a trick, she thought. Another of Nibsy's deceptions, because if it wasn't, everything she had known about Dolph Saunders had been a lie.

PART

VI

THE RIVER

1904—St. Louis

With the brewery in ashes, the Antistasi moved farther out the day after the fire, to a small camp on the banks of the Mississippi just south of town. Without really talking it over or deciding, Esta had gone with them. Harte had followed, but he wouldn't even look at her. He was keeping his distance and making excuses to be anywhere that she wasn't. Not that she completely blamed him, after the way she'd attacked him. Even now, while everyone else was trying to help the newly woken focus on their affinities, Harte was sitting on the bank of the river, his back to her and the rest.

Fine, then. He could sulk all he wanted to. When he got over himself, maybe he would realize that she'd had to at least *attempt* to get her cuff back. She tried not to think about what it meant that she hadn't found it.

Had she simply missed it? Or did Ruth still have it?

But letting her thoughts wander while she tried to help the new Mageus wasn't the safest thing to do, so she forced herself to forget about Harte's clear disapproval and to focus on the task in front of her. Most of the people from the hospital were still processing the reality of their new lives. Born Mageus learned how to use their connection to the old magic as children, and by the time they were grown, it was second nature. But Ruth's attack had been on adults. Learning how to focus their affinities—discovering what power they actually held—was proving to be challenging and frustrating for them.

It wasn't much more comfortable for Esta. The whole thing reminded her of her own childhood—the days she'd spent training with Professor Lachlan. She hated him. She *needed* to hate him, for all the ways he'd betrayed her. But helping the newly woken, she wondered if she didn't also owe him. He'd taught her how to find the spaces between the seconds and had coached her until she could pull them slow with hardly any effort at all. He'd given her Ishtar's Key and the secrets of slipping through time, a fact she didn't want to admit—even to herself. It was as he'd said—he'd made her.

Of course, she reminded herself, the man she'd known as the Professor wouldn't have *had* to do any of that if the boy she'd known as Nibsy hadn't stolen her entire life. Who would she have been if Nibsy Lorcan hadn't killed her parents?

Shaking off the questions of the past, she tried to focus on the man in front of her. Arnie was middle-aged, with a patch of hair on each side of his head and a ragged mustache tinged yellow on the edges. He kept losing focus, and when that happened, flames would burst from his fingertips, startling him and causing him to flail about until he found the pail of water to squelch the fire. If he wasn't fast enough—and he often wasn't—Esta would call one of the bottlers who worked at the brewery, and who was also a healer, to help with the burns.

"Think of it as a connection," Esta tried to explain as he soaked his hands in a bucket of water for the tenth time. "The whole world and everything in it is connected. Magic lives in the spaces between those connections. When you use your affinity, you're pressing at the spaces—reshaping them and manipulating them."

He frowned at her. "How does that help me with the fire? It's just *hot*."

Honestly, she didn't know. Using her affinity, even when she was younger, had always felt intuitive, never dangerous.

"I barely blink and the flames erupt," he complained. "There's no spaces. It just *hurts*."

"Maybe stop thinking of the fire as outside yourself?" she suggested. Fire, since it was a chemical reaction, was aligned with the inert, but time was different. It was Aether. It was everything.

She was a miserable teacher.

"I know you," a soft voice said from behind her.

Esta turned to see the girl from the warehouse staring at her. She looked younger now that she wasn't wearing the stiff, high-necked gray. Her nose was smattered with freckles, and her eyes held an accusation. "No," Esta lied, turning away from her. "You must be mistaken."

But the girl didn't give up. "John. Your name is John," she insisted. "You were there that night."

"No," Esta said, turning back in time to see the moment the girl's understanding clicked.

"You're one of them, and you were there that night," the girl said, her eyes widening. "I saw you. I *talked* to you."

The day was clear and sunny, warm with the heat of summer, but suddenly, there was a burst of icy air, like a blast of winter sweeping through. The tree above them shook with the force of it, and Esta looked up to find the green faces of the leaves crawling with frost.

"You did this to us," the girl said, stepping toward Esta. "I knew it was you. I knew it all along."

"No," Esta said, backing away. But she didn't have the nerve to lie to this girl who looked so scared and broken and angry. "I just—" How could she answer the hate in the girl's eyes? It didn't seem enough to explain that she was just a tool. That she hadn't intended anything, because the truth was that she had. She'd entered the warehouse that night knowing that others might be hurt. She'd chosen Harte and their mission to get the necklace over these people's lives, and it was a choice she would make again.

At least, she *thought* she would.

"Greta, that's enough." It was Ruth, who'd come up behind the girl.

"But he's the one—"

"I said enough. You're one of us now," Ruth admonished. "Calm yourself."

The icy wind died off, replaced by the normal warmth of the day.

Above, frost turned liquid dripped from the leaves, but their faces had gone brown from the cold.

"Come with me," Ruth said to Esta.

Glad to be away from Greta and her accusations, Esta followed Ruth. "She hates us."

"She doesn't yet understand the gift she's been given," Ruth said. "She will."

"What if she doesn't?" Esta asked before she thought better of it.

Ruth tilted her head and gave her the sort of look that Esta imagined only a mother would be able to give. "Would you give up your own affinity?"

"No, but I was born with it," Esta told her. "It's who I am. Greta didn't have any choice in the matter," she said, thinking of Harte's objections.

"Neither did you. Your affinity was bestowed upon you by fate, and yet you've come to see it as essential. In time, Greta will too. They all will," Ruth said.

It was clear that Ruth believed what she said, and her voice was so sure, so filled with emotion, that Esta could almost believe it too. Maybe she had just been a tool, but in the end, no one had forced her to attack Lipscomb and the warehouse full of people. She could have tried to find a better way, but she hadn't. She'd heard Lipscomb talk and she'd judged his life to be worth less than Harte's.

Maybe his life *had* been worth less than Harte's. But watching these newly woken Mageus struggle and seeing the fear in their eyes every time their affinities burst forth uncontrolled, she wasn't sure that she'd had any right to make that decision.

Taking a deep breath, Esta shoved away her doubts. "Did you want something?"

"You've acquitted yourself admirably this past night," Ruth said. "What you did for Maggie and the children during the fire, and here, with the newly woken."

"We told you that we weren't your enemy," Esta pointed out, trying to keep any trace of smugness from her voice.

"Yes, well . . ." Ruth paused, her nostrils flaring slightly, as though admitting as much had been an effort. "With all that's happened, it seems that I must count you as an ally after all," she said, not sounding all that happy about the situation. "With the damage to the brewery and the responsibility here with the newly woken, I need your help."

The words settled something inside of her. *This is it.* "What's your plan?"

"The Society," Ruth said. "I want to make them pay for what they've done to us. I want them to crawl."

"The feeling is definitely mutual," Esta told her. Whatever her doubts, that was one sentiment she could get behind one hundred percent.

"But crawling isn't enough. We need to be sure that they have no recourse left," Ruth said, glancing at Esta from the side of her eye. "The Society cannot be allowed to keep the necklace. I need a thief."

"Then you're in luck. Because I happen to be a damn good one." She gave a little bow. "But I have one condition. If I help you with this, I want what you took from me. I want my cuff."

Ruth was silent for a long moment. "If I don't agree?"

"I'll take it anyway," she said. "I could take the necklace too, before you even get close to touching it. But I'd prefer to work with you. I hope that the fact that I've stayed this long shows you that I'd rather help you than fight you." As she spoke, she realized that she wasn't sure how much of what she said was a lie—and how much was the truth.

"Fine," Ruth said, her jaw tight. "You help us destroy the Society and get me the necklace and the cuff is yours."

But then what? Would she simply steal the necklace too and leave Ruth and the Antistasi behind, as though she hadn't been part of this at all? Or was there a different way forward, a way where she and Harte didn't have to fight alone? The more Ruth talked and explained the Antistasi's plan, the more Esta wondered.

UNTIL THE END

1904—St. Louis

Harte saw Esta coming toward him too late to avoid her. It had been the better part of a day, and as far as he could tell, the power inside of him had settled itself down to a low rumble of discontent, but he didn't trust it. He'd kept his distance, all while keeping her in sight, because he didn't trust the Antistasi, either.

There was no doubt that Ruth was charismatic. She believed in the righteousness of what she was doing. But in Harte's experience, the line between belief and zealotry was often a fragile one, indistinct and prone to crumble when examined too closely. Her idea to give Sundren magic might have been noble had her victims been given any choice in the matter. But Ruth had forced it upon them, had infected them with a power that they neither wanted nor had any ability to control.

He couldn't quite see how that was much different from what the Sundren did by forcing Mageus to hide their affinities. Both sides were driven by desperation and fear, and they seemed to him two halves of the same coin.

As Esta sat next to him, he made sure to focus on locking down the power and was ready in case it decided to lurch toward the surface. It seemed quiet, but that could be just another of its tricks.

She didn't speak to him at first. Instead, Esta picked up a rock and lobbed it into the murky water beyond. The sun glinted off the surface, illuminating the ripples as they grew. For a second he could almost imagine that they were in another place, another situation. His whole life, he'd wanted only to be free from the city. But now that he was, he'd been so consumed with everything else, he'd barely had time to breathe.

"It's bigger than I imagined it would be," he said softly.

He felt her eyes on him. "The river?"

"All of it." He turned to her. "I knew it would be big, but I didn't realize."

She worried her lip with her teeth as she let out a tired breath. "I know what you mean. Bigger and . . . *different* than I thought." She paused, letting their mutual appreciation for the place they'd found themselves in stretch between them. "I'm sorry about flattening you," she told him. "I was just desperate to find the—"

"It's fine," he said, meaning it.

Esta gave him a small nod and turned to look back at the river.

"Ruth asked for our help," she said, finally breaking the heavy silence between them. "She wants to destroy the Society, and to do that, she needs to make sure they don't have the necklace."

Her voice was so hopeful, so determined, but something about it made the power inside of him feel like it was starting to wake again.

"We're not here to destroy the Society, Esta," he told her, his voice coming out more clipped than he'd intended because his attention was focused on Seshat, in case the demon decided to make another play for Esta. "We're here to get the necklace and get out, remember? The rest of this isn't our fight."

"Why isn't it?" she pressed. "We can do something here to *help* people."

"Or we could just make everything worse," he told her. At her agitation, the power seemed to pulse with excitement, swelling and growing. "Look what happened after Ruth attacked that meeting. Look at the people we rescued from the hospital."

"She gave them their power back," Esta said, remembering what Ruth had told her. "She *helped* them."

"She *attacked* them. *Look* at them," he said, turning her back to face the group of ragged-looking victims from the Antistasi's attack. Half were still dressed only in what they'd worn in the hospital. "Really look at them. Do any of those people look happy right now?"

She shrugged away from him. "They will be. Aren't you?"

He laughed. "Happy?" Shaking his head, he tried to figure out how to make her understand. His affinity had driven his father away and destroyed his mother. It gave him power over people, true, but it had also kept him apart. He was always wary, always afraid of getting too close or letting anyone know too much about him. "Nothing about my affinity has made me happy, Esta."

She frowned at him. "That can't be true."

"Let's just go," he said. "*Please.* We still have Julien. He can help us figure out where the necklace is, and then we can get it and get out of this town. We don't need the Antistasi or their grand schemes."

Esta gestured to her arm. "Ruth still has Ishtar's Key, remember? We can't leave without it."

He ran his hands through his hair, trying to keep his frustration in check, so that he could keep the demon inside of him locked away. "She doesn't exactly have a safe nearby, does she? We're in the middle of nowhere. How hard could it be to steal it from her and go? We don't need the rest of this. We don't need to attack the Society—"

"You would just walk away?" Her expression was unreadable, and when she spoke again, her voice came out as barely a whisper. "Even though they burned the brewery?" She met his eyes. "They could have killed *children*, Harte. The Guard knew there were children inside, and they didn't care. They wanted them to die. Because they're Mageus. Because one less Mageus is fine with the Society and the Guard, no matter how old or young."

He couldn't argue with anything she'd said. The fire was nothing short of evil, but the Society was no different from the Order. Now that he was outside the confines of the Brink, it was clearer than ever how pointless it was to think that they would ever defeat them. Crush one roach or one hundred, and there were still a thousand more you never saw, ready to swarm as soon as the lights went out.

Sure, they could help the Antistasi, and then what? The risks were too great, and the good that they might do? He wasn't sure if it was enough to make up for the damage they could cause in the process. "We can't," Harte said finally.

Esta's expression hardened. "It's too late to back out now."

He glanced at her. "What do you mean?"

She met his gaze and lifted her chin, stubborn as she ever was. "I already volunteered our connection with Julien."

Harte's stomach twisted. "You didn't . . ." They'd done enough to his old friend, mixing him up in this mess to start with.

"You already told Ruth we had a way into the Society," she pointed out.

"I didn't give her Julien."

"I know, but . . ." She let out a sigh, and when she glanced over at him, he could see the regret in her expression, but it wasn't as bright as the hope. "He *could* get us in, Harte."

"And then what?" He felt his temper spiking and the power growing alongside it. "We leave, and Julien has a target on his back. I can't do that to him."

"We won't be doing anything to him. Once the Antistasi release the serum, everything will be different. Think about it, Harte. The ball will be filled with dignitaries—representatives from all the Occult Brotherhoods. Anyone with any power at all will be there," she explained. "After the Antistasi set off the serum, the people who make the laws won't be interested in prosecuting magic if they have it them-selves. And this year, the ball has a very special guest—one that Ruth is specifically interested in. . . ."

"They're going to attack the president," he realized, his stomach twisting.

"That's the plan."

"It's a terrible plan, Esta. Can't you see that?"

The spark of defiance was back in her expression. "It might just work, Harte. People love Roosevelt. Someday they're going to carve his face into a mountain."

A mountain? He blinked. "How is that even—" He was getting sidetracked.

But Esta was determined. "No one is going to turn on Roosevelt, even if his affinity is awoken. He could be the solution—"

She'd lost her mind. She was so blinded by the fantasy that she was forgetting the possible cost. "No, Esta. We *cannot* let this happen."

"Why not?" she asked. "It's what Dolph would have wanted. For us to keep fighting. For us to try to actually change things."

"You don't know what Dolph wanted," Harte exclaimed. "*I* don't know what he wanted. No one did. He played everything too close to the vest. Look what he did to Leena."

She was shaking her head. "Maybe I don't know what all of his plans were, but I owe it to him to try to finish what he started."

"You're not Dolph, Esta."

"I know that," she snapped. But she was trembling with emotion.

"And you don't owe him anything," he said, more gently. "You can choose your own path, a different path."

"You just want me to run."

"I want us to *survive*," he corrected. "I want you to be able to look at yourself in the mirror and not loathe the reflection staring back," he told her. "Did you ever stop to think that maybe there was a reason your mother hid you from Dolph? I *knew* your mother. Leena wasn't okay with some of the things Dolph did. She wouldn't have hidden you from him otherwise. She must have wanted something more for you than the endless fighting and violence and death that he would have insisted you be part of."

"He wanted to change things—"

"Dolph might have been my friend once, but he wasn't the saint you're making him out to be. He hurt Leena because it was what he thought was best for her. For magic. For *everyone*. After he took her power, she never completely forgave him. How is what the Antistasi are doing any different?"

She was looking at him with an expression he'd never seen on her before, an expression that worried him, because he didn't know what it meant.

"We have a long road ahead of us," he said, more gently now. "Or have you forgotten what we're supposed to be doing? Nibsy is still out there somewhere, waiting."

"I *know*," she told him, pulling back the sleeve of her shirt.

"What is that?" On her arm were a series of scars that looked like letters. But she pulled away before he could make them out.

"I didn't have it before. We're changing things, and I'm well aware that Nibsy's still out there, waiting. But he's waiting for *me*, Harte."

He hated the sound of pain and worry in her voice, but it wasn't a good enough reason to do the Antistasi's bidding. "We need to get out of this town alive. If we do that, we can go back and fix things. We can make it so none of this—the Act, the Antistasi, none of it—ever happened. We can save people *that* way."

"And what if we can't?" she asked, her voice dark. "What if I *can't* get us back to 1902? What if I can't make any of this right?"

"You will—"

"You don't know that," she snapped. "And neither do I. I need to do this. In case . . ." But she didn't finish.

He started to reach for her. "Esta—"

"No, Harte," she said, standing and taking a step back from him. "I won't force you to help me, but I won't let you stop me either. You're either with me, or I do this alone."

He let out a tired breath. "You know I'm with you," he said.

His words seemed to relax something in her. She gave him a small smile and a satisfied nod before she went off to tell Ruth the news. He watched her as she left, her straight back and her arms swinging as she walked. Strong. Confident. So completely herself. "Until the end," he murmured, but he wasn't sure who he was speaking to as the wind carried away his words.

TABLEAUX VIVANTS

1902—New York

As the carriage rattled onward, Jack crunched two more cubes of morphine between his molars to deaden the pain throbbing in his head and to clear his mind. With the drug coursing through him, he felt like he could breathe again, and as the world came into sharper focus, he took the Book from the inside of his jacket. He used those final few minutes before he arrived at the Morgan mansion to pore over its pages—especially the notations that were in his hand, despite his having no memory of making them. He'd stopped worrying about that particular issue, though, and had decided to take it as a sign that the Book had chosen to reveal itself to him. A sign that he was not only worthy, but *destined*.

That knowledge had buoyed his confidence and made him *that* much surer of his path. He wasn't meant to be meek and obedient. With some help from the Book, he'd managed to take control of planning the Order's little gala so that he could direct the drama of the evening. But with the event only days away, Jack still had one aggravation that he hadn't quite managed to deal with, and her name was Evelyn DeMure.

He knew that the ring the actress wore was something more than it appeared. With the smooth perfection of the stone and the sizzle of power that he swore filled the air when it was near, he would have realized as much even without the details that the Book had revealed to him. The Inner Circle had always kept the contents of the Mysterium a closely guarded secret, known only to the very highest levels of the

Order, but during his nights of study, the Book had handed those secrets over to Jack. So he knew that the ring must be the Delphi's Tear, a stone created by Newton himself. He knew, too, how it had been created—by sacrifice—and what he could do with its power.

That night at the theater, he'd realized what Evelyn was and why she'd been able to defend herself—and the ring—from his advances. But now he had the answer to the problem she posed. The pieces were all coming together, and everything would be revealed at the gala, where Jack would take the ring and deal with Evelyn once and for all.

When the carriage finally stopped at the front door of his uncle's house on Madison Avenue, Jack tucked the Book back into his jacket. There, close to his chest, he could practically feel the power in it, a twin heartbeat pulsing in time with his own. He alighted from the carriage, ignoring the faint throbbing in his head. The morphine had helped with that. So did the knowledge that soon he would have everything he needed—everything he'd ever wanted. He directed the driver to bring in the crate that was strapped to the back of the carriage, a piece Jack had prepared himself for the spectacle of the gala.

He watched as one of his uncle's servants helped the driver carry the crate into the house, and then he followed, feeling more and more sure about what was to come. There was a new maid at the door waiting, a brown-skinned girl who wasn't to Jack's tastes at all. He gave her his coat and hat without a second thought and went to find out how the preparations were going.

In the ballroom, things had progressed nicely from two days before. Curtains of wine-colored velvet cascaded around the large pillars that skirted the room, transforming the open dance floor into four distinct stages, where the tableaux would be displayed.

Tableaux vivants were all the rage in the city. All the most exclusive events seemed to be featuring the often-scintillating displays of art come to life. Even the stuffiest members of society were drawn to the voyeurism of gazing upon their peers in any number of poses reproducing the scenes of classical art. Rumors were already scuttling through the city about which artworks the participants might be creating at the gala. To his aunt's infinite delight, the papers were abuzz about which of the year's debutantes would be involved, and what they might—or might not—be wearing. Reporters at every paper were practically frothing at the mouth for an invite. Just as the Order had hoped.

The Order might have planned the event to consolidate their standing in the city, but Jack would use it to his advantage. He would demonstrate his importance, his *consequence*, once and for all—not only to his family, but to the Order. To the entire city as well.

Evelyn was already there. She was standing on a small stool surrounded by seamstresses who were fitting her in the diaphanous bit of chiffon that she would be wearing in the tableau he had planned for her. She waved at him, and he felt the usual answering burst of lust deep in his gut that he now knew for the feral power that it was. Thanks to a talisman he'd inscribed on his chest that morning, a secret he'd found in the Book, her influence no longer had the effect on him that it had before. At least not from a distance—he still didn't trust her to get close.

He waved back, feigning more interest than he felt as he examined the costume. It was nearly perfect—Evelyn would be portraying the unconscious beauty in Henry Fuseli's enigmatic painting *The Nightmare*. By the end of the gala, Jack had the suspicion that she would find the image she portrayed more than apt.

He turned his attention to the other stages and preparations. He was discussing the best positioning for the Circe tableau with one of the other Order members when he was summoned into his uncle's office.

Jack had only once before visited Morgan's private study, when he'd returned from Greece, weak and broken and an embarrassment to himself and his family. He didn't relish being called back there, but he kept his head high as he entered, remembering that he had the Book and the favor it had conferred upon him.

Morgan's office was an ostentatious place, with burnished wood and vaulted ceilings barreling overhead. It was the sort of place meant for a prince of business, an emperor of commerce, but with the Book's warmth radiating against his chest, Jack barely noticed the grandeur.

Morgan turned when he entered, a look of disgust clear on the old man's face. "How are the preparations?"

"Nearly there," Jack said, confident.

"They should be finished," Morgan told him. "We're only two days away."

He allowed the sneering quality of Morgan's tone to roll off his back. In a matter of days, his uncle would be eating those words and begging Jack to share the knowledge and power he had with the rest of them. And Jack would happily laugh in his face.

He shrugged, hiding his true emotions. "They'll be done in plenty of time."

Morgan's bulbous nose twitched a bit. "They'd better be perfect," he demanded. "Have you seen this?" He thrust a newspaper at Jack.

"Seen what?" Jack asked, trying to discover the source of his uncle's agitation in the equally titillating headlines.

"The one about the fire," Morgan said, leaning over the desk to jab his thick finger at the newsprint. "The damn animals burned one of the stations down on Great Jones Street. That's Charlie Murphy's district—Tammany Hall's territory."

"I don't see how this matters to you—or to me, for that matter," Jack said. Tammany Hall was filled with upstarts, crooked Irish politicians who thought they had a chance at becoming something more than they were destined to be.

"It matters because we have an understanding with Tammany. They've been helping us put pressure on the maggots downtown."

"It's just a fire—"

"It's *not* just a fire," Morgan said, his voice dangerous. "It was intentional arson, and the flames weren't normal flames. For more than an hour, the hoses didn't touch them. The whole thing stank of feral magic."

"So?" Jack asked, not seeing how some decrepit engine company had any impact on him whatsoever. The whole Bowery could burn for all he cared.

"Do you know how bad this makes us look?" Morgan demanded, thumping at his desk. "How *ineffective*?"

Jack wondered how he'd ever been afraid of the old man. With all his bluster, it was clear how weak he was. True power didn't need to rage. It could quietly burn, consuming a place from the inside out.

"It only makes the Order look weak if you and the rest of the Inner Circle fail to answer it," he said. With the morphine in his veins, he was relaxed, his brain clear and sure. "If anything, this only helps our cause. It gives the Order the ammunition it needs to move against the maggots once and for all."

"Maybe, but if Tammany starts making trouble, it could mean problems for the Conclave. They're already starting to make overtures about how powerful they've become in the city," Morgan said. "The other day, Barclay said he heard one of them bragging about how, by the end of the year, the Order would be a nonentity."

"Who cares what one of them said—"

"*I* care," Morgan roared. "The Inner Circle cares. We have three other Brotherhoods coming into the city later this year for the Conclave, and I will not allow the Order to be seen as weak. The Conclave is just the beginning. It will determine who has power in the century to come— and who *doesn't*. It's bad enough that those damn thieves took the artifacts and the Ars Arcana. It's worse that because of *you*, others suspect that we've been weakened. If the Order doesn't claim our spot at the head of the united Brotherhoods now, New York will lose in stature and in *power*. Right now we have the president's ear. If we master the Conclave, we could have the entire country in the palm of our hands."

"I understand," Jack said. Because he *did* understand. He simply didn't have any intention of allowing the old farts that ruled the Inner Circle to be the ones who held that power.

"I doubt you do," Morgan snapped, "but if you screw this up, you will. Some of Tammany's people are coming to this gala, so it's essential that we show them exactly how powerful we are."

"We will," Jack told him, suppressing the amusement that he felt stirring inside of him. At the gala, the entire city would know *exactly* how powerful each of them was, and Jack would be the one on top.

ONCE MORE

1902—New York

With a knife in her hand, Viola could pierce a man's heart from forty paces. Because he wasn't an idiot, Paul didn't often allow her to have knives. Still, as she listened to her brother drone on about her most recent failings, she wondered what damage she would be able to do with the wooden spoon she was currently holding. Certainly, she should be able to do *something* to shut him up.

"I *know*, Paolo," she said, her hands on her hips. "But I don't want to go with John Torrio."

"Why not?" Paul asked, his brows bunching. "You think you're too good for him? Or is there some other reason, some other person I should know about?"

"I don't *like* him, that's why," she said, practically spitting the words.

He lifted his hand to slap her, but she only smiled. "No," he said, gritting his teeth as he lowered his hand. "We can't have you bruised for the gala."

"I still don't see why I should get trussed up for that maiale to drool over. I don't trust him, Paolo, and neither should you. He'll cut you in the back the second he can."

"You think I don't know that?" her brother asked. "Why do you think I want you to go with him?"

"I *know* why you want me to go with him. You don't trust me still."

"I don't trust *anyone*, including Torrio. I need my blade at my side walking into that gala, looking polished and sharp. You'll go with the Fox, and you'll do your duty to me and to the family, or you won't have a place here anymore." His mouth drew up on one side, exposing his crooked eyetooth. "But don't forget, it's not just Tammany's patrols or the boys in the neighborhood you have to watch your back for. I have friends in higher places now too. I'm sure my friend Mr. Grew would like to know where one of the thieves who stole the Order's treasures could be found. I'm sure they'd be even more grateful if I handed her over myself."

She spit on the floor at his feet. "You wouldn't dare," she said. "You'd be dead before you could open your mouth."

"So many threats, sister. And yet here I stand. Still holding your life in my hands." He stalked toward her. "I took you back into the protection of the family because Mamma asked me. Because she doesn't see you for what you are. She never did. You don't think I remember the way she and Papà used to coddle you, leaving me to clean up your messes? All because you were born a monster—a freak. You always thought you were better than the rest of us, as though the rules of this world didn't matter to you. But now you see. Now the rules are *my* rules. The city is *my* city."

She let out a bark of laughter. "Those men *use* you, Paolo. Tammany and the men in the Order both. They don't respect you or your money. It's too new. And it's too dirty for their liking."

His expression was thunderous. "Maybe they *think* they use me, but my money's as good as anyone's, and the country is changing, sister. Soon the age of their purses won't matter as much as what they contain, and I aim to have more."

"Paolo—"

"You go with Torrio, or you don't go at all, capisce?"

Viola clenched her teeth to keep from saying all the things she was feeling. If she didn't need a way into the gala, she would have tried her luck with the spoon. "I understand," she said, turning back to the pot she had been stirring before he'd interrupted her.

"I'll have a dress sent to you. Be ready by six, eh?"

She nodded, not trusting herself to say more, but the minute he was out of the kitchen, she launched the spoon across the room, right at the place where his head had been moments before. She'd do his bidding just one more time and put up with John Torrio's wandering eyes and too-free hands. But only because she needed her brother and his men to get close to the Order. After that, all bets were off.

MAROONED

1902—New York

Logan Sullivan was cold, hungry, and in desperate need of a shower, but at least he was free. In the days since he'd been taken off guard in that woman's apartment, he'd been following her. Rather, he'd been following the stone, and he'd been collecting information.

Now, standing across from the Bella Strega, the witch on the sign stared down at him, as though daring him to run.

Maybe he should. The person Professor Lachlan was in the past wasn't the man Logan had known and come to think of as a mentor—as a father figure of sorts. The kid was barely sixteen and as cagey and dangerous as a feral cat. Going back to him now might be the worst idea he'd ever had.

But what were his other options? He didn't know anyone else in this version of the city, and at least he knew what the boy who called himself James Lorcan would become. If anyone could find Esta and force her to take Logan back to his own time, he would bet money it was the boy who ruled over the Bella Strega saloon.

Besides, now that he knew more about the stone—including where and *when* it would be—Logan had something to barter with. He'd never really paid all that much attention when Professor Lachlan had tried to teach him about the different parts of magic, but Logan hoped that if they could get ahold of that stone, then maybe—just maybe—it would be enough to get him home.

PREPARATIONS

1904—St. Louis

The brush felt cool as Julien dabbed the tip of it against Esta's eyelids, putting the finishing touches on her makeup for the evening. "Just a bit more," he said, his tobacco-laced breath fanning over her face as he dabbed once . . . twice . . . "There. Finished."

She blinked open her eyes and found him looking at her with a satisfied expression. Harte was standing nearby, frowning. "Well?" she asked.

"Perfection," Julien declared, and then he turned to the mirror to do his own makeup.

Esta came up next to him to check her reflection, and her mouth dropped open. Her skin was too pale, and her lips, which were already big enough, looked enormous painted in the orangey-scarlet that Julien had used. He'd lined her eyes with dramatic sweeps of kohl and had painted the lids with turquoise and gold. *Gold.*

"I look like a clown," she told Julien, pushing the long braids of the dark wig she was wearing out of her face.

Actually, she looked like one of the stylized paintings on the Streets of Cairo, but the effect was basically the same. They weren't any more authentic than she was.

Julien glanced at her in the mirror. "That is entirely the point."

"To look like some kind of circus freak?" she asked. Her mouth still felt sticky from the paint as she spoke.

"Don't smear your lips until they're dry," he said, ignoring her outrage as he lined his own with a softer shade of red.

"Why do you get to look like a woman while I have to look like a clown?" she asked. He'd done something to make her features look stronger and more angular than usual, while his own makeup had the opposite effect, transforming the masculine lines of his face into something softly feminine.

He glared at her in the mirror. "Because you *are* a woman. Trust me. No one is going to notice that little fact with your face looking like it is. You look exactly the way you need to look—just like every one of the other men who will be riding on the floats tonight."

She frowned at herself again and then caught Harte's eyes in the mirror. He had an expression on his face that looked like a combination of horror and pain. Which meant that the makeup was every bit as bad as she thought.

He hadn't talked to her since the other day, when they'd argued after the fire, but he was here now. He was going through with things as planned, so she'd won. Somehow, the victory didn't feel as gratifying as she'd thought it would. She'd say it was just nerves, but she made it a practice not to do nerves, especially not before a job as important and as dangerous as this one.

Letting out a frustrated breath, Esta took some more of the cotton batting and shoved it into the overly large corset she was wearing beneath the flowing white dress. It was ridiculous, flattening herself out only to stuff herself back up again just so she could fill out one of Julien's gowns. All because women weren't allowed to actually ride on the parade floats—it was unbecoming or immoral or something. She still didn't understand how a bunch of half-drunk men dressed as women was any better, but at least their hypocritical morality gave her a way into the parade and, even more important, a way to get close to the necklace.

A knock came on the dressing room door. "Your ride is here," Sal called.

"Tell them we'll be there in five," Julien shouted. Then he pulled on his own wig—a black bob that made him look like Cleopatra—and turned to Esta and Harte. "Well," he said. "This is it." He looked nervous. Too nervous.

"Relax, Jules," Harte said, patting him on the arm. "This is no different from any other show. It's all a bit of flash and sparkle, and then it'll be over."

"That's what I'm afraid of," Julien muttered.

He hadn't been happy to see them when they'd gone to him to tell him that they needed his help again. If they hadn't been in a crowded restaurant, Esta thought Julien probably would have laid Harte flat out just to get away. But in the end they'd explained their dilemma the best they could—without telling him anything about the Antistasi. If things went to plan, he'd never have to know—and he wouldn't be in any more danger.

"No one is going to pin this on you, Jules. I promise," Harte said, his voice as steady as his expression. "Ready, Slim?"

"You can stop with that name anytime now," Esta said, but the truth was that it helped. The little spark of irritation it inspired grounded her. "See you at the parade." She tried to give him a smile. Instead of replying, he gave her a terse nod, but his eyes were shaded and his expression was unreadable.

It had been a night not much different from this—and not that long ago—when she and Harte had ridden in an awkward silence to Khafre Hall. Then, she'd planned to betray everyone she had come to admire in New York. She'd had no idea that Harte had plans of his own. He'd been distant that night too, but somehow Harte felt farther from her now than he ever had before—even on that night back in New York when he'd believed her to be the worst kind of traitor.

He'd been pulling back for days now, she admitted to herself. Even before their argument, he'd been holding himself back, and any time they touched or she thought he might move toward her, a look came over him as though it was a mistake—all of it, an enormous mistake. But after the argument they'd had on the banks of the river? The tension between them had been worse.

Esta knew what Harte still thought—that the Antistasi were wrong. That this wasn't her fight. That she would come to regret her actions. But she didn't have time for softness or second-guessing, not with so much on the line. Look what had happened by leaving Jack alive. She'd listened to Harte, allowed him to sway her, and the future had changed for the worse. Mageus had suffered for it. *No.* She wouldn't be weak. Not now.

Dammit. She let out an angry breath and steeled herself for what was to come. In a matter of a little more than an hour, they would have the necklace and the world would be a different place. They would *make* it a different place. Or she would die trying.

She gave Harte a sure nod before she followed Julien through the theater and then out to meet the waiting cab. Guardsmen flanked the doors, so she pulled her magic in, clamping down on it as she climbed into the back of the carriage.

But the carriage wasn't empty as she'd expected. The Veiled Prophet was waiting for them, there in the dark velvety interior, and next to him was Jack.

THE DEVIL INSIDE

1904—St. Louis

After Esta and Julien left the dressing room, with the door closed solidly behind them, Harte had to fight to keep himself from following her. She'd looked up at him in the mirror a moment before, her face painted so that even he couldn't recognize her, and he'd seen more than Esta—he'd seen the woman in his visions, the one with eyes that turned black as night and who screamed and screamed and—

It was a coincidence. Except he didn't believe in coincidences.

He scrubbed his hand over his face and then, with a violence that even he didn't expect, he kicked over the chair next to the dressing table before he swept the rows of makeup and paint to the floor. Porcelain pots shattered and the colors from the different powders splattered in a haphazard mess.

He should have stopped her. He should have tried harder to talk her out of this mess of a plan. She'd been taken in by Ruth and the Antistasi, romanced by their fantasy of a world remade, but Harte didn't have the same stars in his eyes. He couldn't see a world remade and free, not when the voice inside of him promised nothing but destruction and death.

Magic was nothing more than a trap. A *trick*.

Or maybe he should have let her go, as he did. Maybe he *had* to. Who was he to judge Ruth and her Antistasi? Especially not with the power inside Harte trying to make him doubt himself until he was so tied up with fear and indecision that it could break through the final defenses he'd managed to keep up.

Breathing heavily, he stared at himself in the mirror—the dark circles under his eyes, the two days' growth of beard shadowing his jaw. If he looked close enough, he thought he could see the creature inside of him peering out from the depths of his own eyes.

Even now, his fingertips digging into the dressing table, Harte felt like he might fly away if he didn't hold tightly enough. Every day that passed was a day Seshat grew stronger. Every day he had a harder time completely pushing down the voice that was rumbling and gathering its power. She was clearer now—anger and sadness and destruction and chaos was her song, and Esta was the melody she sang to.

She would rip apart the world.

No. He wouldn't let that happen. Harte would do whatever he needed to in order to keep the Book from getting Esta—from *using her.* His visions, whatever they were, would not be his future.

Taking another deep breath, he pried his hands from the tabletop and stepped back. He closed his eyes and breathed deeply, using every last bit of himself to control the power inside of him. Then he moved the panel from the wall long enough to go through it and made his way out the back of the building.

North was waiting for him at the end of the alley in one of the brewery's wagons, which had been painted over to obscure the name. Ever since the fire, things had been easier between Harte and the cowboy, but North's only salutation was a tip of his hat as Harte climbed up onto the driver's bench.

"Your costume's there," North said, pointing toward the burlap sack on the floor.

As they drove, Harte pulled out a cape out and a matching mask. It was a grotesque-looking thing made of papier-mâché, with a snakelike face and straw to cover his hair.

When Harte was done dressing, North handed him a small flannel bag. He looked inside and found the necklace. If he hadn't known it was a fake, he never would have been able to tell. Ruth's people were good—damned good. The metal shone like the platinum of the real Djinni's Star, and the stone in the center of the collar had nearly the same otherworldly depth as the original. "It's perfect."

"Of course it is," North said. "Now, remember, when you switch it with the real necklace, fastening it will prime the activator. When they take it off, that should trigger the mechanism within it. This Julien fellow'll have maybe ten minutes before the acid burns through and the serum vaporizes."

"That shouldn't be a problem." Once Harte switched it off Julien on the float, the next person to touch it would be the Veiled Prophet himself, when he transferred the necklace to the girl who would wear it at the actual ball. According to the plan, that should happen just before the Veiled Prophet escorted the unlucky debutante and presented her to the rest of the attendees of the gala. Julien wasn't invited into that, so he'd be safe. "Everyone should be well on their way back to the meeting place when that happens. You have the bracelet Ruth took?"

"Maggie has it," North told him. "She'll give it to you at the Water Tower once it's all done."

"And then we'll be out of your hair for good."

North pulled the wagon to the side of the street and jumped down from the driver's perch to hitch the horses to a post as Harte opened the back. Inside, more than a dozen Antistasi were waiting solemnly, each dressed in the same costume Harte himself was wearing.

They filed out in silence, one by one, until they were all gathered around North.

"You'll need to make sure you get the right float," North instructed, going over the plan one more time. Distraction was what they needed. Distraction and confusion so that Harte could slip up onto the float and make the switch.

"The Prophet will be near the end of the parade," Harte told them, information Julien had been able to gather. "That's where we need to cause the most fuss."

"We'll do just fine at causing a fuss," one of the snake-people said, and the rest tittered in agreement.

"Remember," North told them, cutting into their laughter, "when the lights go out, you all need to scatter. Ditch the costumes wherever you can, and then get yourself back to camp. Don't go off together, either. Split up. If you get caught, do whatever you have to, but don't betray the rest of us. We'll get you out as soon as we can."

There was a murmuring of assent through the group as Harte pulled on his own mask, leaving it propped up on the top of his head.

"Good luck," North said, reaching out his hand.

Harte accepted the handshake. For a moment he considered pushing his affinity into North, just to be sure that Ruth hadn't made any other plans, but he couldn't afford North suspecting anything just yet. If they wanted to get both the necklace and Esta's cuff away from a pack of other Mageus, they needed the element of surprise.

They studied each other for a second or two, neither one of them willing to be the first to surrender, until Harte decided to let North win.

He released the cowboy's hand and gave him a silent salute as he pulled his mask down over his face. Then he joined the crowd of serpents and went to find the Veiled Prophet, the necklace, and the girl he would never deserve.

THE GALA

1902—New York

Jack Grew stood in the corner of his uncle's ballroom and surveyed all that he had created. Around him, candles glowed and crystal clinked. The low murmur of anticipation wrapped around him like a mantle, fortifying him for what was to come. Everyone who was anyone in New York society was there, including all the members of the Order and a handpicked selection of the press who were most likely to cover the event in the best possible light. In one corner, Sam Watson was chatting with the younger Vanderbilt. Across the room, his aunt was preening over the state of the ballroom. Everyone was happy, content. Including Jack.

He was close. So very, very close.

Watson had noticed him and was approaching from across the room, but Jack pretended not to see. Instead, he ducked behind the nearest curtain that separated the guests from the area behind the temporary stages that circled one side of the ballroom. The mood there wasn't the relaxed, champagne-tinged atmosphere of the crowd. Backstage, the nervous energy of the performers made the air feel almost electric. Anticipation flooding through him, Jack took the vial from his jacket and crunched two more of the morphine cubes. Then he slipped the vial back into his vest, next to the warmth of the Book, and made his way through the preoccupied performers to find Evelyn.

By the time he reached her, she was already wearing the gossamer gown that had been commissioned for her tableau. All the tableaux had been selected for specific reasons, but mostly to portray the strength of science and alchemy over the dangerous feral magic that had once nearly destroyed civilization. *The Nightmare* was to be the final tableau, the finale of sorts. In the painting, a fair-haired woman lay unconscious, draped over a low couch, with her head and hand hanging toward the floor. The way Fuseli depicted her, the sleeping woman might well be dead except for the faint blush of pink across her lips, and on her chest sat a gargoyle-like figure, a succubus that represented the idea of the nightmare, pressing down upon her, holding her in the deathly sleep.

Evelyn had already powdered herself even paler than usual for the tableau. Her skin was so white it practically glowed and was barely different from the ivory gown she wore. She touched up the pale pink paint on her lips in a small mirror, the gown hiding very little. It might as well have been transparent from the way it clung to her curves, and because it was so close to her powdered skin, at first glance it almost did seem transparent. That was all part of the fun, of course. Tableaux vivants were known for being titillating and risqué and for skirting the very edges of propriety.

But tableaux got away with being so provocative because of their subject matter—classical art. The gown Evelyn wore might have been enough to have her jailed on the streets, but for the tableau it was perfect. When she was reclining on the divan, the gown would look very much like the one in the painting, giving the impression of both a nightgown and a burial shroud, to heighten the similarities between the depths of sleep and death itself.

Of course, if Jack's plans came to fruition, those similarities would be one and the same tonight.

On her finger, the ring glinted in the low light. *Soon,* he promised himself as her eyes found him in the mirror and she turned to greet him. *Very soon.*

"Jack, darling," Evelyn purred. "How do I look?" She twirled, allowing the gown to spin.

By now the warm desire she elicited had become familiar to Jack, and with the ritual he'd performed earlier from the pages of the book, it was little more than an annoyance. But Evelyn wasn't the only actor that night. He put on a good show of softening his gaze and stepping toward her as though he wanted to kiss her, rather than wring her neck.

"Ravishing, as always," he said, counting the seconds until the satisfaction on her face turned to fear. "Did you find the wig I sent over?" Fuseli's sleeper was a pale blonde, and Evelyn's violently red hair would disturb the reality of the scene.

"I did," she told him. "I was just about to put it on." She peeked at him from under her lashes. "I also saw the nightmare. You've outdone yourself, Jack. He's marvelous."

"Isn't he?" Near the platform where Evelyn would eventually prostrate herself stood the misshapen figure that would be perched on her chest.

Evelyn walked over to it and ran her hand seductively over the top of the creature's head. "The expression on his face, it's so vital and *alive*. You can almost imagine him haunting your dreams, can't you?" she asked with a sly, seditious smile he'd come to recognize as her trying to manipulate him.

"I can more than imagine it," he said, examining the creature he'd created with his own hands. It had taken more than a few errors to get it just right, light enough to sit on her chest and with enough heft that it would hold up when the time came.

"The audience will be thrilled," she purred.

"Yes. Yes, they most definitely will be," he told her, biting back his anticipation. "Well, if you'll excuse me, I have to check on some other preparations. It's nearly time to begin."

BEFORE THE STORM

1902—New York

Cela tugged at the starched uniform she was wearing. She hadn't been born to wait on tables or clean up after people who thought they owned the world just because their daddies were rich. But she'd promised Jianyu that she would help him get the ring back. It had been a trying week, though, working as a domestic in the Morgan mansion. Every day she watched the preparations for this gala, she'd come to understand that none of these people needed any more power than they already had. They certainly didn't need some magic ring that could cause things to end badly for more than just people with magic. She believed Jianyu when he said that in the wrong hands, the stone in the ring could bring the entire world to its knees.

Cela wasn't built for kneeling.

She straightened her back and got ready. They had a little while longer to wait. The plan seemed simple enough—wait until Evelyn's scene was revealed, and then Jianyu could slide in and take the ring from her finger. If she tried any of her hocus-pocus, she'd have to use it on the whole place or risk exposing herself in the middle of a room full of men whose goal in life, other than making money, was destroying her kind.

Too bad Cela didn't believe anything could go that simply, no matter what Jianyu thought.

But she wasn't alone. Even if he didn't necessarily agree with her, Abe had decided to help. It might have been just to keep her from getting herself into more trouble than she could handle, but she wasn't going to complain. Across the room, he was carrying a tray of champagne. His eyes met hers and he gave a slight shake of his head. No sign of Evelyn yet.

She nodded to let him know that she was okay, and then she went to pick up some more dirty glasses. It was all about to begin.

AN OLD ENEMY

1904—St. Louis

When Esta saw Jack sitting in the gloom of the waiting carriage, she had to force herself to finish climbing aboard. Julien took the seat next to Jack, so she was forced to sit across from him. She swallowed down her nerves and followed Julien's example, leaning back and letting her legs flop wide beneath her skirts—mimicking the man she was supposed to be—and prayed that between the makeup Julien had painted her with and the dim lighting of the carriage, Jack wouldn't recognize her.

"Ah, Mr. Eltinge, and . . ." Jack's voice was expectant as he glanced sideways in her direction.

"This is Martin," Julien said, as though that explained it all. "Martin Mull."

"We weren't expecting anyone else," the man behind the gauzy lace veil told him.

Esta could feel Jack's interest in her, but she kept her face forward and forced herself to *keep breathing* as she met his gaze unflinchingly.

"Martin often serves as extra security for me," Julien explained easily. "Tonight of all nights, I assumed that extra security would be more than welcome. Especially considering what you're having me wear through the streets of the city."

There was a moment of long, tense silence before the Prophet inclined his head, the veil in front of his face waving with the motion. Esta could practically feel Jack's interest in her fade when the Prophet dismissed her.

Unconcerned, he removed a vial from inside his coat, took a couple of small cubes from it and placed them in his mouth, and then, considering it, he took a couple more before tucking the vial away.

It had been only a few weeks, but for Jack it had been longer, and the years showed on his face. He looked older than he had before, and his skin had a sallow and unhealthy puffiness to it. Maybe it was the effects of drinking, but somehow Esta didn't think so. His fingertips were drumming on his leg, and the nervous energy of their soft rhythm vibrated through the air in the small space.

He had the Book. He might even have it with him. He was sitting there, so close, and if she just risked using her affinity, she might be able to lift it from him.

But if she tried—if she managed to get the Book—Jack would know it was missing. His response to that discovery could throw all of their careful plans into chaos—including the plan to get the necklace. Her mind raced, but Esta couldn't see any way to get both the Book and the necklace. Not without putting everyone and everything else at risk. And not before the carriage rumbled to a stop and the door opened.

Outside, strings of electric bulbs lit a staging area that was swarming with people clad in outlandish costumes. Around one float, a band of people with their bodies painted in garish colors were dressed in feathers and buckskin. They stood talking with others dressed in Confederate gray. Around another float, men dressed like sultans, their faces darkened with paint and long false beards glued to their chins, stood laughing and drinking from a shared flask. On top of a miniature replica of one of the steamboats that crawled down the river, people stood in blackface and top hats, waiting for the parade to start.

Esta hadn't been expecting anything enlightened, but her stomach turned at the display around her. It was like the Klan had decided to throw a costume party, she thought, trying to affect bland indifference. She couldn't afford for anyone to notice her disgust. "They do this every year?" she asked Julien.

He nodded.

"Is it always this . . . ?" She was lost for words.

"It's my first year," he told her, frowning at a trio of men who were making lewd gestures to a fourth, dressed as a woman and laughing his fool head off. "But yes. I suppose it is."

They found the float that they were set to ride on—the Veiled Prophet's own. It was designed to look like a larger version of the boats in the Streets of Cairo. It had been built on the back of a large wagon, its sides painted in the same shimmering gold and bright indigo blue that adorned the attraction at the Exposition. On either side of the float, five men waited, oars in hand, for the parade to start. From the fact that they looked completely sober—unlike most of the revelers—Esta suspected they were the Jefferson Guard, added security for the Prophet and the necklace. In the center of the boat, a small raised dais held two golden thrones topped with an ornate canopy of jeweled silk.

A pair of uniformed Guardsmen approached, one of them carrying a small valise.

"Everything go as planned, Hendricks?" the Prophet asked.

The Guardsman holding the case nodded. "It's ready for you," he told the Prophet, offering the case for inspection.

The Prophet took a key from within his robes and opened the lock to reveal a glint of platinum and turquoise blue within. *The Djinni's Star.*

Esta clenched her hands into fists to keep herself from taking it now. It would be easy. Simple. She could get the Book and the necklace both. All she had to do was pull time still, take the necklace, and go. . . .

And Julien will be left holding the blame. He'd brought her, after all. They'd look to him for answers when she disappeared, and when he didn't have any, Esta doubted that it would matter. He'd be ruined.

He'd be lucky if he was *only* ruined.

Never mind that Ruth's people were waiting, ready to put themselves at risk in front of the entire city, most of whom had turned out to watch the parade. And Ruth still had Ishtar's Key. If Esta did anything to put the

Antistasi at risk, it would make it that much harder to get her cuff back.

There wasn't any good option. She'd have to just carry on as planned, even if all she wanted was to reach for the necklace now.

It was too late, anyway. The Prophet was already fastening it around Julien's neck.

"Now, Mr. Eltinge, just as we discussed," the Prophet said. "If anything happens to this during the parade—"

"No one will get past me, sir," Julien told him, his jaw clenching. He glanced at Esta, who glanced away. For an actor, he was a terrible con.

The Prophet nodded, his veil fluttering like an old woman's lacy curtains. "Then I believe it's time," he said, gesturing to the dais.

Julien climbed up first, unaided, and then the Prophet followed. Esta went after them, taking her spot close to Julien. In the confusion, she lost track of where Jack went, but the Djinni's Star was so, so close. And it was still completely out of her reach.

Little by little, the men who'd been milling around in half-drunk groups began to organize themselves, and the staging area grew less and less crowded as the individual floats departed. Esta could hear the thunder of drums as the bands began to move out and then, after what felt like an eternity, the boat lurched beneath her and they were moving.

The parade route was packed with people, each straining to get a better glimpse of the brightly lit floats that traveled through the city. Above them, each float was attached to the electric trolley car lines, the source of power for the electric bulbs that glowed like small suns, hot and dangerous, around the papier-mâché decorations.

As they rounded the corner of Linden and began the slow, steady progression toward the fairgrounds, Esta felt something sharp strike her cheek. She was rubbing the soreness when she was hit again, this time on the arm. "Ow," she said, rubbing at the newly tender place.

"It's just some of the usual trash," Esta heard the Prophet say. "Ignore it."

But the volley of projectiles assaulting them was only increasing.

Two of the men dressed as Egyptian sentries came to attention, moving to the side of the float, where they searched the crowds on the sidewalk below them. A moment later they were pointing to someone, and Esta saw the police who had been lining the route turn into the crowd to find the culprits.

"See," the Prophet said. "A simple nuisance."

The parade continued, and in the distance, Esta saw the arched entrance to the fair. *Soon,* she thought, keeping her eyes peeled for any other sign of trouble. *Harte will be here soon. And then it will be over.*

Or maybe, it will just be beginning?

They were about a block away from the entrance to the fairgrounds when Esta heard a commotion from the crowd. A wild scream split the air, and suddenly masked men emerged from the faceless spectators. They were dressed in dark cloaks, and their masks were made to look like the faces of snakes.

The Antistasi, Esta thought, her whole body feeling warm and ready at the sight of them. Just as they'd planned, and right on time. The men—and women, Esta knew—used the flash powder that Julien had supplied from the theater to distract and blind the line of police before they sprinted for the Veiled Prophet's float. Esta backed up to Julien, pretending to be the security she was posing as, and watched as more than a dozen of the snake-people climbed aboard.

The air was thick with unnatural magic, hot and icy together, as the Antistasi attacked, pulling the oarsmen from their perches and tossing them aside.

"Protect the queen," the Prophet shouted, and the remaining sentries formed a wall around them as the masked Antistasi attacked.

Esta found herself surrounded by chaos as she pretended to fight off the snake-people. But then one of them was immediately behind her, attacking Julien. *Harte.* She launched into the fray, executing the choreography they'd practiced so that their fighting provided the misdirection Harte needed to slip the necklace from Julien's throat and replace it with the replica. He gave her the signal, meeting her eyes with a look of sheer determination—and something else she couldn't quite read—and she did what they'd practiced, fighting him off Julien and pushing him from the float, where dark-suited policemen waited.

She didn't have time to worry about whether he landed safely. She was being pulled back herself suddenly, and before she understood what was happening, the floor of the dais was dropping down and she found herself trapped with Julien in a small cell. The floor above them closed over the top of the opening, and everything went dark.

COLLATERAL DAMAGE

1904—St. Louis

Harte fought against the hold the two police officers had on his arms, but it wasn't long before he was being shoved inside the back of a long, dark wagon with a handful of the other Antistasi. The door shut behind them, and the carriage rumbled on as Harte checked to make sure that the necklace was still tucked into the secret pocket sewn into his shirt.

During the fight, it had taken nearly all of his strength to keep himself from winning the mock battle he'd staged with Esta. The voice inside of him had rallied, urging him on—to take her down, to take everything she was. But that voice was quiet now.

It was a quiet he didn't quite trust. Maybe the power was pulling away from the stone tucked in his pocket, just as it had pulled away from the Book. But it could just as easily be lying in wait, preparing itself for its next onslaught.

Someone lit a match as Harte was pulling off the mask, and the other people in the back of the carriage all looked at each other for a moment. Then someone laughed. "Damn, that was fun," a man with a missing side tooth said as he wiped sweat from his brows and pulled off the gloves he'd been wearing.

Harte couldn't quite agree, not yet, at least. He'd relax when they were free.

When the carriage stopped, he waited, his skin prickling with awareness, until the door opened to reveal a policeman standing there, his mouth twisted in disgust. "Looks like we got us a bunch of Antistasi snakes." Then his expression broke into amusement, and he stepped back to let them out.

Harte released the breath he'd been holding, and he felt the power shift inside of him. It didn't feel half as weak as he did.

He let the other guys go first. His nerves were still jangling from the adrenaline of what they'd just done, and he wasn't in a hurry to get moving, but once he stepped out, he was relieved to be outside the close, stale air of the carriage and into the warmth of the night. Ruth was standing next to the spot where the carriage had stopped, waiting with some of the other Antistasi.

"You made the switch?" she asked when she saw Harte alight.

Harte nodded. "It's done," he said.

Though he still didn't like it. If they couldn't manage to get back to 1902 and to stop all of this from happening—if they were stuck going forward from here, now—who knew what the repercussions could be of an all-out attack on the president?

He pulled out the necklace to show Ruth. "Now your part of the deal. I'll take Esta's bracelet."

"You'll have to wait," Ruth told him, reaching for the necklace.

He pulled it back. "Like hell—"

"Maggie hasn't arrived yet," Ruth said, cutting him off before he could get too worked up. "She should be here any minute."

"Then we'll talk about you getting the necklace once she arrives with the bracelet," Harte said, tucking the necklace into his jacket. Once Esta arrived, Ruth wouldn't get either of the artifacts.

They waited awhile as other people arrived, each breathing heavily and looking absolutely delighted with what they'd just done. Ten minutes passed and then twenty, and with each additional second, Harte grew more and more impatient. *They should be here by now.*

But before too long, the sounds of wagon wheels and hoofbeats quickly approaching signaled an arrival.

Not Maggie . . . *Esta.*

The power inside Harte lurched at the sight of the smaller carriage pulling up next to the brewery's wagon and swelled with need when Esta clambered out of the back before the wagon was even completely still.

But Esta's face wasn't the picture of satisfaction he'd been expecting. "Do you have it?" she asked. When Harte nodded, her expression didn't ease. "They have Julien," she said grimly.

"What do you mean?" Harte asked, stepping toward her and wanting more than anything to wrap his arms around her and pull her to him. But when the voice inside of him rose at that idea, he stopped short.

The plan had been straightforward. Dangerous, but easy enough once the necklaces were switched. The Prophet would take the decoy necklace from Julien and place it on the neck of the debutante who had been chosen as that year's Queen of Love and Beauty, and then the two of them—Esta *and* Julien—would leave.

"They took the Prophet's float off to the side street as soon as the attack happened. They had us in this small holding cell under the wagon's bed, and when we got to the Festival Hall, they let us out. But they took Julien right off—necklace and all. Jack was there waiting for him," she told Harte.

Harte froze. "*Jack Grew* is here?"

She nodded. "I tried to follow them, but the Guards wouldn't let me. Said it was for the artifact's security or something."

Harte didn't like any of it. There was no reason for Jack to go with Julien, unless Jack somehow knew. "Was Julien okay?"

"I don't think the Guards suspected anything," Esta told him. "They seemed more worried about the necklace than about Julien being any kind of threat. I think as long as he stays calm and keeps with the plan, we can go back and get him after they make the necklace switch."

He didn't like it, but things could have been worse. They could retrieve Julien, and maybe in the process, they could get the Book from Jack as well.

Soon they heard more hoofbeats approaching.

"Maggie has the cuff," Harte murmured to Esta as Maggie came into view. She nodded to him, letting him know she understood.

"Tell me you didn't do it," Maggie said to Ruth even before she slipped down from the horse. Then she ran to her sister and grabbed Ruth by the arms. "Tell me it isn't done. That it didn't work, or—"

"Everything went as planned," Ruth told her, frowning.

But Maggie was shaking her head like she didn't believe it.

"It's fine," Ruth told her, gentling her voice in a way Harte had never heard it. "Everyone's safe, and the necklace was switched. All is well."

"No," Maggie said. "*No.* We have to stop it."

"There's nothing to stop," Ruth told her.

"But the serum—it doesn't work."

Ruth frowned. "Of course it works. We saw with our own eyes—"

"They're *dying*," Maggie said, her voice nearly hysterical. "I thought it was just that Arnie's burns were too much for him this morning, but then this evening it was Greta. She's gone already, and the rest are following, dying by their own magic. There's nothing I could do for them. Even Isobel couldn't do a thing to heal them. It's *killing* them."

Ruth's jaw tightened, and her eyes went hard. "That's unfortunate."

"It's not *unfortunate*. It's a catastrophe. They're all dying, and it's our fault. If that necklace detonates, we'll be responsible for the deaths of everyone at the ball. All those people—"

"So they'll die," Ruth said, pulling away. "How many of ours have they killed with their laws and their Guard and their hate?"

"We can't—*I* can't just let this happen," Maggie said, horrified. "This isn't what I intended. This isn't—"

"There's nothing we can do now," Ruth said. "It's already done."

"We can stop it," Maggie told her. "We can disrupt the ball—we can do something to get them out of the building before it's too late."

"I won't risk any of mine for the Society."

"It's not just the Society in there, Ruth. It's their wives and daughters, too," Maggie persisted, not noticing how close to her Esta had gotten.

"Who live off the benefits of the evil their husbands and fathers commit."

Maggie took an actual step back from Ruth and nearly ran into Esta. From the look of horror on Maggie's face, Harte suspected that she'd never quite seen this side of her older sister before. "Ruth," she pleaded.

They had the necklace, and from the look Esta was giving Harte, he knew she'd just lifted the cuff from Maggie. They could go now, before they got caught up in the fallout that was sure to come.

Except that he couldn't. "We can't leave Julien in there," Harte told Esta. Her horrified expression told him that she agreed.

"We can't leave any of them in there," she said, her voice shaking.

"How do you plan to get into the ball?" Ruth asked. "There will be Jefferson Guards at every entrance. Even if you could get past them, you would have to contend with more inside and the president's security on top of it."

"We'll figure something out," Harte said. But short of charging the doors and hoping for the best, Ruth was right. Trying to save the people in the ball was a suicide mission. With all the dignitaries that were attending, they'd never be able to get past the security, and if they did, they'd never get back out again. It was the whole the reason they'd taken the necklace from the parade.

"I can help with that," North said softly.

"I won't allow it," Ruth said. "It's a fool's errand. And you're not going anywhere until I get that necklace," she told Harte.

"You'll have to take it from me," Harte said.

"North," Ruth commanded. "Take care of this."

"With all due respect, ma'am, I'd rather not." North stepped between them.

"What are you waiting for?" Ruth asked the others.

But the men and women who'd dressed themselves as serpents to disrupt the parade didn't make a move to attack. Most of them studied the ground at their feet, their jaws tense and their shoulders hunched against the weight of what they had just helped to do.

"Then I'm done with the lot of you," Ruth said as she reached for her sister's hand. "Come, Maggie. Let's go before we're seen."

"I'm going with them," Maggie told her. She ignored her sister's protests and stepped forward to slip her hand into North's. The cowboy's eyes shone with satisfaction.

Ruth's face had turned a blotchy red, and her expression was a mixture of anger and shock. "Maggie, you'll come now as you're told." Even Harte could feel Ruth's impatience simmering in the air as thick and real as magic itself.

But Maggie looked over her shoulder at her sister and shook her head. "I haven't been a child for a long time, Ruth. I've caused this, and I'm going to do something to stop it."

NOTHING TO FORGIVE

1902—New York

Ruby took another look at herself in the long, mirrored panel of the ballroom's back wall and frowned.

"You don't have to do this," Theo said, frowning at the outfit she was wearing—or perhaps he was frowning at the lack of it.

He had a point. The peach-colored garment she wore beneath the gown might have covered her from neck to toes, but it left nothing to the imagination. She was portraying Circe, from the John William Waterhouse painting of the witch offering a cup of her potion to Ulysses. Over the nearly nude garment, Ruby's diaphanous gown was the color of the sea on a cloudy day. It hung loose over one shoulder, exposing more of her than she would ever have chosen to reveal on her own.

She glanced over her shoulder. "Of course I have to do this," she told him, steeling herself for what was to come. "Being back here gives me access I wouldn't otherwise have."

"I don't like it," Theo grumbled. "It's one thing to pass information on in the hopes of seeing what gets stirred up, but it's another thing altogether to put yourself in the middle of the very storm you've created."

"How am I supposed to know the truth if I'm not in the middle?" she asked, lifting the front of the gown in a vain attempt to get it to cover more. Frustrated, she gave up and let it fall again.

"Last time you insisted on getting in the middle of things, I distinctly remember being shot," he told her, his tone more dry than truly angry.

Still, Ruby felt guilt flood through her. "I don't think I'll ever be able to forgive myself for that," she told him, her voice barely more than a whisper.

His expression softened. "There's nothing to forgive," he said. "I'm alive and well. I just don't want to see you hurt."

Especially since Viola is no longer in our lives. The words hung unspoken between them.

But she wasn't going to think about Viola, not tonight. She'd wasted too much time not writing and not reporting in the last two weeks, and she was practically desperate to get a story that would make her editor look twice at her again.

She'd been rash, maybe, in passing along to Jack the information Viola had given her about Paul Kelly, even if she had sent it to him anonymously. She had thought to stir up the hornet's nest that was the Order to see what happened, but in truth, she'd been acting out of hurt and anger and spite. And maybe she had been impetuous to have Theo talk Jack into allowing her to be part of the tableaux. At the time, though, the Order's gala had seemed like a lifeline, a way back to the person she'd been before she let a pair of violet eyes sway her. But now, it felt like everything she'd once thought she had under control was slipping from her grasp.

She shook off that thought. It was nothing but nerves. Maybe she hadn't completely thought everything through, but at least she was there, as close as anyone could possibly get to the Order's biggest event since Khafre Hall had burned. Tonight, R. A. Reynolds would get a story like no one else's.

Still, the dress was ridiculous. She had never shied away from a little bit of scandal, but now she worried what her wearing it—and wearing it in front of anyone who mattered in her mother's circle—would do to Theo's reputation.

"If you don't want me to—"

Before she could finish, Jack Grew had come around the curtain. He eyed her for a second, looking far too pleased with himself, before he turned to Theo. "Barclay, you're going to have to go. We're about to begin."

Theo gave her a long, unreadable look, and in that instant she thought about changing out of the gown and going with him. But before she could, he was gone.

"You look like perfection, Miss . . ." He frowned. "I'm sorry. I know Theo has introduced us before, but your name seems to have slipped away from me." He gave her a smile that would have been charming had his eyes not been so calculating. "Product of the accident, I suppose—head injuries will wreak havoc, won't they?"

"Reynolds," she told him, wanting more than anything to get away from him and his leering. "Ruby Reynolds."

"Reynolds?" he asked, his expression darkening.

It was the same thing that had happened a thousand times before. If someone didn't already know whose daughter she was, their face would transform itself once they found out. But this was different. Jack's expression was more one of fury than pity, and Ruby realized her misstep.

It had been an Order member who'd ordered her death. *It could have been Jack.*

"Well, then," he said, his face still carefully blank. "You have everything you need?"

She nodded, trying to hide her fear with the brilliant smile she'd learned for her debut. "Yes, thank you."

"Excellent. It should be *quite* the show." He gave her an appraising look, and then he was gone, off to the next set of performers.

Ruby prided herself on being an intelligent woman, one whose intuition had gotten her out of countless scrapes over the years, so she knew she'd made a mistake. She needed to find Theo and get out of Morgan's mansion before anything else could go wrong. She put down the cup and the wand she'd been preparing to carry and started to pull her cloak over the scrap of fabric she was wearing.

"What are you doing, miss?" The costumer was there with a look of horror on her face. "You don't have time for that." The woman was already taking off the cloak and tucking it over her arm before Ruby could argue. "Up you go," she said, leading Ruby to the thronelike seat and handing her the cup and the wand she'd just discarded.

"I need to go," Ruby tried to tell her, but the woman just gave her an impatient *tut-tut*.

"Everybody has nerves. It'll be just fine. You'll see."

The music was already starting on the other side of the curtains, a trilling run of a harp and the soft sounds of a violin, and the woman was leaving with her cloak. And it was too late for Ruby to do anything more than carry on and hope that she was wrong about how badly things were about to go.

BASTA

I t was only the weight of Libitina that kept Viola anchored as she took one step and then another into J. P. Morgan's ballroom. She was on the arm of John Torrio and surrounded by people who hated her, people who would just as soon see her dead or deported as anything else, and it took every bit of her determination to keep the hate from her eyes as she followed Paul through the crowd, nodding and introducing himself to people as they went.

They'd trussed her up again in a corset and a gown covered in silken flounces. A ridiculous thing that did nothing to disguise what she was. Worse, it seemed only to encourage the Fox, who kept sliding glances at the slope of her cleavage above the neckline of her dress. His arm would occasionally rub against the side of her tette, and she knew from the leering look in his eyes that the small brushes were no accident. Had she not needed him—and needed to keep attention *away* from herself—she would have gladly introduced him to her most deadly accessory, the blade strapped to the side of her thigh.

Paul and Torrio made their way through the room, dragging Viola along with them, and as they went, the glittering jewels and perfectly tailored silks of the women all around her only served to remind her of who she was—and who she *wasn't*. She'd never be one of these perfectly coiffed debutantes, so demure that they seemed able to blush on command. She didn't want to be one of them. Even if one of them had a sharp tongue and a nose that crinkled when she smiled.

Basta. She tried to take a breath, but the boning of the corset reminded her that in this world, women were not even supposed to breathe. *Focus.* She needed to figure out which of these preening pigeons had the ring.

The quartet of musicians in the corner were starting to warm up and the other attendees were beginning to find their seats when Viola noticed a familiar silhouette that had her nearly stumbling. Theo was there, talking to an older man who had his eyes. If Theo was there, and Torrio noticed . . .

He wouldn't do anything, she tried to tell herself. Not here, not in the midst of all the men they were trying to impress.

But if Theo was there, Ruby might be as well.

So what? She was done with them, finished. Wasn't she?

She was about to turn away, to settle herself between Paul and Torrio, when she saw Theo give the older man that sad, lopsided grin he'd given at the park. He'd warned her then that it wouldn't turn out well, and she hadn't listened.

None of this was his fault. Ruby had dragged him into this mess and had nearly gotten him killed. But Viola had risked everything to save him once. To simply hand him over to Paul and Torrio now? It would mean that all the hurt and the anger Viola had lived with since Ruby had looked at her with hate in her blue eyes had been for nothing.

Besides, Ruby loved him.

Viola would save Theo for that reason alone. If it was her lot in life to always want and never have, so be it. She was strong and smart and could make her own way. And there were worse things than loneliness. There were the long hours in the dead of night when you had to live with the choices you made.

She excused herself to follow Theo as he headed toward the back of the ballroom. Paul gave her a curious look, but the musicians were starting in earnest now, and he couldn't do much without creating a scene.

It wasn't that difficult to get ahead of Theo before he started back

toward a side hall. When he rounded the corner, she pulled him into an unseen alcove.

He startled, but almost seemed unsurprised to see her. "Viola?"

"Shhh—" She pulled him farther into the alcove, away from prying eyes.

"I didn't really think I was your type," he said, giving her that lopsided smile again.

She opened her mouth to refute his words, her instinct after a lifetime of hiding and denying and refusing. But he wasn't looking at her with the same disgust that Paul or her mother had when they noticed how captivated she'd been with her English teacher years ago. "You're not," she told him, which was as close to an acknowledgment as she'd ever given anyone except Esta.

"Where's Ruby?" she asked, brushing past the moment because dwelling in it was far too dangerous. "Tell me she's not here."

"Of course she's here," he said. "Can you really imagine her missing something like this?"

No. "She has to go. Now."

He looked suddenly confused. "That's not possible. She's playing Circe tonight, and everything is about to—"

The music suddenly went silent, and a man's voice boomed over the crowd to welcome the attendees.

It's too late.

A REUNION OF SORTS

1902—New York

From his place concealed in the corner of the ballroom, Jianyu watched Viola follow the light-haired boy into a side hallway. It had been nearly two weeks since that day on the bridge when he'd last seen her. But in everything that happened, she'd disappeared, and he'd been unable to search. Now he wasn't sure what to make of the fact that she'd arrived with Paul Kelly.

Torn, he considered his options. He didn't know when he'd get another opportunity to speak with her—to explain all that she did not yet know—but he would have only one chance to get to Evelyn while she was at the center of attention and less able to retaliate. On the far side of the room, positioned close to an exit, Cela and her brother were watching the High Princept of the Order introduce the evening's honoree.

Jack Grew.

Jack stepped onto the stage and shook the High Princept's hand, and then he took command of the stage. Harte Darrigan had told Jianyu all about the upstart nephew of J. P. Morgan. He was reckless and dangerous. And he could not be allowed to get the stone.

But even knowing what he knew about Jack Grew, even with the mission before him, Jianyu could think of only one essential thing: *Viola is here.*

THE RIGHT TIME

1904—St. Louis

While North drove them toward the fairgrounds, Esta finished stripping off the Egyptian gown to the men's pants and shirt she was wearing beneath it. She was grateful that she hadn't given in to Julien's pleas for her to leave off the clothing beneath the costume. Using the strips of white linen she tore from the gown, she scrubbed as much of the makeup as she could from her face as the carriage rattled on.

North parked one street over from the fair's entrance and tied up the horses as Esta and Harte climbed out the back.

Maggie, who had ridden up front with North, was frowning, her eyes worried.

"Are you okay?" North asked, looking like he wanted to reach for her.

"Just thinking about Ruth—about how she looked when I walked away."

North's expression softened. "You did the right thing, Mags."

"She's my *sister*, Jericho," Maggie said, her tone dull and hollow. "She's my family, my flesh and blood, and what's more, she raised me like her own daughter."

"She's *used* you," North said, lowering his voice as he took Maggie's chin gently in his hand.

Harte glanced at Esta, his expression impatient as the two talked, but Esta could only shrug. If Maggie didn't make up her mind now, she'd be a liability inside.

"I know," Maggie was saying to North. "I know all that, but it doesn't change what we are to each other."

North took Maggie into his arms for a moment. "Sometimes blood's not enough, Mags."

Maggie's face crumpled. "I know."

Esta understood the emotion in Maggie's voice—the hurt that simmered below the confidence in the words. A betrayal like Maggie's sister's was one that would haunt her, just as Professor Lachlan's betrayal haunted Esta, following her with dogged footsteps. But it had also urged her on—to be better, smarter . . . *stronger*.

"Let's go," Harte told them, apparently done with waiting. "We need to get in there. We don't know how much time we have left. There's no telling when the Prophet is going to switch the necklaces."

But in the distance, the wailing of a siren erupted. The night was suddenly alive with sounds as bells clanged and more sirens droned.

"We're too late," Esta said, as the four of them paused to listen.

"The Festival Hall is on the other side of the fair," North told them. "Even without the crowds, it's nearly a mile from here. But maybe, if we hurry, we can still get some people out—"

"Once the acid hits the serum and the vapor forms, there will be no way in," Maggie said, her voice a strangled whisper.

Esta thought about her cuff and how useless it was in that moment. She couldn't risk using it now, because going back to stop everything meant crossing Ishtar's Key with itself. If it were only her life in the balance, she could have done it to make up for her part in all of this, but it *wasn't* only her life. She'd been so blinded by her own anger, so determined to be strong that she hadn't realized how far she'd veered from what they were supposed to be doing.

Harte had been right—about Ruth and about the Antistasi. They should have stuck with their own plan. They should have grabbed the cuff from Ruth and found the necklace on their own instead of getting tied up into the Antistasi's plot for vengeance. Maybe if she hadn't been so set on being strong—on being *ruthless*—the Antistasi would have had more trouble with their attack. Maybe the innocent people in the ball wouldn't be suffering right now.

She would carry the guilt of her part in the attack with her always, but she would not risk her cuff to change it. Not now. She *couldn't*—Nibsy was still out there, and if they didn't collect the stones, he would. She needed Ishtar's Key, not just for herself, but to stop him from controlling the Book's power.

But North was already taking out his pocket watch. "It's not too late yet," he told them, opening the cover and adjusting it. "They'll have guards all over the place during the ball, but before it starts, we might have better luck. I don't like to go back, myself. Nothing good usually comes from trying to fix what already happened. But I think this warrants it."

"Go back?" Harte asked.

"In time. My mama always used to say I had a knack for being in the right place at the right time," North told him. "I could be out in the streets running wild with the other kids and somehow know that dinner was on. In a blink, I'd be there at the table, right where I was supposed to be, before she'd even called me. If trouble was coming, I'd be out of the way before it ever arrived. Of course, I learned later on that it wasn't just a knack. It was a touch of magic. But I never could control it until I got this." North showed the two of them the watch.

It looked like any pocket watch: brass casing with a scratched crystal cover over the face. The minute and hour hands might once have been painted black, but the paint had rubbed away where North had touched them to change the time. The second hand stood still, and the watch itself didn't make so much as a tick, but Esta could feel the pull of it—the tug in the energy around her that marked it as having an unseen power.

Harte frowned at the watch. "Ritual magic?"

"I don't know about any ritual, but magic it's got," North told him. "I'll just adjust this back a bit. An hour maybe?"

"They might already have the Guard in place by then," Maggie said, worrying her lip.

"Right. Let's go back a few then. Once we're in, I can set us to the time we need," he told her. "If we can get into the building while it's still daylight, we can go forward again, until just before the Prophet arrives. That way, we can be ready for them."

Esta caught Harte's eye. "It will be fine," she said, understanding his reluctance.

But his jaw was tense and his eyes wary. "What about the stones we have?" he asked in a low voice so the others couldn't hear.

"I'll have to leave them here. In the wagon?" she asked.

"You really think that's wise?"

She didn't. It felt like abandoning part of herself to think about leaving the stones behind. But if North could take them back without her risking the cuff..."I don't see that we have any choice if we want to save Julien. We have to try to stop this if we can."

"What about in the wall?" he asked. "They'll be less likely to be found if Ruth comes for the wagon."

He was right. While Maggie was gathering her supplies from the back of the wagon, Harte and Esta found a place close to the wall of the fairgrounds to hide the stones. They buried them, and then Harte used one of Maggie's devices to set a trap. Anyone who might disturb it would get an unpleasant surprise.

"Come on over here." North motioned them around the corner from the gates. "Now hold on." Maggie reached out to take his arm first, and then Esta did the same. Harte hesitated, clearly dreading the thought of traveling through time again.

"If you're afraid ...," North teased.

Harte took hold of North, who only smirked as he clicked the watch shut.

THE ALCHEMIST

1902—New York

Jack took a minute to accept the applause as his due. It rolled over him, a benediction for all he'd suffered and all the plans he'd worked so diligently to put in place. The lights of the ballroom twinkled and shone, winking at him as the morphine coursed through his veins, clearing his mind. Opening him to the possibilities this moment held.

He lifted his hands, gratified to see the crowd follow his directive as he took control of the room and began the evening's festivities.

"Ladies and gentlemen, I cannot tell you what it means to me to be here tonight, honoring the Order's essential work and marking our commitment to the city we love so dearly. I know that for some of us, the past weeks have been a trial. Our newspapers have not always been kind to our esteemed organization or the work that we do to keep our city safe. But tonight we prove the naysayers wrong. *Tonight* we show that the power of logic and science, the enlightened study of hermetic arts, will always be far superior to the craven wildness of the old magic, which once threatened the very essence of civilization.

"Tonight, on behalf of the Order and their Inner Circle, I am honored to present our tableaux vivants."

The orchestra started into their first series of chords, a minor-key piece that sounded as dangerous as Jack himself felt, and the attention of the audience only bolstered him more.

"Without further ado, our first tableau, a painting by the esteemed Joseph Wright, *The Alchemist Discovering Phosphorous.*"

With a flourish of his arms, the curtains on the first of the stages pulled back, revealing the dimly lit scene. Two men sat in the background, leaning over a desk as though doing calculations. In the foreground, J. P. Morgan himself played Wright's alchemist. His uncle was wearing a false beard and his expression was enraptured over the enormous glass flask held on an iron pedestal. Genuflecting before the altar of science, Morgan was dressed in an ancient-looking robe, tied with a sash.

The audience applauded politely, murmuring with amusement to see who was in the first tableau.

"A charming scene, to be sure," Jack told them, anticipation racing alongside the morphine in his blood. "But we can do better, don't you think?"

The crowd murmured and rustled, but he ignored them as he walked over to the tableau. His uncle and the other actors kept their positions, frozen as though they were living, breathing statues. He hadn't warned them, hadn't told them what he would do, because he wanted their shock as well.

"Those who live in the shadows of our city, like rats infesting the very structure of the society we have built here, depend upon feral magic. Weak, unruly power. But see what an enlightened study of the occult arts can accomplish." He lifted his hands and sank into the looseness of the morphine in his veins, and the words he'd practiced in the privacy of his room came from his lips as though he had been born to say them.

The orchestra went silent and the crowd tittered, but Jack barely heard them. He was calling to something bigger, something deeper. Against his chest, the Book felt positively hot.

Suddenly, the chandeliers flickered and the lights wavered. Then, as though they were some sort of fairy creatures, the light from the chandeliers flew toward the dark liquid in the flask his uncle knelt before and set it aglow.

The audience went completely silent as the room went dark except for the glowing flask in the tableau, and then, all at once, they burst into thunderous applause. His blood thrummed, hot and sure. And he had only just begun.

A BRUSH OF MAGIC

1902—New York

The lights flickered back on, and Viola felt the chill of the unnatural magic seep out of the air. She shuddered slightly. "We need to get her now," she repeated to Theo.

He didn't need to tell her that it was impossible. She could see for herself that there was no way to get through the crowd and behind the curtain without everyone seeing her, including Paul and Torrio. When the curtain opened, Ruby would be exposed. Torrio would know the truth of Viola's duplicity, and neither of them would ever be safe again.

Vaguely, she felt the warm brush of magic nearby. At first she dismissed it as more of Jack's tricks, but when it didn't immediately dissipate with the cold power that had flooded the room, she had another thought. Her hand went instinctively to the slit she'd made in her skirts, to take her knife from its sheath and, in a single fluid motion, she held it up to the empty air. "Show yourself."

"Viola?" Theo sounded as though he thought she'd lost her mind, but she ignored him and moved toward the warm energy until it grew denser.

She pressed her knife forward, and in an instant Jianyu was there.

"Viola," he said, his voice every bit as nervous as he should have been.

She didn't lower her blade. Nibsy had indicated that Jianyu could have been one of the traitors, and while she didn't trust the conniving rat, she also didn't trust Dolph's spy, who'd been suspiciously absent for these long weeks. "So you return. Where have you been?"

Jianyu glanced down at the blade at the same time that Theo stepped toward her. But she glared at Theo and then turned her attention back to Jianyu. "You were there on the bridge," she said.

"I was—"

"You weren't any help at all then." She moved the blade closer.

"I was with Darriga—"

The blade went to his throat. "That traitor?"

"He's not the traitor you believe him to be," Jianyu told her.

But she only huffed out a sound of disbelief. She'd been in the Mysterium. She'd been the victim of his treachery. "You expect me to believe that? Where is he now? I'll kill him myself."

Theo made a worried sound, but she ignored him.

"He's with Esta—"

"Esta?" She'd helped the girl escape. Had she been wrong in trusting her, too?

"It is a very long tale, and not one I have time for now," Jianyu said. "One of the artifacts is here."

"I know—the ring. Nibsy told me you would be after it."

Jianyu frowned. "We cannot let him have it."

"I have no intention of letting either of you have it." She lifted Libitina's blade until it was squarely under Jianyu's chin. "Where is it?"

"I know who has it—she is backstage. I was on my way to get it when I saw you and—"

"Backstage?" *Where Ruby is.* "You'll take me." It was not a request.

"As long as you promise that you will listen to reason when this is all through. There is much I need to tell you."

"You'll take me," she repeated. She wouldn't make promises or submit to Jianyu's demands. But she would get the stone, and she would see Ruby safe—whatever it took.

THE VEILED PROPHET'S BALL

1904—St. Louis

Esta's vision went white, but she kept hold of North's arm until she could see again. Her legs felt unsteady beneath her, and her skin was clammy from the magic of the watch.

When the brightness faded, the night had turned to day. In the distance, the sirens had been replaced with the echoes of the Exposition—the hum of the crowd and the far-off melody of a brass band.

Harte let go of North first and shuddered as he stumbled and tried to keep himself upright. "That just feels *wrong.*"

"What does?" North asked, putting the watch back into his pocket.

"You don't feel it?" Harte shivered again. When North shook his head, Harte tried to explain. "Magic usually feels warm, like something you'd want to blanket yourself with. But that? It feels like a shard of ice went straight through me."

"I've never felt anything warm," North said with frown. "And I don't feel any ice either. You, Maggie?"

The girl shook her head.

Esta caught Harte's gaze. North was Mageus—she could feel the warmth of his affinity mingled with the prickling iciness of the watch's magic—but he didn't seem as attuned to his affinity as she and Harte were. Maybe it was because, without the watch, his affinity wasn't all that strong. Or maybe there *was* something to the stories of the Brink—the stories of how it worked to keep magic whole. If she really thought about it, all the power she'd felt on this side of the Brink had been off, mixed with that strange, cold warning that spoke of ritual and decay.

Done with the conversation, North gave a nod, and they were moving. The four of them entered the fair without any problem and then made their way back toward the lagoon. It was still midafternoon and the fair was open, filled with visitors who were there to take in the sights. Boats trailed in lazy paths across the calm waters, unaware that in the span of a few hours everything would change. The lights would turn the water into a glimmering mirror of stars, the white marble of the buildings would glow, and if they couldn't fix this—if they couldn't stop the necklace from detonating or the people from being at the ball when it did—people would die, including the president. Esta shuddered at the thought of what a change like that could do to the future.

The ball was being held in the Festival Hall, the white domed building at the head of the enormous lagoon. Other than the boats, which would have taken too long, there was no direct route there. They had to cut around the buildings that held exhibitions of metallurgy and liberal arts, following the broad paths filled with people until they came to the Festival Hall.

From the gilded dome to the lavish curlicues of marble and plaster, the Festival Hall was a testament to excess. In a city where many of the streets remained unpaved and workers gathered in warehouses to plan their rise, it was unnecessary, this impractical bit of beauty. Everywhere, lush flowers bloomed in perfectly manicured gardens, fountains threw water into the air in elegant looping patterns, and ornate gazebos provided shade from the afternoon sun. It was beautiful and frivolous with its sculptures and carvings. It should have seemed utterly charming and beautiful and feminine, but it was also imposing.

The building stood two stories above the fair on its man-made hilltop like a citadel, with a double row of columns that ringed it like the bars of a cage. Blocking the main entrance was an enormous fountain, THE TRIUMPH OF LIBERTY carved into its base, and on three of its sides were smaller but no less ornate fountains, LIBERTY, JUSTICE, and TRUTH, which all cascaded down to the main lagoon below. And on the top of its gilded dome, the goddess Victory had been wrought in the image of a man. *Of course she had.* Esta wasn't even surprised. The entire building was a statement of the city's power, as though St. Louis could claim its place in the country with marble and water. It was also a statement of the men who'd commissioned it—the Society, filled with the city fathers who ruled from their mahogany boardrooms and marbled halls.

But inside, the hall was mostly a hollow, cavernous space. Though the Guard was everywhere around the grounds of the Exposition, it was too early in the day for them to have taken up their posts for the night, so Esta and the others were able to enter the rotunda of the building, blending in with the other tourists who gazed up to where the daylight streamed in through spotless windows as an enormous pipe organ played a hymn.

They didn't waste time listening the way the other visitors did, though. Esta took stock of the building—hiding places and weak points. The Guard would do the same, and so would the president's security, but it didn't hurt to be aware of the exits in a place.

North led them through the rotunda and then to a small service hall-way near the far side of the building. The door to the service hall was almost unnoticeable because it blended in with the ornate details and the scrollwork of the rest of the building. Once they were in the safety of the hall, they were able to snake through the building unseen.

"The ball will be held in the main rotunda out there," North said, leading the way. He must have seen plans for the building to have such a clear sense of his direction.

"They'll be bringing the parade down the avenue and then around the back, past the Palace of Fine Arts," Esta told them, remembering where the Prophet's float had stopped long enough for the Guard to pull Julien out of the hidden chamber beneath it and lead him away.

"That's just on the other side of this wall here," North said. "When the Prophet's float arrived, did you see where they took Julien?"

Esta shook her head. "They grabbed him and left me behind. By the time I climbed out of the float, he was gone. They made the rest of us leave the fairgrounds from the back entrance, and then I came straight to you all. I don't know where they took Julien."

North considered the question, his eyes unfocused for a second. "The east wing of the building is mostly maintenance and workers, but on the west side, there are some rooms for offices and meetings. They'll want privacy, so I expect that they'll set up for the Prophet there."

With a nod, North pulled them into a broom closet barely big enough to hold them. "The ball starts at ten, when the parade arrives, so we'll need to be a little early to get into position." He adjusted the dial of his watch, moving the minute hand ahead so that it dragged the hours along with it. Then he looked up at them, meeting each of their eyes in turn. "Ready?"

They each took hold of his arm, and once again, the world flashed white.

HUNGRY

1904—St. Louis

If Harte never again had to feel the creeping sense of unease he got when North used that magical watch of his, it would be too soon. He'd thought it was bad when Esta had pulled him through the years, but North's magic was worse. When the world went white, he felt like it disappeared completely and like a shard of ice had stabbed him in the chest. Even once he got his vision back, the cold ache in his chest was still there, like the shard was still melting in the center of his heart.

The voice inside of him didn't like it any better than he did. He could hear it screeching in the hollows of his head, blocking out everything for a moment and reminding him of the vision he'd had of the woman—the demon—in the temple.

But he pushed that voice down until it was a low, constant rumble in the back of his mind and shook off the lingering discomfort of the ice in his chest as he tried to focus.

"We'll need clothes," North was telling them. "Uniforms or something. We don't want anyone to notice us, if we can help it."

"We just need to get Julien and cause a big enough disturbance to get everyone out," Harte argued. "The faster we do this the better."

"We can create a disturbance," Maggie said, taking North's hands.

"Are you sure?" Esta asked her.

Maggie patted the pockets of her dress. "I've got some things with me. Nothing that will do any real harm. Just some smoke and flares to put on a little show, but everyone's already going to be on edge after the attack on the parade. It shouldn't be a problem to clear the ballroom before they get into it. You two get that friend of yours."

North opened the door, and the sounds of the evening came through the crack—the murmuring of voices, the clattering of plates and silver being set, and farther off in the distance, the music of an orchestra. "We'll meet back at the wagon," North told them. "Good luck."

Once they were gone, Harte was alone in the narrow space with Esta. If it had been a challenge before to keep the power inside of him in check, it felt impossible now. Beneath the scent of dust and the sharp bite of some cleaning solvent, he could smell her—the soft scent of sweat, clean and pure on her skin, and the power she carried within.

The thought startled him. It wasn't he who could smell her power. Magic didn't have a smell . . . *did it*?

Her eyes found his in the gloom of the closet, and the power surged again.

"We need to get going," he said, his voice sounding almost unhinged. She heard it too. Her brows bunched over her whiskey-colored eyes.

"Are you okay, Harte?"

He wanted to shake his head. He wanted to tell her to run. But he could only stare numbly at her for a moment, his voice silenced by the effort of keeping the power inside of him in check.

North was right. "We'll need clothes," he said finally, choking the words out like a man drowning. "Something that doesn't stand out."

She studied him a moment longer, a question in her eyes. But she didn't ask it. "Leave it to me," she said.

He didn't argue for once. He didn't want her to go alone, but he needed to get away from her to get the power inside of him back under his control. But a moment was all that he had. She was no sooner out the door than she was coming back, her arms filled with two sets of dark suits and crisp white shirts.

"Do I even want to know?" he asked, trying to make light of the moment. But his voice was too tight, and the words came out as a reprimand he didn't intend.

She cut him a sharp look. "It's not half as exciting as you're thinking. They have a rack of uniforms for the waitstaff tonight." She gave him a shrug as she started unbuttoning the rough-spun shirt she'd been wearing. Beneath, her breasts were bound with wide strips of linen that contrasted with the expanse of tawny skin that was the color of the desert sand at twilight.

He shuddered, knowing exactly where that image had come from. Seshat was hungry. She was tired of his hesitation and his refusal to take what he wanted.

What she *wanted.*

It was easier to turn away from her, to not watch her long, lithe arms disappear beneath the cover of the new clothing. But he could still feel her. Every particle of his being was attuned to her—to the warm magic that was wound into the very center of her being.

Soon, the voice hummed. *So very, very soon.*

They finished dressing, and when he turned back to her, she was wearing a look of determination so quintessentially Esta that he could barely breathe. He wanted to touch her. He wanted to pull her to him and press his lips against hers, but he knew that he'd grown too weak beneath the constant onslaught of the power that dwelled inside of him. If he touched her now, he would not be able to stop, and they would both be done.

"Esta—" Her name came from his lips like a plea, and he could not tell if he was warning her or calling for her or simply girding himself against the power inside with the talisman of her name.

"Not now," she said, her eyes dark with understanding. "Not until we're out of here."

They left the safety of the broom closet and followed the hallway back to where the guests were already gathered in the rotunda. The orchestra was still playing its soft melody from the loft where the enormous organ loomed above them. On the far side of the room, a group of people had crowded around a mustached man with a pair of pince-nez perched on his nose. *Roosevelt.* The dark-suited men near him must have been part of his security detail.

Everywhere Harte looked, he saw the life he would never have. The silks and the jewels, the tinkling laughter. The champagne and the stiff upper lips and the freedom these men had to walk through the world as though they owned it.

He could not even bring himself to hate them for it, because he didn't know, if the tables were turned, that he would be any better. They were, all of them, only what life had carved them out to be.

"I don't think the parade has arrived yet," he told Esta.

"We should figure out which doors they'll use," she said.

"Not those main ones." He nodded to where they had come in earlier and where a steady stream of elegantly clothed people was arriving.

"Maybe in that maintenance hall?" she asked. "There's got to be some kind of delivery door, where they brought all of this in earlier."

"There's only one way to find out."

He straightened his shoulders to match the posture of the other servers, and then the two of them started across the center of the rotunda. At the edge of his vision, movement caught his eye, and he glanced up to see Maggie on the catwalk high above them. *At least that much will work.*

They found they were right. In the east wing, there was a door where various workers came and went. "They'll probably bring them through there," Harte figured. The Prophet still had to make the switch from Julien, who'd worn the necklace in the parade, to the real debutante, whose reputation depended on her *not* displaying herself so publicly in the city streets. The transfer had to be seamless, though. When the Queen of Love and Beauty was introduced to the ball in the rotunda, she would already be wearing the Djinni's Star.

They found a cart laden with stemmed champagne bowls just across from the doorway, and they each took up one of the cloths and pretended to polish the crystal as they watched for the Prophet's arrival. They didn't have to wait long. A few minutes later, the staff around them seemed to noticeably adjust themselves, picking up their pace and attentiveness, and not long after that, the Veiled Prophet came through the door. Behind him, two of the Jefferson Guard had Julien—one holding each of his arms.

Harte ducked his head, pretending to study the glasses, but he used the motion to watch as the group entered one of the unmarked doors in the hallway. Other Guardsmen took up posts on either side of the door.

"You there!" a voice said from behind Harte. "What are you doing? Those have already been polished."

Harte glanced up to find one of the waiters staring at them, his hands filled with a tray of canapés and a scowl on his face.

"Water spots," Esta told him, holding up one of the glasses.

The waiter scowled even more. "You don't both need to take care of water spots," he grumbled. "We need more men on the floor." He came over and thrust the tray toward her. "Take this out there. Roosevelt wanted some of the pâté."

Esta glanced at him. She didn't have much choice but to take the offered tray and head into the rotunda.

"Finish that up and get out there," the man snapped at Harte before he hustled off to reprimand someone else.

Harte kept his head down and polished the spotless champagne bowl in his hand, keeping his eye on the door where the Veiled Prophet had Julien. A few minutes later the door opened and the veiled man exited with a girl on his arm.

No. The debutante must have been waiting in the room. She was already wearing the decoy necklace, and now she was being escorted into the rotunda.

He would get Julien out of there, and then he would go after them.

Harte put the crystal back on the cart and started toward the Guardsmen. He moved fast, pushing his affinity outward as he grabbed one. The other attacked, but not fast enough. A moment later they were both staring, dazed, and making their way like sleepwalkers toward the exit of the building.

Carefully, Harte eased the door open and saw that there was one Guardsman left, looming over Julien.

"I told you, I had nothing to do with the attack." Julien's voice was filled with more irritation than fear, so that was something, at least. "Those barbarians came after me, too. Do you see this? Does this eye like something I did to myself?"

Harte slipped into the room and used the element of surprise to his advantage. He launched himself at the Guardsman and in a matter of moments had wrangled him to the floor. Pushing his affinity through the tenuous layers of skin and soul, he sent the Guardsman a single command. The man went limp beneath him, his eyes open, looking to the ceiling above.

"We need to go," Harte told Julien. "Now."

But Julien was staring between Harte and the incapacitated Guardsman. "You're . . . Dammit, Darrigan. You're one of them," he said, shaking his head as if he couldn't believe it.

"You can hate me later if it means that much to you," Harte told him. "If you don't move now, you can stay here and deal with the Prophet on your own. But I'm leaving."

Indecision flickered in Julien's expression. Finally, he sighed and stepped over the prone Guardsman. "You should have stayed dead," he muttered, but there was no hatred and no heat in the words.

"There are days I feel the same way, Jules." And today, with Seshat already clamoring inside of him, was definitely one of them.

The hallway was empty now, and they had a clear path to the door. They were nearly there when Harte heard the laughter behind him. He turned to find Jack Grew leaning against the wall, his eyes bright with hatred.

"Harte Darrigan," he said, stepping toward them. "Back from the dead . . . again."

Harte stepped in front of Julien, shielding him from Jack. "Go," he urged. "Get out of here, *now*."

"But—"

Harte turned and pushed him through the exit, thankful for the gown Julien was in as he pressed a command into the bare skin of Julien's exposed back. *Leave. Now,* he ordered. *Don't look back.*

Then he turned to Jack.

"I knew you would come to me," Jack said, his voice rough.

Harte frowned. "I didn't come for you."

"Didn't you?" Jack stepped toward him.

"No, I—" But his words died in his throat. There was something shifting in Jack's eyes. Something dark that was looking out at him from inside. The skin on Jack's face flinched, twitching like he'd been struck, and then something beneath it rolled, creeping under the surface like a snake.

Harte reached for the cart of crystal and pushed it over, sending the glasses crashing to the floor as he turned and ran.

The voice inside of him was screeching, and it was all he could do to keep his feet moving as his shoes slipped on the broken glass coating the hallway. He was nearly to the rotunda when Jack spoke again.

"Did you think you could evade me forever, *Seshat?*"

At the sound of the name, the voice unleashed itself, rising in its force until Harte could not fight it. Until he was nothing more than a shell of skin and bone, directed and moved by some unseen power.

THE CURTAIN PULLED BACK

Under the warm blanket of Jianyu's affinity, Viola watched as a second curtain opened, revealing a scene with a boat and sailors, their faces a picture of horror as they tried to escape from three watery maidens dressed in flowing robes who seemed set on capsizing them.

"Hurry," she told Jianyu as he carried her on his back around the edges of the crowd, careful not to disturb anyone and give away his position.

Jack Grew was droning on as they walked, and as much as she would have liked to shut him up, Viola prayed he would keep talking. Four scenes had been on the program, which meant that Ruby could be revealed at any moment.

"Evil creatures, designed and forged to bring men to their knees. Their feral power was once a danger, once unchecked in the face of helpless man. But as time passed, as man learned and cultivated an enlightened view of magic, their time came to an end."

They were at the curtains, and while the audience was enraptured by the sight before them, Viola followed Jianyu as he slipped through the curtain to the area backstage. Jianyu released his hold on the light, and she felt the warmth of his affinity recede as she slid down from his back. "It will be easier this way," he said, before she could argue.

"If you leave with the ring, I'll find you," Viola promised. "And when I find you, it will not be to talk."

Her words didn't seem to have the desired effect, though. Jianyu's mouth curved up at the corners. "We leave here together," he promised. "As Dolph would have wanted."

It didn't take long for Viola to find Ruby, who was sitting on a mirrored throne in front of the closed velvet curtains, wearing a long, dark wig and looking for all the world like she was terrified of what was about to happen. She was dressed in a bit of nothing: a garment that was almost the exact color of her flesh and a scrap of material draped around her that matched the deep blue of her eyes.

For a moment Viola froze. It seemed that her feet wouldn't move and her voice wouldn't make a sound, because all she could do was stare at Ruby, who looked so forlorn and lost and absolutely perfect that Viola could barely breathe. But her hesitation was a mistake. By the time she'd pulled herself together, the curtain was already opening.

CIRCE

1902—New York

R uby lifted the chalice and the wand and raised her chin as the curtain opened, revealing her—*so much of her*—to the audience of Morgan's ballroom.

There was a sudden hush that made her want to drop the objects and run, but she kept herself still, frozen as a statue, just as she was supposed to. Her eyes were straight ahead, searching for some sign of Theo, but she didn't see him anywhere.

"The Order is proud to present to you John William Waterhouse's masterpiece, *Circe Offering the Cup to Ulysses*. Behold the mother of witches, she who would lure men to her cup only to transform them into swine."

To Ruby, he sounded positively angry about the whole thing, as though it were her and not some mythic being that had done the dastardly deed. The tone of his voice sent a chill through her, but she kept her hands lifted, just as the painting depicted, and counted the seconds until it was over.

Without warning, though, the cup she was holding suddenly turned cold, and the bowl of it, which had been empty only moments before, began to froth with a bloodred liquid that dribbled over the rim of the chalice and dripped onto her dress. She glanced over at Jack for some sign that this was supposed to happen, but all she saw was the fury in his eyes.

Before Ruby could figure out what was happening or how she could get away, the curtains closed and she nearly collapsed with relief. She could hear the applause on the other side of the velvet, but she didn't care. She set the bloody-looking cup on the floor and looked at her stained hand. For a moment she was back in that dirty tenement, trying to keep the life from seeping out of Theo. And then Viola was there.

"Come," Viola said, without any sort of preface. "We have to go. *You* have to go."

Viola. Here.

It was so unexpected, so completely unbelievable, that Ruby couldn't quite understand what she was seeing, much less follow the order Viola had just given her.

"Are you okay?" Viola asked when she realized that Ruby wasn't doing anything but staring at her.

Ruby was shaking her head and stepping toward Viola before she knew what her feet were doing. *Viola is here.* The relief of seeing her there was almost too much.

Her hand was still sticky with whatever had burst forth from the cup, but Ruby couldn't stop herself from reaching out to touch Viola's cheek, just to be sure it was really her. The creature in front of her was wearing a silken gown that could have fit in at the opera, along with Viola's usual scowl.

At her touch, Viola went very, very still. "What happened? Did they hurt you?"

But Ruby only shook her head and leaned forward, pressing her lips to Viola's.

The moment her lips touched Viola's, she realized what she'd just done. She started to pull away, horrified that she'd overstepped, when Viola's mouth went soft beneath hers. Ruby nearly collapsed from the combination of relief and exhilaration she felt pooling in her body, heavy and warm and—

Viola pulled away, her violet eyes wide. "Why did you do that?" she asked, her fingertips touching her lips. Her cheek was marred with the red from Ruby's hand.

"I don't know," Ruby told her. "I saw you and . . . I wanted to."

It was the wrong thing to say. Viola took a step back. "This is all a game to you, isn't it?"

Ruby's stomach dropped. Viola had misunderstood. "No—" She stepped toward Viola, but the look on Viola's face had her hesitating.

"What about Theo?" Viola asked, her voice dark.

Theo? "He wouldn't care," she said, knowing it was the truth. The poor dear would probably be relieved.

Viola was shaking her head. "You treat him like your plaything too." Her voice was low and rough. "The whole world, nothing but toys for you because you have nothing to lose. *Nothing.*"

But Viola was wrong. She didn't know, *couldn't* have known that Ruby had already lost everything and had decided that it wasn't worth living life like a mouse, always running. Always afraid. "That's not why—"

Viola's eyes were shining with angry tears. "You play with people's lives because you can and then you walk away and go back to your fancy bedroom—to your maids and your servants."

"No, you don't understand," Ruby pleaded. She wanted to apologize, to explain, but her throat was too tight, and she didn't have the words.

"I understand too much," Viola said dully, taking yet another step back. "I've lived in this world too long not to know how this will turn out. You have to go. *Now.*"

The pain in the other girl's tone pierced Ruby. She took a step forward, her hand raised. "Viola, we can figure this out. It will be okay—"

"It wasn't Torrio they sent to kill you," Viola said, her voice like the knife she'd been holding the first time they met. "It was *me.* I risked too much to save your life then, and I'm risking everything now. So whatever that was, whatever you think is between us, do this for me and leave. Because my brother is out there, and so is Torrio. If they realize who you are—if they see *Theo*—they're going to know. And we will both pay the price for that."

For Viola she would have stayed, she would have risked everything, but for Theo? Steady, innocent, wonderful Theo, who had always been her rock. Who never told her no? She couldn't sacrifice him.

"This isn't over between us," Ruby promised.

"Yes, it is," Viola said, but the shine of tears in her eyes gave away the lie of her words.

In the fraught silence that stretched like a chasm between them, a woman screamed, and on the other side of the curtain, the gala erupted into chaos.

WHAT LIVED INSIDE

1904—St. Louis

The morphine he'd taken earlier was making Jack feel unbearably light, as though his feet were no longer moored to the ground. As though he had already become the god he'd intended to be.

"I knew you'd come for me," he said, and the voice that came from within him was the one he often heard in his mind. That other version of himself that he'd found in Greece, when he'd come to understand what power was and what he might do with it. That other self had guided him, kept him on the straight and narrow, and had unlocked the secrets in the Book tucked close to his chest. It seemed only fitting that his two selves would merge now, that he would become what he'd always intended to be.

The magician no longer interested him. No . . . He desired what lived *inside* the magician. The power that had slipped from his fingertips those many years ago. The demon bitch who had evaded him too many times over the years and centuries. He would have her now. He would take every bit of her power for himself.

Darrigan's eyes had gone dark, and Jack—and the other voice that lived inside Jack—knew it was because the magician was no more than a shell. And Jack would have his revenge. He would destroy Darrigan once and for all.

"Thoth . . ." The words came from Darrigan's mouth, but they were not spoken by his voice.

"Seshat," Jack said, letting the syllables hiss from his mouth, soft as a snake. "You can't win this time. Without the protection of the Book, your power will be mine."

"Protection?" Darrigan's lips curled into a disgusted sneer. "The Book was my *prison*, and now that I am free, I will destroy you."

"You can't destroy me, Seshat. I have become power itself. I have become a god."

"Even gods need a home, Thoth. I will destroy *everything* to ensure that you never again walk free."

SESHAT'S RETURN

1904—St. Louis

Esta was offering the tray of canapés to Teddy Roosevelt himself when the first of Maggie's devices popped, showering sparks over the entire rotunda and spewing forth a fog that wove through the air like a living snake. The security pulled Roosevelt away, making a solid wall between him and any of the other attendees. A woman in the crowd screamed, and the crowd in the rotunda began a panicked stampede toward the doors.

Esta ran in the other direction. She'd heard the crash of shattering glass from the distant hallway, where she'd left Harte, and she'd known somehow that something had gone wrong. But she hadn't expected anything like what she saw when she arrived. Jack Grew was there, and Harte was speaking to him, but their voices were off, eerily inhuman. And Harte's eyes were completely black, with not even the whites showing.

"You had everything," Jack said in that strange, otherworldly voice. "You had the key to all power at your fingertips, the heart of magic at your command. It was yours to control—and instead you tried to destroy it."

"I tried to *save* it," Harte shrieked, his face contorted. "I created the words and the writing of them because I thought it would be enough to stop the eventual death of magic. But I was wrong. The Book was a mistake."

"The Book was a gift," Jack said, stepping toward Harte.

"You had no right to it," Harte spat. "You stole what was not yours to take. I counted you as a friend, and you betrayed me. I revealed my failures to you, and you abused my trust by giving power—broken and debased as it was—to the undeserving who could not appreciate it—all for something as vulgar as fame."

"Why should magic have belonged only to those like you?" Jack asked. "Once, all people could touch the power that threads itself through all of creation. Who were you to keep it from them?"

"Who were you to give it only to the sycophants who favored you?" Harte threw back. "You don't think I know what was behind your rise?" Harte laughed, and it was the high, manic laugh of a woman who had come unhinged. "You don't think I know how you stole the secrets I inscribed and doled them out only to those who could pay, those who could bestow power upon you?"

"I gave them to the worthy," Jack said. "And I was rewarded. You . . . *You* were forgotten."

"Because of *you*," Harte spat. "Because of how you tried to destroy me. But you failed in that, didn't you? You didn't expect that, did you? If you had realized how I had been bound to the Book, you would have destroyed it—and me. But you didn't, and because of your shortsightedness, I bided my time, waiting for someone to release me. Waiting for *this* moment."

Harte lunged at Jack, pushing him backward into the rotunda. Above them, the air was filled with the living plumes of dark smoke caused by Maggie's devices—the distraction she'd promised. Within the depths of it, lights flickered like lightning flashing. Esta could feel the rumble of cold power mixing with the warmth of the old magic, the two battling and warring overhead like some alchemical thunderstorm about to break.

Beneath it, Harte and Jack were grappling with each other, their hands clawing and punching as they rolled across the ground. And the power that came off them was overwhelming, hot as the flames that had consumed the brewery and icy as the Brink all at once, clashing and warring as the two fought. For a moment Esta was sure that Harte would win.

But then something shifted inside Jack and roared up, pinning Harte to the floor. Harte had gone limp beneath him, like he'd lost consciousness completely.

Esta acted on instinct, pulling her affinity close and making time go still as she sprinted to where the two of them were. Shoving Jack off Harte with the bottom of her shoe, she went to Harte and placed her hands on his face. "Wake up," she pleaded. "Come on . . ." She tapped at his cheeks and urged him again.

Without warning, his eyes flew open. But before she could feel the shudder of relief, she realized that it wasn't Harte looking out at her. It was something dark and ancient peering from the coal-black depths of his eyes.

Harte's hand snaked out and gripped her by the wrist before she could even think to back away, and the intensity of the power she felt rise between them shook her so profoundly that she lost hold of her affinity. The world spun back into motion, and Jack moaned softly from where he'd toppled over on the floor.

But Esta didn't notice. The moment Harte had touched her, the moment the power within him had connected with hers, she'd been overwhelmed. And then, the world fell away. . . .

There was a chamber made of stone and clay and the sand of the desert. And there was a woman with eyes of amber, just like her own, and the woman had made a mistake. She leaned over an altar that held the open pages of a book, and her pain and frustration hung heavy in the air. But the woman looked up suddenly and her eyes met Esta's.

"You've come." The woman's voice echoed through the chamber in a language Esta did not know but could understand even so. And though she could hear the woman speaking, her mouth never moved. "The one who can release me. The one who can fulfill my destiny. I knew you would come. I knew you would give yourself over to me."

Esta was frozen in place, moored in time and Aether. She could not move as the woman looked into her very heart.

"I see you so clearly. I see what you desire. The end of this pain and struggle."

Esta wanted to deny it, but she could not so much as shake her head. No, she thought. I don't want this.

"I tried to save it. Magic. Power. The energy that flows between all things. It was dying. It was fading even in my time, as people forgot, divided themselves from each other and from the unity of all things. So I tried to preserve what I could by creating the writing. I thought I could save the heart of magic within the permanence of words." The woman's eyes flashed with fury. "But I was wrong. Creating the power of ritual through writing only weakened magic further. Magic isn't order—it's the possibility held within chaos. Ritual limited the wild freedom inherent in power, broke it apart and kept it fractured. But it also made it controllable, even for those who were without an affinity for it.

"I shared what I'd done with Thoth, because I believed him to be a friend. But he never was. He'd been born weak, and he wanted the power I was fated with. He saw what I'd done, and instead of helping me try to fix my errors, as he'd promised, he took the power for his own. He made a devil's bargain, trading everything we could have been for everything he wanted to be.

"When I realized, I made the stones. I broke magic apart to protect the last pure bit of it. To form a barrier against any who would try to take it.

"But Thoth was never an ibis. He was always a snake, stealing other people's eggs."

Esta saw then everything that happened—the way Thoth had trapped Seshat and then destroyed the stones. He took the Book, but he was a vain and fearful man, so he never stopped running. He never ceased collecting more and more power. More souls and more secrets.

"I put myself in the pages he wanted so badly, but I was trapped by the parchment and vellum I'd written upon in my attempt to preserve magic's true power. Once, I was almost freed again. A man . . . a great magician tried. But he was a coward, unable to contain my power. Now . . . Now I walk in a new body. Now you have come for me, and together we will end him."

How? Esta wanted to ask, but her mouth would not form the words.

"With you, my dear child. With the power inside you, we will end everything."

No . . . *Frozen though she was, the word echoed in her mind.* No. No. No.

But Seshat only laughed, the rich rolling sound echoing around the chamber. *"What did you think you were, child?*

"They hunted your kind—our kind—across eons. Across continents and centuries. They tried to wipe us from the world because they feared us. They were right to. You can touch the strands of time—the very material that carves order from chaos—just as I once could. And like I once could, you can tear them apart.

"Come—" The woman at the altar held out her hand. *"Join me. Release me."*

Looking into the woman's eyes as she pleaded, Esta realized that Harte had been wrong. Seshat wasn't a monster. She wasn't a demon, either. She was just a woman. A woman, like Esta, who had power. A woman who had believed in the possibility of the world and had been betrayed by it . . . And now she wanted revenge for that betrayal. The hurt inside of her, the pain of it was like the same flint that sparked inside Esta. She understood. It burned inside of her, how deeply she understood.

Why not burn it all down and begin again?

Because innocent people would die. She knew it as well as she knew that Seshat had started just as innocent. She knew too, because she herself had been taken in by the anger and vengeance of the Antistasi. It wasn't a mistake she would make again. Esta recoiled at the idea of accepting, even as she felt herself stepping toward the woman.

"Thoth cannot be allowed to continue," the woman said.

Seshat would unmake the world to destroy Thoth. She would sacrifice everyone— everything—to ensure that Thoth, the true Devil's Thief, would die.

"Don't act as though you're so righteous," Seshat chided her. *"You forget that I have already seen the truth of your heart. I have already seen the yearning for retribution. The desire for revenge. The hate that burns brightly inside you can remake the world, my child."*

Yes, Esta had wanted revenge. She'd wanted to make so many pay. But she'd been wrong.

It was too late. Seshat was already pulling her forward, and Esta felt her affinity drawn toward the ancient priestess. She felt Seshat's power vining around her, *but this time it was purer than it had been in the station or in the hotel. This time there was no fighting.*

The world felt like it would fly apart. The darkness, Esta realized, wasn't something that had appeared in the world. It was the world. It was the spaces between, opening and flooding. It was the unmaking of reality.

And there was nothing Esta could do to stop it.

THE NIGHTMARE
COME TO LIFE

T he moment that Jack had planned for weeks had finally arrived. The first three tableaux had captivated the audience, enraptured them with the demonstrations of his and the Book's power—not that they realized that was what they were seeing. He was well aware that they thought the feats he'd accomplished were nothing more than parlor tricks. They were, compared to what was coming.

As the third set of curtains closed, Jack slipped two more cubes of morphine into his mouth before he stepped in front of the final set of curtains. He looked out at the audience as he waited for the room to grow silent. There were the men of the Inner Circle, the High Princept, and the rest of society. Men from Tammany were there as well, and another face, a particular friend he'd invited himself—Paul Kelly, who had turned out to be another disappointment. But Kelly would get his soon enough.

He waited until every pair of eyes was looking only at him—seeing him for what he *truly* was. And then he waited a moment longer, just because he could.

"Ladies and gentlemen, we come to our final tableau. Tonight the Order has presented a veritable bounty of beauty and wonder. You have been transported to the alchemist's laboratory and witnessed the moment when man began to take control of the dangerous powers that surround us. You have seen art come to life, revealing the long and tortured history of feral magic, of those unwilling to control the dangerous power inside themselves for the good of a just and enlightened society. But now our evening is nearly at an end."

He paused, let the anticipation grow in the room until he could practically feel their desperation for the curtain to be pulled back . . . until he had them in the palm of his hand.

"I present to you Henry Fuseli's *The Nightmare*. . . ." With another flourish of his hands, the curtains opened and the final tableau of the night was revealed.

Evelyn, clad in a blond wig and a wisp of a gown, was splayed out on a low couch, just as the woman in Fuseli's famed painting. Her arms arched gracefully to the floor and her eyes were closed in a semblance of sleep. Just as in the painting, sitting on her chest was a creature meant to represent the embodiment of nightmares. Jack had created the figure himself, a gargoyle-like incubus that looked like the image of the one in the painting.

The audience rustled in wonder and in fear. He could tell it was fear from the way the air seemed to go out of the room. It was the most exquisite of the tableaux, the most horrible and beautiful all at once, and it was about to be more so.

"Those who cling to the old ways, who lurk in the shadows of our streets, are a mark upon the perfection of our union. They represent a danger. Like the darkness that creeps into our dreams, those with feral magic lie in wait until we are at our weakest. Like nightmares come to life."

At his words, the incubus began to move, turning its head to stare out at the crowded ballroom, and Jack was more than gratified to hear the audience gasp. The incubus was, of course, no ordinary carving. It was a sort of golem, an impressive piece of magic that had been revealed to Jack during one of the long, morphine-filled nights when he woke with no memory of parsing the Book's secrets. That he'd been given this particular secret was a gift, and he considered it nothing less than a divine sign of what he was meant to do. Evelyn's feral power might affect the flesh and blood, but he doubted it would do much to the misshapen creature he'd fashioned out of clay.

"But nightmares are meant to be tamed, just as those who cling to the old ways must be tamed."

He could feel Evelyn's fear even from where he stood, and that along with the singing of the morphine in his blood only emboldened him.

"Tonight you have seen the wonders of the alchemist's discovery, sirens, and witches, but now I present a *true* siren. A witch who would try to destroy the Order."

At his words Evelyn seemed to sense the danger she was in. She tried to sit up, but the moment she began to move, the incubus caged her with its arms and pressed her back to the couch. Even as she screamed, he could feel the heat of her magic brushing at him, trying to tempt him and sway him from his path, but it didn't touch him. *She* couldn't touch him. He'd learned too much since that girl in Greece. He'd learned too much from the Book.

"Evelyn DeMure pretends to be a simple actress. Perhaps you've seen her at Wallack's Theatre?" From the rustling among the men, Jack assumed that some had more than seen her. "But she, like so many of their kind, is not what she pretends to be. She intended to fell us all. She was there the night that Khafre Hall burned. She thought she could enrapture me with her evil ways, but as you can see, her power is weak compared to the secrets of enlightened study."

He was close—so close—he thought as he lifted his hand, and the clay figure did the same. He brought his fingers together in a fist, and the creature mirrored his action over the tender skin of Evelyn's throat.

By now people were starting to come to their feet. Some were calling for him to stop, but Jack was calm. Allowing the golem to do his bidding, he turned back to the crowd. "But Miss DeMure, as charming as she pretended to be, isn't the only snake in our midst tonight. There is another, one who pretended to be an ally but in truth was doing the bidding of the very people we are trying to protect ourselves from."

He found Paul Kelly in the audience, the low-life bit of Bowery trash who had pretended to befriend him. Kelly had not only allowed Jack's enemy to live but had also aligned himself with one of the people responsible for Jack's greatest embarrassment.

"You all might have noticed that Mr. Kelly is here with us tonight. I'm sure you wondered why someone of his ilk had been invited to besmirch our event," Jack said, watching Kelly's eyes narrow at him. But he dismissed the threat.

This was his room, his moment.

"Officers," Jack called. "If you would be so kind, please escort Mr. Kelly and his colleagues to a more appropriate venue, where they can be dealt with."

A scream went up in the crowd, and Jack turned to see that some of the waitstaff had dropped their trays and were pulling pistols from their dark dinner jackets and taking hostages. Kelly's men. *No. They can't—They are ruining* everything, he thought with a burst of rage.

The Book felt warm against his chest as Jack watched victory slip through his fingers. Kelly simply smirked and darted into the crowd, which had broken down into complete madness.

THE FLASH OF A KNIFE

1902—New York

The room around Jianyu had churned into chaos at the sight of the Five Pointers in their midst. It did not take magic, it seemed, to drive fear into the Order's hearts. A few snub-nosed pistols did the trick just as well. The crowds of the ballroom were trying to shove through a single, narrow exit in an attempt to flee, but Jianyu had his sights set on one thing: the ring.

It was still on Evelyn's finger, but Evelyn was being guarded by the strange beast. From his own vantage point, the cold magic that surrounded the creature was telling. It was not natural, but that was no surprise coming from Jack Grew and the Order.

With light opened around him, Jianyu ignored the noise and the confusion and crept steadily closer to the beast sitting on top of Evelyn. She no longer seemed to be breathing, but the beast still had its clawed fingers gripped around her throat, her sightless eyes staring off into the room beyond.

He was nearly there when he saw Cela moving through the crowd with a single-minded determination. While everyone else was trying to flee, she looked like a koi struggling upstream as she worked her way toward the stage and Evelyn. With his affinity, she had not realized that he was already there.

Before he could warn her, he noticed a flash of dark hair and plum silk and saw Viola coming in the same direction. From the look of fury in her eyes, Viola had seen Cela too.

He had not taken the time to explain earlier, when he could have, he realized with a sick sense of dread. Viola would not know who Cela was. She would only see a stranger after the treasure she had told Jianyu not to take.

It felt as though the moment was suspended in amber and he was viewing everything from outside of it. The flash of Viola's knife coming from the folds of her skirt, the fury in her expression as she screamed at Cela to get away from Evelyn—to leave the ring.

Cela glanced over her shoulder, but she ignored the warning.

Because she did not understand who Viola was. Because she could not have known what would happen.

But Jianyu did—he could see it playing out before it occurred. Viola would launch her knife through the air. She would aim for Cela, and she would not miss.

Letting go of the light, Jianyu did the only thing he could do. Without considering the consequences to himself, he leaped in front of Cela, just as the knife slipped from Viola's fingertips.

The room narrowed to that moment, but even knowing he had been hit, Jianyu did not feel any pain when the knife cut through his tunic and pierced his skin, tearing past sinew and bone to lodge in his shoulder. He felt nothing at all but relief when he landed hard on the floor at Cela's feet.

She was there, standing over him with an expression that told him just how bad it was. Her hands were on his face and her mouth was moving, but he could not hear the words she spoke. When he looked up at Viola, he saw only horror in her eyes. They were rimmed in red as though she had already been crying for him.

Pulling himself up, he took the handle of the knife and pulled it from his arm.

Finally, he felt the pain, the sharp stinging of the blade as it slid from the place it made through his skin. Even with Cela holding a part of her skirt to his wound, trying to stop the blood, he knew that he had to reach Viola . . . had to make her understand.

"We have to get out of here," Cela told him, trying to get him to his feet, but he had to speak to Viola. He had to tell her one, essential thing.

"Come with us," he said, offering her the knife, which was still coated with his blood. His voice sounded far away, even to himself, but he repeated the offer again. "We need you."

But Viola was shaking her head and backing away.

And then Abel was there, hoisting him up to carry him out.

Jianyu didn't know where the ring was, or who had it, but in that moment he knew that it didn't matter as much as making Viola understand. "Come with us," he repeated, knowing that nothing would be possible as long as they were divided.

A MONSTROUS CHAOS

1904—St. Louis

Julien ran from the Festival Hall without looking back. Outside, the crowd that had once been milling about the rotunda was gathered, the women holding one another and the men blustering like fat capons. The Prophet was there, as were others from the Society, all standing and watching as the lights flashed within the Festival Hall and the eerie smoke began to creep from beneath the doors.

He was standing apart from them, unsure of how he got there or what he was supposed to do now that he was outside. He wasn't onstage, so the gown he was wearing and the weight of the wig felt uncomfortable and out of place. Part of him thought that he was supposed to stay, to make sure that Darrigan and Esta were okay, but there was a deeper impulse to slink off into the night. He began to back toward the darkened fairgrounds, out of sight from anyone who might be looking for someone to blame, when an earsplitting scream erupted from the center of the crowd.

It was the debutante he'd met just moments before, the one who'd been selected as the Queen of Love and Beauty. They'd taken the decoy necklace from him and had given it to her, but now a thick, dark cloud of smoke was pouring from where the necklace still perched around her neck. She was tearing at it, trying to get it off, but it was clearly stuck.

I did this, he thought, horrified. He'd only wanted to clear his name, to get Darrigan out of town before anyone knew, and instead, he'd helped them create this monstrous chaos.

People were backing away from the poor girl, terrified of the darkness blooming from the jeweled collar, but Julien found himself walking toward her—toward the danger.

He was there before he could fully think through the consequences. Taking hold of the necklace, he wrenched his arms apart and broke it in two. The girl ran, probably back into the arms of her mother, and Julien hurled the necklace as far as he could, to spew its poison far, far away from the crowd.

But not before he'd breathed in some of the dark fog himself.

NEVER ENOUGH

Margaret Jane Feltz had done quite a lot of things in her life that she wasn't proud of at the moment. Most of those she'd done because she'd believed at the time it was the right thing to do, because *Ruth* had told her that it was, and because she'd wanted Ruth's warm approval more than she wanted the discomfort of standing against her sister.

Maggie might have had an uncanny knack for mixing chemicals and powders—a gift of the kitchen magic that seemed to run in her family—but she hated it just the same. Still, she was grateful for the one incendiary she'd held back just in case. When she saw Ben grab Esta by the throat, she felt the air in the rotunda go electric, hot and bright like she'd never in her life felt it. She pulled the small canister from her satchel and activated the fuse before she rolled it toward them, placing it between the angry blond man in the tuxedo and the two she'd come to think of as friends.

It popped with a violent burst of light, throwing Ben from Esta and knocking him unconscious to the floor.

She ran to where Esta was lying, prone and still on the polished marble floor, and a moment later North was there. They gathered the two of them, and then with a click of North's watch, they were gone.

Between the crowds from the parade and the news that was beginning to spread about the attack on the ball, the streets were in chaos. All of the Antistasi's planning, and for what? The Mageus would now be even worse off than before. Ruth had been wrong—about everything. Maggie had suspected all along, but now she understood.

As they made their way through town to reach the train station, Maggie tried not to think about the fact that she was leaving behind her sister and the Antistasi, who had become her family. But she knew that she'd done all she could here, and now there was somewhere else she was needed more.

She'd tried so hard to do one small bit of good. But it hadn't been enough. It wasn't ever enough. This time, she vowed, it would be.

THE DAGGER

1904—St. Louis

Jack woke sometime in the depths of the night with only a hazy memory of everything that had happened at the ball. Darrigan and Esta had managed to get away. They'd taken the necklace, but they had not been able to retrieve the Book. Instead, they'd exposed themselves, and now the entire country knew about their evil intent. Those mistakes would only help him in the future.

After he'd returned to his room, he'd pored over the Book, looking for some answer, but he didn't recall the words he'd read or how the pages had begun to glow or how he had reached through them, knowing that they would open for him, knowing that his fingers would be able to sink through the paper itself to find the object he'd placed there some months before.

He turned to the vial of morphine and instead found something more. On the table next to the bedside was an ancient artifact—the same one he had hidden inside the pages of the Book for safekeeping so many months ago. He picked it up and turned it in the light, marveling at its appearance as he reveled in the weight of the stone it contained, a sign of the power held within it.

Jack had obtained the artifact itself ages ago—not long after he'd taken the Book from Darrigan. After the Conclave, he'd begun to worry that someone might find it. He'd used one of the spells in the Book to conceal the object within its pages, turning the Book itself into a container for the artifact so that he could carry both with him at all times.

But once concealed, the Book had not willingly given the artifact back. For more than a year now, he'd nearly driven himself mad with the work of trying to force the Book to reveal its contents, all to no avail.

Now, it seemed, his luck had turned. It was as though the Book understood the crossroads he was at, as though it knew that he would need all the power he could harness in the days and weeks to come, and it had given up its contents like an offering. A benediction for the journey ahead—a journey that he was well aware would be difficult but that was his very destiny to fulfill.

SLEEPWALKING

1904—St. Louis

Esta didn't know how they got away from the fair. She remembered pain and a chilling burst of power, and then, little by little, she surfaced from the fog of what had happened. Seshat. Thoth. And the dangerous reality of her own affinity. By then North had taken them forward in time, to long after the fair had cleared out and everyone had gone back to the safety of their own homes.

She moved like a sleepwalker, barely seeing or hearing as Maggie and North led them through the fairgrounds back to the waiting wagon. She almost didn't remember to retrieve her stones—the cuff and the necklace—but Maggie helped with that. Then it was a dash to the station, and before she could process everything, she found herself in a Pullman car, resting next to Harte on the narrow bottom bunk.

Even with everything that had happened, even with her world feeling like it had fallen apart, the sun still managed to come up the next day. It warmed Esta's face through the window of the train, waking her. There was a moment just as she came out of sleep when she forgot where she was—*what* she was. In that moment between sleep and waking, she did not yet remember the night before. She did not think of the mistakes she'd made or the lives those mistakes had taken. She did not yet remember the terrible truths that had been revealed and the heartbreaking reality of what lay before her. Instead, she thought that she heard a woman's voice singing to her, and she thought she could almost remember the words of the song. It must have been a memory from somewhere long ago, when she was nothing but a child with no guilt, only innocence. With the world in front of her, wide and open as a promise.

But the softness and safety of the state between sleep and waking lasted only a moment. The ache in her bones and the pain echoing in her skull returned soon after, reminding her of what she'd been through. She felt soiled and wrung out, like an old rag not worth cleaning to keep. Even her bones felt like they would shatter if she moved the wrong way.

Distantly, she heard the soft snoring of the people in the small berth with her. North, propped awkwardly in a chair, and Maggie in the bunk above her. She remembered lying down next to Harte. The power he carried within him was quiet as she nestled next to him, trying to warm him and waiting for him to wake as she fought her own exhaustion.

But now the bed was cold and empty beside her.

She pulled herself up and looked around the small Pullman compartment, but there was no sign of Harte. After what had happened in the rotunda, North hadn't trusted Harte not to do something rash. He'd lashed Harte to the post of the bunk, but the rope North had used was now hanging empty.

Worse, her cuff—the one that held Ishtar's Key—was gone. In its place was a simple bracelet made of beads: the one he'd bought that first day at the fair. She reached for it, about to tear it from her wrist, but the moment she touched it, a jumble of images rose in her mind, and she felt an impulse so sure and clear that she knew it was a message he'd left for her, deep in her unconscious mind. He'd used his affinity on her, she realized. Rather than leave a note that could have been found or read by prying eyes, he left her a hope and a plea that only she could know.

He hadn't left her completely, then. But he also hadn't trusted himself enough to take her with him.

Cursing Harte for his heavy-handedness and herself for falling asleep, Esta stepped outside into the passage and then out onto the platform, where the prairie grass extended as far as the eye could see.

Harte was gone, but she wasn't alone. There was a long, unknown road ahead of them, one that led to another ocean, a distant shore. She would do what Harte had asked of her, and then, when she found him, she would make sure he regretted leaving her behind.

There was work left to do. A demigod to destroy. There were still stones to gather, a future to make.

And on the inside of her wrist was a scar—a single word in the Latin she'd learned as a child. A command calling her back, to New York and to the past.

Redi.

DISCEDO

1904—St. Louis

As the train marched along the landscape he'd only ever thought to see in dreams, Harte Darrigan watched the horizon turn from the impenetrable blanket of night to a soft lavender glow as the stars disappeared one by one in the creeping light of dawn. He'd dreamed of this his whole life, the impossible open plains and the shadow of the mountains in the distance and the freedom of it all. But now that it was his, he was every bit as trapped—as imprisoned—as he'd ever been, only this time it was a prison he carried with him.

He'd woken in the dead of night when the other train shuddered to a stop at some unknown station. Esta had been curled next to him, her arm thrown over him in the narrow bunk and her face still tense despite being deeply asleep. He could hear the soft, steady breathing of others close by, and for a moment he didn't know where he was or what had happened. Inside, the voice he carried was silent, but he could feel her there, breathing and licking her wounds.

And waiting.

It would have been easier, perhaps, to allow his eyes to close again, to allow sleep to pull him under. It certainly would have been more pleasant to stay there, close to Esta's warmth, breathing in her familiar scent. Letting himself lean on her. But even at the thought of it, the power within him started to rouse itself.

For a moment he allowed himself to nuzzle against Esta's neck and breathe. For a moment he allowed himself to wonder what it could have been like to stay with her like this, as though they were two ordinary people with their lives ahead of them and their whole future as a possibility. But though Harte was a liar and a con, he wasn't good enough to fool himself.

If he stayed, Seshat would do everything she could to take Esta.

If he stayed, Esta would give herself to try to save him.

He couldn't stay. But he would do what he could to save her. To save all of them.

REDITE

1904—New York

James Lorcan held the telegram between his fingertips and read it again, just to be sure of its meaning. Around him, the Aether bunched and shifted, the future remaking itself into the pattern of his design.

His agent in the West had two of the artifacts in their possession, and best of all, they had the girl. It was only a matter of time before everything fell into place.

He lit a match with one hand and ignited the corner of the telegram, watching it combust and transform into a pile of ash. Then he turned himself to the business of the day before him—the business of leading the Antistasi.

AUTHOR'S NOTE

I've tried to depict the 1904 Louisiana Purchase Exposition as accurately as possible in this book. With the exception of the fictitious Nile River ride, everything from the statue on the top of the Festival Hall to the exhibits and layout of the Pike is based on historical maps, original guidebooks, and pictures I found during my research. While the Nile River ride is an invention of my own, I based it on the research I did, especially about the problematic ways the fair represented race and culture. Because the 1904 characters experiencing the fair can't possibly be aware of the future repercussions of the event, I wanted to give readers a better understanding of the Exposition's complexities and contradictions and how they still remain with us today.

The fair had an enormous impact on St. Louis, the Midwest, and the country as a whole. Between April 30 and December 1 of 1904 nearly twenty million people visited the 1,200-acre fairgrounds, which included seventy-five miles of roads and walkways, fifteen hundred buildings, and exhibits from more than fifty countries and forty-three states. A visitor to the fair could have experienced wireless telegraphy, observed fragile infants being kept alive by incubators, watched the first public dirigible flight, or perused 140 different models of personal automobile. Theodore Roosevelt visited, Helen Keller gave a lecture, Scott Joplin wrote a song, and John Philip Sousa's band performed.

From its sheer size, the fair billed itself as the largest and most impressive display of man's greatest achievements. But as I showed in the story, alongside some of the most astounding scientific and technological breakthroughs of the age, the fair also displayed people. In doing so, the fair became part of the larger history of race, culture, and social evolution in America. This was not accidental. The planning committee curated anthropological displays that worked specifically in the service of imperialism and Western exceptionalism.

It's important to note that in 1904 most Americans didn't have access to foreign travel. The Exposition presented a solution—an opportunity to experience the world in miniature. However, the fair presented a very specific version of the world, one seen through the lens of the West. The organizers of the fair did try to separate the serious and "educational" exhibits that were brought by individual nations from the more scintillating and exotic "entertainment" attractions on the Pike, but the average fairgoer regularly confused the two. The effect was that the fair presented a world in which ethnicity and exoticism became a form of entertainment. People and cultures became objects to consume.

As I show in the story, the representation of different nationalities on the Pike was highly problematic, but the rest of the fair wasn't much better. The educational exhibits were purposely selected by the planners as scientific evidence of the natural progress of human history. Fairgoers could understand the superiority of their own culture in contrast to the so-called "primitivism" of foreign cultures. In 1904, anthropology was still a fledgling discipline of study, but the Exposition and other world's fairs like it demonstrated anthropology's usefulness in ordering people. Specifically, the fair helped to justify the dominance of the West and the usefulness of imperialism in scientific terms.

For example, the large Igorot Village exhibit was the direct product of America's recent victory—and acquisition of territories—in the Spanish-American War. Fair organizers brought people from the Philippine archipelago and displayed them as a sort of human zoo. Fashionably dressed fairgoers who observed the villagers' dress and customs saw the Igorots as less modern—and therefore *inferior*.

Another example of anthropology used in the service of Western imperialism was the appearance of Native Americans and First Nations peoples as exhibits at the fair. The fair itself was a celebration of the Louisiana Purchase, the very event that permitted westward expansion and spurred on the ideals of manifest destiny that led to the slaughter and decimation of Native peoples. Harte and Esta see the Cliff Dwellers concession, but those weren't the only Native Americans at the fair. Apache, Cocopah, Pueblo, and Tlingit peoples were also present as attractions. Attendees could purchase an autographed photo from Geronimo himself, who was then still the American government's prisoner of war, or view an operational model Indian School, where children maintained a routine for the viewing pleasure of tourists.

While the fair provided some, like Geronimo, a chance to be entrepreneurs, it also exploited them with unsanitary living conditions and poor compensation. Moreover, the Exposition's display of Native peoples depended on nostalgia and perpetuated the stereotype of a once-heroic and noble people, now defeated and dying. These stereotypes have persisted to this day and continue to cause harm to Native peoples.

Finally, it's also important to note that while the fair displayed diverse people, it was primarily attended by white Americans. When a planned Negro Day to celebrate emancipation was canceled, the chair of the local committee revoked Booker T. Washington's invitation and told him that "the negro is not wanted at the world's fair." W. E. B. DuBois, whose landmark book, *The Souls of Black Folk*, had been published to critical acclaim the year before, was not invited. The Eighth Illinois Regiment, an African American regiment, made an encampment at the fair but were prohibited from using the commissary by white soldiers, who refused to share. In short, the fairgrounds were not a welcoming space for people of color.

Perhaps it shouldn't be a surprise that the Exposition had such a problematic and often offensive relationship to race and culture. It was a product of its time, after all, but it was also a product of larger social forces. Eleven of the twelve committee members who organized and planned the fair were members of the Veiled Prophet Society, including the president of the committee, David Francis. As I reveal in the story, the VP Society's formation was a reaction to the Great Railroad Strike of 1877, a strike that involved large numbers of African Americans and immigrants. The creation of the VP Society and parade was a direct attempt by white city fathers to reclaim racial and class superiority in the city, and much of the design and experience of the fair—both historically and in my book—echoes that same agenda.

For all it might have done to bring technological advances and exposure to foreign nations, at its heart the Louisiana Purchase Exposition cannot be seen outside the larger system of white supremacy and Western imperialism that it helped to perpetuate. It wasn't alone in this project, however. The Exposition and other fairs like it were common around the turn of the century. Their mixture of exoticism as entertainment and cultural exploitation taught white Americans a version of the world steeped in Western superiority. That understanding had far-reaching effects that continue to impact Americans' understanding of race and culture even today.

For further reading:

Whose Fair? Experience, Memory, and the History of the Great St. Louis Exposition by James Gilbert

From the Palaces to the Pike: Visions of the 1904 World's Fair by Timothy J. Fox and Duane R. Sneddeker

"'The Overlord of the Savage World': Anthropology, the Media, and the American Indian Experience at the 1904 Louisiana Purchase Exposition" by John William Troutman

A World on Display: Photographs from the St. Louis World's Fair, 1904 by Eric Breitbart

AUTHOR'S NOTE

ACKNOWLEDGMENTS

A book this big doesn't happen without help from a lot of people.

First and foremost, to my brilliant editor at Simon Pulse, Sarah McCabe, who dealt with missed deadlines and more unfinished drafts than any person should have to read. Her patience and confidence made this book possible, and her keen insights made this book immeasurably better. Thanks for pushing me and for always having the answer. I'm so glad your brain works better than mine.

To the entire team at Simon Pulse, who have been so amazing and shown this series (and me) so much support: Mara Anastas, Chriscynethia Floyd, Liesa Abrams, Katherine Devendorf, Chelsea Morgan, Sara Berko, Julie Doebler, and Bernadette Flinn. Many thanks to Tricia Lin, who read early drafts; and to Penina Lopez, Valerie Shea, Elizabeth Mims, and Kayley Hoffman, whose astute copyedits, proofread, and cold reads made the sentences shine. My heartfelt gratitude to Audrey Gibbons, Lauren Hoffman, Caitlin Sweeny, Alissa Nigro, Anna Jarzab, Christian Vega, Michelle Leo and her team, Nicole Russo, Vanessa DeJesus, and Christina Pecorale and the rest of the S&S sales and marketing teams, who've done so much for the success of this series. Thanks to Russell Gordon and Mike Rosamilia for making the book beautiful, inside and out. And special thanks to Craig Howell, who somehow managed to create art for the cover that outdid his previous work on *The Last Magician*.

I'm grateful to have Kathleen Rushall in my corner. She's a rock star of an agent, and her unwavering support made the whole process of writing this book almost bearable. Thank you for the check-in emails and pep talks. I'm so lucky that I get to work with her and all the wonderful agents at Andrea Brown.

Many thanks to all the wonderful readers, reviewers, bloggers, booksellers, and librarians who put *The Last Magician* on the *New York Times* list last year and who kept me going with their excitement and questions about this sequel. Special thanks go out to the Devil's Own, especially Joy Konarske, Cody Smith-Candelaria, Agustina Zanelli, Patrick Peek, Kim McCarty, Jennifer Donsky, Kim Mackay, Rachel Barckhaus, Ashley Martinez, and Alyssa Caayao, who went above and beyond to spread their love for the series. Thank you for helping to make TLM a success!

Writer friends are the best type of friends. Thanks to all my favorites, especially the amazing women who listened to me complain about *not* writing and then complain *about* writing, who read drafts or helped me brainstorm my way out of corners, and who make the world better with their beautiful words: Olivia Hinebaugh, Danielle Stinson, Kristen Lippert-Martin, Helene Dunbar, Flavia Brunetti, Christina June, Sarah Raasch, Jaye Robin Brown, Shanna Beasley, Shannon Doleski, Peternelle van Arsdale, Julie Dao, Angele McQuade, Risikat Okedeyi, and Janet Taylor.

And last but never least, my family. This book was a beast to finish, and my guys put up with me basically being not present in their lives for three entire months. I know how hard my working so much was on them, but they gave me the time and space and support I can't possibly deserve (but I'll gladly take anyway). To X and H, who are light and joy, and to J, who is everything. Thank you.

LISA MAXWELL is the author of *The Last Magician* and *Unhooked*. She grew up in Akron, Ohio, and has a PhD in English. She's worked as a teacher, scholar, bookseller, editor, and writer. When she's not writing books, she's a professor at a local college. She now lives near Washington, DC, with her husband and two sons. You can follow her on Twitter @LisaMaxwellYA and Instagram @LisaMaxwell13 or learn more about her upcoming books at Lisa-Maxwell.com.